The Pokhraj

Irina Gajjar

Emerald Ink Publishing
Houston, Texas

The Pokhraj
Copyright © 2004 Irina Gajjar

Cover art by Dustin Turnmeyer, Searchlight Graphics, Nashville, TN

Library of Congress Cataloging-in-Publication

Gajjar, Irina N.
The pokhraj / Irina Gajjar
    p. cm.
ISBN 1-885373-44-9 (trade paperback)
   1. Jewish families–Fiction. 2. Fortune-tellers–Fiction.
3. India–Fiction. I. Title.
PS3607.A37 P65 2003
813'.6–dc21

2002153507

Permissions Department
Emerald Ink Publishing
16630 Imperial Valley Drive, Suite 149
Houston, Texas 77060

Printed in the United States of America

Acknowledgements

My first acknowledgement is to you, dear reader, for reading these words. They would be hollow without you.

I also wish to thank the following people who have touched this work and my heart: Navin Gajjar, Chris Carson, Nini Heugle, John Heugle, Ellen Bennett, Diana Benjaafar, Gopika Malhotra, Florence Horowitz, Sita Kapadia, Carol Marver, and Clarissa RamÌrez de Rivera, author of the poem in Chapter 53.

Next, I thank the many people who have unknowingly and unwittingly participated in the development of the characters in The Pokhraj. You all know who you are better than I do.

Finally, I thank my ancestors and the many philosophers, writers and scholars who have contributed to the formulation of the views and feelings expressed in this work. I have tried to do justice to the beauty of their teachings.

The soul of the little boy,
the young man, and the old man
does not change
even though the body changes.
And even if the soul
moves on to another body after the body dies,
the soul stays the same.

Bhagavad Gita, Chapter 2

Book One

1

The Landau dinner party was turning out to be a success. Natalya had planned the evening weeks ago as a surprise birthday celebration for her husband. Victor relished having guests in his home. He basked in their appreciation of his elegant condominium and its view of the city and he was comfortable and at ease on his turf. Thus, tonight, even though he purported to dislike organized festivities–particularly birthday parties, and most particularly his own—he was pleased. Forgetting that he "hated being happy on command" and that he was categorically opposed to gifts, his spirits were high. The group was small enough for intimacy and his guests were good friends, all fun to be with.

They were at about the same place in life as he and Nat were and they shared common interests. The women, like Nat, were attractive and they sparkled with insightful wit. And his presents were to his liking. Besides a broad band gold ring inset with three little diamonds from Nat, he received a bottle of his favorite champagne, Veuve Cliquot, a copy of the Kama Sutra, a dozen glasses with the insignia of Harvard University—his alma mater—Sauvage cologne and The Warrior Angel trilogy on micro disc.

"I'd drive a hundred miles for this dinner," Victor said with a warm smile. His remark was worn with repetition, but it was endearing because its sincerity was fresh. Indeed the meal was superb. Natalya was an excellent cook and she had stayed away from the office this Saturday in order to go all out. She served a salmon baked in pastry, a baby lamb roasted with herbs, a vegetable ratatouille, new potatoes, home baked bread and salad. The birthday cake was Victor's favorite, a babá au rum.

Conversation was animated over the background of string music. Victor and Sunil Khanna were talking about stocks. "I'm betting on a 20 percent gain in the market this year," Sunil said.

"That's unlikely. I'm staying invested because I don't know what else to do, but I'm being selective. It could be a while before we have another real bull run, Victor opined. "The bottom line is that we don't have a stock market any more, only a market of stocks."

Sunil's wife, Jaya, and David Singer were flirting over a discussion of the sexes. Jaya complained, "This is the twenty-first century and the gender gap still isn't closed. After all, Annette, Nat and I work as many hours as you men do, yet we're always trading recipes while you trade football statistics."

"That's because you like trading recipes while we like football statistics. It's not fair to criticize us for doing what we like, while you do what you like."

"I don't like cooking."

"But you like men to like you and your cooking. That's why you trade hair stylists, boutiques, and books about how to become even more appealing than you already are—as well as recipes. And guess what? We like you very much indeed. I personally adore your curries and I adore you. Fortunately, I love Annette or I'd pursue you relentlessly."

As they were speaking, Victor who had been listening to David and Jaya with one ear walked over and interjected, "I hate to interrupt your discussion, but this is not the twenty-first century. It's the year two thousand. The twenty-first century doesn't start until next year."

"That's wrong. Didn't we all celebrate the ushering in of the new millennium at midnight on December 31, 1999?" Jaya asked.

"No, we celebrated the writing of the number 2000."

Jaya pressed on. "That's ridiculous! Everyone knows the new millennium and the new century started this year. What do you think, David?"

"I must agree with you, Jaya. You're too clever and lovely to be mistaken. Besides all the hoopla can't have been for nothing."

Victor pressed on, "A century is the year one to one hundred. The twentieth century consists of the years 1901 to 2000. The twenty-first century and the new millennium begin in the year 2001. It's common knowledge."

"I suppose my problem is I'm not as common as you are," Jaya teased.

"Can you prove your point with something better than common knowledge?" David challenged.

"Very well." Victor pulled Webster's Unabridged Twentieth Century Dictionary off his bookshelf and read, 'The nineteenth century consists of the years AD 1801 to 1900 inclusive.' Would you agree that by extension the twentieth century must be the years 1901 to 2000 inclusive?"

"Whatever." David shrugged his soldiers.

"I guess." Jaya hated defeat as much as any man.

Nat had to call for silence more than once, but eventually she was able to get the group's attention. She switched off the lights and brought out the birthday cake. They all sang Happy Birthday and applauded loudly when Victor made his wish and blew out the candles in one breath. Nat surreptitiously wiped a tear and wondered why the singing of Happy Birthday and the blowing of birthday candles never failed to tug at her emotions. Then, out of the blue, she heard herself saying, "I can't believe all of us are over thirty and none of us are even considering having children yet. Doesn't anybody worry about the ticking of the proverbial biological clock?" As soon as the words were out, she wished she had kept her peace, but the conversational cannonball had started rolling.

Sunil picked it up first. "Jaya is not at all worried. She isn't ready to make a commitment to motherhood. But I think she should be. What's the use of making money if we are not going to be a family while we're young enough to enjoy our children? I'm beginning to feel that my kids will be ashamed of their dad looking like their friends' grandpas."

"That's not true. I am ready to make a commitment, but I happen to know that your mother is already planning to move in with us if we have a baby and that's what I'm not ready for. She keeps telling me how your brother doesn't need her now that his children are all in school and how much she misses caring for babies."

"Mom would never impose. Anyhow, I thought you liked my mother."

"I do. That's the problem. However, I like her in small doses and not under the same roof. She's overbearing. Besides, I can foresee not wanting to slow down and therefore needing help. It's a catch-22. My research is very exciting, and I certainly don't want to stop. I'll also have to keep traveling. So having a baby will mean having your mother too and giving up my privacy."

"I don't get it. Are you saying that your mother-in-law will literally live with you if you have a baby? Isn't she an archaeologist?" Annette was amazed.

"She's retired for the most part. Don't try to understand. It's an Indian thing."

Victor, who hadn't given much thought to babies, felt a prickle of malaise when Nat started talking about them in front of everyone. He was embarrassed and he didn't really know how to take his wife's comment, but he did know that he wasn't ready for the drastic change in lifestyle that a child would bring. He was content with the status quo. His birthday wish had been for his present happiness to continue without any upheavals. It was actually a little prayer of gratitude along with a hope for nothing to come along which might jinx what he had. Jaya's remarks reinforced his opinion that babies were totally disruptive and he was determined to hold Nat off for quite some time to come. His emotions and the lull in the room disconcerted him and he struggled to find the right words to express his feelings.

"These days everyone is having babies later in life. I thought you wanted to wait until you made partner and stopped working over sixty hours a week, Nat," was what he came up with.

⁕⁕⁕

Natalya's heart pounded. She had been off the pill for four months without telling Victor, thinking that he would never be ready to face fatherhood unless it confronted him head on. He was an only child. He was handsome, uncommonly bright, generous, and kind. But he was only comfortable when he was the center of attention. He needed to be the sun around which others, his parents, his students, and Natalya revolved. Like the sun, he radiated warmth and light, yet also like the sun, he could be blinding. Although he had sufficient intellectual fortitude not to feel challenged by his wife's achievements, Natalya worried hard about whether he would handle being upstaged by a baby with equal graciousness. Of course they had discussed having a family someday, but for Victor that day could be postponed indefinitely, whereas for Natalya it was overdue.

"We agreed that our baby would have two parents with equal commitment," Victor had told her the last time they spoke, "and I'm not prepared yet for the responsibility."

"What would prepare you?" she had asked him.

"Time to adjust to the idea and one more book under my belt."

"You'd have nine months. Initially paternal commitment doesn't require the same hands-on dedication as motherhood. You won't be pregnant, even if you're politically correct to consider pregnancy something that happens to us both. You won't gain twenty-five pounds and you won't throw up. You won't have labor pains and you won't suckle our child every four hours for six months. You would have two years or more to adjust and to write. Isn't that enough time for you?"

"Nat, now isn't a good time for this discussion."

"When would a good time be?"

"When you calm down and are willing to look at what a child will do to both of our lives and to our relationship."

Victor was an English professor with a love for literature and a nose for marketing. His book *The Science of Persuasive Communication* had earned him accolades, and more importantly, substantial research grants from the business world. His methodology worked. Victor empowered his students by teaching them how to sell concepts through effective speech and goal-directed writing. Nat met him when she attended one of his seminars. Both the message and the messenger impressed her. Victor couldn't help noticing her and her body language while he lectured. As he was leaving the podium, Nat stopped him to ask a question.

"Do your techniques work regardless of the merit of the ideas we communicate?"

Victor told her he would answer her over lunch and made a date. A week later he intrigued her with his explanation of how concept evaluation was built into the models he had developed. Two months later Victor proposed marriage and Natalya accepted. They were wed within the year.

Now, thinking that persuasive communication sold ideas but couldn't transform attitudes, Natalya responded to Victor's remarks as casually as she could.

"You know I've been cutting back on work for the last few months. Also we have three new associates who are taking on more responsibility. I feel like there will never be a right time to start our family if we don't take the plunge."

Nat had won Victor over by making him feel that he was the beginning and end of her life. But in a way he really wasn't because she had been centered on motherhood for as far back as she could remember. Victor was the one and only man she wanted to father her children. That's why she fell in love with him. His attractiveness to her manifested itself in visions of babies made of his matter: miniature agile Victors with mops of wavy black hair, high cheekbones and warm brown eyes that couldn't hold still.

Once, when she was about twelve, Natalya had gone running to her father to report that her friend's big sister just had a baby. She remembered the letdown her father's response gave her. "Anyone can have a baby. It's no big accomplishment. On the other hand, succeeding in school and becoming educated are impressive achievements. What you should be focusing on is getting ready for a career, not getting ready for reproduction." And she did, earning praise and hugs every time she executed a school project successfully and every time she produced another report card studded with As. Both her father and mother repeatedly reminded her of what her kindergarten teacher had said:

"Nattie should be a lawyer. I've seen many bright children, but never one with such intellectual integrity and such a logical mind."

Natalya wondered how a five year old could demonstrate intellectual integrity, but for better or for worse, her teacher proved to be right. Here she was, highly successful in a career which suited her although so far it had failed to fulfill her.

Natalya was tall and trim with auburn hair, gold-flecked eyes that switched from green to hazel, and a full, determined mouth. She was sentimental and altruistic, but in professional environments her cool, crisp bearing masked her sensitivity. Thus, she won the respect of friends and adversaries alike. Although her eyes smiled, they never lost sight of their objective nor gave ground when confronted by opposition. Her work product was accurate, complete and delivered on time. Her strategies—enhanced by Victor's teachings—generally hit bulls' eyes. Consequently, she was on the fast track to partnership at the premier law firm of Kaplan, McCall and Green. Not that she didn't enjoy her work. She did. It was fun making things come out the way they should according to the relevant facts and legal principles. Her problem was that she felt as if her accomplishments had no substance. Maybe because she never lacked money, she didn't realize what a struggle earning a living could be or how succeeding in the struggle could bring satisfaction. Maybe because she represented large corporations, she missed seeing the effect of her work on real people. Maybe it was just that she was crazy about babies and always wanted to be a Mommy more than anything else in the world. The funny part of it all was that because Nat didn't really care about the results of her work, she didn't stress over it and did an outstanding job. The less she cared, the more she succeeded.

The tension in the room was palpable. Nat tried to deflect it and to distract Victor by questioning Annette and David.

"So do you guys have compatible views on parenthood?"

Neither gave her a direct answer. David said only that he wondered about the wisdom of bringing a child into the world until one had a sense of one's own self. Although the meaning of David's statement was far from obvious, no one wanted to pursue the issue further and the discussion came to an end.

A moment later Jaya turned the conversation to the latest Imax film about extra terrestrial sightings. The shift to less emotionally-charged terrain cleared the air and the party recaptured its lightheartedness.

Later, after their guests left, Victor watched Natalya as she flitted about tidying up. He wished she would stop putting dishes in the dishwasher, but he knew she wouldn't even though it was his birthday. She would say that he could wait but the dishes couldn't because they would crust and come out dirty. Victor didn't think so. He believed the ads for Cascade that promised clean shiny dishes even when they were washed unrinsed hours after use. Sometimes he put dishes that were merely scraped clean in the dishwasher, but Nat always found spots the next day. He hovered about the kitchen confused. If Nat really loved him, he thought, she would understand his feelings and leave the dishes for later. Then again, why shouldn't he be a little patient? Whenever he said something, she asked him if he expected her to get up "afterwards" to clean up the kitchen. There was no way she would leave the mess for the morning. She would tell him to help if he was in "such a rush." Victor couldn't figure out what to do. He wasn't in any mood for housekeeping. It was one o'clock in the morning. Maybe Nat didn't care about making love with him, he thought. Maybe it just wasn't important to her.

The idea that Nat might not want him was unbearable, and Victor put it out of his mind immediately. Another evening he might have made a fuss and punished Nat by going off to sleep but tonight, after the splendid birthday, he decided to wait calmly and to entertain himself by taking a look at the Kama Sutra. He walked into the living room and thumbed through the illustrated section on different forms of intercourse for awhile, but neither the text nor the pictures held his attention. It might be fun to look at the book with Nat some other time before testing a bizarre position or two, but not tonight. He put the book down and walked to the window. He looked out and watched some lights flashing on and off until he lost interest. Just as he was about to head back toward the kitchen to ask Natalya how much longer she would be, he heard her call.
"Victor?"
"Yes, can I give you a hand?" Her voice saying his name had warmed him.
"No, I was just going to tell you I'm finished. I'll leave the glasses for tomorrow."

A pinkish glow bathed the bedroom where Victor sat on the side of their bed watching Natalya slip out of her silk trousers and shell. He thought that nothing in the world could be more arousing than the sight of his wife undressing herself for him. She removed her clothes carefully, placing each item neatly on a chair before taking off the next garment. When Natalya was completely naked, she looked directly into his eyes and smiled at him. Her smile made him feel as if he had conquered the world. Victor was sure that Natalya had never been more beautiful than she was at this very moment. Her lips were wet and her pupils seemed dilated. Her gestures were filled with grace. Her body, though taut, was welcoming and her scent, intoxicating. She emanated vulnerability and a slight tension that enhanced her attractiveness. Victor couldn't believe that just a few short moments ago, this woman was calmly wiping a countertop as if that act were the most important thing in the world. Now her energy electrified him.

Victor took a deep breath to cool the blood coursing through his veins. Then he stood up and slowly approached Natalya. He embraced her and lifted her to their bed. He stared in awe of her loveliness before he lay down beside her and kissed her. Natalya was still for a time to savor the waves of pleasure that were beginning to take over her being. Victor covered her with his mouth, with his hands, with his breath and with his strength, and he watched her, waiting for her to respond. Sooner than he expected, Nat began to answer his kisses and his caresses, loving him in a way that was familiar, yet also new. She was adventurous in her exploration of her husband and her body moved with fluidity, giving little shudders as it thrilled to Victor's touch. Her growing excitement encouraged and emboldened him. In turn, his boldness further emboldened Natalya. Step by step they embarked upon a wondrous journey as they delved more deeply than ever before into the mysteries of lovers' sexuality.

Tentatively at first, and then with greater assurance, they guided each other along paths which gave them more and more pleasure, yet escalated their desire to higher and higher peaks. Initially they were gentle and considerate of one another, but gradually their tenderness gave way to a selfish and demanding urgency, as they became oblivious of everything but their own needs. And as their craving overpowered all awareness, their passion became violent. Man and wife battled against one another and within themselves, mindlessly writhing, panting and shouting in quest of the gratification that eluded them. Yet all the while they understood that it was the very elusiveness of fulfillment which heightened their joy.

Victor's mind flew out of his body. He was no longer a person, but only a bundle of exquisite sensations gathering the momentum that it needed to release the essence of his life force into Natalya. Natalya shamelessly begged for more, more and yet more, fearing that the fire in her loins could never be quenched. In answer to Natalya's demands, Victor's vigorous thrusts became yet stronger and faster. Still she pleaded with him never to stop. Suddenly in a final explosive outburst, Victor emptied himself into Natalya, crying out to God in gratitude and wonder. That instant Natalya, overcome at last by Victor's power, wept tears of happiness and thought that God and her husband were one.

2

Sunday morning, just after ten, Nat was awakened by the sound of Victor's voice on the answering machine saying, "We're either away from the phone or screening calls. Please let us know when it will be convenient for us to call back." Natalya listened for a message, but there was none. No wonder—the recording was rude. From time to time she and Victor argued about it: "I think we should say something more gracious, Victor," Natalya urged.

"There is no such thing as a gracious message on an answering machine. An answering machine is not designed for effective communication. It is a device for playing telephone tag."

"Why not just say, 'Please leave a message at the beep and we'll return your call as soon as possible?'"

"Because we know and they know we won't return it as soon as possible. We'll return it if and when we feel like it."

"Then we should at least thank them for calling. Let's say, 'Thanks for calling. Sorry we can't talk now, but we'd appreciate a message.'"

"I hear those recordings all the time and I hate them. They aren't honest. We don't necessarily feel thankful that whoever called us called, and we don't care about a message because we have Caller ID. The best thing to do is to be truthful. People will appreciate it. I'd appreciate it. If people have something important to say, they'll say it with or without an invitation."

"The other day I heard a funny message. I really liked it."

"How did it go?"

"Something like, 'This is our new customized hot line. Leave a message and find out if you're hot or not.' I can't exactly remember."

"That doesn't sound funny to me. You probably got it wrong. Anyway, cutesy messages are even worse than phony ones. The trouble with supposedly funny or even genuinely funny messages is that they are only funny the first time you hear them. They get pretty stale the fourth or fifth time around. I don't want to be changing the message every day, do you?"

So Victor's recording prevailed.

The tradition in the Landau household was that whoever woke up first on Sunday prepared and served brunch, which Nat and Victor ate in bed while discussing the following week's plans. This custom had started about a year before when the two of them had escaped from Houston for a weekend and were served brunch on a tray in their room at a bed and breakfast. That inspired them to make a big deal of Sunday mornings at home. Their own brunches started out simply but became increasingly elaborate as the Landaus vied with one another, each trying to make tastier, more unusual and more attractively served dishes than the other. And little by little, their talks that at first revolved around practical matters, became more and more searching. The leisure and relaxation invited discussions of hopes and dreams along with plans. Sunday morning was an oasis in their hectic routines as well as the underpinning for an exploration of the deeper concerns in their lives.

As much as she generally enjoyed preparing brunch, this morning in the aftermath of Victor's thirty-third birthday party and the night's lovemaking, Natalya felt drained. Thus she was pleased to note that Victor's side of the bed was empty and she closed her eyes again and pretended to be asleep so Victor could wake her when he was ready. In seconds her pretense became reality and she fell asleep again to dream away her lingering stress.

Last night, within moments of one of the most exciting couplings of his life, Victor fell into a deep, peaceful slumber. In contrast, Nat lay awake for quite some time, reliving what had just taken place because she had the feeling it could lead to the creation of a new life. On one level she considered that her actions and reactions were all part of a divine master plan and that everything would work out well, but on another she was afraid. Then she remembered the importance of stopping alcohol even before conception and she started to worry because she had drunk several glasses of champagne. She wondered why she hadn't thought of that earlier and realized it was because this wasn't her fertile time of the month. At the same time she also recalled reading that women were at their sexiest when the likelihood of conception was greatest.

Natalya's anxious thoughts were spinning out of control. Did her extraordinary sexual experience mean something special? Was it connected with estrous? Perhaps her reactions actually did cause her body to produce a substance which would encourage Victor's best and strongest sperm to successfully penetrate an ovum and start a new life. Surely after this night, Victor could not help but welcome a baby that he had made with such great love. But then probably to him love and sex were not intertwined in the same way they were for her. This insight frightened Natalya. Now she prayed that she wouldn't become pregnant as a result of tonight. In the future she would use protection or else go back on the pill until Victor agreed to become a father. If she conceived now, Victor would never forgive her. He would think she had tricked him. Her imagination created a series of scenarios: Victor leaving her; Victor forgiving her provided she would agree to have an abortion; Victor remaining out of loyalty but withholding love and trust.

While one alarming idea after another paraded through her head, ousting the earlier one, Natalya felt a piercing current that stunned as it flashed before her eyes like a miniature, fiery torpedo. Nat identified the vision as the embodiment of her and Victor's child. But as soon as this concept shaped itself into words clear enough for her brain to process, logic rejected it. Common sense persuaded her that her emotions were toying with her mind. She had never heard of anyone who reported feeling the fertilization of an egg. She was just vulnerable because of the way she lost herself in Victor's lovemaking. Natalya forced herself to be realistic. What happened was nothing mystical. It was just plain good—no, awesome sex—something to appreciate in its own right, something to be grateful for. It certainly wasn't anything to be scared about. She hadn't conceived in four months and chances were she wouldn't for some time, even off the pill. In fact, hadn't she begun to worry that she and Victor might not be able to have a baby naturally at all? If that happened, she had worked out a solution: they would find a way to have a child that was parented by one of them or else adopt. Everything would sort itself out in due time. Somewhat comforted by her return from the world of runaway reveries to common-sensical reasoning, Natalya finally settled down. She lulled herself to sleep by trying to recall the celebrations of her own birthdays, starting with the most recent and going back to her childhood.

⚬⚭⚬❦⚬⚭⚬

Victor startled Natalya when he walked into the bedroom saying, "Time to get up. You have three minutes to brush your teeth and see what's for brunch."

"Wait, I'm in the middle of . . . " Nat mumbled and tried to recapture her dream or at least its memory.

Victor rubbed her shoulders and asked gently, "A penny for your dream. What are you in the middle of?"

"Um, gosh, what did I say?"

"You said you were in the middle of something and I offered you a penny for your dream. What was it about?"

"I don't know. It's over now and buried someplace in my subconscious. What time is it?"

"It's ten forty-five."

"I don't want to brush my teeth. They taste of yesterday."

"You'll like brunch better if you brush."

"What's for brunch?"

"Come see after you brush your teeth."

With some effort Nat got up, washed her face, ran a comb through her hair and brushed her teeth. When she finished, she felt brighter. By the time she got back into bed, there were two trays sitting at its foot. The stereo was playing something mushy from the fifties and Victor announced that the two new crystal glasses with gold ribbon swirled around their stems contained freshly squeezed guava juice. He made a toast to many more nights like last night, and to more years like his thirty-second. In addition to the juice, the trays contained slices of coffee cake, cheese bread, pumpernickel bread, scones, a selection of ham, cheeses and jams, and yogurt mixed with freshly sliced strawberries. The coffee was a plain American brew served with half-and-half. Nat added her own toast to "meaningfulness" in their happy lives. Then, disregarding last night's decision to stop unprotected sex, she proposed a hiatus between the juice and the rest of brunch. Victor declined Nat's offer, but he did so with a gleam in his eye that turned his rejection into a promise.

"Do you have anything pressing to get done today?" Victor asked Nat.

"Mmmn. This is wonderful. Let me think. I put my agenda on mental hold. Oh . . . yes. Tomorrow I have depositions in the Parkway Plaza case. I need to outline some questions, but it's no big deal. I brought the file home and I'll get it done

10

sometime this afternoon. Edward, my new paralegal, organized the documents and I have a pretty good handle on what I need to cover. How about you?"

"I have some essays to correct, but they can wait. Actually I had planned to get together with Linda to outline the research questionnaires we need to send out, but if you're not busy, I'll cancel. I feel like doing something fun."

"Who's Linda?"

"She's my new grad assistant. Her mother's Brazilian. She's working on her Ph.D. in Management and she may use some aspect of persuasive communication as her topic. I thought I told you about her."

"Actually you hadn't mentioned her and no, I'm not busy, so cancel. What do you want to do?"

"Oh, I don't know. Something different."

"Something like staying home and working on our photo albums, or something like going to the movies or out somewhere?"

"Something like going ice skating. It's been a long time since we did that."

"Well, when do you want to go?" Nat asked.

"Maybe at about five." Then we can grab a bite and get home in time for a relaxing evening."

"O.K. But I want to change the subject."

"I've learned to expect non-sequiturs from you, so please feel free." Victor grinned. "What new profoundly thought provoking subject are you switching to?"

"I want to ask you a question."

"So ask before my curiosity turns into apprehension."

"You are reacting negatively for no reason at all. Why would you be apprehensive?" A tiny knot tied itself in Nat's stomach.

"Experience." Victor's grin was gone. Nat had no business telling him he was negative, but he let it slide. "Go ahead."

"What do you think the best part of our lives is?"

"That's your question?"

"Yes." The grin came back. "I don't know. I like everything about our life, but . . . sometimes I worry because I think it's too good to be true."

"You know, Victor, I like our lives too, but I worry for a different reason. And sometimes I am not really happy."

Victor bristled. He was rightly apprehensive after all. He hoped that his wife didn't have an agenda. Trying to mask his irritation he asked, "What do I do to make you unhappy?"

"It's not you. It's me. Everything isn't always about you. Men think that if something's wrong, they can fix it and if they can't, they are to blame."

"That's a very clever little piece of analysis, but the truth is that I'm your husband and it's my job to make you happy."

"Don't be a chauvinist. I can be worried or unhappy all by myself for reasons that I have to work out by myself."

"If you want to be unhappy all by yourself for reasons that you want to work out all by yourself, why are you telling me?"

"I don't know. Sometimes you help me see things that I cannot see by myself. You give me perspective."

That answer soothed Victor somewhat, so he asked, "If you like your life and you are not scared that something will come along to screw it up, what do you think is upsetting you?"

Nat wanted to answer that she wasn't happy because she felt that her life was empty, but then she thought if she said that, Victor would be sure to perceive himself as having failed her. The truth was that she couldn't quite put her finger on what it was that really bothered her.

— ❧ ❧ ❧ ❧ ❧ —

Natalya didn't know that she was already carrying within her the seed—now about eleven hours old—that would become her and Victor's child. She didn't know that before becoming embodied, the soul of this child had hovered indecisively over its prospective parents' spirits for some time. Although it had resisted assuming a physical form, soon it would be compelled to do so. Its window of opportunity to choose the materials and qualities that would define its life was running out. It knew that the Landaus were right for it, but it worried that the timing was wrong for them. It would have backed off, except in the last minute it feared that another soul would grab its spot, so it harnessed its power and willed itself to materialize. En route, it collided with competitors and pushed them away. Then the soul made its mark, at the very moment Natalya had been jolted by the current that she reasoned she had never felt.

Afterwards, while Natalya slept, the finest and most energetic of Victor's five hundred million sperms had swum far ahead of the others, lashing its tail over twenty thousand times, until it penetrated the wall of Nat's ovum and headed for the nucleus buried deeply within. Then in a miraculous instant, Victor's sperm fused with the nucleus of Nat's ovum. Together they formed a blastocyst that contained the blueprint for the soul's new body, its new intellect and its new personality. At rest within the blastocyst, the soul was pleased with the genetic characteristics it recognized in its embodiment. Luckily, the alcohol in Nat's blood stream didn't weaken it. Nat had been drinking very slowly and most of what she consumed had burned out while she was cleaning up after the party. So the freshly merged soul and minuscule body was unharmed and adjusted easily as it began its long journey down Nat's fallopian tube toward her uterus.

The new life defined itself within nanoseconds of fusion and it became instantly conscious of its ambiance and of the chemistry between Nat and Victor, its parents. It hoped it had made a wise choice, because the consequences of a bad one would be painful. It would either proceed to grow and be born, adversely affected by early negative influences, or it would lose this chance at life altogether after suffering considerable pain. Then it would be back to square one.

Embodiment was a risky business. Sometimes an embryo would start in vitro and respond with confusion to its strange home, seeking to transcend the space that separated it from the substance that was its parents. Remarkably, it had capabilities to do that. However, the Landaus' conception was lucky enough not to be faced with a challenge of such magnitude. It was where it belonged.

As Natalya and Victor spoke, the blastocyst that was already their child split into the first of many multiples of itself, all the while fervently checking and copying DNA messages. This hectic activity did not prevent its antennae, composed of pure energy, from registering every fluctuation in the vibrations that swirled around it. It registered the totality of its environment, both inside and outside of Nat's physical body. It understood the tonal quality of her and Victor's voices and of the music playing in the room. It felt the beats of their hearts and the movements of their limbs. Most of all, it felt everything connected with what Natalya and Victor believed in their innermost beings about themselves, about one another, and about the vast universe that existed within and without their souls. During the first three days of its existence, the blastocyst would migrate from its physical and temporal point of origin to the place and time inside Natalya's womb where it would reside until birth. Then its force would gradually dissipate as its expanding body and intelligence merged into the great dance of life. But at present it possessed more cosmic energy than it would ever again possess in a physical manifestation.

⁕⁕⁕

No, Natalya thought. She did not want to share her feelings of emptiness or her regrets over childlessness with Victor. She searched for a way to express the ambivalence in her heart as well as in her head and finally found the words she was looking for.

"I think I'm worried because there is something about my life that doesn't make sense. That's what makes me unhappy at times. I know we are very lucky. We are smart, we have plenty of money, we have love, and we have fun. We're never bored. I think we're pretty decent people. We don't do horrible things and we try to do our bit to make the world a better place, but everything about our life isn't what our life is about."

"Sure it is. We do what we do because we try to be good people. That's what life is about. Being good. Following the golden rule. Doing unto others as you would have them do unto you. Or if you prefer, following Buddha's eightfold path."

"I know that's what your parents probably told you. It's what my parents taught me, but I don't buy it." Nat shook her head.

"What are you saying? Are you saying that life is about fasting on Yom Kippur to atone for our sins, lest we become morally and ethically dead? Or is it about going to church on Sundays to listen to some idiot who is getting rich on the side tell you how to get saved or perhaps confessing your sins every so often so that an anointed human being can forgive you on God's behalf?"

"No, of course not," Nat answered, "but I'm beginning to think that 'God' may be an operative word in the scheme of things."

"I doubt it. You are a nice Jewish girl married to a nice Jewish boy. I don't think our God is in the center of the scheme of things. I see him as more of a traditional and controlling old fellow looking down on the world from the top of a mountain. His primary function is to prevent us from behaving like heathens. He is the rational spirit of virtuous conduct, not a panacea for unhappiness. In any case, I think that the God who presumably created man was in fact created by man or, more likely, by woman first."

Nat pondered her husband's words and then asked, "Why aren't we practicing Jews?"

"Why practice? We've already got it right."

Victor got up and made room on his dresser. Nat followed and put the breakfast trays on the corner her husband cleared. Then they both got back into bed.

13

3

Nat's deposition of Mr. Courtney, the bank officer in the Parkway Plaza litigation, was on track even as her mind wandered. Her client, Pinnacle, was a rapidly growing hotel chain. Pinnacle had entered into a contract with Alpha National Bank (ANB) to purchase the defunct Parkway Plaza Hotel. Alpha had foreclosed on this property over a year earlier. However, prior to closing the transaction with Pinnacle, the bank discovered that it was not in a position to deliver clear title because it had botched up the foreclosure. Alpha's lawyers had not realized the central section of the hotel was built on land the bankrupt former owner had leased, not purchased. This section still belonged to a third party. It contained the café and swimming pool and it cut the property in two.

When ANB discovered the mess, it tried to force Pinnacle to close the deal anyway. Nat had no alternative but to file suit. Although Alpha initially acted out of stupidity, its subsequent dealings with her client were deceptive and coercive. Her aim was to get Courtney, who called the shots, to admit as much. The truth was important because Pinnacle's damages for fraud or deception would far exceed any damages it could get as a result of ANB's incompetence.

After covering preliminary ground, Nat zeroed in on the issues that would give her the evidence she needed.

"Who ordered the title company to forward closing documents to my client on January 2nd, 1999?" was the first question on point.

"I believe I did." Mr. Courtney looked pensive.

"Will you please confirm whether you did or didn't?"

"I did."

"Were the documents in Plaintiff's Exhibit 18 prepared and forwarded to Pinnacle at your direction?"

"Yes."

"On or before January 2nd, 1999, were you aware of exclusion number 2 on page six of the title policy?"

"Can I look at page six?"

"Certainly."

"Please repeat your question."

"Would you please read back the question?" Nat asked the court reporter.

The court reporter read back from his tape, "On or before January 2nd, 1999, were you aware of exclusion number 2 on page six of the title policy?"

"I don't recall." Mr. Courtney shook his head.

Natalya pressed on. "Let me ask you another way and remind you that you are under oath. Do you have correspondence in your file regarding this exclusion dated some time in December, 1998?"

"I don't really recall."

"Is it the timing or the existence of the correspondence that you do not recall?"

"I'm not sure about the date or content of the correspondence."

"Please look at Plaintiff's Exhibit 21 and tell me what it is."

"It's a letter."

"A letter from whom?"

"Alpha Bank."

"To whom is it addressed?"

"To First Title."

"Who signed the letter?"

"I did."

"Please read paragraph two of the letter into the record."

"At this time, Alpha will not take any steps regarding the leased portion of Parkway Plaza. Please forward the documents to Pinnacle and advise Pinnacle that if they do not proceed with the closing on schedule, they will be subject to penalties."

"Thank you, Mr. Courtney. Does this refresh your memory?"

"Yes, it does. Where did you get that letter?"

"Mr. Courtney," Nat replied, "in this deposition I ask the questions and you answer them."

Jack Owen, Jr., the bank's attorney, was surprised by the letter and requested a break to confer with his client. Nat had obtained the letter from First Title. Mr. Courtney had not revealed its existence to Jack, but instead insisted that he did not learn about the title problem until after Pinnacle filed suit.

"I guess I forgot about that letter," he told his own lawyer.

After the break, Mr. Courtney was able to remember much more. He admitted that he knew about the title problem and had made no effort to resolve it but instead tried to hide it. He also admitted knowing that the owner of the unforeclosed portion of Parkway Plaza was about to sue the bank for encroaching upon his land and for back lease payments. Finally, he admitted that he had hoped to catch Pinnacle unaware.

As she left the bank, Nat reminded herself that she was not responsible for what happened to Courtney. Her responsibility was managing her own little family and making her own dreams come true. If only she could handle her personal life with the same ease and detachment that she brought to her work. In some ways she was as dumb as Mr. Courtney.

Dumb and deceptive. Those adjectives applied to Courtney, but they also applied to her. Going off the pill without telling Victor was dumb and deceptive. It didn't strike her that way when she did it, but it sure did now. How could she have been so idiotic? So dishonest? Honesty was what Victor always said he admired most in her and she had failed him. She had failed herself.

Nat needed to talk to someone. Should she tell Victor? No way, she decided. Not until her own head cleared up. Maybe she could speak to Annette Singer. No, that wouldn't work either. As a therapist, Annette was bound by confidentiality, but she wouldn't be talking to Natalya as a professional. It would be as a friend. So there was a risk that what she said would get back to David and then to Victor. She needed her mother. She'd hang in there until Thursday or Friday and then convince Victor to fly to New York for a weekend. At home, she'd make some private time and confess to her mom.

Nat acknowledged to herself that she was feeling funny. In fact she started feeling odd as soon as she finished making love with Victor on Saturday night. They had a wonderful Sunday, but something was weird. Even Victor sensed it.

"You aren't yourself," he told her while they were ice-skating.

"What do you mean?" Nat asked, even though she did feel a bit like a stranger to herself.

"I can't put my finger on it. Something is out of kilter."

"Maybe I'm just tired. You have used up all my energy." Nat smiled.

"No, it's the other way around. I gave you energy. I'm the tired one."

It wasn't until Wednesday that Victor's mind returned to Nat again and he tried to figure out what was going on. It wasn't just that Nat was acting out of character. The air around her was different. Even he felt affected by the change. It was almost as if they both were undergoing an intangible transformation. The idea that crossed Victor's mind was vague and fleeting. Since he couldn't put his finger on it, he dismissed it.

Early in the week he had been busy with the essays he needed to correct. He was also working on a new course he was going to teach on logical communication, which he hoped could become the topic of his next book. Linda Michaels was a tremendous help and he kept his fingers crossed that she would get permission from the Business School to do part of her doctoral work in the English Department.

Maybe, Victor thought, he should agree to teach a course in the Business School—something he had been resisting for a while, but which would probably enhance the sale of his book—and eventually bring in more consulting work. Linda had urged him to do this. "Just promise to think about it," she had said with a twinkle in her eye. She seemed confident that once he thought about it, it would be a done deal.

Both Victor and Nat typically worked late on Monday and Tuesday to get a jump on the week and they fended for themselves at dinner. Nat liked Lean Cuisine and Victor usually had something like cereal and fruit or burritos and salad from Taco Bell. This week, though, he had pizza on Monday. On Tuesday he indulged in two and a half bowls of graham crackers and whole milk instead of his usual Cheerios or shredded wheat squares and skim milk. Nat stuck with her Lean Cuisine, but then she had Häagen-Dazs ice cream both nights. Monday she had Rum Raisin and Tuesday she polished off all the Vanilla Fudge in the freezer.

On Wednesday Nat had to go to a banquet in honor of some judge. She asked Victor to come, but he wasn't up to facing all those lawyers and wanted down time, so he declined. He wasn't too thrilled with the judges he met from time to time, all hungry for contributions to their election campaign fund because Texas judges were elected rather than appointed. Victor thought this system led to biased proceedings. The judges couldn't help remembering lawyers and firms who supported their campaign. Be that as it may, Victor was looking forward to Thursday when he and Nat planned to go jogging together and then have sushi. Victor decided that on Thursday he would get to the bottom of things and clear the air.

By Thursday, Nat had a sixth sense that something was happening to her. She lacked her usual zest and power of concentration. Her keen sense of smell was becoming an annoyance. She kept identifying odors like deodorant, fried foods, and oniony or garlicky breath. She was in a serious quandary and couldn't even formulate her dilemma properly. She didn't know what she wished for anymore and she didn't know what to do. Should she take the pill again? What other contraception could she use without telling Victor? If Victor wouldn't agree to go to New York this weekend, should she go by herself on some pretext?

And, like her dad would say, the sixty-four thousand dollar question: if she was pregnant already, should she consider a quick and quiet abortion? No, she silently screamed. No way. She couldn't do it. In any case, once she told Victor, he would know about her dishonesty and hate her for it. Having an abortion without telling him would be even more horribly deceptive and unfair, even if she could do such a thing, which she could not. She was in love with the baby she and Victor would have some day and she would never kill it, no matter what the consequences. But why was she even thinking like this? Most likely she was suffering from PMS. Once she got her period everything could go back to normal. However, she didn't feel like she had PMS. Well, maybe she did. On the other hand, Natalya couldn't help telling herself if she wasn't pregnant, Victor might not agree to have a child for years. He was just too self-centered. Or too scared. If she gave him an ultimatum, it might be the end for them and then she could never have a baby with him.

All this turmoil disturbed the burgeoning new life which permeated the Landaus' world, but, braced by its courage, its sense of who its parents were, and its ability to visualize the future, it remained free from serious harm. It understood that it would be safe because Nat, in her heart of hearts, wished she were pregnant, even though she desperately feared confronting Victor. It also perceived that Victor was softening and already preparing himself for fatherhood, even though as yet he did not realize what was happening. Thus the newly embodied soul withstood its sail through turbulent waters.

Victor was on edge, too. He could not read the vague and faint clues inside and around him. Nothing made any sense and he was frustrated. Still he determined that he'd stay cool and piece together the puzzle that perplexed him. But as soon as they began running Thursday evening, Nat questioned him about his work and then she attacked him when he talked about his plans to teach a class in the Business School.

"How come you are thinking of doing that when you told me only a few weeks ago that you'd never agree?" she asked.

"Things change."

"Remember how you said that the Business School was too regimented and that you wanted to make a point about your theories being a part of language, and not of business dealings?"

"Well, I think I shouldn't be so rigid. After all, the corporate world is funding most of my research."

"And the funds are going to the English Department, right?"

The best Victor could come up with for an answer was "I'm not so sure that will continue."

"It sounds like you're copping out." Nat stopped running. "I have to catch my breath."

When they resumed their jog, Victor tried to shift the conversation over to Nat's work and to Wednesday's banquet, but Nat was monosyllabic. "Great," she said when he asked how the Parkway Plaza depos went. "OK," she said when he asked how the banquet was. Then she said that she wanted to concentrate on running and that they would talk more at dinner but that she didn't feel like sushi. Victor was dying for sushi, but he didn't say so and pretended not to mind going to Pigalle instead.

After they ordered, Victor was ready to take the bull by the horns. He didn't intend to be confrontational, but at the same time he wanted some answers. However, before he opened his mouth, Nat snatched control of the conversation again.

"Let's go to New York," she said out of the blue.

"When and why do you want to go?" Victor asked.

"Tomorrow night. Mom and Dad are free this weekend. I've been missing them and worrying about Dad a little. Also we promised to go out with Annette and David next weekend to dinner and to this comedy club they said was great."

"I'm sorry, Nat, but this is more than a little sudden. I have work to get done and you know I'm not a last minute person."

"I'm fed up with planning ad nauseam. Why can't we be spontaneous?"

"Nat, I don't know what's gotten into you, but right now you are being extremely unpleasant and I hardly feel like going home with you, let alone sprinting off to New York on a whim." Victor was turning red.

"Isn't that typical? The minute you don't want to do something, instead of giving a sensible reason, you find a way to tell me how horrible I am and how you don't want to be with me."

"Excuse me, but didn't you just say you are fed up with my planning things and lacking spontaneity? Isn't that disagreeable? And while we're talking about disagreeable, I really want to know what bee has gotten into your bonnet. You are not yourself. What's happening to you and to us?"

"You are telling me that I'm so disagreeable that you don't even feel like going home with me. That's what's happening to us. Besides wanting to go to New York, what have I done to tick you off so?"

"You keep bitching about nothing."

"I don't bitch and I don't appreciate your using that word around me. I also don't appreciate your tone of voice. I don't have a problem with your telling me you're upset at me for some valid reason, but right now we're in a public place and you are raising your voice."

"I'll be glad to explain why I'm upset."

"Our supper is here," Nat pointed out. "Your explanation will have to wait."

While Victor busied himself telling the waiter that the roast chicken and Chardonnay were his and that his wife was having the spinach linguini and iced decaf, he thought about how much more he would have enjoyed California rolls and sake. Nat used the moment to try to assess the situation. She was furious with Victor's prying and whining about how something was wrong with her. Nothing was wrong with the way she was acting. If she had a problem, it was a personal matter that she would share with him if and when it became necessary. Meanwhile she was entitled to the privacy of her own thoughts. Being married shouldn't mean having no freedom to think. And why couldn't he agree to something on the spur of the moment just once in his life? If he cared for her, he'd give her a break. But obviously, the minute she expressed an idea of her own and stopped admiring his every move and stopped treating every word he uttered as a kernel of pure wisdom, he got nasty.

Victor interrupted Natalya's train of thought. His irritation was mounting and so was his determination. Instead of answers he was getting a cross-examination. Surely Nat couldn't fail to know that she was being unreasonable. He had to go forward and find out what was behind all this.

"Listen," he started. "Ever since Sunday you have been full of yourself and your off-the-wall preoccupations with finding a deeper meaning in life. You have been totally uncommunicative and insensitive. Now you want me to run off to New York. You couldn't care less about my work or my wishes."

"That's ridiculous. You have lots of flexibility and you can go wherever you want whenever you want. You're the one who doesn't give a rat's ass about me."

"Who's raising her voice and using vulgar language now? What gives you the right to be insulting as well as inconsiderate?"

"My voice is not raised. I'm not insulting. I'm not even responding to your mean and shallow remarks. I'm just stating what appears to be an obvious fact. If you cared about me you wouldn't jump all over me just because I suggest a trip to New York. As far as I know..."

"As far as you know, you don't know anything. You are crazy."

"Must you interrupt to tell me I'm crazy? Can't you even wait to let me finish my sentence?"

"Fine, go ahead and tell me what you think you know."

"As I was saying, I know you love going to New York. Now it turns out that my suggestion is proof that I'm insensitive, that I know nothing and that I'm crazy."

"You really are acting crazy, Nat. Why is it suddenly so important for you to go to New York this weekend which starts tomorrow? You did more than make a suggestion. You accused me of being a jerk when I said no. You didn't think about what I want or need. That's insensitive."

"Why? I could go to New York alone."

"You certainly could, but we could also plan to go together at a mutually convenient time. There is no plausible explanation for your irrational sense of urgency," Victor argued. "I don't want to drop everything and go running off to New York when I'm busy and when we both can easily go in a week or two."

"What you're saying boils down to the fact that I'm irrational for not wanting to wait to a couple of weeks, but you're perfectly rational to refuse to go with me when there is nothing stopping you."

"What I'm saying is that you don't make any sense." Victor put his hands back on his lap.

"Thanks for that insight," Nat retorted. "It'll be a pleasure to go and visit my parents without you. I think we're at a point in our relationship where a couple of days apart will do us a world of good."

"You make your choices, but be prepared to face the consequences."

"What is that supposed to mean?"

"Whatever," Victor said, because he didn't really know.

4

It was nearly one a.m. on the East Coast when the captain of Natalya's flight announced that the plane was making its approach into Newark. In spite of her exhaustion, Nat had been unable to relax or doze because she had to keep climbing out of her window seat over the snoring fat lady in the aisle seat to go to the bathroom. On top of that the ride was bumpy. Nat's gut fear of flying intensified when the seat belt sign was illuminated, and she missed Victor's reassuring handclasp.

Nat had driven to the airport Friday directly from the office. She and Victor spoke little in the morning, avoiding any mention of their Thursday night argument.

"I'll book my flight and then call you to give you the details," she said.

Victor was never ready to pick up and go. He liked to plan, reserving seats in advance and making arrangements at his destination. On the other hand Nat never did prepare ahead of time. She always kept a packed overnight bag at the office. She had a busy morning and didn't get around to telling her secretary to make reservations or to call her parents until after lunch. At three, she left Victor a message, annoyed again at the recording telling her it was screening calls. She hoped he'd get back to her soon. He did.

"I think it's probably a good idea for us to have some private time," he said. "Have a good trip."

"Well, I'll miss you."

"Me too. Have fun. I'll wait for your call tomorrow night. Give your Mom and Dad my love."

Nat walked off the plane looking a great deal brighter than she felt. An application of lipstick and rouge plus the smile she wore to thank the crew as they thanked her for choosing Continental helped, as did the relief she always experienced when her flight touched the ground. She moved briskly toward the transportation counter to catch the last shuttle into Manhattan but stopped abruptly when she heard a familiar voice call out, "Hey, Nattie."

"What on earth are you doing here at this hour?" she asked her kid brother who lived in Paramus, New Jersey.

"A little bird told me you'd be in town so I decided to pick you up and spend a night or two in the city."

"How come? What about Cecily?"

Ronald's smile faded. "It's a long story." He took Nat's bag and gave her a one-armed bear hug.

"Do you want to talk about it?"

"No. I haven't said anything to Mom or Dad either."

"Didn't they ask about Cecily?"

"I preempted their questions. I told them I wanted to see you and that Cecily couldn't make it because she's in rehearsals. What's going on with you? Where's your side kick?"

"Please, Ronald. That's not a nice comment." Nat's expression turned into an unhappy frown.

"Sorry. It's just that you never come here on such short notice and Victor is always with you."

"The truth is that I wanted to come on short notice and I'm upset that he wouldn't come along."

"I was only kidding. Don't scrunch up your face like that. You'll make lines."

"It's OK." Nat smiled again. "I'm just jumpy. I need to have a heart-to-heart with Mommy."

"I wish you wouldn't say 'Mommy.' It sounds ridiculous. You're not six years old."

"Well, that's how I think about her. I don't care how it sounds."

"Just don't say it to people."

"You're not people. You're my brother."

Nat relaxed when she settled into bed a little after three in the morning on Saturday. She set the alarm for 10:30 knowing there was no way her dad would let anyone wake her up. Then, without even opening *The Professor and the Madman*, Nat shut off the light. She fell asleep thinking about her parents' home. It wasn't the sprawling suburban house she grew up in, but it felt equally soothing.

Dora and Harold Rosenbaum lived in an old brownstone in the Village. Nat's bedroom—the upstairs guestroom—was huge. The building had been a loft and her parents decided not to add many walls when they moved in. They had a bedroom and a living room with an open kitchen and dining room on one floor and a huge guest bedroom on top. That was it. Ronald slept in the living room that worked as an extra guestroom. As large as the rooms were, the comfortable clutter that filled them made them cozy. As a rule, Nat didn't like clutter. Neither did Victor. They agreed that flat surfaces should not be resting places for things. An object was either esthetically pleasing, in which case it was placed in a space that showed it off to its best advantage, or it was utilitarian and belonged out of sight. Their taste was the elegant streamlined look. But Nat had to admit that her parents' place was warmly alive. Between Mother, who couldn't toss an heirloom or sentimental souvenir, and Dad, a neatness freak who was cold-blooded about anything that didn't breathe, they had achieved a wonderful balance.

How different the atmosphere in this home was from the one where Victor grew up. His parents' house was tidy and tastefully ornate, but it was also somber and fragile. Only the window dressings were heavy. The senior Dr. Landau, a medical doctor, didn't really fit in the delicate furniture that seemed to have been designed for shorter men. Victor's mother taught language arts in a high school for gifted children. She was an intelligent and well-educated lady. She was also cultured and kind, but she never noticed that her Henry spilled out of the chairs and settees she chose for their rooms. Nor did she notice that her home was gloomy. The upholstery was dark, because bright colors were harsh and pale ones showed spots; bulbs were of low wattage because soft lighting was more restful and calmed the nerves. Rebecca Landau was afraid of light. The sun was her particular enemy. Its glare hurt her blue eyes and its heat burned her pale skin, so she personally avoided it. Its rays faded her carpets and her tapestries, so she shielded them from it. At dawn, Nat's mother-in-law faithfully closed windows and drew curtains. At dusk she always opened them to let in the "fresh" night air. It was an odd environment in which Victor had flourished.

The Rosenbaums spent the better part of Saturday at the breakfast table, letting the hours slip away by default. They had juice, coffee, lox and bagels and then cheesecake and more coffee and finally fruit. Eventually they made plans for what was left of the day: Ronald and his father decided to go to Computer City while Nat and her mother chose to visit the Egyptian Exhibit in the Metropolitan Museum. Dora made reservations for a late dinner at Granada, a new Spanish restaurant and club which was supposed to have great flamenco dancers.

Alone in Houston, Victor dedicated his Saturday to mapping out his first logical communication course. Linda came in after lunch to discuss the teaching materials. Victor's plan was to intersperse the study of formal logic with the study of descriptive linguistics. He explained his theories to Linda.

"In a nutshell, prescriptive linguistics is a futile attempt to preserve language whereas descriptive linguistics captures its evolution."

"Yes, but how does this impact logical communication?" Linda asked.

"Well, it's a question of determining how people speak in different segments of society and then tailoring logical communication to that speech. Fifty years ago, the study of logic was a part of every liberal arts curriculum. Today, logic has become a casualty of the information explosion. But its study has been dropped at a cost. People, even bright people, have no understanding of logic, and as a result they try to sell concepts that don't make sense. For example, take the expression 'very unique.' Older educated individuals find this term illogical because 'unique' means one of a kind. But a younger crowd has no problem with it because it has redefined 'unique' to mean unusual. If the business world applies logic to language within the context of social frames of reference, it can ensure that its messages make sense to targeted audiences."

"Isn't logical communication a lot like persuasive communication? Doesn't persuasive communication have to be logical?"

"Yes and yes. Actually logical communication is an extension of the persuasive communication model. However, logical communication is more precise and quantifiable. Its objectives are narrower."

"This is really interesting." Linda's eyes were wide with admiration. "But how could I contribute to your research?"

"You could begin with gathering examples of advertising messages that are logically flawed in the perception of targeted audiences."

"I see. It would be a two-tiered process. The first tier would be to study linguistic differences. The second would be to see whether or not specific messages are logical in light of those differences."

"That's right." Victor was pleased. "My guess is that our data will have real commercial value."

Victor was having fun, but he was hungry. He wanted to invite Linda to dinner in order to prolong the session, but then thought he'd better not. Linda was too uncomfortably attractive for a time when things with his wife were so unsettling. He had checked his answering machine twice in the afternoon and was disappointed that there were no messages from Nat. Then he became engrossed in his work. Now Victor looked at his watch and, realizing that it was nearly seven, mumbled something about not wanting to keep Linda any longer because it was late. When Linda said she had no time constraints, Victor concocted a prior engagement and began filling his briefcase. Linda said good-bye, she'd see him next week and she'd write up a proposal for her department. Then she reminded Victor about how much it would help if he would agree to do a class in the School of Business.

"Wouldn't you consider giving one course like in communicating through the media, Dr. Landau?"

"That's not exactly . . ."

"It would be a good way to bring persuasive and logical communication to the business community right through the front door."

Before Victor could respond, Linda said, "I have to run," and went out through the front door herself.

When Victor got home, Nat still hadn't phoned and when he called New York, nobody was home. He left a quick message saying that he'd be in all evening and then wished he hadn't because now he was either stuck or else he'd have to leave a second message canceling the first, which would be awkward. He missed Nat and he wished he were in New York with her, but she hadn't given him a chance. He just couldn't react at her lightning speed. It took him a little time to get his bearings and to think things out. He couldn't turn himself on and off like a faucet. Let's go to New York. Let's not. Let's invite twenty people over for a Halloween Party. Let's go to Mexico for New Year's. Let's go to the opera. I want to see *Figaro*. Let's give away our tickets because I have a crisis at work. It made him nervous. The bottom line, though, was that Nat wasn't happy anymore. She had told him that in so many words, and even though she said he had nothing to do with what was bothering her, he obviously had everything to do with it. As a result, he wasn't happy either. The worst part of it all was that Nat couldn't care less about how he felt. He thought she understood him, that they had an understanding and respected one another's differences. What went wrong?

Now here he was at home by himself on a Saturday night, hungry, lonely and with a bulge between his legs. What was he supposed to do? Take a Playboy to the bathroom like some pimply adolescent? Why the hell did Nat have to go off? What was so important that it couldn't wait?

As Victor brooded, the week-old life he and Nat had engendered molded his mind and heart as well as the minds and hearts of its mother and its grandfathers and grandmothers. Transcending physical boundaries, it caused subtle changes to take root in their consciousness. Thus the life that entered their world as a gentle fleeting perception was already evolving into a pervasive bundle of thoughts and emotions.

At the age of eight days, the blastocyst that housed the soul consisted of about two hundred cells and measured perhaps a quarter of a millimeter in diameter. This tiny clump of cells lodged in Nat's body doubled in size every twelve hours and engaged in hectic activity. It secreted mucus that encased it and sheltered it from attack by Nat's immune system and then it sealed off the route to Nat's cervix with a mucus plug. Simultaneously it directed Nat's endometrium to thicken and the muscles of her uterine wall to soften and become more elastic. Blood vessels underneath the endometrium flocked toward the surface to transmit nutrients from Nat's body to the new life. The part of the blastocyst that would become the placenta commenced production of hCG (human chorionic gonadotropin) which notified the ovaries that Nat was pregnant and alerted them to stop ovulation, to stop menstruation and to produce progesterone.

Victor waited to hear from Nat for some time before he gave up and jumped in the shower to refresh himself and clear his head. That was just when Nat called, in between the museum and dinner. She was chagrined when no one answered. When Victor got out, he heard her.

"Hello, Victor. It's me. Hello . . . ? Pick up. Where are you? I thought you said you were staying in!" Nat's voice was followed by a click.

Victor called New York right back, but Nat was already gone. He listened to the phone ring five times. Then he heard Dora's voice, "You have reached 212-676-7767."

Obviously, this is the number I dialed.

"We are sorry that there is no one available to answer your call just now."

If someone were available, I wouldn't be listening to your long-winded speech.

"Please leave us a detailed message including your name, telephone number, the date and the time . . ."

Why don't you get a decent machine that announces the date and time?

". . . and we will return your call just as soon as possible. Thank you for thinking of us and have a very nice day."

Yeah, right, and you're welcome Dora.

"Hi Nat and everyone," Victor told his receiver. "Sorry I missed your call. To answer your question, Nat, I was in the shower. I guess you guys are out to dinner. You must have just left. Bye."

The unsatisfying exchanges with the voices of his wife and mother-in-law irritated Victor. His stomach and his heart were empty and he wanted something that would fill them up. He poked around in the refrigerator and discovered eggs, ham, cheese and asparagus. Thinking that an omelet would hit the spot, he put on some music and poured himself a glass of Chablis.

After dinner he felt better and sat down to do a little more work, but then when he looked at his notes, he couldn't concentrate. It was still much too early for bed, and he didn't feel like reading or watching television. What to do?

He decided he'd label photographs. He and Nat were photograph—not video—people. Neither of them had living grandparents and both were nostalgic over the past. They had each reorganized and made copies of their parents' slides and albums before they met. During their courtship, they spent some pleasant hours smiling over old images with young faces. Beginning with their marriage they memorialized details of their own lives. Now their plan was to go back through their parents' older photos and to write captions for them based on what they knew or could find out about their ancestors. It was an ambitious project that occupied a big armoire in their study.

Victor had fun identifying and dating old portraits and scenes of places visited years ago. These tasks occupied his mind yet left enough room in it for reflection. As he wrote, an insight flashed into his brain. Suddenly everything fell into place and Victor saw exactly what troubled Natalya—no, what troubled them both. Nat hungered for a baby, for a family, and it was high time he stopped fearing the child that deep down he knew he and Nat would have to make some day. His realization made him lighthearted. He wanted to jump to the telephone and leave Nat a message, but he restrained himself. He would wait until she came home and then they would talk.

When should they start making their child? Victor wondered. The best time for it to be born would be the summer after next when he wouldn't have classes. That would be best for Nat too. Lawyers could file vacation letters for the summer months. Things were quieter then and she could get a longer leave of absence. This was April. Nat could go off the pill in August or September. She would be thrilled. So would his parents.

"There's nothing in the world we want except grandchildren," his mother said every chance she got. "Except for that, our life is perfect, touch wood."

"Come on Rebecca, don't nag. Leave the kids alone," was invariably Dad's line.

"Why aren't you honest Henry? Don't you want grandchildren too? Don't you keep telling me about all our friends' grandchildren? Isn't that all they talk about?"

"Rebecca! First you bugged Victor about not getting married. He would never find anyone that suited him you said. You should thank God on your knees that he waited or you would never have been blessed with Natalya. Now you can't stop harping on grandchildren."

Good old Dad to the rescue, Victor thought. But in his father's eyes there was longing too.

"Please, Mom. Give me a break. I can't stand this." Victor's own voice echoed in his memory. "It's not my fault I have no brothers or sisters."

"What's not to stand? Who am I? Am I a stranger? No. I'm your mother. I'm no spring chicken and you aren't getting any younger either. What's the matter with my wanting a grandchild? Isn't it normal? Do you think that such a wish is not for people with college degrees? Do you understand something I don't with your Ph.D.? Tell me, how do you think I should feel? What would you like me to do to make you happy? Not care?"

Now his mother and father would dance with joy.

<hr>

Victor's newly awakened resolve coincided with Nat's realization that she was definitely pregnant. It hit her at Granada's as she watched her brother drinking from a leather pouch. Red wine poured into his throat from the air in a steady stream. Natalya rubbed her eyes. She was exhausted. She took out her compact and peeked at her own image. It looked different. She felt different. She marched to the beat of a new drummer. Only a baby could make changes like that. She would have been thrilled, but for her fear that Victor would reject her as well as their child. She had wanted to speak to her mother in the afternoon, but something had held her back. In the afternoon she didn't yet know for sure that she was pregnant. Now she did. Tonight she would have her talk. Her mother would help her figure out what to say to Victor.

Ronald had mastered the trick of swallowing without putting his lips to the container and without pausing for breath, in the style of Spanish shepherds. People at surrounding tables were clapping. Her father urged Nat to taste the excellent Cabernet he had ordered and Nat made feeble excuses for refusing a sip. Her mother had to say something to make her dad stop. Dad had been in high spirits all day. Love and fun had muted questions about absent spouses. The dinner was superb. All four ordered the specialty of the house, Paella Valenciana, made of saffron-flavored rice baked with meats, poultry and many varieties of seafood. The evening sped by, filled with music, the clicking of castanets and the stamping of feet. Most of all though, the evening was filled with a special sense of wonder.

"Should I come up to say good night, Nat?" Dora asked when they got home.
"Please."
"How would you like some chamomile or apricot tea?" Dora smiled.
"Well, maybe a cup of apricot with just a little honey. I haven't had it for ages."

"This tea tastes of home. It's different when I make it," Nat commented.
"I don't think so. It's just how you feel."
"I don't know. I think the taste of New York water, filled with sediment from pipes that are hundreds of years old comes through. Mommy, I came to New York because I had to talk to you."
"I know. You're pregnant. You have that look. Right?"
"I know I'm pregnant, but I'm not really sure. I mean I'm sure but I haven't taken the test yet. I'm so happy but I'm not really. I'm worried. I'm not making any sense, am I?"
"Yes, you are. You're making good sense to me. Tell me, what happened? Why are you worried?"
"I conceived this baby last Saturday." Natalya's eyes began to shine. They seemed to be filled with a mixture of joyous sparkle and tears. "I'm sure. I knew when it happened and I've felt different ever since then. I already love my baby so much."
"I know."

"Really, do you mean that?"

"Really."

"How could you know?"

"It's the way I felt when Harold and I started you and your brother. But why are you worried?"

"Because of Victor."

"I don't understand." Dora looked puzzled. "Do you have a problem? If you do, how can you be pregnant?"

"Well, we didn't have problems. But now we do. And Victor doesn't know about the baby."

"Obviously he doesn't know until you tell him, but it's great that you decided to have a baby. It's about time. It's wonderful!"

"No."

"No?"

"No. He doesn't want a baby. I went off the pill without telling him."

Dora struggled not to sound shocked. "What made you do a thing like that? It's not you."

"I don't know. It was just something. A compulsion." Nat wanted to cry, but she kept talking. "I don't know what got into me. I didn't worry about it and then last Saturday I felt this baby just landing like it was shooting down from heaven at the speed of light. Then I panicked, and Victor and I have been arguing ever since. So I came to New York. I asked Victor to come with me, but he wouldn't."

"I see." Dora said.

"What do you see? How can I tell this to Victor? I love him so much. I need him. Our child needs him. He's going to freak!" Nat threw her arms around her mother's neck and at last she began to weep.

After some time Dora rustled up a Kleenex from a pocket and handed it to her daughter. She waited for Natalya to wipe her eyes and blow her nose. Then she spoke.

"Victor doesn't freak," Dora told her daughter, "but I'm afraid he won't take this well."

"What should I do?"

"You know you'll have to make that decision by yourself. What are your options?"

"Theoretical options or practical options?" Nat asked.

"Let's say viable options."

"I guess there is no viable option besides telling him the truth."

"You weren't truthful when you went off the pill without telling him," Dora pointed out. "Why not go a little further and tell Victor that you forgot to take the pill?"

Natalya rubbed her eyes with her hands because the Kleenex was a crumpled wad. "I can't. Then I would be consciously lying and I couldn't face myself."

"You're right. You should tell Victor the truth. I know that's what Cecily and Ronald should do. Tell each other the truth." Dora sighed.

"I'm scared," Natalya confessed. "Our marriage is based on honesty and trust."

"Your marriage is based on natural selection, in other words sexual attraction."

"Mommy! You know what I mean. Our relationship is built upon honesty."

"Do you seriously think Victor could stop loving you over this?" Dora asked.

"I don't know." Nat's lip began to tremble, but now she held back her tears.

"I suspect Victor will come round," Dora told her daughter. "He may extract his pound of flesh, but in the end I think you both will find that there is much more to your love and marriage than complete honesty. Still, you know . . . "

"I know." Nat finished her mother's sentence. "Whatever happens, you and Daddy will always be here for me, and that's how it always is."

"Right. And that's how it always is."

5

Sunday, in Houston, Victor listened to music, read, and thought about Natalya. In New York during the morning, Nat, Ronald, Dora, and Harold chatted, smiled some, and laughed a little. When Ronald left for Paramus, about noon, his gait was lighter and he walked taller. Nat went for a short jog. On her way back she purchased an early pregnancy test kit and when she got home she confirmed that she was indeed pregnant. She told her mother to tell her father after dropping her off at Newark, but to ask him to keep the news under wraps until further notice. Then she spoke to Victor. She said she'd be in early, before 6:30, and started to think about getting ready to leave.

Victor made plans to take Nat to see the movie *Siddhartha*, which was playing in the Museum of Fine Arts. Nat's flight was smooth and she dozed through most of it. She landed in Houston right on schedule and she was pleased to drive straight to the museum from the airport. The movie was beautifully done, capturing not only the theme and plot but also the tone of Herman Hesse's novel. After the show, she and Victor had supper at Angelo's. They talked about the film.

"What part did you like best?" Victor asked.

"The part when Kamala told Siddhartha he needed to make money using his knowledge and asked him what he could do and Siddhartha said, 'I can think; I can wait; I can fast.'"

"Me too," Victor agreed. "I also liked the part where he watches his son leave, but it upset me."

"Me, too." Now Nat nodded. "That part made me cry."

"Let's focus on the happier part of the film when we get home," Victor whispered.

"Yes, Victor. But I'm far from an expert at the game of love. Kamala was a courtesan and I'm a lawyer.

"Oh, you are an expert all right. I don't know who taught you, but you are."

"I guess you did. You must have changed your field of expertise without telling me." Nat smiled, but just for a second, before she continued. "The truth is love is too important to be a game to me. Victor, I'm sorry I flew off without you. I missed you so."

"I missed you too, but I had a good weekend and, well . . . I want to talk to you seriously about ..."

"No, Victor. No serious talk now."

"Then when?"

"Soon."

Soon turned out to be a week after Nat returned from New York. It was a week during which she sought inner balance. She wondered what Victor had on his mind and she feared for what he would say about what was on hers. For the first time in her life Natalya felt a need to pray, but she didn't know how to go about it, so she just began holding dialogs with God. She asked Him or Her to please make Victor understand. Then she felt guilty about her request. Even though she had started thinking more about God, she couldn't say for sure if she believed in a universal power and even if she believed, wasn't it wrong not to give God a second thought until you were afraid or wanted something? At the same time, wasn't the very act of asking a sign of faith? If you prayed for something, it meant you thought on some level that God existed and had the power to grant your wish. That made sense, even though Nat wasn't completely sure it was right. The idea of God reminded Nat of the baby inside her. It was everywhere, not just in her womb. It was in her mind, in her heart and in her world. It was a miracle and it proved that God was real.

Things at the office were tense. Over the weekend one of Kaplan, McCall, and Green's bright new associates, Steve Jordan, had inexplicably disappeared. Nat was used to crises, but this one had a nerve-racking spin to it. Still Nat held her own, notwithstanding the fact that she was starting to feel sick in the mornings. She tried to track Steve down and she picked up the balls he had dropped in his wake. On Wednesday, he phoned from Mexico. He said he was in Cozumel, he'd had it and he wasn't coming back. When Nat reported this to her colleagues they seemed disinterested. Meanwhile in the Parkway Plaza case, Alpha National Bank was getting a second wind. After making settlement overtures that were nothing to get excited over, ANB figured it might not be in serious trouble after all if it sacrificed Mr. Courtney. Nat had several meetings with her firm's litigation department to map out trial strategy in light of this development. She had to put in long hours.

Natalya discovered that resting at her desk with her eyes closed energized her and helped her cope with the pressure that was building. If she sat quietly without thinking for only ten or fifteen minutes, she would get a spurt of pep that lasted for hours. At those times she looked inward and felt happy and in touch with her baby and she trusted that the world had to be more than a conglomeration of random coincidences.

⁂

Victor had a busy week too. University politics disrupted his work. He wanted Linda's help and the Business School's endorsement of his course in Logical Communication, but at the same time he decided that he didn't want to teach in the Business School after all. He determined to uphold his conviction that communication and language were as squarely in the province of English as was his class in Philosophical Literature. To the extent that the subject of communication reached out beyond English, it incorporated science, psychology, and philosophy more than it did business. Business was merely an application of his teaching. Victor argued with the dean of the Business School.

"Your students can learn how to interact in the business world from my communication courses, but business concepts do not contribute anything to my theories."

"I'm sorry." Dean Whittaker shook his head. "We cannot justify giving credit to the students for courses taught by the English Department."

"This is going to present a problem."

"Why?"

"I cannot in good conscience pretend that communication is a business course."

"Your empirical studies are in the business arena."

"That's true. At this stage I am working with data derived from business applications. But the theories and the teachings are part of English."

"Can you propose any solutions?" the Dean asked.

"Perhaps," Victor answered, "if we cut the bullshit."

"What bullshit?"

"Pretending that this is about something other than grants. You want the grants I generate to come to the Business School."

"And you want them to go to the English Department."

"I am a professor of English. I have a contribution to make to your students, not vice versa. What I want is to work with people like Linda Michaels who can gather and analyze data, but I cannot teach a business course."

"Well, Dr. Landa . . ."

"Please, call me Victor."

"Yes, if you address me as Paul instead of Dean Whittaker."

"Thank you. I didn't mean to interrupt. You were saying?"

"I was saying let's not burn any bridges. There should be a way to work this out."

"Of course." Victor was happy that he had won this round of chicken, but he realized that if he wanted Linda and more exposure in the business world, he'd have to make some concessions. He'd talk to his chairman and take it from there. "Why don't we both give this more thought?"

Saturday night the Landaus went out with Annette and David Singer. Sunil and Jaya were traveling, attending yet another wedding. The foursome started off at their favorite Mexican restaurant, Conchita's. Later they were going to The Sit Up, a new comedy club that everyone had been raving about. At dinner, Nat had a worrisome moment because Victor couldn't understand why she wouldn't have a Margarita, her all time favorite. Nat had decided to tell Victor about the baby Sunday morning and she didn't want to say anything before that. She was glad that he hadn't noticed anything different about her so far. Well, actually he had. Yesterday he told her that he felt as if they were not alone during their love making, but he made a joke of it. Thinking quickly, Nat said she had put on a little weight and decided to cut back on alcohol and sweets.

"Don't I look like I gained a little weight?"

"No, not really," Annette said. "Well, maybe you do look just a little rounder, but it's flattering."

In the course of conversation and in between discussing dinner options, Nat was taken aback to hear Victor ask David, "Remember when at my party you said you wondered about the wisdom of bringing a child into the world until you had a sense of your own self?"

"Yeah, sort of," David replied.

"What did you mean?"

"I think it's wrong to have a child when you aren't complete and satisfied in your own mind. People shouldn't get married or have kids to fill a hole in their hearts."

"Is that a personal statement or a general one?"

"It's very personal." Annette jumped into the fray. "David thinks I want a child to feel fulfilled and I shouldn't have a baby for that purpose."

"That makes sense, doesn't it?" David asked.

"Not for women." Now Natalya had to voice her opinion. "I think most women are programmed for nurturing. We don't feel whole without a child. On the other hand, most men must feel secure and complete before they are brave enough to have one."

"God help you, Victor," David said. "Your wife's mind is like a vise. How can you ever win an argument with her?" He turned to Nat and continued. "Is that what legal thinking does to you?"

"It's not my legal thinking. It's Victor's persuasive communication speaking." Nat quickly turned her attention to the menu, hoping to quash the subject of children. However, she couldn't help wondering if maybe, just maybe, their baby was putting ideas in Victor's head.

Victor felt good. He looked at his wife and thought she was beautiful. Tomorrow at brunch he would tell her he was ready to make her dream come true. The timing he planned on was perfect. This summer, before Nat got pregnant, they would take a splendid vacation, somewhere far away. Nat was right, a man had to be whole to be a father. And over one weekend, that is what he had become, a whole person. He was a lucky person too, lucky to have a wife like Natalya who trusted him to do the right thing. That moment, Victor silently vowed he would never betray her trust.

The dinners—barbecued baby pork, chiles rellenos, baked snapper Veracruzana, and enchiladas—were all excellent and they put an end to further thought-provoking talk. Instead, Victor led the conversation toward places they might like to visit some day: the Serengeti, Nepal, China, and Rio. By the time the small group got to The Sit Up, everyone was ready to laugh. The place was packed, and with good reason. The show was great. The first act was about a woman at a séance talking to her recently deceased husband.

"Malcolm, Malcolm, do you hear me? Do you hear me?" asked the widow.

"I hear you Evelyn." Malcolm's spirit wheezed. "Do you hear me?"

"I hear you. But your voice is different. It's higher."

"It has thinned out over here."

"How are you, Malcolm?"

"I am very well. How are you, Evelyn?"

"I am lonely. Are you lonely?"

"No, Evelyn. I am not lonely here."

"What do you do all day, Malcolm?"

"I do the same thing every day."

"And what is that, Malcolm?"

"We all do the same thing every day."

"What do you do?"

"I eat a little, and then I have sex. Then I eat a little and I have sex again. Then I rest and have sex again. Then I eat again because I'm hungry, and then I have more sex. That's all I do every day."

"Gosh, Malcolm. I didn't realize heaven was like that!"

"Who said anything about heaven? I'm a rabbit in Australia."

Sunday morning the blastocyst was apprehensive. At two weeks anything could go awry. Through the week it felt content, sensing its parents' love for it and for one another. But now there was electricity in the air. So it huddled inside the watertight sac that was beginning to surround it. The liquid cushioned the blastocyst from physical shocks, but at the same time it amplified the currents and noises swirling outside. Thus the tiny being, barely the size of a pencil dot and shaped somewhat like a microscopic mango, registered both Natalya's anxiety and Victor's excitement.

Natalya was determined to be the first one up this particular Sunday. She had decided to make a brunch that would be the marvel of all brunches. After considerable vacillation she settled on lobster quiche, fruit salad, cappuccinos, and lemon tarts. She had kept all the ingredients ready to go. Thus, when the travel alarm that she buried under her pillow beeped, she quickly shut it off and jumped out of bed. Overcoming a wave of nausea, she freshened up and ate some dry Cheerios. Then she went to work. Forty-five minutes later she was ready and entered the bedroom wheeling a trolley with beautifully arranged trays. On Victor's tray Nat had placed a red rose in a tube. Victor was already wide awake. He was sitting up and looked disappointed.

"You beat me to it," he said. "No fair using an alarm."

"I had to. Otherwise, this would be the third Sunday in a row I didn't get a turn."

"But I had something special planned along with the something special I wanted to talk to you about."

"I have something important to say as well, Victor, but I don't know how to say it."

"Why don't you let me begin. I've been waiting to tell you for a whole week. I think after you hear me, nothing else will matter."

"Well, OK." Nat looked worried. Victor wondered why.

"I came to an important realization last weekend," Victor cleared his throat, "that I think will please you. I am not an impetuous man, but when I make a commitment, I make it in earnest, and I am about to make a big one now. That is, if you agree, we are about to make a commitment that will change our whole lives."

"Victor . . ."

"Don't say anything. Just listen, or I may lose my resolve. No, I won't lose it, but I don't want you to say anything until I'm finished. I have decided that we are ready to have a child. That is, I am finally ready. You have been ready for a while, just like you said to David and Annette last night. But now I am ready too and I want to have a baby with you, Natalya. I want you to be the mother of my child. I have thought about this very carefully and decided that we should start in September. That way the baby can be born next summer when I have no classes. You know how we were talking about places to go? Well this summer we can take two weeks and have a wonderful holiday, sort of a farewell to carefree independence, and then we can settle down and get ready for the rest of our lives as parents. I am nervous, don't think I'm not, but I'm ready because like you said I'm whole."

Nat paled and her eyes welled with tears. "Why are you crying?" Victor asked. "Aren't you thrilled?"

Nat couldn't answer. Instead she asked, "When did you decide all this?"

"Saturday night, while I was working on the photo album it just came to me, like a flash of lightning. It came to me and then I thought of you and I thought of how much my parents needed for us to have a baby. I realized that I couldn't just live for myself. I had to be a mensch and consider you and my parents and the baby that we must have. What's the matter? This is one of your happy cries, isn't it?"

"Victor, you haven't had a bite of quiche. It's getting cold."

"Neither have you."

"OK, I'll have a little. You eat some too. How do you like it?"

"Nat, it's wonderful. It's the best quiche I've ever had."

"Do you really like it? You don't agree with that book about real men not eating quiche?"

"Don't be ridiculous. I love quiche. But why are you still crying? What do you think? What were you going to tell me?"

"I'll tell you. But promise you won't get angry?"

"How can I get angry? I never get angry."

"Victor, I'm pregnant."

"What?"

"I'm pregnant."

"You can't be pregnant!"

"Well, I am."

"Are you saying that you forgot to take the pill and that the baby you and I are having is a mistake? An oversight? I don't want a baby that's a mistake!"

"It's not a mistake."

"What are you telling me Nat? How can you be pregnant with a baby that we haven't planned on?"

"I went off the pill."

"You went off the pill? Without telling me? You thought you would trick me into having a baby? You, the great Natalya Rosenbaum Landau, the woman of integrity I married because I trusted her with my life, decided to cheat on me and to make me have a baby I never agreed to?"

"Please Victor. I didn't think of it that way."

"What way did you think of it?"

"Differently. At first I just thought that if the baby were here, you couldn't help but love it. Then I forgot because nothing happened. And then, I got scared."

"This isn't my baby."

"Of course it's yours, Victor. Whose is it if it isn't yours?"

"I don't know, but it can't be mine. My baby is the child I choose to have. Have you heard of choice? Fathers have a right to choose whether or not they want a child, and I choose no. So it's not my baby!"

"Don't talk like that. The baby will be upset."

"Are you cuckoo? The baby is just a speck. It can't be upset."

"It can too. I can tell."

Natalya was right. The blastocyst was distraught. It was jarred by the harshness of Victor's rejection. It wondered whether the tenderness that Victor had felt earlier was really gone, or whether it was just buried under his anger. If it was gone, the blastocyst would have a tough time. It could become damaged or even lose these parents that it had selected with such care and fought so hard to catch. If it lost them, it would lose itself too. That possibility made it cringe. But then it heard Victor's love. You really had to listen hard to hear it, because his anger was so loud.

"Don't tell me the baby, I mean the speck, is upset!" Victor's voice was harsh. "You tricked me into fatherhood. You probably tricked me into marrying you. I wish I knew how you did it. Here's what I do know though. I know I don't respect you. You have to have what you want. You'll do whatever it takes."

"But Victor, you just said you wanted a baby."

"Yes, I did. That was before I realized I was married to a person who didn't trust me to come around and do the right thing. Now I don't trust you. You're not the person I thought you were. Not at all. I married someone I thought was truthful and honest. Now I find out that you are neither of those things. You're lying when you say you can tell the baby is upset."

Nat was pale and shaking. "I just wanted our baby and I thought that if you knew I was pregnant you would accept it and you wouldn't be able to help loving it."

"You thought wrong."

"But you did accept it. You told me you were ready to have a baby. The baby made you change your mind."

"Nobody made me change my mind. I wanted us to have a baby because I felt we were ready. That was before I realized you were deceitful and selfish. I can't believe you figured you could manipulate me like this."

"I think you're just mad because I stole your thunder. Here you wanted us to have a baby, and I beat you to it."

"That's absurd. I'm mad because you tricked me."

"I didn't realize I was tricking you when I went off the pill. I just felt a compulsion to do it. Please believe me."

"Sure, I believe you, but it doesn't change anything. You are what you are, and that's a liar."

"What are you going to do?"

"I don't know."

"Please Victor, tell me. What are you going to do?"

Victor spoke softly this time, but his voice chilled like a cold wind. "I already answered you Natalya. I don't know. I haven't a clue. When I decide, I'll inform you. Or maybe I won't. Maybe I'll lie. Wait and see."

6

The blastocyst weathered the storm that brewed with increasing fury between Natalya and Victor fairly well. It sought and found the eye of the conflict where there was no turbulence and it took shelter there. And from this vantage point it emitted a powerful positive force. Thus it attained the age of three weeks and the status of an embryo that measured all of two millimeters in length.

The tiny embryo was industrious as well as sensitive. It was in a perpetual state of growth and its genes were hard at work distinguishing the cells that would become its organs. The outer germ or cell layer formed a neural tube that would soon develop into outer skin, spinal cord, and brain. Nerve cells already stemmed from the swelling that was the beginning of its brain. The central layer of cells began to form themselves into bones, heart, and other muscles and into the deeper skin. Blood, lymph vessels, kidneys, and ovaries or testicles would develop from this central germ layer at the same time as the embryo's lungs, intestinal tube and urinary tract would start to form from the innermost stratum of cells. The embryo coordinated all these developments in a systematic manner, using checks and double checks to ensure an orderly and flawless progression.

Meanwhile, Natalya and Victor became warriors in a battle that neither one wanted to fight and neither one could win. How else could they cope with their anger and their pain? At first it seemed that Victor would suffer the fewest wounds because he was better armed. His weapons were silence and rage. However, Natalya had the stronger defense. She shielded herself with inner peace and resilience. Victor's fury burned the guilt that had weighed heavily on her soul and, freed of that burden, she gathered strength. She persisted in her conviction that it was their child who had pierced Victor's heart to prepare him for fatherhood and she absolved herself from having conceived without consulting her husband. It was a thing she had done mindlessly as if forces outside of her had compelled it. Victor was equally guilty, she decided, for shutting her out every time she tried to tell him how she felt.

Victor found no relief whatsoever. He was unable to talk with anyone about the baby. He was unsure about what to do. His blinding anger at Natalya weakened him at the same time that his love for his child kept tugging at his heart. He wondered about the baby and started to worry that maybe Nat was right about its being capable of feeling upset, but then he convinced himself of the absurdity of an idea like that. He refused to question Nat about how she felt or to inquire about her plans. He spoke only when necessary, he buried himself in his work, and he became increasingly miserable. He wondered with whom Nat had shared the news of her pregnancy, but he didn't ask. Finally he fell ill with an intestinal flu. The fever, headaches, and upset stomach were a blessing. They enabled him to suffer in peace.

Nat dissipated some of the tension that pervaded her home with music and flowers. She worked hard, reread her favorite childhood books, and did low impact exercise regularly. She ate frequently and lightly and managed to keep nausea at bay. She slept more and was content to spend time alone. She held herself together, except for empty Sunday mornings when she wept in secret. She made a conscious effort to deflect the missiles of anger that Victor fired at her from his sick bed without physically distancing herself and was somewhat successful. She wanted to sleep in the den but resisted, thinking that it was Victor's place to remove himself if he so desired, and instead, she gargled and took vitamins to prevent catching his bug.

She talked to her baby without words and sang without making a sound. And she listened and heard that the embryo was fine. It was incessantly seeking to balance stability and change, and it was happiest when Nat relaxed. It also knew when Victor thought about it, and it tried to let him know that it was glad its father cared. Victor got the messages, but they confused him. He didn't want to believe that embryo was more than a speck or blob devoid of sensation, but he was puzzled and disturbed by his involvement with it. For some reason, this involuntary preoccupation made him angrier than ever with his wife. He sneaked a peek at her and was annoyed that Nat looked more beautiful than ever. She was a turn on. Sick as he was, he was tense with need and wanted her for relief, but he wouldn't touch her. What a mess!

Victor recovered from his illness and returned to his duties with a burst of frenetic energy. Now he staved off invitations and inquiries by explaining how his illness got him behind in his work. He sounded like a broken record and hoped that what he was saying wouldn't be contradicted by anything Nat said or did. The phone rang. He screened calls. He returned messages that couldn't be ignored and sometimes ran into a human being at the other end of the phone: "Yes, he was much better." "Yes, Nat was fine. No, she didn't catch anything from him. Talk to ya." "There was a virus going around. Sure. Ciao." "Sorry we can't make your dinner." "I'm inundated. I can't see my desk under the papers. Sorry we can't make it. Maybe next week. Bye."

Dealing with Rebecca Landau was tougher. His mother wouldn't leave him alone. Why did she have to torture him?
"Yes, Mom. I'm fine now."
"You sound upset."
"No, I'm not upset."
"Something is wrong. I can tell."
"No. Nothing is wrong."
"I have a feeling that something is happening."
"I can't help it if you have a feeling."

"Nat hasn't returned my calls. That's not like her. Why?"

"Please, Mom. I don't know why Nat hasn't returned your calls. I'll ask her to call you."

"I miss you."

"Mom, I can't help it. I'm really swamped."

"I think Nat is going to have a baby."

"Mom, I gotta go."

Rebecca Landau had started thinking about her grandchild very soon after it was conceived, but she held off saying anything for a long time. She tried to put her finger on what it was that had triggered her feeling, but she couldn't actually pinpoint its source. Maybe it was the tone in which Victor and Nat spoke to her over the weeks. Maybe it was something about Henry. Perhaps it was a forgotten dream. When she spoke to Victor, she hadn't intended to blurt out her thoughts like that, but the words spilled out of her mouth. She was as stunned as Victor to hear them uttered.

The embryo was glad to be acknowledged. It was already four weeks old and six millimeters in length. Its heart had begun pumping blood and it had sprouted tiny buds that would become its hands and feet. Its consciousness was more focused. It wanted to be discussed.

⸺ ⬤⬤⬤⬤ ⬤ ⬤⬤⬤⬤ ⸺

Victor spoke with his department and had several meetings with Dean Paul Whittaker. Finally it was decided that in the fall Victor and Dr. Jack Burgess of Marketing would teach a joint course in Persuasive Marketing for which business credit would be issued, and that in the spring semester, Victor would offer a course in Commercially Logical Communication. This would put pressure on him over the summer, but what the hell; he and Nat certainly wouldn't be taking any fancy vacations now. Paul endorsed Linda's Ph.D. research on 'Logic in Advertising' and agreed Victor could be her primary advisor as long as Dr. Burgess was satisfied with the empirical data. Linda was thrilled that Victor went to bat for her. She was in awe of Dr. Landau. He was everything she looked up to and incredibly attractive. But since he appeared to be happily married, she resigned herself to the role of an admiring disciple.

Neither the ongoing war between Victor and Nat nor their baby interfered with their professional lives, though it was becoming increasingly difficult to keep either matter secret. The Rosenbaums had an idea that things were not too good, but Nat played down her troubles. The Landaus, though, had their receptors finely tuned, and it looked like the egg would soon hit the fan as far as they were concerned. Friends also began to wonder and ask questions. Sooner rather than later something was going to give.

So far, the passing of time had done little to crystallize Victor's thought process. His ambivalent feelings intensified. Much as he tried, he could not fathom the reason for Nat's conduct, conduct he could not see as anything less than a betrayal. If Nat truly loved and trusted him, how could she exclude him from the most important decision she had ever made in her married life, a decision which involved him to the core and which transformed the very fiber of their relationship? Victor asked himself that question over and over again, but he never got the right answer. He completely forgot that every time she had brought up the issue of children, he had avoided it. He forgot that he had said "Let's not talk about this now" too many times and that he had never committed to a time when discussions about starting a family would be welcome, or even possible. He was convinced that sooner or later he would have changed his mind, if only Nat had been patient. The last thing he believed was that the baby inside Nat was what had caused him to take an about turn. Victor's self righteous fury was all he had to cling to, and cling to it he did. But fury did nothing to ease his discomfort every time he stared at Nat, unable to stop wanting to touch her, to feel her and to push himself inside her body. He thought that he would like to rape her and cause her pain, but he couldn't because he knew the minute he approached her, her juices would flow and her taste would be sweeter than honey and there would be no pain and he would have no revenge.

To minimize interaction with Nat, Victor stopped bringing work home and spent most of his evenings in the library or in his office. He left the university in the late afternoon, went for a jog or a quick workout, came home briefly to shower while Nat was still at work and then went out for dinner before going back. Sometimes he stopped at his favorite cafeteria. Other times he did fast food takeout or picked up a salad and sandwich at the university coffee shop. At first Victor was lonely, but then a couple of times he ran into Linda at the coffee shop or the English Center. Linda was fun. Around her, Victor could enjoy himself, become excited about his research, and forget all about Natalya, his mother, and the embryo. He really was pressed to prepare for the new courses he would be teaching while keeping up with his demanding schedule. If he let his productivity wane, he would have a whole new set of problems. Staying productive was the one thing he could control.

Linda was surprised by the shift in Victor's routine and in his state of mind. Almost without realizing what she was up to, she campaigned to attract him with a mixture of admiration, intellectual camaraderie, and feminine wile.

"What do you think, Dr. Landau?" she asked one evening, running her hand through her rich brown hair. "Are you convinced that logic can be a content neutral discipline, or does it have to be grounded in valid concepts?"

"There are several schools of thought. Theoretically, logic is a system of reasoning which can be followed, even given empty premises. However, to reach meaningful conclusions we need valid premises."

"What if we are uncertain about the truth or validity of a premise?"

"Then we have to work on assumptions. After all, a premise is an assumption."

"So logic can be content neutral?"

"It depends. For our purposes we need to demonstrate that our premises are valid. Linda, would you do me a great favor?"

"Of course, Dr. Landau. Anything you say."

"Please call me Victor. You are making me feel old."

"Oh, I couldn't. I respect you too much."

"Well, then I'll have to call you Ms. Michaels. After all, you are a scholar in your own right. In no time you'll be Dr. Michaels. If you won't call me Victor, you must think I'm an old fogy."

"Oh, no! Not at all! You are a perfect age for a man. Experienced enough to trust and admire, and young enough to be full of vigor. All right. I'll say it. Victor, you are a perfect age."

"Linda, you are a beautiful girl. You are bright and sensitive and I appreciate your work. If I were free and a few years younger, I'd make a pass at you."

"Dr. Landau, I mean Victor, I am free and I am only a few years younger than you are, so why don't I make the pass instead?"

"That would be highly improper."

"I love impropriety. Impropriety is my favorite thing." As she spoke, Linda moved to the door of Victor's office and bolted it shut. Then she edged closer to Victor and looked him in the eye. "I'll make a deal with you. I'll stand here and talk to you. I won't move at all. I'll keep on all my clothes." Linda wet her lips with her tongue. "If I see that you want me too, I'll let you kiss me and we'll take it from there. So all you have to do is listen to me for a bit."

"No, Linda. Please! Unlock the door. This isn't right."

"It's right for me. If it isn't right for you, nothing will happen."

"That's not how it works, Linda. Please leave."

"I'm not doing anything, Victor. Look, I'm just standing here wishing the same wish I've been wishing for the last two months. The wish that Dr. Landau would like my work and that because he liked my work he would like me too. That he would hold my hand and draw me to him. That he would press his lips against mine. That he would hold me close. That he would long to see my breasts and that when he saw them he would want to touch them and kiss them. That he would like them enough to want the rest of me. All of me. That he would show me how it feels to be loved by a man. I've only been loved by one person in my life, Victor, and he was a boy. I was a girl. I want a man to make me feel like a woman. The man I want is Victor Landau. Just once is all I ask."

"Damn it, Linda! What are you doing?"

"I'm not doing anything. I'm just telling you what I dream about, and watching you. See? You are looking down at yourself. Now I'm going to make you kiss me."

"I can't, Linda."

"Oh?" Linda took two steps and put Victor's arms around her as she stroked and stood on tiptoes so her mouth would be level with his. Pent up sexual tension made Victor helpless. He returned Linda's kiss and put his hands under her dress. He felt her breasts unfettered by a bra and her stomach and her taut little butt barely covered by a silky strip. Then he pulled away, confused and afraid he would lose control. Linda pulled back too, for another reason. She was unprepared and wanted to run to the bathroom where there was a condom dispenser. This was awkward. She should have gotten the condom before she started fooling around. But everything was so sudden and unexpected. What to do?

"Victor, would you promise not to move? I want to run down the hall. I'll be right back." Before he could answer, she was gone. Victor tried to collect himself and make a conscious decision about what to do next, but his brain froze.

At home, Nat had a headache. It had been building all day. She didn't want to take any medicine, because it wouldn't be good for the baby, but finally she gave in and took Tylenol. She was lying down with a cool cloth on her head and her eyes closed, listening to Brahms and picturing her child and feeling what it was thinking and doing. The embryo, growing at the rate of a millimeter a day and developing moment by moment, was ill at ease. It felt a sympathetic pain in its head as it pondered its father's behavior and tried to mold his thoughts.

Only seven days ago, about five weeks after embodiment, the embryo had measured a single centimeter and its large head was bent forward. Now at six weeks it was over a centimeter and a half long and its head had already straightened up. Its eyes, nose, and mouth were taking shape as well. Its hands with budding fingers were attached to short arms, and rudimentary feet were attached to tiny legs. Its skin was beginning to become downy. The placenta nourished it and filtered waste via the umbilical cord while the embryo's tiny heart fluttered at the rate of about 145 beats a minute. As it began to assume the physical attributes of a human being, its memory of human experiences surfaced and triggered recognition of familiar sensations. Brahms was a familiar sound; a headache was a familiar pain; cool was a familiar feel; thinking was a familiar process; and loving was a familiar emotion. The memories awakened the embryo's consciousness. Nat's consciousness was sharp as well. But this night Victor's consciousness was dulled.

Linda was gone from the room for less than four minutes and when she returned, she was relieved to find that Victor hadn't budged. Nor did he protest when she approached him again, fondling and caressing. Functioning on autopilot, he helped her off with her dress and underwear and allowed her to remove his shirt and unbuckle his belt. Without thought or emotion, he kissed Linda deeply. He responded to her caresses, feeding his hunger with the taste of her, healing his pain with the feel of her, and fighting his battle against Natalya with the encouragement she gave him. He kept on kissing while she stroked him and when she encased him in the condom she brought, he wanted to touch her moistness and he slid his fingers between her legs. For a while they embraced noiselessly in the middle of his brightly lit office, the only sound coming from the hum of his computer. Then Victor sat in his chair and pulled Linda toward him so she could comfortably straddle him. That instant, Victor's eyes met Nat's, gazing at him out of the snapshot on his desk. A second pair of eyes was hidden within Nat's and they penetrated his soul. Victor couldn't go on. He didn't want to go on, so he lifted Linda up and turned away to dress himself. When he was finished, he saw that Linda was dressed too and that tears welled in her eyes. He didn't know what to do, so he spoke the simple truth.

"I'm sorry, but this would have been wrong. It was terribly wrong. You are so beautiful and so refreshing that I forgot myself. Forgive me."

Linda tried to smile, but she couldn't. She walked out without saying a word.

7

During the days following the Linda incident, Victor felt like a displaced person. He was no longer at ease in any physical space; there was no environment where functioned well. The university became uncomfortable. He was embarrassed around Linda even though he appreciated how she kept her cool. She said nothing but instead put their relationship back on the professional footing that had worked so smoothly, until . . . the fiasco. Linda seemed to be able to place the event in perspective, but she had to be upset. It all preyed on Victor's mind and made him want to flee.

At home, things were just as bad. Guilt hammered him over the head. Victor tried to justify his actions to himself, but failed miserably. He became a victim of his own questions. What kind of a person could do what he did? Where was his dignity? How could he continue to be mad at Natalya given his base behavior? It dawned on him that he wasn't even indignant any longer, but he didn't know what to do. For lack of a better plan, he reinforced the wall of silence he had built in his anger and cowered behind it to brood. Then he drilled a tiny peephole so he could get glimpses of his wife and child. What he saw was a growing detachment that frightened him far more than his rage had frightened them.

Nat saw that Victor was no longer making himself scarce and was no longer emitting ballistic vibrations. He had put down his sword and picked up a shield. Sheepishness replaced anger. Possibilities that might account for this change flew through her mind and the name Linda crash landed. Natalyla didn't want to know what was happening. She braced herself not to care.

The embryo, now seven weeks old, also noticed the new climate. Its powerful brain was starting to form concepts and to process sensations, using memories as a database. It worked furiously even as it developed with lightening speed, producing about one hundred thousand new nerve cells every minute. By birth it would have around a hundred billion of them. These cells grew projections that reached out toward one another and tried to touch and to communicate. Some were already connected and had begun to interact. Yet each minuscule nerve cell was a universe in itself.

One Tuesday evening, Natalya had just finished up some interrogatories when Jaya called. Nat resolved that it was time to stop evading her friends and she picked up the phone. Victor was in the shower.

"Hi, Jaya. It's good to hear your voice. Sorry I didn't return your calls, but I just wasn't up to it."

"Hi yourself. I was going to leave you one last message before I came pounding on your door. What's going on?"

"Lots, but I can't talk much. To make a long story short, I decided to come out of hiding."

"Is there anything I can do for you?"

"No, Jaya, not really, except, well, could we get together for brunch Sunday?"

"Absolutely, but I thought Sunday mornings were sacred for you and Victor."

"Not these days. Tell me, how have you been?"

"Not great either, but this isn't a good time to start in with my own problems. We'll talk Sunday."

"Are you sure?" Nat asked.

"Absolutely. By the way, Annette is concerned about you too. She said David called Victor to ask him how things were, but you know guys. They're a dead end. Shall I ask Annette to join us?"

"That would be great. Do you need anything? You don't have a legal problem, do you?"

"No, nothing like that. At least not yet."

"What do you mean, not yet?"

"That was a bad joke, Nat. I just need friendly advice."

"I hope that at least Annette is fine."

"Some stuff is going on with her too, but it'll work out."

"Should I call her?"

"No. That's OK," Jaya said. "I'll tell her we talked. We'll all have a long brunch Sunday. I'll coordinate."

"Thanks a million. Give her my love. I've been so wrapped up in myself; I never stopped to think about anyone else. I'm ashamed of myself."

"Don't be. It's a waste of energy. My messages were vague. You had no reason to think you had to answer promptly. I was just worried because you're usually so quick to get back to everyone. Take care."

"You too. See you."

"OK, lots of love. Bye."

Victor was getting lonelier and lonelier behind the barrier he had built. Now he wanted to climb over it and get out. He mulled things over and over and finally decided to surprise Nat with brunch Sunday morning. He didn't know what he would say or how she would react, but he had some ideas and he hoped that he would find the right language to break the ice. After all, communication was supposed to be his forte.

About nine thirty on Sunday morning, the sound of Nat getting dressed woke Victor up. She looked like she was going somewhere, not to the office, but not for a jog or to the gym either. She was taking care with her appearance and she seemed upbeat. Indeed, Nat was looking forward to meeting her friends and opening her heart to them at last. She was determined not to let speculation about Victor dampen her spirits. The baby needed her to be happy. Ultimately, either things would get resolved, or they wouldn't.

Victor was perplexed and disappointed, but there was nothing he could do, so he stayed quietly in bed and waited for Nat to leave. As she was about to walk out the door, the phone rang. It was the senior Mrs. Landau. Neither Nat nor Victor picked up, but they both heard her message:

"Hi, Victor and Nat. I know you don't pick up the phone on Sunday morning, even if you are home, but please call back this time. Your father and I are worried. We know Victor leaves communicating with us to Nat, but this time the two of you are giving us the silent treatment. Bye."

Nat felt badly for Rebecca Landau. She was shocked that Victor hadn't called her. He owed her that much. Nat made up her mind to phone as soon as she got back from brunch. Inside Nat's womb, the baby's heartbeat accelerated for a bit and then resumed its normal rhythm.

It was just five minutes past ten when Nat walked into the small Cantonese dumpling house that Jaya had picked for brunch. She and Annette were already there and the waiter was serving tea. "Hello. This is a great idea. I love dim sum. And they let you sit around forever in this place. Hey, I'm sorry I've been incommunicado for so long. How are you?"

"We're OK and OK, not great, but OK. The real question is how are you." Annette didn't mention the fact that Natalya's diet obviously wasn't working.

"I'm OK too." She looked from Jaya to Annette and back to Jaya. "How come you're both wearing mauve?"

"Coincidence," Jaya explained. "So, sit down and tell us why you've been playing hide and seek."

"I was going to wear a mauve shell but then I put on this mint colored thing instead." Nat settled herself in her chair and accepted a glass of pineapple juice. "Before I get started, tell me. How long do we have? Do either of you have any time constraints?"

"Not really," Jaya said. "We're having some people from Sunil's office for dinner, but I finished most of the cooking so I don't have to get back until two-thirty, latest three o'clock."

"I'm totally free," Annette said. "Actually, I was thinking of seeing a movie this afternoon. Will you come with me, Nat?"

"What do you want to see?"

"*The Seven Capital Sins.* It's an English remake of an old French film."

"That sounds like fun. I worked over sixty hours this week. I could use a break."

"So," Jaya began, "what has been happening in your life that you haven't shared? Should we worry?"

"Yes and no. I'm pregnant."

"So that's what it is! Annette and I thought you might be, but then we decided it was the one thing you would tell us right away. How come you haven't said anything for so long?"

"It's complicated," Nat answered and once she started, she spoke for over thirty minutes. She told her friends how she had gone off the pill, how she was sure she conceived the night of Victor's birthday which they had all celebrated together, and how Victor had announced his decision to have a baby a year or so down the road. Then she talked about Victor's anger, about the latest change in his behavior and about the embryo who helped her keep body and soul together. She said she sang to it and spoke to it and it was teaching her about God. "I've stopped feeling remorseful and miserable," she concluded, "and I'm prepared for whatever happens."

"Have you been to the doctor yet?" Annette asked.

"No, but I'm going this week."

"Why do you think Victor is suddenly home all the time if he won't talk to you?" Jaya asked.

"I don't know," Nat answered. "I think he either has done something or plans to do something definitive about the situation and he is figuring out how to tell me."

"Such as?" Jaya asked.

"Such as having an affair, or maybe even negotiating a divorce."

"That doesn't make sense," Annette said. "If he were doing either of those things, he wouldn't be hanging around so much. He would stay away. The only thing that makes sense is that he already did something he regrets. The question is what and with whom."

"With Linda, his new grad assistant." Nat's eyes glared—they were at their greenest.

"Then why has it stopped?" Annette asked.

"Who knows," Nat answered. "Maybe Linda dumped Victor. Maybe she gave him an ultimatum. Maybe it hasn't stopped at all. Maybe he's taking time out."

"Taking time out is what men do for three quarters of their lives," Jaya interjected.

"Well, sooner or later I'll know. I'm sure that Dr. Victor 'I cannot tell a lie but I screw around' Landau will inform me when he's good and ready.

"If that's it," Jaya went on, "I mean if Victor admits he was fooling around with Linda and he's sorry and he wants to make up, what will you do?"

"Fooling around or screwing around?" Nat asked.

"Actually," Annette said, "a pretty fine line separates one from the other."

"Sometimes there's almost no line at all," Jaya added.

"I don't know. I can't speculate. I guess it depends on how the baby and I feel. But enough about my problems. You said something on Tuesday, Jaya. What is happening with you?"

"Nothing critical, actually, at least not yet."

"What isn't critical yet?" Nat asked.

"Well, Sunil has been really pressuring me to have a child, especially after Victor's birthday party, and we ended up having a couple of horrible fights. So what does Sunil do? He goes and complains about me to his mother. I understand that Indian families are more involved than American families and all that, but this is going too far. After all Sunil and I were both brought up in the United States with certain expectations of privacy. Even in India there are boundaries. So I think we're entitled to fight without my mother-in-law having to know every detail of what's going on. Unfortunately, Sunil doesn't agree with me. He doesn't see what the big deal is if he feels he has a problem and asks his mother for her advice. So anyway I said, 'You can bet on one thing. I'm not having any children with a husband who is a mama's boy.' So do you know what he said?"

"No, what?" Annette and Nat asked in unison.

"He said 'fine.' He said he wasn't a mama's boy and we both knew it was high time we had a family. He said my fear of his mother taking over our lives if I had a baby was entirely unrealistic. He said that to prove it, my mother-in-law was going to move in with us, and I'd see it would be no problem."

"Oh, my God!" Annette and Nat said, again in unison.

"So now I'm figuring out what to do," Jaya concluded.

Nat swallowed the pork dim sum in her mouth. "I don't know. Maybe you should move out and get your own apartment."

"I thought of that and I told Sunil, but Sunil said it didn't matter; however, if we didn't start trying for a baby within six months he would reevaluate our marriage, whatever that means."

"It sounds to me like his mom cooked up the whole scheme," Annette suggested. "A guy would never think of something like that."

"Naturally," Jaya agreed. "So I'm stuck. I'm ready to scream. Now I feel dumb getting my own place."

"The only thing you can do," Nat said, "is let this drama play itself out without getting lost in every twist and turn it takes. That's the gem I gleaned from my own experience. Become an observer and follow your instinct. If and when you feel like renting your own place, do it. Then after six months, if you still don't want a baby, it will be your husband's problem. Meanwhile, why are you being so nice and making dinner for people from his office?"

"I don't know. I guess I like entertaining. Having guests takes my mind off things. Besides, if I didn't, Sunil wouldn't care. He'd invite everyone out. There's no point in saying no. It's not like anything else is wrong between Sunil and me. There's just his crazy sense of urgency about our having a family and his mother always hovering in the background. And he's right, you know."

"What do you mean?" Natalya asked.

"He's right about my mother-in-law being the main reason I don't want to get pregnant yet. I haven't made any secret about it. It isn't like she's a pain or anything. It's just that she's too much of a factor. My own mom is different. She's just as Indian and she isn't even as sophisticated as Sunil's mother. Still, she's relaxed and laid back. She's always there for us, but nothing seems to phase her. It's weird. Of course, she has my dad, and Sunil's dad died when he was in his teens. So anyway, that's my saga. Now it's Annette's turn to stop eating and start talking."

"OK." Annette polished off a sweet bean dumpling and washed it down with jasmine tea. "Jaya knows some of this stuff, but I'll say it all anyhow. It's funny, but my problems also have to do with babies, and they also started the night of Victor's party."

"I thought as much when we were having dinner at Conchita's." Nat turned to Jaya, "That was the weekend you and Sunil went to some wedding in Dallas or Los Angeles or someplace. So what's wrong?"

"After Victor's birthday party, in the car on the way home I asked David just what he meant by needing to have a sense of your own self before having a child. David freaked and started yelling at me about always disparaging what he had to say. He couldn't see why I failed to understand what he meant. It was obvious, he said, that the reason I suddenly wanted a baby was because I was jealous and insecure and I wanted to be sure I held on to him. I couldn't believe it. Here I thought David was feeling unsure of himself, while it's me he considered 'insecure.' What a crock!"

"How come David thinks you're jealous?" Natalya asked.

"Because four months ago his former shikse fiancée, Chloe, divorced her husband and moved back to Houston. She started calling him and they met for lunch once in a while. David felt sorry for her and he wanted us to be friends. I said that Chloe was bad news and that I didn't believe friendship between us was possible. The reason David broke his engagement with her is that she was two-timing him with the guy she just divorced. Now her husband divorced her because he caught her with his boss. Chloe is your basic slut. I can't understand how David ever got involved with her in the first place. It was a couple of years before we met. So David worked out in his head that I'm jealous. Isn't that wild?"

"It sure is." Nat said. "It's odd that David thinks you're jealous when you're not and it's even odder that he wants to be friends with Chloe now. What's behind this? Does he still have the hots for her?"

"I'm positive David isn't remotely attracted to her anymore. That's why I'm not jealous. Chloe has gotten fat and she's nothing much to look at. She's coarse. Straw hair and nail polish peeling at the edges. You know what I mean. Years ago she was cute in a Barbie dollish way. The thing is she's a lot younger than David is and he has developed fatherly feelings toward her. He is on a crusade to get her into counseling and to get her to finish college. Her parents pleaded with David to please be nice to her because she had no friends, and David promised we would. He said that I'd be happy to work with her in therapy. Can you imagine? Now David's tail is in a crack because he can't deliver. So he's blaming me. He probably thinks he can use my wanting a baby to force me into dealing with her."

"If you're not worried about her and David, then why do you care if David helps her? Why not do what you can?" Jaya asked. "After all, helping screwed up people is what you do for a living."

"Because Chloe is bad news. I'm pissed at the amount of energy David has already expended on her and I don't have room for her in my life. She may have psychological difficulties, in fact I'm sure she does, but the net effect of them is that she's promiscuous and lazy, not miserable. She was pregnant when her husband found out about the affair. She didn't know whether the baby was her husband's or his boss', so she had an abortion, just like that. Besides, my Code of Ethics doesn't allow me to become professionally involved in a situation that impinges upon my personal life."

"So now what?" Jaya asked.

"That's my question, now what?" Annette echoed.

"What do you think would happen if you just played it cool and laid off the subject of babies for a while?" Nat asked.

"Nothing. David would go on trying to help Chloe and he would keep bugging me about helping her too."

"But," Jaya said, "you could explain the professional angle and just say that you don't mind trying to point her in the right direction even though you think it's an exercise in futility."

"I could. But I do mind. I mind a hell of a lot. I don't have time to spend on Chloe. I work long days, I try to stay healthy, I crave more sleep, I keep up with our family, and I run my household as best I can. I want to enjoy every spare moment I can carve out of my schedule. I don't want to waste hours on someone like her who has no morals and no ethics. And I want a baby, I really do."

"That's all well and good, but how long do you really think David would go on being helpful if you play along with him?" Jaya asked. "And suppose you go through the motions of giving her some guidance. Do you think Chloe will want to stick around? No, my guess is she'll get tired of you pretty quick. David may not be interested in her, but I assure you she is interested in him. So before long she'll latch on to someone else and that will be the end of her."

"Jaya has a point," Nat said. "I think you should kill Chloe off with kindness."

"Maybe," Annette replied. "But it won't be easy."

"No," Jaya concurred. "It won't be easy, but it won't be for long."

It was almost one when the waiter brought the bill. *The Seven Capital Sins* was starting in twenty minutes in a theater just a few blocks away. After a little urging, Jaya agreed to go too, even if it meant she'd have to rush when she got home. The film was entertaining. There was a vignette for each sin and it was obvious to the threesome that their husbands had committed more than their fair share of sins, while they themselves were pure as freshly fallen snow.

Natalya got home at about three twenty. When she opened the door, she heard Rebecca and Henry Landau making small talk with Victor in the living room. She took a deep breath, and walked in. Victor was squirming like an animal caught in a trap. His parents looked somber. But as soon as they saw Nat, their mood brightened.

"Hello, my dear." Rebecca said. "It's so good to see you."

Henry got up and gave her a big hug. "Come, sit."

Nat saw a tear run down Rebecca's cheek and then felt her own eyes getting moist. "I'll wash up and be right back," she said and hurried out of the room.

8

In the few moments that Natalya spent washing her face and kicking off her heels, she made up her mind to tell Victor's parents as much as she could about the grandchild she was carrying, about Victor, and about herself. She knew that wouldn't be what Victor wanted, but she didn't care. It was much too late to beat around the bush. She put a smile on her face and returned to the living room prepared to speak. She sat down on the sofa where Henry had patted a space for her.

"Hello Beca. Hi Papa. I can't tell you how glad I am that you came. I'm sorry I didn't call, but I was going to this afternoon, honestly. There's a lot I wanted to say to you, and I didn't know where to begin."

"Begin by saying you are pregnant. You are, aren't you?" Rebecca asked.

"Yes, I am. Hasn't Victor already told you?"

"No. We have been sitting here drinking lemon grass tea for an hour and all I got out of him is that he didn't know where you were or when you'd get back and that he didn't want to discuss anything. We've been talking about the weather and about Fabergé eggs. Did you know that Victor is fascinated by Fabergé eggs? It seems they have quite a history."

"Please, Ma. Don't be facetious. I just told you there was an exhibit in the art museum and that it was interesting."

"And I told you to stop making inane conversation, but you persisted in lecturing us on them." She turned to Henry, a triumphant expression on her face. "See? Didn't I tell you Natalya and Victor were going to have a baby? How long ago was it that I knew? It's been well over a month. Close to two. You're about eight weeks along, aren't you Nat?"

"Exactly. How did you know?"

"It's uncanny." Henry said. "I'm telling you, it's uncanny."

"You know what?" Nat asked. Then she answered her own question. "I think the baby sent you a message. I knew the second it was conceived, and when I went to New York my mother knew, too. In a way, I think Victor knew, because after I got pregnant, and before I told him, he decided on his own that he was ready to become a father. I'm sure he never would have thought that if the baby hadn't made him."

"What I'd like to know," Dr. Landau asked, "is why everyone is sitting around as if this was a funeral instead of just about one of the happiest days of our lives?"

"Because Victor has chosen not to take responsibility for this child I conceived without his blessings. Victor made love to me thinking I was on the pill, and I wasn't. So now he believes that we—the baby and I—are not his concern. He believes in choice, and since he had no choice he feels he can do whatever he wants, acknowledge his child or ignore it."

"That's not how I feel anymore." Victor said.

"Besides," Nat continued speaking over her husband, "matters have become complicated. First there was the question of whether or not Victor wanted to stay married, given what he characterized as my lying and cheating. Now there is also the question of whether I want to stay married to him, given how he feels about me and how he has been behaving lately."

"What do you know about how I've been behaving?" Victor's panic made him pale.

"Not much, but more than enough," Natalya replied.

"Well, well, well. This is a fine mess," Dr. Landau said. "Still, it's a mess that can easily be cleared up. Look at you two. Here you are about to become parents, already parents actually, and behaving like irresponsible kids. I, for one, am not in the least worried. I know my son and I know Natalya. Your natures, your consciences, your upbringing will make you do the right thing. I don't know how you got yourselves into this predicament, but you'll get out of it. Son of a gun. I'm going to be a grandpa! It's about time. Rebecca, let's get the hell out of here."

"Papa, I'm not at all sure we will get out of it. Things may not work out at all," Nat said. "Beca, please tell Papa not to be so confident that everything will be resolved. This whole problem isn't just going to blow away."

"Victor wants it to work out," Rebecca said. "Don't you, Nat dear?"

"I don't know. But I don't hear Victor saying that he does. You're speaking for him. He has a tongue. He has had weeks to tell me that he wants this baby and he wants us to be a family. I haven't heard a thing. What happened to communication? Not logical communication, not persuasive communication, just plain civilized communication?"

"He may not have told you, dear, but he has shown you how he feels. You'll see. Papa is right. You'll do what you have to do and everything will be fine. The baby will fix things. It's such a wonderful baby. Thank you. We really need to go. I brought you a trifle pudding. It's in the refrigerator."

In a flurry of hugs and kisses and mumblings of congratulations, Dr. and Mrs. Landau danced out the door.

After Henry and Rebecca left, Nat and Victor sat quietly, each waiting for the other to say something. Not anything momentous, just something. They were both grateful to Victor's parents for making light of their difficulties, and even though they weren't entirely optimistic about the road ahead, they felt better. After a while their worried silence became tentative and then, almost companionable. Victor got up and played some Viennese waltzes. Viennese waltzes fit with his parents and the mood they left behind. The cheerful music encouraged Nat and Victor to hope a little. Victor hoped that Nat might be able to put what he would have to tell her behind them, and Nat hoped that she would be able to accept what Victor was going to say.

The baby inside Nat also waited. It was aware that its parents were at a turning point in their relationship, it was tense. However, something else also stirred the new life that had just graduated from embryo to fetus. It recognized a special feeling of familiarity, love, and gladness mixed with sadness coming from Rebecca

Landau. That feeling sped up the fetal metabolism and made it turn cartwheels within Nat's womb.

At eight weeks the body of Victor and Natalya's child was still tiny, but it was well-defined. It measured four centimeters in length and weighed only thirteen grams, barely half an ounce, yet it already consisted of many millions of brilliantly programmed cells, each containing about one hundred thousand genes. Furthermore, each and every one of the organs it would need as a full-fledged person was formed and in place. Everything about it was amazing, but its brain was miraculous. About half the size of the body and well irrigated by blood vessels, this brain was a beehive of activity. The axions or projections spun out by the nerve cells in the brain, called neurons, looked and functioned like a sophisticated telephone network. Along the neurons, electrical messages crackled and pulsed as they went about their business of developing and refining human intelligence. And far beyond the wondrous brain, linked to spirit that gave it life, the soul sparked the fetus' mind and made it beautiful.

After a long while Victor spoke. "I had intended to make brunch for you this morning, Nat. But you went out."

"That's nice, Victor, but I'm not a mind reader. I had other plans."

"No, I'm not complaining about the fact that you went out. I'm just saying that I wanted to talk to you. But I wanted to make brunch as a gesture."

"What kind of a gesture?"

"A gesture. A sign. Hell, Nat. It was a way to say I love you."

"Really? You've been acting very strangely for a person who purports to love me."

"I know. It's just that I've been miserable. I've been a fool, a wreck. I didn't know what to do."

"I find that hard to believe, Victor. You've been pretty active up until last week. You were pretty self-righteous and quite cruel, actually."

"How can you say that, Nat? What have I done that was cruel?"

"For one thing you made no effort to understand me or even to listen to me with an open mind. For another you were ready to write off our child. You treated me like some kind of a criminal. Well, maybe I made a mistake, but even the courts consider that absence of fraudulent intent minimizes a crime."

"I never thought you were a criminal, Nat. I just felt horrible because you tricked me."

"Feeling horrible is one thing. Reacting the way you did is another. But anyway, you got even didn't you?"

"What do you mean I got even?"

"You tricked me too, didn't you?"

"What are you implying, Nat?"

"Don't play dumb. I am saying, not implying, that there are more ways than one to cheat. And I'd be willing to bet that you out-cheated me by a long shot."

"How can you say that? What do you think I did?"

"How about you tell me what you did! Then I'll tell you how close I came to hitting the mark."

"I was going to tell you. I didn't plan to conceal anything. I'm just wondering what you think. Why do you think I cheated? I never thought you cheated."

"Oh yes you did. You told me I cheated and lied by going off the pill."

"I thought we were a team, partners, and I thought it was lousy of you to try to change our lives without asking me."

"So now we're back to square one. I was lousy. Well, Victor I think you have been more than lousy. You've been a full-fledged prick. I think you have been hiding plenty. I think you came back to me with your tail between your legs because you got ditched or something like that. I think you're a spoiled, selfish son of a bitch whose ego is his first priority."

"It wasn't like that, Nat."

"Then tell me, Victor. What was it like?"

"I will tell you. First I have to know whether you still love me. I think you do. If you didn't, you wouldn't be so mad. Please tell me. Do you love me?"

"I don't know Victor. I can't judge any more. I tried not to think about it. All I thought about is the baby and that I couldn't let you keep on making us unhappy. Right now, what I have to know is how much you loved making out with Linda behind my back. The other thing I have to know is what made you stop."

"I wasn't making out with Linda."

"You weren't? What do you call what you were doing?"

"Well for a long time I was just working, you know, on the course work. I didn't know what else to do so I worked. And, well, Linda was very nice. And she admires me alot. And I wished you admired me. And I kept thinking about the baby and I wanted it, but I was very angry because I didn't have a chance to decide to have it together with you."

"What a touching story, Victor! Do continue."

"Please don't be sarcastic. I'm just being honest."

"Well, so am I. I'm being honest, too. I'm all ears. Then what happened?"

"Well, um, well one time, just one time I told Linda not to call me Dr. Landau or something like that. I said that it made me feel old, or something. I think I said she was young and pretty and so then . . . Linda sort of let loose."

"Just how loose did she sort of get?"

"She kissed me and started to take her clothes off and to take my clothes off and she got me all excited, but I couldn't do it. I was ready to, but then I saw your picture and I loved you and I just wanted you. And I saw our baby's eyes looking at me from inside your eyes. Its eyes are different from yours. They are deep. The eyes made me stop. And I love you Nat."

After he finished, Victor waited for Natalya to ask another question or tell him they were through, but she just sat there, trying to digest what she had heard. It was strange how she had been so close to the truth and yet so far from it at the same time. She believed Victor. There was no doubt about that. But everything was a crazy paradox. She was horrified at what she learned, but at the same time she was relieved. She hated Victor for what he had done, but a big part of her couldn't help loving who he was. He did not offer her the gift of understanding, but she had that gift to offer and she could not hold it back. Victor's parents were right after all. They would do the right thing, she and Victor. They would get back to some kind of normalcy, not only for the sake of their child but also for their own sakes. It would be very difficult for her to open her heart all the way again, though. Doing it once cost her dearly in pain and humiliation. From now on, she would be more cautious.

Even after reaching her decision, Nat kept her peace. But after a little while she smiled. Victor's heart lifted and he dared ask, "Please, Nat, tell me. Can you forgive me? Can you still love me?"

"I think so," she answered. "I'm going to try."

"How do you feel inside?" Victor probed.

"I feel like I've been hit by a drunk driver. I know I'm going to survive, but I don't know what the permanent damage will be."

"Am I the drunk driver?"

"I guess so. And you? How do you feel?"

"I feel like a fool and an idiot. I'm embarrassed. I want to erase the last few weeks, except for the baby."

"What about Linda?"

"Linda has been OK. She's acting like nothing ever happened. She's a good kid, but I let her get carried away. Do you want me to arrange for her to work under someone else?"

"No, Victor. It's not Linda that bothered me. It's you. The world is full of Lindas."

"So what do we do now?"

"We try to do what your parents said. We try to get ourselves out of this predicament we got in."

"How do we start?" Victor asked.

"With the philosophy of 'as if.' We act as if everything were normal and hope that sooner or later it gets that way. I act as if I forgive you and love you. I try to make you happy. I try not to make decisions for us on my own. You try not to say or do things that make me unhappy. You don't shut me out."

"I always try to make you happy, Natalya. That's what I do. I worried that you didn't care about me."

"I know, Victor. But that's not what I said. Listen. Don't work so hard to make me happy. Just try not to hurt me."

For supper Victor prepared the meal he had intended to serve at brunch: fresh fruit salad, eggs benedict, and polenta. It went over well. As they ate, Victor and Nat talked about their baby, about natural childbirth, about whether or not they wanted to discover their baby's sex ahead of time, about whether they would prefer a boy or a girl, about baby names, and about everything they hoped to do for their child as it grew. The fetus rejoiced.

It had been weeks since Natalya and Victor had touched or spoken to one another. They had fallen into the habit of doing their own thing and had to re-learn how to connect. And of course they had to include a new person in their lives. There was so very much to think about. Where would the baby sleep? Would they move? Would they turn the study into a nursery? How about a nursery/study? What about their jobs? What was pressing? What was the maternity leave policy in Nat's firm? What did they want to do over the summer? How much vacation could they scrounge up? They didn't really care about the answers. The important thing was that it felt good to be asking these questions.

At bedtime Victor wanted to make love, but he was nervous and unsure about how to begin. He was lost without the familiar rituals that signaled mutual interest and triggered romance. What if Natalya rejected his advances? Victor wondered whether 'acting as if I love you' included sex. He was terribly needy. In fact, he thought that lack of sex was to blame for much of how he felt and what he had done. But it was his own fault. He was the one who had let his anger keep him away. It had been a bad move, and now Victor wanted more than to merely fulfill his need. He wanted to make sure Nat felt cherished, not just desired, and he didn't want her to feel used. So he thought about letting it go. He thought he could wait. But when Nat came to bed a few minutes after him, and he felt her breath, like a gentle breeze moving the air, he couldn't keep away. He brushed against her as if by accident and when she faced him, he kissed her lips and pulled her to him.

Nat shared her body with her husband, but she didn't share her mind. It wouldn't shut off, but churned with promise and with fear. Prayers kept swirling in her head. She prayed for her baby's happiness. She prayed that she and Victor were on the right track. She prayed they would be able to bury their unhappiness in future joy. She prayed that her wounds would heal and never re-open. She prayed that her fascination with their baby wouldn't make Victor jealous. Mostly she prayed to thank God for the good that had come to her so far.

Victor caressed Nat and buried himself in her warmth. He felt himself stiffen.
"Is it OK? I mean for the baby?" he whispered.
"It's OK," Nat said and she returned Victor's kisses and caresses. But she couldn't keep pace with Victor, and Victor couldn't hold back. It was just the way pent up tension worked for them. For Victor, it was an accelerator and for Natalya, it was a brake. Still Nat was content to feel her husband close again and she sensed that their baby felt good, too. For her, for now, that was more than enough. But Victor was disappointed.

9

Harmony returned to the Landau home in the weeks after Natalya and Victor's reconciliation. The atmosphere there, free of turmoil but rich in stimuli, encouraged the new life to flourish. It luxuriated in the warmth of the emotions and of the waters that bathed it. The amniotic fluid in Nat's womb was an even 99.5 degrees Fahrenheit. Her body worked to maintain this precise temperature which was ideal for the fetus, although it made her feel hot. She found herself forever turning up the air conditioning.

Much of Nat and Victor's action and interaction revolved around their child. Although Victor couldn't picture his baby as a person, he dwelled upon it and made plans for fathering it. Natalya was consumed with it and Victor tried to imagine the way she felt. Her love was visceral. His was an idea and an ideal. Only the baby's eyes were absolutely real to him. As yet they had no color or shape, but they did have incredible depth and they spoke out to him with eloquence.

As Nat's personal life settled down, pressures began to build in the world outside. Some arose from a change in Nat's attitude. She had the strange sense that the baby inside her was expanding her awareness and fostering the notion that the legal battles she waged were not worth waging. On several occasions she said as much to the partners of Kaplan, McCall and Green, although she knew that voicing her viewpoint could jeopardize her future with the firm. Natalya did not discuss these matters with Victor. Nevertheless, he knew when she was stressed and he kept an extra hug or back rub up his sleeve for those times. Nat came to depend on his affectionate strength and her dependency weakened her resolve to keep her emotional distance. Thus she found herself loving her husband with all her heart again.

⋯⋯⋯

Nat's most recent argument with Mr. Green related to the Parkway Plaza case. She and Jack Owen, Alpha National Bank's attorney, had recently submitted their clients' dispute to mediation. The outcome was a settlement proposal by ANB which was more than fair and Nat advised Pinnacle to accept it. However, Walter Green undercut her recommendation. He urged the Pinn brothers, Pinnacle's major shareholders, to reject the bank's offer and tantalized them with the possibility of a windfall jury verdict. Nat tried her level best to reason with Walter Green.

"Walter," she urged, "ANB has agreed to put the purchase contract on hold pending its getting clear title to the central portion of the property as well as to reimburse Pinnacle for legal fees, to return the escrow with interest, and to pay one hundred thousand dollars in damages up front."

"Nat, I don't think Pinnacle would be well served by settling so soon. What if Alpha doesn't get title?" Green countered.

"If ANB fails to obtain clear title within eighteen months, the bank will pay an additional three hundred thousand dollars in damages as lost opportunity."

"It's not enough," Green said. "The bank has deep pockets and a jury might give Pinnacle a lot more."

"And the court could order remittitur."

"No way. This is Judge Marjorie Janowicz's case. We spearheaded her campaign."

"The problem," Nat pressed on, "is that the jury may find that ANB did not act with willful malice, particularly if the bank proves Mr. Courtney was a loose cannon who acted without the bank's authority. And even if the jury does award punies and the judge doesn't reduce the award, the verdict could be overturned on appeal. What can Pinnacle gain from protracted litigation?"

Mr. Green's response shocked Nat.

"Don't be naive. Are you trying to put yourself out of business? Why shouldn't we go to trial when we have a good case? What difference does it make? If Alpha isn't made to foot our bill, Pinnacle will. No one can fault us for trying our best."

"But this is a waste of time and resources. It isn't right."

"It's a simple case of waste makes wealth," Walter Green explained. "It's right for Kaplan, McCall and Green, so it's right for you."

Nat's worries over Pinnacle paled in comparison to the Home Fitness Trainers case that she inherited from Steve Jordan after he took off for Mexico. HFT, a multi-level marketing company specializing in home fitness equipment, was a long-standing client of Kaplan, McCall and Green. Mr. Kaplan often made reference to his success in defeating the "frivolous lawsuits" filed by disgruntled ex-distributors designated as "trainers." Two former trainers had filed the most recent suit, which Steve was working on before his defection, but the initial two were joined by another four and then three more. All alleged that Home Fitness Trainers induced them to purchase over sixty thousand dollars' worth of exercise equipment, promising them that they could quadruple their money within three months by recruiting other trainers to market the products. The petition further alleged that the equipment was shoddy and that, to the best of their knowledge, none of the "trainers" had ever sold a thing. All they did was recruit more trainers. There were large numbers of trainers throughout the state of Texas and nationwide who had garages full of unsold exercise equipment. This method of operation constituted an illegal pyramid scheme.

The plaintiffs were seeking over four million dollars in actual and punitive damages and it looked like both the number of plaintiffs and the number of dollars could increase significantly. Nat was frustrated and perplexed by her client's lack of cooperation. Among other things, HFT had failed to give her the documents that plaintiffs' attorneys had requested and to which they were entitled. Bart Grady, HFT's in-house counsel, devoted his energy to hiding the ball. Nat was embarrassed at the prospect of finding herself in court on behalf of HFT with no excuse and no information to use in its defense. Unlike the Parkway Plaza matter, this case was assigned to a judge who owed her firm no favors.

In light of her conversation with Walter Green regarding Pinnacle, Nat decided not to discuss the HFT problem with Rudy Kaplan. She suspected Rudy would give her instructions she would not, in good conscience, be able to follow. Nat remembered her mother's oft-repeated statement, "If you ask too many questions, you get too many answers." She also decided she would not do a tap dance before the court to beg for indulgence. Instead, she advised Mr. Grady that she would not oppose sanctions that could be imposed for Home Fitness Trainers' failure to meet its deadlines.

"You know you are risking a lot more than credibility here," she pointed out. "Fines would be the least of your problems. The plaintiff's lawyer, Mr. Jeffrey Dupree, will probably get our defensive pleadings stricken. Then he'll move for summary judgment. Don't let Jeffrey's soft-spoken manner fool you. He thinks his clients have one hell of a case and he's hinting that HFT's officers and directors may be guilty of criminal conduct."

Nat wondered again about Steve Jordan. He was a sincere, bright and hardworking young lawyer. What would have caused him to act so irresponsibly? Could it have something to do with Rudy Kaplan or Home Fitness Trainers? Well, whatever the situation, Nat had no intentions of absconding. She was going to use her judgment and do her job to the best of her ability. If HFT or Rudy didn't like the calls she made, they could assign the case to someone else.

"Hi there, little one," she told her baby, patting her tummy. "I honestly think it's you who made me see past all the fancy footwork I've been doing since I started working here." A wave of approval came back. Then on impulse she dialed her brother's number. Ronald was in his office and as always, not withstanding his horrendously busy schedule, he told Nat that of course he had a few moments. In fact he was ready for a break.

"So, what's up? I'm excited about becoming an uncle and Mom and Dad are delirious at the prospect of grandparenthood. I even think this miraculous baby you're cooking up has done a number on Cecily. Things are a whole lot better between us too."

"I'm so happy about Cecily. She's a little weird, but then we all are. I love her. Tell her I said so."

"But this isn't just a hello call, right, Nattie?"

"Well, yes and no. I'm kind of bugged at work."

"Oh?"

"I think it's part of growing up. I guess I've been pretty slow about noticing what's going on, and now that I'm noticing, I'm bugged."

"Nat, you've never been slow about anything, but you have had some waking up to do. So, what are you noticing now that you're smelling the coffee?"

"I'm noticing that Kaplan, McCall and Green don't admire me as much as I thought they did. And what they do or did like about me isn't what I thought they liked."

"So what do or did they like and admire, and what not?"

"Well, they liked how I logged up billable hours. Look, I know smart hardworking lawyers are a dime a dozen, but I thought I was just a little special because of my . . . I don't know—my conscientiousness and integrity."

"And?" Ronald asked.

"And it's just the opposite."

"How's that?"

"They don't admire my judgment or my opinions. They disagree with me. They just want to use me so they can drag out their cases without looking bad. They don't care about anything except making money. I feel somehow diminished by falling for all the hype and compliments they've been feeding me. You know what else?"

"What?" Ronald asked.

"I feel exploited. As if I were a workhorse with blinders on. I'm well treated and well paid, but an expensive horse is well fed and well treated too. It's an investment. And they dangle suggestions of potential partnerships just like they dangle carrots in front of workhorses."

"So what are you going to do?"

Nat answered with a quick rundown of what had occurred so far. Then she explained her decision to stick it out until things came to some kind of a head. "What else can I do?" she asked.

"Oh, any number of things but none of them would be you. Tell me, are you worried about what may happen?"

"No, not really. It won't be that easy for this firm to dump me. Probably they'd just trim my bonus and try to make my life unpleasant so I'll leave quietly. Things might get a little icky, but I can cope. I'm just upset because I feel dumb. I guess my self esteem is bruised."

"Nat, here's something you have to learn and learn well because you have to pass it along to your kid. Never, ever allow someone you do not respect to affect your self-esteem. Got it?"

"Got it. And thanks. I'll let you get back to work. And, Ron?"

"I'm here."

"I love you. You'll be the world's best uncle. So long."

"Bye, talk to you soon."

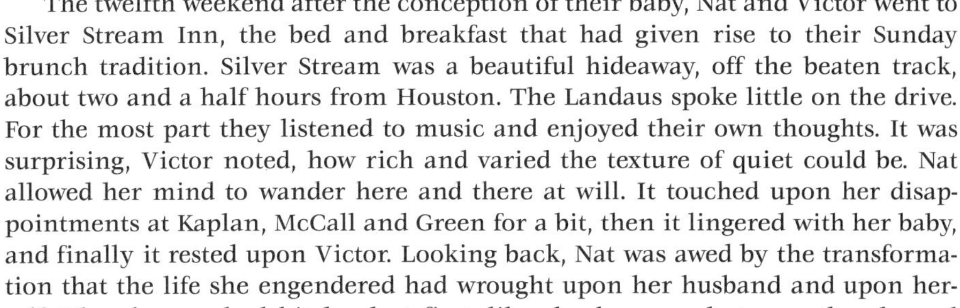

The twelfth weekend after the conception of their baby, Nat and Victor went to Silver Stream Inn, the bed and breakfast that had given rise to their Sunday brunch tradition. Silver Stream was a beautiful hideaway, off the beaten track, about two and a half hours from Houston. The Landaus spoke little on the drive. For the most part they listened to music and enjoyed their own thoughts. It was surprising, Victor noted, how rich and varied the texture of quiet could be. Nat allowed her mind to wander here and there at will. It touched upon her disappointments at Kaplan, McCall and Green for a bit, then it lingered with her baby, and finally it rested upon Victor. Looking back, Nat was awed by the transformation that the life she engendered had wrought upon her husband and upon herself. The changes had hit hard at first, like shock waves, but now they lapped gently like calm ocean waves on a sandy shore.

Nat felt that the fetus relished the ride as much as she did. She knew it was already beginning to look and function like a tiny human being. It measured five centimeters and weighed about one ounce. Its liver and spleen formed red blood cells. Its bone marrow manufactured white blood cells which then moved on to the lymph glands and thymus for further processing. Its immune system, based upon the white blood cells, was beginning to take an active role in protecting the fetus from infection. Its face was no longer expressionless. It frowned, opened and shut its mouth, turned its head, and made movements while it breathed. As the new life developed, its spirit became more and more firmly lodged within its body. Thus the soul of Victor and Natalya's child became increasingly intertwined with its feelings and its mind.

The Landaus arrived in time for a walk in the woods around Silver Stream. As they made their way through winding trails, Nat spoke to Victor about the problems in her office. Victor listened and when Natalya was finished he told her what he thought.

"The bottom line is that you haven't been completely happy with Kaplan, McCall and Green from day one. Actually this may be an excellent time for you to take a break. It would slow down our savings plan but it won't affect our lives."

"What about moving to a house? We won't be able to afford a house we like if my job isn't secure."

"Does that matter?" Victor asked. "Are you ready to give up condo living?"

"No, I'm not." Nat replied. "The idea of a house seems boring."

"Me neither. Buying a big house would make me feel middle aged. I'm more than ready to be a Dad, but I don't want to change my life-style yet."

"Then that's settled. We have plenty of room for the baby. We have two choices. One is to put the nursery in the study and make the study in the dining area. The other is to combine the study with the nursery."

"What about guests?" Victor asked.

"They can share with the nursery. Probably the baby will sleep in our room for a while. It's just that we need a place for its stuff."

"If the baby sleeps in our room, how can we do it?"

"Come on, Victor! When it's old enough to notice, it won't be sleeping in our room. Besides, where is it written that we are restricted to our room?"

After their walk, Nat and Victor went to dinner at a catfish farm adjoining the Silver Springs Inn. Natalya had taken extra pains with her appearance and she looked radiant in a soft flowing dress that brought out the deepest tones of green in her eyes. The restaurant was surprisingly crowded for a spot seemingly tucked away in the middle of nowhere.

"I guess," Nat said, "this place isn't as well kept a secret as we thought."

Over dessert, a fantastic apricot cobbler covered with homemade vanilla ice cream, Nat told Victor how happy she was with life and that a big part of her contentment was rooted in him. She also told him how it had turned out to be much easier than she expected to retrace their steps, just like Papa and Beca said. Then Nat admitted that the prospect of becoming a mother scared her.

"I want this baby more than I ever wanted anything in my life, but I don't want it to become my whole life. I love it more than I love my life, but I don't want to lose my life in it. I want to maintain a balance, not to become bogged down by motherhood."

"You don't look like someone bogged down by motherhood. You're gorgeous and sexy."

"Are you sure you won't mind the baby being Number 1, Victor?"

"I'm very sure. All three of us will be Number 1, you, the baby and me."

"I was afraid you would be jealous and think I'm using up all my love on the baby."

"I expect I won't. Love regenerates itself. The more you expend, the more you have."

"That's a beautiful thing to say. Where did you hear it?"

"Nowhere; at least nowhere I can recall. Maybe I got it from the baby."

Later, lying in bed, Natalya and Victor inspected the tiny mound that was barely perceptible on Nat's tummy. It was exciting to see and to feel the first visible, tangible evidence of their baby's existence. Except for that mound, and her rounded breasts, Nat was slim and Victor couldn't remember when he had found her more alluring than she was right then. Natalya looked at Victor in a new way too. She wanted their child to have his brown eyes, his sensuous wavy hair, and his firm lips. When Victor placed those firm lips on hers and when his eyes penetrated her core, she melted.

That night's lovemaking renewed the passion that nourished Victor and Natalya and tightened the bonds that held them together. Their bodies responded to one another in a way that was familiar, yet filled with surprise. Their minds came to a new understanding of the eternity of sex, an act that mirrored the creation of the world even when creation did not take place. For their child this union and all unions were a memory of life and at the same time an echo of death. As Nat and Victor swelled with excitement, they pulsed in harmony. Their movement was part of an expertly choreographed dance. At the end of the dance, they twirled faster and faster until dizziness caused them to fall into a chasm filled with wondrous emptiness.

The next morning over shirred eggs and waffles topped with strawberries and whipped cream, Nat revisited a subject that she had touched upon before but that now was pressing. She considered how best to phrase her ideas so that Victor would give them serious thought and began with a question.

"What are we going to do about giving our baby a sense of Judaism?"

"Why do we have to do anything? Our parents didn't do anything."

"They didn't have to. They lived Judaism. But even then I feel we're missing out because there is no religious grounding in our lives."

"I don't miss anything," Victor said. "I know I'm Jewish. I'm circumcised because my father thought circumcision was medically sound. I don't even know if I had a bris. I didn't have a bar mitzvah."

"You did have a bris."

"How do you know that?"

"I found a picture and talked about it with your mother. I'm glad you had it."

"Why?"

"Because a bris is a covenant the Jews made with God to circumcise every baby boy on the seventh day after its birth. Our parents, for all their anti-ritualistic talk, respected that covenant."

"So, what's your point?"

"My point is I'm afraid our baby will grow up bereft of its historical identity if we just let the issue of Jewishness slide."

"There is no way Jewishness can slide, Nat. Being Jewish is different from practicing Judaism. It's not a question of following arbitrary rules. It's a question of who we are and how we are perceived."

"Exactly. We are products of a long cultural and religious tradition. We are descendants of rabbis and Talmudic scholars. How can we determine that the so-called rules we have rejected are arbitrary when we don't even know what they are, let alone what they represent?"

"That's a good question, Nat, and I'm not sure I know the answer but I can't see myself doing stuff like not eating bacon just because my ancestors didn't."

"I understand, Victor. But your heritage is more than just not eating bacon. And since we don't even not eat bacon, what do we have to offer our baby?"

"I don't know. But I can't see how not doing something is a particularly worthwhile offering. I'm happy with what my parents passed along to me."

"Which is?" Nat asked.

"Love of learning, respect for family, open-mindedness, the Golden Rule, stuff like that."

"All those things are important, but out of context they are overly broad, and they aren't enough. They don't give us anything we can identify with. I realize that somewhere along the line our elders decided becoming American meant giving up a part of their world instead of adding to it. But that was a mistake. Maybe you don't feel that your birthright is slipping away, but I feel mine is. I don't want to tell our baby that we cannot worship the way our elders did because we didn't think it worth our while to learn how. What I'd like to do is offer our child the gift of its tradition, and then give it the freedom to follow its own light."

"Those are beautiful sentiments, Nat, but I can't translate them into any kind of meaningful behavior. I am Victor Landau. I don't deny Judaism, but I'm not observant either. I eat pork. I do my own thing. I can't pretend that God cares if, when, where, or in what language I pray. I am sure He doesn't care whether or not I learned enough Hebrew to have a bar mitzvah so I could publicly announce, at the age of thirteen, that I was man. Of course, by not having had a bar mitzvah, I missed out on a big party and lots of gifts, but I didn't feel like I wanted five or ten Parker pens anyway."

"Of course I agree that God doesn't care where or how you pray, but I'm not sure about the if. But that's neither here nor there. And I understand that your feelings about God, whatever they are, make you a man I admire and honor, so they can't be without merit. All I want is for you to be open about exploring ways to make our baby know what it means to be a Jew. I want to know myself and I want our child to be proud of being Jewish and proud of its lineage."

"OK, I'm open. You explore. Don't try to change me though. Remember that the man you say you admire and honor is the same guy you married in a civil ceremony. He doesn't like ritual, he adores shrimp, and he is firmly convinced that God doesn't give a damn about color, gender or religious label."

"I'll remember. Still, Annette once told me that making love on Friday nights was part of celebrating Sabbath. Would you perform that ritual?"

"That's one tradition I'll gladly concede to."

10

Though Natalya's womb limited the physical growth of the fetus developing within it, no boundaries contained its flourishing mind. As the tiny being grew and refined the details of its humanity inside its mother's body, its consciousness traveled far afield. Sometimes it returned to the domain it had left when it chose embodiment as Victor and Natalya's child. Other times it dwelled in its memories or drifted into the world of dreams or took off on colorful flights of fantasy. It had many visions. Some were quieting perceptions of universal harmony, but others were thunderous, jolting experiences filled with blazing light and fearful destruction. Whenever it felt afraid, it quickly returned to its present reality where Natalya comforted it with her love and its whole family nurtured it with their joy.

Late in August, halfway through her pregnancy, Natalya spoke to Beca on the telephone. She was inquiring about a photograph when she felt the first stirring of life, a gentle flutter of butterfly wings. She gave a gasp. Before she could explain, her mother-in-law understood what had happened. "The baby just moved, didn't it?" she asked.

"I'm not sure. I think I felt something, but I can't tell."

"Of course you felt something. It's just that the feeling is so gentle, you are uncertain."

"How can you know, Beca? Do you remember?"

"Yes, and I heard you catch your breath. But I also felt something myself, almost as if bubbles were floating around me and inside my head. It looks like the baby is telling us, right on schedule, that she's here."

"What do you mean, she's here? Maybe he's here. What made you say that? I kind of think it's a girl too, but that doesn't mean it is."

"Oh my God! I can't imagine. It just came out." Rebecca Landau was genuinely taken aback by her own remark. "But now that I said it, I'm sure the baby is a little girl. So, what picture were you asking about?"

"The one with a little girl in a pinafore with short curly hair holding the hand of an older girl with long pigtails," Nat said. "Something had to make you think it's not a boy? What could it be?"

"Who knows what? Maybe it's the way you are carrying. Maybe it's a sixth sense. We shouldn't disparage feelings like that. Hmn. A black and white picture of two girls holding hands? I'm not sure I know. Does it have a date or say anything on the back?"

"No, that's why I'm asking. Victor couldn't recognize it either. There are some trees in the background. It came from that shoe box you brought over about six months ago. I'm making an album for the baby."

"That's lovely, dear. Next time I come over I'll take a look. Henry's calling me. Do you mind if I run?"

"Sure. Talk to you later."

"Bye."

Approaching nineteen weeks of age, the fetus measured about twenty-four centimeters and weighed nearly a pound. It was perfectly developed. Its beautifully shaped fingers tipped with miniature fingernails could grasp. It could coordinate sucking its thumb, but, unlike some babies, this one didn't like doing that. It did like to kick its feet, and occasionally, it hiccupped. Its body jiggled and turned somersaults, buoyed by the amniotic fluid around it. Its brain looked like the brain of a miniature adult. Sweat glands formed on its palms and soles, and its skin was thickening into layers. The tiny life was complete with eyebrows and eyelashes; its head was covered with hair. It kept its eyes shut tightly. When the doctor shined a light on Nat's tummy, the fetus' little fists sought to shelter its eyes from the glare. Its ears registered sound vibrations. It paid close attention to the noise of blood rushing through Nat's blood vessels, to the beat of her heart, to the rumblings of her intestines, to the sounds of her and Victor's voices, and to the music they played. Its favorite tune was Brahms' Lullaby. After birth, it continued to love that song coming out of the tummy of a cuddly teddy bear, a gift from its maternal grandmother, Dora Rosenbaum.

Nat and Victor had been undecided about whether or not to find out in advance if their baby was a boy or a girl, and the night before they were scheduled for a sonogram they still struggled to come to a decision. It was two days after Nat's conversation with her mother-in-law, a conversation that annoyed Victor when Nat told him about it. His mother's comment complicated his ability to reach a decision.

"Forget about what your Mother said," Nat told her husband. "Just tell me whether you want to know now whether we're having a boy or a girl, or whether you want to be surprised when he or she is born."

"What do you want to do?" Victor asked.

"I told you," Nat said. "I don't feel strongly, but I would prefer to know. It seems ridiculous for us to just wait for no reason."

"The real question is do you care if we have a boy or a girl?"

"You've asked me at least ten times," Victor complained, "and I keep telling you I don't care. I just want a happy, healthy baby, just like you do."

"I'd like a little girl," Nat admitted. Then she added, "A little boy would be good too, especially if he looks like you. But I think your Mom is right. I think we have a little girl."

"Well, what the hell. Let's stop speculating. Let's find out."

"Good. I'm glad you said that," Nat agreed. "As long as the doctor knows what we have, we might as well have access to the information, too, even if it isn't 100 per cent for sure."

"What do you mean, even if it isn't 100 percent for sure? The baby is either equipped like a boy or like a girl. We get a picture."

"Doctor Hamburg told me that sometimes a little finger looks like a penis, and sometimes the baby is turned around. Jaya said that the doctor told her sister-in-law that their first child would be a girl and it was a boy. Then the second time they told her she was going to have a boy and it was a girl."

"That's crazy. What's the point of finding out if you aren't really finding out?"

"Usually the sonogram is clear and right. So we can plan, but still be prepared on the off chance that there's a mistake."

"OK. Still I don't want to make preparations that are overly boyish or girlish. I hate little girl pink and baby boy blue. Let's go for bright primary colors or maybe a jungle theme."

"Right! Either would be good. Since we decided that the baby's room will be the study, we don't want the place to look frilly or cutesy anyway. We need something that blends. Have you thought about any names?" Nat asked

"No, not yet. But I like names that could be a boy or a girl like Alex or Pat."

"No, I can't stand that."

"Don't you like our names? Vick and Nat could be either a boy or a girl".

"Of course I like your name. I love Victor. But I don't like Vick. And I never thought about Nat being a boy's name too. So what are we going to do about names if we can't agree?"

"We have to agree. There's no way we can pick a name either of us doesn't like. I promise you we'll find lots of names. But that doesn't mean we have to check with everyone and their uncle."

"It would be nice if our parents and my brother like the name, too," Nat said.

"Well, I'm not getting into discussions with everybody. You pick some names, and I'll say yes or no."

"That's fine. But if you get any ideas, tell me."

The next day Victor and Natalya learned that Rebecca was correct. Their baby was a perfect little girl. Though her gender was decided at the instant of conception, the distinctions between her and an emerging male had become apparent just recently. A few weeks ago her external sexual organs were indistinguishable from those of a boy. Now they were visibly female. Her internal organs were already operational as well. The subtler aspects of her femininity could not be captured on a sonogram, but they too were manifest. The baby's grace, her smile, and her responses to the tastes, smells, sounds, and the feel of her environment made it clear that this budding tiny person was going to become a woman.

The knowledge that their baby was a girl impacted Victor and Nat more than they anticipated. Although they were told of the slight possibility of error, they were convinced there was no mistake here. After watching his daughter on video, Victor realized that Nat had been right in thinking that all along he had cared about the baby's gender. Deep down Victor had wanted a son, or thought he had wanted a son. But once he knew their baby was a daughter, he couldn't understand how on earth he could ever have had a preference for a boy. Now he absolutely wanted a little girl. The idea that Nat might be carrying a boy after all became unwelcome. He tried to figure out why, but failing to come up with an answer, he gave up wondering. The explanation though was simple: he had fallen in love.

Natalya was in love as well. She pictured herself nuzzling her daughter and cradling her in her arms. She was ready to begin preparing for the birth in earnest. Coincidentally, she was beginning to show, and that was good, too. Nat could look down at her tummy any time and see her child there smiling or resting or kicking her feet.

The bigwigs in Natalya's firm were displeased with her pregnancy.

"So that's why you deferred your vacation," Walter Green said. "We prefer that our key associates take their vacations in the summer when things are slower."

"The baby is partly the reason. I also didn't think this was a good time to take off. You know how touchy the situation has been with Home Fitness Trainers. There are other serious matters in the pipeline as well."

Green assumed a disgusted expression in preparation for making a comment, but apparently reconsidered. Instead he inquired about Nat's plans. After she told him, he twitched his nose.

"So what do you expect us to do while you are out? We have never had a lawyer on full maternity leave before."

"There is ample time to work that out. I am surprised no one has yet taken advantage of your liberal maternity or paternity leave policies, but they are set forth in your personnel manual. My plan is to work until my due date and then use my vacation plus the three months' paid leave to which I'm entitled."

"I don't know what to say. You are a very stubborn gal. You're bright as a button, but your priorities are misplaced, and you aren't much of a team player."

"That depends on your viewpoint, Mr. Green."

Victor's work was progressing well. Linda behaved as if nothing out of the ordinary had ever taken place. She was grateful to Victor—no, to Dr. Landau—for continuing to work with her even after she had made such a fool of herself. To express her thankfulness, Linda worked extra hard.

As he prepared for the coming semester, Victor lost his apprehension over associating himself with the business school. The course in Persuasive Marketing he was co-teaching with Jack Burgess in September began to take shape. Jack was interesting and resourceful and working with him was fun. However, outlining the logical communication course was more challenging. It was odd, Victor thought, that principles of logic which are virtually self-evident should prove to be so tough to teach from a pragmatic viewpoint. He was glad he had until the spring semester to flesh out his ideas.

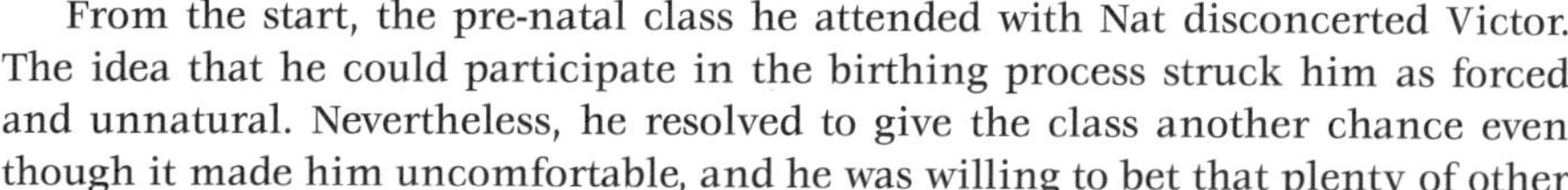

From the start, the pre-natal class he attended with Nat disconcerted Victor. The idea that he could participate in the birthing process struck him as forced and unnatural. Nevertheless, he resolved to give the class another chance even though it made him uncomfortable, and he was willing to bet that plenty of other fathers shared his views.

The next day Victor drove to the grocery store on his way home from the university, proud not to have forgotten the list Nat had given him before she left for work in the morning. In the car he sipped a tepid iced tea and brooded about the class in general and about the disagreeable prospect of watching a birth on film in particular. He was stopped at a red light nursing his malaise when he heard the screeching of wheels and a bump at the same time that he was jolted forward and covered with what felt like blood. Victor panicked for an instant, but then he collected himself and took stock. Nothing hurt, his faculties were intact, and there was no blood, only tea on his chest. He got out of the car and walked to the car behind him. The vehicle that had rear-ended his Jeep was a maroon Honda Accord that looked a lot like Sunil's car. An attractive middle-aged Indian lady dressed in a smart pantsuit approached him. She looked shaken but in control.

"Are you OK?" she asked.

"I'm absolutely fine. How about you? Does anything hurt? Is anything wrong?"

"No, nothing. I'm fine too. I'm sorry. This was my fault," the lady said with a touch of a British accent.

"I may have stopped abruptly," Victor said. "I was distracted."

"I was preoccupied too. Anyway if you rear-end someone, I'm told it's always your fault. How is your car?"

"It's fine. It's a Jeep. It's a tough baby."

"Here's my insurance information." The lady pulled out her driver's license and a card. "My name is . . ."

"Mrs. Khanna." Victor completed her sentence for her. "You don't look old enough to be, but you are Sunil's mom, right?" Victor asked.

"How do you know that?"

"My name is Victor Landau. I recognized your car. Sunil and I are good friends and Jaya told my wife you were visiting."

"To use a trite expression, 'It's a small world, isn't it?' You're right. My first name is Anjali."

"I'm very pleased to meet you."

"You can't mean that, not right now."

"Of course I mean that. You shook me up, but I'm none the worse for it. Besides, my own mom always shakes me up, so this is a familiar experience. Let's take a look at your car."

"Sunil will kill me."

"Don't worry, I won't allow it. He'll be grateful that no one was hurt. Oops! The bumper and right fender are bent. This is one of your typical fender benders. We'll let our insurance companies sort things out. Tell Sunil that what he should do is get a stronger car. Where are you heading?"

"The grocery store. Why were you distracted?"

"Me too. I mean I'm headed to the grocery store, too. Why was I distracted? It's a long story. Why were you preoccupied?"

"That's probably an even longer story. Perhaps I can invite you and Natalya to dinner to make amends."

"Thanks, I'd love a curry. Jaya owes us an invitation anyhow. We better stop chatting, though. We're starting to hold up traffic. Goodbye for now, Mrs. Khanna. Perhaps you'll run into me again at the grocery store."

"God forbid, Victor. By the way, lobster curry is my specialty."

When Anjali Khanna hit Victor's Cherokee, she had been worrying about Jaya's refusal to have a child. Although her extended visit to Houston was a success in terms of what she and Sunil had hoped would happen, their strategy boomeranged. Jaya was happy to have her mother-in-law and expressed no desire whatsoever to move into her own apartment. On the contrary, she allowed her mother-in-law to care for her home, for her husband, and even for herself. As a result, she had extra time and energy to devote to her research and she was turning into a full-fledged workaholic. The excitement she saw in her job and the euphoria she felt at the accolades she was earning were addictive. Consequently,

Jaya became less inclined than ever to entertain the possibility of having a child in the near future. She was too wrapped up in the thrill of the moment to think about tomorrow.

Anjali considered that while there was no real urgency for her son to have children, it was unlikely that even another year or two years would make any difference to his wife. Jaya simply didn't see her life as incomplete or skewed. Sunil on the other hand was becoming increasingly determined and impatient. Now that Jaya could no longer blame her reluctance to start a family on fear of Anjali's intrusion, the true nature of her hesitation became exposed and it distressed Sunil. He had given Jaya an ultimatum and time was running out. Unless something gives, Anjali thought, Sunil will follow through with his threat and file for a divorce.

The temporary truce that her son and her daughter-in-law were enjoying and their powerful love for each other had not softened their positions. Battle lines were squarely drawn and each side was confident of victory. When hostilities resumed, the casualties would be heavy. And Anjali, a would-be peace maker—albeit a biased one with a vested interest—would end up as seriously wounded as the combatants themselves. What could she do?

11

Rebecca Landau was a worrier. She had worried that Victor would never get married, then she worried that he wouldn't have children, and now she worried that something would go wrong in the course of Natalya's pregnancy. If she had her way, she would call Nat five times a day to see how she was feeling, to ask what the doctor said, to inquire about whether she had taken all possible tests, and to give her advice. If it were summer, she would have told Nat to avoid swimming pools and the beach because people urinated in pools, because the ocean was treacherous and because the sun was harmful. Luckily, it was November. Still she wanted Nat to avoid taking baths because soaking in your own dirt could lead to vaginal infections and harm the baby; to avoid strenuous exercise; to be sure to take her vitamins only after meals; to rub perfumed oil on her tummy; and to read poetry aloud. Rebecca realized that if she overdid things, her calls and visits would become unwelcome, so she exercised restraint. But it was hard and she couldn't hold back her most important concerns.

Rebecca's bath phobia irked Dora.
"That's ridiculous," she argued. "You should put your foot down."
"It's OK," Natalya said. "This means so much to Beca and I don't want to upset her. Besides, I don't think the baby likes baths anyway."
"That's absurd, sweetheart."
"I don't know. Every time I get in the water, the baby stops playing."
"Maybe she is soothed and falls asleep."
"No," Nat answered. "When the baby goes to sleep, her movements become slower and softer and then she quiets. This is abrupt. And as soon as I get out of the water, she starts moving again."

Dora changed the subject. "Have you considered any names for the baby yet?"
"Not really. Victor said he liked names that could be boy or girl, but I don't. We thought about naming it after someone in our family."
"Oh, no. Don't do that!" Dora was agitated.
"Why not?"
"Your grandmother was always careful to avoid names of any relatives."
"That doesn't make sense," Natalya said. "I thought Jews honored their ancestors by giving children their names."

"Many do," Dora said. "But my mother believed a child should have its own name so it could start out in life without someone else's attributes. I named you Natalya because I loved the sound and the meaning. You know what Natalya means, don't you?"

"Natalya means birth, doesn't it?"

"That's right. To me your birth was the beginning of wonderful things, and I think your name has colored your character. It's all yours."

"Well, I have to start thinking. Tell me if you have any ideas."

"I think this is something you and Victor should . . ." The phone beeped. "That's another call. I have to go."

"Why don't you hit the flash button?" Natalya said, but her mother had already hung up.

In the seventh month of her life, Victor and Natalya's daughter's eyes were open. The ridges of skin on her palms and soles were fully formed to create the fingerprints and footprints that would be uniquely hers throughout her life. She measured about sixteen inches in length and weighed about three and one half pounds. She responded to physical stimuli. Her vision and hearing extended beyond the womb. Her taste buds were formed so she tasted what her mother ate and she smelled everything Natalya smelled. She enjoyed familiar experiences like Brahms and Bach, olives, Mother Goose, the rhythms of Victor's Jeep and Nat's Comet, the bounces of gentle aerobics, the ring of the telephone, and the lemony furniture polish in Nat's office.

As her awareness developed, the fetus thought about life after birth. She tried to fathom why she had chosen this point in space and time to become a person once again. What connections did she have with the other persons who rode her wavelength and whose destinies most directly interlocked with hers? The unborn girl steeled herself against the pain she knew would accompany birth and life and she reconciled her humanity with the spark of divinity that glowed within her soul. She sought a name, an identity, a self, which would distinguish her from all others and link her to all others as well as to the spark that was the universal spirit of God.

She also thought about the space she would occupy once she was born. She was beginning to feel cramped in Natalya's womb, and it was going to get worse. In the weeks to come, fat would build up under her skin and her weight would increase at the rate of nearly half a pound a week. Additionally, the volume of amniotic fluid surrounding her would increase to two or three pints and would further limit her freedom of movement.

Nat and Victor's preparations for the baby and her room were well under way. They spent a portion of each weekend shopping and decorating, and they converted their study into a nursery/guest room inspired by Mexican folk art. What emerged was an area that could stimulate the eye of an infant or a child, but would also appeal to an adult. A large day bed replaced the old sleeper sofa and desk. Two big bookcases gave way to a crib, a chest of drawers, and smaller shelves. For the first months, the child would sleep in a basket in its parents' room. The Landaus accommodated their dining area on one side of their large living room and moved their desk and books into the former dining area, making that their new study.

Victor stuck with the pre-natal classes for Natalya's sake. The childbirth film made him feel faint, but the other fathers in his group stoically sat through it, so he followed suit. A speaker insisted that the physical exercises and psychoprophylaxis, or preventive psychological training (to prevent what?) would benefit not only his wife and the baby, but him too. He couldn't disagree more and was surprised that Nat, who rarely took things at face value, treated what she learned in the classes as the gospel truth. She didn't feel one bit foolish lying on rubber tubes beside Victor, or even testing various delivery positions. She crouched down on all fours with her stomach barely above the ground, she lay back with her legs up, and she squatted as if she were sitting on an oriental toilet. She refused only to immerse herself in a tub of water.

Nat chatted with other mothers, but Victor couldn't bring himself to make small talk. He was as apprehensive as a white-knuckled flyer during a safety demonstration. It wasn't good form to discuss the significance of the life vests and oxygen masks with one's co-passengers. Nor could one politely rise and say, *"Excuse me, but I think I'd like to deplane now. I'd prefer not to take the chance of having to follow the floor lights to locate the nearest emergency exit."* Nat was thrilled by Victor's cooperation, however reluctant. She wouldn't hear of it when he tentatively suggested she get another coach. "Lots of fathers feel nervous," she said, "but in the end they're glad to do this."

"Which father told you he was glad?" Victor asked.

"Actually Gloria, the short woman with curly blond hair, told me about her husband. This is their second child and Phil was terrific during the birth of their first baby. And they weren't even married then. They had been living together for six years."

"Really!" Victor commented. "What did Phil say?"

"I didn't talk to Phil. Gloria was the one who said he was great. The main thing though is that you are great. If it weren't for you, I know I wouldn't be able to go through with natural childbirth. I'm not getting an epidural, no matter what Dr. Hamburg says. Your being with me makes everything wonderful and I'm not scared."

The words, "OK, OK. You can count on me," came out of Victor's mouth, but he was thinking something entirely different. *"I'm not just scared. I'm petrified."*

The fetus enjoyed the classes. All the parents were behaving like a cast of characters rehearsing a play. Everyone was excited about opening night and wanted to prepare. Yet childbirth was no performance. And even if it were a show of sorts, the star wasn't practicing. No matter, she would know what to do.

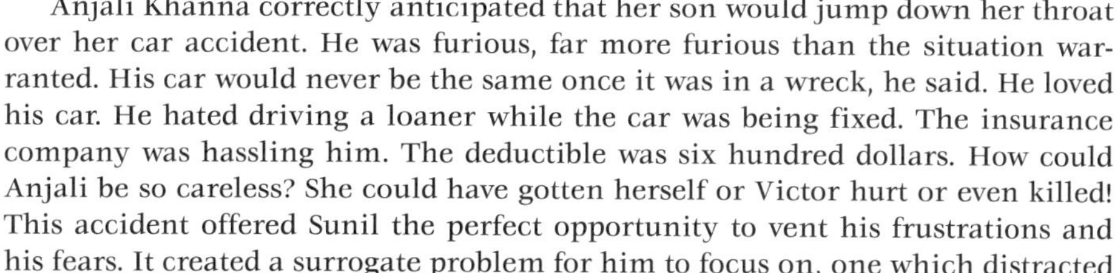

Anjali Khanna correctly anticipated that her son would jump down her throat over her car accident. He was furious, far more furious than the situation warranted. His car would never be the same once it was in a wreck, he said. He loved his car. He hated driving a loaner while the car was being fixed. The insurance company was hassling him. The deductible was six hundred dollars. How could Anjali be so careless? She could have gotten herself or Victor hurt or even killed! This accident offered Sunil the perfect opportunity to vent his frustrations and his fears. It created a surrogate problem for him to focus on, one which distracted him from his real problems: Jaya was unwilling to parent a child; she abdicated her household to his mother; he threatened a divorce he didn't want; he felt guilty because he was making his mother unhappy; he was a wimp.

Jaya had been out of town when the collision took place and when she returned four days later, disequilibrium in the Khanna household intensified. The three members of the small family treated one another with excessive courtesy and each tried unsuccessfully to devise a plan of action which would fit their personal agenda without upsetting the rocking boat in which they sailed. Jaya thought of ways to avoid the issue of children, Sunil thought about ways to force it, and Anjali continued to ask herself what she could do.

Every solution creates a problem, Anjali thought. One morning in the course of her daily meditation, it dawned on her that the most effective thing she could do at this juncture was nothing. Anjali hated doing nothing, but she worked out in her mind that to take a few steps backward under the present circumstances would be an affirmative move. She remembered the passage in the *Bhagavad Gita* where Lord Krishna told Arjun, "I make men and women love each other and have children," and she realized that some things were beyond her power. Thus she decided to leave her son and daughter-in-law to themselves and to entrust their problems to a higher being. For comfort, she resorted to prayer and for insurance she promised God that she would have a puja, a ceremonial worship, to give thanks if Jaya became pregnant.

When Anjali advised Sunil and Jaya of her intention to go to India and accept an invitation to lecture at a conference in Delhi and to spend some time with her sister, they were taken aback.

"I thought you finally retired," Sunil said. "Please, don't go. I'm sorry if I jumped all over you because of the accident."

"But you said you loved being here and helping out," Jaya whined. "How will I manage without you?"

"I'm afraid I just need a breather. It's not anything you have done. I'll be back if you really need me." Mrs. Khanna tried to keep her announcement upbeat. "I'll tell you what. I promised Victor that I'd invite him for a lobster curry. He is very charming you know. Why don't we have a party for the Landaus and your other friends before I go? I don't have to leave for a couple of weeks."

The prospect of a party was a welcome distraction and it brightened everyone's mood. Jaya decided this would be an excellent opportunity to give a baby shower. It would be a dinner shower that included men and it would be a surprise for both Natalya and Victor. Because Sunil's Mom would be an active participant, Jaya thought it would be nice to invite Victor's parents as well and even Nat's mother and father if they could manage a trip from New York. The Landaus accepted with delight, but Harold and Dora Rosenbaum declined. Dora explained that she had recently visited Nat and that she intended to come on an extended visit once the baby arrived. She was thrilled that Jaya was planning the shower and she would be sure to send a gift.

Finding a theme for gifts was the toughest part of the planning because it seemed that Nat had already accumulated everything the baby could possibly need. She didn't register anywhere because she wanted to shop for her daughter on her own. The nursery was almost finished and no one wanted to risk adding something that might not fit in with the decorative scheme. David Singer finally came up with a good suggestion. "Let's give the baby books and micro discs," he proposed and everyone agreed.

Natalya and Victor arrived at the Khanna's on time on the Saturday before Thanksgiving for the promised lobster curry. They rang the doorbell at eight o'clock sharp, and waited in vain for someone to answer. Wondering what was wrong, they rang again more assertively, but this time they jumped back startled when a hand pulled the door open abruptly and a group assembled in the dark shouted "Surprise!"

As soon as the lights were switched back on, big bunches of brightly colored balloons began to float up to the ceiling. "Ronald! Cecily!" Nat screamed when she saw that the hand that had opened the door belonged to her brother and that his wife Cecily was standing by his side smiling.

"Hope you're up to accommodating a couple of house guests in the soon to be nursery," Cecily said with a smile.

"Our day bed is big enough for two, as long as you don't mind snuggling," Nat told her. She tried to hug her petite sister-in-law as she spoke, but couldn't manage. Her tummy had become too big.

"Come on, don't just stand there. There's a party going on," Sunil said, ushering the little crowd that was collected in the entrance hall toward the living room.

As the group moved inside and settled down, Dr. Henry Landau began to puncture the purple balloons using a long pole with a nail on the end of it. One by one, the balloons burst and sent forth a shower of silver confetti that fell like rain on Victor and Nat.

"Our cloudburst of confetti is symbolic," Rebecca said. "It's to shower the three of you with love, blessings and the best wishes of your family and friends."

Conversation hummed in the Khanna's living room. An Indian feast was laid out on the dining table, buffet style, and people were torn between their interest in the food and their interest in the various discussions that were underway. A fair amount of talk centered on the food itself.

"This lobster curry is the finest thing I've ever tasted. Is the recipe a family secret?"

"I usually don't like lamb but this is different."

"I didn't know that saffron was used in rice. I thought it was only for desserts."

"Don't tell anyone, but the eggplants and the nan, that flat bread, come from a restaurant."

"What's in these baked bananas? Are you supposed to eat the skin?"

"Can you buy this stuff in Houston?"

"Grated cucumbers, mustard and yogurt. Hmn. I'm going to try it."

"Remember that you have to put salt in the cucumbers and squeeze out all the water. Do it two or three times."

Anjali was discussing her philosophy of "hands on" parenting with Victor and Rebecca Landau.

"Of course they're adults," she said, "but they're still my children."

"How do you get educated, intelligent adults to pay attention to you?" Rebecca asked. "Victor would run away, wouldn't you?"

"Obviously," Victor answered. "I've been trying to escape from you my whole life, but at the end of the day, here I am, so how far did I get?"

"My kids don't always appreciate my input either. Still, when I've thought something through and I really believe in what I'm doing, I forge ahead," Anjali replied.

"I guess my problem is ambivalence," Rebecca said.

"That and the fact that you always manage to make me feel guilty about something. And your constant worrying drives me nuts," Victor added.

"I've had some blows in my life," Anjali said. "I was devastated when my husband died, but I recovered. A tragedy of that magnitude can teach you to stop worrying about things you can't control."

"I've had tragedy in my life as well, but I never faced up to it. I was too little. What spiritual resources does a small child have?" Rebecca thought, but what she said was, "I could learn a lot from you."

"Let me tell you a little story from Hindu mythology," Anjali offered. "It has to do with mothering and love. The story is about Lord Krishna as a young boy. He was God, and all-powerful, but the human side of Him was always getting Him into trouble. He teased the milkmaids and stole their butter, so His mother decided to tie Him up. The problem was that she couldn't succeed. No matter how many times she tied Him and no matter how strong a rope she used, Krishna could always untie Himself and escape. But one day He saw His mother crying and understood that to make her happy He would have to remain tied up until she untied Him. And He did. The point of the story is that our children can escape from all bonds, except the bonds of love."

"That's a lovely story," Rebecca said. "It's so simple and it says so much."

"Yes, it does," Victor agreed.

"Tell me, Anjali," Victor asked a few moments later, "are all Indian names as pretty as yours and Jaya's? You know Nat asked me to suggest names, but I haven't been able to think of any we both like. I like names that start in 'sh' or 's' like Shenna or Sheena or even Sylvia, but Nat said no to those three."

"I've been thinking a lot about names," Rebecca said, "but I haven't dared open my mouth. I suppose this is an example of a subject where input isn't helpful."

"Yes and no," Victor said. "I have no problem with your making suggestions. The problem comes when you act mortally wounded if I don't take you up on them. See, you already look deflated."

Rebecca mustered a smile. "What does the name Anjali mean?"

"It's the gesture of joining hands in greeting or prayer, like this," Anjali answered putting her palms together. "So you have been thinking about names," she said. "What names do you like?"

"Well, I love Shelly. I don't know a Shelly, but I like it," Rebecca admitted. "You'd probably say it's too common, wouldn't you, Victor? You know sometimes we Jews name our children in honor of an ancestor, but other families say it's bad luck."

"You never told me that. Why would it be bad luck?" Victor asked.

"I'm not sure I know. What if the person whose name we pick didn't have a long or happy life? Why take a chance? Nat told me Dora said a child should be born with a name uniquely his or hers."

"What about Sheela?" Anjali asked. "It's an Indian name if you spell it with two e's—S-h-e-e-l-a. It means having a beautiful nature."

"That's it!" Victor exclaimed. Then he added, "I meant to say that's it if Nat agrees."

Victor was about to seek Nat out, but before he could get up Sunil clanged on a glass with a tablespoon.

"Sorry to interrupt your conversations, but we have some gifts for Nat and Victor's baby girl. So please make yourselves comfortable and quiet while I get them. Nat and Victor, please sit in these two chairs in the center of the room so everyone can see you. Thanks. Dessert, which is ice cream cake, will follow."

A minute or two later, Sunil wheeled in a tea trolley filled with many carefully selected and attractively wrapped books and micro discs. It took nearly an hour to open them all, because Natalya and Victor savored each one, flipping through the books and talking about the discs. The book most prized was *The Country of Thirty Six Thousand Wishes*, which Dora Rosenbaum managed to find in good condition in a rare bookstore. It had been Nat's favorite when she was a child and it was many years out of print. Her own copy, inherited from Dora, had disintegrated from being read so many times. The other books were wonderful too: a complete set of Dr. Seuss, an exquisitely illuminated copy of Mother Goose, a book of Russian children's stories with drawings by children, two big Richard Scary books, several books of fairy tales all beautifully illustrated, collections of classic favorites like *The Little Engine That Could*, books about animals, a book about fishes that was a work of art, and the Indian epics, *The Mahabharata* and *The Ramayana*, written for children.

The micro discs were special too. Nat and Victor loved all of them, especially *Fantasia, Noah's Ark, The Baby Kings, Flying On Top of the World*, and Isaac Asimov's *Robot Dreams*. But their favorite was *Mirrors,* ten stories about children who saw reflections of the world inside themselves and discovered that everything they saw was real.

Victor did not get the courage to ask Natalya if she liked the name Sheela until much later that night when they were in bed. That name, he felt, suited their little daughter perfectly. He wanted her to have it so badly, that he was afraid to hear his wife's answer.

"Yes," Natalya said. "Sheela spelled with two e's. Of a beautiful nature. It is the perfect name."

"Sheela," Sheela thought. "I am Sheela." Sheela smiled and gave her parents a gentle kick of approval.

12

Sheela, Nat, and Victor were impatient for birth to take place. They wanted to be together in the outside world. Moreover they were uncomfortable. Nat's stomach exerted pressure on her insides. Sudden leg cramps during the night disturbed her sleep. Sheela was squashed. Victor had a knot in his stomach. He wanted the process of birth to be over and he wanted Nat's body back to himself.

Both Nat and Victor's days were full; they worked long hours so they would have less to do once Sheela was born. After work they finished Sheela's room and assembled the tiny garments and items that she would require for the first few months of her life. The photo album was up to date. So far it had pictures of five great grandparents, of all four grandparents, of Victor and Natalya, and of Ronald and Cecily. There were also pictures of Sheela's sonogram and of the growing bulges she made inside Nat's tummy. All the photographs were annotated with dates, or approximate dates, and legends. The album would be complete when Sheela was born.

⚬⚬⚬❊❉❊⚬⚬⚬

The morning after Sheela's shower, Nat and Victor broke their Sunday brunch tradition to take Ronald and Cecily out to the River Café, which specialized in crepes. The foursome ate and conversed with gusto.

"I can't believe I'm eating so much, especially after yesterday's banquet," Cecily said. "Since Ronald and I made up, my appetite has gotten out of control. I'm going to have to go on a diet if it doesn't taper off on its own."

"What helped you make up?" Natalya asked. "I mean besides the fact that you love each other."

"I stopped hiding behind the curtain," Cecily said. "I realize that what I do isn't just my business. It impacts Ronald and now I tell him the truth, the whole truth and nothing but the truth about what's going on in the theater."

"And I've come to terms with Cecily's devotion to the theater." Ronald volunteered.

"Is there any chance Sheela can look forward to having a cousin any time soon?" Nat asked. "You guys are her only shot."

"We talked along those lines," Cecily answered. "But first we want to have some fun times. The last eighteen months have been from hell. We want a year of heaven before we think about parenthood on earth."

"Is that what you think, Ronald, or is your wife speaking for you, like mine tends to?" Victor asked.

"I don't."

"You don't agree!" Cecily exclaimed. "How can you say that? We talked about this on the plane."

"No. I meant I don't think."

"See? Here I am accused of speaking for Ronald, who told me clearly that he wanted a year of quality time before starting a family. Didn't you, Ronald Rosenbaum, tell me that in so many words?"

"I guess I did. But I didn't think."

"I rest my case," Cecily concluded.

* * *

Natalya and Victor usually spent Thanksgiving in New York with the Rosenbaums, but traveling was out of the question this year. Instead, Nat planned to have it at home. In the end she wasn't up to that either. After some discussion, it was settled that Rebecca and Henry would prepare dinner using the Rosenbaum recipes since Rebecca's turkey and stuffing admittedly didn't hold a candle to Dora's. There would just be the four of them, but the meal would still be a full-fledged affair with all the trimmings.

Henry did not habitually get involved in cooking and marketing, but this occasion was an exception. He took it upon himself to personally ensure that all the preparations were correct and he couldn't remember when he'd enjoyed a project so much. He insisted on doing the marketing alone and he enjoyed the challenge of locating each item on his list in the labyrinth that was the grocery store. He mumbled to himself, almost audibly, as he trekked through the crowded aisles and filled his shopping cart.

"Cranberry sauce, ah, here it is. I'll take two cans. Oops, that's not Ocean Spray. It has to be Ocean Spray and jellied. Right, there it is. And marshmallows for the sweet potatoes. Here they are. But they come in two sizes. Nat didn't tell me whether I should get the regular or the miniature size. I'll get a pack of each."

After two hours and fifteen minutes, Henry was finished. He returned home and helped Rebecca set the dining room table with their finest china and silver so they wouldn't have to do it tomorrow. Everything was under control. Rebecca had already baked pumpkin, apple and mince pies.

* * *

"This is without a doubt the best turkey I have ever eaten," Henry proclaimed, "and I've enjoyed it in the company of the three people I love most in the world."

"I'll second that statement," Rebecca added. "Except there are four of us here you love most in the world."

"Yes, and the littlest seems to be dominating the occasion. We've hardly talked about anything but Sheela," Nat said.

77

"I stand corrected. I guess I didn't count Sheela separately because even though I think of her all the time, I don't have a picture of her in my head. Who do you think she looks like?" Henry asked.

"Like Victor," Nat replied just as Victor said, "Like Natalya."

"I was thinking," Nat said later in the evening, "that we shouldn't put up a Christmas tree this year."

"Why not?" Rebecca asked. "Christmas trees aren't Christian. You know they are an old pagan tradition."

"Because even if they aren't originally Christian, today they symbolize Christmas which in turn is the celebration of the birth of Christ. I want Sheela to know she is Jewish."

"Of course she's Jewish. That has nothing to do with Christmas or Santa Claus. Christmas is hardly a religious holiday any more," Rebecca argued.

"I think Nat's right," Victor said, to his wife's surprise. "It's funny. I agree that Christmas has been commercialized and secularized beyond recognition. And as a kid I was thankful that you and Dad let me have a tree and presents. I felt sorry for the other Jewish children whose families wouldn't let them. I appreciated having enlightened, broad-minded parents. Still, deep down there was a part of me that didn't feel right. It felt like I was betraying something even though I didn't know what."

"With me it was the opposite," Nat explained. "My parents didn't allow Christmas trees and I resented not having them. They never could give me an explanation as to why we couldn't put a tree up. After all, Jesus Christ was Jewish, and he was a great person if not a saint. So what was wrong with a Christmas tree? My father only said that my grandmother wouldn't have liked it, but my grandmother wasn't alive. It didn't make sense to me. Ronald told me that we couldn't be sure that Grandma wouldn't know. I asked my mother if she thought maybe Grandma could see, and she said it didn't matter. What mattered was that she wouldn't have liked it. My mother couldn't even say why she wouldn't have liked it; she just knew she wouldn't have."

"So why don't you want to have a tree now?" Henry asked his daughter-in-law.

"Because Christmas trees celebrate the birth of Jesus Christ the savior, not Christ the man or Christ the saint. The essence of Judaism is the belief that Christ is not the Messiah, but that the Messiah is yet to come. Christmas is the pivotal distinction between Judaism and Christianity."

Rebecca corrected Nat. "That's only the dogmatic distinction between the two faiths. The real distinction is multi-dimensional."

"I'm sure you are right, but I still think we should pass on Christmas celebrations now that we have Sheela," Victor reiterated.

"What will you say to Sheela," Rebecca asked "when she goes to kindergarten and wants to know why Santa Claus won't come to her house? You asked me, Victor, if Santa Claus wasn't visiting the other Jewish children because they were naughty."

"How did you answer me?"

"I said Santa Claus didn't visit children who didn't believe in him."

"Then that's what we will tell Sheela when she is in kindergarten," Natalya said. "Plus I'll out-do Santa at Chanukah and Purim. But when Sheela gets older I want her to understand what being Jewish really means."

"Do you understand what it really means?" Rebecca asked.

"No," Nat answered. "I honestly don't, but I intend to learn and I bet you can help me."

⸺ ⚬⚬⚬⚬⦿⚬⚬⚬⚬ ⸺

Sheela was "due" on January 7, 2001, but she didn't want to wait that long. Ever since she had turned herself around so her head pointed downward in Natalya's uterus, she felt ready to make the journey out into the world. Now she was ill at ease. There was little to see. Victor and Nat only played music or read to her in the evenings. It was no fun lying there, on top of her mother's bladder, barely able to move. She weighed six and a quarter pounds and she was eighteen and a half inches long. Her skin was red and smooth. It looked polished under the cheesy splotches of grease that covered her. Her head was thick with two inches of gleaming black hair. Her big almond shaped eyes were a deep dark blue with a greenish tinge. Her fingers and toes were long and wrinkled. Both her fingernails and her toenails needed trimming. She was supposed to gain a few more ounces and grow a few more fractions of an inch, but couldn't she do that just as well after being born?

⸺ ⚬⚬⚬⚬⦿⚬⚬⚬⚬ ⸺

Like most people who had exhausted their enthusiasm on the year 2000, Victor and Natalya made no spectacular plans to usher in the new millennium, not that Sheela would have let them do much even if they had wanted to. At first they considered going to The Houston Symphony's New Year program with the Singers, but then even that seemed like it would be too stressful. They thought the loud noise might bother Sheela and Nat could barely sit for an hour without going to the bathroom. Since Christmas, she had been experiencing occasional irregular contractions which made her tense. Thus the Landaus decided to stay home and celebrate with their favorite cold cuts and a plum pudding.

The morning of December 31st Nat woke up feeling surprisingly energetic and well. She went to the grocery store and purchased whatever was still needed for supper as well as provisions for the next few days. After returning home she prepared and froze lasagna and a pot roast for future consumption. Later in the afternoon she decided to take a short walk in Hermann Park. As she was struggling to reach the Velcro fastening on her tennis shoes, Rebecca called.

"How are you, Nat?" she asked.

"I'm fine. I made lasagna and a pot roast to freeze and I was just going for a walk in the park. That is provided I can get to my feet to close my tennis shoes. Are you sure you and Papa won't join us tonight?"

"Yes, we want to watch the Boston Pops. But we may not be able to."

"Why not?"

"Because Sheela may decide to be born tonight. The burst of energy you got today is a common sign that you are ready to go into labor."

"I never heard of anything like that," Nat said.

"Well, I could be wrong. Maybe it's just an old wives' tale. Still, you might pack your bag and tell Victor to be sure his camera is ready."

"The baby isn't due until January 7th and first babies are usually late, aren't they?" Nat asked.

"They often are," Rebecca answered. "You never can tell."

79

"But why do you think I suddenly got so peppy? There has to be an explanation. You know, I just thought of something."

"What's that?"

"I read that when a baby is ready for birth, its levels of adrenaline surge like crazy. Maybe some of that is passing through to me. That would explain the old wives' tale. It's probably true."

"That makes sense, dear," Rebecca said. "Let's just wait and see. How is Victor holding up?"

"He's fidgety, but he tries to be supportive. His back rubs are more like back pokes. He keeps worrying that the baby isn't moving as much as it did and he watches me like a hawk."

"I thought all those classes you've taken were supposed to calm him down."

"They were supposed to, but they didn't."

"I'm sure the baby is anxious too," Rebecca added.

"Why?" Natalya asked.

"Just imagine, being squeezed upside down, with your hormones out of whack. How would you feel?"

"I didn't think of that. What should I do?"

"I guess just tell Sheela you love her."

When Natalya related her conversation with Rebecca to Victor, he panicked.

"There's no way you can go for a walk," he said. "What if you go into labor while you're out? What if your water bursts? Let's pack your bag. Please."

"It will take me five minutes to pack my bag, Victor," Nat answered. "It's no big deal. I may not go into labor at all. This is just speculation. I don't feel like staying cooped up in the house. I want to go for a walk. It's good for me."

"What about me?" Victor asked. "What should I do?"

"Don't do anything, Victor. Relax. Get your camera out. I gassed up this morning. There's nothing else to do."

"Well, I could come for a walk with you."

"That would be nice," Nat said. "A walk would do you good too."

"But I need to get my camera ready and we need to pack your bag."

"No, we don't need to do any of that. We don't have to go to the hospital until the contractions are six or seven minutes apart, and that takes a while even after they start, which they haven't."

"But if your waters burst, then we have to go right away."

Nat packed her bag and Victor took his loaded camera out of the drawer. Then he was hungry, so he had a bowl of soup. At last, they set out. They walked for forty minutes and returned home refreshed, but with no indication that Sheela intended to make her debut into the world on the first day of the new millennium. That would be neat, Nat thought. Victor worried about tracking down the obstetrician on New Year's Eve. He called Dr. Hamburg's office and was reassured that the good doctor carried his pager wherever he went. Since he was already on the phone, Victor asked the voice at the other end how he could tell when labor was about to begin.

"You've been over that more than once, sir," she said.

"My wife has been extremely active," Victor explained.

"That's quite typical before labor," the voice commented.

"How much time before?"

"It varies" was the extent of the answer Victor could extract. Before he thought to ask the voice if she was an answering service, she hung up.

Victor was helping Nat set up for supper when Nat felt the onset of a pain in her lower back. She waited to see if she could feel a contraction or an easing of the pain, but she couldn't. Her uterus seemed to tighten without relaxing. Simultaneously Sheela felt the pressure of a discomforting constriction and she tensed up too, causing Nat's tummy to harden. These sensations didn't really fit in with anything Nat had been anticipating, so she tried to ignore them and to proceed with preparations for the evening. However, after a few minutes, she had to tell Victor that she couldn't go on. Not wanting to risk Victor rushing her to the hospital for no good reason, Natalya played down her pain.

"I'm sure this isn't labor. I just ache a bit," she said. "I'm sure it will pass if I lie down and rest for a while."

"I think we should call the doctor's office and find out what to do," Victor said.

"That's silly. You know we're supposed to call and go to the hospital when the contractions are about seven minutes apart, ten minutes at the earliest, or if the amniotic sac ruptures. Anyway, all we'd get is the answering service."

"I know, but they didn't say anything about what to do if you ache steadily."

"Let's just wait a little longer. I'd hate to have a false alarm, tonight of all nights."

Lying down felt worse, so Nat decided to take a hot shower. The warm water coursing down her body helped, and after some time Nat felt well enough to dress and think again about supper. But after a few moments the ache intensified. She let out an inadvertent gasp.

"What should we do now?" Victor asked. He started to reel and took several deep breaths. In his head he had planned that when the time for Sheela to be born came around, he would take charge of matters, at least to the extent of delivering his wife safely to the maternity ward. It was the part after that which terrified him.

"I need to walk. I've got to keep moving."

Nat started pacing in her home. She walked to the nursery, moved a stuffed parrot from the day bed to a shelf and then put it back on the day bed. Then she walked into the kitchen and wiped countertops that were already immaculate. Then she went back to the nursery. Victor felt a wave of nausea and then stomach cramps. He rushed to the bathroom. When he emerged, Nat was pale. Victor was relieved that she didn't seem to notice what he looked like.

"Now I think I'm feeling contractions," Nat said, "but I can't keep track of the time. Maybe we should go the hospital after all."

The Landaus arrived safely at Hermann Hospital shortly after 9:00 p.m. Nat was wheeled to a birthing room and within moments nurses and residents took over the show. They felt and probed at Nat and Sheela and hooked them up to machines. They gave Nat hot tea. Victor stood uncomfortably to the side and was frightened to learn that Sheela's heart was beating almost twice as fast as Nat's. Eventually someone said "Yes, that's normal. They're doing fine." Somewhere along the line, Nat felt gushes of water wetting her bed, and someone told her that was good. Victor kept trying to find a chunk of time in which to hold Nat's hand and to say "Breathe . . . Now relax . . . Another deep breath . . . that's great," just like they had practiced, but there was no opportunity. When he approached Nat she screamed and asked him to rub her back. But when he rubbed, she said he wasn't doing it right and made him stop.

"I can't handle this! It's awful! They didn't tell me! It's not fair!" Nat yelled.

When Victor couldn't stand it any more, he walked out of the room. As soon as he stepped outside into the hall, Nat called for him.

"Victor! Come back! Please! Don't leave me! Help me!" she shouted, and Victor came back in and took her hand. Nat squeezed his hand to a pulp. It hurt for a week afterward.

Sheela hurt too. Her head throbbed and she was red and breathless, but she was strong. She forged her way forward and downward, rotating herself well into Nat's pelvis. At one point Rebecca and Henry came in for a second and their gentleness soothed her. It won't be much longer, Sheela thought, and the thrilling prospect of finally being caressed by Nat and Victor kept her going.

Dr. Hamburg arrived all chipper at three o'clock in the morning. "How do you feel?" he asked Nat.

"Like I'm trying to . . . Owwww." Nat's face contorted with pain and stress. "Owwww!"

"Come on, Nat, breathe. More. The baby needs the oxygen."

"Ok. I'll breathe, but please tell that awful nurse to stop counting."

"She'll stop if you breathe," Dr. Hamburg said. "You're at nearly four inches, fully dilated," he said. "It's time to start pushing. Come on, Natalya. Sit up. Push! Good. Now breathe. Push again. Harder! There, I can see the head. Does your daughter have a name?"

"Uhh, ennhh. Ohhh." Nat replied.

"Her name is Sheela," Victor volunteered timidly.

"What are you hiding from?" Dr. Hamburg asked Victor. "Look, Sheela has the longest black hair I've ever seen on a newborn. Take a picture."

Victor attempted to do as he was bid, but the second he saw Sheela's head, covered with blood, trying to work its way out of his wife's body, he felt faint. He greened and then staggered. Luckily, the counting nurse who had been watching caught him and lowered him gently to the floor saving his head from a bad blow. His camera wasn't quite as lucky. When it fell out of Victor's hands, it hit the floor with a bang and crashed to smithereens.

Book Two

13

Sheela Landau was born at 3:50 a.m. Monday, January 1, 2001. The shock of exposure to the outside world dazzled her, momentarily blocking her awareness of her surroundings. But her senses were aroused as soon as she successfully inhaled and then exhaled her first gulp of air. The world was cold and weird and Sheela cried. She stopped when she was laid on Nat's body to feel the familiar beating of her mother's heart, to absorb her mother's joy, to touch her skin, and to inhale her scent.

Victor suffered more embarrassment than regret over missing the final moments of his daughter's birth. He regained consciousness seconds after he had passed out, but didn't move because his legs felt like jelly and his brain was fried. He floated in a state of vagueness. However, Sheela's first lusty cry made him want to get up.

"I didn't really faint, did I? It's a girl, isn't it? Everyone is fine, right?" He fired questions at no one in particular and no one answered until Natalya called out.

"Come and see us."

"I feel ridiculous," he mumbled.

"You'll be fine," Jennifer, the counting nurse said, helping him to his feet. "You're not our first paternal casualty. Go ahead, say hi to your daughter."

Victor had been bracing himself for the fact that Sheela might look funny. Many newborns, he had been told, look beat up. Their eyelids might be swollen or their eyes reddened, as if they were hung over. Their faces could be puffy, or blotched, or their skin scaly. Sometimes their heads were elongated. But nothing prepared him for what he would see and how he would feel the first time he laid eyes on his daughter.

She was exquisite. Her black hair gleamed. Her head was round and her hair-line was in the shape of a heart. Her eyebrows were the same design as Natalya's. Her mouth was a miniature version of his. It was firm, but full and topped with two peaks on the upper lip. She had a single dimple on her right cheek, a marking all her own. No scientific explanation could account for such perfection. Victor vowed that from this instant forward he would do everything within his power to shelter Sheela from sadness and from harm. The very idea that anyone could ever dare to cause her even the smallest iota of pain caused a streak of fury to flash through his being. But it quickly passed and he smiled as he leaned down and embraced his beaming wife. Then he gently stroked his daughter's cheek and spoke to her softly.

"Hello, Sheela. I'm your Dad and I love you."

As soon as Sheela heard those words, she opened one of her deep ocean blue eyes and winked. When Sheela opened her second eye, she saw the imprint of Victor's love on his face and she was glad.

Then her mother spoke to her for the first time since she was born. Nat's melodious voice was familiar.

"Welcome to the world, Sheela. We're going to have fun."

Sheela turned her head. Her gaze met Natalya's and Sheela saw her own blue eyes shine back at her from within her mother's hazely green ones. The green eyes enveloped Sheela in their warmth and told her that she was cherished. They smiled as Nat puckered her mouth and gave Sheela a soft kiss on her cheek. Sheela liked that and she puckered her mouth too and snuggled at Nat's breast. Nat puckered her mouth again, and Sheela did it again, too.

"Look, Victor, Sheela is copying me," Nat told her husband.

"That's impossible. It's your imagination," Victor responded.

"No, it's not. You hold her and watch."

Victor's strong arms lifted his daughter in the air and embraced her. Sheela liked how she felt and she puckered her mouth in approval. Victor laughed and then he opened his mouth wide and Sheela opened her mouth again. Then Victor stuck out his tongue and thought he saw Sheela stuck out her little tongue as well.

Sheela heard her brain beeping as it registered her new surroundings. She felt stickiness, warmth, coolness, wetness, and dryness. She flinched at a bright light and relaxed her eyes when they fell upon softer tones. She saw shapes and colors and tasted the salt and the sweetness on her mother's skin. She felt the texture of her mother's nipples and the strength of the muscles in her father's body. She smelled his cologne mixed with the odor of his masculinity and his excitement. She listened to familiar and unfamiliar voices and she heard herself cry.

All this tired Sheela, and finally, having spent the flood of energy that her body produced for her birth, she slept her first sleep after being born. And while her body and brain rested and her mind dreamt, her spirit fathomed its connection with eternity.

⁂

The Landaus left the hospital for home on January third, when Sheela was two and a half days old. Henry used a disposable camera to take snapshots of the event. These snapshots would complete Sheela's album. There were no photographs of her being born since Victor's camera broke when he fainted. Natalya wondered what Sheela would think about this story when she grew up. Would she be relieved or would she regret not having her entry into the world documented for posterity?

Rebecca, it was decided, would stay and assist in caring for Sheela until January fifth, when Dora was scheduled to arrive. She was happy as a lark to have been asked. Victor urged his father to stay as well.

"I'm being overtaken by women. I need moral support."

"You want me to sleep with Rebecca in the nursery? Two grandparents snoring in one tiny bed?"

"It's not a tiny bed. You'd easily fit. Or else, you can snore on the sofa. Besides, how will you manage without Mom?"

"I'll be fine. I have work to do for an article I'm writing."

"I didn't know you were writing an article. What is it about?

"It's about the long-term effects of early tonsillectomies. Anyhow let me leave Rebecca to her granddaughter and let me sleep in my own bed. I'll be by tomorrow."

Sheela liked home better than the hospital. Victor carried her on a tour of their condo and showed her every nook and cranny. Sheela paid attention to what Victor said and peered around. She liked what she saw. The shapes in her room intrigued her and she spent a long moment staring at a stuffed brightly colored parrot who would become her companion for years to come. She also examined with interest a pair of tall silver candlesticks that stood on the dining table and a big mirror in the hall. After a while she pressed her mouth against Victor's chest and he handed her over to Nat. Nat took her to a sliding chair and Sheela nursed. Then Rebecca put on music and took her. She bundled her, burped her, put Sheela on her shoulder, and patted her on the back until she fell asleep.

The picture of his mother caring for his daughter with a glow of contentment on her face moved Victor to wonder. *How can she love Sheela so much? She probably loves me just as much. Is it possible that she and Dad care about me as much as Nat and I care about our daughter? My God! I should try to be less abrasive with Mom and less neglectful of Dad,* he told himself, overcome by a sense of guilt. *But she drives me nuts,* he thought to justify his behavior. Then his conscience told him, *That's no excuse. You can't punish her for being who she is or for loving too much.* In his heart Victor acknowledged that Rebecca had been a fine mother and he hoped he and Nat could do as well by Sheela as their parents had done by them. *Will Sheela think Nat or I make her crazy when she's an adult?*

Victor needed to connect with Rebecca.

"Mom, would you like a cup of tea or something, maybe a glass of wine?"

"A glass of wine would be delightful. It's a bit late for tea. Nat suggested that we have the New Year's Eve cold cuts for supper unless you want the lasagna or pot roast she froze. Or would you prefer that I make something else?"

"The cold cuts would be great. There are frozen bagels and fresh German pumpernickel and I could bake a loaf of French bread. I'm going to check on Nat and then I'll open a bottle of a great Chilean Merlot I discovered."

A few moments later Victor was back with two glasses of wine. "Nat's taking a nap. Cheers, Mom. And, uh . . . thank you for helping with Sheela."

"Cheers and blessings. Here's to the new millennium heralded by Sheela Landau! Listen, I'm not ungrateful, but please don't thank me for doing something that gives me so much happiness."

"Why not, Mom? I'm glad you're here with us, participating and helping with Sheela. Nat's so tired, and I feel helpless."

"That's good to hear, very good. But 'thank you' makes me feel that I'm here doing you a favor rather than because I belong here. I want you to take it for granted that I'm part of Sheela's life."

"OK." Victor moved to give Rebecca a warm embrace. "Let's just share a moment of mutual appreciation. But I have to tell you that this means a lot to me. Having Sheela and watching you with her and with Nat has opened my eyes."

"I'm sure it has," Rebecca mused. "You know, fatherhood is the biggest change that ever happens in a man's life. It's a more comprehensive change than marriage. I think that while motherhood completes a woman, fatherhood transforms a man."

"I hope the transformation is a positive one."

"It is, but being a father sometimes comes at the expense of light-heartedness. Things that never bothered a man before bother him when he is responsible for a child."

"I guess. You know, Mom? The second I saw Sheela, I felt angry at the world. The feeling just lasted a second. Then it went away. But it was there."

"What were you angry about?"

"About the fact that there might be someone or something out there that could cause Sheela to suffer," Victor replied.

"There will be things out there, and I'm sure you'll deal with them. But the important thing is to give Sheela every possible opportunity to deal with them herself."

"I guess that won't be easy," Victor remarked.

"No, it won't. It will make you different. I used to wish that our children could know us the way we were before we became parents. But then I remembered how I felt about my own mother and father. I realized that I would never have understood them anyway because kids cannot see their parents as real people with personalities, problems, and joys. To kids the only point of a parent is that he or she is a parent and the only reality of the parent-child relationship is how it impacts them."

Natalya and Victor had their first spat over Sheela in the two-hour window between Rebecca's departure and Dora's arrival. Nat was cranky. She was sick and tired of being cooped up in the house. She wanted to take Sheela and drive with Victor to the airport, but Victor said no.

"It's cold and rainy. There's no reason for me to be worrying about driving with you guys on the slippery highway just because you want an outing. Besides, being alone with Sheela for a couple of hours will do you good."

"It's not just that I want an outing. Change is good for babies. We're going from a heated house to a heated car and it's not all that cold anyway. Do you think babies who live in Chicago, where the wind chill is 20 degrees below zero, don't go out?"

"I'm sure they don't go to the airport at the age of five days."

"Well, Victor this isn't Chicago and it's forty degrees above zero here."

"I wasn't the one who brought up Chicago, Nat. You did."

"So? That doesn't tell me why I can't surprise my mother. I want to go with you. Are you suddenly scared of driving in the rain? If anything happens to you because of the rain, I'd just as soon it happened to all of us," Nat said.

"I'm not afraid of the rain and nothing is going to happen to me. But it is lousy out and if there's a traffic jam or a thunderstorm, it would be a mess with you and Sheela in the car. You're staying home and that's that."

"Since when do you tell me what I can and can't do?"

"Since I have become a father. But, hey, I'm always willing to listen to reason. Do you think your mother would approve of your dragging Sheela out in this weather simply because you'd enjoy the ride?"

"She'd be surprised and excited to see her," Nat answered.

"That wasn't my question, Natalya. I asked whether she would approve. Would your mom think it's a good change for her five-day-old granddaughter to be stuck in a traffic jam or waiting at the airport on a miserably rainy day?"

"I don't know. Maybe she wouldn't. But Victor, I've got to do something. I'm down in the dumps. How can I feel this way when I have everything I ever dreamed of? I love Sheela so much and she is doing so well, touch wood. I thank God a hundred times a day, but I still feel like shit."

"You have post-partum depression caused by hormonal changes. It's all in the brochure you made me read. Your body was used to having a baby inside it and now it's sad because the baby is gone. Plus here are some other reasons you feel like shit, as you put it: you haven't been getting enough sleep and the sleep you have been getting has been broken up; you want to make love; you are bored without the stimulus of your usual hectic life; you haven't had a chance to gossip with your friends; you still hurt from the episiotomy and your hemorrhoids; you would love a couple of glasses of wine and can't have more than a sip because you're nursing; much as you want your mother to come, you miss your privacy. Does that cover it?"

"Actually there's more. I thought you had no clue about what I was feeling so I wasn't going to tell you. But you really understand."

"I always understand," Victor said. "So what else is there?"

"I'm worried about not being free again until I'm practically an old lady. I feel fat. We haven't found anyone we can trust to take care of Sheela when I go back to work. I worry about you resenting the fact that I don't pay any attention to you and that you have to make do, you know, with whatever we can do."

"OK. Now does that cover it?"

"Yeah."

"So besides lugging Sheela to the airport which is out of the question, what do you want to do?"

"I want to cry."

"OK, cry."

"I can't," Natalya said. "I love you."

Still, when Victor said, "I love you," and gave Nat a wonderful deep long kiss, Nat began to bawl and soon after that she felt better.

Sheela adjusted easily to the switch in grandmothers, although the way she felt about them was as different as night and day. Rebecca Landau understood her like Natalya's mother never would. She anticipated her every need, her every worry, her every joy. There was more than love in her translucent blue eyes. There was recognition. But her voice, even when she carried Sheela in her arms and spoke or sung directly into Sheela's ear, was always followed by an echo that came from far away. Dora Rosenbaum, on the other hand, was cozy and relaxed. She thought Sheela's life was going to be a piece of cake. She smiled readily and showed Sheela tricks like putting a teddy bear who could play Brahms' Lullaby on your tummy and then bouncing both you and the bear up and down on her knees.

Although Sheela didn't like to cry, every day she cried a little more than the day before. Before being born, she could take care of herself. Now, unless she cried, Natalya didn't think of letting her nurse and unless she cried, no one picked her up and cuddled her, or talked or read to her or showed her anything interesting. When she was in Natalya's womb, she always heard everything her parents said. Then she could even read minds. But that wasn't so easy any more. One of the bad parts of being born was that other people decided what you wanted and what to do about it. Sometimes they couldn't get it right. Especially in the evening when no one realized how tired you were and how crying made you swallow air and then gave you a tummy ache. Then the only thing that helped was when Dora wrapped you up tight in a blanket and danced with you until you fell asleep.

Victor couldn't stand it when Sheela fretted. By the time she was two weeks old, it seemed that she cried non-stop every evening for two or three hours. Actually, his daughter was a pretty good baby, but she was exceptionally alert and active and she had a tough time winding down after her six o'clock feed. He felt that there should be a way to make her stop instantly, so when Natalya or Dora took too long to get her to settle down, he tried to take over. Invariably, the minute Victor picked Sheela up, his frustration made her scream louder than ever. That was bad for his ego. It was Victor's first lesson in recognizing the fact that he could not always alleviate his child's discomfort and it was a hard lesson to learn.

"What's the matter with her?" Victor asked Dora one evening, handing Sheela back to her grandmother. "Why won't she stop crying?"

"Nothing's the matter. She's just tired and uncomfortable. It's best to keep calm and try to help her quiet herself down," Dora answered. She walked and gently jounced her granddaughter as she talked.

"We must be doing something wrong. She shouldn't be crying so much."

"You aren't doing anything wrong. Sheela is a demanding child. She expects attention and wants to be comforted when she's on edge."

"Why does she expect attention? How can we stop her from being demanding? There has to be some explanation," Victor insisted.

"The answer to your first question is Sheela expects attention because she knows she is entitled to it and because she will thrive on it. The answer to question number two is we cannot stop your daughter from being demanding and we should not even try. To be demanding is a good thing in life. When Sheela is older, you can guide her so she makes wise demands. As for your third point, there is a very good explanation. Babies are people. They are born with personalities and we have to honor their personalities if we want them to flourish."

"So what should we do?" Victor asked.

"You should notice when Sheela is uptight, respect her right to feel that way, and then let her unwind at her own pace."

"It's odd," Natalya remarked, "that Beca said something similar to Victor when she was here."

"What did Rebecca say?"

"She told him that things are going to come along that will make Sheela unhappy and that his job was to let her deal with them herself, as far as possible."

"Yes, that is exactly what I believe," Dora whispered because Sheela was sound asleep.

14

Sheela smiled when she was five weeks old, the morning of the day Dora returned to New York. She had been bathed and fed and was propped up on the sofa with Dora and her parrot.

"We need a name for your parrot," Dora suggested. "He is rather handsome, isn't he?"

"Aaa-oooo." Sheela opened her mouth wide and then closed it in a circle as if she were about to whistle.

"What do you mean by that?" Dora asked. "You do agree that the parrot is handsome and needs a name, don't you?"

"Eeeehhh." Now Sheela looked as if she was preparing to cry.

"Hey, that's nothing to get upset about. What do you think about calling the parrot Pete? That's a cheerful easy name. Or maybe Pedro fits him better."

"Aaa-oooo," Sheela said again, this time aloud.

"Are you trying to tell me the parrot's name is Aa-Oo?"

Sheela smiled a real smile and for the third time told her grandmother "Aaa-oooo."

Prettied up in a smocked yellow dress given to her by Rebecca, Sheela and her paraphernalia—including Aa-Oo—went to the airport with Natalya to bid Dora farewell. Sheela gurgled at Dora throughout the drive and paid close attention while her grandma showed her the parrot's eyes and beak. She also glimpsed the scenery fleeting by, but everything was too far away to come into focus. At the airport, she took in all the exciting sounds, faces, actions, and smells. There were lots of people around but most of them paid little or no attention to her. It felt odd to be ignored. In Sheela's experience she was always the center of interest. Occasionally, though, someone would walk up and peer at her face. Then they would say "How cute!" or else ask Natalya "How old is she?" When that happened her mother looked all mushy and happy and replied "Thank you" or "She's five weeks."

When it was time to board, Dora gave Natalya and Sheela a huge hug. Her eyes misted because she didn't want to go, but she walked away anyhow. Then she turned back and waved. Natalya waved back and helped Sheela wave as well. Sheela could tell that her mother was about to cry so she cheered her up by saying Aa-Oo several times. On the drive home Sheela fell asleep trying to put her new experiences into context.

Back home, the house felt empty. It was time for Sheela's evening meal. Nat changed her into a T-shirt, fed her, burped her and put her in her crib along with Aa-Oo, a new terry cloth music box that played "It's a Small World After All," and her overhead jungle gym from which a mirror and many interesting shapes and colors hung. Then Nat headed for the kitchen so she could rustle up supper for Victor and herself. However, the moment Nat stepped out of the room, Sheela started to cry. Instead of fixing dinner, Natalya picked Sheela up and tried to lull her to sleep, but Sheela remained wide-awake and inconsolable. By the time Victor got home, mother and daughter were distraught.

"She misses her grandmother," Natalya said, almost in tears. "I think Sheela is more comfortable with my mother than she is with me."

"I'm sure she misses Dora," Victor agreed, "but she's probably crying because she senses that you are sad and that you aren't quite at ease with her this evening. Here, give her to me."

Victor and Sheela paced the floor until Sheela's screaming subsided. Victor didn't put her down, but continued to walk and talk to her until he could tell she was completely relaxed. Then he put her in her crib, but the moment he started to walk away, Sheela screamed again, so he had to pick her up and talk to her some more. When she got cranky again, he burped her, wrapped her up in a light blanket, and put her over his shoulder while he walked humming Brahms' Lullaby over and over in his deep baritone voice. At long last Sheela fell asleep. Victor was content because he had succeeded in calming his daughter where her mother had failed. He was also very happy to be alone with Nat for the first time since Sheela's birth.

Nat prepared trout sautéed with almonds in a lemon caper sauce and an accompaniment of rice, beans, and salad while Victor tended to their daughter. She too was happy to have her privacy back. To celebrate, she chilled a bottle of white wine and allowed herself one small glass.

At 7:45 the Landaus sat down and lifted their glasses to make a toast. Consistent with Murphy's Law, the telephone rang that very second.

"Let's turn down the volume and catch the messages later," Victor suggested.

"What if it's from New York?"

"Call back after dinner."

"You know I still can't stand the message on our machine. It discourages people from saying anything."

"Please, Nat, let's not get into that now," Victor replied.

"OK," Nat said, but she didn't lower the volume and she and Victor couldn't help hearing the message.

The caller was Jaya and she sounded dejected.

"Hi Nat and Victor," her voice said. "This is Jaya. Sorry to call when you are probably having dinner, but I'm getting ready to work out, and then I'm going back to the lab to check on an experiment. I need to talk to you, Nat. It's about

Sunil. Also, my mother-in-law sent a card for Sheela to my address. She didn't have yours. Can I come by after work tomorrow? Please leave me a message."

"What do you suppose is going on with Jaya?" Victor asked after he got up and silenced the recorder.

"I don't know, but trouble has been brewing for some time," Nat replied. Then she added, "I hope they make it."

"How can they not make it? They're a perfect couple. Anyway I thought Indians were more traditional than Americans and didn't separate at the drop of a hat. Sunil was telling me that even today, even in America educated Indians entered into arranged marriages and they succeeded because of strong family values and minimum expectations."

"Well, it's a long story..." Nat started to respond, but Victor interrupted.

"Never mind. That was a rhetorical question. Let's not get into other people's problems this second. Wouldn't you rather talk about us?"

"I seem to have forgotten how to do that."

"I'll start," Victor said. "Hasn't it been long enough yet? When do we go back to a normal life?"

"Well, I guess our life is normal now, but normal has changed."

"No. That's not what I mean. I mean normal including Sheela. Like when can we go back to . . . Hell, you know what I mean."

"Oh, that."

"Right, that," Victor said. "Hasn't it been on your mind at all?"

"Very much so," Natalya said. "But I still look horrible and I'm afraid you'll hate my swollen boobs, especially if they spritz milk on you. Every time Sheela cries, they start to flow."

"Won't bother me. They could spritz spinach juice for all I care. Every time I see Sheela feeding, I think what a good time she is having, at my expense."

"It's not at your expense, Victor."

"Sure, it is. The look on your face tells me you are enjoying yourself, that you're completely fulfilled. You don't miss me or anything."

"It's true that I'm fulfilled and that I love nursing Sheela. But I still think about making love and about the whole rest of my life. Right now though, Sheela is consuming all my energy. We're just beginning to get into the semblance of a routine. I told you the nannies I interviewed have all been weird. I plan to talk to a few more people soon. I think I'm going to concentrate on Hispanics. They seem sweeter somehow. I also thought that the exposure to Spanish and Mexican culture would be good for Sheela."

"That's a great idea," Victor said. "So who's lined up?"

"One woman from an agency and Annette's cleaning lady Rosario's cousin, Lulu. And, well, the doctor said we can go back to having sex after my six week checkup, if everything is OK and if I feel well."

"So, do you feel as well as you look? I don't know why you think you look horrible. You look very sexy to me."

"Really?" Nat asked, reaching over to hold Victor's hand.

"Really."

"For the last two nights Sheela has slept for six hour stretches so I'm not as frazzled as before. I'm not at all sore anymore either. Also, I'm ready to start working out. A girl in our pre-natal class who had her little boy two weeks before we had Sheela told me about a great video. It's called *Shaping up New Moms*. I'm going to begin with that. By the way, the class is having a reunion next week. Do you want to come?"

"Thanks, but no thanks. I'll volunteer to baby-sit instead."

'"No, we take our babies and show them off."

"Well, then I'll spend the night alone and reminisce about the good old days while you tell everyone what happened to me during the birth."

"Do you miss the days before Sheela?"

"Of course not. I was just trying to be clever. So when are you going in for your six-week check up?"

"Next Thursday."

"So are you saying that we can do it Thursday night?"

"Yes. But I won't be on the pill yet and while chances are I won't get pregnant while I'm nursing, it's not a hundred percent sure. I was going to ask you if we should figure something else out."

"Nah," Victor said. "I'm willing to live dangerously if you are."

"Sure," Nat said. "The worst case scenario is that Sheela gets a little sister or brother before she has a chance to be jealous, but I doubt that will happen."

"A little boy would be good."

"What if we have another girl?"

"I guess we could go for a third round."

"And if that's a girl too?"

"I suppose we'd call it a family and quit. I could live with three little girls."

Sheela didn't realize that Dora's departure would be permanent. She fully expected to see her the next morning and to play like they always did after her bath. She tried crying and she tried saying "Aa-Oo" over and over, but Dora still didn't come. Finally Nat put her in her basket and carried her into the study.

"You'll have to amuse yourself, Sheela," she told her. "I have some paper work to take care of. I'm right here, and I'm putting on some music, so take it easy."

Sheela associated her yellow dress with Dora's departure and would never wear it again.

A little later, Beca and her grandfather Henry came to see her and they talked and played with her for a long time. Her grandfather tickled her with his funny old-fashioned handlebar mustache and he called her toes little piggies. Then he showed her where her tiny belly button and her eyes, nose, ears and mouth were. He also showed her his own great big eyes, nose, ears and mouth. It was lots of fun, especially when he made her nose beep and then he made his own nose beep. He'd say 'beep beep beep' in a nasal twang that sounded like a bell. Sheela wished he would bring the parrot so he could show her its beak too. She told Henry Aa-Oo, but he didn't understand.

Beca read Sheela the story of *The Little Engine That Could* and showed her the pictures in the book. When Sheela got tired of that, Beca talked to her. She told her about things that had happened long ago and stories that she invented. Or maybe she already knew them in her head. One was about a cheerful little country house. The city grew all around the house so there was no more room for the children in the family to play and the pond where ducks used to paddle and say 'quack quack quack' dried up. The family moved away and the house was locked up and left all by itself. It was very sad and lonely. Then one day the great-grandchildren of the family that used to own the house came to look at it. A person called a developer wanted to buy it and tear it down. The great-grandchildren didn't want the house torn down and they didn't know what to do. Then one of them had an idea. They decided to take the house and move it back into the country so they could live in it when they were on vacation. They moved it on a big platform. Soon it was all set up on a pretty hill with flowers and another pond.

Sheela wondered if children swam in the pond with the ducks. She was sure she wouldn't have done that. Once her mother tried to give her a bath in a bathtub with a lot of water and she cried, even though Natalya went into the tub with her. So Nat went back to bathing her in the kitchen sink. That was fun. Nat held her firmly with one hand and she put soap all over her with the other, then used the sprinkler on the sink to rinse her off. She wished her mother would put powder on her like Dora wanted to, but Nat said no. She had read that inhaling particles of talcum wasn't good for babies. After her bath, Natalya always dried her off in a big Turkish towel with a hood. The towel was white and soft and Nat gave her a nice rub-down which made her tingle. Even without the powder, Sheela loved the way she felt when she was all clean and fresh. She didn't even cry when her hair was shampooed. Her mother's hand felt so nice. Once her father gave her a shampoo and he tickled her.

While Beca told Sheela about the little house, Natalya talked to a thin woman. Then she brought the woman to see her. Her name was Marielos, which was Spanish. It was a shortened form of Maria de los Angeles. Maria de los Angeles meant Mary of the Angels, but this lady didn't look like an angel at all. Angels had a kind spirit and you could see this lady's mean spirit in her face. Her eyes were beady and she made a noise with her nose, as if she was sniffing the air. Marielos smiled at Sheela with her mouth, but her eyes didn't smile, so Sheela made a sour face and was just getting ready to cry when the woman went away with Natalya.
"Thank you for coming," her mother said. "I'll get back with you if we are interested."

"I'm really getting depressed with all these would-be nannies," her mother said to her grandmother. "This one came from an agency and she had fabulous references. I can't imagine anyone leaving a child with such an unpleasant character. If Rosario's cousin is horrible I don't know what I'll do. The office called today and they need me to go in for a couple of hours next week. Do you suppose you could come by for a few hours on Tuesday or Wednesday?"
"Of course I can. I'll be glad to come both days, or if you prefer I'll stay over night," Beca answered. "And I bet Rosario's cousin will be perfect."

When it was time for Beca and her grandfather Henry to leave, Natalya told them that Sheela looked like a doll in the yellow dress they gave her.
"Would you like me to put it on her so you can get a picture?" Nat asked.
When Sheela heard that, she started to cry.
"She may be a little hungry," Natalya said.
Actually Sheela wasn't hungry but nursing was cozy so she drank up some milk while she and Natalya slid in their sliding chair. But when Nat picked her up and put her over her shoulder to burp her, Sheela spit up all the milk and made a

mess. Natalya had to wipe it and then she had to wash, change, and soothe Sheela. After a little while Sheela's eyes became heavy and she fell asleep.

⸺ ❧❧❧ ⸻

In the evening Jaya Auntie came to visit. Jaya was Indian. She looked sun tanned and she had big brown almond shaped eyes. She was really beautiful and she smelled of fresh flowers. She wasn't afraid to pick Sheela up. She brought Sheela a floor mat for a present. The mat had all kinds of fun things on it, like pockets with little dolls that could go in and out, trains, balloons and little doors that opened and shut. Her mother put her down on it and she played for a little while, but playing alone wasn't much fun.

Although Jaya usually spent time amusing Sheela, tonight she just said hello and started talking with Natalya. Sheela started to cry as soon as she got bored with the mat. She cried and didn't let her mother and Jaya have any peace until her father came home.

"I'll take Sheela and leave you two ladies to your own devices. I missed her today."

"This is her cranky time," Natalya explained. "I guess it's my cranky time too, because I'm tired out."

"Don't you take a nap during the day?" Jaya asked.

"I'm not a nap person. I try to rest after lunch, but I can't really sleep. Anyhow, tell me what has happened. I've been worried about you. Can I get you something? Tea? A glass of wine? Sherry?"

"Maybe a small sherry, if you'll join me."

"I can't. I'm nursing. On the other hand, a tiny sherry might be calming for both Sheela and me. I'll be right back."

"I'll plunge right in," Jaya said as she accepted the golden sherry Natalya brought her, "because I don't know any good way to lead up to this. Sunil got a job offer in San Diego and he said that if I don't go with him and if we aren't pregnant right away, we're through."

"I can't believe it. Is your mother-in-law behind this craziness? I can't imagine it, not after meeting Anjali. She is really a fine lady."

"No, that's the odd thing. You are right. She is great. I was wrong about her. It's Sunil. I don't get it. He just doesn't realize how much my job means to me. And you know the funny thing? Once Anjali left, I really started thinking about having a baby. Sheela was a big part of it. I saw how wonderful she is and how happy you are. I know your work matters a lot to you and I realized that a hiatus wouldn't be the end of the world. But now Sunil has gone and done this crazy thing. His new job doesn't even pay as well as his old one."

"Why don't you tell him you are ready to have a baby, but that you guys have to stay in Houston?"

"I tried but he won't listen. He doesn't believe me. He started screaming that it's too late. And he said that I would lie about trying, which I would never do."

"What if you tried to get pregnant but didn't succeed right away?"

"I asked Sunil that and he answered that it was my problem."

"Do you think some of this has to do with Sunil knowing that I didn't tell Victor I was off the pill?"

"That could be part of it, but you didn't actually lie. You just didn't tell Victor because he refused to discuss the subject. And I have always been honest with Sunil. I've probably been too honest."

"So what are you going to do?"

Jaya gulped a mouthful of air and rubbed her eyes. "I'm not going to do what he wants. I can't. He can't force me to get pregnant by shouting ultimatums at me. That's no way to start a baby."

"I agree, but you have to understand that you have been difficult and career crazy lately. You have to make room in your heart for him and for a family."

"I know. I've been talking to my parents and to my mother-in-law and they said the same thing. But they also realize that Sunil isn't handling this thing in the right way."

"Is there any point in our saying something to him. Maybe Victor can talk to him?"

"No, Sunil told me point blank that he didn't care what I said or to whom I said it but he did not want to hear one word about this from anyone. He won't let his brother or his mom mention the situation. He said that if I didn't give notice before he left next month, I'd be hearing from his lawyer. So now I need a lawyer. I don't want to be a sitting duck waiting for him to lower the boom."

"I don't think you should do that."

"No? Why not?"

"Because it doesn't really matter who files for divorce first. If he does it, you're the good guy. Just sit tight and see what happens. If you're served, I'll find you someone who is top notch. To tell you the truth though, I honestly can't see Sunil going through with this. He loves you too much."

"Is your advice personal or professional?" Jaya asked.

"It's both."

"I considered trying to get pregnant before Sunil leaves," Jaya continued, " but like I said, I decided that was a bad idea. No one should have a baby to bolster a marriage. It would be irresponsible and unfair to the baby."

"You're right. I just wish there was something I could say or do. But in my heart of hearts, I think everything is going to be all right."

"I wish I were as confident as you are, Nat. Well, I have to go. I just wanted to ask you about a lawyer. I wish you did family law."

"Even if I did, I couldn't represent you, since both you and Sunil are such good friends. But you know what? I'll call you tomorrow with a couple of names. Maybe you could talk to one or two people just so you're not scared. That way, if Sunil does go through with anything, you'll be prepared. But let him take all the initiative. You be reactive, not pro-active."

As Jaya took her leave, she remembered the card Anjali had sent for Sheela. "Here is something for your daughter," she told Nat. The card Anjali sent was a birthday greeting. It was filled with smiley faces in all the colors of the rainbow. The legend said, "We all started smiling when you were born." Anjali added a personal note. It said:

Dear Sheela,

I ordered a horoscope from India as a special birth gift for you. Remember, horoscopes are meant only for fun. Astrology is more of an art than a science so it is to be taken with a grain of salt. I hope to visit Houston soon again to deliver your gift to you personally.

Love to you and your parents,

Anjali Khanna.

15

The first time Nat and Victor made love as parents was Friday, a day after Nat's six week checkup. Thursday at bedtime, Victor was excited. However, to his surprise and chagrin, shyness hit him and his overtures were clumsy. Natalya was no help.

"This doesn't feel right, Victor," she said.

"It's the nursing and your preoccupation with Sheela. You're freezing me out."

"No, Victor, that isn't the problem. But today, after lying with my legs in stirrups and being poked at, I'm not in the mood."

"So when will you be in the mood, Nat? Maybe you will never be in the mood now that motherhood has taken you over."

"I will be."

"When?"

"Not at any special time, just at the right time. Soon, but not by appointment."

The following evening was Sabbath. Victor arrived home with a dozen long stemmed red roses and a chilled bottle of champagne. He felt sheepish and afraid that his gestures might seem calculated, but he didn't know what else to do.

"Wow, Moët et Chandon," Natalya told him. She looked beautiful in one of the kimonos she had been wearing around the house after Sheela came.

"I love you," Victor said. "This isn't a come on. We can wait a few more days if you aren't ready. The truth is I feel a little strange too, almost afraid. I see you lit candles and set the table. It looks beautiful. How was your day?"

"It was an average day until this second when it turned lovely. I made a chicken pasta for dinner."

"How did you get the time? I thought you were going to the office."

"I did go in for a deposition. I took Sheela over to your mom's after lunch. But everybody was stalling and wasting time, and I started to get full and to leak, so I adjourned at 4:30."

"What about your clients?"

"They weren't there. It was just experts and lawyers. I figured, too bad for them. I'm not officially working anyway."

"And Sheela?"

"She was fine. I brought her home and fed her. Afterwards she played quite happily for a bit and now she's napping. With luck she'll let us have dinner before she wakes up and starts screaming."

"What are we doing for an appetizer?" Victor asked.
"Since when do we have appetizers?"
"As of this moment." Victor took his wife in his arms.

In their bedroom where Sheela slept making soft cooing sounds, Victor unwrapped Nat's kimono as he kissed her and felt her swollen breasts under her nursing bra. He released the hooks and let the bra fall to the floor. Then he pulled down Natalya's panties, the same ones that used to delight him when they were dating. Victor remembered those days as if they were yesterday, but his memory got lost in the intoxicating present and he forgot time. Nat's breath mingled with his own and then replaced it. Victor struggled to remove his own clothing without letting go of Nat, but he couldn't manage. In the end he had to release her and she helped him and kissed him and stroked him all at once, before she lay down on their bed. Victor remained standing to marvel at the beauty of Natalya's darkened areola and at the firm, rich fullness of her breasts. When Nat saw his delight, her eyes beckoned and Victor fell on top of her. He tasted the sweet milk that nurtured their daughter and then he savored all that was his alone. He did not last very long, but his vigor filled Natalya and she was sated and spent.

The Landaus were groggy and limp when their daughter began to stir. Sheela started to kick and whimper. She was ready for attention.

Victor saw that his daughter was in need of an immediate change and bath and he went to tend to her so Nat could rest a little while longer. He too felt like he needed a quick shower and he decided to carry Sheela into the stall with him. At first Sheela sputtered when streaks of water ran down her face, but she soon got the hang of closing her mouth and started to enjoy herself. It felt like being out in the rain, except that she was inside the house and the water was warmer and she smelled soap instead of wetness. Sheela remained quiet and cheerful until she was dried and dressed, but soon the evening blues attacked again. By the time she settled down so her parents could enjoy their dinner, it was past ten o'clock, but they didn't mind at all.

⚬⚬⚬⚬●⚬⚬⚬⚬

At three months, Sheela was a 12 pound, 24 inch long alert little baby who had a deeper grasp of life than most people recognized. Her limited verbal and motor abilities had no bearing upon her capacity to understand or to communicate and she interacted with fluency. Thanks to Rebecca's words, or to their own wisdom, Natalya and Victor treated their daughter like a miniature person, rather than like an infant who didn't understand the world around her.
"Remember," Rebecca repeatedly told them, "her body is small, but her will and her understanding are boundless."

Sheela's colic had subsided and she was comfortable most of the time. Her needs were generally anticipated and when they weren't, she resorted to the many tones in her repertoire to publicize them. Her cries let you know if she was

100

hungry, bored, burpy, frustrated, angry, or sleepy. When she was having fun, Sheela laughed, gurgled, and squealed. She was also a hard worker, and she practiced steadily to hone her skills. By early April, she sat propped up holding her head steady. She followed moving objects. She rolled on the floor. She brought her hands together. Sometimes she could grasp and hold things and she was learning to reach out and grab. She recognized her family and friends and she welcomed the attention of kindly strangers. She listened to music and to the sounds of voices, of familiar and unknown footsteps, of bells, and of miscellaneous clatter. She loved adventures like going for rides and on shopping sprees.

Her life and that of her family settled into a routine.

Beca and Grandpa Henry visited often and once in a while Sheela went to their house to play. They lived in a place called "The Village." But it wasn't a village at all. There were no tiny houses or children playing on narrow streets amidst dogs and chickens. "The Village" in Houston was a part of the city near the university where her Daddy worked, and it took only about ten minutes to get there from the high-rise building where Sheela lived.

Sheela missed Dora and her yet to be met Grandpa Harold who lived in New York. Oddly enough, the Rosenbaums' home was also in a "village," Greenwich Village, and coincidentally—or not—it was on a street named Houston. Her parents pronounced it "Howston Street." Her mother hoped they would visit New York soon, and Sheela hoped so too. Natalya was trying to arrange a trip for a long weekend or maybe even four or five days if it wound up becoming a business trip.

Once Victor called Dora and Harold "Sheela's other grandparents," but Natalya got upset and said that her own mother and father weren't the "other" grandparents at all. They were just her grandpa and grandma, the same as Beca and Henry, and they would be just as close, even if they lived in New York. Natalya was going to see to that. Aunt Cecily and Uncle Ronald lived in New York too, but not in the Village. Sheela remembered their voices from the time they visited before she was born.

Starting in the middle of March, Natalya spent most days at her office. Every morning Sheela cried because she didn't like to see her mother go, but then she would settle down. Her crying didn't make Natalya stay home, but she cried anyway to let her mother know she was upset. As a rule, once the front door closed Sheela played with Victor for a little bit and then her friend Lulu would come to take care of her. The day they met, Nat told her Lulu's name. Sheela pronounced it Oo-Oo with the stress on the first syllable like she said Aa-Oo, but that was wrong. Then Lulu, whose real name was Lourdes, said "No, Lulu." Sheela understood and got it right. She said "Oo-Oo, Oo-Oo" over and over again, with the stress on the second syllable, and she laughed. Lulu smiled and called her "mi amorcito" which means my little love.

Lulu was very cozy and quite pretty. She was the same color as Jaya Auntie. Her cheerful eyes hid behind a pair of red rimmed glasses and her nose had a groove in it. Her short hair was soft and curly from a perm. It was mostly black, but it had a few streaks of gray in it. Lulu's mouth was curvy and gentle. When Sheela was hungry, Lulu gave her a bottle and her mother's milk came out of it.

The milk tasted fine, but it smelled of plastic. Still, Sheela drank it if she was hungry. Lulu always held her and talked to her in Spanish while she gave her the bottle. At first, the constant jabbering distracted Sheela, but little by little Sheela began to understand what Lulu said and to enjoy listening to her. Lulu spoke English quite well, but Sheela's parents wanted her to learn Spanish.

A favorite game of Sheela and Lulu's was for Sheela to sit in Lulu's lap on a chair facing the big gold-framed mirror in the Landau's entry hall. Lulu made faces and gestures, and Sheela copied them. Sometimes Sheela would go first. The game was Sheela's idea and she taught Lulu how to play. For several days she cried and made Lulu carry her all over the house until they came to the mirror. Then Sheela stopped crying and started babbling. As soon as Lulu walked away from the mirror, Sheela started crying again. Finally Lulu learned to bring a chair so she could sit down and put Sheela on her lap. The game was a good way for Sheela to practice clapping her hands and making noises and faces while she studied the expressions that the mirror reflected back to her.

Sheela loved that mirror. It captured moods and showed you what they looked like. It mimicked everything it saw. Of course it couldn't copy noises, tastes or smells because it didn't see them. It felt funny too. The images inside looked soft and warm, but when you touched them they were hard and cold. Sometimes the mirror played back things you thought or remembered, but you had to look extra hard to find those things because they were hidden inside. The mirror had pictures that came from when it used to belong to Beca. It was Sheela's now because her grandmother had given it to her parents as a wedding present.

⸻ ❈❈❈❈❈❈❈ ⸻

From time to time the Landaus remembered the horoscope that Anjali Khanna had promised to bring Sheela. They thought she might have forgotten or changed her mind about getting it done. It looked like Anjali wouldn't be visiting Houston anytime soon, now that Jaya and Sunil had separated. Sunil had moved to California, but so far he had not initiated divorce proceedings.

One afternoon Jaya told Natalya that she and Sunil knew they had incompatible charts when they decided to get married but that neither they nor their parents had cared.

"Do you think Anjali wishes she had paid attention to your charts now?" Nat asked.

"I doubt it," Jaya replied. "My mother-in-law has always been adamant about not basing serious decisions on what some astrologer says. Astrology is just a hobby with her. She said it has nothing to do with our destiny. I am the one who is beginning to wonder."

Natalya repeated her conversation with Jaya to her husband. "Do you still want to see Sheela's horoscope? Aren't you a little scared?" she asked.

"No, I'm not scared. I don't care either way," Victor answered. "It's no big deal. I don't believe in astrology, but like Anjali said, it may be fun."

"Don't you think the planets have a bearing on our lives and personalities?"

"Possibly. I don't know enough about the subject to have a valid opinion. Besides, I'd guess ninety percent of the world's so-called astrologers are frauds, so I'd never take anything they said seriously."

"Maybe," Nat answered. "But my parents are against our even looking at Sheela's chart."

"How come?" Victor asked. "I would have bet they'd be cool about stuff like that."

"They think an astrological reading can end up becoming a self-fulfilling prophecy. So, according to my mother, there is a danger there."

"Hmmn. I wonder what my parents think."

"I asked. Your dad said he had no opinion. Beca thinks astrology may be accurate about the past, but that future predictions are unreliable. She said human destinies are so intertwined that she can't see how it is possible to anticipate the myriad of possible outcomes of any particular life. In her opinion, life cycles are repetitive, like the astrological cycles, and certain patterns repeatedly give rise to certain lives, or something like that."

"I would guess that our lives are the result of our characters and that characters are the product of experiences we have had in other lifetimes," Victor said.

"Are you telling me you believe in reincarnation?"

"Maybe. I never thought about it until this second, but I don't want to speculate."

"You are speculating, Victor," Nat pointed out. "Sheela makes us both speculate."

The only thorn in Nat's life was her career.

"To put it bluntly," she told Annette, "my job sucks. The firm wants to get rid of me, but it needs me to crank out the work and put out fires. Besides, too many clients like me. I want to quit, but I don't want to shoot myself in the foot. If I don't get a decent recommendation, I'll have problems finding a good job in another firm. It's a standoff."

A few days after speaking with Annette, Nat heard a surprising message on her home machine.

"Hi, Nat," it said. "This is Steve Jordan. Sorry to bother you, but I don't have your private e-mail. I don't blame you for not answering your phone. Maybe you won't want to talk to me at all, but I wanted to let you know I'm back in Houston. I think I owe it to you, if not to anyone else at my illustrious former law firm, to tell you why I took off. I respect you and your judgment and would appreciate hearing from you. You can reach me at 713-686-5686."

16

The trip to New York never materialized because of problems in Natalya's office. Instead, Dora and Harold Rosenbaum came to Houston. They rented a car and drove in from the airport. They were all set to do things on their own and with Sheela because Nat and Victor were so busy. The Rosenbaums intended to take dancing lessons, something they had never gotten around to doing in New York. For Sheela, Dora was full of plans. One was to get her started at Water Babies where they taught children under one year old how to swim, but Victor had said no way. Then Dora got a better idea. She and Sheela were going to investigate a new infant school called Infantasy which had classes, games, and exercises for babies starting at four months. The point was for them to have fun, to achieve learning readiness, and to interact with their peers.

Sheela had listened to her parents discussing all this one Sunday morning while they were having blintzes with sour cream and red caviar in bed. She was playing in her crib while they ate, and then they brought her into the bed with them.

"Don't you think Dora is going a little nuts with some of this stuff?" her father asked.

"No, I don't. I always did neat things when I was young. I went to a nursery school where they let us paint the walls and run around with no clothes on."

"I draw the line at Water Babies. Sheela won't even get in the bathtub. I suppose there is no harm in taking a look at Infantasy though. Let's just make sure it isn't totally crazy or a disguised daycare which we already decided is out of the question."

"It's not a daycare. Babies go there with their parents or nannies," her mother explained.

"Then, assuming it's worthwhile, how will we transport Sheela back and forth? Lourdes can't manage."

"Actually Lulu can."

"How? You wouldn't trust her to drive with Sheela would you?"

"No, but Infantasy is pretty near, and I was thinking that you could drop them off and pick them up during lunch once a week. On Saturdays either you or I could take Sheela."

"I don't know how Dora finds all this out living in New York." Victor shook his head.

"I don't either," Nat said. "But she has her ways."

The Saturday after the Rosenbaums came, Victor and Nat had a party. Sheela had to get all dressed up in a new dress, and everybody took pictures of her. She posed alone, with each of her parents, with both of her parents, with each of her grandparents, with each set of grandparents, with all four grandparents, and with the friends who knew her. Grandpa Henry even took a video. Sheela did not like being photographed at all, but she didn't cry because she didn't want to upset anyone and because her dress was very pretty. It was mint green with darker green buttons in front and fruit all over it. Dora had brought it from New York.

When they weren't busy making her look at the camera, her grandparents and friends played with her. Together the grandpas taught her to hold a rattle in one hand and then to move it to the other. She had a lot of fun, and then she decided to drop it on the floor to see what happened. First, Harold picked it up and gave it back to her to drop again and then Henry picked it up. The three of them did that for quite a while.

Just before dinner was served, Victor came to talk to her. He looked worried.

"There are so many people here that you are forgetting your daddy," he said. Sheela raised her arms for him to lift her up and he did.

"Da-da-da," Sheela said. That got Victor excited. He carried her all over the room and told everyone that she could say "Daddy." He made her repeat "Da-da-da" over and over again.

Sheela knew most of the guests, but not all. Uncle David and Aunt Annette were there. Jaya Auntie came with a man Sheela had never seen before. He was blond and very tall. His name was Zigfried because he was Swiss. Zigfried talked softly and Jaya seemed to follow him all around the room. She laughed a lot. It seemed as if she was just pretending to have fun.

Sheela liked the music that was playing for the party. Her favorite song came from the movie *Casablanca*. While it was playing, Beca danced around the room with her singing, "A kiss is just a kiss; a sigh is just a sigh; the fundamental things apply; as time goes by." Sheela was sure she remembered *Casablanca*, even though her parents had never played that CD for her before. How could they have? Uncle David and Aunt Annette had just brought it this evening as a present.

A great deal of food was served and the guests talked about how wonderful it was. Dora and Natalya had cooked during the day while Victor and Grandpa Harold took care of her. The "boys" took her to the grocery store and then they hung around and watched TV. They saw three series of shows: Bewitched, I Dream of Jeannie and I Love Lucy. They all laughed their heads off during I Love Lucy, especially in the episode where Lucy was in Italy and she was crushing grapes with her feet. While Sheela was laughing, she opened her mouth wide. That was when Grandpa Harold noticed that there was a hard white spot inside her mouth. He rubbed his finger on it and said, "She's getting a tooth!" Victor thought that getting a tooth so young was pretty amazing, but her grandpa said that a baby's first tooth could appear at any time between the third and the twelfth month. He said she needed a teething ring to chew on and that he would get her one tomorrow. Then he took her to Natalya and Dora so they could see the beginning of her tooth too.

The menu for the party was stuffed veal, potato dumplings, mushrooms cooked in brandy, sweet and sour red cabbage with bacon, cucumber salad, and onion bread. The guests raved about everything. They said the stuffed veal was a masterpiece. Beca brought her famous trifle pudding for dessert and gave Sheela three licks on her finger. Dora's specialty was lemon meringue pie, but they were having that another day.

Right after dinner, while the party was still going on, Sheela got very hungry. She didn't want to make a fuss, but she couldn't wait any more. So she started to cry and Natalya came right away. Nat asked to be excused and then she invited Aunt Annette to come inside and talk to her while she nursed Sheela.

"I'd love that. Of course I won't feel as if I'm missing the party," Aunt Annette said.

Once they were in the bedroom, Sheela started gulping her milk so quickly that she kept coughing and gagging until Natalya made her take it easy. As soon as she slowed down, Aunt Annette started talking.

"Like I told you the other day, I followed the advice you and Jaya gave me. I've even managed to be somewhat nice to Chloe."

"So what happened?" her mother asked.

"Pretty much what you and Jaya predicted. Chloe lost interest in David and she acquired a new boyfriend."

"So where does that leave things?"

"At a pretty good place, except that David is deflated. Chloe's mother keeps complaining that the new boyfriend is a bum and that he's taking advantage of Chloe."

"What's to take advantage of? I thought you said Chloe doesn't have two nickels to rub together and that she's brassy and overweight."

"I guess her mother means that he's sleeping with Chloe. The good news is that Chloe is moving to Louisiana with the guy."

"So?" Nat asked.

"So as of last week we're working on getting pregnant."

"That's something I missed out on. It must be fun."

"It's not bad," Annette said, "not bad at all."

After several days of phone tag, Natalya and Steve Jordan made voice contact.

"I don't really want to discuss anything on the telephone," Steve said, "because I'm not sure about what all I can tell you without putting you in an awkward position. My plan was for us to meet and sort of feel our way along."

"I'm not worried about my position," Nat replied. "To be honest, I'm no longer the shining bright star I was when you left Kaplan, McCall and Green. When would you like to meet?"

"What's a good time and place for you?" Steve asked.

"Anywhere is OK with me. Mornings are best. I usually start my day pretty early. I have a new baby girl so I'm usually antsy about getting home in the evening. At lunch I try to squeeze in a quick workout."

"Don't advertise that you're seeing me," Steve advised. "After we talk, you can decide how to proceed."

The meeting was set up for 6:45 in the morning on the Wednesday after the Rosenbaums' departure. When Nat arrived, Steve was drinking a huge latte at The Milan, a funky Italian bakery.

"You're ahead of time," she said.

"I just got here. It's amazingly crowded, even this early. I guess everyone knows this place never closes. What can I get you?"

"I'll help myself."

"No, this is my treat. You hold the table," Steve said.

"OK. A decaf cappuccino and a cranberry scone," Nat requested.

Nat waited for Steve without thinking of anything in particular. She felt at peace. She relaxed with her eyes closed and decided to re-incorporate her self-designed meditation into her life even if just for 10 or 15 minutes a day. Soon Steve was back with a loaded tray.

"Here's your coffee and scone. I also got a breakfast frittata to share."

"Thanks. It's good to see you," Nat said. "Are you back in Houston permanently?"

"Yes, I am. I'm going to take a stab at practicing on my own. However, before I say anything else, congratulations! After we hung up, I realized that I never even asked you what your baby's name is. And here's a small gift for . . ?"

"Sheela," Nat said. "But you didn't have to do this."

"It's just a little something. Sheela is a beautiful name and I'm sure she's a beauty if she looks anything like you. Go ahead. Open it."

Inside the package was a book called *Little Children from Foreign Lands.* "Where did you find this?" Nat asked. "It's lovely."

"At the River Oaks Bookstore," Steve answered. "I'm glad you like it."

"So why did you take off in such a hurry and go to Cozumel of all places?" Nat asked. "And why did you stay away so long?"

"I'll answer the second question first," Steve said. "Once I was gone, I decided to make the most of being in Mexico. I studied Spanish and made friends. Then I was asked to teach some courses in Business Law at the University of the Americas near Puebla. It was a good experience. But eventually it became time to come home. As for why I left Kaplan, McCall and Green, the answer is I had no choice."

"What do you mean, you had no choice?" Natalya asked.

"I was given two options," Steve answered. "One was to leave immediately and make it look like I'd flipped under pressure, for which Mr. Kaplan promised to give me a plane ticket and thirty thousand dollars. The second option was to be fired, in which case he promised to ruin my career. I picked option A. Anyhow, I've always been interested in Mayan ruins."

"Are you serious?" Nat asked.

"This isn't something I would kid about."

"What led up to Mr. Kaplan forcing you out of the firm?" Nat asked.

"I'll try to make a long story short," Steve replied. "The first part is personal. Maybe it's of no consequence, but it's background. You know that Kaplan, McCall and Green only hires the crème de la crème, so, like you, I seemed to be right:

Order of the Coif, Editor of the Law Review, presentable and all that. But the truth is I was a lousy fit. I'm not your run of the mill associate. Until my senior year in high school, I wanted to be a priest. Then my confessor seduced me and I learned that I'm gay. I lost all respect for the Church and had a tough time respecting myself. However, I eventually realized that if I believed I was created in God's image, I had to accept my orientation. I decided I could still seek God's grace as a lay person by living a life of abstinence and doing my best to understand and fulfill His purpose."

"In college, my English professor steered me toward the law. He thought my analytical and verbal skills along with my philosophical bent would make me a fine lawyer. My law school performance proved I had the ability to succeed in our profession. But for a while there Kaplan, McCall and Green made me wonder if I wanted to."

"When I was hired, the firm assured me that I would be allowed to do pro-bono work, that it would steer me toward appellate work, and that it measured performance by quality, not billable hours. They weren't serious about those things and probably thought I just mentioned them to sound politically correct. When I started raising issues, the partners assured me that I was doing a fine job and that I should give them time. Gradually, I realized that I was in the wrong law firm. My conscience was pricked because, although I was doing my best, what I was doing wasn't good. Just about then, the HFT case came along. I thought it gave me an opportunity to make a difference. I made up my mind that I would get to the bottom of whatever it was our clients were covering up and that I would then convince them to come clean and settle the case. What a joke!"

"I have a comment before you go on," Nat interjected. "Do you mind?"

"Of course not," Steve answered. "I'm rambling."

"No, you are decidedly not rambling. I wanted to say that you are giving me a preview of coming attractions. We seem to be on different time lines but on parallel careening career paths."

"I'm sorry." Steve commented.

"It's nothing to be sorry about. I have understood for quite some time now that I was hired as a brainy—but dispensable—drone at Kaplan, McCall and Green. The partners took it for granted that I would be too enthralled with the intellectual challenges and inflated paychecks to question their directives. And if I wasn't, no matter. After all, bright young lawyers are fungible. But please continue. I didn't mean to interrupt."

"No, what you said is interesting. Two wave-makers at Kaplan, McCall and Green. They must wonder how they could have screwed up so badly. Anyhow, as you now know, Bart Grady, HFT's in-house counsel, and the whole Home Fitness Trainers' management team are masters at burying the ball and at buying time, which they use to shove it deeper and deeper into the ground. But now their strategy won't work."

"Why not?"

"Because HFT is under investigation by the Office of the Texas Attorney General and Grady has concealed this vital information from the plaintiffs. But the plaintiffs' lawyer, Jeffrey Dupree, knows. He has already been in touch with the Attorney General and he plans to nail HFT and their officers and directors."

"This is news to me, but it explains a lot of things such as why Jeff has been so patient with our stalling tactics," Nat commented.

"Everyone has different reasons for keeping you in the dark." Steve continued. "HFT thinks you would take steps to inform the court and Dupree wants to maintain the element of surprise."

"Doesn't Bart Grady realize that he's plugging up the dyke with his finger?"

"Nope. Bart Grady is sure he'll come out of the investigation clean and the plaintiffs will never find out a thing. He's confident he'll win this latest legal battle too."

"How can he be so dumb?"

"He's not dumb; he's arrogant. His arrogance makes him underestimate his adversaries. Besides, Jeff is playing his cards close to his chest. He still needs more information and he is digging faster than Bart is burying. The thing is that no one—except me and now you—knows that Jeff knows about the investigation. I only found that out after I got back in town. It was happenstance. I have a good friend who has a friend whose wife works as a paralegal in Dupree's firm."

"So why were you asked to leave?"

"Mainly because of some sensitive information that Home Fitness Trainers inadvertently made available to me when I reviewed their files. Most of the stuff they turned over was junk. They claimed all their other documents were disposed of in the ordinary course of business. However, someone in the office left a needle in HFT's haystack. One of the eight boxes of papers they sent me to send to the plaintiffs contained a folder that was a bombshell. That folder, which was believed to be well-hidden in Bart Grady's great big desk in his great big office under lock and key, ended up in a carton on the floor of my cubicle. When I insisted that I wouldn't be a party to suppressing responsive information given to me, Mr. Kaplan and I had a showdown."

Steve paused to let what he had explained sink in. Nat was quiet for a few moments and then she simply said, "I see."

Steve looked at his watch and commented, "It's getting late for you. You probably should be heading for the office. Besides," he added, "this is a good place for me to stop. You can mull things over and do what you have to do. I told you enough to put you on guard, without giving you any specific information you would be ethically bound to disclose. The bottom line is that HFT will go up in smoke. The only question is, how badly will Kaplan, McCall and Green be burnt by the fire?"

"I suspect they'll be burned quite badly," Nat said. "Moreover, I'm probably at risk of getting charred myself. Thanks for warning me. I really appreciate it. I don't know what else to say."

"No need to say anything. Thank you for hearing me out."

"Well, good-bye," Nat said as she got up and quite spontaneously gave Steve a quick but warm hug. "I'll contact you and keep you posted. As of this second, I have no idea what my next step should be. Hopefully once I digest this information, something will come to mind."

"Yes, I have something in mind already. But for now just play this tune by ear."

17

The world of destiny exists beyond fantasy and beyond fact. Sheela visited that world many nights. She soared over the earth and high above the clouds until she reached the point where her soul imagined itself once again disembodied. In this unencumbered state, it severed its ties with space and traveled freely between the past and the future. Determined by the past, destiny redesigns itself in accordance with events that occur in the fleeting ever-changing present. Thus, destiny's forms become perpetual blueprints for the future and because time jumbles human experiences, Sheela's reveries were predictions as well as memories.

Sheela traveled alone in many of her dreams, but was not lonely because she was part of a whole that shared its mind with her. However, there was a recurrent dream from which she always returned feeling incomplete. In it she saw herself aloft maintaining her balance by means of two long pigtails stretched wing-like, one above each of her ears. She was drifting toward a globe encircled by many halos. As she approached her destination, another being beckoned, causing her to change direction and to fly toward him instead. He was tiny and his features were indistinct. Yet he emitted a powerful magnetism and Sheela tried to get close. But she was too slow and her movements were disoriented, so she had to abort her journey and turn back.

In subsequent variations, when the being appeared in the distance, Sheela quickly focused and gathered momentum. She commanded her pigtails to point her toward her objective and then to align themselves with her arms. Obediently they rotated her and fell to her side so as to compress and elongate her body. Transformed into a sleek and swift airship, Sheela aimed herself at the being's aura and propelled her mind toward him with lightening speed. But each time she was almost near enough to discover who he was, something caused the dream to dissipate. Once, the being exploded into a myriad of stars. Other times she lost power and fell to earth or was swept into darkness by a huge wave. In yet another dream, the being waited for her, but then at the last minute he became frightened and fled. Most recently, just as she was about to capture his essence, Sheela got trapped inside the pattern of a huge kaleidoscope.

The dreams were awesome until they came to the end. Sheela cried the moment she felt them dissolve and called out so Aa-Oo would know to come to her rescue. He was the anchor that helped her make the transition from slumber to wakefulness and back to slumber. He softened the jolt she felt as she returned from her journeys and helped her realize when and where she was. Nat always heard the crying and she always went to check on Sheela, but by the time she got there, Sheela would be sound asleep once more. Wondering if she had imagined the sound, Nat would bend down and give her daughter a kiss that made her smile as she snored little palatal baby snores.

When she slept or mused, Sheela was unconstrained by her limited verbal skills. Her concepts were the stuff of perceptions and recollections, and her communications were telepathic. Thus, even when she didn't dream, Sheela's mind was filled with richness.

Her favorite experience was the visualization of God. Sheela saw the Creator as the One who made the music to which life danced. Life was the dancers as well as the dance. It was both one and many. Together the dancers choreographed the world that Sheela pictured as a great dancing net. Every step a dancer took was intricately connected to countless other steps, just as each brainwave inside her own head was linked to countless other waves. The net's every movement was simultaneously a stimulus and a response. Not even a flicker of thought could materialize without changing the structure and essence of the net. Nor could a fraction of a movement occur which was not in tune with God's music because every dancer was also a musician. There was not an iota of life that did not contain some of God's music within itself.

The music that caused Sheela to select Natalya and Victor as mother and father also determined many of the steps they would perform in the life dance. These steps were both their roles and their duty. With respect to Sheela, her parents' duty was to nurture her body, her mind, and her personality so that she might become all that she could be. Nat and Victor's capacity for love as well as their intelligence willed them and enabled them to excel at this responsibility. In exchange, one of Sheela's duties, for which she was well equipped, was to awaken her parents' spirituality. But notwithstanding the talent that these three Landaus brought to their respective tasks, only time would reveal the obstacles on the road ahead, and only time would provide a yardstick that could measure their success.

⚹⚹⚹

Sheela's days were zestful and stimulating. They were also predictable. Routine and repetition made her cozy and helped her flourish. Wednesdays, Thursdays, and Saturdays were her interesting days. She loved Wednesday because Grandpa Henry, whom Sheela now called Appa, was off from work. He would come for her and Lulu and take them to his house for the day. Beca came home in the afternoon and then Lulu left. Wednesday evening, on her way home from the office, Natalya came to get her. Thursdays and Saturdays were Infantasy days. On Thursday Sheela went there with Lulu and on Saturday she took whichever one of her parents was less busy at work.

111

Mondays and Tuesdays were uneventful unless Lulu planned a surprise, like the time she brought a niece to play. Friday they had dinner with Becca and Appa or at home. Victor and Natalya would be in a good mood and they often let her stay up late to listen to music, to read a story, or even to watch a micro disc. Sundays varied, except for the mornings which she spent playing and chatting with her parents in their king-sized bed. Sunday morning was probably her favorite time in the whole week.

Every Thursday, Victor left the University and came to pick Sheela and Lulu up at exactly 10:45. He was always on time so Sheela and Lulu waited for him in the lobby of their building. To be on the safe side, they had to be a few minutes early and while they hung around, they visited with Martin March, the fat red-faced concierge who treated Sheela with respect and never talked down to her. The opening lines of their Thursday conversations were scripted.

"Good morning, Ms. Landau. It's a pleasure to see you this morning," Martin began.

"Goo," Sheela usually replied.

"How do you like the weather today?"

"Ain," Sheela would say if it was raining. If it was sunny, she would say "Goo" again.

"So what's new today?"

"Ooo." That was Sheela's response ever since her tooth made its appearance. She opened her mouth wide and pointed inside.

"Wow! That's a fine tooth. Show me Aa-Oo's tooth."

"Ooo" Sheela repeated pointing to Aa-Oo's beak. Just about then her daddy would pull up and honk.

"Bye now!" Martin March would say waving.

"Ba," Sheela said, waving back.

Then Sheela and Lulu would come out. Her daddy always stepped out of his car and gallantly opened the back door for Lourdes. After that he carried Sheela around to the front of the car and together they honked the horn three times until Martin March came out from behind his desk.

"Remember now. Have fun and don't do anything I wouldn't do," Mr. March said and then he marched back inside.

Finally, Victor settled Sheela in her car seat in the back. They got to Infantasy just before 11:00 o'clock and at precisely 12:25 Victor would be outside ready to drive them home. The ride back home was quiet because Sheela was tired. When they'd got to the driveway of her building, Sheela and Lulu got out of the car and went right into the elevator and rode up. Anyway, Martin March wasn't there because he was on his lunch break.

Ms. Meredith, the teacher of Sheela's group, was in charge of sixteen babies. She planned their activities and made sure the morning went smoothly. Her ideas were interesting and everything she did had a purpose. Ms. Meredith was quite strict with the babies and with their adults. Everyone had to arrive and take a seat on the floormat by 11:05. Then, when the rustling stopped and you could hear silence, Ms. Meredith said, without so much as a how do you do, "I want everyone to concentrate." After a short pause, Ms. Meredith continued, "Please begin as usual. Close your eyes and picture something pleasant that gets you in touch with your inner serenity and generates positive energy. When your picture makes you smile, open your eyes and look up." Next Ms. Meredith turned on music and switched off the lights. As people looked up, they saw a painting or colored pattern projected on a big screen in front of the room. The projection always fit the music as well as the picture Sheela had made in her head. It also complemented the special incense that had been selected for the session.

Once Sheela saw a vaguely familiar design on the screen. Perhaps it was something real she had known, or maybe it belonged to the past or the future or to a dream. The day's scent was eucalyptus and the music was spirited and jingly. In Sheela's mind the crisp design flashed and twirled as it expanded and contracted and then expanded itself again, changing yet remaining unchanged. Another day, Sheela heard music that seemed to sway as it wove through the sandalwood perfumed wind. The picture on the screen was a field of golden wheat stalks curving in the breeze. Sheela couldn't remember such an expanse of wheat. In her picture, the stalks were stick people performing a flowing dance in perfect harmony. When the lights came back on, the people faded into the clouds.

After the opening picture, Ms. Meredith "moved on" to the activities. There were three types of activities at Infantasy, not counting the closing that was meant to instill learning skills. Although the activities—music, exercise and play—were for the babies, they were also supposed to teach the caretakers how to enrich their charges' lives.

During music, people listened to musical compositions. Sometimes they clapped or beat out the rhythms on little drums that Ms. Meredith passed out from time to time. One day, a baby cried in the middle of music. Ms. Meredith made a stern face and said, "There is no crying permitted here. You will have to leave." Sheela never cried. She knew she was not allowed to because she had heard Natalya warning Lulu.

"You have to make sure that Sheela isn't tired or hungry before Infantasy. If she cries, they won't allow her to stay in the program. Change her diaper just before you leave and try not to give her a bottle while you are there."

"What do I do if Sheela does number two? Do I change her diaper or let her stink?" Lulu asked a bit sarcastically.

Nat ignored Lulu's tone. "I guess you can quietly take her to the bathroom if you have to change her."

Exercise came after music and rhythm. To warm up, the babies were massaged with aromatic oil from a tiny tube. They were given a fresh tube, coordinated with the incense, each time. Ms. Meredith believed in aromatherapy, which meant that good smells made you feel well and affected your mood. After the massage, Lulu wiped off the excess oil with a baby wipe. Then she helped Sheela with the exercises, which consisted of stretching, lifting, pulling, and wiggling different parts of the body.

Play was the last activity before closing. It was divided into two parts, free play and games. In free play the babies could roll or creep around anywhere they felt like over the big mat. They could look at each other and touch each other's fingers or toes. Even Aa-Oo was allowed to join in. Games were structured. The adult/baby pairs divided into four groups and they rolled balls, picked up small toys and threw them in a pile, played peek-a-boo, or built towers with blocks and then knocked them down.

At the close of each Infantasy session, Ms. Meredith read a poem or sang a song accompanied by gestures. Everyone was supposed to copy the gestures and try to say the words or sing the song. The adults were expected to learn them and then practice at home with the babies. Sheela knew some of the rhymes like Pat-a-Cake from her Mother Goose book, but others, like Little Bunny Fufu, were new. A few songs were in Spanish and other foreign languages. Lulu knew all the Spanish ones and had sung them to Sheela. Their favorite was La Cucaracha, except Ms. Meredith changed the ending. It was supposed to go like this:

> La cucaracha, la cucaracha
> ya no puede caminar.
> Porque no tiene, porque le falta
> Marijuana que fumar.

In Infantasy the last line was "nadie con quien jugar."

After the reading or singing was over, Ms. Meredith rang a bell. That meant the class was over. Everyone had to keep quiet in case Ms. Meredith had announcements to make. The very last thing that happened was that Ms. Meredith waved goodbye and Sheela and everyone else waved back. You were not allowed to say goodbye out loud. If anyone did, Ms. Meredith frowned because she wanted the group to make a quick, orderly and quiet departure.

⁓◦◦◖◗◖◗◦◦⁓

Beca did not approve of Infantasy, but she didn't say a word because she didn't want to interfere in something that Dora Rosenbaum had come up with. Dora Rosenbaum was charming and very bright, but she was an adamant nonconformist. Beca thought that sometimes Dora did things for effect. After thinking that, she felt guilty. She didn't want to be unfair, but at the same time she worried that having such small babies in close contact with each other would increase their chances of catching diseases. Lulu was an ally, because she too believed the whole business of Infantasy was nuts. Some lunatic with a yen to get rich thought up classes for babies so people with money could waste it!

Sheela could see Lulu and Beca's point of view. After all, she played games with Lulu that were just as entertaining as the Infantasy games. Actually, they were more entertaining, especially the mirror game. Still, Sheela loved the outings. And it was really fun to daydream and match the pictures in her head with music and pictures on the screen. It was also nice to have a chance to see other babies and to study their personalities.

Everyone who knew Sheela thought she had a fine personality but deep inside, in her heart of hearts, Sheela wasn't so sure. She was good in Infantasy. She never cried or fidgeted. But that was because she was interested in the goings on. At home, if things didn't go her way, or if she got bored, she could make quite a fuss. She had to have what she wanted when she wanted it. Luckily everyone around her understood her wishes and always jumped to do her bidding. Once Sheela heard her parents discussing having another baby, hopefully a boy. Sheela didn't want them to have any more children. She liked being the center of their universe and she didn't want to share her space, her possessions, or her family. She knew

114

that her parents' love would grow if they had more babies, but she also knew that the time and attention at their disposal was limited. More important than everything else, Sheela wanted to fill her family's hearts and souls all by herself, without interference and without competition.

Sheela displayed her capacity to create a scene one Wednesday when Nat came to pick her up from her grandparents' house. Sheela didn't want to leave; it was only seven o'clock and she and Beca were busy. As a matter of fact, they were in the middle of playing the piano. When Beca was young, she had contemplated becoming a concert pianist, but then she changed her mind. The music Beca played was hauntingly beautiful. It evoked memories of joyous candlelit dinners, animated conversations in the midst of sweet smelling pipe tobacco, and shelves crammed with colorful books. Just as Beca was coming to the end of a movement, Natalya barged in saying, "We have to get going." Beca didn't reply. She kept right on playing.

"Sit down a minute," Appa said to Nat. "Look at them. Can you believe Beca has been playing like that with Sheela in her lap for over a half hour?"

"I wish I could," Nat replied, "but we really have to go. I've got three motions to get done."

"You'd better stop, honey," Appa said to Beca. "Natalya is in a hurry."

As soon as Beca stopped playing, Sheela began to scream. Nat took her out of Rebecca's lap kicking and yelling.

"I'm sorry, sweetheart. We have to get home. Daddy's waiting," Natalya explained, but it didn't do any good.

Sheela kept right on crying hysterically. Nat called Victor on the car phone, but she couldn't hear because Sheela's screaming was so loud. Victor was worried, and he was downstairs waiting when they drove into the parking garage. He carried Sheela upstairs, but she kept on crying. Beca called to see if she had calmed down, but she hadn't. Nat couldn't get any of her work done and neither she nor Victor had dinner. The drama lasted until after nine o'clock when Sheela quieted down from mere exhaustion. By then she was ready to be fed. Nat still nursed Sheela once in the evening, before going to bed, and once in the early morning, before work. Starved, worn out, and perplexed at her mother's utter disregard for her feelings, Sheela clutched Aa-Oo and began suckling. After her tummy became a little dome filled with milk, her eyes closed. Natalya gently burped her and laid her in her crib.

18

After he learned the details of her meeting with Steve Jordan, Victor advised Natalya to resign from Kaplan, McCall and Green. However, Nat's fighting spirit wouldn't let her quit.

"I have to stick it out," she told Victor, "until matters come to a head. I have nothing to gain by precipitating a crisis. Sooner or later something is going to snap and my options will clarify themselves."

Nat advised Home Fitness Trainers, Inc. to settle, insisting that the trainer/dealers who sued had the upper hand in the litigation. Not surprisingly, Rudy Kaplan and HFT's management disagreed with her assessment.

"The information the court ordered you to provide is incriminating." Nat concentrated on keeping her voice low-pitched. "It shows HFT made money from product that filtered down the dealer hierarchy without ever getting into the hands of consumers. It also proves HFT earned millions of dollars by front loading. It induced its dealers to purchase demos they could never sell. Over thirty percent of them wound up in bankruptcy. Home Fitness' Board can be found personally liable. You are on the Board, Rudy, aren't you?"

"Relax," Kaplan insisted. "Dupree is spitting in the wind. The most he can prove is a technical illegality. He'll never show a nexus between the bankruptcies and the inventory purchases."

"Trust me when I tell you that Mr. Dupree has the motivation, the resources, and the intelligence to dig out anything you may try to conceal," Nat told Mr. Carson, Home Fitness Trainers' Chief Executive Officer and Chairman of its Board of Directors. "He has to know a lot more than he is letting on."

"Rudy and Bart assured me that I do not have to answer any questions that are not directly on point or about which I don't have firsthand information. They said you are going to drown Dupree in objections." Horace Carson countered with bravado.

"I am the lead attorney in this case and I'm advising you that you will have to disclose all information that could lead to the discovery of relevant evidence. I'm further advising you that if your interests are separate from those of Home Fitness Trainers, you should get another lawyer. I represent the corporation, not you individually."

"What could happen to me as an individual?" Carson fiddled with his bow tie.

"I told you in several memos directed to you and copied to Mr. Kaplan and Mr. Grady. You could be jailed for perjury; you could incur criminal penalties. It depends on what you are found to have done wrong."

"That's the key. It depends on what I am found to have done wrong." Carson smirked.

The time was ripe for Jeffrey Dupree to hit Home Fitness Trainers with a few of his bombshells and he used the Carson deposition to do it. For two days he pelted Horace Carson with questions. For every answer that was "I don't remember" Dupree had a barrage of further questions.

"Who on this list might remember?

"What documents on this list might help you recall?

"Which persons on this list have discussed this matter with you?

"Have any of the following persons contacted you in the last ninety days?"

Suddenly it became clear that the grave Home Fitness Trainers had dug to bury evidence would be used to bury them instead. It also became clear that Rudy Kaplan had at least one foot in that grave too. Everyone at Kaplan, McCall and Green was nervous. HFT had been one of the firm's biggest clients for years. Now it owed a lot of money and it was not going to pay. Rudolph Kaplan, who had assured his partners that there was absolutely nothing to worry about, had split.

The Carson deposition was transcribed within days and as soon as a copy was forwarded to Nat, Jeffrey contacted her.

"Please tell Mr. Kaplan that it would be in his and your firm's best interest to hear me out before the egg hits the fan. If he is interested in talking, let me know within three days."

"Rudolph Kaplan is in London," Nat told Dupree. "He said he had pressing business there and would be absent and unavailable for an unspecified period of time."

"I see. In that case I'm going to do what I have to do. But you're a straight shooter. I think your best bet would be to withdraw from this case as fast as you can."

"I'm the attorney of record. The judge will never let me off the hook."

"She might since I won't object. You have earned her respect."

"Aren't you hurting your clients by suggesting that I withdraw? If I do manage to get off the case, HFT will request an extension of deadlines."

"That doesn't worry me. I'll fight their request, but even if I lose that battle, I'll win the war. Anyway, my stuff will keep. It may even get better."

"I'll give your advice serious consideration. I appreciate it. Thanks."

"Will you let me know what you decide within the week?"

"Absolutely, Jeff. Thank you again."

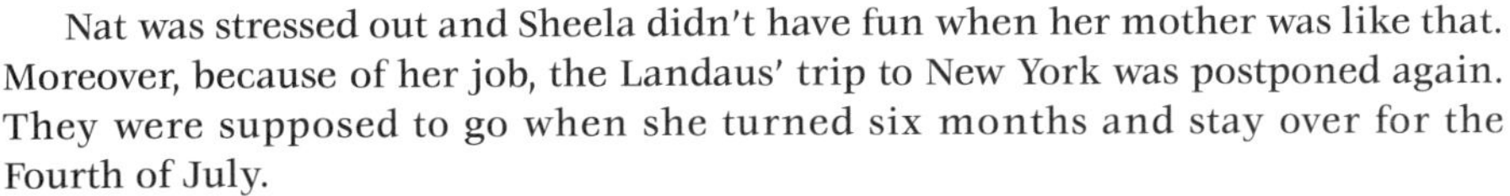

Nat was stressed out and Sheela didn't have fun when her mother was like that. Moreover, because of her job, the Landaus' trip to New York was postponed again. They were supposed to go when she turned six months and stay over for the Fourth of July.

Instead, Sheela got a private half-year birthday party at midnight of July 1. Nat baked half a chocolate cake. Sheela got a little bite of the cake with a big lick of icing, a sip of champagne, and a set of nesting dolls that came from Russia. They were so beautifully hand painted that Natalya put them in the living room. There were eleven dolls and the littlest one was just a tad bigger than a grain of rice. Sheela and Victor put it under a magnifying glass and they could see how well crafted it was. It was balanced to stand upright and it had a pretty face with sparkling brown eyes and long delicate eyelashes.

Victor made two quick trips to New York on his own. Both were for business. One was for a meeting and the other was to give a lecture. From the first trip, he brought Sheela a little suitcase, and the second time he brought her a teddy bear.

"I know you're devoted to Aa-Oo, and that you have Brahms," Victor said, "but every person needs a big shaggy, cuddly, light brown teddy bear. So, do you like him?"

"Ike," Sheela answered.

"Is that a yes or a no?" Victor wanted to know.

"Ike," Sheela repeated, nodding her head.

"So, what shall we call him? Ike?"

"Rrr. Ike Rrr."

When Victor stuck Rrr in her arms, Sheela beeped his nose, just like Appa had taught her. But Rrr couldn't make her forget that she didn't get to go to New York.

Nat worked late the night Jeff Dupree spoke with her about withdrawing. She reviewed her docket and sorted the piles of papers on her desk according to deadlines, while in her mind she tried to figure out what to do. After some time, she resolved to have a frank talk with Green and McCall. She was between a rock and a hard place.

"Well," Nat told herself, chewing on a bagel, "You were the one who wanted to wait until something snapped. So now it has."

When she got home, Sheela was asleep and Victor was watching the evening news. "Do you need to talk?" he asked.

"No, not yet." Nat replied. "But things are boiling. Any messages?"

"Yes. I didn't erase them."

"I'm surprised anyone bothers to leave a message with the recording we have," Nat muttered when she was out of Victor's earshot.

There were six callers: her brother Ronald—the only person in the world who still called her Nattie—left a message just saying hi; Beca asked if Nat needed any help with Sheela; her mother wanted to remind her that working out was a great stress reliever; Steve Jordan was returning Nat's call; Annette Singer, who sounded depressed, asked her to call back even if it was late; and Jaya said that her mother-in-law was visiting her and had Sheela's horoscope.

Nat was worried about both Annette and Jaya. Annette was frantic because her attempts at getting pregnant were unsuccessful. Jaya was a mess. Although she said she was happy without Sunil, she was too skinny and in a perpetual nervous rush. Her brief fling with Sigfried had come to an abrupt halt. Jaya explained that he was exciting, but undependable and he had a touch of body odor. Besides she needed a respite from men. Natalya was glad that Anjali was in town and that she hadn't abandoned her daughter-in-law. She decided to call Jaya first.

"Hi, Jaya." Nat said to the voice on the line.

"Hello," was the reply. "This is Anjali Khanna, her mother-in-law. Can I take a message?"

"Hello, Anjali. This is Natalya. I'm sorry to be calling so late. Is Jaya OK?"

"She's so-so. It's not that late, but I insisted that she have a decent meal and lie down with a book, so she fell asleep. You probably know that Jaya hasn't been doing too well since Sunil went to California."

"Yes, I do know that and I'm glad you're here. Do you think you'll be able to knock any sense into their heads?"

"I don't know, but I'm going to try. Sunil is pretty miserable too, but he's stubborn and things have gotten complicated. Anyway, I guess you gave up on Sheela's horoscope, but I didn't forget. I finally was able to get it done by the woman I wanted. She has wonderful insight and she writes beautifully. I'm looking forward to showing it to you. When would be a good time?"

"This weekend. Why don't you come over Sunday for dessert and coffee?"

"Wouldn't Sheela prefer an outing? Come here for high tea instead. How does five o'clock sound?"

"It sounds fine and very English."

"It's Indian too," Anjali said. "See you then."

"I'll just check with Victor. If there's any problem I'll call back in five minutes. If you don't hear from me, we'll be there. And thanks. I'm excited."

"Bye, then."

"Bye. And give my best to Jaya."

Next Natalya called Annette who picked up the receiver on the first ring.

"Thank God you called! I've been sitting here by the phone waiting to hear from you."

"What's the matter? You could have called me at the office if it was urgent."

Instead of a reply, Nat heard sobs on the line. "Please," Nat said, "take a deep breath and talk to me."

"I got my period again." The sound of nose blowing trumpeted through the receiver. "It was a week late and I was *sure* this time we made it."

"Hey, Annette. Don't take it so hard. It's just been a few months. You know I was off the pill quite some time before I conceived Sheela."

"What will we do if we can never have a baby?"

"Isn't that worry premature?"

"Maybe," Annette conceded, calmer now. "But I need a backup position."

"I'll tell you what. Let's do lunch on Saturday and talk about possibilities. How is David?"

"He's upset. That's one of the things bothering me. Once he made up his mind, he expected he'd impregnate me at the first shot. He feels demasculinized."

"There isn't really any word like demasculinized and the concept is absurd."

"Maybe not Nat, but that's the way David feels, and I feel defeminized."

"You're both reading your own mind sets into each other and upsetting each other. You're too anxious. That's why you guys aren't getting pregnant."

"Where should we go for lunch?" Annette asked.

"Someplace where they have frozen golden Margaritas. How about Las Palmas?"

"I'm not drinking and it will be tempting and depressing since my abstinence is in vain. Let's just go to Foo's Kitchen in The Village."

"Foo's Kitchen it is. I'll see you there at twelve thirty."

"Should David come too?"

"Absolutely not. Tell him to go work out. He can afford to lose a couple of pounds."

"Actually, we've been having so much sex that we both lost some weight."

"That could be the problem. There isn't enough time for David's sperm to replenish itself."

The next day Nat made an appointment to meet with Walter Green at 2:20 p.m. Since Mr. McCall had no interest in what she had to say, he deferred to his partner. At 2:19 she knocked on the door and Walter invited her right in. Nat told him about her talk with Jeff and asked him how he felt about the HFT case and about her withdrawing.

"This is my decision," Natalya explained, "but I would appreciate your input."

"Do whatever you want," Walter replied. "If you'll excuse me, I have a client waiting."

At 2:27 Nat was back out in the hall.

By 3 o'clock Natalya finished her emergency motion to withdraw on the catchall grounds of lack of communication with her client. She set the motion for hearing the following Tuesday, sent a memo to the firm, and called Jeffrey to let him know what she had done.

Although she was confident that she had taken the correct step, Nat was wary. Green's words "Do whatever you want" set off alarm bells in her head. They sent her back to her childhood when, at the age of five, she learned how dangerous those words could be. Today, decades later, she again saw herself dressed in green overalls that camouflaged the grassy stains that covered them. It was a sunny Saturday morning and she had been sliding backwards down a slide in the park. Her mother told her to stop, but she was determined to go on. She begged and begged Dora to let her slide backward "just two more times." Dora was reading and she was irritated by Nat's whiny insistence.

"Natalya, do whatever you want but stop bugging me."

"Yeah!" Nat shouted to a playmate, "My mom said I could do it again!"

Natalya climbed up the slide and gleefully slid down backward as fast as she could. She landed squarely on her head. Eight stitches and a partially shaven head were her penalty. In retrospect, the worst part of the whole affair was not the pain she endured, nor the panic she felt when she saw blood pouring out of her skull, nor the shame she suffered during the weeks she looked like a freak. The worst part of it was the distress she had put her mother through. It was upsetting then, and it was even more upsetting now that she was a mother herself and understood how Dora must have felt.

Her renewed sense of guilt reminded Natalya of Dora's opposition to even *looking* at Sheela's horoscope. She didn't want to see that horoscope without her mother's blessings and she didn't want Dora to say "do whatever you want" again. Nat decided that she would discuss this problem with Anjali Khanna.

Sheela had a fun weekend. She and her parents spent Friday evening with Beca and Appa. Her grandparents had fallen into the habit of lighting candles and preparing a traditional Shabbat dinner after Sheela was born. Victor, Natalya, and Sheela had a standing invitation every week and they accepted about half of the time. Sometimes Rebecca and Henry invited friends, but even if there were no guests, the dinner was always a white tablecloth affair.

The elegance and warmth of her grandparents' dinners made Sheela happy. Beca said that on Sabbath everyone had to look their best and that gave Sheela a chance to wear the pretty clothes that she outgrew almost as soon as she could fit into them. Sheela sat in her high chair between Natalya and Appa and she admired the pretty flowers and china and the shiny silverware. She listened to Appa make the Hebrew blessing which he called Kiddush and waited for him to give her a tiny sip of his sweet red wine. Then she nibbled at the heel of braided challah, slurped a teaspoon of comfortably familiar chicken soup, and checked out some of the other dishes. Every time she drank the soup, Appa made sure she had a bite of a matzoh ball.

"You know, Sheela," he always said while Beca beamed, "your grandmother makes the best matzoh balls in the world. There are matzoh balls that are like rocks. Those are too hard. There are matzoh balls that crumble. Those are too soft. Then there are Rebecca's matzoh balls and they are just right."

On Saturday, Sheela went to Infantasy with Victor. Natalya had to go out to lunch with Aunt Annette, who was waiting impatiently for a soul to pick her and Uncle David for parents. Sheela and her father were both glad that her mother wasn't going in to the office. Nat was more relaxed than she had been for a long time. Sheela listened carefully to her parents' conversation.

"I'm not complaining, but I am curious about your good mood," Victor had said. "And I'm glad you finally made some time for yourself and your friends. What happened? Did I do something right?"

"I would say so," her mother answered. "This weekend got off to a very good start. Last night was pretty terrific."

Sheela saw Victor puff up even though all he said was "Oh."

Saturday evening the three of them stayed in and relaxed. They all watched *Fantasia*. Then Natalya read *The Little Engine That Could* to Sheela who made all the "Chug, Chug, Chug" noises while the Little Engine climbed over the mountain, saying "I think I can, I think I can, I think I can." She clapped her hands when all the children on the other side of the mountain got their toys and the lovely fruit and candy that the Little Engine brought them. However, Sheela thought it strange the toys didn't know the Little Engine would make it. It was right there in the picture. After thinking about it, Sheela realized that they couldn't see over the mountain, and so to them, what was going to happen was in the future.

After *The Little Engine That Could*, Natalya looked at a fashion magazine while Victor and Sheela played with the Russian nesting dolls. They lined them up and then they put them back inside one another. Sheela thought the dolls should each have a name, but she didn't want to choose so many names by herself and her Daddy didn't know what she was thinking.

Sunday morning, Natalya prepared a meal for brunch because they were skipping dinner altogether. Instead, they were going to have tea and food and see Sheela's horoscope. Nat served creamed mushrooms on biscuits with French beans and orange and coconut salad. For dessert she made warm apricot cobbler with fresh apricots and cappuccinos stirred with swivel sticks covered in brown sugar, except Victor said the brown sugar was really plain sugar colored brown by coffee.

Nat brought out the brunch on two new Japanese lacquered trays that had cherry blossoms painted on them and that came with matching napkins. Sheela wondered if she would get a tray too when she got bigger. Right now there was no point; she got only little tastes of grown up food. Her own diet consisted mostly of milk, which she liked in a bottle, pureed fruit, juices, cereal, Zwiebacks, and once in a while a mashed vegetable. She wasn't crazy about vegetables except for carrots and asparagus tips. Occasionally she ate a scrambled or soft-boiled egg. She couldn't eat much more than that because she couldn't chew very well yet. So far she just had four and a half teeth, two and a half on the bottom and two on top.

During brunch, Natalya told Sheela and Victor that Anjali had called earlier to say that she had spoken with Dora and Dora said it would be OK to give them Sheela's horoscope because it didn't say anything scary. It just talked about what effect her character was likely to have on her life. It also discussed her past.

The past and future were mixed in Sheela's mind because experiences from long ago played hide-and-seek with her memory. She saw the perfection of a ballerina's arabesque and she heard the loud, wet rat-tat-tat of rain beating on her windows. She listened to herself whispering secrets to Sweak, her friend who hid in corners. He was bluish and always exactly her size. He wore a brown beret and a tan and green plaid scarf and he smoked a mellow pipe. Those remembrances were sharp and bright. On the other hand, other fuzzier voices, fragrances, flavors, colors, shapes and textures—forgotten yet ever-present in her mind—taunted her. Would her horoscope cast any light on the mysterious hodgepodge that was many yesterdays old but would live for many tomorrows?

After brunch Dora phoned to tell Natalya how much she appreciated Anjali's input and how glad she was Nat cared about her concerns.

"I didn't want Sheela's horoscope to wind up becoming a horrorscope," Dora said. "But Anjali put my mind at ease. Did you know that Indian astrology is quite similar to American astrology?"

"No, I didn't," Nat answered. "I never gave the subject much thought."

"There are some interesting differences though," Dora explained. "Anjali faxed me an article. It says there are no references to the planets Neptune or Uranus, probably because Indian astrology was developed before those planets were named. Instead, there are mentions of the influence of Rahu-Ketu named after a demon. Rahu is the demon's head and Ketu is its tail. The days of the week represent the other planets. Sunday is the Sun; Monday is the moon; Tuesday is Mars; Wednesday is Mercury; Thursday is Jupiter; Friday is Venus and Saturday is Saturn. There are also signs that are more or less parallel to the signs of the zodiac. For example, Virgo is called Kanya or bride and Aquarius is Kumbh, which is a water jug. But the signs follow the lunar calendar so their dates aren't fixed. They also vary in accordance with the location of the sun and the other planets. I should think that makes for greater accuracy."

Between brunch and the anticipation of going out to tea and to get her horoscope, Sheela had a tough time settling down for her nap. She lay down, as was her routine, with her head in Victor's lap and with Aa-Oo in the crook of her elbow. She rubbed her thumb against her father's palm. Some days she would fall asleep in minutes, but on days like today she needed to be eased into slumber. If she were with her mother or Beca or Lulu, she would have listened to them singing to her, but her father's specialty was talking in Gibberish. Sheela loved it when he did that because she understood every word he said. Today Victor talked and talked and talked until his tongue thickened from the effort of forming so many elaborate sounds.

"Kapachoola paka, coliandel, rumbalooplursky? Noh! Noh! Noh! Akaploochakap, lednialkoc, rulplabmursky. Aha! Aha! Aha!"

"She's finally asleep," Victor told Nat after nearly an hour. "The thing that amazes me is that while Sheela wouldn't go to sleep, she didn't want to get up either. She wouldn't let me stop speaking. Otherwise I would have just let her stay awake."

"She needs that nap. She would have become impossibly cranky without it."

"So what do you want to do now?" Victor asked.

"Let's us take a nap too."

"That's an excellent idea, Nat. After all, we need to make sure we don't become impossibly cranky either."

19

Anjali and Jaya were ready and waiting when the Landaus arrived at four minutes before five, bearing an imaginative mix of purple gladiolas and brilliant orange birds of paradise, with centers that echoed the tone of the glads.

"I'm sorry we're early," Nat said. "My mother taught me that it is good manners to arrive five or ten minutes late, but Sheela has been eager to come ever since she woke up from her nap. She's been tugging at my finger and saying 'Yaya, Yaya.' At first I thought I was imagining it, but she kept on and on, so we gave up and left too soon."

"Yaya, Yaya." Sheela confirmed when Jaya took her and gave her a tight hug.

"The flowers are beautiful. You didn't have to do that," Anjali said. "Are they from that street of flower shops near your building?"

"Yes. They're from my favorite florist who has three-year old identical twin boys named William and Walter. She can't tell them apart when they're dressed so she calls them both Willy-Wally."

Anjali took the flowers. "Why don't you settle down in the living room? I'll put the flowers in a vase and bring the reading. I think you will be pleased. It will be a surprise even for Jaya. After you've read it, we can have tea and discuss what we think it means. Will that be fine?"

"Fine," the little group replied in unison, except for Sheela who said "Ine."

"What?" Anjali asked, turning toward Sheela. "I didn't hear you clearly."

"Ine," Sheela repeated.

"Did you hear what I just did?" Anjali asked.

"Yes. I think," Jaya replied, "that the Landaus have a seven and a half month old baby who understands everything and who communicates responsively. Do you realize how unusual that is? She must be extremely precocious."

"Sheela is precocious," Anjali said, "but babies do understand much more than we think."

"Here it is. Why don't you read it out loud, Natalya?" Anjali suggested when the group was settled. Sheela sat primly next to Natalya with Aa-Oo in her lap.

"I'm too excited. Victor, you read it." Nat said.

"OK. Here goes."

"This reading is for Sheela Landau, a strong girl born in Kumbh Rashi (sign of the water jug). The time and place of her birth—3:50 a.m., January 1, 2001, Houston, Texas, USA—indicate that she would benefit from a name that begins with the sound Sh, S or G.

"Sheela comes to her family with a strong need to complete the development that was cut short in her last life. She has chosen parents that have the power and intelligence to help her, but to use their power to the fullest, they will have to find ways to cope with Sheela's stubbornness.

"In her most recent previous life Sheela belonged to an educated and religious family that lived in a large city on the eastern coast of America. She had one half-sister and no brothers. Her father was an immigrant who left the country of his birth at a young age. He died prematurely, and his baby daughter was raised by a loving stepfather. Her mother was conceived in Europe, but was born in America. The mother was a professional and her insistence on working outside of the home, even though she had a well-to-do husband and children, created something of a scandal in her time.

"Sheela was lean, agile, and graceful. As a child, she silently longed to study ballet, but she never expressed this longing to her parents because she thought she was too tall to become a dancer. Her dream of becoming a dancer was one of many unfulfilled dreams.

"In her present life Sheela will reunite with two souls remembered from at least one earlier life. These souls and Sheela's soul will meet again in at least one more future incarnation.

"Sheela has many feelings that linger from her past. Recollections that should have been shed when she shed her body remained attached to her soul. Thus she fears and avoids large bodies of water, she has a great love of music and dance, and she seeks fulfillment in the traditions of her religion. However, in this embodiment her intellect will lift her beyond ritual to philosophy and spirituality.

"Sheela's present birth is in a cultured and gracious family. Sheela will bring good fortune to her entire family. As she grows, she will blossom into a tall, slender, shapely and very beautiful woman. Her appearance and her demeanor will reflect her high self-esteem. Thus Sheela will maintain her good looks throughout her life and into her golden years. The influence of Shukra (Venus), Ravi, also called Surya (the sun), and Chandra (the moon) contribute to Sheela's personality. She is intelligent—indeed brilliant—determined to the point of stubbornness, self-confident, ambitious, hard-working, and energetic.

"Following the example of her mother, Sheela will conduct herself with propriety, with sensitivity and with an awareness of the circumstances in which she finds herself. She will have an excellent command over language. She will become a highly analytical thinker with interest in logic, philosophy, and law. These interests will direct her career. Sheela will also prove to be a very talented actress, but acting will be a hobby, not a profession.

"Sheela will enjoy good health, prosperity, and comfort due to the position of Chandra (the moon) and Shukra (Venus) and she will achieve academic excellence due to the influence of Guru (Jupiter). Thus she will earn well, travel widely, and have a happy life overall.

"Her relationship with both her mother and father will be very good. Sheela will be especially precious to her parents because she will have no siblings. This can be determined from the position of Surya (the sun), Budh (Mercury), and Ketu, the Demon's Tail (perhaps Neptune and/or Uranus.)

"Although the position of Mangal (Mars) indicates a late marriage, probably between the age of twenty-seven and twenty-nine, Budh (Mercury) and Shani

(Saturn) point toward a happy married life. Sheela and her husband will have their first child shortly after their marriage and they are likely to have several more children thereafter. Her husband's name will begin with the sound A.

"Sheela's chart is vibrant with positive forces. She is blessed. Her life will be a joyous journey with only a few dark passages. Throughout this journey she will strive for and achieve excellence. Sheela will brighten the lives she touches."

Victor read the last paragraph with a catch in his throat. Natalya listened with moistened eyes. At the end, mother and father turned toward their daughter. For an instant, she appeared not to see them. They felt her to be tuned in to a mysterious universe that existed beyond all known dimensions. But by the time Natalya embraced Sheela and dropped a warm tear on her cheek, Sheela was back and she gave her parents and her friends a delicious, self-satisfied smile.

Nat was the first to speak. "It's just so beautiful. I don't know what to make of it, but the part about being an only child, I don't think that's going to turn out to be true. We are planning to have more children as soon as possible," Nat said.

"That part probably isn't right," Anjali agreed. "Like I told you, a horoscope is an opinion, like a doctor's opinion. There are often more ways than one to interpret the signs. The predictions are not cast in concrete."

"But I wonder," Jaya commented. "The horoscope was very clear about Sheila being an only child. Why would they put that in there if it wasn't pretty definite?"

"Well, if we do turn out to have more children, does it mean that the rest of the horoscope is wrong too?" Nat asked.

"No," Anjali said." The least reliable parts of horoscopes are the specific future predictions. The most reliable portions are those that describe a person's nature."

"Well, I don't disagree with the description of Sheela's nature," Jaya said. "She has to turn out to be pretty terrific. She is quite extraordinary already. Besides, heredity is a given and Sheela is her mother's daughter."

"And her father's," Nat added.

"Whichever way you consider the nature versus nurture debate," Anjali said, "Sheela was definitely born with many good things going for her. Her genes are good and she will get the best possible upbringing. So I guess a lot of what her horoscope anticipates is a given."

"You know something?" Natalya pointed out. "This horoscope assumes that reincarnation is a fact. What if there is no past life?"

"You're right that Indian astrology takes the matter of past lives for granted," Anjali answered, "and if you don't accept reincarnation, the horoscope doesn't make much sense. I suppose allusions to earlier lives would seem eerie to someone who isn't comfortable with the idea of reincarnation."

"Is belief in reincarnation a tenet of Hinduism? Victor asked.

"Not exactly," Jaya explained. "It's more of a starting point, a premise. There is no paradigm that Hindus must believe in, but reincarnation which incorporates the concept of karma is the philosophical foundation of Hindu belief."

"So what do Hindus believe?" Nat asked.

"A better way to answer would be to explain Hindu thought because no two Hindus believe precisely the same thing."

"Well then, Jaya, can you explain Hindu thought simply?"

"She can," Anjali piped in, "but while she explains it, I'm going to set up our tea."

"Give me a second," Victor said. "I left Sheela's bag of toys in the car. Let me get them for her. They'll hold her interest while we talk."

"OK," Jaya began a few moments later, "I'd say the most important idea in Hinduism is that life's goal is to know the Truth, with a capital T. You could say that Truth is God. Knowing Truth is an all-encompassing reality. It's everything: the essence of immortality and liberation. *The Gita*, which is a distillation of the Hindu scriptures, explains that there are three paths to reaching Truth: learning or gnana yoga, worship or bhakti yoga, and action or karma yoga. Since Hinduism presumes that it is impossible to attain knowledge of Truth in one lifetime, it becomes necessary to accept reincarnation."

"Where does karma fit in?" Victor asked.

"Karma is intertwined with reincarnation. Karma means destiny that is neither random nor arbitrary. Together karma and reincarnation answer the human question of why things happen as they do. We know from science that physical phenomena are the result of cause and effect. If we drop a glass, it will break. If we see a broken glass on the floor, we know from experience that it fell or was dropped. We know precisely what caused the glass to break, even if we didn't see how the glass got broken. Hinduism maintains that everything in life is the effect of a cause. If something happens in this life, it has to have been caused by something that happened before, either earlier in this life or in an earlier life. It makes no difference whether or not we know or acknowledge a cause. Just as in physics every action mandates an equal and opposite reaction, in life every cause mandates an effect. Not remembering the cause is analogous to not seeing the glass break."

"You just gave a lucid and logical explanation of something that I always believed was muddled or complex," Victor said.

"It's food for thought," Nat said. "I guess believing in karma and reincarnation is like believing that what goes around comes around. Perhaps it does take more than one lifetime to play out a cycle. So, even if you don't believe in reincarnation as an empirical reality, you'd have to say it's plausible."

"It's a hypothesis which somewhat explains the mysteries of life, death, and suffering," Victor suggested.

"That's true," Jaya agreed. "Those mysteries are in part what I meant by the 'human question of why things happen as they do.' And that's precisely how many Hindus view reincarnation, as a hypothesis. I personally think that even if it cannot be categorically proven, reincarnation is more plausible than not. Besides, believing in it gives my life direction. It's a lodestar which guides my conduct."

"I hate to interrupt, but could we please transport this conversation into the dining room," Anjali came back to say. "Otherwise everything will get cold."

"I'll quickly change Sheela and be right there." The moment Nat spoke, Sheela came crawling to her from across the room with a grin on her face.

High tea was an elaborate cross between hors d'oeuvres and breakfast. Along with cardamom-flavored English style tea, Anjali brought out sliced mangos, samosas—fried triangular pastries filled with spicy peas and potatoes—and assorted sandwiches—cucumber and onion, minced ham, tomato and cheese, and green chutney—all on thin slices of white bread with the crusts cut off. She also served Indian style vegetable cutlets and a savory mix made of puffed rice and wheat flakes with cashews. Finally there were shortbread fingers, gingersnaps and chocolate-topped butter cookies. The gingersnaps were Sheela's favorite. They were zesty and perfect to teethe on. From now on, she would make sure that her parents kept them on hand.

As always, the combination of good food and good company proved to be relaxing. Jaya ate instead of picking. Everyone laughed. Talk was lighthearted. Victor, Natalya and Sheela assimilated some of what they had learned. Victor especially enjoyed himself, never noticing that he was surrounded by women. Anjali and Jaya thought about their problems in the light of karma, something they took for granted but didn't necessarily consider in their daily lives. Sheela's blessings had already touched the people gathered around the table.

The following Tuesday at 2:15 p.m. Natalya, Defendant Home Fitness Trainers' in-house attorney Bart Grady, and Plaintiffs' counsel Jeffrey Dupree met in court for the hearing on Nat's emergency motion to withdraw from the HFT case. They didn't chat in the hallways, as lawyers often do, because there was nothing to chat about. Instead they sat in the courtroom listening to the other disputes as they waited for their turn. Their case was the seventh on the afternoon docket and it was called at 3:10 p.m.

Natalya, as movant, spoke first. She explained that although she was attorney of record, Rudolph Kaplan who was a partner in the firm that employed her had, until recently, played a very active role in this litigation.

"Mr. Kaplan has gone to London, Your Honor," Nat said, "without giving any indication of when he plans to return. Meanwhile, I have had problems persuading my client to follow my recommendations. Furthermore, on several occasions HFT has given me instructions which I believe conflict with my professional and ethical responsibility."

When the judge invited HFT to comment, Grady asked the court to deny Ms. Landau's motion.

"Your Honor," he said, "we are shocked by Ms. Landau's intention to abandon this matter at the eleventh hour and offended by her insinuation that we have done something wrong. We ask that her motion to withdraw be denied. In the alternative, we ask you to give us thirty days to find other representation and to abate all pending matters for sixty days in order to give our new attorneys an opportunity to review the files."

"What is Plaintiffs' position in this matter, Mr. Dupree?" the Judge asked.

"We do not oppose Ms. Landau's Motion to Withdraw, Your Honor," Dupree replied. "However, we object to the extension of any deadlines. This case is set for trial next March and we ask that the existing Scheduling Order remain unaltered."

"Ms. Landau's motion is granted," the judge stated. "This Court cannot understand why HFT wishes to compel a reluctant lawyer to continue to represent it. Since Mr. Rudolph Kaplan, a partner in Ms. Landau's firm, is in a position to replace Ms. Landau as attorney of record, there will be no extensions of existing deadlines. The existing Scheduling Order continues in effect."

"Thank you, Your Honor," the three lawyers said in unison, although only two of them meant it.

"I have an Order for your signature," Natalya said, "but it needs to state that the existing Scheduling Order remains unchanged."

"That's fine. I'll pen that in," said the judge.

When Nat returned to her office, she found two envelopes on her desk. Both were sealed and marked "Personal and Confidential." Nat opened the top one first. It contained a memorandum signed by Mr. McCall on behalf of the firm. The first paragraph regretfully advised Ms. Natalya Landau that the Limited Liability Partnership of Kaplan, McCall and Green was in the process of being dissolved and that therefore Ms. Landau's services would no longer be required. In the second paragraph, Mr. McCall was pleased to inform her that pursuant to her employment contract, she was entitled to six months' severance pay in the event that the firm dissolved. The monies would be forwarded to her at the time of distribution of the partnership assets. In the third paragraph, Kaplan, McCall and Green wished her the best of luck in her future endeavors.

The second envelope contained a note from Mr. Green. Walter asked Natalya to meet with him at her earliest convenience, but in any event before the end of the week, in order to discuss the handling of pending cases and to work out timing and other details pertaining to her orderly departure. It would be greatly appreciated the note added, if she would make an appointment through his secretary without mentioning the nature of her business and also if she would be kind enough to refrain from discussing this development with anyone else until after they had an opportunity to talk.

Natalya smiled. She put the letters in her briefcase and took everything else out. Then she left for the day.

20

Although Sheela couldn't understand the words in her horoscope, she loved their cadence and she could tell that they fit her feelings. The reading validated her choice of Victor and Natalya as parents. It defined the hollowness she identified within her soul as yearnings born in the past. It breathed life into her strange memories. It uplifted her spirit. It also caused her to wonder whether she could give up her stubbornness without giving up a piece of herself in the process.

The horoscope suggested that Sheela's life before she was Sheela was a mystery that she would seek to unravel in the years to come. Who was the person who longed to dance but was held back by unknown forces? Now new forces propelled Sheela toward new horizons. She would marvel at the artistry and power of words and become their master. She would use speech to make her imprint on the world, to sway the universal net that danced to the music of God.

As Sheela matured, she worked on her motor skills, especially verbal communication. She also learned about herself. When she was alone, she meticulously explored her mind and her body. She fine-tuned her senses and discovered that she had the ability to manipulate them. She could control what she saw by looking in one direction or another, or she could shut out visual stimuli altogether by closing her eyes like Ms. Meredith taught her at Infantasy. She could touch softly or with vigor or not touch at all if that was her preference and she could feel textures and density with her hands, her face, or her body. She could move her muscles and wiggle her toes. She could identify different tastes and she could eat, or close her mouth, or spit. Sounds and smells were more difficult to control. She was somewhat at the mercy of her environment, but she could muffle noise by covering her ears and she could block odors by closing her nose and breathing through her mouth.

As interesting as all those powers were, the most exciting was her power over her mind. Sheela's mind was the master of all her senses, yet she was the master of her mind. She could direct it here or there. And by controlling her mind, Sheela could make herself feel happy or sad. She could process the information that she gleaned from her other senses and thus tune in to the vibrations that came to her from near or far. And in her mind she could assume any form she wished, and she could place herself at any point she wished in time or space.

In the course of her self-examination, Sheela discovered a special place between her legs. If she gently rubbed herself there in a certain way, she found that she could awaken extraordinary sensations. The sensations were so intense that Sheela dared not let anyone see her in their grasp. What she did to herself was her secret, something private she saved for the times that she cuddled Aa-Oo early in the morning or after her nap when everyone thought she was asleep. She thought of it as bursting because after touching herself or scrunching herself until she could bear it no longer, she felt as if she were bursting inside. Then she collapsed with relief. But her physical delight often ended in loneliness and fear of discovery.

"What if my parents see me?" Sheela asked Aa-Oo once after she had almost been caught by Natalya. "Or even worse, what if Lulu or someone else finds out about my secret?"

"It would be embarrassing," Aa-Oo replied. "Better make sure no one finds out."

"How can I do that?"

"You have to be quiet as a mouse, even quieter," Aa-Oo suggested. "And I'll listen and tell you if I think anyone is coming."

"Do you think I'm doing something wrong?" Sheela inquired of her parrot.

"Bursting is not wrong," Aa-Oo pronounced. "It gives you feelings that are a part of you. But it has to stay a secret because it is very personal."

"Do you think it's personal like Sweak?" Sheela asked.

"No, that's entirely different. Sweak isn't a secret. He is only private because no one would believe you if you talked about him," Aa-Oo said.

Sheela considered Aa-Oo's explanation and decided that it made sense. Then she asked, "Are you like Sweak?"

"No, of course not," Aa-Oo replied indignantly. "I'm physically tangible. Sweak has no body. He is an idea and only you can hear or see him."

"You are just finding another way to tell me Sweak isn't real. I think you are jealous of him."

"Not at all," Aa-Oo answered. "Why would I be jealous? I feel very secure. It's not my fault that Sweak is invisible."

"I can describe him perfectly," Sheela retorted, "so he is not invisible. He is bluish and he smokes a pipe and he speaks in his own special voice."

"What does he say?"

"I'm not going to tell you if you think Sweak has no body. What's the point of telling you something so important if you can't even see Sweak."

Sheela was upset after her quarrel with Aa-Oo. She turned over in a huff and tried to go to sleep, but she couldn't. She would have taken comfort in telling her parents or Lulu about the fight, but she wouldn't know how. Anyway, she couldn't trust them to understand. After all, they were grown-ups. So she hoped that Aa-Oo would make up with her. And luckily after a few minutes he did.

"You never have been so angry with me before," Aa-Oo told Sheela.

"Because you never said anything so horrible to me until now," Sheela said.

"I didn't mean it." Aa-Oo explained. "I was just reflecting your own ideas back to you. Please tell me what Sweak says."

"OK," Sheela said, "I'll tell you some day. But I won't tell you now."

"Please tell me now," Aa-Oo said. "I'm anxious to know and I hate to wait."

"I can't because we had a fight."

"But we are friends again, aren't we?" Aa-Oo asked.

"All right, I'll whisper it in your ear." When she was finished, Sheela gave Aa-Oo a big hug as they both shouted "ugatak ugatak ugatak" just as Lulu came in.

Later that evening Lulu told Natalya what she had heard, and Nat wondered about it but couldn't decipher the words.

"It's probably Gibberish," Nat concluded. But a few days later she heard it herself and asked Victor if he had any idea what Sheela was saying. Victor thought for a while and then his face broke out in one of his wonderful smiles.

"I figured it out," he said to Natalya. "I'll give you a hint."

"Just tell me!"

"No, this is too delicious. That's why I'm giving you a hint. You have to figure it out for yourself. Here's the hint: It's something you say all the time."

"I never say ugatak."

"Sure you do, Nat. Why don't you repeat what Sheela said in the exact tone you heard her say it."

"OK. Ug a tak; ug a tak; ug a tak."

"And what was Sheela doing when she said it?" Victor asked.

"She was hugging Aa-Oo. Oh, I get it." Nat chuckled. "It's hug attack, hug attack, hug attack."

Natalya's meeting with Walter Green was more cordial than expected. Nat thanked him for not putting her in the position of having to demand the severance pay that she was entitled to as well as for his good wishes.

"I didn't think I was appreciated around here, so your letter made me happy," Nat said.

"The firm has been under a tremendous amount of pressure for some time now and the partners haven't been seeing eye-to-eye. But that's water over the dam. We have straightened out our accounts, and with Mr. Kaplan out of the picture, we can fulfill our commitments. However, we do have one expectation."

"What's that?"

"That you refrain from working with any of the firm's clients for two years. Mr. McCall and I are forming a new Professional Corporation and we will need all the business we can retain to make it fly. I recognize that, except for HFT, the folks you have been working with think you walk on water. We will have to come up with some excuse about why you are leaving and cannot continue to represent them."

"That won't be a problem. I'll give you a letter stating I need time to be with my daughter. That's a fact. I also need a chance to grow up, to find myself, so to speak. I can't remember when I ever had more than a few weeks off from school or work."

132

"Logistically, how can we work out the mechanics and the timing of the transition?" Green asked.

"I'd like to talk to our clients over the next two weeks," Nat said. "I'll say that I'm familiarizing you with the details of their cases and that you will be filing substitution of counsel notices with the court on their behalf. I don't think anyone will object or go elsewhere."

"Two weeks is a long time," Green said. "I was hoping to get this sewed up within a few days."

"I'd like to take a quick overdue trip to New York and then come back and wind down."

"Can I ask you to please postpone going out of town? I need to get our new company up and going before we get hit by the fallout from HFT."

"All right. You have given me a nice incentive."

"Thanks, Natalya. I think you understand why my new firm can't re-hire you. You have unwittingly become involved with too many sensitive problems."

"Yes. I also recognize that you consider my philosophy detrimental to your bottom line."

"I don't know how to respond to that," Green said, shaking his head, "but you may have made some dents in my thinking."

"No response is called for. It's 3:30. I'll give you a quick write up on my cases this evening and attach the docket sheets."

"How many active cases require immediate attention?"

"Twenty-seven."

"That many!"

"Edward has been a great help. I hope you will keep him. He's energetic, smart and discreet."

"He'll probably quit and decide to go to law school after he hears you are leaving."

"No. He works as an apprentice chef evenings and weekends. He's saving to open up his own restaurant."

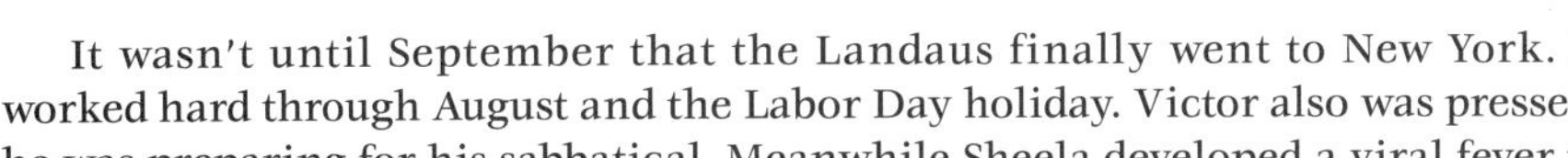

It wasn't until September that the Landaus finally went to New York. Nat worked hard through August and the Labor Day holiday. Victor also was pressed as he was preparing for his sabbatical. Meanwhile Sheela developed a viral fever that made her cranky and restless. Soon after she recovered, she acquired a throat infection. Rebecca was on summer vacation and she spent most of August keeping Sheela company and trying to keep Lulu from going nuts.

Rebecca and Lulu both blamed Infantasy for Sheela's ailments and they discussed the absurdity of sending Sheela, or for that matter any baby, there.

"It's crazy," Lulu said. "Small babies should not be around so many other babies. If one baby gets sick, they all get sick."

"I know," Rebecca agreed. "But I'm only one grandmother. The other grandmother thinks Infantasy is wonderful. She is a very smart lady, but she is a little crazy herself, so I cannot say anything. What do you do in Infantasy, anyway?"

"Nothing. Lights come off and lights come on. Ms. Meredith opens her eyes and closes her eyes. She is, what do you say? Yes, she is frustrated because she doesn't have a good man or children of her own. The babies go bang, bang, bang on drums and they crawl around and grab each other's toys. Sometimes they pull and push. One baby boy, whose name is Mark, makes número two," Lulu held up two fingers. "My amorcito is the smartest baby there."

"Maybe I should take Sheela once and see for myself," Rebecca suggested.
"No," Lulu said. "Infantasy has a strict policy. Only people on its list can bring the babies. If you are not on the list, you cannot come."
"Who is on the list?" Rebecca asked.
"Only Mr. and Mrs. Landau and me."
"Well, I'm Mrs. Landau."
"No, the list says:

> Natalya Landau, Mother;
> Victor Landau, Father
> Lourdes Santos, Nanny."

Rebecca was no earth mother. Her bones poked when she hugged her granddaughter and she jerked when she walked her, but she was soothing none the less. Beca told Sheela things and did things with her that made her forget all about her headache or wanting an outing, so she thrived and got well.

One morning Rebecca joined Sheela and Lulu in their favorite game of making faces in front of the mirror and she added a new twist. She taught them how to make faces with names like happy face, smiley face, sad face, scared face, angry face, silly face, and so on. Sheela couldn't say the names of the faces properly, but she always could make a face that matched Beca's description.
"I used to play this game all the time when I was a little girl," Beca said to Sheela, somewhat wistfully. "And you know what? This used to be my mirror, but your daddy and mommy loved it so I gave it to them when they got married."
"Wid Ooo?" Sheela asked, wanting to know with whom Rebecca used to play. But Beca misunderstood. She hunted for Aa-Oo who had fallen under the crib and brought him over to participate in the fun.

Her grandfather Henry helped her get better too. He was strong and soft at the same time. He could carry her for hours without getting tired and he made Sheela laugh. He could make her fever drop just by patting her head, but the problem was he didn't stay with her as long as Beca did. Sheela asked Aa-Oo whether the reason she always felt fine around Appa—whom she just renamed Gappa—was because he was a doctor who knew how to cure sick people.
"No, that is not the reason," Aa-Oo answered. "After all, your pediatrician cures sick babies and he can't make you better by patting your head. Gappa just has a way about him. You could say he has a magic touch."

<hr>

Almost as abruptly as it began, the avalanche of activity and tension in the Landau household abated. Sheela was fine, Rebecca returned to teaching and to her Henry, and both Victor and Nat finished up their work. They had three empty days before they had to leave to visit the Rosenbaums. They resolved to keep to themselves for those days and to refrain from discussing any issues of consequence. They also decided not to make any plans for the future until after they returned from their ten-day stay in New York.

"I want a holiday from thinking," Nat said.

Victor agreed. "Let's just sleep, cook, eat, work out, entertain Sheela and fool around with our photographs."

"And make up for the times we've been too stressed to make love," Nat added.

"I wanted to say that, but I was afraid you would think that's all I think about."

"Is it?" Nat asked.

"No, but I think about it a lot."

"And you think I don't?"

"I don't think about whether you think about making love."

"You don't?"

"Well, maybe sometimes. But then my thoughts turn into fantasies."

Natalya and Victor marked and labeled photographs for hours on end. Meanwhile Sheela, enjoying the cozy atmosphere, calmly watched *Mirrors*, her micro disc pick of the month, or played alone. But occasionally, she scooted over to her parents, wanting to sit in one of their laps for a bit while they worked. Then Victor or Nat showed her some of the snapshots, commenting on the people who stared or smiled out at her.

"This is your Great Uncle Albert Landau. He was a respected rabbi," Victor said about a picture of an old man with a long white beard. Then he pointed to a photo of a little girl whose head was covered by a potty. "This must be Beca when she was a baby. She put the potty on her head because she didn't want her picture taken. Isn't that naughty?"

"No, no," Sheela replied. She thought the grown-ups who took the picture were the naughty ones. She didn't like having her picture taken either.

The evening before the flight, while her parents were packing, making phone calls and attending to last minute details, Sheela wanted to read *The Country of Thirty-Six Thousand Wishes* which Dora had given her before she was born. Neither Victor nor Nat could understand why, when they had all the time in the world, Sheela required almost no attention, whereas now when they were busy, she suddenly became impossibly demanding.

"We have a lot to accomplish," Nat told her, "because we are going to see Grandma Dora and Grandpa Harold bright and early tomorrow morning."

"Boo, boo," Sheela whined, pointing to the bookcase.

"Not now. We have a flight to catch. You can see that I am busy."

Nat gave up. She read several chapters of that marvelous book to her daughter until she put her head on her lap and rubbed her palm. Sheela's eyes closed just at the part when the fairies were getting their wings.

After putting Sheela in her crib, Nat wearily placed *The Country of Thirty-Six Thousand Wishes* in an oversized backpack along with Aa-Oo, *The Little Engine That Could*, Sheela's floor mat, *Mirrors*, extra diapers, bottles, formula, snacks, and a change of clothes. The backpack weighed more than Sheela, so Nat removed *Mirrors* because the disc couldn't be played on the flight and the floor mat because Sheela probably wouldn't miss it. But a few moments after packing those items in the to be checked bag, Nat took them out again and replaced them in the backpack. Sheela liked holding the disc and looking at its cover. And she just might want to sit on her torn and faded floor mat, even if it had to be folded to fit on the seat or on her or Victor's lap.

21

The Landaus left for the airport in a bad mood. Nat, who never used to worry about preparations, found that traveling with a baby was different. She packed the previous night and set her alarm at 6:15 a.m. for their 9:05 flight. Even so, getting out of the house was difficult. Sheela wouldn't leave without her big teddy bear Rrr, Brahms, her It's a Small World After All music box and the suitcase which Victor had brought her from his trip to the Big Apple. Figuring out what all Sheela wanted was a production and carrying everything was awkward. Victor got annoyed by Nat's "lack of planning." The family set off late, in a rush and irritated.

On the drive to Intercontinental, Nat remembered that Victor had forgotten to change the message on their answering machine. Now it was her turn to criticize.

"Since you plan in such an exemplary fashion, how come you didn't plan to change the message on our machine?" Natalya inquired. "It's not like you did anything else to get ready for this trip. I packed my stuff and all of Sheela's stuff; I got up almost an hour ahead of you; I got Sheela ready; I made our breakfast; I cleaned up; and I took care of all the details like stopping the paper."

"That was your choice," Victor answered. "You could have asked me for help."

"Are you kidding? And get a lecture? Not that I didn't get one anyway. I don't see why we couldn't let your parents drive us instead of having to park and all. They wanted to and you refused for no reason. This way it will take us an extra 20 or 30 minutes to get checked in."

"No it won't. It's just 10 or 15 minutes extra and it's much less coordination."

"You could have used those 15 minutes to record a civil message."

"There's nothing wrong with our message," Victor insisted.

"It's a rude message, and now that we're out of town and haven't left our number, we'll have to check the machine twice a day."

"So we'll check. It's no big deal!" Victor's loud voice caused Sheela to start crying.

After a few moments of smoldering, Victor admitted that he didn't really think Nat had planned badly. What bothered him, he explained, was that she was so uptight.

"Why didn't you say that in the first place instead of jumping all over me?"

136

"I just figured it out," Victor admitted. "Let's start over. We're making good time and we won't be late. Don't worry about the machine. We'll pick up messages and answer whoever calls. Most people who matter know we're going anyway. Right?"

"Right." Nat smiled. Then she looked over her shoulder at her daughter and told Sheela that everything was fine. "No more crying, OK?" she asked.

"OK," Sheela answered breaking out in a teary smile of her own. For good measure though, she reconfirmed, "Rrr? Aa-Oo? Bams?"

"Yes," Natalya replied. "We have Rrr, Aa-Oo, Brahms, and your bag. But I hope they let us take all that on the plane."

"OK," Sheela responded. "Ike Aa-Oo, Rrr, Bams,"

"Wow," Nat told her. "That's very good. You like Aa-Oo, and Rrr. Can you say 'like?'"

"Ike Aa-Oo, Rrr, Bams," Sheela repeated extremely pleased with herself. After a moment she added, "Ike Dada; ike Ma," but she said it so softly that she wasn't heard.

The flight was fun. Sheela was excited and she loved the attention she got from the cabin crew. They gave her a dinosaur puppet to play with and her parents entertained her with it as well as with her books, with snacks, with Brahms and with her music box. Rrr slept in the overhead bin. For a while, Sheela and Nat played peek-a-boo and pat-a-cake. She didn't need her floor mat after all.

Less than an hour before touchdown at La Guardia, Sheela fell asleep, but as soon as she felt the bump of her plane landing she woke up again, delighted and full of chatter. She babbled on and on, although everyone around her was too engrossed in the disembarkation process to pay attention to what she was saying. Her parents were busy gathering their paraphernalia and smoothing themselves and Sheela. At last they went through the passage that connected their plane to the terminal gate. Within seconds Sheela was accosted by Dora, Harold, Ronald, Cecily, and a bunch of wild flowers. Still in Victor's arms, she didn't know which way to turn.

Dora recognized Sheela's consternation. She took Sheela, helped her get ahold of Aa-Oo, and gave Cecily the flowers to hold after Sheela had a nice whiff.

"When we get home," Dora said, "we all want to play with you. We've missed you so much. Do you know that I think of you at least once every hour of every day?"

By way of an answer, Sheela blew a round of kisses. She thought about Dora a lot too, not every hour of every day, but still, a lot. Sheela wondered if every hour included the night, and Dora seemed to read her thoughts.

"During the day I think about what you must be doing. Your mother keeps me posted you know. I hear that you have a nice vocabulary and that you are a star pupil at Infantasy. At night, I dream wonderful dreams about you."

It was mid-afternoon by the time everyone was home and settled. Her parents had some fruit salad and open sandwiches. Then Grandpa Harold said that the Landaus were tired and they would have a late night, so he sent Sheela and her parents upstairs to take a nap.

Sheela wasn't sleepy. She was eager to play in the teak crib that had been her mother's when she was a baby. She looked at the crib's sturdy yet gracefully curved rails and thought she could manage something that had been on her mind for a while. She was going to pull herself up without help and see if she could take a few steps. Then she had second thoughts. She wanted no witnesses to failure and no assistance, so she decided to wait and remained seated. However, after a few minutes, she got bored. Her parents were reading on their own. Her music box had sung five times, but then Victor said, "Enough is enough."

Sheela whined in response, but Nat just scolded.

"Come on, sweetheart, let's quietly do our thing for a little while, OK?"

"Ike Aa-Oo, Rrr. Ike Dada. Ike Ma." Sheela calculated that this litany would get her more positive attention. Nat and Victor perked their ears and turned toward her, so Sheela treated them to an encore. "Ike Aa-Oo, Rrr. Ike Dada. Ike Ma."

"Ma and Dada like Sheela," Nat replied to her daughter.

Sheela held out her arms so as to be transferred to the big bed where she could cuddle between her mother and father and listen to Natalya read more of The Country of Thirty-Six Thousand Wishes to her. After ten minutes of attentive listening and some discussion over the beautiful illustrations, mother and daughter simultaneously fell asleep. Seconds later Victor dozed off too, with his open magazine resting face down on his forehead.

Sheela was the first to awaken, a little after 5:30. Her stirring aroused her parents just as Dora knocked on the door.

"Come in," Nat said. "We're getting up."

"I was thinking that it would be fun to give Sheela a bubble bath downstairs," Dora suggested. "If she's uncomfortable with me, Nat can bathe her and I'll watch."

"That's probably not a very good idea," Victor, said. "Sheela hates baths."

"Noooooo," Sheela remarked.

"See?" Dora answered. "She said no, she doesn't hate baths."

"I don't think so," Nat explained. "I believe that no means Sheela doesn't want a bath."

"Well, how on earth do you get her clean if she won't take a bath?" Dora asked. "Besides, I never heard of a baby who doesn't love bubble baths. You adored them when you were little, didn't you Nat?"

"I did and I still do, but Sheela isn't me. She has a thing about bathing."

"How can a baby develop an attitude about baths? It's crazy. Maybe it's something Rebecca put into her head. Didn't Rebecca remove all the bath tubs in her house and replace them with shower stalls?"

"Yeah, she did," Victor said. "My mother is nuts, but then again, whose mother isn't nuts? She never bathed Sheela though. This is my child's personal phobia."

"I'm Nat's mother, and I'm not nuts, am I?" Dora asked with a sheepish grin.

"Well, I love and admire you more than words can tell," Nat said, "but you aren't exactly your run of the mill normal parent."

"Well, perhaps I am a tad eccentric. Anyway, how do you wash Sheela?"

"One of us takes her into the shower with us." Victor explained.

"Have you ever tried a bubble bath?"

"No, we never did," Victor answered.

"Let's take her down and see what happens." Turning to Sheela, Dora asked, "Would you like to come and look at a bubble bath?"

Sheela answered by shaking her head up and down and back and forth as if she were saying yes and no at the same time. She didn't mind looking at the bubbles but she did not want to sit inside a tub. So Natalya undressed her and wrapped her in a fluffy white towel with a hood. Then Victor carried her downstairs and marched into the master bathroom followed by Nat and Dora. Dora filled her large circular mauve tub with water and bubbles. Sheela plopped her hand inside and swished the bubbles around. But when Victor tried to lift her in, she began to scream. Then Nat carried her back upstairs and the two of them showered together in the guest bathroom.

"This evening we're splurging," Harold announced to his family when everyone had settled down with a glass of red wine and sips of grape juice for Sheela.

"Splurging in what sense?" Natalya asked.

"In the only meaningful sense. We're having an unhealthy dinner."

"Which is?"

"Veal cordon bleu with cornflake crumbs, stuffed with ham and cheese, and sautéed in pure butter. Also salad with homemade Roquefort dressing, baked apples, mashed potatoes, and dilled peas, not to mention rolls and apricot upside down cake."

"OmyGod!" Nat said.

"How on earth did you get Dora to do that?" Victor asked Harold. "I thought she swore off high cholesterol menus years ago."

"The only way I know how," replied the paunchy patriarch of the Rosenbaum clan. "I threw a tantrum."

"And it worked?" Victor asked.

"It did. Tantrums can be very effective as long as they are used sparingly."

"Doesn't veal call for a white wine?" Cecily asked.

"Never mind," Ronald said. "This Australian Cabernet is to die for. I'm not switching."

At dinner Sheela sat in a high chair, just like she did at Beca and Gappa's house, and she behaved as well as she did at Shabbat in Houston.

"Sheela, you are a very good girl," Cecily smiled at her niece.

"Goo," Sheela agreed. She clapped her hands.

"Our daughter is at her best when she is the center of interest," Victor noted.

"I have to compliment you," Harold said, "on Sheela. You certainly have done a good job with her."

"Except for the fact that she won't take a bath," Dora pointed out.

"That's not anything we did," Nat said. "This started when Sheela was a tiny baby. In fact, she squirmed every time I took a bath when I was pregnant. Don't you remember my telling you?"

"I do, now that you mention it," Dora acknowledged. "But at the time, I thought it was your imagination. I still can't understand why Sheela feels the way she does."

"It has to be something that goes beyond either genetics or rearing," Cecily suggested. "It proves there is much more to human nature than we can even begin to understand."

"You are certainly right," Harold said. "The source of Sheela's aversion to baths is a mystery. On the other hand, her brightness is the product of both genetics and a superior upbringing. You know, I was always sure that a child's intelligence could be cultivated so it expands, but it wasn't until well after Ronald and Nat were grown that my theory was confirmed and explained."

"What is the explanation?" Ronald asked his father.

"Human intelligence is a function of connection or interaction between brain cells. So, although we are born with virtually all the neurons we're going to get, they aren't connected. The connections start building in the womb and the process continues through infancy. A single cell can connect with up to fifteen thousand other cells that in turn connect with fifteen thousand others and so on. By the age of three, a child's brain can have as many as one thousand trillion connections. But infants and young children need to be stimulated in order for the connections to be formed."

"That explains a fantastic program I saw about ten years ago," Ronald said. "It was about hydrocephalic babies—those born with water on their brains. They used to die, but then doctors started putting in shunts that diverted the water to the latter half of the body. When the first children who had shunts grew up, they televised cat scans of their brains. You could see that the kids had almost no brain cells. Their skulls were hollow except for small clusters of cells on the outer rims. Still they had high IQ's and were completely normal because the few cells they did have built enough connections to make up for the others."

"The brain starts disposing of unnecessary connections at about the age of eleven, but it retains those that have been reinforced through childhood stimuli," Harold pointed out.

"That's amazing," Cecily remarked.

"It is," Victor said. "We get these brochures from Infantasy which bases its program on this stuff."

"All this detailed information didn't exist when any of us were babies and there were no Infantasies," Ronald pointed out, "but we were all stimulated the same way you are stimulating Sheela. That's what's really amazing."

"Right!" Nat said. "Parents instinctively do the right things. You know, Ma, I still remember how you told me that babies in orphanages who had no one to love them and carry them died from lack of attention. Didn't you volunteer to cuddle and play with abandoned infants?"

"Yes," Harold answered on his wife's behalf. "Your mother has always been a step ahead of science and a pushover for babies."

After dinner Victor could not keep his hands off Natalya.

"There's something about being here with you in your parents' house that's a humongous turn-on," he whispered as she was settling Sheela for bed. In between words, he blew gently in her ear and caressed her upper arm until he felt goose bumps. "I feel deliciously wicked. It turns me on."

"Please," Nat responded. "Sheela will hear."

"Don't be silly," Victor urged. "Look at your daughter. She's three-quarters asleep. The minute I put her in my lap and talk to her for thirty seconds, she'll be in dreamland."

Victor was half right. It was well past midnight, and as soon as she was settled and her Daddy opened his mouth, Sheela began to snore softly. When Victor placed her in her crib, she didn't stir. Nevertheless she was far from unaware of what was going on.

"This doesn't seem right," Nat said while Victor's hands roamed and tugged at her clothing. "How can we be sure she won't know what we're doing?"

"We can't be," Victor answered. "I don't expect that anyone will publish a paper entitled 'Subliminal Effects of Witnessing Parental Intercourse as Reported by Babies under One' in the near future. On the other hand, if Sheela does notice something, she won't be the first baby in the world to have done so. For all we know, we saw our parents making love too. Maybe it's a healthy thing."

"I don't think I can relax."

"Why not?" Victor asked. "It's not like we never did this before with Sheela around."

"I know, but Sheela suddenly seems much more alert."

"She has always been alert," Victor mumbled while his trousers dropped to the floor. "It's just that she expresses herself more effectively. But don't worry, she still can't tattle on us."

Nat started to speak, but Victor's mouth pressing firmly on hers stopped her. Within moments, his tongue teased her and made her forget what it was she was going to say. Soon they both lost track of everything except the demands of their excited bodies. Only in the end did Victor think to muffle Nat's moans with a pillow.

Although the first days at the Rosenbaums seemed as long as a week, the Landaus' ten-day visit flew by. Ronald and Cecily returned home and Dora scheduled the remaining days, causing them to merge into one another until suddenly none were left. There were outings for Sheela to Central Park, to the Metropolitan Museum of Art, to the Museum of Natural History, to the Museum of Modern Art, to FAO Schwarz, and to the Bronx Zoo. Her parents thought it would be too much and that Sheela wouldn't appreciate the museums, but they were wrong. She lapped it all up. Of everything she saw, she loved the Degas exhibit at the Museum of Modern Art most. She looked at the ballerinas with intensity and started to cry when Dora finally made her leave that hall. The catalog of the exhibited works which her grandmother bought for her finally consoled her and lived on to become a prized volume in her library.

For Nat and Victor there were tickets to the theater to see Mikado and to hear the new Liza Minelli concert honoring her mother, Judy Garland. The tickets guaranteed Dora and Harold at least two evenings alone with Sheela, and they eked out one more by persuading her parents to try a new Thai restaurant. Then there was an afternoon and evening at Ronald and Cecily's, a small dinner party for old family friends, and a night out at Granada, where Nat had dined the last time she visited her parents, just after Sheela was conceived. This time Sheela, who had barely napped during the day, slept throughout dinner on two chairs and awoke just in time to climb into Harold's lap to see the flamenco dancers. After the show ended and the little group was finishing dessert and coffee, Harold asked "What does Sheela call her other Grandfather?"

"Gappa" Sheela replied.

"What is she going to call me?"

"Pappa," Sheela said and she jabbed her finger into Harold's chest with all the strength she could muster.

Their last evening in New York, Natalya felt sorrier to be leaving than she had expected.

"It's like we hardly had any time at all," she said.

"Actually," Dora remarked, "we've had quite a lot of real quality time. I should think you'd be happy to get back home to your own turf. Aren't you anxious to figure out your professional life?"

"Well, yes," Nat answered, "but I'm uneasy too. I've had a couple of messages from Steve Jordan, the guy who went to Mexico that I told you about, and I think that he may have some collaboration in mind, but I'm not at all sure that's what I want."

"What else is happening on the Houston front? How about your work, Victor?"

"My work is going well. By the end of my sabbatical I expect to have the first draft of my new book on logical communication ready. I hit some rough spots, but now it's shaping up. My association with the business department has turned out to be a positive. Not to change the subject, but this chicken pie is out of this world."

"It's better than mine," Nat said. "I don't think I put in enough mustard."

"I'm sure you do dear," Harold said. "It just seems different because your mother made it."

"And the crust is lighter," Nat added.

"No," Victor said concurring with his father in-law. "This is excellent, but Nat's pie is too. The problem is she hardly ever makes it."

"And you never made us stuffed peppers or New England boiled dinner," Nat complained.

"There wasn't enough time," Dora said.

"That's what I told you in the first place. We've hardly had any time at all." Nat reiterated. "Right, Sheela?"

"Ike Door, Pappa," she replied, blowing kisses in the air.

"Who likes Dora and Pappa?" Harold asked. "Do you have a name?"

"I Sheea," Sheela replied pointing to herself.

"I thought babies didn't say 'I'. Don't they usually say 'Sheela likes this or that?'" Harold asked.

"Yes, but Sheela's linguistic abilities exceed the norm for her age," Victor proudly answered. "Most babies barely make meaningful sounds until they're about one year old. And typically, once they start stringing words together, they use the third person to talk about themselves until they're about two and a half or three. But we say 'you' and not 'Sheela' whenever we talk to her directly, and we told Lulu to do the same."

"Does Sheela understand any Spanish?" Dora asked.

"Yes," Victor said. "Lulu speaks only Spanish to her." Turning to Sheela he asked, "Will you speak in Spanish for Dora and Pappa?"

By way of response, Sheela spilled her cup of chocolate milk and loudly said "Ay-ay-ay; ay-ay-ay."

Sunlight filtering through the miniblinds woke Victor the day the Landaus were returning to Houston. No alarm was needed because this time they didn't have to leave until after noon. Their flight was at a comfortable 1:45 p.m. Harold was taking them to the airport, and packing to return home was a no-brainer. Victor looked at the bedside clock and saw that it was 8:10. Then he turned to check on his wife and on Sheela. Nat was sleeping soundly, but Victor was astounded to see his daughter standing upright, clutching the rails of her mother's crib and taking carefully measured steps without making a sound. Not wanting to break her concentration, Victor quietly tapped Natalya. But when Natalya sat up, Sheela began to cry.

"My goodness!" Nat said to her daughter. "Look at you. Standing and taking steps all by yourself. That's wonderful! Why are you crying?"

Sheela's cries became louder and louder.

"What should I do?" Victor asked. "Should I call Dora and Harold to see?"

"No," Nat said. "Sheela has learned to stand and walk with something to hold on to, but she has a major problem."

"What?" Victor asked as Sheela continued to howl.

"She doesn't know how to sit down," Nat explained. "You'd better rescue her. Then we can see if she'll do it again."

Victor picked up his daughter who clung to him for dear life and refused to return to the crib, much less to stand or walk any more. Later, at home, she mastered the art of using the large coffee table in the living room to pull herself up to her feet and, most importantly, she figured out that she could plop herself back on the floor without hurting her well-padded rear. With these skills in place, she merrily walked circles around the table, picking up speed and stopping to sit or crawl away whenever she chose.

22

Back home in Houston, Natalya wondered how she had ever managed her old job. Since activity expands to utilize all available time, caring for Sheela filled Nat's days and consumed her energy, even with Lulu's help. Victor was taking this opportunity to concentrate on his writing without sharing much responsibility for his daughter. Sheela was growing more mobile and interactive by the day. She couldn't handle the word "no" unless it came out of her own mouth. She wanted lots of outings. She scooted all over the house, touching and tasting and feeling everything in order to become familiar with its properties, oblivious of danger to herself or to anyone or anything else. She maintained constant dialogs in English, Spanish, and in her own brand of gibberish. She even talked in her sleep.

For the first time in recent memory, Nat had discretionary weekday hours at her disposal. She made good use of them. She lunched with former colleagues. She cooked. She took Sheela to Infantasy, to Hermann Park, to the Children's Museum and to the zoo. She read voraciously; she shopped at leisure; and she went to the beauty salon. She completed the albums with Sheela's photos and with the photos of her own childhood.

As she did these things, Nat wished she would conceive again soon, a little boy if possible, but another daughter would be great too. A splendid son is a pride and joy, but a fine daughter is a friend and a comfort. Nat considered the warmth of her relationship with her mother and both Beca's and Dora's struggles to stay in tune with their boys who had become men. How did that jingle go? "A son is a son 'til he takes a wife; a daughter's a daughter for all of her life."

Although she had hoped to conceive in New York, it didn't happen then. Nat remembered the sensation Sheela gave her when she began, and it was missing. Occasionally, she thought Sheela's horoscope might prove true and feared she would never again experience the wonder of making a baby with Victor.

Nat would like to have spent more of her leisure with Annette and Jaya, but both of them were working overly hard, perhaps compensating for their troubled minds. Annette's distress over failing to become pregnant was growing and strain-

144

ing her relationship with David while Jaya's self-confidence was eroding in the absence of any foreseeable reconciliation with Sunil.

One afternoon, while Nat was watching Sheela go round and round the coffee table, almost but not quite letting go of the rim, the phone rang. She picked up the receiver and heard Steve Jordan's voice asking, "What do I have to do to get you to come in for a serious conversation?"

"Hi," Nat said. "I heard your question. I'm not sure how to answer it."

"Would tomorrow be too soon?"

"Yes, for a serious talk. I'm not ready to think about my future career. I need a few weeks longer."

"I already waited a few weeks longer. Aren't you going stir crazy by now?"

"No, not yet. I'm worried about how I am going to be able to do justice to two demanding masters, my family and my profession, without shortchanging one or both. Sheela needs more attention now and I plan to have another child."

"If I promise to address those concerns, will you hear me out? I'm desperate," Jordan pleaded.

"Since you put it that way, I will. I'm a friend."

"Thank you," Steve said. "I'm a friend too, one who respects and admires your abilities. Let's do this. Let's meet a week from Wednesday. That'll give you some more time to mull over the prospect of a career step. All right?"

"OK." Nat's smile came through in her voice.

"I'll see you," Steve confirmed, "on October 31st at 12 noon."

"October 31st is Halloween."

"Well, wear a costume to lunch. That's fine by me. Come to the office so you can get to know my small but excellent staff. We'll order in."

Nat was excited by the prospect of taking Sheela trick or treating this Halloween dressed up as a clown in purple tights, an old white shirt of Cecily's with multicolored dots the size of silver dollars, a plaid vest, tennis shoes, a green baseball cap worn backwards so her shiny black hair would show in front, and a painted face.

After the trick or treating, Nat thought it would be neat to do something different. Perhaps she could convince the Singers and even Jaya to go out wearing something outrageous. Something sexy that would show off the women's good looks and trim figures, but what? Maybe they could bar hop in the guise of hookers and pimps. Her parents had a picture of themselves dressed like that. It was taken at a bar hop masquerade ball on a cruise ship and had earned them first prize.

Nat was figuring out how she was going to fatten Sheela the Clown when Jaya called.

"Hello, Nat," she said in a heavy tone followed by a pause.

"You don't sound well. What's going on?" Nat asked.

"Something terrible happened."

"Where are you?"

"Home."

"Good. I'll be over in about twenty minutes. Sit tight until I get there. OK?"

"All right. Thank you." Jaya said.

Within the half-hour, Nat knocked on Jaya's door and waited worriedly for her to open up. After a few moments, Nat heard her footsteps and called out, "It's me, Nat."

Jaya was ashen but dry-eyed. She invited Nat in and when they were seated she asked,

"What time is it?"

"It's twenty to five," Nat answered, looking at her watch.

"Would you like a glass of sherry or tea or something?" Jaya offered as if she just remembered her manners.

"No," Nat said. "Tell me what's wrong."

"It's Sunil. He had an accident."

"Where is he now?"

"He's in intensive care. The hospital called. He told them to call me."

"Well then he's not unconscious. That's a good sign, right?"

"I don't know," Jaya replied.

"Do you know whether the accident was his fault or the other driver's?"

"It wasn't a car accident."

"No? What kind of an accident then?"

"He fell off his balcony last night. He rents this apartment on the second floor. They think he climbed up on a stool to change a light bulb on the balcony and lost his balance. He was drinking, alone."

"Let's both have that cup of tea now," Nat suggested.

Two hours later Nat, Victor, Annette, and David were seated in Jaya's living room. They had called the hospital, which described Sunil's condition as "fair." He was off the critical list and "resting comfortably." He was "very lucky." He had suffered a concussion and fractured his right arm and both legs. Additionally, he had assorted internal and external bruises, but there was a good chance of a full recovery. He wanted Jaya to come to him. Jaya started to shake. Her eyes, which had been glazed by dread, now sparked with anger as she spoke.

"Why should I go to California? After all, Sunil left me. Am I supposed to be heartbroken because he made a mess of himself? What about my job?"

"What did the nurse say, exactly?" Nat wanted to know.

"Hell," David intervened. "What difference does it make? The guy wants her to come. He practically killed himself. Isn't that enough?"

"The nurse told me," Jaya replied, "that Sunil wanted me and that it would make a difference to his recovery if I came."

"I guess, Jaya, you'll have to figure out what feelings are pushing and pulling at you and then decide what to do," Annette interjected. "You're in a tough spot. I don't want to influence you, but I suspect that you will never forgive yourself if you don't go."

"I agree," Nat said. "The bottom line is that you and Sunil still love each other. I think you have already made your decision. It's just a question of your coming to terms with it."

"Why do you think that?" Jaya asked. "I haven't decided anything yet. I just want to do what's right. When I heard about the accident I was petrified. Now I'm furious, but I can't be responsible for Sunil's not getting better."

"Precisely," Nat agreed.

At that moment there were several impatient knocks at the door.

"Will someone please get rid of whoever it is?" Jaya asked.

"It isn't anyone," Victor said walking to the door. "It's pizza and beer, arriving two seconds short of the forty minutes after which it would be free. Who's hungry?"

<hr>

Nat woke up on October 31 eager to take Sheela out for her first Halloween, and disappointed because neither Victor nor David could be persuaded to make a public appearance as pimps escorting hookers. David didn't feel like partying and Victor refused to make "a spectacle" of himself. So the four of them were going to stay home and have a quiet supper. Nat said they all made her feel old, but she agreed to fix pork chops and sauerkraut and bake a pumpkin pie.

Later in the morning, as Nat was getting ready for her meeting with Steve Jordan, she was surprised to note how much she was looking forward to the luncheon. Steve had been right, the extra time made a difference. She was almost ready to walk out the door when her telephone started ringing. The answering machine caught the message and she had no time to chat so she listened:

"Hello, Nat. Hope I can catch you before you set off for my office," Steve's voice said. "I'm stuck in court trying to forestall a temporary injunction. We were set for nine o'clock and I thought there would be plenty of time, but today seems to be crazy. Please give me a rain check. Talk to you soon."

"Darn," Nat said out loud. "Here I am, all dressed up with no place to go! Not until my 3:40 appointment at Infantasy."

Nat's meeting with Infantasy got off to a bad start. She arrived late because she forgot she had to get gas. Meredith Coolidge, Sheela's teacher was understanding but Dr. Anthony Campobello, Infantasy's director, was irked.

"Our appointments are at twenty minute intervals," Dr. Campobello began.

"In that case we had better get started right away, hadn't we?" Natalya retorted.

After some hemming and hawing, Ms. Meredith began, "Your daughter is exceptional. . . "

". . . but exceptional children can be difficult children," Anthony Campobello finished the sentence.

"Dr. Campobello, are you suggesting that there is some problem with Sheela?" Nat asked.

"No, not at all," he quickly responded. "Please call me Mr. Anthony. I apologize if we have given you that impression."

"Words like 'difficult' worry me. Now, Dr. Camp, uh, Mr. Anthony, please explain how my daughter is exceptional and how exceptional children can be difficult children."

"Very well." Mr. Anthony's tone was cool and his speech was clipped. "Exceptional children can be difficult because they see through our efforts to control their behavior. Sheela is not only bright, but she is extremely determined and she cannot be easily distracted. At home, babies learn that crying or acting cute produces results. Here they learn it doesn't and they learn to cope with disappointment. Social behavior among babies isn't a matter of generosity and sharing. It's a question of grabbing and hanging on. The naked laws of the jungle prevail up to the age of two or two and a half. In this jungle, Sheela is the fittest, the quickest and the deftest. She survives and ends up with all the toys she wants, while the other babies end up learning to manage their frustration. Do you see?"

"Yes," Natalya conceded. "To an extent I've been concerned about Sheela's unwillingness to share and I'm happy for your explanation, but I don't understand your point. Are you saying you don't want Sheela here any more?"

"Oh no," Ms. Meredith smiled. "She has captured our hearts. I'm afraid Anthony sometimes lacks tact, but he means well and he is impressed with your daughter too."

"Then do you have any suggestions about managing her?" Nat asked.

"Not really," Ms. Meredith smiled. "You seem to be doing very well. We just wanted you to be aware of why your daughter behaves as she does and of the challenges ahead."

Nat glanced at her watch. "If there isn't anything else, I'd better be going."

Anthony and Ms. Meredith shook Nat's hand.

"Thanks," Nat said. Then, thinking she should be more gracious considering these people's value to Sheela, she added, "Your program is outstanding. I'm happy Sheela has the opportunity to be here."

"We feel privileged to have her here," Dr. Campobello said.

On the drive home, Natalya decided that though Ms. Meredith was a gem, Anthony Campobello could be irritating. Still, he irritated in a nice way. He was pompous because he took himself and Infantasy too seriously, but then again a lot of people probably disparaged his efforts. And he worked on the cutting edge of child development and enhancement. Most importantly, both he and Meredith appreciated Sheela.

23

After she came home from her meeting with Infantasy, Natalya busied herself cutting up a big pumpkin, which she turned into a Halloween jack-o-lantern with a candle burning inside. Then she started dinner preparations. When the pork chops were ready to put in the oven, Natalya called her daughter. "Come on Sheela! For your first Halloween you will be transformed into Sheela the Clown."

Sheela was frightened when she heard she was to be "transformed." She had no desire to become anyone else. Why did her mother want her to be a clown? Clowns made people laugh, but lots of times they were sad in their hearts.

Even before Nat told her she was to be changed into a clown, Sheela had been upset. She wanted to hear what Ms. Meredith and pudgy Mr. Anthony said about her, but Nat didn't tell. Then she wanted to show how she could go around the coffee table without holding on, but Nat didn't give her a chance. Now Sheela worried that she was being transformed because there was something the matter with her, like there was with the poor pumpkin who was changed into a jack-o'-lantern.

Sheela began to cry as her mother carried her into the master bedroom where all the mismatched clown garments were assembled. She wept and wept, and Natalya couldn't imagine what the problem was.

"Stop fussing, sweetie," Nat said "We're going to have such a lot of fun."

"No, no," Sheela answered.

"Are you hungry? You had a nice lunch, and milk and fruit. It's too early for supper. Beca will give you soup after we finish trick or treating around her house. OK?"

"No, no, no, no, no," Sheela replied.

In the end, Sheela tired of crying in vain so she just kept still while Natalya dressed her and tied a pillow around her tummy. The only nice thing was that the blouse she wore smelled of Aunt Cecily. Then Nat got out face paint and spent a long time carefully putting it all over Sheela's face. Sheela feared that if she cried again something terrible might happen, so she concentrated on eating a gingersnap. When Natalya finished drawing and painting, she helped her daughter walk to the big hallway mirror to meet Sheela the Clown. Sheela was surprised to see the reflection that stared back at her. It had a remarkable face, but the face wasn't hers. It was white and pasty and it had a curious, questioning expression. It didn't show that Sheela felt miserable. Sheela tried to take it off but couldn't because it was stuck. That made Nat laugh. Then Victor came home and took pictures and they set out.

Beca greeted Sheela the Clown with a hug asking, "Why are you so solemn? Clowns are supposed to have fun. Well, maybe not. They're supposed to make the people around them have fun and it looks like that's what you're about to do."

"OK." Sheela was grateful for Beca's empathy.

"She cried the whole time we were getting ready. I don't know what the matter is," Natalya explained to her mother-in-law.

"She's hot and bothered. Even under that face I can tell she's out of sorts. It looks like Halloween isn't a big hit with her."

"Maybe she's too young," Victor suggested.

"No," Beca answered. "I don't think that's it. She's old enough to know what she likes and this isn't her cup of tea. You never cared much for Halloween either."

"Well that could be because you didn't encourage him," Nat said. "I loved it."

"I know, dear," Beca responded.

"And now Victor thinks it's fun, too." Her mother-in-law's remarks made Nat uncomfortable. "Well, we'd better get going. Maybe once we start seeing people Sheela will perk up."

"No, no," Sheela repeated softly, but only Beca heard.

Victor, Natalya, and Sheela returned in about thirty minutes. Henry was home and eager to see his granddaughter's get-up. He got upset though when he heard her crying. "What's the matter?" he asked.

"It's a long story," Beca answered.

"She was fine for a while," Victor told his father, "but now she's upset because we said she can't eat any of the candies in her bag until later."

It's not fair, Sheela thought as she calmed down so Gappa could kiss Sheela the Clown. She wasn't going to eat a single sweet later just to make her parents understand that timing is everything. After soup, when Nat unwrapped a miniature Mars bar, Sheela threw it on the ground. Then she tore at her clothes and rubbed at her face with her hands, crying "No, no, no," louder than ever. Finally Beca rescued her.

"Why don't you let me wash her face?" she asked. "I don't think Sheela is comfortable looking like a stranger to herself."

"I guess that will be fine," Victor told his mother. "What do you think, Nat?"

"All right," Natalya agreed. "Maybe Sheela is coming down with something. I don't know why else she could be so cranky."

When Sheela returned after a few minutes with a clean face and a flat tummy, she was chipper. However, when Nat tried to pick her up to go home, she again said "No, no. Dan, dan." This time Nat understood and put her down on the floor, trying to take her hand. But Sheela pulled away and much to everyone's surprise she took four careful steps all on her own. Gappa rushed to get his video camera, but by the time he got back with it Sheela didn't want to walk any more.

————— ·:•❊❂◉◉❂❊•:· —————

When Annette and David came over, instead of meeting Sheela the Clown, they found plain Sheela dressed in her favorite pajamas full of smiley faces. There were four different expressions on the faces. One looked dapper, one was a know-it-all, one was surprised, and one had a whimsical look. At first Annette and David didn't pay attention to the pajamas because they were busy listening to Victor tell about how Sheela the Clown didn't enjoy trick or treating. When the story ended, Sheela and Aa-Oo climbed into Aunt Annette's lap and showed her the four faces. Aunt Annette named them, calling the dapper face Emil, the know-it-all Philip, the surprised smiley Steven, and the whimsical face Peter. Sheela gave Aunt Annette a hug and a kiss. Aunt Annette squeezed Sheela and then suddenly burst into tears. Natalya stopped fussing with dinner and came over to hug her and to take Sheela off her lap.

"Hey, take it easy, Annette," she said. "Here's a Kleenex."

"I'll never have a baby of my own," Annette said.

"She's being a defeatist," David said. "We're doing everything possible and the doctors say there is nothing wrong with either of us."

"If there's nothing wrong with us, then why aren't we getting pregnant? Why not? That's what I'd like to know," Annette replied, blowing her nose. "Other people get pregnant without doctors pumping air into their tubes. Other people don't have to take their temperature every day. Other people don't have to have sex on a schedule. I hate all this. And David acts as if he couldn't care less."

"Hold it, Annette. You sound uncaring. And why are you and David talking about each other as if you two weren't in the same room. What's going on here?" Victor asked.

"I honestly don't know," David said. "I feel like a creep because I can't make a baby and I don't know how Annette expects me to act. Does she expect me to pretend I enjoy squeezing my ejaculate into a jar so a specialist can determine whether my sperm is healthy and mobile? Or does she want me to complain because I feel like shit?"

"I don't want you to feel miserable or responsible. I want you to care and not to blame me. I feel guilty as it is. I'm sure it's my fault that I just can't conceive. I want you to love me anyway and to be honest."

"Here's honest," David said. "I love you, but I hate what's happening to us. I can't take much more of this. I just want a normal life. I can't stand your mourning over every period as if it were a death in the family. I won't put up with it because I can't."

"Normal," Annette said, "is to be a family with kids. If we don't have one soon, I want to try in vitro and if that doesn't work I want to adopt. But David won't do it."

"See?" David asked. "Listen to yourself. You're talking about me in the third person again."

"Well, it's true isn't it? Annette insisted. "Will you try in vitro? Would you adopt if that doesn't work?"

"No and no. No way, José."

David's response made Annette cry again, but Sheela stopped her. She climbed on the sofa, put her head in Annette's lap and started to rub her thumb in her palm.

"You are a real sweetheart," Annette told her. "I love you."

"Sing to her," Natalya suggested "or tell her a story."

"Once upon a time," Annette began, but when she looked down at Sheela, her eyes were closed.

When Nat took Sheela to her bed, Annette followed. "I don't know what to do," she said. "I'm losing it. Maybe I should talk about this to a therapist."

"No," Sheela said from her crib, which was now in her room.

"Is she saying no to me?" Annette asked, "Or is she dreaming?"

"I don't know. Sheela mumbles in her sleep. Maybe she's thinking of Halloween," Nat replied. "But I agree with her 'no.' The last thing you need is to rehash all this with a stranger. You're a therapist yourself. You know what's really happening. This is transactional. Try to stop dwelling on your own misery and consider David."

"My hair is falling out too. I'm going to wind up sterile and bald to boot."

"You're crazy," Natalya said.

"That's why I need analysis."

"No, you're not nuts crazy. You're unreasonable crazy. You're not thinking. You've got to realize that this is not your opportunity to take out all your frustrations—old and new—on your husband."

"Well, shouldn't we try in vitro?" Annette sat on the day bed. Sheela's room was lit by a soft night-light.

"I don't know. You and David don't need the hassle now. You need to be happy, with or without a baby. A baby is no good if you two aren't good together."

"What's your opinion about adoption?"

Before Nat could answer, Victor came in. "We're starved," he said.

"Everything's ready. Why don't you get the water? We'll be right out," Nat told him. Then she answered Annette, "I'm not sure. But I think you should do things David's way. Give yourselves some time, say a year, and agree to revisit the subject if nothing has happened by then. Meanwhile, live it up. Look at what's happening to Jaya and Sunil and at what almost happened to me. And take vitamins. They'll stop your hair from falling out and strengthen your nerves."

At dinner, Annette smiled. "We're going to do it your way," she said to David. "I guess a good, smart friend is worth a thousand therapists."

"It takes two friends," David said. "One to speak and one to listen."

"Thanks, David, for saying that; thanks, Nat, for being a friend. From now on I'm going to try to forget about babies. No more visits to doctors' offices. No more medically prescribed sex. We make love when we feel horny or romantic and we use any position we feel like, period."

"I don't want to hear another word about periods," David said.

"All right. No discussions about periods, period," Annette agreed, trying to be amusing. But she wondered how she could she stop her arms from aching to hold an infant. She couldn't forget that she wasn't getting any younger. Still, Natalya was right—she was going to have to pull herself together, for her husband's sake, for her marriage's sake, and even for her own sake.

"I believe," Nat said, "Sheela picked us when she thought we were ready for her. Maybe your baby is out there on some cosmic plane waiting for you."

"That's not even plausible," David argued. "There is no baby before fertilization."

"It is plausible," Nat explained, "if the baby is a soul seeking an embodiment."

"Where did you come up with that?" David asked.

"I don't know, but I think embodiment is a part of the soul's destiny and everything has to fit. Either the soul that is right for you isn't ready, or you're not ready for it."

"We might never be ready," Annette said.

"Since the doctors say you're both fine, chances are that you soon will be."

"Assuming your explanation is right, Nat," David asked, "how does it account for adoption? To tell you the truth, I don't think I'd ever want to adopt a child."

"I haven't thought about that," Natalya answered, "but why can't a soul's destiny be to be born to one set of parents and to be raised by another?"

⁂

Natalya rescheduled her meeting with Steve Jordan for Friday. She arrived at his office on Austin Street, barely two minutes away from her condo, at noon. Steve had remodeled an old building that had once been a beautiful home but subsequently fell into disrepair. Now, like other houses in the vicinity, it was reborn as a law office.

"Welcome," Steve said as she was buzzed in. "I'd like you to meet Georgia Lindstrom, the firm's legal secretary, receptionist, and office manager. Don't be fooled by her appearance. I'm not exploiting minors."

"Hi, Natalya," Georgia said. "I hope you don't mind my using your first name. Steve talks about you non-stop and I feel like we're already friends."

"And I'm John Bloom," a young man with a dimpled chin said, coming down the stairs. I'm the law clerk. I'm a senior at University of Houston. I don't usually work Fridays, but I'm here to make a good impression on you."

"Well," Nat replied. "I guess there's no need for me to introduce myself. It's good to meet you both."

"Now," Steve said, "let me give you a quick tour before lunch."

Nat trotted along behind Steve. She was shown Steve's office, a staff office, a file and copy room, a vacant office, and a well-equipped kitchen downstairs. Upstairs there was a library, a conference room, and two additional rooms that could be used as more offices, or meeting rooms, or whatever. The entire building was elegant and restful, a cross between a modern no-nonsense place of business and a cozy country cottage.

"This is a welcoming place, Steve," she said. "Who designed and decorated it?"

"Norman Larsen, my first client, with help and input from me. I did some hands on supervision and a part of the donkey work personally," Steve proudly replied. "Norman is an architect, an acquaintance of an acquaintance, who wasn't paid by some people for whom he did a large restaurant. We made an old fashioned deal based on a handshake. I would try to get him his money and he would design and oversee this job, an inadvisable arrangement, but I trusted my gut reaction to this guy and you are looking at the story's happy ending.

"Now that you've had the grand tour, let's go into the kitchen, my private conference room. Lunch is courtesy of Louise, Georgia's sister who loves to cook. We have home-baked bread and brownies and chicken salad made from scratch."

"Don't forget the grapes and cheese," Georgia said.

"What do you think of my set up?" Steve asked, putting a sprig of mint in a large jug of iced tea. "Don't you think you could be happy working here? You could have a baby-sitter watch Sheela in one of the upstairs rooms whenever you wanted."

"I'm impressed by the tastefulness of everything. It's very well planned. I'm flattered by your attention. Georgia and John make a fine first impression."

"But?"

"I didn't say but."

"No, you didn't. I heard a but in your voice. So tell me what it is."

"All right," Nat conceded. "I guess the 'but' is I feel pressured."

"I can't help it. I have to pressure you because I believe in our chances as a team," Steve said. "I like you tremendously and admire you and I feel you respect me. More importantly, I'm convinced we could both become successful if we work together. I think there is an opportunity for you here and I don't want you to brush it aside lightly. So a lot is at stake. Today I could have pretended to be cool, or I could be honest. I picked honest. You'd see through pretense anyway."

"I see; I mean, I understand. But you have to understand that I'm not ready to make any commitment."

"Until?" Steve asked.

"Until I've considered all my options."

"But you're ready now to consider your choices and get back to work."

"Yes, now I am."

"In that case, I have a fair shot and you will hear me out, right?" Steve asked.

"Right." Nat's tension dissolved into a smile.

"So," Steve continued, "I am going to tell you how I got started, what I'm doing, where I'm heading, and how I think we could structure our relationship. Please interrupt any time to ask a question or interject a comment. Then you can tell me that you're not interested or else that you'd be willing to consider my proposal or a modification thereof, subject to whatever. Fair enough?"

"Fair enough. But I don't want to mislead you."

"You won't mislead me," Steve said. "If I'm misled, it will be my own doing, so here goes: When I came back from Mexico my father told me, out of the blue, that he wanted to help my career in a material way. He admitted he had not been supportive in the past. During my absence he had a heart attack that changed his perspective about many things, including me. I thanked my father and told him I'd consider how to put his offer to good use. Then once I decided to hang out my own shingle and started looking at offices to rent, I drove past this building. I couldn't stop thinking about it. To make a long story short, my father bought it for me. So here I am. It's mine, mortgage free, lock, stock and barrel."

"That covers how you got started," Nat said. "Now tell me where your practice stands and where it is heading."

"My practice is past the crawling stage. It's toddling and requires all the energy that any toddler takes. I have about twenty-five clients by now, all small and medium sized entities with business problems. I represent individuals, partnerships and closely held corporations in matters ranging from real estate and contract issues to fraud and bankruptcy. I would love appellate work, but I guess I have to wait for some of my cases to be appealed."

"Or," Nat said, "try to market the firm to other attorneys who shy away from appeals. So how do you get your clients and how do you expect to grow?" she asked.

"Long ago," Steve answered, "I read a book by Joe Girard. He was a car salesman who was in *The Guinness Book of World Records* for selling the largest number of cars ever. I think Girard's book was *How to Sell Anything to Anybody*. The point was that to sell, you have to like people and you have to make them know you're out there offering a valuable service or product. Girard did stuff like throw bags full of his business cards in the air at football games. I just wrote to everybody I know asking them to give me a try and to spread the word that if anyone needs a lawyer, I am available. I tell people that my goal is for our dealings to leave a good taste in their mouths. Clients refer other clients. I belong to the Rotary Club and I'm on a few committees. The main thing is that I'm not shy about asking for business."

"How do you bill?" Nat asked.

"Flexibly. I explain that my range is generally from two hundred to three hundred dollars an hour, depending on the nature of the work and the client's ability to pay. If we represent plaintiffs owed monies, I'm open to working out a contingency or partial contingency fee arrangement. If we're defendants, I sometimes do an hourly rate plus a cap on the total fee. When someone comes in, I hear them out and then, based on their circumstances and the nature of their case, I propose a fee arrangement. I also tell clients that they can save money by doing their own word processing and copying. People like that because they feel involved and in control and I like it because it frees up the office so we can handle more cases without increasing overhead."

"It seems you're in great shape, so why do you need me?"

"Because I'm working 80-hour weeks. I'm exhausted and the work isn't something just anyone can help with. But more importantly, I want to develop this into a substantial and reputable Houston firm. You and I are like-minded attorneys. We can help folks and make good money in the process. Look, Nat, if you go on to another firm like Kaplan, McCall and Green, you'll make much more at first, but you don't have the stomach or the meanness to get to the top. Besides, here you would be your own boss. Make your own hours. Be able to take care of Sheela. I'm not saying you won't work just as hard or even harder, but you'll be working for yourself. It's a wonderful feeling."

"What arrangement do you have in mind?"

"A partnership. For the first year you get a clean thirty percent of everything either of us makes. All expenses are on me. From the second year on we share everything, expenses and earnings fifty-fifty. Here, I prepared a copy of my financial statements for you to take home and look over."

"Thanks. But what happens about decisions? What if we disagree?"

"We try to agree. If there is a dispute, the nay sayer prevails. Each of us has full veto power so we don't get into anything either of us is uncomfortable with."

"This is a lot to consider," Nat said after a pause. "I've been talking to some legal placement firms, but you've made this sound good."

"Then," Steve suggested, "let me stop while I'm ahead. Get back to me after you review the numbers and talk this over with Victor."

"When?" Nat asked.

"Whenever," Steve replied. "It's not like I have sixteen other people lined up. Maybe you can do this in two stages. Tell me if your answer is no within a week. If it's maybe and you have questions, we can regroup. OK?"

"OK."

"This feels right," Steve said as he walked Natalya to the door.

24

On her first birthday, Sheela woke up excited. The night before, she had gone to bed early, before her parents' open house. Then, as promised, Natalya brought her out at midnight to welcome the year 2002. Sheela intended to stay awake until 3:50 a.m., her birth hour, but after hugging and kissing her mother and father and blowing kisses to the guests, she said "Enuf" so Victor put her back to bed. There she waited for the guests to leave and for her parents to go to sleep. As soon as the house was dark and quiet, she wished for Sweak to appear and the second she saw him, the two of them climbed out of her crib and went to watch "Mirrors."

Aa-Oo, resembling a penguin in a black coat and white jacket, was already in front of the television waiting for the disc to fast forward to 'Snow.' Sheela and Sweak sat down beside him, silently hugging their knees. When the music rolled, Varkin appeared on the screen. Varkin was a boy who roamed the world seeking his origin. One day, in the course of his quest, he saw his reflection shimmering in River. He quickly called on River God to come and take him to his first birthplace.

"Very well," River God said and he lifted the watery reflection from River and poured it into Varkin. Then he whisked the boy to a snowy mountain peak. Varkin searched all over the mountain for his source, but to no avail. His great sorrow over his failure made him cry so many tears that he shrank to the size of a pea. That night the sky crystallized Varkin into a beautiful snowflake and carried him to heaven. At dawn, Varkin floated back to earth and settled on the tip of the peak. However, when the sun came out, he melted and got lost in a waterfall that rushed from the mountain peak downward toward River. He traveled in River for many seasons until he came to the place where he first saw himself. There, River God released Varkin from his reflection and cast him ashore.

After 'Snow,' Sheela wanted to watch more "Mirrors" stories, but Sweak told her she had better get back to bed before daylight. Sheela obeyed and when her eyes opened hours later, the sun was shining brightly, yet a bittersweet taste lingered in her mouth and sorrowful notes rang in her ears along with joyous ones.

"What do you think the matter is?" she asked Aa-Oo.

"Maybe you had a frightening dream last night," Aa-Oo suggested.

"No, I didn't dream," Sheela said. "When 'Snow' ended, I went right to sleep. Nothing else happened."

"Were you afraid when Varkin got lost in the waterfall?"

"Only a tiny bit, but it was awesome. And I knew Varkin would come back. Anyhow, 'Snow' is a fairy tale and Ma says fairy tales aren't real."

"How does your Ma know that?" Aa-Oo asked.

"She knows a lot of stuff. But I'm not sure what 'real' means. I'm too small to understand."

"Shh," Aa-Oo whispered. "Here come your parents. Let's hide under the blanket."

"Oh my," Natalya said as she came into the room. "I thought there was a little girl here. But there isn't. There's no one here at all. Victor, hurry up! Sheela seems to have disappeared. And on her birthday too."

"Well, that's just awful," Victor said rushing into the room. "I'd better have a good look. Did you check under the bed?"

"Yes, I did." Nat said. "I couldn't find anything, not even a dust bunny. Try tickling the blanket.

"OK. Here I come. I'm going to attack! But wait! I feel something squirming. What's this? It feels like a nose. I'd better tweak it to make sure."

"No, no, no!" Sheela squealed as he pulled off her blanket.

"It's the birthday girl hiding from her birthday!" Victor yelled. "Let's sing."

"Can her first surprise, who hid from Sheela all last night, come in and sing too, or must she wait for the party?" Nat asked.

"Now, now," Sheela demanded, and in walked Dora with a ribbon fastened in her hair to join Nat and Victor in singing Happy Birthday.

"Since it's your birthday today, you get to do whatever you want, well, almost," Nat told her daughter when her diaper was changed and the singing was over. So what do you want to do first thing?"

"Door." Sheela replied.

"Do you want to play at the door?" Victor asked.

"No, Door," Sheela repeated poking her grandmother and raising her arms to be carried.

"Door! I like that," Dora said.

"What would you like us to do, after breakfast?" the newly christened Door asked.

"Mrr," Sheela replied.

"She wants to play in front of the mirror," Nat explained. She loves making faces and watching herself."

"Is that something they do at Infantasy?" Dora asked.

"No, actually she and Lulu figured the game out. It's fun. Go ahead and play."

"Maybe Sheela got the idea from her *Mirrors* micro disc."

"No," Natalya said. "She hasn't watched *Mirrors* for weeks."

For a while Sheela and Door made faces and played pat-a-cake and peek-a-boo, watching their mirror images mimic their actions. While they played, Sheela stared at her own face because lots of times she would forget what she looked like, although she remembered the looks of everyone else. Sheela's reflection showed her a swirl of shining raven colored curls that framed her face and almost hid her flat ears. Under gracefully arched eyebrows there was a pair of deep blue almond-shaped eyes with a tinge of green peeping out from behind the blue. Inside the mirror eyes, Sheela saw her own eyes shining with the knowledge that they alone had vision. Sheela's reflection showed her a small full mouth, with two little peaks on the upper lip. The mouth, half-closed with determination, was a tad too close to her nose, which had the beginnings of a tiny groove in the middle. And from the mirror, a single dimple twinkled at Sheela whenever she laughed.

Sheela's birthday party was scheduled from 3:00 to 6:00. The invitees were the Landau family and close friends, Mike Hansen and his grandmother, and Angela Campos and her parents. Mike and Angela were two of Sheela's Infantasy classmates. Mike had turned one a few weeks earlier and was already in the one to two-year-old class which Sheela would be starting when Infantasy reopened after the Christmas break. Angela was going to be one in February. Sheela had taken a liking to these two and the Landaus had exchanged occasional pleasantries with their parents. The Campos were both doctors. Mike's mother and father owned a small gallery that specialized in Native American art. They were busy but happily agreed to send their boy with his grandmother, especially when they learned other grandparents would be at the party.

"Do you know who is coming to celebrate your birthday?" Victor asked his daughter while helping her dress.

"OK," was Sheela's reply.

"You're starting to sound like your mother, a specialist in non answers," Victor told Sheela. "I asked a question which takes a yes or no answer."

"No," Sheela said.

"No, you don't know or just plain no?" Victor asked and then, seeing that the conversation was losing focus, he added, "I think we're mixed up. My question is, do you know who all are coming to your birthday party?"

"Ya," Sheela said.

"So let's go over everyone's name, OK?" Victor asked.

"OK." Sheela looked smug. She was thinking, "That's what I said in the first place."

"Let's see. There's you, of course, the birthday girl. Then there's me and Ma and Beca and Gappa and Dora."

"No," Sheela piped in.

"No? Those are people you adore."

"Ya, Door," Sheela explained to her father, giving him another huge smile. "Me, Ma, Dada, Beca, Gappa, Door."

"Right," Victor said. "But there's more. There's Uncle David and Aunt Annette, Lulu, Angela Campos and her Mommy and Daddy, and Mike Hansen and his Grandma Ellen. Sunil Uncle and Jaya Auntie can't come because they are in California. We'll miss them, but still it's going to be a terrific party."

"Uncateeve?" Sheela asked.

"Who?"

"Unca Teeve." Sheela repeated.

"Oh, Uncle Steve," Victor said. "He doesn't really know you or us all that well. He's Mama's new business associate."

"Unca Teeve, Unca Teeve, Unca Teeve," Sheela insisted, losing her composure and gathering strength for what promised to become a battle.

Natalya had begun working with Steve Jordan in early December, after interviewing with several law firms. Most of them came through with offers, but they all reminded her of Kaplan, McCall and Green. The salaries offered were inversely proportionate to the flexibility she would have in managing her practice and to the firms' friendliness. So Nat didn't say 'no' to Jordan. Instead, she proposed that after Thanksgiving she would help out until the end of the year to get a sense of what working with him would be like. If it felt right, they would sign an agreement after the New Year.

Victor had reservations about Nat associating herself with Steve. He told her that their arrangement lacked professionalism. But the truth was that Jordan's office was too cozy for comfort and he didn't buy this business of Steve being an abstaining gay person.

"It's not that I'm a bigot," Victor had explained, "but something here doesn't compute."

"And what might that be?" Nat tried to keep a challenge out of her tone, but did not quite succeed.

"Well, we've only met once not counting the Christmas party, but Steve strikes me as straight. Maybe he thinks he's gay but isn't really. Lots of guys go both ways."

"Are you saying you're jealous?"

"No, I guess not," Victor answered with more restraint than truthfulness. Steve was too nice, too smart, too well built, and too handsome for his taste.

"So what would you like me to do?" Nat went on. From Victor's perspective the trap was closed. What could he say? He countered with another question. "Since when do I have the right to interfere in your professional life? You already know how I feel."

"Well, of all my choices this one seems to be the best fit, so I guess I should give it a try."

"I wish you the best of luck."

"Nat? Would you please come here?" Victor called.

"Coming," Nat answered as she walked in the room.

"What's the matter?" she asked taking in the agitation in Victor's voice and Sheela's stern expression.

"It seems that . . ." Victor started, but before he could finish Sheela interrupted saying "Unca Teeve, Unca Teeve, Unca Teeve, Unca Teeve, Unca Teeve" like a loud broken recording.

"Hush, Sheela," Nat said to her daughter. "Let Daddy talk and we'll see if we can fix your problem. After all you're a birthday girl today and you should have no reason to fuss. So be quiet a second, OK?"

Sheela nodded tentatively.

"As I was saying," Victor continued, "it seems that Miss Sheela wants *Uncle Steve* to attend her birthday party. Would you kindly explain how come she is suddenly so inordinately attached to him and how you plan to handle this development?"

"Sheela," Nat said picking her up firmly, "I'm taking you to play with your Grandma for a bit while Daddy and I talk about Uncle Steve coming to your party."

After depositing Sheela with her grandmother, Nat returned to Victor. "I don't exactly know why Sheela decided she wants Steve at the party, but like I told you she's been to the office with Lulu a couple of times. There's an empty room up there and everyone in the office has brought a toy or two for Sheela to play with. I guess she and Steve just hit it off."

"Oh, I see," Victor remarked, although he didn't. "So now what?"

"I guess I'll call Steve and see if he can make it. That's fine with you isn't it?"

"No, it's actually not, "Victor answered, "I don't like mixing our personal lives with business, but I guess I don't have too much of a choice."

"Thanks. You're a sport." Nat sealed her appreciation with a warm and promising embrace that foreclosed further discussion. "Now I hope I can find Steve. He's probably working in the office. I feel sorry for him. I think he misses having a family."

"I'd like nothing better than to come to Sheela's birthday party. I'm honored," Steve told Nat when she honestly explained what prompted the last minute invitation. "Thank you for asking me."

Nat had worked out the logistics for the afternoon in great detail. Some of the meticulous planning paid off, but for the most part, Sheela's party took on a life of its own. The arrival of Beca and Henry with red balloons, pink streamers, candles, and the other items on Nat's list kicked off the festivities. Lulu appeared a few minutes later insisting that she was not a guest but a part of the family and that she was not going to sit and make conversation but that she too would help. She brought a red and purple piñata that vaguely resembled a fat burro and crepe paper to decorate a chair for Sheela to sit in. Although it was barely two o'clock, Victor popped a bottle of champagne and the fun began.

By a quarter to three the living area was a riot of red balloons floating amidst swirling pink streamers. The dining table was covered with a red paper tablecloth draped to the floor and Nat placed a large arrangement of pink roses in the center. Sheela's special chair awaited her at the head of the table. In a corner, a round table was covered with gifts. The piñata hung from a ceiling hook, displacing the plant that had been there moments earlier. Sheela, in a brand new red dress with a floral trim, matching floral jacket, coordinated socks and red shoes, clapped and smiled prettily, though she turned away when the camera flashed in her eyes or a video pointed at her. Natalya beamed, Victor preened, Rebecca and Dora rejoiced, Henry gloated and Lulu chirped.

At three, the other guests poured in all at once. They filled the Landau home with more happy noise and piled more presents on the gift table.

"It seems we never went home last night," David said, accepting a mimosa from Victor. "Yesterday I thought I had enough champagne to last throughout 2002, but this hits the spot."

"Just orange juice, please," Annette said. "I'm not drinking, just in case."

While Mike and Angela scampered after musical balls rolling around on the floor, Sheela flitted cheerfully from guest to guest, until she realized Unca Teeve was not yet among them. Luckily, before she could react, the bell rang and

Rebecca ushered Steve Jordan in. He was carrying a big brown carton tied with a bright violet ribbon.

"Hi," he said. "Sorry I'm late, but finding the right gift took longer than I expected."

Sheela's eyes jumped from Steve to the box.

"I'm Rebecca Landau, Sheela's grandmother," Beca said. "Sorry we couldn't come to the Christmas open house at your office, but we had guests that evening. Natalya tells me you have a very nice set-up."

Everybody was too busy chatting, playing with the toddlers, or sampling the food which had been temptingly set up at one end of the table to notice the arrival of a man in tails and a top hat until he was well in their midst and Nat announced, "I am happy to present to you Ivan Ivanovich, the Russian Master of Magic. He is currently on tour and performing at the Library Club. I pulled some strings to get him to come here this afternoon, so please be seated and welcome him with a big hand."

As her guests arranged themselves on the sofa, chairs, or on the floor, Ivan Ivanovich opened up his trunk and set up a table covered with a big yellow cloth. When the clapping began, Ivanovich removed his hat and put it on the cloth. Then, taking a bow, he pulled a bright blue scarf out of his pocket and placed it on the hat. With all eyes riveted on him, he slipped off the scarf and lifted the hat to reveal a large bowl full of apples, bananas, and tangerines. Next, showing the empty hat to his audience, he put it back on, only to scratch his head and remove it again, this time pulling out an old-fashioned wind up teddy bear which banged on a tin drum. He gallantly presented the toy to Sheela, who clapped with glee. Before Mike and Angela could begin to whimper, he quickly reached further into his hat and produced a bear for each of them.

The Master's next trick called for someone in the audience to think of a number from one to ten. When Henry volunteered and said that the number was one, Ivan invited him to step forward. "Please lift your left foot and look at the sole of your shoe," he instructed in a heavily accented voice.

"Here goes," Henry said, raising his leg with a flourish. Stuck to his shoe with scotch tape was a folded piece of paper. Henry detached and unfolded it and then read the note penned on the paper out loud. "You picked number one," it said, "because today is Sheela's first birthday."

The magician followed the number trick with more sleights of hand that amazed and delighted everyone present. He pulled balloon animals out of his ears, he transformed a dozen wet paper napkins into beautiful silk scarves which he presented to the ladies, and he poured a glass of milk into his hat wherein it disappeared. For his finale, Natalya stood by while Ivan slipped under the table. After a few moments, Nat whisked off the table cloth to reveal the magician's trunk, securely closed and padlocked. Nat then removed the padlock. Moments later, the Russian Master stepped out, doffed his hat, and bid the group farewell.

Next, Mike's grandmother broke the piñata. She had Mike in tow but dispensed with the traditional blindfold and the grown-ups as well as the children scrambled for the chocolates and candies that fell out. The cake ceremony followed. Propped on a big pillow on her fancy chair, Sheela gazed at the two candles flickering on her cake, a pink one for being one and a red one for good luck. They burned brightly while "Happy Birthday" was sung to her for the second time that day.

Afterwards she puffed and blew both candles out in one go. However, in the midst of the applause she caught Nat wiping a tear and her own eyes began to mist as well. Victor lifted her up and explained, "Sometimes your Mommy cries when she is happy." When Sheela smiled again, Victor took her little hand in his big one. Then, both hands encircled a knife festooned with curly ribbons and cut the cake.

The rest of the party was about eating ice cream, chocolate cake and marzipan roses, and watching Sheela open her presents. She wanted to begin with the big carton, so Natalya cut off the purple bow and gave it to Angela, who had been eyeing it for some time. Then Nat helped Sheela open the lid and lift out a small wicker rocking chair and a crocheted coverlet.

"Say thank you to Uncle Steve," Nat instructed, but Sheela blew him a kiss.

"A smile or a kiss is better than a thank you any day," Steve said.

Sheela rocked for a bit and then hopped back into Natalya's lap, pointing to a box with Pooh wrapping. Nat started to remove the paper, but she was interrupted by Mike who darted over and began to shriek as loud as he could. Ellen Hansen came after him, apologizing profusely for her grandson's behavior.

"It's OK," Nat said. He can rock.

"OK," Sheela repeated, pushing Mike into the chair at which point his cries grew more piercing.

"I think we'd better leave," Ellen remarked, embarrassed. "Mike must be tired or hungry."

"No, no, no!" Mike shouted.

"See, see!" Sheela said, tugging at the rocking chair carton which lay on its side and made a perfect cave. Still sobbing, Mike crawled inside. When he was comfortably settled, his howls became whimpers and finally stopped.

The Pooh present was a xylophone from Lulu, who was rewarded with a clang and a great smile. Next Sheela picked a smaller package that had been sent by Jaya and Sunil. It contained a pair of silver anklets made of tiny bells. After tinkling the bells, Sheela opened Annette and David's gift, a dozen bars of transparent soap formed around dinosaur toys. Sheela kissed each bar before moving on to Angela's package, a "pitty" smocked denim dress.

The next item to be opened was from Victor and Nat. They had made Sheela an album filled with photograph collages of her first year, a sequel to the album that they gave her at birth. Sheela looked at several pages with a perplexed expression on her face and then put the album down and grabbed a bright red bag that looked like it had a pile of laundry inside. Victor helped her open the drawstring and pulled out a bean bag coil that turned out to be a big snake with shiny maroon eyes. Mike saw the snake too and he wanted it, so he came out of the box in which he was hiding and tried to yank it out of Sheela's hands. Sheela held fast, but Mike kept pulling until all ten feet of the creature uncoiled. At that moment Sheela made a loud hissing noise that sent him scampering to find his grandma. Then she turned her attention to his present, *Alice in Wonderland*. Sheela gave the Queen of Hearts a kiss.

Nat was glad that the grandparents' gifts, which were bound to be special, were saved for the end. The box in which Harold and Dora's present came was the size of a large shoebox, while Rebecca and Henry's gift was a smaller oblong package. Sheela chose the bigger box first. Inside she was amazed to find a doll, her exact likeness, wearing a red dress and floral jacket that matched hers perfectly.

"Sheea?" she asked this miniature replica of herself.
"No, Dolly," it replied, but only Sheela heard.

Beca and Gappa's package, the last one to be opened, was heavy and covered by a floral wrapping. A well-crafted oblong teak box was inside the paper. Sheela stared at the box for some time and then, with a far-away look in her eyes, she deftly slid the lid off. The box was lined with felt that protected a set of shiny black obsidian dominoes with silver dots, the same ones that Victor played with when he was a boy. He had used the dominoes as building blocks to make bridges and skyscrapers much before he learned to count dots. After a long moment, Sheela turned the box upside down and emptied it on the rug on the floor. She picked up two tiles and held them in her hand absorbing their cool, smooth feel, before laying them down, one on top of the other. Then she tried to fit the dominoes into the box again, but she couldn't so she called Beca. Together Sheela and her grandmother put them back, face up, row by row, and when the box was full Sheela carefully replaced the lid in its grooves and closed it.

25

"What is Sheela doing?" Victor asked Nat one Sunday, several weeks after their daughter's birthday. Nat had just served chicken and mushroom pastries with a mushroom sherry cream sauce accompanied by a peach compote for brunch.

"I get nervous when she's this quiet."

"Relax. Your daughter is in the closet happily playing with my shoes and making a mess. I'll have to straighten up later, but it's worth it."

"I don't want her touching shoes. That's unhygienic. What if she puts them in her mouth?"

"She doesn't do that. She's trying them on, lining them up, and fiddling with the straps, trying to get them into the buckles."

"It's still gross. Make her stop."

"Come on, Victor," Nat said. "Let her be. I'll wash her hands afterward. Besides she'll scream and that will be the end of our Sunday morning. And I went to all this trouble."

"Sheela has to get used to the fact that screaming isn't a helpful technique for getting her way. In fact, she has to learn that she can't always have everything she wants."

The morning turned into a fiasco. Victor stomped off to get Sheela, leaving brunch untouched.

"No, no, no, no, *no!*" Sheela cried, clutching a pair of patent leather heels that Victor tore away from her. Then he took her into the shower because the shoes were "very dirty" and "dirt can make you sick."

The age of one was becoming stressful from Sheela's viewpoint too. Although she could do and say more and more, things weren't nearly as cozy as they had been before. Her parents no longer considered her every wish a command. They had agendas of their own. They helped her when she wanted to do things for herself. They wanted her to finish her block puzzle, or to tell what noises all the animals made when she didn't feel like it. They even interrupted her when she was busy, or scolded her for no reason at all. Like today, Natalya let her play with the shoes and then suddenly Victor made her stop and when she cried, he lost his temper. Then in the afternoon, Sheela took off Dolly's clothes because she wanted to see her belly button and her dress tore and one shoe got lost. So her ma got angry, and she took Dolly away and put her up on a shelf.

"You're too little to appreciate your beautiful Sheela doll," she said. "First you messed her hair and now you ripped her dress. I hope I can find the missing shoe. You can play with her when you're older."

There were other things too. For example, Sheela loved going to her ma's office on days when she didn't have Infantasy and it wasn't Gappa's Wednesday off. Staying home all the time was no fun. Uncle Steve said she should come whenever she wanted to, but she hardly ever got to go.

Then there was this business about her milk. Lulu gave it to her slightly sweetened in a bottle so she could drink it sitting in her rocker with Aa-Oo in her lap. But her parents made her drink it in a cup without even a drop of sugar. They said the bottle and sugar were bad for her teeth, but Sheela remembered that her baby teeth would all fall out anyway and she would get new ones when she was bigger. Her parents knew that, didn't they? So why wouldn't they let her enjoy herself? It just didn't make any sense.

Often her parents didn't understand what she was trying to say. Maybe she wasn't too clear, but then again they didn't always listen very well either. Instead of pausing to consider things from the perspective of a one year old, they hurried her and rushed off to get on with their work or their lives. Perhaps when Sheela's verbal skills caught up with her intuitive abilities, communication would become more of a two-way street. But would it? Would her parents heed her voice or would they overpower it with their own voices? And would she embrace or resist their opinions?

The Thursday after the shoe incident, Sheela got upset at Infantasy. She still went to Ms. Meredith's classes on Thursdays and Saturdays, but now they were in the afternoons from 2:35 until 3:20. That particular afternoon Ms. Meredith read a picture book to everyone. While she read aloud, a screen in front showed the story in words and pictures. The story was called "Bobby," and it was about a boy and his birthday wish. In the story, when Bobby blew out the candles on his birthday cake, he wished for a baby sister and his wish came true. No one had told Sheela that you were supposed to make a wish before blowing out birthday candles. The picture of Bobby closing his eyes so he could wish with all his might disturbed her. She wondered what happened when you didn't make a wish.

Lulu was at a loss when Sheela started to cry during the birthday story. It was the first time she had ever misbehaved at Infantasy and had to be removed from class. What an unfortunate blot on a heretofore perfect record! When Victor came to drop Lulu and Sheela back home, Lulu told him what had happened.

"Sheela just started to cry, for no reason, and we had to wait for you in the hall," she explained.

"She seems fine now," Victor said "What did you do?"

"I gave her a drink and changed her diaper. I asked her why she was crying and Sheela said 'Bobby.'"

"Maybe she was thirsty," Victor suggested.

"No," Lulu replied. "Sheela doesn't cry when she is thirsty. She says 'wawa,' 'mik' or 'joosh.'"

"Please, Lulu," Victor reproached, "Don't use baby talk around Sheela. I've told you that a hundred times."

"Sorry," Lulu said laughingly. "OK. Sheela is a big girl now. She says 'water', 'milk' or 'juice' if she's thirsty and she says 'yum' if she wants to eat."

Sheela didn't like Lulu talking over her head, so she started to cry again. Victor still didn't ask her what the matter was. Instead he raised his voice and said, "Sheela, I want you to stop this nonsense right away. No more crying. OK?"

Sheela stopped crying, and tried to make her point another way. "Bobby, Bobby, Bobby, Bobby, Bobby, Bobby, Bobby, Bobby," she repeated all the way home.

When they pulled up to the entrance of their building, Victor unlocked the car and let them out; he had to go on. However, he promised they would talk about Bobby later.

It turned out that Victor didn't keep his promise. Something was wrong with his book, which meant he had to work late. And Nat was no help either because as soon as she got home, Lulu had to leave. As a result Lulu had no time to explain what had happened. Besides, Natalya's mind was on other things like her speeding ticket, her bulging briefcase, and Annette Singer's message.

Natalya showered and changed Sheela without wasting any time or words and then she set about preparing supper. Tonight she would not be a companionable playmate or a soothing parent. Instead, she would probably let Sheela watch a laser disc or amuse herself with the pots and pans in the bottom kitchen drawer. Usually Sheela was happy with those things, but when she was uncomfortable, she didn't want to be left to her own devices. So, after supper, Sheela pushed away her bowl and thought about starting to cry. Luckily Nat noticed her scrunched up face and said, "I heard you had an upset at Infantasy today. We'll see if Ms. Meredith can help clear things up after class on Saturday." Suddenly Sheela felt a whole lot better. She relaxed her face and when Nat asked, "What would you like to do until bed time?" she answered "Anpans."

"OK," Nat agreed. She opened her briefcase and took out her papers while Sheela matched pots and pans with lids, wore the pots on her head like helmets or banged on them with a spoon as if they were drums. "The noise doesn't bother me, but you know we can't do this when Daddy is home, right?" Nat asked.

"OK," Sheela answered, because it really was OK and she was fine. After a while she climbed into Nat's lap and let her head droop so her ma would know that she was ready for bed.

⁂

"It's happened!" Annette said as soon as she picked up the phone and heard Nat's "Hi, it's me."

"I guessed! Congratulations! That's wonderful. When did you find out?"

"This morning. I wasn't going to tell, but then I had to."

"Why weren't you going to tell?" Nat asked.

"You know, because it might be unlucky. There's a higher than average risk of a miscarriage at my age, and I had such a tough time conceiving. Then I figured it was silly to think that keeping the baby a secret would make a difference. I'm going to be devastated if something goes wrong anyway."

"It's unlikely that anything will go wrong. Don't even think about it."

"I'm not," Annette said. "That's why I decided to call."

"So when is the baby due?"

"That's the thing. I don't know. I've been irregular. Even though I've been hoping this was 'it' for a while, I waited to take the test, in case my feeling yucky was wishful thinking or the stomach flu. Anyway, this morning I took it. I didn't say anything to David until after the result came out positive and then we went a little crazy, but we had to pull ourselves together for work. Now I'm floating on cloud nine."

"When was your last period?"

"I stopped keeping track. It was before Sheela's birthday. I feel silly saying this but I think maybe the baby got started on her birthday."

"Wow! Then you're nearly two months along. I'm really excited for you. I'm excited for me too. It'll be fun talking about our children and letting them hang out together."

"How is everything at your end?" Annette asked.

"Good, but Sheela is getting to be difficult and Victor and I don't always see eye to eye when it comes to managing her. It's nothing major. And work is good except that Victor resents Steve Jordan. He doesn't buy into the idea that Steve is gay and he imagines that one of these days we're going to fall for each other. I think it would help if we got pregnant again soon."

"Aren't you the one who says that a baby never solves marital problems?" Annette asked. "I think it's too early for you two to have another child. What you guys need is a vacation, a second honeymoon really."

"Now isn't a good time. I'm picking up momentum and Victor is being hyper about his book. It's supposed to go to the publisher next month. By the way, I spoke to Jaya a couple of days ago."

"Do you know when they're returning to Houston?" Annette asked.

"I think probably in May. But it's not certain. Jaya is on leave of absence until then. Sunil is fine and working again, but he wants to quit and get his old job back. If he gets it, they'll come. Otherwise, they're both going to try to find new jobs wherever. I'm keeping my fingers crossed that everything will work out here."

"Are they trying to have a baby after all this?"

"Not yet," Nat said. Jaya told me things between Sunil and her were great and that they both want to start a family but are going to wait until their work situation is settled. Their house is rented until May. If they don't come back, they're going to put it on the market."

"I would think Jaya is going nuts without her work," Annette remarked.

"She is working. She has access to a lab and is doing research on her own; plus, she has a part time job as an instructor at a health club. She's having a ball."

"That's great! I'd better let you go but let's plan on getting together soon."

"All right. Bye. And congratulations again."

Ms. Meredith was helpful in trying to find out what caused Sheela to lose it during the previous Infantasy session. "Did you cry in the middle of class last time you were here?" she asked.

Sheela didn't reply, but she nodded her head and started sniffling.

"Use words," Ms. Meredith told her.

"Bobby," Sheela said.

"Did Bobby make you cry?" Ms. Meredith continued.

Sheela nodded again.

"I told you to use words," Ms. Meredith repeated.

"Bobby," Sheela repeated.

Ms. Meredith took the Bobby story off the shelf and turned the pages for Sheela to look at. "Show me the part that made you cry," she said. Sheela stopped her at the picture of Bobby closing his eyes while he was wishing for a sister.

"There's something on this page that really bothers her," Ms. Meredith explained to Natalya. "Isn't that right Sheela?"

"Ya," Sheela said.

"I'm going to read this page and you say the word that made you cry, OK?"

"OK," Sheela said solemnly. Ms. Meredith read the page and when she was through Sheela said "Ish."

"Ish?" Nat asked.

"No! ish, ish," Sheela said emphatically closing her eyes like Bobby was doing in the picture.

"Oh! I see. You mean wish, right?" Ms. Meredith asked.

"Ya," Sheela replied, her face brightening. "Ish."

It turned out Sheela was worried over her failure to make a birthday wish like Bobby did on his birthday. Nat wondered what to do and finally she had an inspiration.

"We all wished when you blew out the candles," she said. "We wished for you to be a very happy girl and to have lots of fun. But we couldn't say anything because birthday wishes are always secret. Bobby didn't tell anyone that he wanted a sister. That's why his wish came true. And your heart made a wish even if your head forgot."

Sheela watched her mother's demeanor and listened to her tone of voice attentively. When Nat stopped speaking she said "Oh" and smiled.

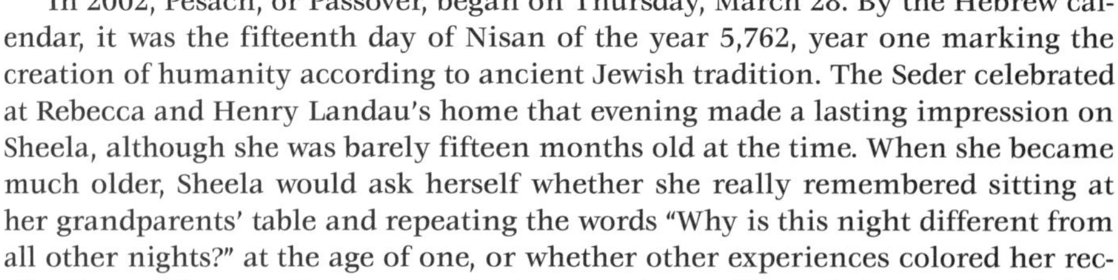

In 2002, Pesach, or Passover, began on Thursday, March 28. By the Hebrew calendar, it was the fifteenth day of Nisan of the year 5,762, year one marking the creation of humanity according to ancient Jewish tradition. The Seder celebrated at Rebecca and Henry Landau's home that evening made a lasting impression on Sheela, although she was barely fifteen months old at the time. When she became much older, Sheela would ask herself whether she really remembered sitting at her grandparents' table and repeating the words "Why is this night different from all other nights?" at the age of one, or whether other experiences colored her recollections. Whatever the answer, the images, the smells, and the wonderful feelings that the occasion evoked would live in Sheela's consciousness forever.

Thursday turned out to be a beautiful crisp spring day. The air was fresh after an early morning shower, and the weather was cooler than usual for Houston. Sheela and Lulu skipped Infantasy to spend the day in The Village. Sheela loved everything about Beca's home: the delicate furniture, the rich fabrics, the shiny piano that sang to Beca's touch, and the deep red Bukhara carpet with squares that were such fun to play on. She often tiptoed around the house listening for secrets that lurked in corners. Sometimes, when no one was looking, Sweak would surprise her by jumping out from under a pillow or from behind the curtains to play a quick game of hide and seek.

The hours flew by. Sheela had brought her dominoes, and she and Gappa built and demolished domino towers. She helped Lulu shine a candlestick and ate a piece of matzoh with peanut butter and jelly. Then she took a nap in the middle of Beca and Gappa's big bed. When she woke up, Gappa dressed her, his big fingers deftly slipping the tiny buttons on her dress into even tinier buttonholes. "This is the first time I have ever dressed a little girl," he said, "and even if I say so myself, I did a pretty good job." By the time her parents arrived looking splendid, Sheela was ready to greet them. And a few moments later she pranced around Aunt Annette and Uncle David who had also been invited, along with their baby who wasn't big enough to be born yet.

"Thanks so much for asking us," Uncle David told Rebecca and Gappa. "This Passover is special for us."

"It's our pleasure. We thank you for coming to share in our blessings," Gappa said to them. "A Seder is meant for company."

At the table, Henry Landau distributed yarmulkes to the men and welcomed his visitors. "As you know," he said, "Passover commemorates the Jews' Exodus from Egypt," he said. "However, this festival also reminds us that liberation is ongoing. In the Haggadah, which guides this evening's rituals, it is written 'In each generation, Jews must regard themselves as if they personally had been delivered from the hands of the Egyptians.' That is why, along with the feast that is now before us for our enjoyment, we eat special foods that symbolize the miracle of the Israelites' redemption from Pharaoh's tyranny: hard-boiled eggs are a reminder that life transcends death; sprigs of parsley represent the eternal hope of spring; the brown roasted egg represents ancient temple sacrifices; salt water stands for the tears of the Hebrew slaves; bitter horseradish brings back the bitterness of servitude; and the matzoh is the unleavened bread that the Jewish people ate on their way to freedom. The cups of wine beside your plates represent our joy and thankfulness to God for saving us and blessing us throughout the ages."

The ceremony followed. Dinner and conversation were interspersed with readings and the eating of symbolic food. As the youngest child seated at the table, Sheela was responsible for asking, "Why is this night different from all the other nights of the year?" four times. She babbled the questions and Victor translated into English. The answer unfolded as the evening progressed. At the culmination of the ritual, Henry opened the front door to invite the prophet Elijah into his home. Elijah brought the news that at last, after long years of waiting, liberation and freedom were at hand.

26

In coping with the demands of parenting, Natalya discovered an unexpected source of help in Rebecca. When Sheela's behavior de-calibrated her household, Nat often turned to her mother-in-law for advice.

"It seems like every day we have a new crisis," Nat told Beca one Wednesday evening when she came to collect Sheela. "One day it's bedtime. Then it's mealtime. Then when it looks like Sheela has settled down, it's something else. Yesterday she started screaming and kicking when we put on her diaper, yet she won't use the potty."

"Sheela is conflicted," Rebecca explained. "She has discovered courage at the same time she has found fear. She wants independence, yet understands she is dependent. She is developing likes and dislikes over which she has no control. All this has to be as frustrating for her as it is for you. Children grow in spurts. Stable times are periods of equilibrium. Turbulent times are periods of growth. All you can do is stay aware and manage the situation in as matter of fact a way as you can."

"I try to be calm and detached," Nat replied, "but Sheela's swings are wreaking havoc on Victor and creating problems between us. He blames himself and me when Sheela acts up."

"Sometimes I think it's unfortunate," Rebecca remarked, "that today's fathers are expected to share such a big chunk of responsibility for rearing young children. Their help often becomes interference. Often men view uncooperative children as a challenge. You have to help Victor realize that he cannot control Sheela with logic or persuasion and that it's no one's fault if things don't always go smoothly."

The day after a particularly harrowing evening, Nat complained to Rebecca that Victor refused to let Sheela sleep in their bed.

"It shouldn't have been such a big deal," she said, "but lately every little thing is an issue."

"You are both under such pressure between your work and your commitment to Sheela that you neglect each other. As a result, you make noise when you should be making music."

"What do you mean?" Nat asked.

"Music is harmony. Noise is cacophony. In both cases different instruments play their own tunes, but in music every instrument is in tune with the others."

"Well, I'm willing to compromise, but compromise is a two-way street."

"Harmony isn't compromise," Rebecca suggested. Harmony is agreement. Compromise is concession and a recipe for dissatisfaction. Imagine you wanted to vacation in Mexico and Victor wanted to go to Canada, and you compromised on

Kansas which is in between. It would be dumb because you both would have an awful time. But if you explored, you would find out why you like Mexico and why Victor prefers Canada. Then you would discover a third place that meets both of your requirements. Or else you would determine whose needs are greater and go along with that one's preference."

"How about what Sheela wants?" Nat asked.

"The same principle applies. Sheela may be little, but her needs are just as great as yours."

Later, Nat thought about Beca's words and tried to make up with Victor, but he was tired and out of sorts. He didn't care that Sheela was sound asleep in her own room. Maybe tomorrow he would be in a warmer mood. Maybe then she and he would succeed in starting a new baby.

⁂

Natalya used to wonder what made Victor's father so totally devoted to his wife. Now she saw Beca's qualities emerge, like colors in a child's paint-with-water book. Beca was attractive, but petite and fragile. She was almost mousy. Yet she had depth and strength that bolstered and energized Henry. She was the source of his gusto, a gusto that overshadowed her tentativeness. And although she seemed to hide a secret sadness, she loved her husband, her life, and her home. It was a home that Nat considered somber, yet it glowed with graciousness, and it was filled with wisdom. Rebecca had depth and intelligence. Henry believed that he held the key to his wife's balance in his hand and Rebecca's gift to him was the preservation of that illusion.

⁂

Sometimes Nat talked with her own mother and she was surprised to note that she often gave her the same advice as Beca, though her mother was less guarded.

"I can't believe you are telling me this!" Natalya exclaimed one day after Dora criticized her for refusing to go with Victor to a University reception. Sheela was feverish and Nat didn't want to leave her with Lulu. Victor was angry and hurt and Nat thought his behavior was selfish and childish.

"You should have bundled her up and taken her over to the Landau's. Her grandfather is a doctor, after all. I think you are a tad jealous of Sheela's attachment to them."

"That's a horrible thing to suggest! It's not true! I told you I was worried."

"I'm sorry, sweetheart. I'm just trying to make you see that you can't ignore Victor when he needs you more than Sheela. Every time you do something like this, you pay for it."

"Pay for what? I didn't do anything! Staying home with my sick baby isn't a crime. You sound like Beca who thinks I send Sheela to Infantasy because I feel guilty about neglecting her. She thinks you're strange because Infantasy is your thing."

"That remark," Dora said, "isn't worthy of you, Natalya. It's unkind and unfair."

⁂

Several weeks later, Nat and Victor took a Saturday walk in Memorial Park. "I've been wondering about something," she said.

"What's that?"

"You always told me your parents were against rituals, like mine, but from what I see, that's not at all the case."

"I guess they changed," Victor said. "At the time I was growing up, my parents viewed rituals as divisive. They were Universalists. They believed the world could and should become one giant melting pot. Gradually, it dawned on them and on like-minded thinkers that in the process of giving up tradition, they were giving up their legacy. Now that Sheela has come along they want to make sure she doesn't miss out on her heritage."

"My mother and father aren't moving toward reconsidering anything. I guess they were never as grounded in their underlying Jewishness as yours must have been. But I'm still surprised that Beca let you have a Christmas tree when you were little."

"It's not that surprising. Look at it this way, Nat. Your parents were vague and insecure about Judaism, so they felt uneasy about a Christmas tree. My parents were fundamentally comfortable in their beliefs, so the idea of a tree, which is not even originally Christian, didn't threaten them."

"I guess," Nat said, "your parents basically considered Judaism pivotal to their lives whereas my mother and father treated it as an accident of birth, yet didn't feel right about their own attitude. They are actually a paradox. Although they think being Jewish isn't important, it defines who they are."

"Perhaps it's their resistance that defines them," Victor suggested.

"To an extent," Nat said. "But resistance is just a part of their Jewish consciousness."

"Would you say your parents' Judaism is mostly tradition or mostly faith?" Natalya asked.

"Today it's some of both. But when I was a boy, they gave me the sense that Judaism was a code of conduct, something like an intellectualized and legalistic framework that puts life in context. But my parents disparaged restrictive observances like keeping kosher. Their focus was always on upholding affirmative values like education and doing good deeds. The day I started first grade my father put honey on a corner of my notebook and told me to lick it so my first taste of learning would be sweet."

"That's beautiful. Let's do the same when Sheela starts school. To me Judaism is primarily an identity. This identity offers us riches that we have to preserve for future generations; maybe we even have to find a way to make the riches grow."

"That was a great walk," Victor said as he and Nat rode up in the elevator. "Why don't we do this more often?"

"Because things don't always fall into place. The weather was perfect, we had a free afternoon, and Beca wanted to take Sheela to play with her neighbor's grandson who is in from out of town. They're bringing her back after supper, at about eight."

"A free afternoon, huh? Sheela isn't coming back until eight. Are you saying your dance card is empty?" Victor snuggled up to Nat while they walked out of the elevator.

"Someone may see," Nat said, but she didn't pull away. Then she added, wistfully, "Yes, my card is empty but it's the wrong time of month."

⊷⊶⊷⊶⊷⊶

Natalya had been in a quandary about whether or not to mention Annette and David's baby to Sheela, just in case something went wrong, but then Sheela picked up on things and Nat didn't like being evasive with her. So just before Passover she carefully explained how "Maybe there was a baby growing in Aunt Annette's tummy."

Overlooking the 'maybe' Sheela responded, "Ya, boy," as if she already had the inside scoop.

"We aren't even sure yet that the baby is there and we won't know for a while if it's boy or a girl," Nat answered. "So far it's a secret."

The miracle of conception touched Sheela. It evoked a fading memory of her own embodiment, the magical moment when she left the pool of spirits still seeking a suitable material life and plunged into the world to become a person. She empathized with the soul that had chosen the Singers as mother and father. She was eager to meet the new life and she already felt the warmth of its companionship.

After Passover, Sheela decided that the Singer baby's name was Bobby, like the boy who made the birthday wish, and she added Bobby to the list of people with whom she carried on telephone conversations, using the phone on the night table next to Natalya's side of the bed. A couple of times she tried the Playskool phone that Victor had given her, but it didn't work. One day Nat overheard her and asked, "Who is Bobby?"

"Bobby Ananet baby," Sheela answered.

Nat held off telling Annette about Sheela's talk with Bobby until a sonogram confirmed that he was indeed a healthy boy.

"Wow!" Nat said on the Saturday that Annette gave her the good news over a lunch of bagels with assorted fancy fillings. Then she added, "You're going to think this is crazy, but a few weeks ago I heard Sheela pretending to talk to your baby on the phone. She named him Bobby, after a boy in a story she heard at Infantasy. Remember I told you about what happened with the birthday wish problem. The boy's name was Bobby."

"That's impossible," Annette said.

"I know it seems impossible, but it's true."

"Well, I can think of a reasonable explanation for Sheela imagining the baby is a boy," Annette suggested. "She is at the age where the difference between boys and girls intrigues her. So she wants us to have a boy because it would be much more interesting. And Bobby is a name she knows."

"So why did you say it's impossible?"

"Because Bobby, short for Robert or Roberta, is one of the names David and I have been seriously considering. I know you don't, but we like names with nicknames that are the same for boys and girls."

"I didn't before, but I like them now."

"Don't you wish Jaya were here?" Annette asked after a few moments. "It feels strange having a conversation like this without her."

"I know," Nat agreed. "Sheela cried when we drove past her house and I told her that Yaya Auntie wasn't coming back. Somehow I was sure she and Sunil would end up returning to Houston."

"So was I," Annette said. "I guess we're no different than toddlers thinking that reality equates with what we want."

"On the other hand, starting fresh in a new place may be what the Khannas really did want and need. Here they have had bad memories to unload and Jaya's job would continue to pose a problem. Now she won't have to travel as much."

"You may be right, Nat, but I think it's hard to say what's best. Sunil and Jaya had a lot of good things going for them in Houston too. I hope everything works out and I hope they don't freeze this winter. I don't think I could stand the Chicago weather."

The next time Sheela met the Singers, she snuggled up to Annette's tummy and said, "Hi, Bobby." Then she put her ear where her mouth had been and listened for his answer.

"What did Bobby say to you?" Dave asked.

"Hi," Sheela replied. Then she patted the large tummy that was Bobby's temporary home and a protruding elbow acknowledged her caress. Sheela kissed it and listened once more.

"Did Bobby say anything else?" Nat asked.

"Ya," Sheela answered.

"Can you tell us what he said?" Nat persisted.

"OK." Sheela said.

"Did he say OK?" Victor asked.

"No." Sheela replied.

"What did Bobby say?" Victor asked.

"Bobby goin' born," Sheela solemnly explained.

Robert Daniel Singer's bris took place on October 8, 2002, the same day that Victor's second book, *The Art of Logical Communication*, was published and the same day Nat took on a case which would consume her for the next few years. It was the eighth day of Bobby's life. His ritual circumcision on this day celebrated the Jews' covenant with God and established his place in a tradition that began with Abraham. The atmosphere in the Singer household was festive, but tense. Annette was recovering from the caesarian section that had to be performed at the last minute. She cowered in a corner of her living room, burying her head in Nat's shoulder and clenching her mother's hand. David, proud but also nervous, gathered the small group of men which was assembled for the occasion: his father, Irwin Singer; his father-in-law, Jeffrey Loeb; his friends, Victor, Simon Weiss and Michael Segovia; Dr. Henry Landau and Dr. Joseph Kantor, Bobby's pediatrician who was also licensed as a mohel and was to perform the circumcision.

The procedure took almost no time at all; it was over before Bobby began to cry. By the time Annette reached her son's side, his screams had softened into whimpers. Thus, the room was quiet and joyful as David recited the benediction that praised God for instructing him "to bring this child into the covenant of Abraham our father" and the guests responded, "May the boy grow into the life of Torah, marriage and good deeds."

After the blessing, Annette took her son into the bedroom to nurse. Twenty minutes later, she came out again to rejoin the party. Her make-up was refreshed, her hair shone, and she looked radiant.

"Bobby is asleep. My incision doesn't hurt any more," she explained. From the sofa she directed Nat and her mother, Renee, to serve the food while she talked with Simon's wife, Elaine. On the other side of the room, the men laughed and then quieted to hear Dr. Kantor's third mohel joke.

"An American Jew," Joseph Kantor said, "was walking in Tel-Aviv, and he saw a big sign over a show window filled with watches and clocks. 'What does the sign say?' the American asked his Israeli cousin. It says 'mohel,' the Israeli answered. 'Why on earth would a mohel display watches and clocks?' the American asked. 'What else could he display?' the Israeli retorted."

The Art of Logical Communication was a success; Victor was elated. He had been waiting nervously for the response to his second book during a period of time that he had little work to do. Victor devoted his free hours to worrying about how his work would be received. At last, accolades began to trickle and then pour in from scholars and from industry. These accolades guaranteed his reputation, his tenure and a promotion to full professor. They meant he would be able to dedicate himself to the business of teaching and to pursue further research at his pleasure and they ensured that he would continue to be in demand as a consultant. *The Science of Persuasive Communication* placed Victor at the threshold of distinction, but *The Art of Logical Communication* enabled him to cross it.

Natalya was proud of her husband, but she was not surprised by his accomplishment. She took it for granted that his work would be applauded and had no idea that Victor had fretted over the possibility of it ending up as a flop. Only after that specter was gone did he admit to Nat that insecurity had been eating away at him.

"I can't begin to tell you how relieved I feel." Victor showed Nat a pile of print-outs of his congratulatory e-mail. "I was really nervous."

"Why?" Nat asked. "It's not like you didn't know the book is excellent."

"That's not the point," Victor said.

"What is the point?"

"It's that I went out on a limb and could have fallen on my ass. The fact that I believe in what I say doesn't guarantee that either the academicians or the business community will accept it, let alone both. I took English and made it the crux of marketing at a stage when the study of language arts is at an all time low. And I said well-known and arguably effective advertising is illogical because it uses bad English. Imagine "We Do More" as a hospital slogan! More what? More unnecessary surgery? More dangerous procedures? There are dozens of examples like that one that premier advertising agencies have come up with."

"Why didn't you tell me?" Nat asked.

"Because I didn't want to be a wimp and I didn't want you to worry. That's why."

27

Nat vacillated between worrying about Power Industries and reminding herself that this was a case she would have regretted turning down for the rest of her career. She had persuaded Steve to take Power on, but on hectic days like today she wasn't so sure it would be manageable. She was overloaded and her juices had stopped flowing. So, at about 6:45, she wearily grabbed a few files, just in case she could squeeze a little more work out of herself at night or early in the morning, and headed for home.

A little before 7:00, Nat rang her own doorbell and when no one answered, she let herself in with her key. She rushed to the refrigerator and smiled at the note Victor had attached under their four leaf clover magnet, "Giving Lulu a lift and Sheela a ride. Bringing supper from The Mandarin. Back by 7:30. luv." Twenty or thirty free minutes were a bonus. Nat decided to spend them listening to her voice mail. Since the recording on the answering machine had been replaced by the opening bars of Schubert's Unfinished Symphony and a beep, Nat felt the messages she received were warmer and fuller. The flashing indicator showed three messages and Nat pressed the play button.

"Hi. It's Annette," the first caller said. "Could you guys come over for dinner the 31st and help with giving out candy to the trick or treaters? We're all fine, but I'm going crazy and David won't go with me. Ha, Ha. Sorry about the lame joke. Oh, remember you were telling me that Lulu had a sister-in-law who might want to work as a nanny? Please ask Lulu about her. Call as soon as you can, because I need help and Rosario is fresh out of relatives. Bye."

The next message was from her mom: "Hello kids," it began. "This is Door. I was wondering whether you would consider spending Christmas, New Year week, and Sheela's birthday here in New York instead of coming for Thanksgiving. It would give us more time together and a chance to host Sheela's party. Give this some thought and let us know. Ciao."

176

The final message was the most newsworthy. "This is Cecily," it began. "This morning we found out we're pregnant. The baby isn't due until early June. Ronald is happy, but I'm confused. On the one hand, I love this baby so much it hurts, but on the other I'm not prepared to deal with it. I hope it's a girl, like Sheela. If it is, we've already picked out her name, Sylvia. We don't have any boys names lined up yet. Any suggestions? I haven't figured out my life yet, but we just closed *Apples and Oranges,* and I'm going to ask my agent if there is a part for a pregnant lady out there. Staying home would drive me nuts. Oh, and by the way, don't say anything to your parents. We're meeting for dinner Saturday and spending the night in the city. We're going to tell them then."

This news made Nat wish she were pregnant, too. There was no reason for her not to have conceived by now. Her doctor said that everything was fine. Nat quickly reprimanded herself for thinking selfishly instead of rejoicing whole-heartedly for her brother and sister-in-law. After all, she reminded herself, she had Sheela and Victor and they filled her life completely. It was 7:30, she noted, and they should be home any minute.

At 7:40, when her family still hadn't made it back, Natalya tried Victor's cell phone only to get a recording stating he was unavailable. At 7:48, the bell rang. Nat rushed to open the door, and her heart lifted when she heard Sheela call out, "Ma! Open!" As soon as she was inside she started to cry.
"What's the matter, sweetheart?" Nat asked.
"Ooo," Sheela sobbed.
"What happened?" Nat asked Victor.
"I have no idea," he replied.
The minute she witnessed her parents' concern, Sheela stopped crying. Instead she gleefully pointed to an almost invisible scrape on her knee and demanded a "kith."

Sheela's second Halloween was far better than her first, when she had been frightened to see herself changed into a clown. This year, October 31 came on a Thursday and there was a party at Infantasy. Thus Sheela understood that wearing special clothes was something you did for fun. Her costume was better too. Instead of being transformed into a clown, Sheela wore her own face and a long soft blue dress that enhanced her deep blue eyes. A tiara perched over her black curls indicated that she was meant to be a princess.

Sheela's friend, Angela, was a black cat with whiskers painted under her nose. She was dressed in black leotards and her brown hair was hidden under a cap with two protruding ears. A tail had been attached to her tights, but it came off when a zebra in striped pajamas pulled at it. Angela crawled around on her hands and knees saying "meow, meow" to everyone. Mike Hansen was a pirate. He had a patch over one eye and a cardboard sword covered with aluminum foil that he waved in the air. There was one outfit, however, that Sheela couldn't fathom. It belonged to Johnny Borden. Sheela recognized his hazel eyes, which peered out at her from two holes cut into a white sheet that covered him from head to toe. Johnny ran around making strange oooh, oooh-like noises that sounded as if he were wounded, and when he stood in front of the class, Ms. Meredith said he was a ghost. Sheela understood that Johnny was a goat. His costume didn't make sense to her because goats had ears and four legs and they said naaa, not oooh. However, Sheela didn't give this problem much thought as she was used to grown-ups not making sense.

At dusk, the Landaus took Sheela to see Gappa and Beca who confirmed that she made a beautiful, huggable princess. They thought her glittery nail polish and lipstick were appropriate for a princess and said that the chocolate milk that had dripped on her skirt and been sponged off by Nat could not be detected. They looked at the Halloween pictures from Infantasy, but only one showed Sheela clearly. In the others she either placed herself behind another child or had her hands covering her face. Victor surreptitiously got a couple of good shots of his daughter while Gappa or Nat distracted her. Afterwards, he and Sheela went trick or treating at several neighbors' houses in the immediate vicinity. Nat stayed behind to make a jack-o-lantern to take to the Singers.

Sheela had fun. She rang bells and when doors opened to greet her, she smiled regally and said, "tick o teak" before putting the candies into her sack. Their last stop was the Singers. After hugging Aunt Annette, Sheela went to check out Bobby's costume. He wasn't wearing any clothes except for a diaper with a leaf stuck on it.

"Why baby Bobby nakit?" Sheela asked.

"He's supposed to be Adam," Annette explained.

"Oh," Sheela said. Then, watching Aunt Annette change his diaper, Sheela pointed to Bobby's penis and solemnly announced, "Bobby boy. See?" At that moment Bobby validated Sheela's observation by showing off. He made a big effort to produce a forceful spray and succeeded in wetting the bodice of Sheela's princess gown. Instead of impressing or shocking Sheela, Bobby's accomplishment merely provoked her disdain.

"Oh, I'm so sorry," Annette apologized on behalf of her son. "Let me take off your dress and wash it out and clean you up. You can wear one of my tee shirts. Here, this one with the hearts is perfect. The neckline isn't too big because it has a button and it will look just like a nightgown. OK?"

"OK." Sheela shrugged her shoulders. She was tired of being a princess anyway. Then she explained the accident. "Baby Bobby teeny weenie pee pee wet."

That night Sheela dreamed she was a teacher and that all the boys in her class had jack-o-lantern heads. The girls were attached to large fairy wings that kept them afloat under sparkling halos. Sheela's name was Ms. Varian and Aa-Oo, her teddy bears, and the people in her family were all in a story she was reading to the class. She couldn't really recognize anyone specific, but collectively everyone was there. The story was a little confusing because suddenly the characters jumped out of the pages and became pieces in a musical puzzle. Then, as Sheela was about to wake up, Sweak came into her dream and rearranged the pieces into a picture of *The Little Engine That Could* filled with candies and other goodies. Sheela herself was in the picture, pushing the train over the mountain. As it chugged along, the little blue engine sounded like a clock saying "tickoteak, tickoteak, tickoteak" instead of "I think I can, I think I can, I think I can." But when it finally crossed the peak and slid down the other side, only one lonely child who looked exactly like Beca was waiting for it.

"Why did you change my dream?" Sheela asked Sweak, trying to stay asleep so she could preserve the fading vision of her grandmother as a little girl.

"It got stuck in the wrong place," Sweak replied.

"Well, now you woke me up and it doesn't make sense any more," Sheela complained.

"It does too," Sweak explained. "You just weren't watching the right channel. Besides, I didn't wake you up. Your *rem* stopped."

"I don't know what *rem* means," Sheela countered testily.

"Sure you do," Sweak said. "At least you used to. Your *rem* is your magic. It means remembering the rapid eye movements you make while you dream."

Victor didn't want to miss the holiday season in Houston and Natalya was eager to spend Thanksgiving at her parents' home as she had done most of her life. So they stuck with their original plan. Sheela loved Thanksgiving in New York followed by the thrill of Chanukah, the holiday spirit and the celebration of her birthday back home. She also accepted the let-down that followed on the heels of these events, when the very air around her seemed to have lost its tingle. The green lights that outlined all the skyscrapers Sheela could see from her living room window disappeared. On the eighth night of Chanukah, candles of hope were extinguished, not to be re-lit until next year. Christmas trees in her building lobby, in her Mama's office and throughout the city were denuded of their splendor and taken away to be burned or left to dry up and die. Pianos and carolers departed from banks, grocery stores, and public halls. Footsteps, which had been light and full of hope, became weighted with the burdens of their owners' lives.

The theme of Sheela's second birthday party was polka dots. Nat thought of it when she took her daughter shopping for her party outfit and Sheela chose a cream dress covered with tiny peach colored spots. Sheela was attracted to its crinoline underskirt because it crackled when she moved about. Once the polka dot idea was established, Nat decided to create a mood. She ordered orange cake with butter icing decorated with M&M's and found a party store which provided polka dotted balloons. Sheela's invitations said:

Sheela Landau invites you
to attend her second birthday party
on January First, 2003, at three o'clock p.m. at her residence.
The party will be polka dotted with fun and games.
We would love you to wear something polka dotted as well.
A scarf or tie will do.
Please do not be extravagant with gifts.
Something wearable would be most appreciated.
Polka dotted wrapping paper is enclosed for your convenience.

Regrets Only

Except for Cecily and Ronald and their unborn baby, just about everyone accepted her invitation, including the Khannas who flew in from Chicago. Veterans of last year's festivities said they wouldn't miss the occasion for anything and told the new invitees to expect something special. Ms. Meredith—who wouldn't be

Sheela's teacher anymore because Sheela was now too big for Infantasy—said she would be delighted to come. Moreover, she also agreed to put on the entertainment, a puppet show. It turned out her hobby was puppeteering.

The polka dots sparked the party. Everyone was interested in everyone else's polka dots. The plaque for 'the most creative use of polka dots,' went to Mrs. Hansen, Mike's mother. She looked magnificent in a sleek black skirt, a white blouse with black polka dots, and a turban with the same pattern in reverse. Others won scrolls acknowledging the biggest polka dots, the smallest polka dots, the most polka dots and even the least polka dots, so no one was let down.

"The extraordinary thing about Sheela's parties," Steve Jordan told Beca, adjusting his neon green ascot with purple polka dots, "is the interaction between children, parents and grandparents. Everyone here is comfortable being at a party with two year olds. It's not like the adults are bringing the children. They are participants and they're actually mingling with the kids as well as with each other and having a blast."

And he was right. From Bobby who observed the goings on with deep concentration to Dr. Henry Landau and Lulu who insisted on joining in the 'children's game' of musical chairs, everyone contributed to the fun. And this time, when the crowd finished singing Happy Birthday, Nat, blinking away a tear of happiness, reminded Sheela to make her secret wish before blowing out the candles.
"I membered," Sheela said.

Sheela's favorite gifts were those from her family and the tiny gold monkey pendant from Jaya Auntie and Sunil.
"The monkey's name is Hanuman," Jaya explained. "He is very brave and he fought demons in Sri Lanka." Door and Pappa gave her a pair of opera glasses that could be worn on a chain around her neck. Sheela peered through them and giggled because they made Harold's nose look big. Her parents gave her a gold and enamel ladybug pin that looked real. Cecily and Ronald sent her a shoulder bag filled with fun things including a small polka dotted heart with a key you could wind to play "If you're happy and you know it clap your hands," a lip gloss stick, and a little woolly lamb which said "baa" if you rubbed its head. From Beca and Gappa, Sheela received a medallion with photographs of themselves at the ages of three or four.

⸎⸎⸎

"We were little children too once upon a time," Beca told her.
"Ya," Sheela agreed. "Beca cute."

Two days after Sheela's birthday, Dora and Harold left, and the night after that they called to tell Natalya that Aunt Cecily had to stay in bed to try to stop her cousin from being born before it was big enough to stay alive. When Natalya took her daughter in her lap and quietly told her that "Aunt Cecily's baby was thinking about maybe not being born after all," she was non-plussed to see Sheela close her eyes and then open them again and nod before she said, "I know."

180

28

Sheela missed Infantasy. Kinderland, the bilingual play school in which she was enrolled for Monday, Wednesday, and Friday mornings wouldn't have an opening until March. Her parents believed Kinderland was worth waiting for and even Beca agreed. It was owned and run by the University's Department of Education and its teachers were graduate students specializing in preschool education. Ms. Meredith and Mr. Anthony had recommended Kinderland because Infantasy's program was geared to flow right into theirs.

Kinderland took children starting at the age of two if they were toilet trained, and Sheela was. She had been using pull up diapers for several months, but now she didn't even need those, except at night, just in case. Lulu told her about a little boy she took care of before Sheela who at three still wore diapers day and night. His mother was a child psychologist and she was against toilet training. "Apestaba," Lulu said holding her nose."

"What's his name?" Sheela asked.

"Se llama Peter."

"Peter mamá loca," Sheela concluded.

"Sí, la mamá de Peter es loca," Lulu agreed.

As an interim measure, Natalya took Sheela and Lulu to the office with her two or three times a week. Victor said nothing until one dreary Saturday morning when he exploded.

"Not only don't I get to see you, but when I come home during the day to see Sheela, she isn't here. Steve Jordan won't give up until he breaks us up!"

"The only thing that could break us up is your craziness," Nat yelled back. "What on earth has Steve done to make you this crazy?"

"That's what I'd like to know! What has he done to you? What does he do that I don't?"

"For one thing, he doesn't scream irrationally. I can't believe this. You're jealous, jealous of a gay person."

"An allegedly gay person," Victor yelled. Then, lowering his voice a notch to sound more reasonable, he added, "I can only address what I see and this is what I see: Item, you don't just work in your office; you camp out there, with Sheela, Lulu and the works; even your friends visit you there. Item, you come home so full of Power and Jordan's opinion of Power and everything else that goes on in that office, you have no interest in me or my work. Item, you're never tired and I have to ask myself what energizes you. I can't stay awake long enough to wait for you to come to bed. No wonder we can't have another baby. Now this is my question: How come you are so energized? What's in it for you? It can't be the money. You make half of what you made with Kaplan, McCall and Green."

"Will you calm down and listen to me, Victor?" Nat asked.

"What do you mean calm down? Who just accused me of being crazy? It sounded an awful lot like you."

"OK, I'm sorry about that but when you talk about 'breaking up' it tends to unbalance me," Nat said. "And what I mean by calm down is . . ."

"I don't want to know," Victor interrupted. "I am perfectly calm."

"Well, since you asked, I'm going to tell you. Your rhetorical questions are insulting. By 'calm down' I mean control yourself so that the veins in your forehead stop throbbing. So please take a deep breath and listen to me."

"Sorry, I don't feel like listening or discussing this further right now. Maybe later. I have work to do."

"It's unfair of you to raise an issue and then decide to drop it after making absurd accusations, but that is your style, isn't it?" Nat stomped out of the room, happy to have come up with a rhetorical question of her own.

After that argument Natalya decided to go into the office, although she had planned to work a little at home and then see if Victor wanted to join her when she took Sheela for a run in the new three-wheel stroller that was designed for joggers' kids. That would wait for another day. Nat showered and dressed and then asked Victor whether she should wake Sheela and take her along, or leave her with him.

"For God's sake!" Victor answered. "You want to wake up your daughter just so you can get to the office early on a Saturday? Leave her alone. You can trust me with her. I'm her father, remember?"

Natalya had the office all to herself. Steve would probably come in later. Nat reviewed her docket and updated her list of things to do. She prepared a note for John Bloom setting out several tasks for him, then she ate her heart out. Finally, she meditated in an attempt to dissipate her anxiousness and her hostility. At the end of twenty minutes, Nat felt better. She thought of dropping in on Annette to talk about what had happened and then she thought about going home to try to make up with Victor before his fury had a chance to fester. But in the end she decided to go to the gym.

Working out and in the sauna, Natalya had a serious heart to heart talk with herself. She acknowledged that while Victor was crazy to suspect something was going on between her and Steve, he was right about her having neglected him. Perhaps not all infidelity was sexual in nature. The truth of the matter was that Nat loved Steve's company. He challenged her intellectually and they had their work in common. The very fact that Steve was gay warmed their relationship. He was a man with particular sensitivity to a woman's way of thinking. He was soothing. Victor, on the other hand, was strong and charming, but he was also wrapped up in himself. He was needy and demanding, too. Then again he had always been that way. It was she who no longer strived to satisfy his needs and demands. For the first time in her life, she found her work empowering and challenging; for the first time in her life, she believed she could "make a difference." It was an absorbing, heady experience. Plus she had a child who always beat Victor in the race for her attention.

In effect, Nat didn't need Victor's strength like she used to and that unbalanced their relationship. Furthermore, the sexual cravings that had been so dominant in her life before Sheela was born had abated somewhat. While she still thought of having a second child, she had stopped caring too deeply about her failure to conceive. At the same time, there was no way that Natalya could envision her life without Victor. He still made her heart sing when they were both relaxed. She loved him with all her soul and she was frightened by his sudden and unexpected anger. His jealousy was childish and infuriating; however, it was symptomatic of a much more serious problem: his dissatisfaction with their marriage.

Nat recognized that she was at fault for failing to nurture her husband. When she pampered Victor, Nat herself blossomed in his appreciation. Being with her husband, focusing on him and sharing fun with him refreshed her and made her receptive to pleasure. Lately, her absorption in her career hadn't left time for that. Things would have to change.

During the drive back to her condominium, Natalya considered how she would go about recapturing what was slipping away. Suddenly she felt very tired and understood that nervousness and excitement had been fueling her for weeks. She realized that she had to take time to relax for her own sake as well as for Victor's. Then she pondered the more immediate question of how she should behave toward Victor today. Should she tell him she forgave his absurd outburst while reassuring him of her love? Should she be apologetic? Should she pretend their argument never happened? It depended, she decided, on how he acted.

When Nat got home, Victor and Sheela were playing dominoes on the floor. They were taking turns building towers. As Nat walked in, Sheela jumped up and came running to say, "Mama, wait!" Victor followed behind her.
"Hi," Nat said, assessing the atmosphere as she bent down to give her daughter a hug and kiss.
"Ma, Daddy not mad," Sheela volunteered. "Daddy upsept."
"That's right," Victor said "Daddy is not mad. Daddy is only upset."
"Ya," Sheela repeated. "Daddy is oney upsept."
"I'm sorry I upset Daddy," Natalya said. "I love him very much, and I am going to stay home more now and make him feel better."

Nat's resolution was easier made than carried out, but that afternoon she took a step in the right direction. She called Rebecca to ask if it were possible for Sheela to spend the night. It would be the first time she slept away from her parents, but she thought Sheela wouldn't mind and if a problem should arise, Nat or Victor could come right away and get her. Rebecca and Henry readily agreed and Natalya broached the subject to Sheela.
"How would you like to sleep at Beca and Gappa's house tonight?"
"Wif Aa-Oo and Bams and Rrr?" Sheela asked.
"Yes, with Aa-Oo and Brahms and Rrr," Nat conceded.
"An wif dominoes? "
"OK," Nat said.
"An wif Dolly?"

"No, Dolly has to stay home and watch your bed." Nat realized Sheela was on a roll that might get out of hand if not arrested.

"OK." Sheela knew she was pushing it and she really wanted to spend the night with her grandparents.

Next Nat called Annette and asked if she would mind terribly if she and Victor took a rain check and didn't meet them and their friends for dinner as planned.

"I need time alone to sort some things out with Victor," she explained.

"No problem," Annette said. "Bobby will miss being entertained by Sheela, but he'll survive."

With those arrangements out of the way, Natalya approached Victor.

"If it's OK with you, I'd like to go on a date with you this evening. Your parents are keeping Sheela for the night. They are all excited."

"What about the Singers? Aren't we supposed to meet them at Churrasco?"

"They gave us a rain check."

"So, what do you want to do?" Victor asked.

"I thought maybe we could go out for dinner alone somewhere expensive and elegant so I can wear that black dress I bought last month."

"I don't know if we can get a reservation at the last minute."

"I already checked. Cafe Annie's has an opening at 8:30," Nat replied. "You can always get a reservation at a pricey restaurant. It's the good, yet reasonable, places that are always booked."

"All right." Victor was less enthusiastic than Nat had hoped, but at least he didn't say no.

The evening was somewhat forced, especially at first. Victor had clearly done some serious thinking, too, after their morning's quarrel. But he was still uptight, and Nat was visibly trying too hard to enjoy herself. Both of them were excessively polite. Still, Natalya did look ravishing, and Victor was proud. Heads turned when they walked to their table. The dinner and wine were wonderful, and although Nat had her hand phone by her side, there were no calls from her in-laws. Victor deflected all talk about their relationship or Steve Jordan. Instead, he spoke of his work. Nat was amazed to learn that WOW Technologies was planning to endow a chair at his university and that her husband was certain to win it. What a funny title for Victor, "the WOW Professor of Business Communication!"

"Will that chair take you squarely out of the English Department?" Nat asked.

"No. That's the great thing. English and Business are sharing the endowment."

Victor also talked to Nat about wanting a bigger place.

"One of our problems," he said, "is that we have no space at home. Sheela's room doesn't work for us any more. That's why we both spend so much more time away at our offices. We have stopped doing our albums too. It's no fun because there's no way we can spread the photos out and leave them.

"Where were you thinking of moving?"

"Nowhere yet. I've been waiting for an opportunity to talk to you to see what you think."

"I love our condo," Nat said, "but I agree it's cramped."

"So do you have any ideas?" Victor asked.

"I guess the only logical place to go would be around your parents' house. It's close to everything and not too far from my office, but I don't think we can afford that yet."

"There are some really nice townhouses coming up right around the corner from us. Maybe you can talk to a realtor."

"I'll do that." The last thing in the world Nat wanted to deal with at this point in her life was moving. Still, Victor made sense and, since house hunting was clearly her department, she added, "I'll find out what we can get for our condo too."

"We have to count on sending Sheela to private schools," Victor said as an after-thought, "unless we move to the suburbs."

"God forbid!" After all, Nat had been raised in New York City.

"Yeah, God forbid." Victor's thing was being close to his students and the university libraries.

During dessert, Victor introduced another subject, one that sat much better with Nat than the prospect of leaving her beloved high-rise. He started off with a question. "Do you know how long it's been since we've had a vacation?"

"Well, we were in New York for Thanksgiving," Nat answered.

"That was a family affair. I mean a real vacation, just the two of us."

"I can hardly remember. I guess it was when I was pregnant and we went to the Silver Stream Inn, but that was just a weekend. And before that it was when we went to Hawaii for our third anniversary."

"That's right, Nat. Don't you think it's time for us to give ourselves another holiday?"

"I guess so. I didn't think we could get away, but now I suppose we could man-age if your parents would be willing to keep Sheela for a few days. Lulu could go over there and help out instead of coming here."

"What about your office?" Victor asked. "Can it survive without you for a week or so?"

"Of course." Natalya ignored the dig. "It would take a little planning, that's all. When can you get away?"

"Spring Break. That's the week of March 17."

"It sounds good. But where do you want to go?"

"I'd like to go on a cruise. Where would you go if it were up to you?" Victor asked.

"On a Caribbean cruise." Natalya's eyes began to sparkle. "Remember, in Hawaii we decided that was next thing we had to do."

"You mean that, don't you?" Victor asked. And then he answered his own ques-tion. "You still want to go to the Caribbean. You aren't just saying it because you think it's what I want to hear. I can tell."

That night, for the first time in quite awhile, Victor's desire to make love to his wife was more than perfunctory. He and Nat were eager to retrieve the romance that had evaded them in recent weeks, but they also felt shy. So, after returning from dinner, Victor put on some fifties' music and poured two cognacs into crys-tal glasses. For a while they sipped their drinks in silence, thinking of the night ahead. When the glasses were empty, Natalya took them into the kitchen and rinsed them out. Then she started walking toward their bedroom, but Victor stopped her. "Let's go to the entry hall instead," he said, and Nat nodded her assent.

In the morning, Natalya prepared a brunch she knew Victor would love. She made grilled cheese sandwiches on freshly baked baguettes covered with tomatoes and bacon, seasoned with a touch of red pepper and fresh dill. The sandwiches were accompanied by wild mushrooms cooked in sherry. A pot of steeped English breakfast tea and a raspberry cobbler topped the meal off. While they ate, Nat and Victor talked about the cruise they would take in March.

"Are there any islands you particularly care about seeing?" Victor asked.

"No," Nat answered. Then she said, "I take that back. Everyone says we can't miss the Virgin Islands, but I think almost all the cruises stop there anyway."

"And you are sure you wouldn't rather fly to Paris or London?"

"Yes, I'm sure. That would be fun some other time, but now I'd rather we just relaxed. There's too much to do and see in Europe."

29

During the weeks before the cruise, Natalya worked long hours to reduce the burden her absence would place on Steve and she worried about leaving Sheela. Victor continued to mistrust Steve Jordan. He recognized that his suspicions might be groundless, but that was as far as he went. Possibility was no certainty. His mistrust gave Nat second thoughts about her responsibility for her husband's jealousy. It also revived her anger at Victor's former entanglement with his grad assistant Linda. Now, three years later, Nat began to brood.

"No wonder he questions me," she thought. "If he's the kind of person who could become involved with another woman, he's bound to doubt me." So now, although Linda had moved on to the University of Chicago and a fiancé, a scar that Natalya didn't even know she had itched.

Sheela fretted at her parents' unrest and thought it was her fault. One evening while Nat was working at home and Victor was jogging, she asked, "Mama, am I good?"

Nat's answer, "Absolutely, sweetheart. You are a very good girl," gave Sheela more comfort than she imagined.

⁂

Tiffany Power Jackson and Randolph Jackson owned Power Industries, a company that manufactured high-pressure industrial steam cleaning equipment. At the time the Jacksons purchased the company, it produced a single model of propane gas cleaners and its aging owners barely eked out a living. Over several years, Tiffany and Randy improved the existing cleaner and added new models to the product line. They expanded and modernized their factory and began to bid for military contracts. Four days after they won their first large contract, they got a visit from the Department of Defense liaison officer in Houston.

"Congratulations," he told them. "I hope this award doesn't land you in bankruptcy."

It didn't. The Jacksons read their contract carefully and took its terms, however absurd, literally. They performed and made a substantial amount of money on their first and subsequent contracts for machinery built to government specifications.

However, one morning Power Industries' factory, housing one thousand partly built pressure washers for the U.S. Marine Corps, burned down. The units were to be shipped within three months. The Jacksons had already collected close to a million dollars in progress payments for them. Now if the machines could not be rebuilt and delivered on time, or an extension negotiated with the Marine Corps, they would have to repay those monies plus fines and penalties.

Tiffany and Randy rented a facility. They needed only a few extra weeks to rebuild the machines, but the Marine Corps was unwilling to grant an extension. And Americana, the Company's insurance carrier, refused to pay for the damage on the basis that they suspected the Jacksons of arson, notwithstanding the fact that the fire occurred on a Sunday while Tiffany and Randolph were at church.

Steve and Nat both met with Tiffany and Randy the first time they came in to talk about their problems. Steve's opinion was that the case would be too time consuming for their small firm, but Nat disagreed. Eventually she persuaded Steve to change his mind.

"I am confident you can eventually collect actual damages from Americana," Natalya explained the day Power signed on with the firm. "The problem is that current legislation permits insurance companies to withhold payment pending any inquiry. Therefore, unless we can show bad faith, they'll stall you forever. We'll have to prove that Americana's investigation is an unreasonable and deliberate pretext to avoid paying up. Can you think of anyone who would want your factory destroyed?"

"Not really," Tiffany said, "except for some disgruntled employee. But no one comes to mind."

"Well," Nat said, "you had no motive since you were doing well. The insurance company knows that. But they figure that if they hint around at implicating you in arson and scare you enough, you'll agree to a greatly reduced settlement. I guess our work is cut out for us. We'll tackle Americana. We'll also put some pressure on the Marines."

The Friday before Natalya and Victor took off, they planned to have Sabbath dinner at the senior Landaus and settle Sheela in. Friday afternoon, Nat packed Sheela's bag under her daughter's close supervision while Victor hovered in the background. He had already packed his suitcase, but Nat hadn't even begun to consider what to take. As a matter of fact, she still had several motions to draft and e-mail to the office and she was prepared to do with very little sleep that night. It made Victor nervous.

"Can't I help with something?" he asked.

"Please, relax," Nat answered. "Everything is under control."

"Have you got the list of phone numbers for Beca? Should I check it over?"

"No," Nat said. "I gave it to her a few days ago."

"I want Dolly." Sheela piped in.

"Dolly doesn't like being in a suitcase. We'll carry her, OK?" Nat asked.

"No K, No," Sheela answered, so Nat took out some clothes to carry instead. Sheela expressed her gratitude with a big squeeze.

⚬⚬⚬⚬⚬⚬⚬

Sheela's time with Beca and Gappa was a magical interlude during which life revolved solely around her. It was a lovely state of affairs, albeit one that would not work well on a permanent basis. She felt cozy. Beca posted her parents' itinerary as well as a schedule of when they would call on the refrigerator, and they always phoned when they were supposed to. "What are you doing?" one of them would ask.

"Noffing," Sheela answered, "I'm busy."

The second question was "Are you too busy to talk?"

"No. I love you," Sheela replied. Then it was her turn to ask, "Are you axing?"

"Yes, honey, we are relaxing," Victor answered. When her ma answered, she said, "Yes, sweetheart, we are relaxing, but we miss you."

Instead of good bye, Sheela went "Mmmvsh, Mmmvsh" because that was how you sent kisses far away.

Every evening Sheela called Door. Calling Door was important, Beca said, because the Rosenbaums were upset about "losing" Ronald and Cecily's baby who would have been her cousin. Sheela couldn't explain that babies didn't get lost. They surrendered their embodiment when their bodies didn't match their souls. Then they returned to the world of the pre-conceived and waited for another opportunity to become a life. When everything fit together, the right soul would find Ronald and Cecily. The only thing Sheela could say was, "I'm getting anover cousin soon."

The routine at the senior Landaus was pretty much the same as at home. Monday, Wednesday, and Fridays were Kinderland days. She went in the same van that picked her up from her condo.

"I'll see you in front of your grandma's house next Monday at 9:30 sharp," the driver had told her on Friday."

On Monday morning, Lulu came at 7:45, just like she always did. Lulu got Sheela dressed and, if it wasn't Tuesday or Thursday, she packed her backpack and placed it over Sheela's shoulders. Sheela always checked to be sure it contained an extra change of clothes, a bottle of water, and a snack for the juice break.

In the evenings Beca played songs on the piano and they both sang. Sometimes Gappa joined in, but only Beca and Sheela knew songs like 'Marsie Doats' and 'The Nickelodeon.' Playing dominoes with Beca was special too. Sheela started learning to count the dots and one time Beca built a house that was exactly like the one Sheela saw in her head. Then Sheela told Beca, "Make paper babies" and Beca knew exactly what to do. She cut out paper dolls and put them in the domino courtyard to play.

Sheela had no time to watch her micro discs because when they weren't singing or playing, her grandparents read to her. Sheela brought the Mother Goose book Beca had given her before she was born. Beca was quite upset when she saw that two of the pages were torn. She fixed them with scotch tape.

"You have to be more careful," Beca said. Her displeasure brought tears to Sheela's eyes.

"Don't cry," Beca told her. "It was a mistake, but you have to have respect for books. They represent one of the most beautiful parts of life—learning. OK?"

"OK." Sweak had scolded her for tearing the book too.

After that, Beca and Sheela read and looked at the pictures and acted out the jingles. One of Sheela's favorites was 'The King of France.' They recited in sing-song voices while she and Beca stomped up and down in the living room in rhythm to the words they repeated over and over again:

> The King of France
> With forty thousand men,
> Marched up the hill
> And then marched down again.

From the moment they stepped aboard the Silver Maiden, Victor and Natalya could tell their voyage would exceed their expectations. But Nat was exhausted and she disappointed Victor by sleeping and catnapping for the first couple of days when they were at sea. Victor read, exercised in the ship's gym, swam in the pool and wished Nat were out and about rather than dozing in her cabin or in her deck chair. After they touched their first port of call, the beautiful island of Antigua, Natalya perked up. Victor was ready for her companionship. There wasn't a lot to do in Antigua, but they roamed on the beaches, chatted with the friendly people and poked around the simple handicrafts.

Refreshed and at ease, Nat was looking forward to formal night that evening. She put on her white crepe sheath with spaghetti straps that dated from before she got pregnant with Sheela. Victor took in her suntan, her perfect make-up, her silver heels, and her pearl choker. He got a whiff of Gio and said, "I'm glad we have a table for two." The Landaus walked into the Silver Maiden's glittering dining room hand in hand. Nat saw admiring eyes looking in her direction and she felt vibrant and alive. Lately she had imagined that she was losing her glamour as well as her interest in sex, but now she realized that she had been mistaken.

Under the spells of the sparkling ambience and of her own sparkle, Natalya inhaled Victor's maleness, and felt her pulse quicken. Victor brushed against her before he pulled out her chair and he didn't miss the quiver her body gave when his electricity shot through it. Then he moved across the table and sat down facing his wife. His eloquent smile told Nat "tonight you will discover pleasure you never dreamed existed" and it told every man who glanced at her, "Eat your heart out; she belongs to me."

The remainder of the cruise was a blur of sun, sand, crystalline waters, excellent dining, and dancing—all preludes to making love. By the end the Landaus were sated, renewed, and eager to get back to Sheela and their lives.

The last night on board Nat packed their bags and put them outside the door for the stevedores before retiring. In the morning Victor discovered that his wife had not left out a pair of trousers for him to wear.

"I've told you over and over," he scolded, "that you shouldn't leave things until the last minute. What am I supposed to do now?"

"This has nothing to do with the last minute." Nat said. "I thought your slacks were hanging in the closet along with your green shirt and my dress."

"Why would you think that?"

"I guess I goofed," Nat replied.

Nat explained her situation to the Silver Maiden's office and listened to laughter coming through the receiver. Victor's suitcase was retrieved from the dock and returned to their cabin. The slacks were removed and the bags taken off the ship and cleared through customs a second time. Nat and Victor were the last passengers to go ashore. As he walked down the gangplank, red-faced, Victor had to grin at the crew's farewells:

"We're so pleased to see you're wearing pants. Have a safe trip home."

"So glad you have your trousers, Dr. Landau."

"It's good to know you're wearing the pants in the family after all."

30

The vibration of Nat's beeper scared her, interrupting the rhythm of the deposition she was taking.

"Could you please read back that last answer?" she asked the court reporter.

The long-winded response to her simple question was evasive and an appropriate follow-up failed to pop into Nat's mind even after she heard it again.

"Thank you. I need to take a ten-minute break. My beeper just went off and I'm concerned about my daughter."

Even before checking the number, Nat knew the call was from Kinderland. Sheela had awakened cranky and refused to eat her cereal. But she hadn't felt warm to the touch and when Nat suggested that she stay home with Lulu, she threw a tantrum.

"No, no, no! No, no, no-oo!" she cried in a cadence she had refined over time. "I hafta finich my pitcher, I hafta."

"Why don't I call Ms. Molly and tell her to save it carefully for later?" Nat suggested.

"No, no, no! No, no, no-oo!" Sheela shrieked again. "Later is summer. Kinderland is closed."

"Kinderland isn't closing for the summer until next week," Nat explained, wondering what she would do with Sheela between mid-June and mid-August.

"I hafta hafta finich today," Sheela said between sobs so Nat yielded.

"This is Nat Landau, Sheela's mother. You beeped," Nat told the unfamiliar voice that answered the phone saying "Kinderland, can I help you?"

"Just a moment please." The voice cut Nat off with a click. Its owner didn't hear her plead, "Please don't put me on hold." After two interminable minutes, Molly Goode came on the line and said, "Don't worry, but you have to come get Sheela because . . ."

"The words 'don't worry' scare me," Nat interrupted, unable to contain her anxiety. "Please tell me what's wrong with her."

"I was just going to," Molly patiently answered. "She has chills and is getting a fever. She quote 'feels like a porpupine' unquote."

"I don't understand," Nat said.

"She's got goose bumps and she's horripilating."

"Oh my God!" Nat said. "What's that?"

"Don't you know?" Molly asked with a soothing chuckle. "It means her hairs are standing on end. She's asking for you, but she's in good spirits."

"Oh. OK, I'll be there as fast as I can."

Six men waited impatiently for Nat to return to the conference room and resume her questioning: the deponent who was testifying on behalf of Americana, his counsel and co-counsel, a Marine Corps Captain in full uniform who had flown to Houston from Quantico, Virginia, to observe the proceedings, the Marine Corps attorney who expected to cross-examine the deponent, and Jeremy, her favorite court reporter. Except for Jeremy, the group was antagonistic. Perhaps they would profess to understand her personal emergency, but Nat knew they would debit her cutting the proceedings short to an unwritten account and gain concessions down the road. She braced herself and marched down the hall to make her excuses.

Several hours later Victor, Nat, Beca, and Henry stood in an uneasy cluster around Sheela who looked small and fragile in her parents' bed with Aa-Oo lying askew near her head. She had grown too big for her crib and slept in the day bed now, but in the middle of the night she would often crawl in with Victor and Nat. This night though, she wouldn't have to make the trek because she'd get to sleep "in the middle" all night. But she was too sick to appreciate the treat. Sheela's good spirits dampened when her fever rapidly climbed to 105 degrees, leaving her limp and weepy. Although baby Tylenol and a cold water rub had brought her temperature down to 102 and let her fall asleep, she was restless and mumbled unintelligibly. Even her parrot looked peculiarly forlorn.

"Her throat and tonsils are extremely inflamed," her grandfather said. "They must hurt a great deal. But it's certainly nothing serious. It doesn't appear to be strep throat, but we've taken a culture to make sure. In any case, she's on antibiotics. High fevers aren't at all unusual in little children."

"If it's nothing serious, why do you look so gray?" Victor asked.

"Because I feel helpless and I can't stand seeing Sheela like this." Dr. Henry Landau hunched his shoulders and covered his eyes with his palms.

"I think we should leave now," Rebecca said, "and let everyone rest."

Nat tried to move, but Sheela clung to her so she gently shook her husband's shoulder. Victor jumped up with alarm. "What's wrong?"

"Sheela feels hot and she was crying in her sleep. She won't let me get up."

"I'll bring the thermometer. What time is it?" He switched on the light on his side of their bed.

"It's 3:15."

"Here it is." Victor handed the thermometer to Nat and Nat placed it in Sheela's ear.

"Did you have a bad dream, Sheela?" Nat asked. "Why were you crying?"

"Cause," Sheela answered.

"Because you had a bad dream?" Nat persisted.

"No, cause no one came."

"It was just a dream and I'm here."

"No, before," Sheela explained. "And my froat and head hurt."

"There's medicine that will make you feel better, OK?"

"Bad medicine?"

"No, good medicine, and a little 7-up."

"Her temperature is 103. Can you bring some cold wet cloths for her tummy and her forehead and give her some more Tylenol? She isn't due for the antibiotic until six," Nat said to Victor.

"I'm not a hundred and free, I'm two and a half," Sheela thought. "Aa-Oo is a hundred and free."

Within a half-hour Sheela was snoring softly but neither Nat nor Victor could go back to sleep. "I guess Sheela's over the hump," Victor said.

"She looks peaceful enough now, but this has been an unsettling experience. I'm still rattled. But you know what?"

"What?" Victor asked.

"I walked out on a deposition which a Marine Corps captain from Quantico flew in to observe."

"Couldn't Steve have taken over for you?" Victor asked.

"No, he was in court. But anyway, I couldn't have filled him in quickly enough. From now on, I'm going to have a contingency plan in case something unexpected happens and one of us has to get to Sheela in a hurry. And next time I'm not letting Sheela go out if she isn't up to par, no matter how much she fusses. I should never have sent her to Kinderland yesterday."

"Sheela has handled herself like a trooper though, wouldn't you say?"

"She certainly has. She's a brave little thing. Do you know what she told Molly when her fever started to climb and she had the chills?"

"How could I know? No one told me," Victor answered.

"She said she felt like a porpupine."

"That's a terrific description. I'm pretty proud of Sheela. She's smart, she has a great handle on language, and she's spunky. I think you and I have done pretty well."

"You and I and God." As an afterthought, Nat said, "I bet you don't know what 'to horripilate' means."

"Of course I do. It means your hairs are standing on end."

During the hot summer months of 2003, Nat made trips to a fertility clinic and learned that she was fine, but that causeless secondary sterility was a fairly common phenomenon. Sheela's horoscope loomed in the back of her mind and dissuaded her from involving Victor in any tests and from pursuing extraordinary measures to become pregnant. Victor was happy with just Sheela, but she missed a little brown-eyed boy. She believed he belonged in her life, but by now doubted that she would ever have him. Still Nat refused to complain, even to herself, lest God think she wasn't grateful for the many wonderful things in her life and lest Sheela sense that she did not make her mother's happiness complete.

Between work and family commitments, Natalya house-hunted. She disliked her realtor who was considered the best in the business. The man, tall, white haired, handsome and soft-spoken was, in her opinion, an idiot who made Nat feel guilty every time she didn't like a home, which was all the time. Since he spoke little, Nat didn't zero in on his incompetence until after they had spent days looking. By then it would have been bad form to dump him for no reason that she could put her finger on.

"You seem to have trouble finding something within your price range," Paul Rutherford, *II* suggested.

"I don't quite agree with that assessment," Nat said. "The houses we're looking at are all appropriately priced and in acceptable locations, but they just aren't right."

"Perhaps you could give me additional parameters that would assist me in identifying properties that you might consider suitable," Paul said condescendingly.

"Perhaps," Natalya agreed. "I require a home where the master bedroom is not isolated from the remaining bedrooms. Also we need a large study and a kitchen with lots of storage space. We would like big windows and a small yard. Most importantly we require a home filled with good, happy vibes. I'd be thrilled if you could direct me to such a home without wasting any more of your time or mine. What do you think?"

"I'm sure that if we persist, you will find the perfect place," Paul said. Because he could see his commission being flushed down the toilet, he refrained from asking what "good, happy vibes" meant.

While Nat stressed, Victor worked enthusiastically on outlines for two new classes he would be teaching in the fall: The Evolution of Business English and The Business of Shakespeare. They were fun and promoted his conviction that success in communication was at the heart of success in business. The chance to incorporate such courses into the curriculum was one of the perks that came from the acclaim won by his second book.

By August, Victor became impatient with Nat's inability to find a single potentially acceptable house, so he decided to take a look for himself. For starters Nat gave him a list of her five "least undesirable" rejects and her realtor's phone number. When Victor called, Paul was pleased. Now that a man was taking over, he expected to emerge from the ordeal of coping with "the professor's wife" unscathed.

A few days later, Paul showed Victor all five of the homes he had asked to see. In Paul's words, they were respectively "elegant," "high-class," "dignified," "top-drawer," and "refined." Back in his office after the tour, Paul made his fingers into a pyramid and squinted his eyes just a tad as he prepared to speak.

"I suggest, Professor Landau, that you take the reins in this situation."

"Indeed," Victor remarked encouragingly.

"Consider," the broker continued, "one of the homes is already under contract and the others won't last long. This is a seller's market. I'm sure you can make a decision and manage Mrs. Landau. I don't want to be critical, but she is rather flighty."

"You're right, Mr. Rutherford," Victor answered watching Paul swell like a turkey. "I can make a decision and I can manage Mrs. Landau. As a matter of fact, I am making my decision right now. Neither of us likes any of the houses you showed us and neither of us wishes to deal with you any further."

"So," Nat asked her husband later that evening. "What do you think?"

"I think the houses are all awful. I also think you are a saint to have put up with that moronic broker as long as you did. I told him not to darken our doorstep again."

"You did?" Nat asked incredulously.

"Yup," Victor answered.

"Wow!"

"Uh huh. The WOW professor has wowed his wife."

"So, where do we go from here?"

"I think we have to consider a fixer-upper or else build."

"Oh God," Nat said. "I don't think I could stand that."

Rebecca, who was free over the summer, took up the slack when Kinderland closed. On Tuesday and Thursday mornings, assisted by Lulu, Beca ran a kind of informal playgroup. Three or four neighboring children and Lulu's four year-old nephew Hector romped on her covered porch or in the shaded yard where they splashed around with buckets of water.

On other occasions, Beca dropped Sheela and Lulu off at Nat's office or took Sheela for outings. Sheela's favorite visit was to the Butterfly Center in the Science Museum where brilliantly colored butterflies flew freely in a miniature tropical rain forest within a glass enclosure. Alone at home, Beca and Sheela sang the age-old songs that were born anew as each English speaking generation entered child-hood. Sometimes Beca taught Sheela verses that she had learned from her own mother which were not in today's' 'toddlers' repertoires or Sheela, in turn, taught Beca ditties that hadn't been around when she or Victor were young. But Sheela's favorites were the silly duets Beca made up on the spur of the moment:

> Bi g, not small, tra-la-la,
> Short, not tall, ha-ha- ha.
> High, not low, ho-ho-ho,
> Fast and slow, go, go, go!
>
> Tra-la, ha-ha.
> Ho-ho, go-go.
> Go, go, go, go!

One afternoon, after Sheela yelled "Go, go, go, go!" for the umpteenth time, Beca finally said, "That's enough. We have to stop now."

"No, no, no, no!" Sheela replied.

"Why?" Beca asked.

"Cause," Sheela replied, and merrily repeated, "No, no, no, no!"

That event inspired Beca to come up with "whisper time." During "whisper time" Sheela was allowed to play quietly with her dominoes, to read, to work on puzzles or to color under Beca or Lulu's supervision. She could speak in whispers if she had something important to say or a secret to share. She could watch her reflection or her shadow coming and going. Soft instrumental music was allowed but television and micro discs were not. In short, everything was permitted except sounds made by vocal chords. Sheela enjoyed the enforced periods of quiet which gave her a chance to live in her own imagination as much as the grown-ups around her enjoyed the resulting calm. The only problem with "whisper time" was that Sheela insisted it only applied at Beca's house.

Dora came to Houston at the end of July. She wanted ten days of quality time with *her* granddaughter. Beca was ready for a break and she happily suspended her playgroup and surrendered Sheela to experiences that were new and exciting. Door took Sheela to tea and out for sushi. She took her ice skating at the Galleria. They went shopping and bought several outfits each, as well as an enormous clay kit with which the two of them constructed a menagerie of dinosaurs. One afternoon they went to Computers Are Toys and bought Sheela her first computer and several CD-ROM game disks. Another afternoon Dora made Nat play hooky and the three of them went to see the new cartoon version of *Red Shoes*. Over the weekend Sheela, Nat, Victor and Dora all went to Galveston where they saw the French Mime Circus and frolicked on the beach. But as much as Dora tried to persuade Sheela to play in the waves, she couldn't. The child insisted on remaining where the sand was dry.

Sheela's love for her two very different grandmothers was quantitatively equal, but qualitatively very different. Beca was molded to her soul; her universe was familiar and comfortable, even if it was sometimes a little sad. Dora, on the other hand, turned Sheela's life into one big adventure. But Dora's world could be scary because it had yet to be conquered. Sheela described her feelings for Beca and Door to Aa-Oo: "Beca is from before and Door is from after."

On the last Friday of Dora's visit, she and Sheela both helped Beca prepare Sabbath dinner. At sundown Victor and Nat came over. Dora had a far more interesting and happy time with her "in-laws" than she expected to. It was a lovely conclusion to a wonderful trip.

Three days before Kinderland re-opened for the fall, Sheela and her father heard a knock on their door. They were rustling up supper because Nat was working late. Victor went to open up, wondering why security hadn't phoned ahead to announce a visitor.

"Who is it?" he asked, looking through the peephole at a mop of red hair.

"We're your new neighbors. I'm . . ." a soft low-pitched voice started to answer as Victor opened the door.

"Oh, *my*!" Victor said to the anxious face under the dark red hair and to the two miniature versions of the same face that were standing on either side of the slinky young woman.

"I'm Naomi and these are my twin daughters, Lillian and Gillian. I call them Lil and Gil."

<h1 style="text-align:center">31</h1>

Ronald and Cecily's son, Alexander Roth Rosenberg, was born a week past his due date on July 5, 2004 in the afternoon. Sheela was right outside the birthing room with Door, Pappa, and Aa-Oo waiting for him to be born. Cecily's Mama, Evelyn Roth, was there too, but her Dad, Joseph Roth, couldn't come because he was dead. Aunt Cecily said that she often felt that Joseph's spirit was "alive and kicking" inside Alex's body while Alex was inside hers. Ronald disapproved of that kind of talk because it wasn't respectful.

"Nonsense," Aunt Cecily told him. "Who is to say where my Dad's spirit is?"

As soon as the doctor came out to get the family, everyone rushed to greet the newcomer and to congratulate the parents. Ronald was fine; he didn't faint like Victor did when Sheela was born. Instead he looked proud and said, "I'll be darned. He looks like a miniature Joe Roth."

"That's because my late husband had a pudgy baby face," Evelyn remarked. "Actually Alex has Cecie's eyes and your chin."

"I fink," Sheela said, "he looks like himself."

Sheela had been in New York since mid-June when Kinderland closed for the summer. At first her parents didn't want her to go, but she went on and on about how "Door promised."

"When did your grandmother make a promise like that?" Nat asked her.

"When she didn't come in my birfday, member?" Sheela said.

Indeed, Nat and Victor had decided to celebrate New Year and Sheela's third birthday privately. There was simply no energy for a party, so they planned an outing to Silver Stream and invited family and Sheela's special friends for an "after birthday supper" the following weekend. That was when Dora and Harold had told Sheela that they couldn't come but hoped to have a special surprise for her in the summer.

"Where is the surprise coming?" Sheela had asked.

"To New York and we want you to come too."

"I wish," Victor said, "Dora wouldn't make arrangements pertaining to you without checking with us first. There's no way you can go to New York."

"Why?" Sheela asked. "Why? Why?"

"Because this isn't a good time for me or Mommy to fly off to New York with you."

"No, no, no-oo," Sheela said. "Door didn't say you and Mama. I hafta go because Alex is being born. I hafta show him stuff."

"Well, how will you get there by yourself?" Natalya asked.

"Wif a tickit like Lil and Gil. Like a company mine," Sheela explained.

"What?" Victor asked.

"A company mine," Sheela repeated. "When Lil and Gil go to see their Daddy in LA, they go a company mine wif a tickit on their neck."

"Oh, I see!" Nat exclaimed, "An unaccompanied minor."

"Yea, a company mine," Sheela said, brightening. Seconds later the smile which was about to form on her face, reversed course.

"Now what's the matter?" Victor asked.

"If I go a company mine will you and Mama cry? Lil and Gil's mama cries."

"No. We won't cry. We'll be fine. We'll miss you this much," Nat stretched her arms, "but we'll take some down time."

"Time isn't up and down," Sheela said. "It's all around."

"That's true," Victor acknowledged. "Time is all around, but we call resting down time."

"Oh," Sheela said, and rushed to the phone.

"What are you doing? You know you aren't allowed to call New York without asking if its OK."

"I know," Sheela said smiling again. "I'm calling Lil and Gil. Now I can be a company mine just like her and her."

"You should never have programmed that phone," Victor complained.

"It wouldn't make any difference," Natalya replied. "Sheela has known her numbers for some time now."

Murphy's Law thwarted Natalya's hopes for taking things a little easy during her daughter's absence. Just two days after Sheela left, Steve Jordan flew to Hawaii because his father got himself in a pickle. As a result, Nat was stuck with a double workload for the better part of two weeks, just when she was trying to get her ducks lined up for the Power trial. Eventually Nat learned that Fred, the elder Mr. Jordan, had invited a much younger lady to share a romantic getaway with him on the Big Island. There, the mismatched couple took a hike into the crater of a volcano where Steve's dad stumbled on some rocks and fractured his ankle. He had to be evacuated by helicopter to a hospital in Honolulu. Meanwhile, his companion decided to take a hike of her own, with the contents of Fred's wallet. As a farewell courtesy, she left him a note. She wrote:

Dear Freddie,

I am sorry I couldn t wait for your ankle to get better. The thing is, even if it becomes as good as new, what good will it do?

You said you felt like a kid again around me, but I didn t feel anything, even though you secretly popped Viagra pills, which was no secret as far as I was concerned.

I borrowed your credit card and a few hundred dollars and I took your ticket which I cashed in, because when I get back home I don t think my boy friend will want me any more. I figured you wouldn t want me to be destitute after all the favors I did for you and your popsicle including getting down on my knees which I have never stooped to do for any other gentleman.

Yours truly,
Poopsie

PS. My real name isn t Juliet Marlow, so don t bother to try to find me.

When Steve called Nat from Honolulu he asked her to be discreet. "I thought about not e-mailing that note," he said, "but then I figured I owed you, since I left you high and dry."

"Well," Nat said. "This does explain the problem. It would be hilarious if it hadn't created such a mess. At first I thought the volcano had started to erupt or something. Anyway thanks. I appreciate it. Is it OK if I show the letter to Victor?"

"Sure. He's probably furious at me for dumping everything on you. It might help."

As Nat tried to dig herself out from under the avalanche of work in her office, even skipping a Sunday brunch, she thought that Sheela's being away didn't make things any easier. Tension over her inability to find a new home was escalating. Victor couldn't take the clutter that had accumulated as Sheela grew. It made him crazy and far more ready to compromise than Nat was. He did his best to be patient and understanding, but, as he saw it, Nat was "totally unrealistic."

"Either look for a house further out, or make up your mind to bite the bullet and settle for remodeling or, even better, building around here."

"That would be a disaster waiting to happen," Nat argued. "I read that eight percent of all divorces arise from building or remodeling. Look, we've been through this a hundred times. Nothing we've seen sits right and I have a feeling that the perfect place will come up if we just wait a little longer. I have several agents combing the multi-list."

"Frequently the best properties aren't on multi-list. Someone has to drive around and look for 'for sale' signs," Victor commented.

"I've done that too, off and on but there aren't enough hours in the day. Why don't you see if you have any luck?"

"OK. I'll drive around inside the loop and I'll tell my parents. But if we don't find something by the end of the year, I want your commitment that we'll build or remodel. All right?"

"I guess," Nat said.

Naomi Gleason was another issue. Nat didn't dislike her, nor was she jealous. What annoyed her was the woman's neediness. Naomi was a divorcée with a haunted look enhanced by artfully applied eye shadow. She worked as a surgical nurse in Houston's main medical center and had few interests outside of herself and the operating theater. Since she talked about both subjects non-stop, Naomi lacked friends and had to hunt for companionship. Using her adorable daughters as bait, she found the Landaus easy prey. It seemed that whenever Victor and Nat sat down to read, or work, or spend a few moments with Sheela, or simply chat over a glass of wine, Naomi dropped in to ask a question, or sent Lil and Gil to see if they could stay while their Mommy went to the store, or ran down to borrow a cup of something, or phoned for directions to somewhere. "I know you're there," she said one evening, "and screening calls, but I'm sure you don't mind little me. Please pick up for just a sec. I'm having trouble finding Albans Street on the key map and the twins want to visit a friend there."

"In my opinion," Annette Singer told Natalya, "what really bugs you about Naomi is that fact that Victor isn't bugged."

"That's true. But whenever Naomi shows up, he walks out of the room and leaves me to deal with her. But she's not that bad, so why am I so bothered?"

"Because she spoils moments and moods and like I said you resent the fact that Victor doesn't resent her. It's no fun feeling antagonistic toward someone all by yourself. If Victor felt like you do, the two of you would put an end to Naomi's nonsense."

"I don't feel antagonistic toward Naomi."

"Sure you do. She uses people and plays on their sympathy and sense of guilt. She wants you to feel responsible for her loneliness. Naomi is the sort of person to whom you have to say, 'If you have nothing to do, don't do it here.'"

"I can't really say that to her," Nat explained. "I have to get along with her because of the twins. They're a big part of Sheela's life."

"So, what are you going to do?" Annette crunched on a carrot.

"I don't know," Nat stretched her arms. "Right now all I can think of is chocolate mousse pie. Will you split a piece with me?"

"No way. I worked too hard to get my figure back and if I start on chocolate I can't stop."

"That's another irritating point about Naomi. She eats like a pig and is skinny as a rail."

Sheela hovered over Alex, mothering him, chattering to him, and filling him with her love. The Rosenbaums and Evelyn Roth expected her to be affectionate, but Sheela's effusive attentions exceeded anything they could anticipate or understand. They didn't appreciate the extent to which Sheela was enchanted by the wholeness of Alex's spirit, by the energy emanating from his mind, and by the minuteness of his body. How could they know that when Cecily let Sheela hold him in her lap, she saw in his soul reflections of worlds beyond life? How could they understand that those reflections revived Sheela's fading memories of events preceding her own birth? How could they imagine that Alex brightened Sheela's inner vision of the universe she had left behind when she herself chose to become embodied?

"Aa-Oo and me are all set," Sheela told Dora when she saw that Alex and Cecily were ready to leave the hospital. "I don't need my soupcase."

"Of course not sweetheart," Dora explained. "You're coming home with Pappa and me."

"I can't, I can't," Sheela insisted. "I hafta go with Alex."

"I'm afraid that won't be possible," Door said. "Cecily is too tired to take care of both you and the baby."

"But you said I'm a big girl. You said I help," Sheela argued. "I'm free and a half."

"Of course you are a big girl compared to Alex and you are a big help, but you still need to be looked after. Anyhow, this isn't my decision. Why don't we ask Cecily?"

"Aa-Oo and me hafta come, we hafta," Sheela plead. "We hafta to tell Alex secrets. And he has to tell us about before he was born."

"You could talk to him before we go and then come visit." Cecily suggested.

"And you can stay overnight when Alex has his bris."

"No, no, no-oo! I hafta bond."

"What do you mean?" Cecily asked.

"Ma said if I come to New York I could bond so Alex members me."

"I don't know. Uncle Ronald has to go back to work and Alex and I will sleep a lot. You'll be all alone."

"You said Ma Roff is coming. I can talk to Ma Roff when you sleep."

"What if she sleeps too and you are wide awake?"

"I can watch Alex sleep and I can talk to Aa-Oo and read my books and do pujjles."

"I really don't know. Now, tell me again," Cecily said, "How old are you?"

"Free and a half," Sheela solemnly said.

"That doesn't sound right. You have to say 'three and a half.' Stick your tongue between your teeth like this," Cecily demonstrated. "Then say 'three.'"

"Thh . . . ree?" Sheela asked.

"That's right. Now what you have to do is ask my mother. You should say, 'Ma Roth (with your tongue stuck between your teeth), I'm three and a half and I want to come to help you take care of Alex. May I?' And you have to promise not to cry or make a fuss if she says no."

"Will Ma Roff, no, Ma Roth, say yes? Will she? Will she? Will she?"

"I can't be sure. So can you promise to be good if she says no?"

"No, no, no-oo. I can't." Sheela shook her head from side to side. "Cause if she says 'no' my eyes would cry."

"That's a problem. We can't have you making a scene in the hospital."

"Even if my eyes cry, I won't scream." Sheela was desperate.

"Do you promise?" Cecily thought her niece was quite a negotiator.

"Promise what?" Strategies swirled in her brain.

"Promise me that if Ma Roth says no, then, even if your eyes cry, they will cry quietly and you won't make a fuss. Can you do that?"

"But if I say 'Ma Roth please, please, say yes,' I fink she could say yes."

"Say think," Cecily suggested.

"I think she could say yes."

"I think so too," Cecily agreed.

<hr>

Alexander's room adjoined Cecily and Ronald's and it was decorated like outer space. There were stars and planets that glowed at night on the ceiling and a child's bed that looked like a spaceship stood in the middle of the floor. Since Alex was still too tiny for his bed, he slept in a basket in his parents' room with Robo. Sheela slept in his spaceship with Aa-Oo.

Robo was Sheela's birth gift to her cousin. She and her mother found him in FAO Schwarz standing with a group of make believe aliens. Sheela picked him out because Robo was the only real alien there. His three eyes flashed when she looked into them and, unlike make believe aliens, he got warm when she held him. When you rubbed Robo's head, his stomach said, "I am power. I am peace."

The last night Sheela slept in the spaceship, Sweak fell out of a star and got in bed with her. He told Sheela and Aa-Oo that Robo came from the planet of Diamon in the galaxy of Brillian.

"How do you know?" Sheela inquired.

"Simple. I asked," Sweak replied. "Robo told me that everyone in Diamon has three eyes. One is for seeing light, one is for seeing darkness, and the third is for seeing truth. And Robo's whole name is Robo Obor Draziw. In Diamon, everyone's first and middle name is Robo Obor.

"Cool," Sheela remarked.

"Cool," Aa-Oo parroted, because he was, after all, a parrot.

"Do you suppose," Sheela asked Aa-Oo and Sweak in a whisper, "that Robo Obor Draziw would take Alex and us to Diamon?"

"We don't know," Sweak replied, "but there is a way to find out."

"What's the way?" Sheela asked.

"Simple," Aa-Oo replied.

"Oh, I get it," Sheela said. "Ask."

Sheela and her friends snuck out of the spaceship and into Cecily and Ronald's room. Cautiously, they approached the basket where Alexander and Robo lay, peering at the darkness. "Robo," she whispered, "Can you take us to see Diamon?"

"You take oath. I take you." The alien lowered the volume of the transmitter in his navel so as not to wake Cecily and Ronald, asleep in their big bed.

"What oath?" Alex asked. He couldn't use words, but everyone understood the question.

"Secrecy oath," Robo answered.

"All right," Sheela said in hushed tones. She placed her right hand over her heart and promised, "I will never tell anyone about Diamon, ever." Next Alex repeated the words in his mind while Sheela placed his hand on his heart for him. Finally Sweak and Aa-Oo together said, "We will never tell anyone about Diamon, ever." Sweak stretched his right arm up to his heart and Aa-Oo touched his heart with his beak.

"Secrecy oath accepted," Robo announced.

Even as Robo spoke, a purple beam emerged from his head. It bathed the group in an ephemeral light.

"What's happening?" Sweak asked.

"Travel in time," Robo answered. "Spirits leave bodies."

In an eon's moment the time travelers found themselves standing on a field of clay. Clusters of craters were visible far in the distance. The only sounds they could hear were the sounds of their own voices. The only stimuli they could sense were waves of harmony that felt like nothing and everything at the same time.

"Where are the others?" Sheela inquired of Robo.

"No people here," Robo replied. "All Robo Obors."

"I know that. I meant other Robo Obors."

"Inside third eye," Robo Obor Draziw answered.

"What are those craters over there." Aa-Oo asked.

"Robo Obor houses," Sweak said.

"Are they really?" Sheela asked.

"Big ones temples. Little ones houses," Robo replied.

It was still dark in New York when Sheela's essence reentered her body. After making sure that Alex and Robo Obor Draziw were safe in their basket, Sheela picked Aa-Oo up from the floor and hurried back to bed. Sweak darted off without saying a word.

"You know what?" Sheela asked Aa-Oo.

"No," Aa-Oo said.

"'Do you wanna know?" Sheela continued.

"Yes," Aa-Oo replied.

"Well, ask."

"What?" Aa-Oo asked.

"I looked inside myself and I saw all the Robo Obors."

"Where were they?"

"Everywhere," Sheela said. "They were outside on the clay, and inside the craters and up in the sky. And they talked to me. One of them who was real cute reminded me of someone I used to know. He called me Robo Obor Aleesh. It was weird. I told him I wasn't a Robo Obor. Then he said that he wasn't one either. He said he was a visitor just like me but that while we were on Diamon, we were Robo Obors like everyone else there."

"Did you find out his name?"

"Yes. I asked and he said Robo Obor Liera."

32

"Señora, Nat," Lulu said, several weeks after Sheela returned from New York, "I think Sheela changed over the summer, no?"

"Yes, I think so too, Lulu," Natalya replied. "She has grown up a lot."

"She changed too. She is different."

"What do you mean, different?"

"I don't know how to say it. She is more herself. She is not so many questions and too many answers."

Later that evening, Nat repeated the conversation she had with Lulu to Victor, but Victor was disinterested. His mind was on something else. After mumbling something to Nat, he plunged right in.

"Today I saw a for sale sign on a house that looks like it has possibilities, at least from the outside. Here's the phone number." He handed Nat a napkin with the number scribbled on it.

"Where is the house?"

"On Sunset Boulevard."

"That's a pretty ritzy street. I bet the price is ritzy too. What if we can't sell this place for a decent amount?"

"Let's cross that bridge when we come to it," Victor said.

"I disagree. I think we need a strategy so we know what we're doing."

"Look, Natalya," Victor said, reining in his own agitation in an effort to dissipate her resistance, "we already know what we're doing. Just give the owner a call and look at the house. OK?"

"Don't talk down to me," Nat answered. "*We* don't have a strategy. *We* don't know what we're doing. If you do, I would expect you to have the courtesy of sharing your knowledge with me."

"This is a diversion. You fully understand our finances. You know that I've been doing pretty well, even if your earnings are iffy. And we already discussed renting this place if we have trouble selling. So far we don't even know what the price of the Sunset house is or if it would work. Just make an appointment to look at it and find out the asking price. Then we'll sit down and talk."

"I get it!" Although Nat tried to keep her voice low, it became high pitched. "Now that you are making more money than I am, you decided you can push me around."

"Don't raise your voice," Victor responded.

"Don't accuse me of shouting, because I'm not."

"True, you aren't shouting but you are speaking at twice your normal speed and in a very unpleasant tone. In any event, this isn't about money. It's about our moving to a place than can contain our life in an orderly fashion. It isn't my fault that I'm doing well and you aren't. You chose to work with Steve Jordan."

"If this is really only about finding a house, why are you bringing up Steve? What has he got to do with anything?"

"Nothing except that he dominates your life. However, please make time to look at the house and find out the price before the weekend. OK?"

"Fine," Nat answered in a huff, "I never said I wouldn't."

Sheela missed Sweak who never appeared to her after Alex was born. She figured he had stayed behind in New York. Aa-Oo agreed.

"That has to be what happened," he said.

"Is Sweak taking care of Alex now?" Sheela asked.

"I think so," Aa-Oo replied. "We can't ask, right?"

"Right. Alex wouldn't tell. Sweak should have said good-bye."

"How could he," Aa-Oo asked, "when he never said hello?"

A few days later a new being came into Sheela's life. The first time Sheela saw her was after the twins told her they were moving to Nebraska. Sheela started to cry and then she went to find her reflection in the hallway mirror. She wiped her eyes and thought about what to do. Instead of wiping its eyes, too, her reflection smiled. Then slowly and gingerly it stepped out from its two-dimensional prison, creating a flurry of airwaves that made Sheela feel as if a cloud was embracing her.

"My name is Leela," the image whispered. "Sweak sent me."

"Hi," Sheela whispered back to Leela. "Are you my dentical twin?"

"No," Leela replied. "I'm your clone."

"That's the same thing," Sheela argued silently. "You look zactly like me and Lil and Gil look zactly like each other. They are dentical twins and they are both going to be four on Halloween, except Gil is ten minutes older and they are moving to Nebraska. I'm going to be four on New Year. How old are you?"

"I have to go—your mama is coming," Leela answered and disappeared back into the mirror.

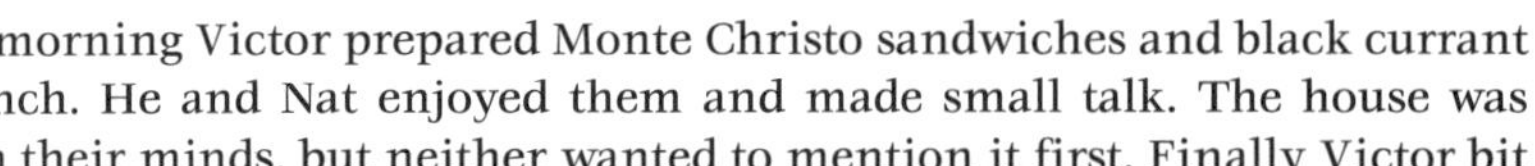

Sunday morning Victor prepared Monte Christo sandwiches and black currant tea for brunch. He and Nat enjoyed them and made small talk. The house was foremost on their minds, but neither wanted to mention it first. Finally Victor bit the bullet.

"Did you get a chance to check on the house yet?" he asked.

"Yes," Nat replied. "I said I would and I did."

"Help me out here. What did you think of it and how much are they asking?"

"I didn't like it, but I didn't hate it either. The asking price is $460,000 and it's in pretty bad shape. Of course the location is great."

"That's a start," Victor encouraged. "Let's talk about what you didn't like and about what it would take to fix it up, OK?"

"Fair enough. It has a good floor plan. The kitchen has new appliances. The bathrooms and the floors need re-doing and the house has settled. That's par for the course in Houston. It can be jacked up."

"Go on," Victor said.

"What else should I say? I think you should see the place. Considering the condition it's in, I don't think it's worth the asking price."

"Let's make an appointment and see it together." Victor suggested.

"No, I'd rather you checked it out on your own. Then we can talk some more. Let's do something agreeable now."

"We can't. Sheela could trot in any minute. You know she rarely naps any more and today she slept in."

"That's not what I was thinking of."

"A pity. So what were you thinking of?" Victor asked.

"The photographs. Sheela may want to help if Naomi doesn't park Lil and Gil here after church."

"Don't answer the door," Victor proposed. "No one else comes unannounced."

"I hate doing stuff like that. It's sneaky and Naomi will know. Besides, they are leaving in a few weeks."

"If she knows, it isn't sneaky, and a few weeks is a long time."

"What if Sheela runs to the door and starts shouting?" Nat asked.

"Then you can explain that you were busy. Or you could say we were naked and making passionate love hanging from the chandelier."

"Sometimes, Professor Landau," Natalya said putting her arms around her husband and rubbing herself against him "you surprise me."

"Mama, Daddy, come! Hurry!" Sheela shouted breathlessly from outside the bedroom.

"Coming honey," they both replied. They knew from experience that Sheela was about to share something she saw on the disc with them.

"Watch!" she said. "See Kaeeisha?"

"Yes," Nat and Victor answered in unison.

"She's looking at herself in a mirror, and she is going to melt inside it. I want to try that."

"I don't think you can," Natalya replied. "Remember this is a fairy tale. It isn't real. If you try, you'll break the mirror and hurt your head."

"No, not that way. I have to find another time byte like Kaeeisha. She never touched the mirror. Can I try if I find another time byte?"

"I don't know. What do you think, Victor?"

"You can try when you are asleep. But only if you promise not to touch the mirror while you are trying. OK?"

"I promise. But Daddy?"

"What?"

"You know Varkin?"

"Let's see?" Victor was in a mood to tease. "Isn't that the story about the little boy that fell into a lake because he loved himself?"

"No, Daddy! That's Narcissus."

"Oh, right. Varkin went to the top of a mountain and became a snowflake."

"Yea," Sheela answered, adding, "I know how come he didn't fall in the river like Narcissus. Wanna know how come?"

"Absolutely," Victor replied.

"Because he never fell in. God poured the river into him and then he fell out," Sheela said. Then she asked, with a worried expression on her face, "But Daddy, is loving yourself like Narcissus bad?"

"No, it's good to love yourself, but you have to love other people too. Narcissus fell in the water because the nymphs loved him and he didn't love them back."

"Oh. But then he came alive again as a flower, right?"

"Right!" Victor was relieved to see twinkles back in his daughter's eyes.

The rest of Sunday was mellow. Naomi never did appear. Nat wanted to organize pictures of Sheela, but Sheela refused. Instead she studied the photographs of Beca and Gappa. Sheela learned Beca was born in Chicago but grew up in Houston and that Gappa was from New Orleans. He came to Houston to go to medical school and that's when he met Beca. Then Sheela wanted to see pictures of Nat and Victor when they were children. Eventually Victor said the three of them needed to get out and get some exercise. Just as Nat was putting on her jogging shoes, it started to pour. Nat was pleased. She and Sheela stayed home and played on Sheela's computer and Victor went to the new gym their building had just put in on the second floor. Later they went out for supper to a South Indian vegetarian restaurant. After returning home, Sheela read *The Country of Thirty Six Thousand Wishes* with Victor and went to bed early. Natalya and Victor took a shower together and retired too, but not to sleep.

⸺ ❦ ⸺

Monday morning Nat was ten minutes late for her meeting with the Jacksons. She ached and had a strawberry mark hidden under her neckerchief. But as always, the moment she stepped into her office, her attention directed itself completely to the business at hand.

"Here's where we are," she began. "Americana Insurance has admitted you are not suspected of malfeasance with respect to the fire; however, it has evidence of arson and is continuing its investigation. It's using this situation to stall. It alleges that by the terms of your policy it can withhold payment until its investigation is closed. I don't read the policy that way. Bottom line: Americana may or may not be off the hook for punitive damages, but Power Industries will eventually get paid for all actual losses that you can substantiate and quantify."

"What can we do to get the maximum as soon as possible?" Tiffany asked.

"Stay the course," Natalya replied. "The ball is in Americana's court. We have made our demand and we have proof that it is acting in bad faith. The longer Americana drags its feet, the better our chances become. If we don't reach an agreement by the time of trial, we let the jury decide how much you are entitled to. And you should get your money after trial, unless of course Americana appeals."

"This could take years," Randy exclaimed.

"Theoretically," Nat said. "But Americana doesn't want to waste time and money on an appeal it is apt to lose. This brings me to another point."

"What's that?" Randy asked.

"Americana has moved the court to order mediation. I don't think we should object."

"Why not?" Tiffany asked.

"Because an objection wouldn't do us any good and it would irritate the judge. Also, the process just might give Americana a wake up call. At a minimum, mediation will ensure that someone in a position of authority at Americana realizes that this case isn't going to go away."

"I'm worried about Lone Star Bank," Randy said. "They may not renew our note."

"Americana has agreed to give us a letter confirming you are no longer suspected of any foul play," Nat said. "Maybe this will persuade Lone Star to work with you. It would make sense for them to do so. After all, you cannot pay them back now and they have nothing to gain by forcing you into bankruptcy. Like my mother says, 'you can't squeeze blood from a turnip.' You could offer the prospective insurance award as collateral. That would allow the bank to intervene in the lawsuit and put additional pressure on Americana."

"We have already pledged a big chunk of the Marine Corps payments," Randy said, "but it's a smart idea. It just might work."

"As for the Marine Corps," Nat continued, "they asked me how soon you could begin shipping units."

"We can start Monday," Tiffany said. "But until we are back in our own factory, we won't be in a position to bid on other contracts."

"I need specifics on the contracts you are unable to bid for and I also need your costing for rebuilding the factory. I want to give that material to our expert to incorporate in his report and also to include in our mediation notebook.

"What's a mediation notebook?" Randy asked.

"It's a big loose-leaf notebook which sets forth everything we want Americana and the mediator to keep in mind. I guess this covers most of what I wanted to tell you. Do either of you have any questions?"

"You have a knack of answering my questions before I have a chance to ask them," Tiffany said "and I agree with your recommendations. Randy, how about you?"

"Just one. When are we getting Americana's letter saying they know we didn't set the fire?"

"By the end of the week."

"Thanks," Randy said. "We should get going."

After the Jacksons left, Natalya worked nonstop on other matters and ate a quick sandwich at her desk for lunch. She went home via the gym and got in just in time to tuck Sheela into bed. Victor was OK. He had prepared a stir-fry and listened to Sheela read *The Little Engine That Could* to him. She had it memorized and didn't miss a single word. After supper, he mentioned that he had made an appointment to see the Sunset house on Wednesday.

33

Friday, after Sabbath dinner, Victor described the Sunset house to Henry while Sheela and Nat helped Beca clear the table.

"I think," Victor told his father, "the place could be fixed up for about $80,000, if we're careful. It meets all our requirements. It's pleasant, spacious, and well situated. The reason it's on the market is that the sellers are moving to Seattle."

"What does Natalya think?"

"She agrees that it's the best thing we've seen so far."

"The best of what you have seen or the only thing you've seen that has potential?" Henry asked.

"I guess that depends on your point of view. But . . ."

"Activate the screen. Hurry!" Beca shouted running in from the dining room followed by Natalya and Sheela.

"Why?" Victor asked, as Henry switched a button on his remote. Suddenly a panel pulled back to reveal a noisy and chaotic scene. Sirens screeched, lights flashed, and crowds shoved.

"What's going on?" Victor repeated.

"Helen from across the street called to say President Gorham has been shot." Beca's eyes welled with tears.

"With a gun?" Sheela asked. "Is he going to be dead?"

"Hush," Nat told her daughter. "We don't know what happened yet."

"But Beca is going to cry." Sheela insisted. "We love the president, even though he isn't in our family. Right?"

"Right," Victor said. "He's the best president America has had in a very long time. But let's all be quiet and pay attention."

Within moments SBS's Vanessa Lewis came on the air. The Landaus listened, frozen, as she spoke, her engaging voice somber and clear:

"Satellite Broadcasting System has just confirmed reports that President Gorham, shot eight minutes ago at exactly nine o'clock Eastern Standard Time, in Cambridge, Massachusetts, is alive. He is in a helicopter that is about to land at Massachusetts General Hospital. Details regarding his condition will be released pending authorization from Vice President Barry Mayer. President Andrew Gorham was leaving Harvard University where he had spoken to a national gathering of high school principals in opposition to the incorporation of prayer as a feature of morning assemblies, when a figure in a stocking mask emerged from behind a tree and fired three shots. The White House reports that although several threats were investigated earlier today, none of them appeared to pose any unusual danger and Gorham refused to take extraordinary precautions.

"Within seconds after the shooting, SBS itself received communications from spokespersons purportedly representing the predominantly black American Muslim Brotherhood and the White Christian Moralists. Each of the spokespersons claimed credit for this heinous deed. Excuse me . . ."

The screen went dead. Vanessa returned after a few seconds and continued.

"I have just been advised that there will be a total news blackout regarding this incident. The Vice President will address the nation at 11:00 p.m., Eastern Standard Time. Until then, we resume our regular programming."

"I can't believe this." Nat shook with fear and rage. Our President has been shot and we don't know what his condition is. Aren't we entitled to know? I hope to God he'll make it. How can the government muzzle the press? I don't think it can legitimately do that."

"It certainly is a first," Victor agreed, "but it's about time."

"Maybe," Beca suggested, "the press was not muzzled. Perhaps the satellite and network stations voluntarily agreed that this blackout is in the interest of national security. Lately the press has been blamed for every problem we've had, from earthquakes to the Majority Leader's bisexuality. Yet it has never jeopardized or even been accused of jeopardizing national security. Who knows what has *not* been conceded in the past?"

"You have a point," Victor conceded. "We may have gone too far in making reporters our scapegoats, but the fact remains that they have caused a lot of trouble by proliferating rumor and speculation."

"We better take off so we can be home in time to hear Mayer's speech," Natalya said. "I don't know what to think."

As soon as she was buckled in, Sheela shifted gears and asked her parents "What's a Sunset House?"

"It's a house on Sunset which is the name of a street." Nat's mind was on Gorham and she missed the anxiety underlying Sheela's question. "We are thinking of buying it and living there so that we can have more room."

"No, no, no! We can't live in a Sunset house! We live in my condo! It's a sunset condo. I watch my sunset. I never said we could live in a Sunset house. No, no, no!" Sheela screamed, rapidly losing it. By the time Victor pulled up to their building, she was hysterical.

"Hey, honey, chill," Victor said, carrying his squirming, teary daughter toward the elevators.

"Hi, Sheela" the night concierge said to her as the troubled family waited for an elevator to come down, but Sheela buried her head in her father's shoulder and didn't reply. "Cat got your tongue?" he then asked. Instead of answering Sheela opened her mouth and began to bawl in earnest.

"The President has just been shot," Nat explained over the screaming. "And we have a crisis on our hands."

The elevator door opened as she spoke and she followed her husband and daughter inside, thankful that it was empty.

Sheela cried, screamed, kicked and banged her head for the better part of an hour. Nothing Victor or Nat said or did could calm her. The Vice President's speech was recorded for later viewing while Sheela lay on the floor having a tantrum. Fury and despair wreaked havoc on her emotions and dissolved her reason.

"Talk," Nat urged her child. "Use words," but 'no' was the only word that Sheela could utter. Finally, at eleven fifteen Texas time, Sheela asked for Aa-Oo who had been forgotten at her grandparents' house.

"I guess I'd better go get him," Victor offered.

"No," Sheela said between sobs and gulps of air. "I wanna sleep with Aa-Oo at Beca's house."

At her wit's end, Natalya called the senior Landaus just as they were going to sleep. Henry immediately volunteered to come over and get his granddaughter.

"What are we going to do?" Victor asked, after he deposited Sheela in his father's car. "There is no way a three-year old can determine whether or not we move."

"I suppose Sheela will eventually listen to reason and accept the inevitable," Nat said, although she wasn't at all sure it would work that way. "Meanwhile I'll explain that we haven't decided anything yet."

"I thought we did decide to make an offer," Victor pointed out. "I don't approve of misleading Sheela with false hopes."

"We did sort of, but we haven't settled on how much and the sellers may not accept a low ball offer."

"Well, a few thousand here or there isn't that critical. I'm confident that we will come to terms. You're not thinking of flipping on me, are you?" Victor asked.

"No, I'm not. Not unless a better option miraculously falls into our laps."

"Good," Victor said. "I'm rewinding. Let's watch Barry Mayer."

No one had paid much attention to Gorham when the National Party nominated him their presidential candidate for the year 2000 because no one appreciated the depth of America's disgust with both the Democrats and the Republicans. Gorham and his Jewish running mate, Mayer, campaigned on a shoestring, using radio addresses, taped presentations and question and answer sessions to educate voters. They maintained that a vulnerable America was losing political, ethical, and economic supremacy in the world community and they mapped out a plan to regain lost prestige, power, and muscle.

Thus, while the Democrats and the Republicans worked to discredit one another, the Nationals asked Americans to endorse their "holistic" platform based on humanism, centrism and responsibility. While the Democrats promised opportunity and freedom of choice and the Republicans promised prosperity and morality, the Nationals promised only to protect the nation's interests and to strive to raise its consciousness. When the Democrats and the Republicans sought larger and larger contributions and thanked their donors with galas, the National Party asked for loose change and thanked its donors with plastic buttons. Only the Nationals were naïve enough to believe that every quarter collected represented a vote and that the poor felt better when they gave than when they received, particularly if what they received were false promises.

Until the eleventh hour, the polls indicated that the Nationals could not win. The analysts' consensus was that Dr. Gorham was a philosopher and that a leader of his ilk didn't have "a snow ball's chance in hell." But when the votes were counted and re-counted, astonishingly, Gorham and Mayer won the election. In addition to the presidency and vice presidency, the Nationals won three congressional seats from California, New York, and Wisconsin as well as two senatorial seats, one from Gorham's home state of Pennsylvania and the other from Maine.

The United States advanced under the Gorham-Mayer watch. Its voice resonated more forcefully throughout the world. The public became better educated and the number of people living below the poverty level was reduced. As the government stopped spending, the public started saving. Not everyone was pleased, but because the displeased were splintered, it now appeared that Gorham and Mayer would remain in power for a second term.

"Fellow citizens," Vice President Mayer announced. "I thank you for your patience in waiting for my address and I tell you with deep regret that while President Gorham is alive, he is in a coma and unable to act as our leader. Therefore, I will perform his duties until further notice."

"At this time the doctors have been unwilling to commit to any prognosis. They have advised me only that the president's condition is precarious. I have been given three scenarios. The best scenario is the possibility of a full recovery. A second scenario is the possibility of death. A third scenario is a partial recovery the extent of which cannot be determined while he remains unconscious. We have no idea how long Andy Gorham will continue to be in this coma, but we do know that the sooner he regains consciousness, the better his chances are for a total recovery."

"To those of you who support our party's continuing efforts to elevate America to the greatness it has known in the past, I say we will not give up our struggle and we will fight to win the upcoming elections, whatever the outlook for President Gorham. His mission and his vision are greater and more enduring than his person. To those of you who rejoice in this setback, I say, beware.

"Our friends of the press have rallied and agreed that they will not report any news pertaining to the president's condition or to our investigation of this tragic attack without my personal authorization. They are doing this in order to protect the president's privacy and to enable the National Party to respond to this threat. I thank them and I thank you for your understanding. I will speak to you again as soon as I have something to report. Good Night."

"You notice how Mayer didn't ask for our prayers?" Victor pointed out.
"That's true. I didn't pay attention, but now that you mention it, it's interesting," Nat answered.
"What will happen if Gorham doesn't recover? There is no way a Jew can become president. Or is there?"
"I don't think that's an issue. The anti-Semites are already anti-National.

Sheela returned home Saturday afternoon subdued, but unrelenting in her determination never to leave "her condo from before she was born." Victor was at his wit's end and told Natalya, "Look, I can't deal with her. You talk to her. But don't give in. She has to learn that things can't always be the way she wants them to be. That's lesson one. Lesson two is her parents are wiser than she is and she has to accept the fact that we see the big picture."

"Have you learned those two lessons?" Nat asked.

"Not necessarily, but my parents haven't given up trying to teach them to me and I'm a grown man. However that's not the point."

"What is the point?"

"It's that we're moving and Sheela is moving with us. The only question is how miserable she is going to be as a result. So your job is to help her accept the inevitable with good cheer. Is that fair enough?"

"No, it isn't. It's not fair to say that because Sheela is little, her feelings don't count. On the other hand, she has to realize that life isn't fair."

"We have to talk," Natalya told her daughter Sunday after brunch, "about the Sunset house. OK?"

"I told Beca and Gappa," Sheela said.

"What did you tell them?" Nat asked.

"That our condo will be sad, like the house in the story. You know?"

"Yes, the little house that moved from the city to the country. What did Beca and Gappa say?"

"They said you should talk to me."

"Well, that's what I am doing. So do you understand that we can't fit in this condo any more?"

"We fit. We are here."

"That's true," Nat admitted. "We are here, but we have no room. Mommy and Daddy need a place to work that is different from your room. You need a place to be and to play that is all yours. And look, you need a bicycle and you can't have one while we are here because there is no place for it. And you need a special place for your clothes. Right now they are squished in with Mommy's. And I was really hoping to get a piano."

"Why don't we make this place bigger?" Sheela asked.

"How can we do that?" Nat asked. "We only own this one condo."

"We could own anover condo and mix it together with this one," Sheela countered.

"My God," Nat said, "that's a good idea. Who gave it to you?"

"Martin."

"Martin the concierge?" Nat asked.

"Yea," Sheela answered.

"When did you talk to Martin about this?" Sheela inquired of her three and a half-year-old.

"A lady told Martin."

"What did she tell Martin?"

"She said to put two condos to make one big one," Sheela explained, using her fingers to show Nat what she was talking about.

That night, Victor asked his wife whether she had spoken to their daughter about the Sunset house.

"Yes," Nat answered him, "I did talk to Sheela."

"Am I right in supposing that the conversation went well? Sheela was very chipper tonight. That's why I thought maybe you hadn't gotten around to saying anything yet."

"Well, whether you're right or not depends on what you want to do."

"Don't play the enigma game with me, Nat." Victor began to feel nervous. "It's not what I want to do, it's what we have to do to live like normal human beings."

"I realize that and I agree that we absolutely must have more room. So bear with me, OK?"

"OK." Victor calmed down a bit. "What I would like to know is whether you succeeded in getting this concept across to Sheela."

"Yup. Sheela realizes full well that we need much more room. So she came up with a suggestion."

"What did Sheela suggest that will get us more room without moving to a bigger place?"

"I think her exact words were, 'We could get another condo and mix it with this one.' She got the idea when she overheard someone tell Martin that she was buying two units and combining them."

"So what I did," Nat continued, "was look in the Sunday paper. I found out that Coldwell Banker has a high rise department and I asked if there were any units for sale in this building. And guess what?"

"What?" Victor duly asked.

"The unit right above ours just came on the market."

34

The celebration of her fourth birthday was the first specific recollection Sheela had of her childhood. It was thus a landmark and a point of departure. From the age of four onward, Sheela understood that many of the strange yet familiar vignettes that periodically flashed before her mind's eye were separate from her present life. Sometimes the flashes vanished abruptly, leaving only a smile or a scowl behind, but other times they faded slowly, leaving a cloud of doubt in their wake. Such subtleties taught Sheela to distinguish between fantasy and actuality, though to her, both were equally real and equally true.

Sheela also realized at four that life could be confining and lonely. Now she no longer traveled through time and space, except in her dreams. Sweak abandoned her and even Aa-Oo only spoke when Sheela put words in his mouth. Of her inner friends, Leela alone remained and she was a tease.

"I'm your clone and your very best friend," she would say one day, but then other days when Sheela stepped in front of her mirror, Leela hid away and Sheela saw nothing more than her own reflection staring back or silently mimicking her actions.

All told, four was a challenging age. Sheela could no longer live within the sounds and images that filled her mind; she had to try to separate her first hand memories from narratives that touched her life as well as from the collages of disjointed experiences and premonitions that were her brainchildren. She was not always successful. Her private reveries were numerous and rich. It took little to trigger them. A word, a sound, a shiver, a scent, a taste, a shape, or a color could evoke a world that danced within the world inhabited by Sheela Landau.

Sometimes visions struck Sheela unexpectedly when she heard an odd remark, or saw a familiar sight. At other times she summoned them. Sheela gazed at her reflection or her shadow; she daydreamed; she gathered Aa-Oo in her arms, she helped Beca bake brownies; she blew out candles; she rearranged her collection of frogs. When she did things like that, she never knew where they would lead.

The purple amethyst frog Lulu gave Sheela for her fourth birthday became another clear memory. It started her collection. The frog was purple because purple was the theme of her birthday. Purple was going to be the predominant color in her new room. Sheela picked it over blue and green, which were the two colors her mother suggested. Sheela called the frog Alvin, after the chipmunk. Her frog reminded her of Alvin the Chipmunk, even though she knew full well that a frog was an entirely different creature.

"*Alvin no es una rana,*" Lulu protested.

"*Ahora sí es. Mi rana se llama Alvin.*" Sheela insisted.

Subsequent frogs' names followed the alphabet, so the next frog, one that Victor brought her as a present for no reason, was called Boris and so forth. When on her fifteenth birthday Sheela received an exquisite jade frog, a tiny rose quartz one, and a malachite frog that looked real, she named them Zachary, Amaryllis and Bethsheba respectively. Thus the first twenty-six frogs in her collection were males and the rest starting with Amaryllis were to be females.

"What are you going to call your fifty-third frog?" Natalya asked her.

"Who knows," Sheela replied. "If I don't think of something, you will."

Sheela's fourth birthday party took place at her grandparents' home, because her condo was suffering the throes of remodeling. When everything was finished in February or March, the Landaus would have an upstairs and a downstairs. The kitchen, the living room, and the dining room were going to stay downstairs and incorporate Sheela's old room. Victor and Nat's former bedroom was to be a den. A spiral staircase would connect the downstairs living room to the large library/ study upstairs. Three bedrooms were to be upstairs as well. Although Natalya insisted that all the walls throughout the house had to be white, Sheela's bedroom was going to have a light purple bedcover with complementary colored cushions and dark purple mini-blinds. The master bedroom would have black and rust accents and the guestroom tones would be aqua. No rooms were planned for future children.

The constant presence of workers and the abundance of dust, of noise and of general confusion was great fun from Sheela's perspective, but her parents felt differently. They were bothered by the disorder and by the need to constantly move their furniture from room to room while walls were being torn down and put up again. Her father especially needed peace and quiet. He also minded that he and Natalya couldn't get anything accomplished at home and had to spend extra time in their offices. As a result they often resorted to sending Lulu and Sheela off to the senior Landaus. This made Victor feel guilty about neglecting his daughter and about imposing upon his parents even though neither they nor Sheela minded in the least.

Although Victor was frequently annoyed, he sincerely tried to hide his bad moods. He understood that most of the burden of getting the remodeling job done fell upon Nat and she was as busy as he was at work. Also, even though he didn't admit it, he was thrilled at not having to move from his high rise. Besides, he appreciated Nat managing problems that he couldn't handle because he always lost his temper with the contractors.

When the mess and disorder were at their peak, Victor received a commendatory letter from the White House Press Secretary which greatly improved his humor and almost calmed him down.

⁕⁕⁕

According to medical science, President Gorham's recovery from his injuries was nothing short of miraculous. The bullet fired by the stocking-masked gunman had lodged in his skull, just grazing the left frontal lobe. The doctors who removed the bullet feared for the American president's life, but they feared an incomplete recovery even more. Most of all, they feared the consequences of any mishap that might arise as a result of their removing the bullet.

The President remained in a coma for a few hours after the bullet was extracted. During that period of time no news bulletins were issued. Even after Gorham regained consciousness, the White House remained worried and fearful. Vice President Mayer and the handful of individuals who needed to be fully informed of every detail and who kept making and remaking contingency plans were most fearful of all. Their alarm bordered on panic. Why? Because the briefing they received from the doctors made reference to a bizarre accident that befell one Phineas Gage in 1848.

Gage was foreman of a quarrying gang who was injured by gunpowder. In the course of his work an explosion blew a metal rod through his cheek, up through the left frontal lobe of his brain and out of his skull. He miraculously survived and his wound healed. However, the accident caused his personality to undergo a radical change. Before the occurrence, Phineas Gage had been a considerate, easy going, and apparently contented individual. After it, he became stubborn, moody, and prone to using obscene language. Medical history touted Gage's transformation as evidence that the front of the brain is linked to the human personality. Recent studies, the doctors said, confirmed that brain injuries produced behavioral problems.

Twelve hours after the surgery, President Gorham was conscious and out of critical danger. Twenty-four hours after the surgery he appeared to be lucid and physically unimpaired. However, the tale of Phineas Gage loomed in the back of the minds of his team like a time bomb. Vice President Mayer told the American people that the White House was now cautiously optimistic about the President's prospects for a full recovery. Eight hours after that, Andy Gorham, his head swathed in bandages, insisted upon addressing the nation himself. His close staff held its collective breath.

"My fellow Americans," Dr. Andrew Gorham said, "I want you to see for yourselves that I'm alive and well and I want you to know that our Government has credible information which will soon enable us to apprehend the perpetrator and the other persons responsible for the attack that was made on me and on our country. We will disclose all the details to you after these persons are taken into custody."

"The healers hovering over me here have given strict orders that I am to rest under their care for a few more days, and as I owe my life to them, I feel obligated

218

to do as they say. Thus I will not perform any presidential duties this week and continue to leave my responsibilities in the capable hands of Barry Mayer. But next week, rain or shine, in the oval office or in a hospital office, I'll be doing my job and Vice President Mayer will be doing his. And if you'll have us, we will both be working for you for the next four years to build a strong nation conscious of its actions, conscious of its power and conscious of its honor."

The speech was well delivered and apparently well received, but Gorham could palpate the tension hovering over him. He disregarded it, waived away his staff and napped. When he awoke, he summoned Barry Mayer and asked to be left alone with him. Then he said, "I know what's bugging you."

"Nothing at all is disturbing us," Mayer retorted flushing as he spoke.

"You're a lousy liar, Barry," the President said. "You know how I feel about lies. For politicians we have done a fairly good job of sticking to the truth and between us there is no excuse for mincing words. Besides, you are red as a beet."

"I apologize, sir," Barry said. "There is something, but I'm afraid it is not anything I am free to tell you."

"Cut the sir and the crap," Gorham told his Vice President and good friend. You don't have to tell me a thing. I'll tell you what's going on. The doctors have warned you about possible effects that this accident might prove to have on my personality. I heard them muttering and I learned about that Gage fellow when I was in high school. What was his first name? Wasn't it something like Finnicus?"

"It was Phineas Gage."

"So what are you going to do?"

"I'm going to tell the docs and the need-to-know guys that there's no way you have changed in any respect at all. I'll tell them you saw right through us. The official word now is that you are on your way to a full recovery and that your injuries have caused no lasting damage."

"What if they don't believe you?"

"It makes no difference," Mayer answered. "This administration doesn't respond to beliefs. People are entitled to their opinions, but credence is given to facts. And your speech was a fact."

In November, Gorham and Mayer won the election by a landslide. Eighteen National candidates were chosen to represent their districts in the House of Representatives and of the seven Nationals who entered the Senate race, six won.

⁓⁓⁓ ❊❊❊❊❊ ⁓⁓⁓

The letter of December 8 that Dr. Victor Landau had received from the White House read as follows:

Dear Dr. Landau,

It is with great pleasure that we acknowledge the value of your work to the National Party. My office has stressed the importance of persuasive communication and logical communication to our speech writers and public relations personnel, as our job is to communicate our purpose to the American people and to reach their minds and hearts.

President Gorham considers that your books have made a significant contribution to the success of his campaigns.

Please keep our office in mind in the event that you ever require information or assistance.

Sincerely,
Donald Rufus
White House Press Secretary

When Natalya told her mother-in-law that she was considering holding Sheela's party at Tumble Tots, Beca volunteered her house.

"Why not use our terrace and back yard?"

"That's sweet and generous, but I think your offer goes way beyond the call of duty. You don't know what you would be in for."

"Sure I do. It can't be much worse than the chaos we used to go through when Victor was a boy. For his fifth birthday, all his friends came dressed as animals and the boys behaved accordingly. That party was a true zoo. It rained at the last minute and I wasn't prepared. I covered the furniture and rolled up the living room carpet, but I had to have the walls repainted. This wouldn't be as bad."

"You want to bet?" Nat found it difficult to visualize a youthful Rebecca Landau with a houseful of rambunctious boys. "Sheela wants to invite just about everyone in her class plus Bobby. I think it will be too much."

"It'll be fine. You must be going crazy with the dirt and the disturbance and with keeping Victor sane. Victor doesn't do too well when he is surrounded by commotion, you know."

"I do know, but the end is in sight," Nat said. "What will we do if it's cold?"

"We have space heaters. Your invitations can indicate that warm clothes for an outdoor party are in order. If it's freezing or wet, I guess we'll be redecorating next."

"Maybe if your parents find out that we're hosting the party, they will get inspired to come," Beca suggested.

"No, they want to spend this holiday season in Austria. It's been my mom's dream for years. She wants to hear the Vienna Boys' Choir and go to the opera. The Rosenbaum gang will visit when our house is ready. My mother is excited about helping with the finishing touches and she will try to stay longer than usual."

Rebecca tried not to show she was pleased. She would have graciously included the in-laws in the festivities, but it was nice to know for sure she wouldn't be upstaged by Dora.

The first of January, 2005 turned out to be a comfortable and sunny winter day. The party took place in a tent filled with purple balloons. They floated near the ceiling and bounced on the floor. The laughter of boisterous children, the rustling of gift-wrap, and the popping of balloons stayed in Sheela's head for several months and then faded while her memory of the taste of Welch's grape juice, her grandmother's purple dress, her grandfather's loud purple flowered Hawaiian shirt, Alvin, and the scent of lavender perfume sharpened over time. *The Purple Cow and Other Preposterous Poems* sent by Dora and Harold would live in Sheela's night table for the rest of her life. Beca and Gappa's gift, a mauve pastel of two girls holding hands would hang in her room always. But the feelings the pastel evoked would endure beyond forever.

35

The day Sheela took *The Purple Cow* to Kinderland for Show and Tell, she wore purple jeans and purple ribbons in her black braids.

"Where did you get this book?" her teacher asked.

"From Door," Sheela replied opening the book to show her grandmother's inscription. "Door is my grandma's name," she explained. "I got it in my purple birthday."

"That's intriguing," the teacher said.

"No, it was very fun," Sheela retorted.

"Intriguing means very interesting and fun," the teacher explained. Then she asked, "What would you like to tell us about the book?"

"I can say a poem," Sheela replied and began to recite:

> I never saw a purple cow,
> I never hope to see one,
> but this I ll tell you anyhow,
> I d rather see than be one.

Sheela's classmates and Ms. Molly enjoyed the brief recital. Most of the children had attended the purple party and appreciated the verse. Sheela's performance was impressive as well and prompted her teacher to invite her to do an encore. Luckily Sheela knew another preposterous poem, a green one. This time as she recited she shook her head vigorously from side to side, both for emphasis and to feel her braids swish.

> Green tea ice cream s not for me.
> I like hot black tea you see.
> But if you like it, do feel free
> to eat green tea and disagree.

When she was finished, she announced, "That's all I know."

"Let's put our hands together for Sheela and show her how much we enjoyed her preposterous poems," Ms. Molly said and the class clapped enthusiastically.

Sheela loved giving her first solo public performance. Standing before an audience with all eyes upon her empowered her and she ate up the applause that followed her success. Even though she had started off a little bit afraid, conquering her fear was part of her triumph. Her tummy felt tight, almost like it did when she sat on top of the high seesaw in New York, but not exactly. This feeling was even more exciting.

⊹⊶⊰⊱⊷⊹

Natalya's parents hadn't called for several days. The last time Nat talked to them was when they had just returned from Europe. They told Nat they had thoroughly enjoyed their trip. Budapest was fascinating. Vienna and the Boys' Choir were spectacular. The city was filled with history and coffee shops where they had pastries every afternoon and ate a ton of whipped cream. It was everywhere: on cakes, on puddings, on fruit and in coffee. But they were glad to be back home. They were also glad that the woman who shot Gorham was found sane and would stand trial. Yes, they knew she belonged to a neo-imperialist group that the United States Government had been trying to penetrate for some time. They missed everyone, especially Alex who had grown a great deal. He seemed fretful though, probably due to teething. They were eager to come to Houston.

At first Nat attributed Dora's silence to preoccupation with her grandson. However, when four or five days passed with no further news, she was concerned. She e-mailed and phoned and when there was no response, her concern became fear. She did the most she could which was to leave voice messages on her parents' and on her brother's machines.

"This isn't like you guys," she said. "I'm the one who hasn't always been prompt in getting back to you. I'm sorry. I hope you aren't trying to give me 'a taste of my own medicine' as you used to say. Please call right away because I'm nervous."

Nat's mother didn't call back. The message Natalya retrieved at ten o'clock that evening came from Ronald.

"We got your message. Please call at 212-525-5555, even if it's late. Don't worry, we'll explain."

Nat was petrified. A bone-chilling ache resounded through her body. She felt alternately hot and clammy. Her shaking fingers could barely punch out the numbers on her telephone and the tightness in her chest almost suffocated her. She counted while the phone rang four times. Finally a crisply efficient voice said, "Mount Sinai, Intensive care, can I help you?" Nat's brain lost its connection to her vocal chords, leaving her suddenly tongue-tied. Her empty breathing caused the voice to ask, "Who is calling?"

"This is Natalya Landau," Nat managed to get out. The simplicity of the question helped her regain her speech. "My brother, Ronald Rosenbaum, said my family could be reached at this number."

"Just a moment, and I'll get Mrs. Rosenbaum for you," the voice said.

"What happened. Who is in intensive care?" Nat rasped.

"It's your father, sweetheart. He had a heart attack, but he'll pull through," Dora answered.

"When?" Nat asked.

"Two days ago."

"How could you wait two days to tell me?" Nat asked. "How dare you do that!" Anger took over, a blessing that distracted her from fear and pain.

"We didn't want to worry you needlessly," Dora replied. "You are so stressed already, trying to juggle all the balls in your life without dropping any and there wasn't anything you could have done."

"You had no right to keep me in the dark! No right!" Nat hung up. Moments later she re-dialed and apologized to the voice, "I'm sorry. I accidentally disconnected. Could I please speak to Mrs. Rosenbaum again?"

"Are you positive Daddy is going to be OK?" Nat asked her mother.

"We think he will be fine," Dora replied. "Right now he is sedated and hooked up to all kinds of monitors. He survived the initial attack but the doctors are afraid of secondary attacks. Ultimately he will need bypass surgery."

"But there is a possibility he will die, without my ever having a chance to see him again. You made a unilateral decision to keep me away. I'll never forgive you for doing this."

"Look, Nat," Dora said. "This decision was mine to make. It took everyone into account. Your presence would make your father think his condition is worse than it is and alarm him. It would disrupt your life and serve no purpose. We hope and expect him to get well. Anyhow, right now is not a good time to have this conversation. I'll have to hang up in a minute."

"I'm coming to New York in the morning, on the 7:00 o'clock flight. If something happens, I'll never speak to you again. You should have given me the option of coming or not. I would have thought you cared about having me around. You told me that families should be there for one another in times of trouble."

"Sweetheart," Dora tried to explain. "Anything can happen to anybody at any time. Daddy is getting excellent care. Nothing is going to happen. I wanted to wait until tomorrow to talk to you. The doctors said that if he's still stable, they can pretty much promise a full recovery."

"Pretty much isn't good enough," Natalya said. "You may not care about me, but I care about Daddy and I'm coming."

"Please, Nat," Dora pleaded, hoping her daughter couldn't tell that she was crying, "not yet."

Nat listened to the silent phone for a few seconds and then placed it back on its base. Steeling herself, she went to tell Victor who was reading in Sheela's room that she was going to New York tomorrow on the first flight out.

"Shh," Victor whispered. "Sheela just fell asleep."

"Please come outside, I have to talk to you." Nat said.

"In a minute," Victor mumbled, and he fell asleep as well.

An hour later, Victor woke up and headed to the bedroom. He was surprised because Nat was packing. Since she left her old firm, she didn't travel as much as she used to and she no longer kept a bag ready to go.

"What is going on here?" he asked.

"I tried to tell you, but you fell asleep. Nobody cares about me except for Daddy. To hell with everyone." Nat threw herself on the bed.

"Hey," Victor said. "Take it easy. Talk to me. What happened?"

"I'm going to New York." Nat stood up again and resumed packing.

"I'm sorry." Victor embraced his wife. "Something is very wrong. I didn't realize. Please tell me what the matter is."

"I'm going to New York early tomorrow . . ." Natalya concentrated on remaining dry eyed and coherent, "because Daddy had a heart attack."

"Oh my God! When? How is he?"

"Two days ago and I don't know how he is," Nat replied.

"How come you just found out?"

"Because my mother didn't want me to know. She doesn't want me to go to New York. She didn't call at all. Ronald did after I left a message. He left the hospital number and I called and found out that Daddy is in intensive care."

"I'm sure your Mom expects your Dad to be fine and she didn't want you worrying." Victor reasoned.

"You always take her side."

"That's not true. I don't take sides. Anyhow you, your mother and your brother are all on the same side, scared and trying to do what's best, trying to cope. Please stay calm and think. Don't blame Dora for wanting to spare you."

"I want to go and see Daddy. I can't stand being away. My mom should know that."

"She knows, but she isn't thinking primarily about what you want. She's thinking about what your father and she and you need. She's worrying about Harold and using her energy to give him strength. She's a wife and a mother, doing what she considers best, which is not necessarily the same as what she or you or anyone else wants."

"My energy could help Daddy get better too. Why am I excluded from my family?"

"You aren't excluded. This is a matter of timing. You should go to New York when you are needed."

"Well I think I'm needed now, and I intend to go now," Nat insisted.

"Why don't you take time out," Victor suggested, "then decide. If you still want to go to New York early, I'll drive you to the airport. But perhaps you could be more helpful and supportive by doing what your mother asks. Look, it's human to be anxious and mad, but don't take it out on Dora. Don't act in anger. OK?"

"OK. I guess I wasn't very nice to my mother. I'll call and talk to her again."

"I'd like to say a few words to her too," Victor added.

Nat called the hospital, and a new person identifying herself as Yolanda answered the phone. When Nat asked for Mrs. Rosenbaum, Yolanda said, "Dora Rosenbaum is sleeping on the sofa. This is the first rest she has had in over two days. Do you want me to wake her?"

"No, I guess not," Natalya answered. "How is my dad doing?"

"He's holding his own. Is there anything else I can help you with?"

"I guess not," Nat said. "Thanks. Well, maybe when my mom wakes up, you could tell her that I called."

"Is there any other message? She seemed pretty upset. I talked to her at the beginning of my shift."

"I guess not, except, well, can you tell her I love her?"

"I certainly can. She'll be happy to hear you said that."

"Thanks a lot, Yolanda. Good night."

"Good night. And have faith. Your dad knows he has a lot to live for and he's pulling hard."

"I'm going to lie down," Victor said. "You can wake me up if you need to talk or anything. I feel sure your father will be just fine. The doctors have to be careful.

They can't give assurances, but Dora has to know in her heart that Harold is going to come through with flying colors and that he will need you later on. Otherwise she would have called and told you to come now."

At about two a.m. Victor felt Nat struggling to get comfortable. "What is it?" he asked sleepily. "Is there some news? Have you figured out what you want to do?"

"No, not really," Nat said. "It's just that I can't sleep. I didn't want to disturb you."

"Move over here and let me hold you. There, now, that feels better doesn't it?"

Nat nodded, and closed her eyes, but Victor could see wetness seeping out from under her lashes so he held her tightly and inhaled her salty breath. "Open your mouth," he whispered.

Nat opened it and started to speak, but Victor covered her words with kisses. Then he paused for a moment.

"It's OK to make love at a time like this. It's better to feel love than anything else," Victor said and Nat allowed herself to relax.

They slept for two hours, until the alarm Nat had set for five a.m. rang.

"I guess it's time to get ready if I'm going to make the early flight," Nat said, snuggling up to Victor. "I don't know what to do yet, but I feel much better. Thanks."

"Don't thank me as if I did you a favor. Making love to you isn't among the things I do to be noble," Victor said. "I'll put on coffee while you gather your thoughts."

"There's plastic all over the counter. The coffee pot's in the refrigerator," Nat explained.

When Victor returned carrying two steaming cups, Natalya gratefully took one and asked, "Why do I feel like you're humoring me?"

"Because I know you better than you know yourself. I know how you feel and what you are going to do and I'm waiting for you to work things out and then to come to terms with your decision."

"So what am I going to do? I have my reservation and I'm all packed and ready."

"I see that. You can catch the seven o'clock flight if you hurry or you could get on a later flight after Sheela wakes up and you say goodbye to her, that is if you are certain that you want to go to New York today."

"I definitely want to be by my father's side. Why can't I just do what I want and make sure he's going to be OK?"

"Probably," Victor suggested, "because you know it wouldn't be the right thing. You are anxious and even resentful, but this is too serious a matter to decide on the basis of anxiety and resentment."

"Yeah. I'm going to wait to talk to my mother, right?"

"Right," Victor said.

"So, do you want to go back to sleep or what?"

"I want to do whatever you're doing," Victor answered.

"I want to call the hospital, but I think it would be better to wait until a little later. I can't sit still, so maybe I could make us pancakes."

"The kitchen is a mess. I could go out and bring something."

"No place good is open this early. I can make pancakes on a hot plate.

"I don't see how," Victor said, "but I'd love that."

"The air around me feels lighter," Nat said as she and Victor finished off the blueberry pancakes, except for two little ones they were saving for Sheela. "Do you suppose it could be because Daddy is getting better?"

The phone rang before Victor could answer Nat's question. It was Dora. Her 'Hello, Nat?' sounded upbeat.

"Yes, it's me," Nat said.

"Yolanda gave me your message. I appreciate it. I worried about waking you, but I wanted to catch you as early as possible," Dora said. "Daddy had a good night. They're moving him out of intensive care today. Why don't you let us call you this afternoon, when he is settled in his room? You can talk to him then and decide when to come. How does that sound?"

"OK, I guess. But is Daddy out of the woods? Is he definitely going to get well?"

"You know there is nothing definite in this life. I could be hit by a car tomorrow; but yes, he is going to get well."

"Victor wanted to talk to you a second, so I'll say good bye. Tell Daddy I love him. And use my hand phone number and call as soon as you can. And I'm sorry I behaved so horribly. Here's Victor."

"Hello, Door," Victor said. "I don't want to keep you. I heard Nat's end of the conversation and I can see from her face that Pappa is on the mend. You know you can always count on both of us. Take care and get some sleep."

"Thank you, Victor. I will. I know you helped calm Natalya and I really appreciate it. You're good for Nat and for all of us."

"That's nice of you to say. Uh, I'd better let you go. Bye."

At about seven o'clock Sheela padded into her parents' room asking, "What happened in the night? What are you putting in the soupcase?"

"Mommy is going to New York," Nat answered, "because Pappa is sick. He's in the hospital."

"No-o!" Sheela cried. "Pappa isn't sick any more. You can't go to New York, Ma, New York without me. What did Pappa say?"

"Well, sweetheart," Victor answered, "Pappa didn't say anything. He was too sick to talk. But he's better now and we can call him this afternoon."

"Ma don't go to New York. Don't! Don't! Don't!" Sheela cried, her dimple quivering. "You have to finish fixing our condo. It's all broken."

After a moment Sheela asked, "Did someone shoot Pappa, like the President? Was it on TV?"

"No," Victor replied. "Pappa just got sick like you did. Remember the time you got sick?"

"No," Sheela answered.

"You don't remember when your throat hurt you?"

"I didn't stay in a hospital," Sheela answered.

When Lulu arrived, she was surprised to find Sheela still in her pajamas with her teeth unbrushed and her hair a mess. Victor had left for work and Natalya was dressed in a pantsuit. Her suitcase was parked by the front door.

"*¿Qué pasó?*" she asked.

"*No voy a Kinderland,*" Sheela answered.

"My father had a heart attack. He's going to be fine, but I may be going to New York," Nat explained. "Sheela doesn't want me to go or else she wants to come along. I can't deal with this. I have to get to the office and clear up a few urgent things."

"When did it happen?" Lulu asked.

"A few days ago, but I just found out. My mother didn't tell me right away."

"Why not?"

"Because she didn't want me to come to New York and she didn't want me to worry. She said she knew my father would be OK."

"So why did you pack your suitcase?"

"Because I thought my mother needed me and I wanted to see Daddy."

"You were scared," Lulu stated.

"Yes, Lulu I was very scared," Natalya agreed.

Sheela, who had calmed down and was listening intently, suddenly piped in asking, "You aren't scared any more, right?"

"Right," Nat answered. "Pappa is going to get better."

"Then you better stay here," Lulu decreed.

"Please, Lulu," Natalya said. "You shouldn't mix in. This is a family matter and you are just complicating everything."

"Excuse me, Mrs. Landau. You are right. This is none of my business. I am very sorry." Although Lulu apologized, she didn't sound contrite, just offended. "Come on, Sheela. Get dressed and comb your hair. Oof, you didn't even brush your teeth. They will all turn black and fall out and you will look like a witch."

Nat hated it when Lulu told Sheela nonsense like that. This time she didn't say anything, even though she worried that Sheela would become frightened when she started losing her baby teeth. Nat felt awful for putting Lulu down too. She wondered about taking Sheela in to Kinderland late, but decided against it. Instead she followed Lulu and Sheela into the bathroom to say a quick good bye. Sheela had pink toothpaste in her mouth and laughter in her eyes.

"I'll unpack my bag tonight," Nat said.

36

"Where did we live before I was born?" Sheela asked Beca with all the solemnity of an almost five year old. The two of them were making gingerbread boys. Beca cut them out with a cookie cutter and Sheela put on raisins for the eyes, noses, and mouths. She looked up from her work while she spoke. Her deep blue eyes penetrated her grandmother's soul.

"Right here in Houston," Rebecca answered. "You were in your mommy's tummy living with her and your daddy in your condo. They were here when they ordered you from God."

"They didn't order me," Sheela corrected. "I ordered them. But where did we live before?"

"First you stayed in your parents' room and then in the study. Now you moved upstairs. Gappa and I lived in this house all along."

"No, no. Not then. I know that part. When I was bigger, before I was born."

"I don't know," Beca said, taken aback.

"Yes, you do. You hafta know," Sheela insisted. "Before, when I was bigger where did we live?"

"Hmn, let me think a minute," Beca stalled. "Did you talk about this with Mommy or Daddy?"

"No," Sheela answered. "They weren't with me."

"I'm not sure I know either." Beca's heart began to pound. A million doubts clamored in Beca's head, but one tiny kernel of truth drowned them out.

"I don't remember."

"You do! You do! You do!" Sheela insisted in a loud and demanding voice.

"Please, don't shout, Sheela. It isn't nice and it upsets me."

"OK, but you remember."

"Well," Beca took a deep breath. "I might remember, but I'm not sure and I'm not allowed to tell."

"Why?"

"Because it's a secret."

"Am I allowed to tell?" Sheela loved secrets and she was satisfied with Beca's reply, but she wasn't quite ready to end the exchange.

"You can tell me what you remember," Beca suggested, "if you're sure."

"I'm sure but I can't tell because I remember the pictures, not the words," Sheela explained.

"What makes you remember the pictures?" Beca prodded. This time she was the one who didn't want to let the subject rest.

"When I look at myself in the big mirror which used to live in your house, I see my face and I remember when I used to be big. And sometimes when I'm not looking in the mirror too." Sheela sniffed the air. "I smell the gingerbread boys. Are they cooked?"

"Yes, I think this batch is baked to perfection," Beca replied.

"I want to eat one with a belly button," Sheela said.

Natalya went to New York in the fall for her father's triple bypass. The surgery was successfully performed on November 8. She expected to stay with her parents through Harold's recuperation and Thanksgiving. Sheela and Victor planned to join her for the long holiday weekend. Although the Power Industries case was set for trial during the last two weeks of November, the odds were against it being reached since there were quite a few cases ahead and Thanksgiving fell on November 24th, right in the middle of the docket. Nat's preparatory work was behind her and she was looking forward to a quiet holiday. This year they had a lot to be thankful for.

However, on Thursday, November 17th, she was shocked to get a call from Steve Jordan. Steve told her the court coordinator had just phoned and told them to be ready to pick a jury bright and early the next morning and to give opening arguments in the afternoon. That way they could begin with the testimony on Monday and wind up before the holiday recess. Their case had been assigned to a visiting judge, Charles Allbright from San Antonio.

"That's crazy!" Nat exclaimed. "Two days ago we were sixth on the docket! And we estimated five days for the trial!"

"Well, three cases settled, two were continued, one is being heard, and Charlie Allbright was called to expedite things," Steve said. "And he slashed our time to three days max — two for us and one for the defense—as soon as Lone Star Bank confirmed that it will not participate in the trial. There was no need, the bank's lawyer said. He paid us a compliment. He said Lone Star had confidence in the strength of our case and in our ability to win it."

"So what do you think?" Nat asked. "Should we try for a continuance?"

"On what basis? I don't want to object to this judge."

"On the basis of a family emergency. I'm the lead attorney, and my father had open heart surgery," Natalya answered. "The point is would it be a good idea?"

"I don't know," Steve answered.

"Let me digest this news," Nat told him, "and call you back within the hour. Right now my brain is in low gear."

Nat was befuddled. She was mentally and emotionally a million miles away from a Houston courtroom. 'Natalya Landau, wake up,' she told herself. She willed herself to concentrate. Twenty minutes later, Nat realized she had no choice. She would have to return to Houston tonight on the red-eye.

She called Steve, then the airline, then Victor. Then she told her parents and started packing. She didn't feel good about what she was doing. Her mother and father understood, but Victor didn't. And he was right when he told her Sheela would be devastated. She was counting the hours until she could see Alex again. She would have to find a way to make this up to Sheela.

"Don't get upset, dear. This was something we all knew might happen, even though we thought it was unlikely," Dora said when Nat closed her suitcase. "Anyhow, I have a brainwave: you all can come the first weekend in December and we'll have a late Thanksgiving. Maybe you can stay longer than four days."

"Maybe," Nat said gratefully, giving her mother a quick hug that made her feel weepy. "Thank you. Thank you a lot. What would I do without your brainwaves?"

By evening Natalya began to pick up mental speed. Her body was still in New York, but her mind had returned to Power Industries. As soon as she was headed for the airport, an idea began to take shape. She called Steve again on her hand phone.

"I thought of something," she said when he came on the line.

"You'll miss your flight if you don't leave right away," Steve said.

"I'm already on my way. I am calling from my cab. Listen, why didn't Americana file a motion for a bifurcated trial? Aren't defendants always adamant about separating damages from liability issues?"

"Of course, "Steve answered, "but in this case Americana expects to lose on liability. They owe the money. They acted wrongfully. We already discussed the fact that the whole thrust of their defense will be to minimize damages."

"Precisely!" Nat agreed. "So *we* should file a motion to bifurcate. We can request it as a matter of right. Our reason for doing this at the eleventh hour is that three days isn't enough time to cover the complex question of damages. Denying our motion could end up as reversible error."

"That's good; it's damn good," Steve said. "I'll get the motion out right away."

"And suggest that we can rest our case by mid afternoon Tuesday. That way Americana has to finish by noon on Wednesday and the jury can have Wednesday afternoon to deliberate."

"Done," Steve said. "See ya."

Victor could not understand why Natalya and Steve didn't ask for a continuance. He thought it would be impossible for them to gear up for a major trial on such short notice and he thought they were doing their clients a disservice by trying. He hoped this decision wouldn't result in a fiasco. But in a small place within his heart, a place well hidden from his conscience, he also thought that if this error of judgment caused the firm of Jordan and Landau to wind up with a goose egg, it wouldn't be too terrible. Then Nat and Steve's partnership might fizzle and Steve Jordan would be out of his life. Then he wouldn't have to listen to Sheela jabber on and on about how she "helped Uncle Steve today." If they didn't win the case, Nat wouldn't earn a bundle and she would continue to be financially dependent on him.

❈❈❈❈❈❈

Friday morning Judge Allbright granted Power's motion for bifurcation over Americana's vehement objection.

"If the plaintiffs prevail, I see no problem in reconvening the jury after Thanksgiving to hear evidence on damages. However," he pointedly said to Americana's attorneys, "if you lose on the questions of liability and wrongful conduct, I would hope your clients have enough sense to make a reasonable offer of settlement."

Steve and Natalya were pleased with the court's ruling and remarks. They sensed that some of the wind had been taken out of Americana's sails, but they knew better than to allow this small preliminary victory to make them complacent. Regardless of the merits of any case, a trial was a gamble.

Jury selection proceeded expeditiously. Neither side wasted time. Americana tried to empanel as many unsophisticated jurors as possible, thinking such jurors would become bored by the details of a case that was only about money and would be less likely to award a sum that struck them as extravagant. Conversely, the Jackson's team tried for a more educated group of people who could identify with economic disaster. Ultimately a fairly even mix was selected, including a lawyer, a doctor, and two owners of small businesses. One of them said he resented this "waste of his time" when he had his own problems to worry about, but Nat's jury consultant felt he would nevertheless be an asset. She was right because he wound up as the foreman.

Nat's opening argument went well. Steve watched the jurors and saw that she held their interest. She had a knack of presenting facts in a straightforward and simple fashion. This case was easy, she explained. Her clients owned a successful business making equipment for the United States Armed Forces. One Sunday, while they were at church, a fire started in their factory. The Jacksons had insurance for which they paid handsomely, so they called their insurance company, Americana, and reported the incident to them.

When Americana received notice of the fire, what did it do? Instead of paying according to the agreement that it had with the Jacksons, it decided to blame the fire on them. It figured that by really scaring Tiffany and Randy, it could get away without giving them any money at all. If push came to shove, Americana thought, it could give them a token sum along with a promise not to file criminal charges.

Did Americana succeed in doing what it set out to do? Yes indeed. The Jacksons were scared even though they had done nothing wrong. And they are still scared, because unless this insurance company pays for the damages and for the harm its delay has caused Power Industries, Tiffany and Randy will be in big trouble.

Natalya then asked the jury to pay attention, because the next thing she had to tell them was important. Americana never did file any charges against anyone connected with Power Industries, she said. It couldn't because there wasn't a single shred of evidence pointing to her clients. Americana admitted that the Jacksons had never, *never,* she stressed, been suspected either of arson or of instigating arson. But did Americana then offer to pay what its agreement with the Jacksons promised? No, not at all. Why not? Because it argued that by law it didn't have to as long as it held its investigation open. And for how long had the investigation remained open? It was still open, Nat explained. This is the reason we are here, several years later, asking you, the jury, to tell Americana that it has to honor its agreements. It has to pay the monies it owes to the Jacksons who own Power Industries and it has to pay for the harm it caused by its inexcusable delay.

Originally Nat had planned to summarize the damages suffered by Power Industries, but now this was reserved for the second phase of the trial. Therefore, following the advice of a wise teacher who said, "When you are finished, stop," Natalya thanked the jury and moved toward her chair. Then almost as an afterthought, she added, "I don't know what Americana will tell you it can prove, but I assure you it won't be that it doesn't owe my clients money."

Considering the strength of Nat's opening, Americana's lawyer responded effectively. He said pretty much what Natalya and Steve expected and what they would have said had they been in his shoes. Using brevity to his advantage, he agreed with Nat that this was a simple case. However, he explained, the lawsuit was not about whether or not Americana was obligated to pay Power Industries for the damage caused by the fire. It was about whether or not Americana could be faulted for duly investigating the fire before making a settlement.

Nat worked throughout the weekend with Steve and the Jacksons. Saturday morning she was out before Sheela woke up.

"This house feels funny," Sheela said to Victor.

"How is it funny?" Victor asked.

"It feels like Ma's mad at us, even though she isn't."

"That's a good way of putting it," Victor agreed. Mommy is very busy with her trial and she is nervous."

"I'm nervous too," Sheela said.

"Don't be silly," Victor told his daughter. "You are a little kid. Little kids don't get nervous. You can't even explain how nervous feels."

"I can too," Sheela argued.

"OK, then tell how you feel when you are nervous."

"I feel like I'm in a hurry, even when I'm not."

Victor conceded, "I guess kids can get nervous after all."

"What would I like to do today?" Sheela asked.

"You tell me," her father answered. "Tomorrow you are going to Beca and Gappa's, but today they are busy."

"Today I planned to go shopping to the Galleria and to Gymboree and to eat."

"When did you plan that?" Victor noted that Sheela had at least one of his traits. She preferred structure to hanging loose.

"Just now, when I asked you."

"I wish I could take you, but I can't because I promised Mama I'd stick around in case she needed some help. In a little while I'm going to her office to see what's up."

Partly because Victor didn't want Natalya and Steve spending all weekend without him, and partly to assuage some inchoate feelings of guilt that plagued him, Victor had volunteered to help with last minute details like double checking exhibits.

"I wanna go and help too," Sheela whined.

"Not this time," Victor said. "Lulu is coming over to stay with you."

The finality in her father's tone let Sheela know that today was not a day to press any points. She felt a lot like crying, but decided to hold back her tears because if she cried now it would just make Victor angry. So instead of fussing, she asked Victor in a small voice, "What could I do?"

"You could watch your micro discs, or read with Lulu, or play with your puzzles, or paint, or color, or cut. I can help you with your great big floor puzzle if you want until it's time for me to go."

"No," Sheela decided. "I wanna play with pots and pans."

When Victor arrived at Nat's office, he saw that everyone was harried and engrossed in some document or other and no one had time to delegate any jobs to him. Not knowing how else to help he asked, "Can I get anyone something to eat or drink?"

"That would be great," Steve said.

"So who wants what? Victor inquired.

"Anything, it doesn't matter," Nat said. Then she remembered to ask, "but first could you see what's pouring out of the fax machine? We're being drowned in garbage."

"The garbage you are being drowned in is from Lomax, Cushman and Sweeney," Victor said. "There are three settlement offers here, for three million dollars, for four million dollars and for five million dollars, respectively. Maybe someone should pay attention."

"What?" Tiffany asked.

"The last settlement offer is for five million dollars."

"Forget it," Nat said. "We can't respond."

"Why not?" the Jacksons and Victor asked in unison.

"Because we sued for twenty-five million and if we get bogged down in talking settlement now, we'll get distracted from getting ready for the trial."

"How much would you settle for?" Victor asked.

"Somewhere around fifteen million," Steve replied. "That might be the most we can get. If a jury verdict comes in above that figure, there is a chance the court would reduce it. But Nat's right—we can't consider any offers now."

"So is this a tactic to make us bungle our preparation?" Randy Jackson asked.

"Maybe, maybe not," Nat answered. "Bottom line is we don't think about anything except the trial until Monday."

"I'll be back in about a half-hour with something good to eat," Victor said walking out of the room.

37

When Natalya and Steve walked into court Monday morning, they saw that Americana was serious about settlement. Its lawyers arrived early and upped their offer to seven million dollars.

Tiffany and Randy were psyched to go to trial and urged Nat and Steve to play hardball, notwithstanding Judge Allbright's admonitions about the parade of horribles that was apt to ensue if Power and Americana didn't come to an agreement. It seemed to the Jacksons that everything terrible that could happen had already happened and they wanted their day in court. Meanwhile, Americana was losing its nerve and its patience with the firm of Lomax, Cushman and Sweeney. Its lawyers had milked this case for all it was worth and failed to wear the Jacksons down.

Seven million dollars would compensate Power Industries for actual losses and legal fees. It would bail the Jacksons out, but that's about all it would do. Several years ago it would have been more than adequate. Today it wasn't enough. Nat obtained authority from Tiffany and Randy to settle for twelve point six million dollars and she put that demand on the table. Americana agreed in a heartbeat.

Sheela started to cry when she learned that her Mama and Uncle Steve got a lot of money for their office.

"This is good news, sweetheart," Natalya said. "Why are you crying?"

"Cause," her daughter answered.

"Because what?"

"Cause your office is going to get big and you are going to put a lawyer in the room where Uncle Steve lets me keep my toys."

"Maybe," Nat said. "But then you are getting big, too. You'll be going to school soon and you won't need that room. You'll be big enough to sit in my office or to study in the library without Lulu. Right?"

"I don't know," Sheela answered, unwilling to let go of a part of her life that was slipping into the past.

Nat empathized with Sheela. She understood her resistance to change engineered by outside forces. She also recognized that Victor was afraid of the quality of change this victory would bring about. Strangely enough, even in her own heart she found a grain of sadness. A trying but thrilling phase of her life had just come to an end.

"We all are a little afraid when we see that things are going to be different," Nat told Sheela. "But nothing stays the same and usually things get better. So it's best to enjoy the present and not to worry about later on."

"What present?"

"The present means right now."

"Oh! I know poem about the present. Can I tell you?"

"I'd love that," Natalya said.

In one breath Sheela recited:

> Yesterday is history.
> Tomorrow is a mystery.
> Today is a gift, so we call it the present.

Several days after the Landaus returned from their belated Thanksgiving celebration in New York, Nat asked Sheela a question.

"Would you like to spend your fifth birthday in Chicago with Jaya Auntie, Sunil Uncle, and Sunita?"

"Is Sunita really Jaya Auntie's baby, even if she's dopted?" Sheela asked in lieu of responding.

"Of course. An adopted baby is just like any other baby."

"So how come she is dopted?"

"The word is adopted," Nat clarified. "She's adopted because she didn't live inside Jaya Auntie's tummy before she was born. Her mommy and daddy picked her when she was only three weeks old.

"No. She picked them," Sheela argued. "They picked her name."

"So would you like to have New Year and your birthday in Chicago?"

"And with everybody else too?" Sheela wanted to know.

"Aunt Annette, Uncle David, and Bobby would come, probably a day or two after us, and Aunt Cecily, Uncle Ronald and Alex can come."

"And Beca and Gappa and Door and Pappa?"

"No, they couldn't come, but they will send presents."

"Maybe Beca would feel sad if we go."

"I know," Nat said. "That's why you have to choose."

During the night Sheela dreamt she was floating over the ocean in a glass house, except Aa-Oo told her it wasn't really an ocean; it was just a very big lake.

"It isn't a lake, cause it has waves and a beach just like Galveston and it's blue. Anyway, I don't care because I'm not going in the water. I'm staying in this house."

"It's not a house. It's a great glass elevator like in the book." Aa-Oo was annoying Sheela. He contradicted everything she said. "And if you don't care about the difference between a lake and an ocean, you should."

"Why?"

"It's a fact, that's why. It's a Great Lake. Ask anyone."

"No, I'm cold. Let's go home," Sheela said.

Aa-Oo was ready to go home too, but the glass house didn't want to take them back. It floated for a while and then it careened downward. Just before it crashed into the water, it evaporated and Sheela began to fly, propelled by her pigtails. After some time a handsome lad with chestnut colored hair joined her.

"I'm keeping my promise," he said, "but this isn't when."

"Me too," Sheela vowed.

The morning after her dream, Sheela woke up with a strong wish to go to Chicago after all, but she didn't want Beca to feel bad. She asked Victor to ask Beca what she thought.

"That isn't a very good idea," Victor said. "It's your birthday after all and your decision."

"If it isn't a very good idea, it's a little bit good, isn't it?"

"No, actually it's a bad idea. Saying something isn't a very good idea means it isn't good at all and so it's bad. It's just more polite to say it that way."

"OK, I have another idea," Sheela volunteered, her hands folded in her lap, her lips pursed and her perky dimple out of sync with her furrowed brow.

"And what is your new idea?"

"Promise you won't say it's bad."

"I can't promise that. I'll be honest. But if it isn't good, you can think up as many ideas as you want and I'm sure one of them will turn out to be good. Will that work?"

"I can't think of so many ideas," Sheela solemnly answered.

"Well, let's hear this one and then if it's bad, we'll figure something out together."

"OK, this is my idea. Let's send Beca an e-mail."

"Why? It would be easier to just pick up the phone and talk."

"Cause then you could help me say the right words. That's a good idea, isn't it.?"

Victor considered the proposition carefully, before he replied. "Yes, it's a fine idea."

The final version of Sheela's e-mail said the following:

Dear Beca

Here is my question. If I go to Chicago to see Jaya Auntie and Sunil Uncle s new baby, Sunita, would you be upsept? If I don t visit Sunita she maybe would feel bad because she is adopted.

What is your answer? Please say yes or no.

Love,

Sheela

And please tell Gappa too.

In the evening Victor printed out Beca's answer and read it to Sheela after she found the words she could read herself, like *I, love, birthday,* and *Beca.* But she couldn't find *yes* or *no,* so she held her breath, and listened intently to her grandmother's words spoken in her father's voice.

Dearest Sheela,

Your question about whether I would feel bad if you go to Chicago for your birthday cannot be answered in one word because my feelings are mixed. I wish that you could be in two places at once. Since that isn t possible, except in your heart, I want you to go. Chicago is a wonderful city. I lived there when I was a little girl.

Gappa and I will miss you and your birthday very much, but we still want you to go.

I know Sunita loves you and will feel glad that you came.

love, XXX s and ( ) ( ) s from Beca.

"I want to go to Chicago," Sheela announced.

"Done," her father said.

"Could you show me Chicago now?"

"It's too big, but I can show you a map on the computer," her father answered.

"Could I see if there is a Great Lake that looks like an ocean on a map?"

"Sure, you can see that. Who told you about the Great Lakes?"

"I don't know." Sheela shrugged her shoulders. "I just remembered."

In a few moments Sheela was seated on her Daddy's lap looking at the Great Lakes. "Wow!" she exclaimed. "There are five of them and they look like fingers."

"That's quite right. The lakes' names are Lake Erie, Lake Huron, Lake Ontario, Lake Michigan and Lake Superior."

"And Lake Michigan is in Chicago, right?"

"That's right. I can't believe you know that."

Sheela looked crestfallen. "I do too. You hafta believe me," she said.

"I do believe you," Victor clarified. "I'm just surprised. 'I can't believe you know that' is an expression. It means, 'Wow!'"

"Oh, like a present means now."

"Yes, just like that," Victor agreed. "Since you know so much, say what state Houston is in."

"Texas," Sheela shouted anticipating a game in the making.

"And New York City?"

"New York!"

"And Chicago?"

"Michigan!" Sheela answered gleefully.

"Gotcha!" Victor said. "Chicago is in Illinois."

"That's not fair." Sheela's pride was wounded.

"Maybe not," Victor said, "but it's a fact."

<hr>

As soon as she walked into the Khannas' living room, her ears popping from the elevator ride up to the forty-first floor, Sheela hurried to the windows and stared at the panoramic view.

"The Great Lake is all white!" Sheela exclaimed. "It's supposed to be blue."

"It is blue, but now it's covered by a blanket of white snow," Jaya explained.

"My grandma lived in Chicago when she was little, but not in this house. But the lake was here when she was little, wasn't it?"

"Of course. Chicago was very different when Rebecca Landau was a child. But it was as cold, windy, and beautiful as it is now. Chicago has kept a lot of its old flavor. It was considered a modern city a long time ago because it was rebuilt after a big fire and it is certainly a modern city today."

"I know," Sheela agreed.

That evening Sheela and her parents went to see the Nutcracker Suite, just the three of them. The Singers and the Rosenbaums weren't arriving until the next day and the Khannas stayed home with Sunita. Sheela watched the ballet spellbound. The charm of the music and the dance were familiar, like old friends, but the performers and the audience generated excitement that was all new. When the cast took its final bows, Sheela cried. She didn't want the performance to be over.

When the others arrived the next day in time for an at home New Year's Eve celebration, Sheela was beside herself with joy. She adored being with Alex who was as determined not to let go of Sheela as she was to remain close by him. Alex brought Robo along so he could play with Aa-Oo. Bobby was a handful. He was jealous of the attention Sheela paid to Alex, but Sheela pacified him by handing him M&Ms whenever he threatened to cry. She also allowed him to chase her, and each time she was caught, she let him give her a hug.

Sunita was one quarter from India, one quarter Scottish, one quarter Chinese and one quarter Polynesian. She had been born in Hawaii, and when she was barely three weeks old, the Khannas flew from Chicago to Honolulu to get her. Her hair was the color of copper; her skin was the color of gold; her wide eyes were hazel and her mouth looked like a dark red rosebud. Sunita gurgled and cooed at Sheela. The second Sheela saw her, she knew that being adopted was good. Still, she had a worry.

"Why didn't her tummy mommy and daddy keep her?" she asked Jaya.

"We don't know," Jaya answered.

"Sunita knows," Sheela said, "but she will forget when she is bigger. How will you tell her what happened if you don't know?"

"The answer is in an envelope in a safe place in Honolulu. When Sunita is eighteen, if she wants to find out how she came to be our daughter, she can write a letter and someone will show her the envelope where it is all explained," Jaya answered.

⁂

Jaya arranged Sheela's birthday party late on the evening of the first. Bobby and Alex were deprived of naps and tired out to ensure that they would go to bed early.

"You are going to be five," Jaya explained, "so you are old enough to have a grown-up party. And you took a long nap, so you won't be sleepy. We'll give Bobby and Alex their favors tomorrow."

Since the group was small, the Khannas arranged an elegant sit down dinner. Everybody was dressed up. Sheela wore a new velvet dress in a color the saleslady called "aubergine." The menu included Sheela's favorite dishes: grilled cheese sandwiches, sweet and sour chicken, noodles and fruit salad. The combination was a little off, but Jaya made it work. The table was beautifully set, with crystal glasses and Jaya's gold rimmed bone china. To the right of each plate was the favor that the Landaus had brought for everyone: money clips for the gentlemen and perfume bottles for the ladies.

After Sheela cut her strawberry ice cream birthday cake, the grown-ups presented a show. She laughed and clapped while her elders danced, sang, and told jokes. The program ended with a short play about a little girl who lost her birthday but found it again hiding under her pillow. When the birthday was discovered, the performers brought in Sheela's gifts.

Dora sent Sheela Natalya's old but well-preserved Barbie and Ken dolls with whole new wardrobes; Beca and Gappa sent a ballerina in a glass filled with golden snow. It was an antique that looked familiar to Sheela though Victor assured her she had never seen it before. Lulu's gift was a box of jungle animal puzzles, one of which was a parrot who looked a lot like Aa-Oo. Natalya and Victor gave her a palm held computer which carried on conversations; Alex, Ronald, and Cecily presented her with a play tea set made of real china. From the Singers, Sheela got two new games that she could play either on her computer or on television. Steve Jordan had insisted that Nat take his gift to Chicago. It was a tiger-eye frog Sheela named Donald. The last box to be opened came from Sunita and her parents. Inside it, stood an exquisite Indian bride doll wearing an embroidered red silk sari and real gold jewelry.

The birthday girl had a hard time falling asleep after her party, even though she stayed up until nearly midnight and snuggled between her parents in the big bed in Jaya's guest room. Nat felt Sheela twist and turn.
"Are you sad because your birthday is over?" she whispered.
"Only a little. But that's not all." Sheela whispered too.
"You did like your birthday and you are glad you came, aren't you?"
"A lot, but my eyes are crying."
Nat caressed Sheela's face and felt wet tears on her fingers. "Do you know why your eyes are cying?"
"I can't remember," Sheela said. But telling her mother how she felt comforted her. Nat held her and stroked her head. In a few minutes, she saw that Sheela's eyes were closed and dry.

Book Three

38

At nearly sixteen Sheela was beautiful, intelligent, graceful, and talented. She smiled at the world with poise and confidence. Her beauty and strength were true reflections of her self, but her poise masked inner turmoil. Waves of turbulence often swelled in Sheela's mind and heart when she was alone. Sometimes her mother almost sensed that Sheela was not at peace, but Nat brushed that vague notion aside, attributing it to her imagination. Only Beca, her father's mother, noticed when Sheela was guarded, or her eyes shone too brightly, or her thoughts were detached from her actions. Rebecca knew the source of the torment that intermittently troubled her granddaughter, but her knowledge mandated silence.

Sheela tried to hide her deepest, most perplexing emotions from others and even from herself. She was like an incompetent oyster unsuccessfully attempting to cover a troubling grain of sand with a pearl. One day, when the sand touched a tender spot, she confided in her mother's friend, Annette Singer, a therapist.

"Sometimes I feel like I'm losing it, Aunt Annette," Sheela confided. "Why don't you give me a Rorschach test or something?"

"I wish I could," Annette replied, "but we can't treat or counsel people we know. It's against our professional oath. I could refer you to someone else."

"No way," Sheela said. "My parents would freak. You know they think one good friend is worth ten psychologists. I was just kidding anyway."

"Why don't we talk? I am a good friend and I am not obligated to disregard my knowledge and experience, you know."

"Well . . . there isn't really anything to say, Aunt Annette," Sheela pointed out. "It's just that I feel scared and alone. A part of me is linked to shadows."

"Don't we all feel scared, alone, and linked to shadows?" Annette asked by way of response. "That's normal unless our feelings impact our capacity to be happy. If you aren't willing to explore your emotions, you have to acknowledge them and accept them for what they are."

"Yeah," Sheela said. "I know."

Annette's advice gave Sheela insight into herself and helped her far more than Annette could imagine.

Up until the summer she was fifteen, Sheela's trials and tribulations appeared to be the normal—albeit frequently dramatic—ones that accompany girlhood and adolescence: tiffs with parents to test boundaries, overreactions to occasional facial eruptions, and the pain of friendships gone sour. Her closeness to family and dedication to intellectual development compensated for the fact that there was less giggling and more solitude in her life than her elders would have liked.

At school Sheela was hurt when classmates resented her achievements and wept when they accused her of being a mama's girl for not wanting to go to summer camp. And she fretted over her disinterest in the boys who awkwardly sought her friendship and a little more. "Maybe I'll never fall in love," she thought to herself. "Something must be wrong with me." But after some time she joined the drama club, she made new friends with girls and boys whose interests and ambitions were in tune with her own, and she put romance on the back burner.

Dora worried. "Things are going too smoothly with Sheela. She is too low key. One of these days something is going to give."

"Don't be silly." Nat denied the possibility of a problem. "You are just a sophisticated worrywart. You worry because things are going too well. You didn't have any more problems with me when I was a teenager than I have with Sheela."

"You have a short memory," Dora said.

"You had problems with Moi?" Natalya feigned indignation.

"Yes, you," Dora answered. "You were bolder than Sheela and more interested in material things, not to mention fascinated by boys. In junior high you succumbed to the influence of a rather shallow circle of friends who believed that self-worth was defined by parental net-worth and confirmed by the price tag of the clothes one wore. That was before school uniforms were the norm. We had scenes because I refused to finance the Calvin Klein label on your butt. You wanted a job so you could buy your own clothes, and you thought I was horrible because I wouldn't allow it. You couldn't appreciate the idea that your job was to become educated and cultured. I couldn't see providing a rapidly growing girl with six or eight pairs of expensive blue jeans that all looked alike. I was blind you said. The jeans were *completely* different you said. Some looked worn in the knees and others were stone washed, and yet others had God knows what. *Everybody* wears them you said."

"Really?" Nat interjected.

"Really. Then there were the gatherings in your friends' houses. You were furious because I wouldn't let you go until you were sixteen. You said it made you an outcast. Have you forgotten the time you made me think you were spending the night with Gloria Epstein, but you both went over to Janet's house? She was having one of those psychedelic parties. I found out when I called Gloria's mother. Your father and I left a dinner engagement and came to haul you home. You were dressed like a little slut in someone else's clothes. But you looked like an exquisite nymphet. When I saw that some of the guys were much older, I panicked, even though deep down I trusted you. It was the boys I didn't trust. You screamed at me in front of your friends and accused me of being archaic. In the end though, you confessed that the party was awful and you felt we had rescued you. Has all that slipped your mind?"

"I guess," Natalya said. "I didn't think I was that bad. I can't believe that I lied to you."

"You didn't lie, as such. You merely manipulated my assumptions. You were clever."

"How horrible," Nat remarked.

"In truth I suppose it wasn't all that horrible," Dora said. "It was the times and you liked to take chances. Still, you were basically a fine daughter and look how marvelously you've turned out. You are probably right. I'm just an aging worrywart."

⸎

Between her sophomore and junior years, Sheela originally planned a trip to Europe with a youth theater group, but then, at the last minute, she canceled out. No one could understand why. Even Sheela herself had no explanation. One minute she was excited about the trip, which had been mapped out months in advance, and the next she was overpowered by the need to stay put in familiar surroundings.

That summer Sheela read, exercised in the gym, and worked in Nat and Steve's office, now a thriving boutique of eight lawyers. The firm of Jordan and Landau was well settled in the contemporary re-designed space on the same site where it had started out well over a decade ago.

During her plentiful free time, she lived in virtual reality. Sheela's cyber world consisted of a large family, the Stellars who lived in Karmatica, a place that existed both in today's world and in the hereafter—or the herebefore—where the present, past and future merged. Sheela's Karmatic Avatar was Sarah. Sarah was Sheela's age. She had brown eyes, was petite, and was a magnificent ballerina. Sarah had recently competed in the annual Dance Expo held in Madrid and had won a silver medal. As for her relatives on the net, Sheela suspected that many of them had recreated their characters to a much greater extent than she had. She thought Gregory Stellar, her father figure, was an oldish lady in her sixties or seventies.

Natalya worried that Sheela's involvement in virtual life might damage her in some way, though Victor assured her that enough research had been done to confirm that interaction in web families was harmless at worst and creative, enriching and even therapeutic at best.
"It's just like anything else," he said. "Everyone finds his or her own level. Someone like Sheela is going to hook up with people of her caliber. The creeps will find other creeps. Besides, Sheela has plenty of outside interests. There's no danger of her becoming addicted."

Sheela began to change after a dream tha came when she had been out of touch with the Stellars for over a week. She had been busy helping with a petition to be filed in federal court. Jordan and Landau's clients were suing a cosmetic company, Beauty Teen, on behalf of thirty-six thirteen and fourteen-year olds who had collectively spent over seventy-six thousand dollars on the Company's products over a period of several months. The petition alleged that Beauty Teen engaged in false and misleading advertising that promised its creams and cosmetics improved users' appearance and self-image. These expensive products were worthless at best. A number of the teens who bought them wound up with deteriorating complexions and thinning hair resulting in nervous collapses.

Although Sheela agreed that the ads exploited the vulnerability of the young, she believed that kids should have the same right to waste their money as adults. Why be patronizing and unduly protective of them? Moreover, the chemical analyses of the products could not confirm that they directly caused hair loss or acne. On the other hand, experts were prepared to testify that Beauty Teen's advertising campaigns were designed to be psychologically destructive.

"It's a kind of voodoo," Natalya explained. "Any kid who is fundamentally insecure and unpopular and exposed to these ads is afraid not to buy the stuff."

"I don't know." Sheela wasn't convinced. "Isn't this one of those things you call a slippery slope? Remember the time we went shopping and the salesman tried talking you into buying me an outrageously expensive aqua dress. He said, 'You really should let her have the dress; your daughter is worth it.' So you answered, 'I have no doubt that my daughter is worth it. It's the dress that is over valued.' Still, you didn't sue the salesman."

"Life and law are both slippery slopes," Nat replied. "But in this case Beauty Teen has made a concerted and wide scale effort to induce teenagers to buy its products, knowing that they are entirely worthless. And they didn't use generalities, like 'You're worth it,' they made specific representations like 'Beauty Teen products will fix your skin, fix your hair, make you slim, and turn you into a Dream Teen. If you don't buy them, forget the prom.'"

That night Sheela was up late thinking that had she not backed out of the European tour, she would be in Madrid for a Garcia Lorca festival with her friends. They were all having a blast. She wondered what on earth had prodded her to remain in Houston. Her musings gave way to a sharp and unexpected pang of worry. Was it a premonition of some kind? Was something going to happen to someone she loved? Beca hadn't been feeling well recently, but everyone else was fine. "God," she prayed, "don't let anything happen. Especially not to Beca. No, I take that back. Not especially not to Beca, not to anyone. Please, God."

Hoping that a hot shower with an aromatic gel would be soothing, Sheela selected a raspberry-almond scented packet. But instead of calming her down, the cascading water suffocated her and the bittersweet scent of the shower enervated her. She rinsed herself off and cuddled into an old flannel nightgown. Then she turned up the air conditioning and climbed into bed with Aa-Oo who was faded and had a loose beak.

Sheela thought she would be twisting and turning for hours, but she fell asleep almost as soon as her head hit her pillow. Except that she didn't fall asleep. She felt herself plunged into a murky darkness where she became totally unable to breathe. She fought the demons that pulled at her, turning her legs into lead. For a time she tried to shout, but no sounds came from her mouth. Then suddenly the darkness channeled itself into a tube and she was no longer bogged down. Instead she flashed through the tube at an unimaginable speed and she soon emerged into light that lifted her out of her body.

Looking down she saw the place where her body had been left behind and she saw another strong and beautiful body, that of a boy-man who was swimming in the darkness and tugging at her lifeless shape. Sheela called out to him again and again, pleading with him to join her in the beautiful light, but he didn't. Gradually he became fainter and smaller until he faded from view.

Far away, in another place, there were many more people sitting on the floor sobbing and chanting a name that she couldn't make out. One little girl in particular could not be consoled. Sheela tried to tell her that everything would be fine, but the child didn't understand. She hugged her small narrow shoulders and wept silent, copious tears—so many that she filled the room where she huddled in puddles of water. From where she floated, Sheela saw that the girl was making paper boats and sailing them in the puddles, but soon that vision faded as well.

In the morning, a single beam of light filtered through a gap in her blinds. The light had an unusual quality. It touched Sheela's memory and brought back faint images of the trip that her mind had taken during the night. She was overwhelmed with longing. She tried to put her thoughts and feelings into some kind of context but couldn't do it. Then she concentrated as hard as she was able to in an effort to convey her questions telepathically to Aa-Oo, like she had done when she was little. In those days, Aa-Oo always had answers. But now, her old parrot was silent."

Sheela wasn't a morning person so she was surprised to find herself awake at only 6:30, particularly after a late night. And she felt anxious and hungry, empty really. And she needed music. So she was eating a third piece of French toast when Victor discovered her in the kitchen. A transparent thread hung from her head and she was swaying to the beat of something playing in her ears. Victor tapped her on the shoulders and she gave a little start and unplugged herself.

"Earth to Sheela," Victor said, looking puzzled. "I thought something smelled good. What has gotten into you? Up at dawn and cooking up a storm? Are you my one and only daughter Sheela, or are you an imposter? Usually it takes an act of congress to get you to the breakfast table."

"To tell you the truth, Daddy, I can't understand it myself. I feel like Serena."

"Who?" Victor asked.

"You know, Samantha's cousin on *Bewitched*, the antique TV show."

"Oh, *that* Serena," Victor said. "I see. Well, to be honest, I don't see."

"Well, I feel like my own alter ego. I'm not myself. Something is weirding me out. Instead of Samantha who has it together, I'm Serena, the kook who's lost it."

"Nah," Victor said. "You're one of the Tabathas. Did you know she was played by twins? Ma is Sam, I'm Darren/Dum dum, Beca and Gappa are Mr. and Mrs. Stevens, and Door is a perfect Endora. Harold is a tame version of Maurice. Right?"

"Daa-deee," Sheela retorted impatiently.

"What's really wrong?" Victor asked.

"I'm just hungry, that's all," Sheela said. "It's nothing."

"What is nothing?" Nat asked barging in on the tail end of Victor and Sheela's conversation. Nothing is always the wrong answer."

"And good morning to you too, Mama," Sheela replied. "Would you like a cup of tea? First Daddy, and now you are interrogating me simply because I decided to have breakfast."

"You look odd." Nat ignored Sheela's irritation. When Sheela got up to get a glass of milk from the refrigerator, she added, "You look taller too."

"That's ridiculous, Mama. I've been almost 5'4'' tall for the last two years. I've stopped growing. Lulu measured me just last week because she thought I looked taller too. Can I use the big video conferencer today, Ma, if no one needs it? Please?"

"I don't know," Natalya replied. "It's pretty expensive and it isn't something you should take for granted."

"On the other hand?" Sheela prompted.

"On the other hand . . . . ,"

"Thanks a lot Ma," Sheela interrupted, giving Nat a quick tight squeeze.

Sheela started her conferencing with New York. First she visited with her maternal grandparents and then with her cousin Alex, and while she didn't ask outright, she was reassured to know that everyone was well. Door and Harold looked fit and relaxed. Alex, browned and skinny, was safely back from his canoeing trip. Sheela cringed when he went on and on about how much fun he had when their canoe turned over. Ronald and Cecily were fine, he said. His Mom was excited about a play she was going to direct and in which she was also playing a neat minor role. His Dad was working a lot, but he was making time to play tennis with Alex. His six-year-old brother Jimmy was fine too. He was going to day camp, and he insisted there were alligators in the stream that ran through the woods.

Next Sheela connected with Sunita in Chicago. Her parents were both at work. Jaya usually worked out of her home, but today she had a live meeting downtown. At eleven, going on eighteen, Sunita was a young lady. She had shed most of her baby fat and was bouncing with excitement because she was getting ready to go to India for three weeks with her grandmother, Anjali Khanna. She promised to bring back tons of bangles, sparkling forehead tikkies, and everything else that had become the rage. One of her cousins was getting married in Bombay so she was going to spend a week there and be in Delhi the rest of the time. Her cousin was having eleven different functions in the course of the week and Sunita was attending all eleven.

"What are the functions going to be?" Sheela asked her god-sister.

"Let's see," Sunita said. "There is the wedding, of course, and the next day is the reception. Before the wedding, there is a morning party where everyone gets mehndi, you know henna, put on their hands. Then there are two concerts, the bride's and the groom's, the two nights before the wedding. They aren't actually concerts. They're more like shows. Everyone puts on skits, but there is also music and singing. How many is that?"

"That's five," Sheela answered.

"OK, then there is a dinner the bride's family gives for the groom's immediate family. Oh, and there is a dance performance and a Latin American party and there are three different lunches given by the bride's relatives. Is that eleven?"

"That's what I counted. Are you sure you aren't going to get fed up?" Sheela inquired.

"I'm sure," Sunita replied. "I need a different outfit and jewelry for every occasion and my gran is making sure I get them. She's ordered most of the stuff for me already, and I get to bring it all back."

"What all are you going to wear?" Sheela asked.

"Different things. Tight pant and loose pant outfits and long skirts, and maybe a sari at the reception. No western clothes, except for the Latin American dancing and maybe one or two of the less formal lunches."

"Wow!" Sheela said. "That's quite something."

"It's terrifical," Sunita agreed.

"Well, I'd better disconnect," Sheela finally said. "Someone else needs the conferencer at ten and I should make myself useful. So let me know what's up. OK?"

"OK. Love," Sunita said.

"OK, I'm signing off. Love."

Sheela wished she could see Bernie, but Bernadette Williams didn't have access to a viewer over the summer and she wouldn't be in anyway, so Sheela just left a voice saying, "I'm thinking of you. Actually, I really miss you. OK, bye."

After putting down the receiver Sheela had another fleeting wish, but even before the wish materialized it evanesced and left her feeling lonelier than ever.

39

Sheela's friendship with Bernadette, a true eccentric, grounded her. It showed her how much she could love and respect someone whose opinions, predilections, and personality differed from hers. The girls were unalike. Sheela — not withstanding her love for solitude — was gregarious whereas Bernie was a genuine loner. Sheela was her only friend. Bernie didn't mind being disdained as a brain, while Sheela down-played her intellect. Sheela enjoyed being attractive, but Bernie did her best to hide her looks. Sheela stood 5'5" tall as confirmed by Natalya who measured her, insisting that she had grown, overnight, so to speak. Bernie was a petite 5'1½" freckled redhead with long, out-of-control frizzy hair and intense brown eyes that peered out from behind fogged black spectacles. Sheela's gleaming black curls always fell into place, and her ocean blue eyes reflected within them the objects at which she gazed with perfect vision. Bernie refused to wear contacts. Her glasses were a shield so people couldn't see her thoughts, she said. And they complemented her style. Bernie *liked* looking like a mini bag lady in oversized clothes that hid her delicate hourglass figure.

What Sheela loved most about her friend was that Bernie never exacted confidences. She was the only person in the whole world who was close to her yet didn't pry. Sheela's other friends always wanted to know what Sheela thought of people or things Sheela either hadn't considered or else didn't want to discuss. Her parents forever wanted to understand her when Sheela often couldn't understand herself. Her grandparents were subtler, but it was the same thing. They noticed nuances in her moods and believed there was a discoverable reason for every little thing she did.

Sheela was interested in the secrets of life. She believed in karma and rejected the idea that the world was the product of random destiny. At the same time, she felt it was pointless to try to figure out hidden answers to formless questions. Either you knew stuff or you didn't. Bernie didn't dwell upon esoteric mysteries. She was an open-minded Catholic who took the teachings of her church with a grain of salt, yet was filled with faith. Bernadette neither agreed nor disagreed with Sheela's views. She said she didn't worry about whether or how predetermination affected free will, and she trusted that the details of her life and after life would take care of themselves.

"I'm confident that God or some equivalent coordinator watches how you play the hand you are dealt," she said. "However we came to be, we are here. It's what we do that matters."

During the summer, while Sheela's thespian friends traipsed through European theaters, Bernie worked in the New York ghettos with street children. Bernie believed in hands on social reform. She was going to be an educator. Therefore, the last thing in the world Sheela expected was for Bernadette to return in August looking more frizzy and bedraggled than ever to announce, "It's happened."

"What happened?" Sheela asked.

"The L word."

"What?" Sheela didn't get it.

"I like someone." The short sentence resounded in Bernie's own ears. Her confession was the first time she had ever verbalized her feelings and she felt as if she were speaking a foreign language. "So there is hope for you. But since I promised myself not to say a word to a single soul about HIM, this is all I can tell you for now."

"I guess you know what you're doing," Sheela remarked, "although it sounds as if you don't."

"Actually I don't," Bernie admitted. "I'm addled. I think it might even be the big L. It hit me like a bomb. Sixteen is a lot older than people think. How old were Romeo and Juliet when they fell in love? Fourteen, fifteen?"

"Something like that," Sheela said. "So how does this affect your life?"

"Well," Bernie answered, "I have to get into Harvard even if it kills me."

Bernadette's excitement and purposefulness made Sheela think about her own ambitions.

"I'm going to UT and then UT law so I can come home to Houston a lot. Maybe some day I'll be a judge. Do you think I could ever become a Supreme Court Justice?"

"Sure you could become a Justice if you really want to and if you get lucky. But you'd have to be political," Bernie said.

"Yeah, that wouldn't be much fun." Sheela looked wistful. "Whatever I do, I'd better have a good career, in case you are wrong."

"Wrong about what?" Bernie asked.

"Wrong about there being hope for me. I'm scared that I'm never going to like anybody, let alone find someone I could love. I have a thing about a man in my head and he's nothing like anyone on earth. Sometimes I hate him because he's spoiling everything else for me. How can you love a person you haven't even met and hate him at the same time?"

"Are you asking me or telling me?"

"Whatever," Sheela replied.

Dwayne Houseman, the well-built blond senior class president, didn't take rejection well, although he dished it out with impunity. He was tired of his current steady, doe-eyed, curvaceous Minnie Tampawn who oozed come hitherness and last year had made him the envy of just about every guy in the junior class. Over the summer Minnie gained a little weight and her face became blotchy. Her hair lost its sheen, too. Dwayne no longer felt that having her by his side was a badge of glory. She was becoming a drag. In fact only a few days ago someone teased him about her name. His eye was on that junior, Sheela Landau, who had calculus with him every other day at 11:00 a.m. Now there, he thought, is a class act.

Sheela had lots of friends who were guys, but she didn't have an exclusive boy friend. To Dwayne, that meant he wouldn't have the satisfaction of winning her away from someone else. On the other hand, maybe she was chaste. That would be exciting. There weren't all that many chaste girls around any more. Almost every girl he ever dated could show him a thing or two about how to have a good time. But Sheela was different from the others. It wasn't that she was cold or aloof—on the contrary—she was warm and friendly. He tried to put his finger on what it was about her that moved him and decided it was her innocence.

Obviously Sheela had yet to encounter a Mr. Right who could show her the heights to which she could ascend on the upward drift of surging hormones. And Mr. Right is yours truly, Dwayne told himself. I'm a handsome, bright and experienced guy, not some clumsy groper. I know what it takes to make a female tingle. Even without help. Of course it would be easier if he could get Sheela to imbibe or inhale, but he doubted she was the type. Anyway he wasn't big on stuff like that. And he didn't necessarily care about making Sheela go too far. He just wanted to be the one to bring out the woman in her. She would thank him for that.

Dwayne knew he was lucky because he had been well coached by his older half-brother, Edgar.

"You have to get inside a female's head," Edgar told him, "before you start with them. Femmes are funny. They look at you, a handsome hulk who can really take good care of them, but what they see is someone who needs their help. So you like play along. And they like to talk, especially about feelings."

"What is there to say about feelings?" Dwayne asked.

"You don't have to say much. Just ask a femme how she feels. Even better, ask what she imagines you feel. Then she'll tell you and all you have to do is agree."

"What if she doesn't?"

"They always do. You can bet on it," Edgar said.

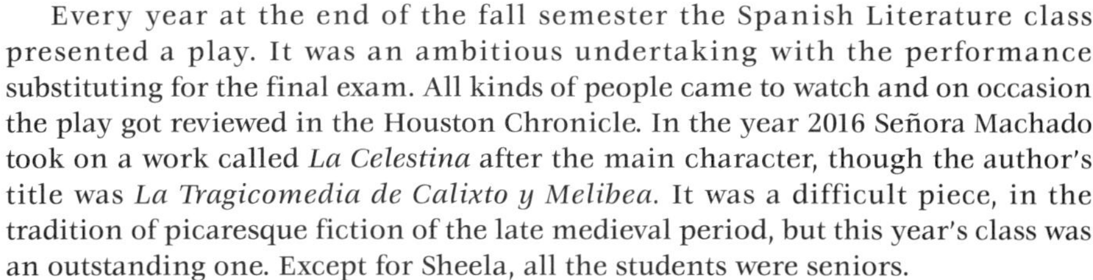

Every year at the end of the fall semester the Spanish Literature class presented a play. It was an ambitious undertaking with the performance substituting for the final exam. All kinds of people came to watch and on occasion the play got reviewed in the Houston Chronicle. In the year 2016 Señora Machado took on a work called *La Celestina* after the main character, though the author's title was *La Tragicomedia de Calixto y Melibea*. It was a difficult piece, in the tradition of picaresque fiction of the late medieval period, but this year's class was an outstanding one. Except for Sheela, all the students were seniors.

Sheela wanted to play the lead, not the wimpy role of Melibea that Elena Machado had hinted would be perfect for her, though the final decision wouldn't be made for another week. Celestina was an evil old procuress whose many talents included the mixing of love potions, the aiding and abetting of petty criminals, and the restoration of virginity by means of little pouches made of entrails filled with chicken blood. Celestina was not a good person, but she was a tough, resilient maneuverer and her cleverness was appealing. Sheela found the challenge of portraying such a character irresistible. She was willing to learn the lines and determined to find a way to get that role.

Two days before the formal try-outs Sheela marched into Señora Machado's Level 4 Spanish class three minutes late. She wore pasty make-up, a long faded full black skirt, a shawl and a wig. She felt sick to her stomach and feverish, but she had a plan and she pushed herself to execute it. As yet unrecognized, she began to recite some of Celestina's best lines, which she had memorized and practiced extensively in front of her beloved hall mirror. After she finished the soliloquy, she removed her wig, wiped her face with a wet towlette, and was about to take a seat to assess the impact of her performance. Instead she made a beeline for the trash bin in the front of the room, reaching it just as she started to heave and throw up.

By the time Victor got to school, Sheela was stretched out on a cot in the nurse's station. She had barely managed to walk there, helped by two students. Between the make-up and her own pallor she looked like a ghost. Victor was frightened. The school nurse had been about to call for an ambulance, but Sheela had begged her to wait for her mother or father to get there.

"She has all the signs of appendicitis," the nurse said. "She has a fever of 100.5 degrees and her stomach is tender to the touch. I think you should get her to a hospital. It could be an emergency."

Four hours later Sheela started to regain consciousness in the recovery room of Hermann Hospital. She was confused. Her mind was still inside a canal filled with moisture. She wasn't sure of her identity, but whoever she was had been trying to push its way through. She couldn't remember why she was struggling so hard. Nor could she remember why she had left the wonderful vaporous place she had been visiting in order to make such an arduous journey. Her eyes fluttered as she tried to put the pieces of this strange jigsaw puzzle together. She remembered herself looking like a hag and became frightened. Then she heard a familiar voice whisper "Sheela" and she knew herself again. But where was she? Why was she so wrinkled and dressed so shabbily? What was she doing in the dusk on cobblestone streets? Ah, she thought, I'm an actor in a tragic comedy. I wonder how I escape from here. It wasn't until she opened her eyes and recognized Dr. Henry Landau that she remembered the present. Henry's thick white hair fell into his eyes as he looked down at his cherished granddaughter.

"Dr. Young took out your appendix just in time. A couple of hours longer and it could have ruptured. You're going to be fine."

Sheela didn't feel fine. She was groggy, thirsty, and terribly mixed up. Her head continued to swim from the effect of the anesthesia, but her body was beginning to shrug it off and to hurt. She had no voice and she had no words. Without words she was a disempowered bundle of sensations because her thoughts had no meaning. She felt like a lump of clay floundering in a vast, hollow universe. Soon she visualized a specter-like reflection of herself wafting in space. It hovered over her for a while before it descended and merged with her body. The reunion buoyed Sheela and enabled her to fall into a deep dreamless sleep.

The next time she awoke, Sheela found herself in a pale green hospital room with bright flowered curtains. Her mother and Beca were seated forward and to the right of her bed, so Sheela would be sure to see them when she opened her eyes. First her gaze fell upon her mother. Nat's head was bent forward. She was reading some legal papers using a highlighter to make corrections. Sheela remembered that her mother liked printed copies of things. She couldn't get the feel of a document from a computer screen. Sheela found the recollection of that concept and the ability to formulate it in her head comforting. Then she focused on Beca who was sitting quietly, doing nothing, just watching, waiting for Sheela's eyes to make contact with her own. When they did, Beca smiled and Sheela smiled back even though her stomach and throat hurt badly and she felt woozy. She decided to see if she could talk, so she said "Hi" in a weak, throaty voice.

"Hi, there," Beca responded, getting up to stroke her head. "You gave us a scare, but you're going to be fine. Would you like a sip of water?"

Sheela nodded and then she made another smile for Natalya who brought her a glass of chilled water and fed it to her with a teaspoon. After drinking a few sips she closed her eyes again and tried to replay the sequence of events that landed her in the hospital with her tummy swathed in bandages and a head filled with visions of other worlds. It wasn't easy, but in the end Sheela got it right.

⸺⸺ ❊❊❊❊❊❊❊ ⸺⸺

Dwayne was disappointed to learn that Sheela was recuperating from her appendectomy just when he was ready to make a move. He was all set to ask her to the senior mixer. Now she wouldn't be in any condition to go, which meant he would have to go alone and let it be known that Sheela would have been his date had she not fallen ill.

Dumping Minne had taken longer than he had expected. Every time he proposed they broaden their social lives, she started to cry.

"But you told me you feel differently about me," she moaned. "You said I'm not like the others."

Dwayne didn't recall saying anything like that, but he had to be cautious. He didn't want Minnie spreading around the word that he was a heel. Something like that would be sure to get to Sheela and spoil everything. He had to keep up his reputation as a kind, sensitive guy. The problem was that Minnie had lasted much too long. He planned not to get tied down like that again, except perhaps with Sheela. She was special and deserved the best. Maybe he would stick with her all through the year.

"Of course you're different," he said to Minnie each time she complained. "You are terrific. I just want to be fair to you, that's all. We'll go on being exclusive as long as you want."

In the end Dwayne got his friend Irwin Dershowitz to bail him out.

"Shit, I'm not interested in Minnie," Dersh had said.

"But you said she was the alpha femme of our class," Dwayne reminded him.

"That was last year, before the sun made her face peel and before she bloated."

"I'll give you ten crisp green hundred dollar bills if you manage to get Minnie off my hands. She's on a diet and her face is smoothing out," Dwayne offered.

"Deal," Irwin said.

Sheela missed twelve school days following her surgery and during that time she drove her parents and Lulu, who had just gotten her driver's license, up the wall.

"You're crazy," Natalya told her when Sheela insisted that she had to go back to school two days after she came home from the hospital.

"I'm going to ruin my GPA. I have to go to school; I absolutely have to," Sheela said. "I feel fine. If you cared about my grades you'd let me go."

"Your teachers have e-mailed all your assignments and Bernie has brought you all her notes," Nat said. "If you get septic or run into any other problems, *then* you'll ruin your GPA. You have to learn to deal with an occasional setback in life. Grow up."

"You don't understand anything!" Sheela's voice became increasingly high pitched and she spoke quickly in a staccato mode. "School isn't like it was for your generation. It isn't. Things move at a faster pace. I can't afford to stay home. You can't make me."

"No, I can't lock you up, Sheela," Natalya responded softly and legato, "but if you defy me and go against the doctor's orders I *can* make your life quite unpleasant. You have been a very sick young lady and you don't realize how much of a problem you created for us all by hiding the fact that you were sick. And at this moment you are being extremely inconsiderate. I would have expected some graciousness from you."

"I hate it when you whisper at me like that. And you're making snake eyes at me. You don't love me, you don't!" Reduced to tears, Sheela turned away with a parting shot, "You're not fair. You're totalistically unfair. You don't care that I want to be valedictorian. You just don't want to bother because of your stupid cases. You wouldn't care if I flunked. You wouldn't."

"You're out of line," Victor said when Sheela told him "Mama is clueless," and begged him to drive her to school for a couple of hours.

"I think you were rude and unkind to your mother. You owe her an apology," he added.

"It's hopeless. Everyone is hopeless," Sheela muttered in reply. She went off to her room in a sulk, trying unsuccessfully to walk upright. Her medication was wearing off and her incision was beginning to hurt.

"Estás loca," Lulu said, when Sheela tried to circumvent her parents and begged to be driven to school just for one hour. "Totalmente loca."

Ultimately Beca and Gappa made peace between a resentful, homebound Sheela and an angry, hurt Nat.

"Look, Sheela," Dr. Landau explained. "You feel OK, but your body hasn't built up any resistance. Your defenses are down. You need rest. You're a bright girl, extremely bright, but you still have lots of growing up to do. Trust us. Upsetting yourself will only delay the healing process."

"Every sickness has two components," Beca said, "a physical one and a psychic one. The very fact that you got sick means you needed a little hiatus from your routine."

Finally a contrite Sheela apologized tearfully and embraced those who loved her. Inside she felt her appendicitis was a test that she had failed miserably.

40

"Hi, Sheel," Dwayne said one Tuesday afternoon, several weeks after Sheela's appendicitis. "Where are you heading?"

"Hi, and it's Sheela with an A at the end," she replied. "I'm going to the communications center. How about you?"

"Actually I was following you. I wanted to ask you something. Is it OK if I walk along with you?"

"Sure," Sheela answered. "It's a free country. So what do you want to ask? Is it about calculus?"

"No, nothing like that. I wanted to invite you to the new Rocklyn Stevens Imax with me this Friday night. It's supposed to be his best yet."

"I don't think so. I'm really not into dating."

"Not into dating me, or not into dating anyone?"

"Not anyone. The whole scene isn't for me," Sheela said.

"It's a great scene. You really should give it a chance. Your parents wouldn't stand in your way, would they?"

"To tell you the truth Dwayne, I don't know. It just hasn't come up. My crowd is into group stuff. I move with Janice, Sidney, Bernie and kids in the drama club. We do things together, your know. We have a great time and that way there isn't any pressure."

Dwayne was at a loss for a moment, but he was a quick thinker.

"What are you guys doing this weekend? Anything cool?" he asked, though he doubted it with the dweebs in Sheela's circle. Once she realized what he and his pals were like, she'd lose interest in them fast.

"I'm not sure yet. I have Spanish play rehearsals all day Saturday. The performance is the weekend after Thanksgiving, just a month away. I'm really excited about it."

"I bet you have the lead and it's the part of a real beauty. You're made for roles like that."

"You are half right." Sheela smiled. "I have the lead, but I'm an old hag."

"Well, OK. I'll be seeing you," Dwayne said, proud of himself for keeping a level head. He was evolving a strategy.

"OK, thanks anyway for asking," Sheela said as they approached the communications center.

Dwayne is really not so bad, Sheela thought to herself. And he's good looking, not to mention in superb shape. He was an A student and president of the senior class too. Her gut tried to tell her that something about him was fishy, but she didn't listen. Instead she reprimanded herself. Her fundamental problem, she told herself, was her total disinterest in the opposite sex. And to look at Dwayne, you'd expect him to be pushy, but he wasn't. Sheela appreciated the fact that he accepted her refusal like a gentleman. So when he phoned Thursday evening she was happy to speak with him.

"Hi, Dwayne, what's up?"

Dwayne took a deep breath. He couldn't answer because he had been fantasizing about Sheela all day. Now the sound of her voice and his take on her question gave him a sudden erection. It was a good thing he wasn't using a conferencer.

"Are you there?" Sheela asked.

"Sure, I'm here," Dwayne finally said.

"So how come you called?"

"I had a thought," he gulped.

"So, what is your thought?" Sheela wondered what was going on. Dwayne wasn't the type to be at a loss for words.

"Uh . . . would it be OK with you and everyone," Dwayne asked, "if I came along with you and your friends tomorrow to wherever you decide to go? You all TGIF, don't you?"

"Yeah, I do," Sheela said, "but not the way you think. We're Jewish and as a rule my family celebrates Sabbath on Friday nights. I normally go out with my friends on Saturdays."

"Oh." Dwayne was settling down. He didn't realize that Sheela was Jewish, but that was no problem. He wasn't prejudiced. After all he was friends with Irwin, wasn't he? Dersh didn't practice his religion, but still. It would be neat, Dwayne thought, to get up front and personal with a real Jewish girl. He wondered if she would be different from the other femmes that he had let into his life.

"Hello?" Sheela prompted after a second or two of silence.

"So are you going to do something this Saturday?" Dwayne continued.

"Maybe after rehearsal. We were thinking of going to Miller Outdoor Theater. They're having a Thai dance performance. It's right across the street from where I live," Sheela said.

"Can I join in?" Dwayne asked. Thai dancing wasn't his idea of a thrilling evening, but in the Miller Outdoor Theater he'd have a chance of easing Sheela away from the group.

"Sure," Sheela said. To say no would be rude.

After she hung up the phone, Sheela went to find her parents. She was thinking of mentioning something about Dwayne, but they were in the den engrossed in photograph albums. It didn't feel right to talk about him right then. Why should they care if he came along with her other friends?

"Come on in, Sheela," Natalya said. "We were just looking at pictures of your bat mitzvah. There aren't that many. I thought we had more."

"Oh. Do you guys have photos of yours and of Dad's bar mitzvah?"

"Well, no," Natalya answered.

"How come?"

"Actually it's a long story."

"So, I have time. Tell me about it." Sheela sat down.

"Let's see," Nat started. "The story goes something like this. When we were thirteen, our parents thought rituals didn't make sense. They were liberals and believed in loving your fellow man and universal goodness. So our parents and we strayed from many trappings of Judaism. We didn't realize that those trappings were like clothes. Being without them was like being naked. We didn't understand that we needed them and that they fit us well, like a fine tailored suit."

"I can't imagine Beca and Gappa and Door and Papa thinking that way." Sheela was incredulous.

"It was a phase," Nat answered. "Your grandparents believed their children should decide on their own how they felt about religion."

"When I was thirteen," Victor volunteered, "a teacher I respected said that I would look ridiculous announcing 'I am a man' in a crackling soprano, and I bought it."

"Rabbi Morgenstern explained that in the olden days people got married much younger and that they were required to take on responsibilities early," Sheela said.

"When I was turning thirteen," Natalya added, "bat mitzvahs for girls weren't that common anyway. The first bat mitzvah wasn't held until 1922. It took some time then for them to catch on."

"If bat mitzvahs weren't traditional," Sheela asked, "why did you encourage me to have one?"

"Traditions are very important," Nat replied, "but they shouldn't be cast in concrete. They should evolve with the times. Through most of the last millennium women didn't have the same education, the same opportunities and the same responsibilities as men, so there wasn't much point in having a bat mitzvah. Today there is. Do you see?"

"I guess," Sheela said, "but I have two questions."

"Ask and ye shall be answered," Victor said, adding "if possible."

"First, who had the first bat mitzvah?"

"That's easy," Victor answered. "It was held for Judith Kaplan, the daughter of Mordecai Kaplan. He started an American Jewish movement called Reconstructionism which views Judaism as not just a religion, but a total civilization."

"OK," Sheela said, "but we're not Reconstrucionists, right?"

"Right," Victor said. "Strictly speaking, Reconstructionists think God is just a moral force. We think He . . ."

"Or She," Nat piped in.

"Or She," Victor agreed, "is more than that. Next question."

"My next question is, when did you and Ma change? Like when did you decide to be real Jews?"

"We were always real Jews, but we gradually became more observant. Your Mother eased me into it," Victor said.

"It was you who made me appreciate our heritage," Natalya told Sheela. "I began to feel the need to study and practice Judaism when I conceived you."

Sometimes Sheela wished she could discover the true identities of the Stellars and of other Karmaticans, although obviously she would never try. And even if she were the sort of person who might attempt something like that, it would be practically impossible. All virtual reality people affirmed that they would not reveal themselves under any circumstances. Furthermore, even if anyone ever did, there would be no way of knowing whether that person was being truthful. Some people had more than one virtual avatar in any case.

Whoever they were on earth, the virtual people of Karmatica constituted a colorful kaleidoscopic society filled with characters from diverse cultural and ethnic backgrounds, and from all periods of history, even projected futuristic eras. They adhered to a wide variety of religions. There were Christian and Jewish families, eclectic families, atheists, individualists, and families or solos who followed any number of Eastern, Western, and ancient creeds.

Sheela through Sarah became fascinated by *Caodaism*, a Vietnamese religion. Caodai means 'high tower' or 'palace' and Caodaism became popular in Karmatica and other virtual worlds. It began as a sect in the late nineteenth century and became an official religion in Vietnam in 1926. Its doctrine blended Mahayana Buddhism, Taoism and Confucianism and its believers communicated with the spirits of many famous humans including Shakespeare, Joan of Arc, René Descartes, Victor Hugo and Louis Pasteur.

<hr>

"Why are you letting Dwayne the Pain come out with us?" Bernadette asked Sheela when she heard that he was crashing their Saturday night program. "If he comes, I'm staying home."
"Come on, Bernie," Sheela coaxed. "It's good to get to know new people. Anyhow it's not like you to be calling people names. Dwayne is a pretty nice guy."
"He is not. I don't see why you didn't just say no."
"I couldn't see any reason to say no when he asked if it would be OK. And you've hardly ever talked to him, so on what basis can you decide he isn't nice?"
"On the basis of the way he struts around. I can tell he thinks he's God's gift to women."

In the end Bernie stayed home. The rest of Sheela's friends ignored Dwayne and enjoyed the music and dancing. Sheela had a horrible evening. In some respects it was the worst evening of her life. Dwayne had a wonderful time. He was confident of having latched on to a very good thing.

Throughout the performance, Dwayne sat uncomfortably close to Sheela. Every time she inched away, he inched right after her. They were on the lawn and it was crowded, so there wasn't that much room to maneuver. Eventually, Dwayne's arm slipped behind the small of her back. His fingers began to stroke. Sheela imagined thick slimy worms crawling all over her body. It was difficult for her to do or say anything because she didn't want to make a scene. When Dwayne asked if she would like to walk toward the food stalls and get a soda, Sheela was relieved at the prospect of distancing herself from him so she readily agreed. Dwayne took her hand in his thick sweaty one. She tried to pull away, but he held firm.
"Please, let go of my hand," she said.
"If you insist," Dwayne agreed. "I always accommodate a girl who insists."

"Thanks," Sheela said. When Dwayne let go he put his arm on her shoulder instead, but Sheela let it ride since it was the lesser of two evils and they were almost at the refreshment stands anyway.

"What'll it be?" he asked.

"I'll get a Dr. Pepper," she replied, "and some Fritos."

"No you won't," Dwayne said. "It's my treat and my pleasure." Dwayne got the Dr. Pepper but no Fritos and Sheela didn't comment.

They hung around drinking their sodas for a bit and then Dwayne asked Sheela to wait a second, so Sheela waited. After about seven or eight minutes, just as she was beginning to become impatient, he returned, looking flushed.

"There's something I would like to show you," he said. "Come on."

"Please," Sheela said, "let's go back. I don't want to miss any more of the dancing. Besides, everyone will wonder where we went."

"It'll just take a second," he said. "This time *I* insist."

"Just for a minute," Sheela agreed because she couldn't think of how to say no quickly enough and she didn't realize what Dwayne was up to.

Dwayne led Sheela to a tree and said, "Here is what I wanted you to see."

"What?" Sheela asked.

"This," Dwayne said, grabbing her hand and placing it at his crotch. Then, before Sheela had a chance to react he swirled her around. He pushed her body against the big tree trunk, pinned her hands down behind her, and plastered his slobbery lips on her mouth. His body pressed against her. Sheela couldn't breathe or move. When Dwayne came up for air, she said "Stop!" and he pulled away.

"I never force my attentions on a girl," he said calmly. Next time, he thought, when she gets a taste of my tongue, she won't be so quick to say stop. Dwayne belonged to the school of thought that believed if a lady says no, she means maybe, if she says maybe, she means yes, and if she says yes, she is not a lady.

When they rejoined the group and sat down again, Dwayne kept his hands to himself. Sheela shivered and hugged herself. Dwayne saw her and assumed that she was enjoying the memory of his embrace. He was smart to let her feel his hardness before he kissed her, he thought. She had to have been proud of herself when she saw the effect she had on him, even without fooling around. Dwayne was proud of himself too for having thought ahead and taken the edge off his excitement before getting close to her. He was right to realize that he'd have no problem getting stiff again. Dick never let him down. If he hadn't done what he did, something embarrassing might have occurred the second he made contact with Sheela's breasts. All in all he was glad that things had turned out the way they had. He thought maybe he should put his arm around Sheela's shoulder again, to let her know he appreciated her, but then decided against it. That way she would be more eager next time.

Sheela thought she would die of shame. She felt dirty all the way to her bones. At home, she took a hot shower and scrubbed herself with a scrungy until her skin was red, but it didn't do any good. She still felt soiled. Then she went to sleep hoping she would dream something that would make her feel better the next day, but if she did have any dreams, she couldn't remember them. If anything she felt worse when she woke up.

Sunday morning Sheela had brunch with her parents in their bedroom as usual. She wished she could climb into their bed like she did when she was little. Instead she sat on the wicker lounge chair and tried to behave normally. Victor had prepared green chilaquiles. They were like enchiladas but with the corn tortillas broken up instead of rolled and filled. Sheela said they were delicious because they probably were, though they could have been made of plastic as far as she was concerned. Her taste buds were non-functional. She just ate to avoid a long discussion about why she wasn't eating. Food always produced a discussion it seemed. Her parents noticed exactly how much she ate and generally it was either too much or too little. Either way one of them would point out that she was eating like a bird or like an elephant and try to determine why. It was bad enough before her appendicitis, but now every time she wasn't hungry they thought she was feeling sick and not telling. This morning she really did feel sick, but not the way they would think. And she couldn't possibly explain.

The rest of the day Sheela brooded. She couldn't concentrate on her schoolwork, she didn't want to face her friends, she didn't want to talk or conference with anyone, and she had no desire whatsoever to get involved with her virtual family. She wished she had confided in Ma, but there was no way during brunch and now Natalya was working. Anyway, even if Ma were home, what could she say?

Sheela finally decided that Dwayne kissed her the way he did because he thought she wanted him to. She probably gave out the wrong signals. It was all her fault. Maybe a part of her did want Dwayne to do something. Once she read a book where a character was "Sweet Sixteen and Never Been Kissed." Well, that wouldn't be her any longer. Except these days most girls got kissed by time they were twelve. By sixteen they were a lot more than just kissed.

But Dwayne truly disgusted her. When he put her hand down there, she felt like . . . like, she couldn't describe it. She was afraid he would unzip himself and that she would catch leprosy. That part of yesterday was something she could never talk about. And then when he squished her and kissed her it was awful. And to think that she left her friends to walk with him, and let him buy her a Dr. Pepper, and then waited for him, and followed him when he said he would show her something! How could she do that? She was crazy if she thought she could talk to her mama. Her mama wouldn't scold or punish her or anything like that. She would do what hurt Sheela most. She'd flash her eyes and say she was disappointed.

No one she knew—not a single person—thought kissing was disgusting. Not even her mother. Not even her grandmothers who got married in their teens, for heavens sake. She was sure her mother had boyfriends in high school. Door had even talked about it. Girls who had boyfriends got kissed and touched and liked it. Now even Bernie who had said she never wanted to like anyone was practically in love. Imagine Bernie, the confirmed solo. How ironic! Maybe she could talk to Bernie, Sheela thought. Bernie would just blame it all on Dwayne being a creep. But it wasn't as simple as Bernie would make it.

The hardest part of all was that Sheela longed to like a boy. She wanted to fall in love and have babies. That was a part of what life was all about. At least that's what she thought until last night. Now she wasn't so sure. And there wasn't a soul in her whole real or virtual world who could understand.

41

Monday morning, Sheela's alarm startled her into wakefulness and the realization that she didn't want to go to school. She didn't want to face Dwayne Houseman or her friends. Texas International High was a bad place for her to be with loathing and shame stuck in her throat. Thinking about the day ahead made her sick with worry. What should she say to Dwayne if he talked to her? What should she tell her friends about Saturday? How could she face Bernie? Bernie wouldn't say 'I told you so,' but the words would be there in both of their heads. Sheela had no intention of revealing any gory details and Bernadette wouldn't ask, but she would know anyway. Maybe everybody would know. Sheela felt as if her disgrace showed, like a brand mark.

Before her appendix nearly ruptured, it would have been easy enough for her to say she wasn't feeling well and stay home, but now her parents would give her the third degree. And *La Celestina* was only weeks away, the Friday after Thanksgiving weekend. Señora Machado was beginning to get paranoid. She would lose it if Sheela were absent. Tension over the upcoming performance was beginning to get to Sheela too. She didn't practice her lines on Sunday. Hopefully she wouldn't screw up.

It turned out school wasn't bad after all. In calculus Dwayne acted as if Saturday had never happened. Things went OK with her friends too. Only Janice was free for lunch at the same time as Sheela and talking to her wasn't so bad.

"Is that all you're having for lunch?" Janice inquired. "Black tea?"

"Yeah,"

"So..." Janice had asked. "The program was neat wasn't it?"

"Yes," Sheela answered.

"I can't believe Dwayne Houseman of all people would have been interested in that sort of thing. I guess his real interest was you, though."

"Yeah," Sheela said.

"He seemed nice enough. What happened?" Janice asked.

"He was gross," Sheela blurted out. Actually saying it felt OK.

"So you don't want to discuss it, right?"

"Right," Sheela responded.

"That bad, huh?"

"Yeah," Sheela answered. "Could we drop this subject?"

"Sure," Janice said and she let Sheela be.

Bernie smiled at her during English and then said a quick hi and bye on her way to bio, but she and Sheela didn't really have a chance to talk until after school, while they were heading for the buses.

"Sorry I missed you at lunch," Bernie said. "I didn't track you down because I knew you were practicing for Spanish during your free."

"It's OK," Sheela replied.

"I don't think so," Bernie said. "You didn't answer your phone all day yesterday and you didn't get back to me."

"I mean it's OK that you didn't find me. I got your message. I'm sorry. I should have called."

"Don't worry about it; we'll get together tomorrow."

"Thanks," Sheela said.

The rehearsal went very well too. Elena Machado was calmer. It had dawned on her that her students were as committed as she was to *La Celestina*'s success. After all, they had studied their lines for days, had told the whole world about this endeavor, and were sending out invitations to everyone that mattered in their lives. Sheela in particular had invested a great deal of her time and energy in this role, giving up a part in the Drama Club's Christmas show. She wouldn't let herself or anyone else down.

Then Sheela amazed her. Elena closed her eyes for a second and imagined that an old Spanish crone was speaking, not a young American teenager. And Sheela inspired the rest of the class as well. Calixto, Melibea, their parents, the servants, everyone was great. The play was finally coming together.

Sheela felt better after the rehearsal. Her mind no longer replayed Saturday over and over again like a retarded disc. Maybe what felt like an open wound to her spirit would turn into a scar and stop hurting, the same way her appendectomy stopped hurting. That scar was healing. It was no longer an angry red. It was starting to look like a pink railroad track. Dr. Young said it would turn into a faint line. He said she could even wear a string bikini if she wanted. But Dr. Young, notwithstanding his name, was almost Gappa's age. He didn't realize no one wore bikinis any more.

It all depended, Sheela figured, on Dwayne not getting near her again. If he stayed away, she could stop feeling so guilty and so cheap. And she could stop being afraid. Yes, she was afraid. When that perception flashed into her head, Sheela made a deal with God and herself. If Dwayne just stays away from me, she promised, I'll tell Ma everything. And, she added, I'll never keep anything from her again. And I won't be yucky to her, even if she asks me a million questions.

⸺⸺⸺ ❧❦❧ ⸺⸺⸺

"A new Chinese restaurant has just opened on Montrose," Victor said to Sheela later that evening. "Your mother and I are going there for dinner. Would you like to come along and talk Thanksgiving plans?"

"Sounds good," Sheela answered.

"What did Sheela say? Is she coming?" Natalya asked Victor when he called her at the office.

"She said it sounded good," he replied. "She didn't seem as upset as she did in the morning."

"That's a relief," Nat said. "I can't imagine what the problem was and I don't dare ask. And don't you say anything either."

"Are you kidding? I don't want to get pounced on," Victor agreed.

"Although," Nat said, "I don't see why two parents can't ask their only daughter if something is bothering her."

"Maybe we are being overprotective," Victor said.

"Or maybe we hit a communication gap," Nat suggested.

"More like a generation gap," Victor countered. "Actually the generation gap begets the communication gap. Then the two gaps merge into one humongous gap."

"Maybe so, but gap or no gap, if Sheela's moodiness persists, we have to get to the bottom of it. Sheela is a great kid and a fine human being. Still, she is only fifteen and we can't let her flounder with worry or be sick in secrecy just because she believes that it is her prerogative to be left alone."

"Well," Natalya said as she sipped her hot and sour soup, "I guess we plan on Thanksgiving in Houston, what with your play and all, unless you will be able go to New York after all. Will you?"

"I don't know yet," Sheela said. "Mmn. This soup tastes yummy."

"I can imagine," Victor pointed out. "It's probably the first thing you've eaten all day."

Sheela let her father's comment ride. "Señora Machado told us in the beginning that we wouldn't have to rehearse over Thanksgiving if we were in good shape by then, but I was talking to Melibea, that is to Marjorie who has Melibea's part, and she said maybe she wanted to stay and practice even if we didn't have to."

"Then we should forget about New York. We won't get tickets at the last minute," Nat said.

"But Ma, I want to go," Sheela whined. "I miss everyone."

"Let me remind you of an old adage," Natalya said.

"I know," Sheela said in a sing song, "You can't have your cake and eat it too."

"But in this case," Victor proposed, "perhaps Sheela can have and eat half a cake. Actually I have been baking a surprise."

"What?" Nat and Sheela asked together.

"It looks like Dora and Harold can visit Houston and stay through *La Celestina* and that Aunt Cecily and Alex could come the weekend of the performance. Uncle Ronald would come too, but he has to fly to Toronto on Friday. Jimmy is going to stay with Aunt Cecily's sister."

"Cool," Sheela said, smiling for the first time in forty-eight hours, "That makes four out of six, two thirds of a cake."

On Thursday, Dwayne stopped Sheela on the way out of class. "So, what's up Saturday?" he asked.

"I have to stay home with my parents," Sheela replied, her heart pounding. She hated lying, but she couldn't think of anything else to do. "We have company and I have to help. Sorry," she added, struggling to keep her voice steady. "I have to hurry to my next class."

It wasn't until the following Tuesday that Dwayne found out from Dersh that he'd been given a brush off.

"Minnie and I ran into Sheela and Sydney and some other guys last Saturday at the new Rocklyn Stevens Imax," Dersh informed him. "I was surprised you weren't there."

"Hey," he added with a smirk. "There is plenty of honey left in Minnie's pot. We have to do business again soon."

"I know, I didn't feel like going," Dwayne responded with as much bravado as he could muster. "Me and Sheela wanted to do our own thing, but she was committed this time. And listen," he added as if it were an afterthought, "I'm glad things worked out with Minnie."

The longer he mulled over what Irwin Dershowitz told him, the more Dwayne seethed. He couldn't believe it. First, Minnie switching her affection to Dersh without missing a heart beat. Now Sheela, the conniving bitch, telling him she had to help out at home and then going out with her dweeb friends to see the movie *he* told her about. How dare she lead him on and then give him the cold shoulder? Unless, he considered, she was doing it to heat up his blood. Well, if that was her plan, it was working. He *was* getting hot. As a matter of fact, his thermostat was on boil. Nobody ever teased Dwayne Houseman and left him standing on one foot.

The best approach, Dwayne decided, was to say nothing. He would go to the auditorium Saturday and see the rehearsal. Watching Sheela act would be a nice prelude to what he was planning. Maybe if she noticed him, she would be inspired. On the other hand, the sight of him might get her skittish and make her try to sneak away. He'd be safer if he stayed in the shadows. That way he'd surprise her before she could react. Sheela said she had an old woman's part. That would be something to see. A preview of Sheela at sixty. Weirdness. But when the play ended, he'd restore her youth to her just like in a fairy tale.

After the rehearsal, he had to find a way to get her into his car. Then he would take her someplace nice and private. Finally, he would thaw her out. There were only two details he had to work out first. One was how to persuade Sheela to take a ride with him. That might present a problem because if she screamed, someone might hear. Two was where to take her. Once he had these matters ironed out, everything else would fall into place. It was the domino effect. Another lesson Dwayne had learned from his half-brother was that if you took care of the details, the important stuff took care of itself.

A little serious thinking led Dwayne to conclude that the only way to make certain Sheela would quietly sit down and buckle up inside the passenger seat of his six month old Fiat was to frighten her a bit. Not that he would actually hurt her. He didn't hurt femmes. And this wasn't the nineteen hundreds or even the early two thousands when high school students carried guns to class and shot people. Like he always told his parents, the world was getting better. His generation wasn't like theirs. It was civilized. All he intended to do, if necessary, was to show Sheela one of those charged disposable knives the Zbras used to carve Zs on their cheeks. That would ensure her silence and compliance.

As for where they should go, Dwayne resolved that too. He'd take Sheela to the Econolodge near Kirby and Main. It was nicer than a Motel 6. He'd pay for the room in advance. No sweat. He still had over three hundred dollars left from his summer job. Hell, he'd even put some Dr. Pepper for her in the refrigerator and have some chips handy in case either of them got hungry.

⁕⁕⁕

Thursday's conversation with Dwayne made Sheela anxious, but she managed to focus on *La Celestina* and on keeping up with the rest of her schoolwork. The play was consuming most of her time and energy. Her role was by far the largest and hardest, but everybody else was getting intense too. Friday afternoon's rehearsal was going to run into the evening, so Sheela was skipping Shabbat and having pizza with the rest of the cast and crew. Saturday morning they would work out some kinks and Saturday afternoon would be the first dress rehearsal. No formal rehearsals would be held over the Thanksgiving holiday, so this weekend was going to be critical. It would be Señora Machado's first opportunity to see the production as a whole. Hopefully it would be good and nothing would have to be changed.

⁕⁕⁕

The five days from Tuesday to Saturday were among the longest in Dwayne's recent memory. Waiting for what he wanted wasn't his forte. At long last Saturday morning arrived. Dwayne was more excited than he had been in his entire life, and with good reason. Today was going to be a big day for him, the day he transformed Sheela Landau from an ice maiden into a woman. He would be doing her and the world a big favor. It would be like the classic movie, *Pretty Woman*, where Julia Roberts started out as a hooker and then became a lady, but in reverse.

His sources told him the dress rehearsal was starting at 1:30, but they didn't know when it would end. He estimated at about 3:30 or 4:00. To be on the safe side he had to be in the auditorium by 2:30, 3:00 at the very latest, and wait it out. That gave him plenty of time to get a haircut and to get everything ready, including washing and polishing his Fiat. He wanted to impress Sheela.

Luckily for him, the plans he had put in place were working without any unexpected hitches. At 2:45 Dwayne was seated in the last row of the dark auditorium watching *La Celestina*. It was a hoot. He knew a little Spanish and between that and the English narrator who came running out in tights before every scene to give a short outline of the plot, he got the gist. There were these two kids, Calixto and Melibea, who were secretly in love and Sheela was a facilitator for their affair. He couldn't recognize Sheela, but he knew she had to be Celestina. At the conclusion of the play everyone ended up dead. It was pretty funny.

265

Dwayne wondered whether Sheela was going to leave the auditorium in her costume or change. He guessed she would change, and he was right. After the curtain, there was a pause. Then the cast came out in their street clothes and talked with the teacher for a while. Then they started to walk up the aisle toward the exit.

By the time Sheela reached the door, Dwayne was ready for her, but then he got a sudden attack of nervousness. If things didn't work out according to his plan, he'd be in trouble. Big time. He might not get into Yale and his life could be totally screwed-up. But it was too late in the game to do anything except go with the program.

"Hello, there," he said stepping right in front of Sheela and blocking her path.

"What are you doing here?" Sheela asked him in a panic.

"Picking you up," Dwayne answered as he grabbed her hand and pulled out his knife. He held it up against her cheek. "You're coming with me, nice and easy," he continued, "that is unless you'd rather join the Zbras."

Sheela took in Dwayne's demeanor, his words, and the tone of his voice and she detected his fear. It encouraged her and helped her gather herself together. In a split second, her own panic evaporated. She was in control.

"So what's with the knife?" she asked. "Did you think you needed it to make me come with you? I'm surprised you don't have more self-confidence than that."

For a moment Dwayne was speechless. Then he mumbled, "I wasn't sure. Not after I found out you went out on Saturday without me."

"Only because I didn't know how to reach you," she said with a smile. Sheela was a talented actress after all. "My parents' company canceled out at the last minute so they said I might as well go to the Imax."

"Oh," Dwayne said, and put the knife back in his pocket.

It occurred to Sheela this might be a good moment for her to scream and run, but what if no one heard and then Dwayne caught up with her? She decided it would be better to play along with him instead. "So where are we headed?" she asked.

"It's a surprise," Dwayne answered as they approached his car. "Here's your chariot. Climb in and fasten your seat belt."

It took about ten minutes to get to the Econolodge. Sheela kept the conversation going. She told Dwayne she really admired his build and asked him where he worked out. Then she asked him what career he envisioned for himself. As she spoke she reached into her purse and removed her card phone. Dwayne answered unenthusiastically. He worked out at Titan. Sheela slipped the phone into her pocket. He was considering dentistry. Dwayne sensed something was wrong, but he couldn't put his finger on it. He was in a quandary.

As they pulled up to the parking space marked 34, Sheela saw Dwayne pat the side of his pants that held his knife. He didn't seem to realize what he was doing. Then he reached into his back pocket and pulled out his wallet. He took the room card out from one of the flaps and put the wallet back into his pocket. Sheela willed herself not to shudder, at least not visibly. She took a deep breath and remained seated, with her belt fastened, waiting for Dwayne to tell her what to do. Dwayne pulled his keys out of the ignition and said, "We're here. Follow me." Then he walked on ahead. Sheela quickly dialed 911. She said Econolodge, Kirby &

Main, Room 34, hurry. Then she disconnected. Dwayne was still at the door fiddling with the card. Room 34 was on the ground floor. It took several tries until the green light flashed and the door unlocked. He turned around and saw that Sheela hadn't budged.

"Hey, come on gorgeous," he said. "What are you waiting for?"

42

At 5:45 Saturday evening, Natalya sat in the kitchen listening for the phone or the front door. Her concern over Sheela's failure to call was deteriorating into full-fledged worry. She had expected a call by about 5:00 or 5:15 to find out if Sheela had a ride home or needed to be picked up from rehearsal. Even if she had forgotten to call, which wasn't like her, she should have been home by now. Nat was about to go up and interrupt Victor's reading when at last she heard her daughter's key unlock the door to their condo. She took one look at Sheela's reddened eyes and ran to embrace her.

"What happened, sweetheart? What's the matter? Why didn't you call?"

"It's a long story, Mama." Sheela was white and she spoke in a whisper. "I'll tell you everything, but first you or Dad have to take me to the police station. Here's the address. We have to speak with Officer Sanchez. He's real nice."

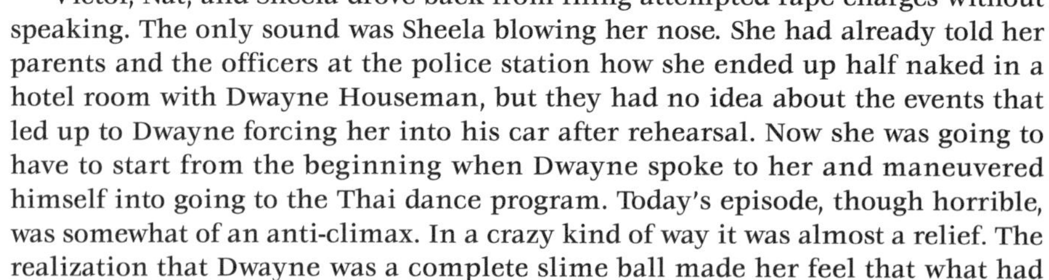

Victor, Nat, and Sheela drove back from filing attempted rape charges without speaking. The only sound was Sheela blowing her nose. She had already told her parents and the officers at the police station how she ended up half naked in a hotel room with Dwayne Houseman, but they had no idea about the events that led up to Dwayne forcing her into his car after rehearsal. Now she was going to have to start from the beginning when Dwayne spoke to her and maneuvered himself into going to the Thai dance program. Today's episode, though horrible, was somewhat of an anti-climax. In a crazy kind of way it was almost a relief. The realization that Dwayne was a complete slime ball made her feel that what had happened hadn't been entirely her fault. And she had nothing left to fear. The hard part was going to be explaining it all to her parents.

At headquarters Dwayne's lawyer warned the Landaus that if Dwayne ended up going to trial, they would all regret it. Every piece of dirt that could ever be dug up against Sheela would become public.

"And don't kid yourselves. There is always dirt," he added.

"Hah!" Sheela blurted out, with a spurt of spunk.

"You don't know our daughter," Victor said, proud in spite of himself.

"Be our guest," her Ma replied. "Remember, Sheela is fifteen and Dwayne has already turned eighteen, hasn't he? You'd better start thinking about a plea bargain if you want your client to have even a semblance of the rest of his life."

Back home Sheela wanted a shower, her father's checkered flannel shirt to use as a nightgown, and Beca's ultimate remedy for emotional ailments, hot cocoa with marshmallows. She wanted to talk to Mama alone.

"Ma can tell it to you later," she said to her father. "It's not a secret or anything."

"Sure," Victor agreed. "I'm a guy. I don't think I could handle this anyhow."

After cocoa in the kitchen, Sheela and Natalya went into Sheela's bedroom. They both sat on Sheela's bed. Sheela spoke, holding her mother's hand, for over an hour. Natalya barely said a word. Off and on Sheela couldn't push back her sobs and Nat had to hug her tightly before she could go on. Several times she said, "I'm sorry Mama. I know I really screwed up." When she had nothing left to tell, she begged her mother, "Please don't stop loving me! Please don't say you are disappointed or that I let you down or that you think I'm sleazy!"

"I'll never stop loving you Sheela," Natalya said. "That's an impossibility, no matter what you ever do; you aren't sleazy either, nor could you ever be, but I need you to stop crying now and listen to me very carefully. If you can do that, then perhaps all of us will eventually be able to put this nightmare behind us. OK?"

Sheela nodded her head, but Nat insisted that she "make an audible response" so Sheela whispered, "Yes."

"All right," Nat began. "Now, I wish I could say that I am not disappointed in you, but I am. You made your father and me feel that we have not done a very good job of parenting. Do you understand?"

"No," Sheela whispered, choking back her tears. "You are the best parents in the whole world. Please don't say you aren't! What happened isn't your fault. It's mine."

"No, Sheela, it is all our faults. If your father and I had done better, this incident could have been prevented. We let you let us down."

"I don't understand." A fresh stream of tears rolled down Sheela's cheeks.

"You did not let us down because of what Dwayne did. As a matter of fact you handled today's situation like a mensch. I am proud of you for that, but you let us down by being secretive and not confiding in us. You knew something was wrong, but you didn't trust us. Instead of sharing the truth, you gave us 'butt out, this is my own business' signals. Our mistake was heeding those signals, instead of stepping in and giving you the guidance we should have."

"As for you, you had no business going out with an unknown character and without permission, especially when your gut feeling told you he was bad news. But you did and you let one deception lead to another. Instead of telling us that Dwayne forced himself on you, you moped around and tried to cope with the situation alone, something you were not equipped to do. Your father and I noticed your acting as if the weight of the world was on your shoulders, but you made it clear we wouldn't get very far if we tried to find out what your problem was. Unfortunately we were unwilling to let another huge scene disrupt our lives. If you had been forthright, we would have told you how to prevent what happened today. Dwayne is not unique. He is a type with predictable behavior.

All this isn't the first example of your poor judgment. You were sick with appendicitis and didn't tell us because you were afraid we would interfere with the scheme you cooked up to get the lead in your Spanish play. That decision put us all through another kind of hell.

It is disrespectful, even unkind, to hide things from your parents. It's also stupid. Believe me, sooner or later mothers find out everything. That is a fact of life. And the later we find out, the worse it is for everyone. Whatever your problem, the earlier it is admitted the more easily it can be resolved. Otherwise it will only grow larger."

By this time Sheela could no longer contain her sobs. She cried softly but steadily. Her eyes puffed up and her nose turned red. She buried her face in her hands. Natalya longed to stop and comfort her daughter who had already been punished enough by the consequences of her actions, but there was more to say, so she continued.

"Look at me while I speak to you."

Sheela uncovered her face and grabbed another wad of tissues.

"While I don't think you will come out from this experience unscathed, you do have the opportunity to emerge stronger and wiser, provided you learn from it. Whenever you are caught in a situation that doesn't feel right, you have to heed your instincts. You and even your friends had the right feeling about Dwayne from the outset, but you didn't listen to your inner voice warning you that he was bad news. You ignored it and ended up knee deep in muck."

"There was a tiny part of me," Sheela forced herself to admit, "that wondered what it would be like if Dwayne kissed me. And it was awful. Maybe even worse than today. Everybody says kissing is so neat. I don't think I'll ever let anyone kiss me again. I am so mixed up. I'm weird, Ma."

"You're not weird. The piece of you that wanted to experience romance and sex is not in the least bit responsible for what Dwayne did. He alone is completely responsible for that. You are responsible only for hiding what was going on from us and for not listening to your own instincts."

"I'm afraid I'll never find romance or love."

"I think you will. I think you'll find a man to whom you are ready to entrust your spirit and your body and you will yearn for him and love with all your heart."

"Sometimes I dream of that person. I feel like I already know him, but I am sure I haven't met him yet."

"You have to wait until your Prince Charming comes along," Natalya said.

"The man I remember is real. He's not a fairy tale prince. I hope he doesn't want any other girlfriend. I hope some day I'll see him and recognize him."

Nat gave Sheela a hug and dried the teardrops that lingered on her daughter's cheeks. "Who said fairy tale princes aren't real? Your lover must be out there searching for you just as eagerly as you are waiting for him. And if I were to bet, I'd bet he will not give up until he finds you."

Natalya and Victor had a much rougher night that Saturday than their daughter did. For Sheela, her near rape was the denouement of an episode that some day would lose its importance and leave a mixed legacy: hurt and healing; guilt and redemption; diffidence and self-esteem. It also gave birth to hope: hope that her prince charming would indeed ride into her life like a knight on a white horse and rescue her from the prospect of a loveless existence. On the other hand, for her parents Saturday marked the end of Sheela's childhood and proved they no longer had the power to shield her from the ravages of life.

Sunday Sheela prepared brunch. Her labor was one of love and gratitude. Besides, puttering around with a purpose comforted and distracted her. Sheela enjoyed cooking when she was in the mood. She had her mother's magic touch combined with her father's penchant for orderliness. Thus she worked slowly, but her kitchen was always spic-and-span at every stage of her preparations, and her dishes—from elaborate curries to simple fruit salads—were always delicacies.

This morning Sheela decided to fix eggs poached in wine. She had set her alarm at eight to make sure she would have things under control before either of her parents ventured into the kitchen. After drinking a cup of tea she checked out supplies and, failing to discover anything special, opted to fall back on eggs. The idea of poaching them in wine came from a magazine. Sheela was no pack rat and she hadn't kept the magazine. Rather than looking for an alternative recipe in a cookbook, she adapted what she remembered. She made a sauce with sherry and tarragon and substituted Thomas English Muffins for fried bread. For an accompaniment she sautéed shiitake mushrooms. Then, thinking that something was missing, she made a garnish of chopped apples, apricot jam, powdered red pepper, mustard, and curry powder. For dessert she iced canned litchis. Finally she boiled water for tea. By the time everything was either done or ready to go, it was past ten. Still in her father's shirt, Sheela sat down to read the Sunday comics while she waited for someone to emerge from the master bedroom.

After about ten minutes Victor came out. He headed toward the kitchen wondering what he would make for brunch. It would have to be something soothing. He and Nat both felt like they had been through the wringer, but at least Nat had been able to do something. She talked to Sheela and made her feel better. He, on the other hand, was helpless in the face of his anger and fear. Victor was angry with Sheela for putting herself, her mother, and him through all this for no good reason. He was afraid for her too. Mostly he was enraged at a social code that didn't permit him to beat Dwayne to a pulp.

"Hi, Daddy," Sheela said to Victor as soon as she saw him. He was disheveled and forlorn. He looked worse than Sheela felt. She wondered what he would do or what he would say, but he just stood there. Sheela didn't know what to do or say either so she just went to him, arranged herself so he could embrace her, and buried her head in his neck. Victor thought Sheela looked like a little girl lost in an oversized shirt. Still, she was big enough to squeeze his heart, but that had been the case from the moment she was born and she was a lot tinier then. After a few seconds, Sheela looked up.

"I made brunch," she said. "I'll bring it in when Mama is awake."

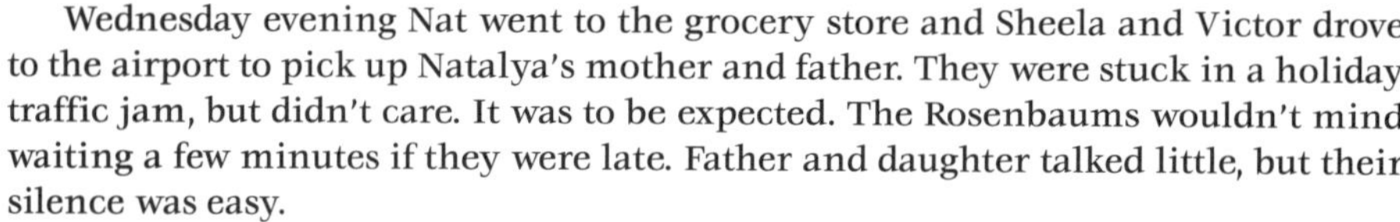

Wednesday evening Nat went to the grocery store and Sheela and Victor drove to the airport to pick up Natalya's mother and father. They were stuck in a holiday traffic jam, but didn't care. It was to be expected. The Rosenbaums wouldn't mind waiting a few minutes if they were late. Father and daughter talked little, but their silence was easy.

Sheela felt better than she had since her appendicitis. She assumed that Nat had told Door all about everything and that Door had told Pappa and probably even Ronald and Cecily. Same thing with Beca and Gappa. That was the way things worked in her family. She used to wish they were different, but this time she didn't really mind. She was sure no one would say anything though because her mother would have explained that there was nothing left to be said.

She was OK with "the incident" as she dubbed it. Except for the fact that she had upset her parents so much, it hadn't really been that big a deal. Of course she still got the creeps when the memory of Dwayne's slobbery choking kiss sneaked up on her and she still broke out in a sweat when the picture of him holding that knife near her cheek forced itself into her mind. However, the image of him, standing shriveled up without his clothes and with his hands handcuffed behind his back was somewhat of a cheerer upper. So was the knowledge that he had plead guilty to attempted rape and was going to spend thirty days in jail and the rest of his senior year under house arrest. Sheela figured that was enough punishment for him. It was his first brush with the law and she felt pretty sure it would be his last.

Earlier Nat had said, "I'm going all out this Thanksgiving because we have a great deal to be thankful for."

"You and your mother go all out every Thanksgiving," Victor countered. "You make yourselves and me crazy."

"That's because we have a great deal to give thanks for every Thanksgiving. Anyway, I love doing this."

"So what are you making?" Victor asked. "Why don't you try something different?"

"We can't have anything different. Thanksgiving has to be the same, something we can count on."

However, in the end, Nat was forced into making some concessions.

"Homemade mince and pumpkin pies with Häagen Däzs French Vanilla ice cream on the side are nice," Victor said, "but I personally love my mother's apple strudel."

"What are we having with the turkey?" Sheela had wanted to know.

"Same as last year," Nat told her, "celery stuffing, candied sweet potatoes with marshmallows, waldorf salad, mashed potatoes, baby peas with butter and dill, jellied cranberry sauce, and biscuits," Nat replied.

"I think we should use the packaged Idaho potatoes. They're yummy. And let's have peas and carrots, not just plain peas," Sheela proposed.

"Oh my God," Natalya said. "I can't believe this. My own daughter wanting to deviate from a tradition that has survived unchallenged for two generations."

"And you call me rigid!" Victor said. "Be rash, have peas and carrots!"

"Without dill," Sheela added. "And tell Beca to bring an apple strudel."

"OK," Nat said. "If I am going to be defeated, I'll be gracious about it. But that's as far as it goes. You both have to promise you won't ask me to change anything else."

By the time Sheela and Victor arrived at Houston Intercontinental, Door and Pappa were waiting by the curb.

"Perfect timing," Dora said. "We just got here."

"Hi, honey. The sight of you makes my old heart sing," Harold said to Sheela. "Hello Victor, I'm so glad we could come. We are going to have a wonderful time."

"We're having Shabbat with Beca and Gappa on Friday and we have tickets for Swan Lake for Saturday," Sheela said. "My friend Bernie is coming too and spending the night."

"A young man is spending the night?" Pappa asked.

"Nooo, Bernie is Bernadette. She's a girl. She's fantastically smart and fun."

"Harold, I told you about Bernadette," Dora scolded. "You are either getting old and forgetful or you're an impossible tease."

43

Although the Rosenbaums' visit, the Spanish play, and finals occupied Sheela's mind, the Dwayne fiasco still had a hold on it.

"Of course it's still in your system," Bernie said when Sheela complained of the images that kept cropping up in her mind. "For better or for worse, what happened is now part of your history, but talking about it will only blow up its importance in your head," she said.

"For worse. The thing is I want to get it out of my system."

"It's healing," Bernie continued, "to define a problem. That way you face it and put it behind you. But to deal with an issue that's over and done with is counterproductive."

"What about my parents?" Sheela asked. "They aren't an issue that is over and done with. Their attitude is ongoing. They love me and all and they don't think I'm responsible for what happened, but they are disappointed in me."

"Maybe, but mostly they are disappointed in themselves. They think what you did is their fault."

"Yeah," Sheela said. "It's weird. That's what my mother told me."

The remainder of 2016 flew past Sheela like a combination phoenix rising from the ashes and bat fleeing from hell. Thanksgiving was splendid as always, though less quality time was spent with Door and Pappa than usual. *La Celestina* was a glorious if short-lived triumph followed by hellish semester exams and project deadlines. Never had Sheela been so unprepared. She had good excuses, but excuses wouldn't help her grade point average.

There were holes in her preparation for calculus, geohistory, and science.

Besides Spanish, only English was smooth sailing because of the reading she had done while recuperating from her appendectomy. So, as Sheela awaited the New Year and her sixteenth birthday, she was in a state. Grades wouldn't be distributed until after the holidays and Sheela knew that if she missed a single A, she could kiss her chances at being valedictorian goodbye. As it was, competition was stiff. Last year two students shared the honor. Sheela prayed, but a knot in the pit of her stomach told her it was unlikely she'd pull the points she needed to attain her goal.

"Look," Natalya told her, "we go through this every semester and you always ace everything."

"This is different," Sheela said. "This time I know I didn't ace calculus and I omitted a couple of important points in my geohistory essay question."

"I'm sorry," Nat said. "I should have helped."

"No, there isn't anything you could have done. It's my mess and has nothing to do with you," Sheela said, but instead of smiling or something, Nat turned white and walked away.

⋯⋯ ✦✦✦✦✦ ⋯⋯

Nat and Victor tried to figure out how to make New Year's Eve and Sheela's birthday special, but they were fresh out of ideas. She didn't want to go out of town and she didn't want a bash. It would be hard to organize a party anyway. The Rosenbaums had come and gone and Bernie was in New York. The senior Landaus' rabbi had invited them to a retreat and at everyone's urging, they went. The Singers were on a cruise and the Khannas couldn't leave Chicago because they had a houseful of visitors from India. Sheela refused to go to the Museum of Science party with her friends.

"We wouldn't mind, honey," Victor urged Sheela. "It's OK if you spend New Year's Eve with your own crowd."

"I just don't feel like making merry with everyone and their uncle with a huge dinosaur skeleton looking down on us," Sheela said.

"I'm afraid," Victor said, "you don't feel like making merry at all."

"I'm not merry or un-merry," Sheela explained. "I just want to be mellow."

In the end Sheela spent the first hours of her sixteenth year sleeping. Her parents ate melba toast with caviar and drank iced vodka while they watched the New Year Sound and Light Performance transmitted live from the recently opened Gorham Planetarium in Washington. The show was as close to miraculous as art could be and it filled the Landaus with wonder. After the midnight finale, which was at 11:00 p.m. Houston time, they switched to brandy and Donna Lisa chocolates. Filled with salt, sweetness, and beauty they greeted 2017 making love.

While Nat and Victor reenacted the ritual that gave their daughter life, Sheela dreamed her death.

Without seeing, Sheela saw herself in the moonlight. She was young, about the same age she was now, and she was as tall as she was now. Her mouth and chin and dimple were familiar. So was her hair, almost ebony colored with a heart shaped hairline. She kept swishing her head back and forth to feel her curls bounce. Occasionally she rubbed her neck. It seemed naked, as if it were missing something. Maybe she had just cut off a ponytail or pigtails. She recognized her eyes too, except instead of being ocean blue they were hazel and filled with gold flecks that you could tell would glitter in the sun. She was wearing a halter and shorts so the tiny oval mole perched just above and to the left of her belly button was showing. It was dark, like it always got in summer.

At the beginning of her vision, Sheela was sitting on the edge of a lake humming a song that went:

275

The y try to tell us we re too young,

Too young, to really be in love,

They say that love s a word,

A word we re much too young to know . . .

She was interrupted by a magnificent boy who ran up behind her and put his palms over her eyes. In a voice filled with promise he asked, "Guess who?"

The girl who was Sheela didn't guess. Instead she asked, "Who loves you more than God?"

"Someone who always answers a question with another question. The impetuous, irresistible Sarah Fine, that's who."

Sheela was surprised. This wasn't Karmatica where Sarah Stellar lived. It was Camp Chicopee where she was a counselor. Who was Sarah Fine? She tried to tell the boy that her name was Sheela, Sheela Landau, but she was tongue-tied.

Sarah Fine unclasped her knees, hopped up, and turned to face the boy with the grace of a gazelle. Then she put her arms around his shoulders and kissed him with frightening hunger. Barely pausing to catch her breath she asked, "Did you get it?"

"I got it," the boy answered, "but I didn't bring it."

"Why, Danny, why not? You promised," Sarah Fine said. Her lower lip drooped, leaving a gap between it and the two peaks that formed the top half of her mouth. Droplets fell from the corners of her eyes.

"Please, darling," Danny urged. "Don't cry. We have to wait. This isn't how it should be. We have to wait."

"But I can't wait." Sarah spoke in a hoarse voice. She was choking on her words. "You said yes. I'll die if you make me wait, I just know I will."

"No, Sarah. No one ever died from not making love."

"People do, too, die of broken hearts."

"I'm not going to break your heart. I love you too much."

"I feel like something horrible is going to happen if we wait. I'm so frightened," Sarah pleaded. "We won't get married for years and years."

"We won't wait years and years," the boy called Danny said, "just a little while longer. I'm going to figure everything out and make it beautiful. I don't want us to be afraid of being found out."

"I don't care about that," Sarah said.

"You do care about disappointing your parents. And what about Ruth? How would she feel if your parents tell her that her big sister has dishonored the family. You know that's just what they will think and say."

"That wouldn't be fair," Sarah said.

"Maybe not, but that's what would happen."

"What are we going to do?" Sarah asked.

Daniel wiped her tears with his hands. "It's a beautiful night. We're going to go rowing under the stars. But first I'm going to give you a present, if you promise not to cry. OK?"

Sarah nodded even though her heart was beating like a jungle drum broadcasting the news that her love was slipping away. Then she put her arms around him and made him kiss her. He was the most beautiful man the Lord had ever created.

Daniel Ariel Reuven was faithful to the moral code etched in his soul. He wanted Sarah more than life, but he wanted her openly, not furtively wearing a rubber shield around his manhood. He wanted her forever, not for a few hours stolen from the night.

Still Sarah tried to make him abandon his resolve. She didn't care that he had no protection. She lay down on the grass and pulled him down after her. She kissed him until he returned her kisses and caresses and slipped his hands under her halter. She felt his ring with the yellow-gold stone his grandfather gave him for his bar mitzvah against her breast and wished it would adhere to her permanently. She looked in Danny's eyes. For a moment they suggested he would succumb and fill the emptiness that tortured her, but he didn't. Instead, when Sarah felt his hardness, he turned away.
"Wait; please don't; I'm sorry," he moaned.
Sarah knew that he was sorry for going as far as he did, not for leaving both of them so alone.

Sarah inhaled the night air in place of the breath of her beloved. She breathed deeply and forced herself not to weep. After one or two minutes that were an eternity, Danny faced her again and kissed the tip of her nose. He smiled from the center of his heart. Sheela didn't smile back. She took his hand in hers and kissed his ring, as if she were paying homage to a king. Daniel saw her pain, but he could not do what they both wanted. He only had words with which to console her.
"I don't just love you, Sarah, I see God shining in your eyes. I see God within myself through you. I could not be with you and then let you go. Making love to you will be sacred, not just once, but always. That's why we must wait. Please don't be sad."
"I can't help it. I'm afraid we will be forced apart."
"I'll never leave you, Sarah. I swear it. I have a gift for you, look!"

Sarah opened the tiny white box that Daniel handed her. It contained a gold chain with a small heart pendant. Daniel put it on her and the heart fell right in the hollow of her neck.
"It fits you just like I thought it would," he said.
"It's beautiful."
"Promise you'll wear it always."

Transfixed, Sheela watched the remainder of the scene unfold before her eyes. She saw Danny and Sarah get up, walk to a deck, untie a rowboat, give it a shove and climb in. Danny grabbed the oars and started rowing. In the middle of the lake Sarah suddenly stood up, took off her halter and shorts, and dived in. Danny quickly jumped in the water after her. The rowboat drifted away. Danny and Sarah swam until they could no longer be seen. Lake Chicopee glistened silently in the light of the moon. Hours later a head appeared bobbing toward the shore. Sheela felt the hairs on her arms become erect. She saw Danny slowly approaching, weighted down by Sarah's body which he pulled behind him. Eventually they reached land. Danny lifted Sarah and placed her on the grass. Then he began to pump her body. Gallons of water gushed out of her, yet she remained listless. He breathed into her mouth, tears streaming down his face until he himself had no breath left and dawn began to battle with the moonlight.

When Natalya looked in on her daughter at about nine o'clock in the morning, Sheela pretended to be asleep, a ruse she had adopted early in childhood. She felt guilty about this small deception, but she needed it to make the transition from sleep to wakefulness.

"Is she still asleep?" Victor asked. He was eager to get started with Sheela's birthday, and hoped she would be in good spirits. "She went to bed so early."

"Not really," Nat replied. "But she isn't ready to face the morning yet. And we don't know that she went to bed early. All we know is that she went into her room early. And even if she went to bed, that's not to say she went to sleep. You know bed isn't synonymous with sleep."

"I'd think for a single person it would be."

"No way," Nat answered. "There are lots of fun things to do in bed alone."

"I'm glad I wasn't alone last night," Victor said. "I'd say that on a scale of one to ten, last night was nine point seven."

"When was ten?" Nat asked.

"Ten is yet to come," Victor said. "Nine point nine was the night we made Sheela and nine point eight was on our cruise. Our average is at least a nine point five."

Forty-five minutes later when Natalya peeped into Sheela's room again, she saw her daughter sitting at her dressing table arranging her hair into two braids.

"That's cute," Nat said. "So, good morning, Happy Birthday and Happy New Year. Sheela jumped up and hugged her mother so tightly for so long that Natalya had to push her off in order to catch her breath. "Your birthday brunch will be served in our bedroom in an hour. Would you like some juice or coffee or something beforehand? "

"No, thanks Mama. I'm fine," Sheela said. "And Ma?"

"Yes, sweetheart, what is it?" Natalya asked.

"I think I'm ready for the rest of my life. I can forget about what happened and I can live with not graduating first in my class, as long as you and Daddy won't be too let down. I just want you to be proud of me."

"We are so proud of you, we could burst," Nat said. "But we can't help being upset and worried when you aren't happy."

"Please Mama," Sheela said, "I need you not to carry everything I do and everything that happens to me on your shoulders. It rattles me horrifically. You guys do everything parents could do, but no parent can do it all. And..."

"And what, Sheela?"

"And what happened, you know, that wasn't your fault either. Please don't think it was."

At a quarter to eleven, Sheela knocked on her parents' door. Victor immediately came to open it. Before he could say Happy Birthday, Sheela buried her head in his neck.

"What's the matter, honey?" Victor asked. "I'll fix it, whatever it is."

"Nothing is the matter," she said. "Can't a girl hug her father?"

"What's with the pigtails?" Victor asked as soon as his daughter moved far enough away from him so he could get a good look at her.

"Braids are easing their way back in style," Sheela answered. "A couple of kids have been wearing them, with pom-poms and stuff at the ends."

Brunch, served on lacquered trays, was an assortment of Sheela's favorite foods: chilled amaretto sour, with just a splash of amaretto and extra almond flavoring, grilled cheese sandwiches topped with mushrooms, a beet and pineapple salad, biscuits, and blueberry cheesecake birthday cake.

After the cake was cut and Nat and Victor sang, Nat opened the top drawer of her dresser and brought out a Florentine leather jewelry box.

"It's beautiful," Sheela said, as Natalya handed it to her.

"Your mother didn't wrap it," Victor explained, "because it is the wrapping. Your gifts are inside."

"Thank you," Sheela said, staring at the box.

"Well, open it up," Natalya said.

Inside Sheela found an array of gold jewelry. There were four bangle bracelets from her parents. From Bernie, there was a snake shaped gold ring. From Steve Jordan there was a toe ring. From the Khannas and the Singers combined there was a gold armlet. Door and Pappa gave her a pair of dangling earrings and Ronald, Cecily, and the boys gave her a chain link anklet. Attached to it was a note that said,

"This gift comes from the FIVE of us. Guess what? Alex and Jimmy will have a little brother or sister next June. This is our official announcement, so feel free to spread the news. The boys are happy but shocked that at our age we still engage in behavior that makes babies."

"Wow!" Sheela said after reading the note.

"What?" Victor and Natalya asked in unison.

"Here, read this," she answered, passing the note to her parents, who seconds later echoed Sheela's "Wow!"

"There is another level underneath," Victor told Sheela. "You lift the top part off by the tabs."

Sheela pulled and found two small boxes, white and tan, remaining in the jewelry case. She opened the tan one first. It contained a tiny turquoise frog.

"That's from Lulu," Nat explained. "When I told her about the birthday gift theme, she thought about giving you a single earring for the top of your ear, but then she decided you had to have a frog."

"I'm glad. This frog is exquisite. Look, it has gold chips for eyes! I hereby dub it Felicia. There is just one box left, so it must be from Beca and Gappa, right?"

"Indeed it must," Victor agreed. "Beca said to tell you it's a family heirloom."

Sheela's hands trembled when she picked up the box and removed the lid. Inside, resting on a wad of cotton, she found a freshly polished gold chain threaded through a beautiful heart shaped pendant. Sheela tried to put it on, but she couldn't manage, so Victor lifted her braids and fastened the clasp behind her neck.

44

Sheela loved performing, but she had disliked posing for photographs ever since she was a child. Moreover, she was embarrassed by pictures in which she appeared as a crying clown, or sticking out her tongue, or lifting her dress to cover her face. The antics her parents thought cute were actually efforts to deter them from snapping their camera. When she was about nine or ten, Sheela had asked her parents not to present her with her any more birthday albums commemorating the year gone by.

"These photos are memories," Victor said.

"I keep my remembering in my heart," Sheela explained. Nat and Victor continued making albums, but lined them up on shelves instead of giving them to their daughter.

"You'll be happy to have these one day," Natalya told Sheela some years later when she complained about the amount of time her parents spent messing around with the boxes of photos that flooded their study.

"You waste all your free time working on those stupid pictures," she said. "Every time one album gets finished, five more boxes filled with photographs, mostly of me, appear. It's like they reproduce by mitosis."

"When you get older you will appreciate what we are doing," Victor said.

"Maybe." Sheela forced herself to be tactful. She hated hearing about how she would change when she was older.

"Perhaps we should just stop taking pictures altogether if they upset you so." Victor was hurt.

"That isn't what I mean, Daddy." Sheela knew how much pleasure photography gave both of her parents; it's just me. "Once I read that some people still believe being photographed is a bad omen. They think it's like having their soul stolen. I can identify with that viewpoint."

"I'm sorry." Nat's apology was a reprimand. "I cannot respond to your belief that your father and I are stealing your soul by keeping pictures of moments that have given us such great happiness."

"I didn't mean to upset you. Please, Ma. Please, Daddy, don't take it that way." Sheela regretted her remarks. "You know I am really happy that we have such good pictures of our ancestors. They mean such a great deal to me. I realize someone had to take them and someone had to pose or they wouldn't exist."

The word "happy" was an understatement when it came to the way Sheela felt about the old family photos in black and white and sepia that Natalya and Victor had lovingly assembled and restored over time. Snapshots from the late eighteen and early nineteen hundreds moved her profoundly, but a few—mostly the unidentified ones with no labels—did much more; they gave texture to a reality that lived in Sheela's inner being.

Cecily and Ronald refused to predetermine a girl and they didn't want to know whether their child was male or female, until the actual moment of birth. Sheela adamantly agreed with letting nature take its course, but she didn't get her Aunt and Uncle's refusal to learn whether Cecily was carrying Mark or Renee. The last two times they wanted to know as soon as possible. Now her Aunt had to have a sonogram because she was over forty, but Cecily instructed the doctor not to reveal the baby's sex to her or to her husband or to anyone who might spoil their surprise.

Sheela wanted three or four children, but she feared she might never find a man she would love enough to have them with. This fear had been a part of her for as long as she could remember. While her friends worried that this boy or that boy didn't like them, Sheela worried that she didn't like anyone at all. At school many a classmate approached her, but no one touched her emotions or made her tingle, not even a little. It was only because Sheela thought she might not be giving the boys a fair chance that she had gotten herself into the biggest mess of her life. After Dwayne, she thought she would rather live a life of chastity than allow anyone less than the man of her dreams to touch her. She decided love at first sight was the only trustworthy love.

Bernadette's romance confirmed Sheela's belief that true love comes in an instant. Cupid's arrows have to pierce your heart, just like on Valentine Day cards. Bernie was lucky; she had never given boys a thought. She just happened to meet her fiancé and fall in love. And she certainly had never worried about future children. As a matter of fact, at one point Bernie had considered the possibility that she might be a latent lesbian even though girls didn't attract her any more than boys did. At a minimum she figured she had no libido at all.

"You certainly are a tomboy and a little odd," Sheela had told her, "but that doesn't make you a lesbian. And I don't think you lack sexuality. Your biological alarm just hasn't given you a wake-up call yet. Either that or you are looking for someone who can see past your camouflage. I think you are fortunate."

"Why?" Bernie asked.

"You are your own person. You are happy and you feel whole."

"At least so far," Bernadette said. "But sometimes I wonder about whether something is wrong with me. You know I wouldn't care if I ended up in love with a woman, but I'd hate to miss out on what everyone thinks is such a big deal."

And then boom! Out of the blue, Bernie met Will, actually Dr. William Jenkins who was twelve years older and an assistant professor at Harvard. He had a Ph.D. in political science and a JD and he and Bernadette were in love. It was official now. They had met again in New York over the Christmas holidays. Will was from the Big Apple and Bernie's favorite cousin lived in the city, not far from Sheela's grandparents. Will proposed to Bernie on his knees and she accepted the one and a quarter karat diamond ring which he placed on her finger. Now it sat in her parents' safety deposit box because she could hardly wear it to school.

Her parents freaked at first. She was still a few months shy of eighteen, arguably too young to know what she was up to, but she stuck to her guns and eventually her father and mother came around. There was really nothing for them to object to. This wasn't the nineteen nineties when people didn't get married until they had a history. She wasn't stopping her education, and Will wasn't a person you could complain about. There was absolutely nothing wrong with him. Besides, her own father was ten years older than her mother too, and he had been divorced when he and her mom met. Will, on the other hand, stayed single because he was waiting for someone like Bernie to come along.

Now Bernie glowed. She was beginning to look beautiful. Her hair was still long, curly, and out of control, but it was shiny. Her clothes were still a tad too big for her, but she wore them with grace. And although she still couldn't tolerate contacts, she had new flattering frames and special-ordered extra thin lenses. She and Will were going to get married as soon as Bernie finished her first year of college.

"Maybe I'm dreaming," Bernie had said to Sheela. "I feel like I'm living a fairy tale from the Middle Ages."

"Fairy tales are eternal," Sheela declared. "Where is it written that they cannot happen in the twenty-first century?"

⁓⁓⁓ ✦✦✦✦✦✦✦ ⁓⁓⁓

Sheela had been right about her grades. She ended up with a B+ in calculus and an A- in geohistory. She had an A in everything else and an A+ in Spanish. An A+ was rare and given only for extraordinary work and this was her only one. Thus, even Natalya had to concede that Sheela's chances of standing first in her graduating class were slim.

Nat had a problem too, one that touched Sheela. The Federal Court in Houston dismissed the Beauty Teen case, granting Defendant's Motion for Summary Judgment. That meant the matter would not make it to trial. Judge Hardmon ruled "even if all Plaintiffs' allegations were true, Beauty Teen's ads, while deplorable, did not rise to the level of false and misleading misrepresentation." Consequently, after spending tens of thousands of dollars on discovery and expert opinions, not to mention time and effort, the firm of Jordan and Landau ended up with a big fat hickey.

Sheela was upset because she had invested personal energy in this case when she was working in her mother's office over the summer. At first she had doubts about its merits, but after meeting some of the young plaintiffs, she changed her mind.

"I don't get it," she told Nat. "How could the judge say that?"

"The pendulum is swinging again. We're reverting to the old doctrine of caveat emptor."

"That means buyer beware, right?"

"Correct," Nat answered. "The courts are making it easier to cheat. What with physical stores, virtual shops, and interactive marketing, it's too much of a burden to police sellers. Remember, you started out saying the kids should be responsible for their own purchasing decisions? I guess you were right."

Only Victor's professional life was progressing along a smooth course on a gentle upward slope. He was content. His tenure was secure, his work was appreciated, and the flow of royalties from his publications was steadily growing.

⚜

The Landaus' successes and defeats lost importance when Beca suddenly fell ill. At first only her husband, Dr. Henry Landau, worried about the hacking cough and low-grade fever that bothered his wife. Henry was now fully retired, but he knew this year's Asian flu was a nasty piece of work. And Beca was frail. Moreover she had been behaving strangely ever since their return from the New Year Retreat. While she wasn't depressed, she lost interest in life and she appeared to have become detached from him and from the things that had always mattered to her.

In the course of a few days the fever passed and the cough eased so Henry told Victor that his mother was making some progress. However, when he added that she wasn't up to celebrating Sabbath and categorically insisted that "no one should come to check up on me, especially not the children."

Victor was shocked. "Maybe if I had known, I would have understood my mother better. Mom did tell me once that she had a half-sister who died, but she wouldn't discuss it."

"That's true," Henry concurred. "Rebecca was a small girl when it happened. Soon after that, the family moved from Houston to Chicago. I'm going to check up on Beca. you can wait if you want."

"Yes," Nat said, "I'll make us some tea."

After several days, Victor and Natalya decided they could not continue to accept a dictate that banned them from visiting home.

"What do you expect me to do?" Victor asked his father. "How can I tell Nat and Sheela that Beca doesn't want to see them? What is really wrong?"

"I wish I could tell you," his father answered. "Your mother is an unusual person and although I've generally known how to deal with her, I am now at a loss."

"But she's feeling OK, isn't she?" Victor persisted.

"I'm not sure," Dr. Landau replied. "Like I said, her cough and fever have subsided, but she is congested and weak. This strain of the flu is weird. It has been known to cause some serious problems."

"What serious problems?" Victor asked. "How serious?"

"Quite serious," his father answered. "I just keep praying that Beca will snap out of this. She could, you know, if she wanted to."

When Victor relayed his conversation to his wife and daughter, Natalya insisted that the three of them go see Beca immediately.

283

"But Beca doesn't want us over," Sheela argued. "How can we disregard her wishes?"

"She isn't well," Nat explained. "How can we ignore that?"

"When a person is too sick or too old or too young to stand up for herself is when we should pay most attention to what she wants," Sheela insisted.

"But Beca hasn't said what she wants," Victor pointed out.

"Yes, she has," Sheela retorted. "She has said she doesn't want us to see her."

In the end Nat and Victor insisted on going to The Village.

"You don't have to tell Mom we'll be over," they said to Henry. "At least we can talk to you."

"All right," Henry conceded, "but understand that your mother doesn't want you to see her in her present condition. She's not herself."

"We understand, but we also need to see you."

"There is nothing to see," Henry said. "I look like a wreck. Almost worse than Beca."

"All the more reason why we need to come over," Nat insisted. "We need to touch you and hug you and get a sense of what's happening. Then we can decide what to do."

Beca was asleep when Victor and Natalya arrived, and heeding Sheela's admonition they refrained from asking to sneak a look at her.

"You're frightened, Gappa," Nat said as she fell into the tight bear hug she got from her father-in-law. "You shouldn't be dealing with this yourself."

"I am helpless," Victor's father replied. "Rebecca is a wonderful woman, but she is complicated and full of secrets. I think . . ." Henry choked on his words and rubbed his eyes.

"You can't be thinking maybe she is going to die." Natalya finished his sentence.

Henry nodded.

"Why?" Victor asked. "You said she could get well if she cared to enough. And if she is so sick, why does she want to keep us away? Have we done something to upset her?"

"No," Henry said. "There are things," he added, "that go around in her head, things that lurk under the surface of her consciousness. Maybe she believes it would be best that they not be brought out into the open and she's scared that someone will ask questions."

"I can't imagine that Beca has ever done anything she is ashamed of," Natalya remarked.

"Not things she has done," Henry explained, "things that have happened and ideas she has. Maybe something has made her feel they are in danger of becoming known, and the only way to ensure that they don't is for her to go."

"That's crazy," Victor said.

"It might be crazy," his father acknowledged, "but I'm afraid it's true."

"And you know these things?" Natalya asked.

"Only some of them," her father-in-law replied. "They started way back. Beca always avoided talking about her childhood. It was filled with tragedy. And then, before we had Victor, we had a stillborn daughter. Your mother never talked of her and she never recovered from that loss. I didn't allow her to see the child. I thought it would be best, but it was a mistake. God should have given me more wisdom."

Victor was shocked. "Maybe if I had known, I would have understood my mother better. Mom did tell me once that she had a half-sister who died, but she wouldn't discuss it."

"That's true," Henry concurred. "Rebecca was a small girl when it happened. Soon after that the family moved from Houston to Chicago. I'm going up to check on Beca. You can wait if you want."

"Yes," Nat said. "I'll make us some tea."

Beca's head was spinning; she lay in bed, lost in a Picassoesque world of colors and forms that refused to cohere. She was exhausted and she wanted peace. Her only worry was her family. She wanted them to let go and be happy, but she feared they wouldn't. They would want to understand and they would pry, and if she told them the truth, they would think she was crazy.

"Hello, my love." Henry was pleased to see his wife was awake and that her gaze met his. "Are you feeling better?"

"Tired," Rebecca whispered. "Please . . ."

"I'll do anything you ask," Henry quickly said. "But first let me bring you a cup of tea, all right?"

"Yes," Beca rasped. "Tea."

Henry turned his head so Beca wouldn't see that his cheeks were moist and walked downstairs into the kitchen.

"She agreed to drink a cup of tea," he told Nat and Victor. "She had a few sips of orange juice this morning, but that's all. I thought of putting in an IV or even a feeding tube, but I couldn't do it. It would strip her of her dignity and impose my will on hers."

Henry held the teacup to Beca's lips and she took a few sips before she spoke.

"Make Victor and Nat understand. Sheela already does."

"Have a little more tea," Dr. Landau urged, "and then tell me what Victor and Nat must understand."

"Not . . . ask questions," Rebecca said. She made a real effort to drink and managed two thirds of the cup. Henry hoped against hope that if he could set her mind at rest, she might rally. He didn't know how he would survive without her.

"They want to see you," Henry explained. "They think it's their fault that you won't let them come."

"Tomorrow," Rebecca said. "No questions."

The next morning Rebecca was weaker and gasped for breath, but she smiled and ate a Marie biscuit dipped in tea. Henry sponged Rebecca and dressed her in a kimono. She felt brittle and light, as if she were about to break. He put a little lipstick and a dab of rouge on her and lovingly carried her downstairs to the living room. The bedroom had a sick smell.

Victor, Natalya, and Sheela arrived together. Even from the outside, the home that until recently had been a source of nourishment to the three of them looked empty. Forewarned of Beca's insistence on "no questions," they entered tentatively, not knowing what to expect. Together they said hello and hugged Gappa and walked toward Beca. One by one they each gave her a gentle embrace and a soft kiss on the cheek. Then they sat down, Victor in the easy chair, Nat on the love seat next to Henry, and Sheela on the sofa with her grandmother and the pillows that propped her up.

Silence severed the bond that had united the small family until this moment. Rebecca smiled, but her smile did not connect to those who had always turned to her for sustenance. They all looked upon Rebecca's illness and her admonition in different ways and these differences created a wall of isolation. Henry, his son, his daughter-in-law, and his granddaughter all recognized that Beca was thin as a reed, exceedingly weak, and unable to reach them, but they experienced separate realities. Rebecca herself wanted to leave a legacy of peace, but pressure was squeezing the life out of her and she could not speak. Though she willed her spirit to convey the message trapped in her heart, she felt her effort failing.

Henry watched the scene in his living room like a theatergoer watching a play. His brain and his soul could not process what was taking place and he gradually became overcome with numbness. He stopped feeling, thinking, and moving. He wondered if he would ever be able to see or hear or walk or touch or eat again.

Victor couldn't understand why his mother had chosen to desert him. Instead of fighting for her life, she was willing to surrender it, heedless of the burdens she was leaving behind and utterly heedless of his feelings. He wondered why she insisted on no questions. Was she playing some kind of cruel joke on him? What questions was she thinking of? He hadn't had any questions until she brought up the question of questions. Now he was filled with them and they would churn in his mind forever. Victor was afraid and he was angry with Rebecca for provoking his fear. He suddenly felt older and uncomfortably aware of his own mortality. Mixed with Victor's anger were feelings of guilt and inadequacy. He should have been a kinder son. He should have been capable of making his mother care enough about life so as not to succumb to the aftermath of a stupid flu.

Natalya saw her mother-in-law as a shadow of her former self, a person no longer in full possession of her senses, even considering that Beca had always been a little strange. Nat asked herself what could possibly be flowing through Beca's mind. What was she bent on hiding? Rebecca had been a steadfast support in Nat's life and she had loved her daughter-in-law with all her heart. Nat hoped she might still recover, but it didn't seem likely. Thus she worried about how her husband and Sheela would react to the loss of their mother and grandmother. And she worried about Henry who looked like a zombie. What if Beca survived, she asked herself, but remained unbalanced? That would be the worst possible scenario. Nat knew that deep down, her real worry was that her own life would now become more difficult and she was ashamed of her selfishness.

Sheela no longer saw her grandmother as a physical being. She recognized that Rebecca Landau had cut her ties with the world and that her body just barely contained her soul. She also saw the joys and sorrows of lifetimes flickering in her Beca's pale blue eyes. Sheela shared some of those joys and sorrows and she knew that without Beca they would live alone in a hollow place in her heart. She tried to hold back her tears afraid that they would disturb her grandmother's reverie, but she couldn't. It didn't matter. By the time the first salty droplet fell down her cheek, Beca had stopped breathing.

45

Sheela was salutatorian of her graduating class. At seventeen, she was also the second youngest graduate in her school and winner of the Texas Annenberg Foundation prize for the most promising high school graduate in the state. At first she didn't want to participate in the competition, but she did because her parents wanted her to.

Natalya and Victor also wanted Sheela to apply to Ivy League colleges like Harvard or Stanford.

"At least apply," Nat suggested. "You don't lose anything by applying. Bernie is trying for Harvard and the two of you could be together."

"Please Ma." Natalya made Sheela nervous. "This is pressure. We've had this conversation a thousand and one times. Bernie has always had her heart set on Harvard and now she is even more determined, with Will teaching there. Thank God she'll probably end up as valedictorian, since it's going to make a difference. On the other hand I never wanted to go anywhere but the University of Texas. It's close and it's a first class school."

"But what harm is there in applying?" Victor asked. "You can always say no."

"It would be a waste of time and a dishonest thing to do. I don't need the glory of being accepted just to say no. Like I told you, I want to be a lawyer and I want to practice in Houston. In this day and age it's helpful to have home turf connections and with luck I'm going to build them. If Jordan and Landau won't have me, I'll get a job in another firm."

"You're a long way from being a lawyer," Natalya said. "You're just graduating from high school. I think making such long term plans is silly."

"I know you think that," Sheela acknowledged. "You told me so repeatedly. At the same time you always managed to make me feel like you want me to be a lawyer. Anyway, I don't see anything wrong with long term plans as long as they stay flexible. They set goals that provide energy and motivation. I don't want to end up with a career that falls into my lap by default. I prefer to make conscious decisions. If something happens to make me change my mind, I'll change it."

"Wouldn't getting into Harvard qualify as something which could make you change your mind?" Victor asked. "What your mother and I would like for you to do is to keep your options open."

"No. What you and Mama would like is to be able say your daughter attends Harvard. That definitely would not qualify as something which could change my mind."

"So what *would* qualify?" Natalya asked.

"Someone or something that changes it."

Another thing Nat and Victor could not accomplish was to get Sheela to attend her own graduation. She had no desire to flaunt her achievements and she thought marching in a black cap and gown in the hot midday sun would be exceedingly and pointlessly uncomfortable.

"Why do you want me to stand around for three hours just to walk up and grab a scroll that's a blank piece of paper, since the real diplomas won't be ready?"

"Because it's a moment to remember. An honor," Natalya answered. "Because Gappa and Door and Pappa would be proud to be in the audience when your name is called and your honors are announced. As salutatorian you would give a speech. You could say something meaningful."

"There will be hours of boring speeches for the audience to squirm through."

"You have made us proud," Victor said, "and we would like to celebrate."

"It should be enough that you are proud. Besides, I'd hate for Gappa to be thinking how happy Beca would be to see this moment. And Gappa and Door and Pappa shouldn't be outside in Houston in May. It's unhealthily hot and humid and if it rains, things will be a mess."

"No they won't," Nat said. "Everything is covered."

"Still, it gets muddy," Sheela continued. "And it's quite a walk from the parking lot to the seating. Anyway, I don't like public ceremonies. They're silly."

"The fact that you don't like them," Victor pointed out, "hardly makes them silly."

"I stand corrected by the world's expert in logical communication," Sheela snapped. "They are silly *to me.*"

"I wish you would think about how much pleasure your being part of the commencement would give us," Natalya said. "We were so looking forward to putting your graduation picture in the album."

"Is that what this is really about?" Sheela asked.

"Not entirely," Nat honestly answered, "but yes, that's a part of it."

"Then I have good news for you." Sheela grinned. "There's going to be a photography session. I really didn't want to attend, but I could. We'll be wearing our caps and gowns and holding our quote diplomas unquote. The honor students will be photographed shaking the principal's hand. And parents are invited to attend and snap to their hearts' content."

Victor and Nat couldn't figure out what to give Sheela for the graduation she declined to celebrate. For her seventeenth birthday, the first one without Beca, they took her to Hawaii. She seemed to have a good time, even though she didn't swim and she didn't run into any young people. She said she loved the Big Island and Maui. At seventeen, Nat thought, she wouldn't have particularly enjoyed spending ten days with just her mother and father, but then Sheela was much more of a homebody.

That holiday was a healing one. The aftermath of Beca's death had been difficult for them all. Victor had taken his mother's passing badly. He was just coming around. He didn't say much and he evaded Natalya's attempts to understand him or to console him. Nat herself missed her mother-in-law much more than she had expected to. She knew Beca had loved her, but she didn't realize how deeply rooted her own affection lay. Nor did Victor or Sheela, so neither of them offered Nat much consolation. Sheela was the most dejected of the three. She tried not to show it, but she felt as if a part of herself had been cut out of her. Like her father, she did not speak of her sorrow and like him she didn't realize that it was so palpable. Natalya and Victor both felt their child's pain even more intensely than their own, but they were helpless.

Sitting Shiva to mourn Rebecca's death had given no relief to the Landaus. Instead of bringing peace, the silence and covered mirrors sharpened their sense of gloom. However, little by little, this small family came to understand that its loss was one each of them would have to cope with alone and that time would assuage their grief.

Dr. Henry Landau came to a different understanding. He felt time would never ease his suffering. It would remain sharp for the rest of his days, that he hoped wouldn't be too many. But he appreciated the need to maintain a brave front so as not to burden his loved ones, and he tried to act as if being alive without Beca was bearable.

Alone, he said Kaddish for the soul of his wife, whom he knew as Rebecca Gershwin, although she had been named Ruth at birth. Rebecca was her middle name, given in memory of her mother's grandmother. Beca confessed this to him some years after they were married.

"Why don't you use your first name?" Henry asked.

"I'd prefer not to say," Beca replied.

Rebecca left no will. That was a deliberate judgment she had made when she was quite well. She knew her property would go to her husband, if he survived her, and then to Victor and his family and she had no wishes, other than those she had relayed to Henry. He knew she would prefer cremation to burial, so she had been cremated and her ashes stored in a crematorium. The vault that contained the urn where her physical remains would rest indefinitely was inscribed:

Rebecca Landau née Gershwin, Beloved wife of Henry Landau,

Mother of Victor Landau and his wife Natalya Landau,

Grandmother of Sheela Landau.

Now, more than a year after her death, a new routine was established in the lives of those Rebecca left behind. Natalya and Victor prepared Sabbath dinners whenever possible. They always invited Henry and sometimes they asked the Singers. Not infrequently Steve Jordan and other non-Jewish friends or colleagues or Sheela's friends would join them because the dinners Nat cooked were delectable and the mood in her home was welcoming. On the Friday nights Dr. Landau spent with his children, he relished their food and basked in their warmth. For a few short hours he could ignore the hurt that never let him rest. And during those hours he was grateful for the tradition that was his legacy. That tradition hadn't been much help in dealing with death, but it made dealing with life much easier.

"Perhaps," Natalya suggested to her husband, "we should give Sheela a trip to Europe as a graduation gift. Remember how before her junior year she missed out on the drama club tour? What do you think?"

Victor thought it an excellent suggestion and he presented it to his daughter a few days later.

"Even if you refuse to attend your graduation," he said, "we would like to do something special for you. The problem is we don't know what would please you. We've looked into some student tours of Europe. Here are the brochures. If there is any particular tour that appeals to you, we would be happy to send you."

"Thanks Daddy," Sheela said. "That's really nice of you. So, I'll look them over and think about it, OK?"

"OK. But let me know soon. The bookings are getting tight."

Over the weekend Victor raised the subject of the tours again.

"So?" he asked. "Do any of the packages look good to you?"

"Actually," Sheela replied, "I'd rather go to Europe with you and Mama. We'll have some quality time together before I leave home, and I'm sure the accommodations and the food will be much better. That is if you two can swing it."

"Sure we can swing it. It's just that we thought you might get bored with two old fogies like us. Wouldn't you rather be around younger folks?"

"Not really, but if you don't want to go with me, it's OK."

"We'd love to go with you," Victor said. "Nothing could be more enjoyable from our viewpoint. Your mother worries, though, that you don't socialize more. She thought this might be a nice opportunity for you to maybe have some fun with people your own age."

"And you don't worry?" Sheela asked.

"Well," Victor admitted, "just a tad."

"But I have enough friends, boys and girls. I don't need to get involved with any more Dwaynes."

"That's just the thing we worry about. We don't want one bad experience to be a turn off."

"No, Daddy," Sheela said. "It won't be. But I'm not interested in flirting around with just anyone."

"You shouldn't flirt with just anyone," Victor explained. "Look, this isn't the kind of thing I'm good at discussing. Your mother would know what to say."

"You are doing great. Go on Daddy," Sheela encouraged.

"Well, what you should be doing is meeting lots of nice young men and enjoying yourself in a lighthearted way. But hey, we'd love to take you wherever you wish to go: Europe, Asia or the moon."

"Thanks. I'd love Europe, and I want you and Mama to pick where. And Daddy?"

"What, sweetheart?" Victor asked.

"Thanks for caring. Sometimes I worry too, but I can't force myself to enjoy guys drooling over me. If and when I do like someone, I'll know. But it isn't something I can practice for and it isn't something I can make happen by running to more and more parties where I have a horrible time."

"Sure," Victor said. "Maybe in college you will go to parties where you don't have a horrible time. You might even run into some guy who is nice, like me, with whom you can have a good time. But you have to give him a chance, OK?"

"I'll try," Sheela answered.

The Landaus went to London, Florence, Madrid and Granada. They decided there was no way to do more without chasing around like the characters in the remake of the movie *It's Tuesday So This Must Be Belgium*. London and Florence were places Nat and Victor adored and in Spain, Sheela she could use her Spanish.

The trip was a success. Everything was perfect, including the weather. There were no misplaced pieces of luggage, no fouled-up reservations, no favorite haunts closed for renovation, and no lost travelers' checks. The itinerary was ideal for a leisurely two weeks. At the end, they couldn't say which city was the most enjoyable. Their experiences in all four were equally wonderful.

In Europe, Sheela realized that her adolescence was over. Suddenly, she had stopped arguing with her mother or father. Not once did she become defensive or feel that she wasn't getting through to them. Not once did they talk down to her, as if she were too young to understand something. And what they said made perfect sense to her. Her newly found maturity endowed her parents with wisdom. She also noticed what great company her parents were and understood this was one of the reasons she hung around home and family so much. Compared to them, many of the teenagers and young adults she knew were dull. Her relatives and family friends were smart, vivacious, and full of ideas. It was much more entertaining to hang out with them than with the average Joes of her own generation. Except for Bernadette and a handful of others, her peers didn't have a thought in their heads beyond their grades, their appearance, their dates, or their status. They talked a great deal, but they had no conception of what it was like to have a conversation.

⸻ ❈❈❈❈❈ ⸻

Two days before flying off to Harvard, Bernadette spent the night with Sheela. Sheela was driving to UT with her father a day later. She was going to live in a dorm in a single room that was somewhat larger than a cubicle. She won her scholarship, and her parents agreed to spend a portion of the money the scholarship saved on a communication center to die for. Bernadette was moving into an apartment with a roommate.

"I think Helen, that's my roommate, will be smooth," Bernie said. "She'll be a sophomore so she can teach me some of the ropes."

"How come you aren't going to live with Will?" Sheela asked.

"I don't think I could handle the pressure of Harvard, of being away from home and of washing someone's dirty socks all at once, even if the dirty socks are Will's."

"He could wash his own socks," Sheela pointed out. "I don't know, but if I were in love like you are, I couldn't bear living apart."

"The thing is," Bernie volunteered, "we haven't made love yet; we're waiting."

"Waiting for what?"

"For a special occasion. We may go to the Cape or something our first time."

Sheela didn't understand. Not knowing what to say, she kept quiet and Bernie took the opportunity to ask her the question that had been weighing on her mind, "Did your mother ever tell you not to have sex before marriage?"

"No," Sheela answered, "she just told me marriage made sex special. She said even though a wedding is only a ceremony and words on a piece of paper, it makes a difference. The words represent a commitment, just like a diploma represents an achievement. Of course the commitment is already there, but saying the words out loud in front of witnesses like a rabbi or priest, or even a judge makes the commitment sacred."

"Do you agree?" Bernie asked.

"I don't know. I never loved anyone, but I can't imagine waiting for a wedding if I did. Anyway my mother didn't say to wait, she just said marriage made something wonderful even better."

"My Mom actually expects me to practice total abstention until after my wedding!" Bernie said.

"How does she define *total* abstention?" Sheela asked.

"She doesn't."

"I think the reason my parents never said anything like that to me is that they didn't abstain themselves. But I don't get the point of abstaining if you are committed."

"Will and I are totally committed. We aren't getting married yet because my mother and father wanted us to wait until after I finish my freshman year, and we said OK to keep the peace."

"Well, you are pretty young," Sheela said. "I'm not getting married until I'm a lot older, if ever."

"How do you know that?" her friend asked.

"Because," Sheela answered, "when I was a baby Sunita Khanna's grandmother got my horoscope read in India and that's what it said."

"Sunita is that girl who lives in Chicago, right?"

"Yeah, our parents have been friends forever. Sunita's grandmother said that not everything written in the horoscope will necessarily prove to be true, but I believe most of it. Sunita said her mom thinks that if we believe our horoscope, sometimes we act in a certain way to make things happen according to what it says. I don't know."

"Neither do I," Bernie agreed.

"Anyway, I made up my mind about some stuff," Sheela added. "If I don't get married to someone I adore, I'll never have any children; and if I ever really fall in love, I'll be too frightened to wait."

"What would you be frightened of?"

"Maybe one of us would die. Or maybe something would happen to separate us forever. Is that macabre?"

"Not in your case," Bernadette replied. "When you finally find the thief who has stolen your heart, it's natural that you'd be scared to let him so much as breathe until he gives it back."

46

Life at the University of Texas overwhelmed Sheela. She was homesick and had difficulty identifying kindred spirits. In retrospect she decided her peers at Houston International High, whom she had considered shallow, were at least innocuous. On the other hand, the UT climate was purposefully arrogant. The student body for the most part was materialistic and Texas-proud of its conservatism. That meant they supported reviving the death penalty and killing any program that might uplift the disadvantaged.

While older faculty members were still committed to ongoing reform, many younger instructors and much of the student population believed the Gorham-Mayer years were the beginning of the downfall of America and blamed the conquering of Aids for social corruption. They also believed they were going to become rich because they were deserving and they couldn't see why they should pay taxes to a government that supported the undeserving. Since she knew arguing about politics didn't change minds, Sheela kept her views to herself. However, she was shocked by the mindset around her. She decided she had been brought up in an ivory tower.

She wondered how she would survive in this hostile environment. Her skin crawled at remarks like "If we don't watch out, our next chief will be as black as the ace of spades" or "Jewish, female, and homosexual politicians have sent our great country on a downward spiral. It's time to act!" The makers of those statements didn't expect a response. Thus Sheela kept her silence or else simply said, "Many of our great nation's greatest citizens have been Jews, females, blacks and gay persons," and walked away.

Though the most vociferous students were those who believed God smiled on the wealthy, disdained the poor, and gave the powerful an entitlement to impose their personal views on the weak, alternative groups did not strike Sheela as particularly attractive either. The state of Texas had banned fraternities and sororities, maintaining they encouraged "unacceptable gender discrimination and dangerous behavior, particularly but not exclusively in initiation practices." The slack left by these institutions was taken up by a plethora of "societies" whose members represented diverse and incompatible clusters of undergraduates.

Sheela was bombarded with leaflets asking if she qualified for societies like Americans for America, Judaism Reborn, Islamic Revivalists, Hispanic Power, Ebonic Culturists, United Asian Americans, and so forth. 'Yuck,' she thought!

Her parents offered her little sympathy.

"Are you saying," Natalya asked her, "that no one at UT is good enough to be your friend? This is the university of your choice. It has over fifty thousand students; surely a handful of them would be worthy of your consideration."

"My problem," Sheela explained, "is finding the handful among the fifty thousand. It's like finding a needle in a haystack."

"Look," Victor said, "types like you are watching and waiting and keeping to themselves just like you are. The noisemakers are the insecure students, the ones who feel threatened. They have always been around. America will not falter because of them. You do your thing and before you know it, you and other young men and women with values like yours will gravitate toward one another. You can bet on it."

Among themselves, Victor and Nat worried.

"What is the matter with our daughter?" Natalya asked her husband. "Do you think she is just a snob, or is she disturbed or what? Maybe she is just spoiled. If we had been able to have another child, Sheela would have learned to bend a little."

"That wouldn't have changed things," Victor said. "Sheela would still be a snob. She doesn't think she is a hot shot, but she avoids people with whom she can't immediately identify. On top of that she hasn't quite recovered from stuff like Dwayne, and Beca's death. She and Beca had a thing. Beca shouldn't have died like that, leaving us all hanging in thin air."

"It's not fair to blame Beca for passing away and for being close to Sheela. It doesn't help us or Sheela at all, Victor."

"Well, you asked what the matter is and I think my mother is part of it. She encouraged Sheela's idiosyncrasies and she's one of the reasons Sheela is spoiled."

"Hey, if she is spoiled, we should blame ourselves more than anyone else. We did the best we could and so did all her grandparents. This isn't anyone's fault."

"You are probably right," Victor agreed. "I might as well face it. I'm projecting my own stuff with my mother to my daughter."

"So do you think Sheela will snap out of all this?" Natalya continued.

"Of course. It isn't like Sheela is doing anything wrong. Her attitude is only a problem because it makes her unhappy."

"I guess," Nat mused.

"Hopefully," Victor said, "she'll learn to take people as they come. I used to have a tough time making small talk and letting people be. I was well out of college before I figured out that if Jack Jerk is a good tennis partner, to hell with his ideology. I just play tennis with him and enjoy that."

"That goes without saying. No one can be all things. Maybe we should have a talk with Sheela about lightening up."

"No way," Victor told his wife. "We can't teach her how to make friends."

"I hope Sheela doesn't wind up a dried up old maid," Natalya suddenly blurted.

"That's what really scares you most, isn't it? You think she is so picky that she'll never find someone good enough for her and that she'll be miserable and you'll never become a grandmother."

"Yes, that's part of it," Natalya acknowledged.

"Well," Victor admitted, "I've thought of that too. But then again, I never wanted to get married either. I couldn't see myself stuck to a bimbo for the rest of my life, and look what happened to me. So I think the best thing we can do is chill."

Dissatisfaction with her social life didn't stop Sheela from enjoying the academic challenge of her classes. She studied hard and began to attract favorable attention from faculty and from peers. Because she was not competitive, but merely tried to do her best, she shared her notes and thoughts freely. In the process she acquired a few grateful admirers and many angry rivals.

"Stop helping Lauren and those guys," an irate classmate complained. "You are going to ruin the curve by your volunteer tutorials. It's not fair!"

"It most certainly is fair," Sheela retorted. "If others do poorly, it doesn't mean you have done well. You can take your curve and put it where the sun doesn't shine. And have a nice day."

Before Sheela knew it, it was time to start preparing for semester finals. The first round of college grades gave freshmen a reputation that was apt to stick until graduation. Sheela focused on her work and stopped worrying about the principles that circulated in the university community. As a result, she felt less lonely and sorry for herself. When her parents drove up to see her for a weekend—actually to check out how she was doing—they found her in better spirits. She seemed to be interacting with other students and she didn't complain.

"I'm getting caught up so I don't have to slog over the Thanksgiving holiday," she said. The thought of Thanksgiving lightened her spirits.

In two weeks and three days she would take the new bullet train to Houston. She looked forward to speeding over the Texas countryside at more than three hundred kilometers per hour. When she got home, she would have a wonderful time helping Ma prepare Thanksgiving dinner and then she would sleep in her own bed for four heavenly nights. When she returned to school, she decided, she would bring Aa-Oo, her old parrot, along. He might make her room in the dorm feel cozier.

Sheela took heart in the knowledge that—as always—the two weeks between Thanksgiving and Christmas vacation would flash by at the speed of light. At UT she would have a few days of review sessions, a couple of dead days for preparation, and then finals. After that, at long last she would spend the Christmas/Chanukah break, the beginning of the year 2019, and her eighteenth birthday in New York.

⁕⁕⁕

Sheela hadn't been with the Rosenbaums in a fulfilling way for ages and she was counting on making up for lost time during this coming visit. She could hardly wait to cuddle Re, by now a ham with a coquettish smile guaranteed to get her whatever her heart desired. She loved conferencing, and she worked hard at perfecting her communication and enunciation skills. The last time they talked, Renee told Sheela to "Come now now," and after waving good-bye with gusto, she said "Re luv She."

It wasn't only Re whom Sheela missed. She also was eager to roughhouse with Alex and Jimmy who were different every time she saw them. Alex's most recent thing was magenta colored hair to which his parents finally consented as a reward for a prize-winning biology project. And Jimmy was growing his hair long because he was impressed by *Samson and Delilah*, the latest Broadway hit.

"If Alex can dye his hair, I can let mine grow long," he argued. "I got good grades and it isn't my fault we didn't get any projects. If we did, I'd win a prize too. And I'm the second most ahead in math in my whole section. I'd be aheadest except for that dumb Helen Kovack who does nothing but math her whole life. Besides, lots of people have long hair. Kultar Singh in my class isn't even allowed to cut his hair because of his religion. And Jews like us, you know Hasik Jews, have long hair too because Samson was Jewish."

"Hasidic Jews," Cecily corrected. "We aren't Hasidic and I doubt that their long hair has anything to do with Samson."

"OK, Hasidic," Jimmy said. "But they are still Jews and so are we, and anyway it's my own hair on my own head."

"It isn't quite that simple," Ronald explained to his son. "Like it or not, we are responsible for your health and hygiene and for your appearance. But as long as you look tidy and civilized, we agree that you should have a right to make as many personal decisions as possible."

"Yeah," Jimmy said.

"I'm not quite sure that magenta hair could pass for civilized," Cecily interjected.

"It's more civilized than having a scar sliced into your cheek like Barry Chow," Alex retorted. "Especially if your face is all pimply. Barry's mom is one of your best friends, right?" he asked.

"That's neither here nor there," Cecily replied.

Who could imagine that the boys were already fourteen and eight? Sheela remembered Alex's birth with the sharpness that time gives images you replay over and over in your head. Robo, her birth gift to him, still occupied a position of honor in his room. Robo had survived the years much better than Aa-Oo; he was made of a more enduring fabric. Sheela decided to take Aa-Oo to New York to see if the toy hospital attached to the Children's Wellness Center could restore him.

Sheela's Thanksgiving, Chanukah and eighteenth birthday/New Year celebrations turned out to be everything she had hoped for and more, except she missed Gappa. He seemed to have aged a great deal just since she left for college and he didn't feel strong enough to face the cold so he stayed in Houston.

Door and Pappa on the other hand were as chipper and upbeat as ever. Knock on wood, the years had been kind to them. Door could still carry off a wardrobe of young-looking brightly colored clothes, Pappa still could arm wrestle with Ronald and win, and both of them could entertain their grandsons for days on end without tiring. Only Re was a bit too much for them, but then she was a bit too much for everyone.

The Rosenbaums cooked up a small but splendiferous bash to celebrate Sheela's becoming of age. It was family only with the exception of two surprise guests who qualified as relatives: Lulu and Sunita Khanna. Those two were the first to greet Sheela when she came to the city the afternoon of the thirty-first, after having spent two days in the suburbs with her cousins. Sheela saw them—Sunita unbelievably foxy and Lulu looking like a dumpling—as soon as she walked in the door and she let out a big whoop, leaving Ronald and the rest of his family waiting outside in the hall for a good three minutes. It was a fitting opening scene for a grand evening.

Once the hellos and how are yous and wows were dispensed with, everyone except Sheela went to work. While the birthday girl hung around aimlessly, the others scurried, busy with preparations. Re was unavailable because she was taking a nap. Alex and Sunita, in charge of decorations, moved almost in unison preening and glowing, magenta hair and clanging bangles making contact whenever possible. Thirteen and fourteen, Sheela thought, feeling matronly. As the two worked, the walls of the Rosenbaum living and dining rooms became hidden behind multi-colored metallic streamers. Then Jimmy joined in and the threesome let loose a hundred transparent helium balloons with silvery tails that turned the party area into a dense forest of moonlit vines suspended in thin air. Walking through the long shimmering curls was like wafting in an optical illusion.

In the kitchen, the others prepared canapés, chilled champagne, tended to a roasting lamb, and made Rebecca's trifle pudding which they iced like a cake in a bowl and studded with nineteen as yet unlit candles, eighteen for Sheela's years plus the one for good luck. Everything looked, smelled, and sounded festive. But there were no piles of presents, no rustling of wrapping paper, and no whispered secrets to suggest that a special gift was yet to come.

"You don't have to sit like a bump on a log," Door told Sheela. "Wander around the house, feel free to see if you find anything interesting; or watch the entertainment. Use the communication center or call Bernie. Do whatever gives you pleasure."

Sheela had already spoken with Gappa who was spending the evening with friends and with Bernie who was in Houston with Will. On the entertainment center nothing could hold her attention given the excitement that tingled around her. Finally Jimmy was sent to distract her.

"Daddy told me I should play with you," he announced.

"Thank you," Sheela said. "You don't have to play though; you can do whatever you want."

"OK," Jimmy agreed.

"So what do you want to do?" Sheela asked.

"Nothing," Jimmy replied.

"That's good," Sheela said. "Here sit with me. It's what I'm doing, nothing."

"How come grown-ups get mad when you do nothing?" Jimmy asked.

"I don't know," Sheela answered.

"Well, you're grown up, aren't you? Isn't eighteen grown up?"

"It's supposed to be grown up or practically grown up," Sheela said. "But I think doing nothing is great. It's when you get your best ideas."

"Yeah," Jimmy agreed.

It was late in the evening before the party started. Intoxicated by the joyousness around her, Sheela forgot her worries. She forgot about college life, about exams, about Gappa, and about her dismal inability to become attracted to guys which was the cause of her loveless existence. For the moment, the love surrounding her was more than enough.

Talk, meaningful and idle, made the hours fly. Nat and Victor took stills with their new concealed palm camera. Ronald took moving pictures with his new chip camera. A selection of music to suit all tastes played in an order masterfully arranged by Alex. Re chirped and danced and insisted on being filmed in three or four of her favorite hats. Everyone looked dazzling. Sheela had never been more beautiful. Before she knew it, it was time for dinner.

At the table there were favors for all present, carefully selected by Nat. Even Sheela got one, a translucent white onyx frog, number 41, which she named Olivia.

After dinner Harold Rosenbaum carried out the trifle pudding cake blazing with candles. Everyone sang Happy Birthday, Natalya got tears in her eyes like always and Sheela made the same wish as always. After Sheela cut the first slice, Victor announced that it was now time for the birthday present.

"Technically, Sheela wasn't born until almost 5:00 a.m. tomorrow, New York time," he said, "but that's too late for us all to wait. So what we are going to do is put on our coats and go downstairs. We can all crowd in Ronald and Pappa's cars since we aren't going far. We'll eat the cake when we come back."

As they bundled up, Natalya said, "It's just one gift from Gappa, my parents, Ron and Cecily and the kids and from us. The Khannas and Lulu have provided the extras. Still, I'm sure you won't be disappointed."

"There's no way I'd be disappointed," Sheela said. "I have the best communication center in the world. There isn't anything else I want. At least nothing material."

"Nothing material?" Nat asked.

"Not really," Sheela honestly replied. But she wasn't thinking.

After a two-minute journey, the Rosenbaums, the Landaus, Sunita and Lulu reconvened at a garage several blocks away from the Rosenbaum residence. Ronald used his genie to open the door and a bright light automatically switched on. Sheela's mouth opened and drooped. She tried to speak, but her excitement tripped the fuse that linked her brain to her vocal cords. After a short while the reset kicked in and she screamed, "Oh My God!"

A brand new two-door, top-of-the-line sports model Vixen, the same color as Alex's hair, sat awaiting Sheela's approval. It seemed to stare at her. Sheela stared back. It was her absolutely most favorite car. She had loved Vixens ever since she saw them, the first year they came out, which was in 2012. MMC—Millennium Motorcars—took on the big boys of the automotive industry that year and they succeeded right from the start. Young people loved Vixens, old people loved them, and middle-aged people loved them. Males wanted to possess them and females identified with them. They had what you could call "universal appeal." Why? Maybe because of their daring colors; maybe because of their smooth handling; maybe because of their sleek lines. There was nothing you could put your finger on, except perhaps that the positioning of the lights and the eyebrow like design above them, along with the mouth-like shape of the bumper gave the Vixen an almost human look.

"So?" Door asked. "How do you like it?"

Sheela hugged her and hugged everyone in sight by way of response.

"Here are the keys," Lulu said. "The key chain is my gift." It was a big solid silver ring, bigger than a bangle bracelet, with a whistle at the end.

"It's beautiful," Sheela told her and hugged her all over again. "And it's practical."

"Listen to the whistle," Lulu said, blowing hard. The shrieking sound was piercing and deafening. "It's special. Made to scare burglars."

"Look at the 3D decal," Sunita said. "I picked it in Chicago and had it shipped for your grandparents to get put on. They're shooting stars. They had gold and silver and I thought gold, but then I decided silver. There is real silver in them."

"They're gorgeous; I love them," Sheela said and grabbed Sunita and hugged her until she begged to be let go."

"The color was chosen by a unanimous vote," Cecily volunteered, "based on our preference combined with our understanding of your taste. The fact that it seems to match Alex's hair is purely coincidental."

"Alex car hair," Renee volunteered.

"Hey," Alex said. "Did I or didn't I say that the *only* possible color was magenta? Isn't it totally in?"

"It's perfect," Sheela said and started yet another round of hugging.

"Well, take her for a spin," Natalya proposed. "Alex, Jimmy, and Sunita can go along. After you're done, park here. Cecily can drive you home. The cake is waiting."

47

The second semester of Sheela's freshman year was an improvement over her first. Returning to college was like returning home now. Although her college home wasn't as comfortable, physically or emotionally, as the one she had grown up in, the space in the dorm room had become more her own. Aa-Oo, in refreshed colors and with a mended beak, dominated the décor. A few possessions from home plus some new acquisitions like a tie-dyed bedspread and a red glass bowl filled with odds and ends brightened the room and Sheela's mood.

In part because her grades put her almost at the top of her class, Sheela found herself in demand. She opened up a little to students who approached in a gentler way and she developed a cordial relationship with an assortment of people. Abigail, Lauren, Charlie, Martin, or Joshua often met with her to have lunch or a pizza or to hold an informal study session. She still missed Bernie and the rest of her high school gang and wished that at least one of them had opted for UT, but, unlike her, and quite like her parents, they all thought that the east and west coasts of America offered the greener pastures.

Now that she was settled in, Sheela visited Houston more often. Steve Jordan sent her two round trip tickets on the bullet train as a belated birthday gift and she used them to good advantage. On one visit Victor told her, "I think you're here more to see your Vixen than you are to see us. I guess it was worth our driving it home all the way from New York." On another occasion Sheela met with her grandfather in Hermann Park for a Saturday noon picnic and a heart to heart talk.

"I'm awfully worried about you, Gappa," she began.

"What's there to worry about, sweetheart? I'm an old man. The worst thing that could happen to me is that I will die. Actually that would be a blessing."

"Don't say that. You have a lot to live for," Sheela told him.

"Such a cliché from a bright girl who should know better than to make canned statements," Henry retorted.

"No! It's the truth. Truth often comes in clichés."

"So tell me, sweetheart, what is the so much I have to live for?"

"What did you live for your whole life?" Sheela asked.

"Now she answers a question with another question," Dr. Landau mumbled, taking a sip of lemonade. "This lemonade I made is good, even if I say so myself. And your mother's tuna salad sandwiches are almost worth living for."

"Well?" Sheela insisted. "So tell me what your life was about before."

"It was about my work. It was about praying that my son would be a happy man. It was about you. Mostly it was about making Beca happy. So now I have done all those things. I have no more agendas and I'm not having any fun. I miss your grandmother and I want to join her. What is so terrible about that?"

"How can the main part of a life be wanting to make someone else happy?"

"Another question! My answer is simple. It's 'I don't know.' Maybe it was my destiny: Beca and you. There was something about the two of you. But I've done what I could and I have no more obligations."

Sheela was quiet for some time after her grandfather spoke. It was hard to admit that he made sense. But then she realized that he was right and it was OK. Why shouldn't Gappa wish to die? Wasn't it a blessing to greet death with hopefulness rather than with terror? When a few moments passed and Henry added nothing further, Sheela finally said, "I love you Gappa and I need you, but I think I understand."

"I'm glad you love me Sheela," Gappa said. "And I'll tell you a secret. Much as I want to die, I'm a little scared."

"What are you scared about?" Sheela asked. "I read that we fear death because it is an unknown."

"In my case that isn't so," Gappa explained. "I'm scared of something else, something you can help me with. Will you do that?"

"Yes, I will, Gappa. I will if you tell how I can help."

"You can help me make peace with your parents. They haven't forgiven your grandmother for leaving so suddenly and I'm afraid that if I go too, they will be angry. I want their blessing so I can remind God that I'm waiting for Him to take me whenever He thinks the time is right."

"What you ask is hard to do," Sheela said.

"It's not so hard," Gappa urged. "You don't have to do or say anything yet. You just have to understand. Then when you need them the right words will come to you. After all, who knows when God will decide it's time? It may not be for years."

What Sheela heard from her grandfather on this occasion saddened her a little, but it also clarified her perspective of life and death. However, what she heard from her mom's good friend Annette Singer in the course of the same weekend shook her up.

Annette's son Bobby was a tall and handsome boy exactly one year and nine months younger than Sheela, which made him sixteen. Sheela had always thought of him as Baby Bobby and that's what she had called him through most of her childhood. Then one day when he was about nine, Aunt Annette took her aside and told her he ranted and raged after every meeting with her, but he would never explain what bothered him. Annette wondered if Sheela could figure out what the problem was. At first Sheela was as puzzled as Annette.

"All we did was play chess. Baby Bobby even beat me one time out of three," she had said on that occasion. "He's quite smart you know."

"Bingo," Annette said. "I bet you called him 'Baby Bobby' to his face.

"I always call him Baby Bobby," Sheela admitted. "It's kind of a joke."

"I'm sure he doesn't find it amusing. To a growing boy being big is a big deal. You've got to stop."

Sheela made a few slips but pretty soon she learned to skip the "Baby" part when she spoke to her young friend. As she and Bobby grew, meeting frequently when their families got together and even doing things on their own like going to the movies or skating, their friendship blossomed. They chatted about their parents, their schoolwork, and their other friends.

In his teens, Bobby had become a soccer player and was much sought after by femme teens he disdained. Sheela could understand why.

"I know exactly how you feel," she told Bobby. "When those self-appointed he-men try to fall all over me, I want to become invisible."

Although Bobby never found out the details of the Dwayne incident, he had heard rumors and he hurt for Sheela. At the same time, though, he was encouraged by the fact that she had rejected Dwayne like she rejected every other guy who tried to be more than a friend. He himself had harbored a consuming crush on Sheela for as long as he could remember. Some day, he told himself, she'll notice me and both of our lives will fall into place. Once when he was about twelve he had said to Sheela, "I'm going to be bigger than you when I grow up."

"No way," Sheela had responded. "I'm always going to be almost two years older."

"Yeah," Bobby said, "but I am going to be bigger and taller and stronger so I can take care of you."

"How would you take care of me?" Sheela had asked.

"I'll give you whatever you want and I'll do whatever you want and I'll beat up anyone who is mean to you," he replied.

Bobby never did beat up Dwayne, but only because he never got the opportunity.

After returning from the picnic and dropping Gappa home, Sheela learned from Natalya that Annette wanted to meet her in the afternoon for a cup of tea.

"What?" Sheela asked. "I don't have cups of tea in the middle of the day. I was going to drive to the outlet mall and I was hoping you'd come along."

"Well, then call up Aunt Annette yourself and make your excuses. She said it was important."

Sheela did call Annette, but instead of going to the fashion outlet as planned, she ended up driving to the Galleria with her mother's friend wondering what on earth was up. Annette wouldn't say right away. They browsed a little at Swinger's and Annette bought her a transparent vest. Then they found a table at the August Moon where they shared a pot of jasmine tea and some almond cookies. Finally Annette got to the point.

"I can't believe that you and Bobby have a romance going," she said.

"What?" Sheela was astounded.

"A romance," Annette repeated. "This has come as somewhat of a surprise to me, although not an unwelcome one."

"That's crazy," Sheela said. "Bobby and I are buddies. We've known each other our whole lives."

"What do you mean by buddies?" Annette asked.

"I mean friends, like cousins or brother and sister. We're pals."

"If that's the case," Annette said, "you had no business leading my son toward thinking your relationship was of a different nature. There is a difference between the way you act with a friend and the way you acted with Bobby. You know how much I love your mother and I've adored you ever since you were born, but to be very honest, at this moment I am at a loss. I don't know what to think of you."

"You don't have to think anything," Sheela said, beginning to shake. "It's unfair of you to come to conclusions and to judge me. I've never led Bobby on. You have no right to accuse me of something like that."

"Are you calling my son a liar?" Annette asked.

"I'm not saying anything," Sheela answered in tears. "I don't know what gave him the idea that I care for him that way."

"According to Bobby," Annette said, "you kissed him and you told him you love him. Besides, neither of you has ever hit it off with anyone else. This explained a lot to me."

"No," Sheela insisted. "We never touched or kissed and I never told Bobby I cared for him. No way. Why would I say that if it isn't true! You have to understand."

"What is there to understand? I'm getting two wildly different stories from two people who I thought were honest. You know I would be delighted if you were to confirm that what Bobby said was true. There would be nothing wrong with that. According to Bobby, he has been carrying a torch for you ever since he knew about the birds and the bees, if not before."

"How can I confirm something that's totally off the wall?" Sheela struggled to regain her composure. "How can you expect that of me? I can't even believe we are having this conversation." After a pause she said, "Excuse me, I have to wash my face."

When she returned, Sheela asked, as calmly as possible, "When did Bobby tell you I said I loved him? And, according to him, what did I do make him believe something as wild as that?"

"He told me this morning," Annette replied. "My son said the two of you were together last night, after dinner. You were in your room."

"Oh my God!" Sheela said.

"Why Oh my God?" Annette asked. "What were the two of you up to?"

"We weren't up to anything, Aunt Annette. After we cleared up the table when you guys were talking, Bobby said he wanted to hear my new Cobalts' disc so I said OK. Then he asked what I thought of the Cobalts' blue hair and I said they looked OK but I preferred normal hair. I said that my cousin had magenta hair and that in my opinion it made him look immature. Then Bobby asked, 'So what could I do to make you think I look mature and to make you love me?' So I said, 'You don't have to do anything. You're quite mature for your age and I already love you.' And I gave him a hug and kissed him on the cheek. It was a sisterly hug, like the ones I give my cousins. God! I never dreamt that he was thinking of *love* love."

"I see." Annette masked her fear. She wanted to deny the possibility that her son was the victim of a crazy passion that led him to misconstrue Sheela's affection. She wanted to ignore the fact that she herself had been totally taken in by wishful thinking. However, Sheela's subsequent remarks forced her to accept that reality.

"I'm sorry you are mad at me." Sheela swallowed a new set of tears. "You can think whatever you want, but I didn't do anything wrong. Anyway, I can't cope with guys who throw themselves at me or think that I love them just because I'm friendly. You know what happened with Dwayne. If Bobby is going to turn out like that, I never want to see him again. I don't care. You're a therapist. You're supposed to understand stuff. I always trusted you. Well, I don't trust you anymore. So I'd appreciate it if you ask for the bill and I'll drive you home. And you can return this vest. I couldn't wear it now."

This time it was Annette's turn to ask to be excused to the lady's room. She doused herself with cold water and powdered her nose. Then she told herself, 'You're an idiot, a raving, lunatic idiot.' When she returned to the table where Sheela sat staring at a bamboo screen, Annette spoke softly and slowly.

"Please," she said. "I listened to you and now I'm asking you to listen to me. I may be a therapist but I'm human. I love my son and I love you. So when Bobby told me his version of what took place, I believed him. Maybe I thought it was too good to be true, but if it were true, it would be the most wonderful thing in the world. I should have realized that things that seem too good to be true usually are just that, not true. I should have listened to my muted inner voice that held just a trace of suspicion. I should have talked to you more gently. I should have asked you what happened before jumping to conclusions. Excuse me." Annette paused to rub her eyes. Then she went on. "But I wasn't thinking, at least I wasn't thinking straight. It was callous of me not to keep in mind what you had gone through with that low-life Dwayne. I was afraid for my son. I'm sorry. Please forgive me and forgive Bobby for his foolishness. I beg you, don't equate Bobby with someone as horrible as that creep Dwayne. Bobby would never hurt you. Not in a million years. If you believe anything, you have got to believe that."

"I do," Sheela interjected.

"This is my fault; I never considered how vulnerable you still must be. So please forgive me. Please." Annette stopped and hid her face behind her hands.

"Don't cry, Aunt Annette," Sheela said. "I understand. It's OK. Remember, it's like the Baby Bobby thing when we were little."

"Not exactly," Annette said, "except that probably even then Bobby wanted to be big because of how he felt about you."

"That's what I meant," Sheela said.

"So you'll keep the vest?" Annette asked.

"Sure," Sheela answered.

"And can we keep this conversation between ourselves?"

"Of course. But I don't know what to do about Bobby."

"You don't have to do anything until the next time he does or says something. I'll drop some hints about how he might have misunderstood you."

It was about six when Sheela came home. Although she wanted to confide in her mother, she didn't. She showed Nat her new vest, mentioned that Aunt Annette wanted some advice about Bobby, and left it that.

When Sheela returned to UT, an interesting voice message awaited her. "My name is Zyan," it said. "I just found out that my grandparents know Anjali Khanna who is the grandmother of one of your friends. I think your friend's name is Sunila or something like that. So my grandmother told me to call you up. She seems to think that this connection means we'll like each other, which may or may not be the case. Anyway if I don't meet you and report back she'll keep bugging me. My number is 512-687-6887. By the way I'm a junior at UT. I'm a liberal arts type and . . ."

"Hello, it's Zyan. Your machine cut me off, rightfully so. I'm always too long-winded. What I want to say is I'm not being forced to call you. You sound neat from what I heard. Bye. Oh, I'll repeat my number just in case you missed it: 512-687-6887 and my mail is Zy@intnet.edu. Bye for real."

Sheela thought Zyan sounded like a fun person. But she wasn't sure if the person was a guy or a girl. She couldn't tell from the voice, which was husky but also sounded congested. Zyan had the ring of a female name so it was probably a girl. On the other hand, there were some foreign names that you would think belonged to girls but were really boys' names. She wondered if Zyan's family was from India.

It took several days of missing one another before Sheela and Zyan made contact and by then Sheela was too embarrassed to inquire about Zyan's ethnic background or gender.

"This is Sheela," Sheela finally said the first time Zyan answered the phone in person.

"Hallelujah!" Zyan sounded extremely hoarse. "I can't talk much," she explained. "At the risk of stating the obvious, I'll say I have a horrible throat. But I don't want you to think this is how I always sound."

"That's OK," Sheela said. "I didn't really call to chat. I thought we should try and get together and talk in person."

"Right," Zyan said.

"So," Sheela asked, "what do you think? What do you like to do?"

"Oh anything at all. Are you pretty busy?"

"Sure," Sheela said. "But everyone is busy. I'm staying in Austin this weekend though. Maybe we can meet then."

"Lamentably, I'm not. I am going to New Orleans," Zyan croaked, "to see this clerk I know who works for Judge Flickhauser who just got appointed to the fifth circuit. I want to be a lawyer so I'm starting my networking early. But next week would be good."

"I want to be a lawyer too. My mom's a lawyer," Sheela volunteered.

"The more the merrier," Zyan said. "So let's talk after I get back which will be Sunday evening."

"Good," Sheela said. "Should we make an appointment to talk, or just continue with our hit and miss strategy of trying to reach one another?"

"Hit and miss is good," Zyan said.

The second time the two linked up, Zyan was sick with laryngitis and could barely speak at all.

"I should have listened to my mother," Zyan whispered. "I shouldn't have gone to New Orleans."

"I guess not; so let's get in touch when you feel better," Sheela proposed.

"Right," Zyan rasped.

The morning following that conversation, Sheela's radio jolted her out of a bizarre dream. She was walking in circles in a tropical jungle amidst a myriad of brilliantly colored macaws busy preening their feathers. However, instead of flying and making human or bird-like noises, they were hopping and croaking like frogs. Sheela was trying to find Aa-Oo in the melee, but Bobby kept stepping in front of her.

"You'll get hurt," he said. "Wait here, I'll find Aa-Oo. I'll turn myself into a frog and call until he answers."

"No, *I'll* go," Sheela insisted. "Aa-Oo is expecting me. These are parrots, not frogs. Don't think they are going to turn into princes."

"What is Aa-Oo doing here anyway?" Bobby asked.

"He came down to see Zebara, his sweetheart," Sheela replied. "She isn't a zebra though. She's a cyborette."

"How did she get here?" Bobby asked.

"She just flew in from the Orient. Or, maybe she rode in on the Orient Express. That's the new trans-oceanic bullet train, you know."

"Of course I know," Bobby Singer replied. "I'm not a baby any more."

"No, but you're stil . . ."

Before Sheela could finish her sentence, her alarm jolted her awake. She was upset because she knew she could have located Aa-Oo in a few more seconds, but then she saw him right before her eyes, looking dapper and smug.

At last Sheela and Zyan connected via insta-mail. They arranged to meet on Friday at 8:00 p.m. at a new booth parlor called Clementine's. These parlors were opening up all over the place. Door explained to Sheela that they were a modern version of old diners, which used to have little coin operated jukeboxes in each booth. The new parlors had small entertainment boxes instead which could be activated by special cards.

"How will we recognize one another?" Sheela typed.

"I'll be wearing something brown," Zyan wrote back. "What about you?"

"I guess I'll wear brown too. I have lots of brown."

"Brown is the 'in' color," Zyan agreed. "Anyway if everyone else is in brown, we'll just ask around. I'm signing out."

"OK and ditto." Sheela confirmed.

Sheela thought Zyan had to be a girl, but she hoped against hope she was wrong. Whatever, she told herself, I'll soon find out. I hope Zyan likes me, because I already like her or him. This is the sort of person I just know I'll click with.

48

Sheela decided to wear a slinky skirt that zipped just below her navel and a long sleeve knit top that zipped just above it. She debated about putting a little sticky with glitter in her navel, but decided against it, because she wasn't sure about just how people dressed at Clementine's. Besides, if Zyan turned out to be a guy after all, she didn't want him to think she had gone all out for him. As she got ready, Sheela remembered her horoscope and figured that even if Zyan was a guy, he probably wouldn't be her prince charming after all because she was destined to remain unmarried for about another decade. Of course she might end up having a ten year long affair or else getting her heart broken, the more likely scenario.

Sheela walked into Clementine's a few moments after eight and looked around for someone who could be Zyan. It took a few seconds for her eyes to adjust to the dim lights, but then she noticed that brown was everywhere. She wished she had clarified whether brown meant some brown or everything brown. After a quick scan, Sheela's eyes fell upon a blond boy wearing boots and a brown shirt with jeans. He was sitting alone and seemed to be waiting for someone. Sheela tentatively walked up to him and asked, "Excuse me, but are you Zyan?"

"Who?" he asked.

"Zyan. Is your name Zyan?"

"Bryan?" His face broke out into a broad smile.

"No, Zyan."

"Uh uh, but I wish it were Zyan instead of Bryan," he said, "if that's who you're looking for."

"It is," Sheela said. "Sorry to have barged in on you." Bryan was nice looking, but not devastatingly handsome. "You are wearing brown and you seem to be waiting for someone."

"I am," he replied. "A blind date. I should never have let my friends set me up. I hate blind dates. But for a second there, when I thought you might be her, I started to rethink."

As they spoke, a tall anorexic looking female in a cream pantsuit, a brown jacket, and wearing glitter in her short blah-brown hair approached. Sheela held her breath and told herself there was no way that creature could be Zyan, no way.

"Hi," the girl said. "Bryan?"

"That's me," the young man replied, looking as dejected as Sheela looked relieved. "You must be Cynthia."

"So long, Bryan," Sheela said and scurried toward the door. She glanced at her watch to check the time and as she registered that it was eight minutes past eight, she bumped into a softish body.

"Excuse me," a deep but definitely feminine voice said.

"Gosh, I'm sorry," Sheela apologized. "I was looking at my watch instead of where I was going." She looked up at a dark eyed young woman with golden brown hair done in an up-sweep. She was wearing a long flared brown skirt and a soft brown shell.

"No, no," the girl said, "it's totally my fault. I'm late and . . hey, you're all in brown. Are you Sheela?"

"Zyan," Sheela said, "I'm so happy to meet you at last."

"So," Zyan explained over a shared carafe of sparkling red wine, "Gramp Jake, my grandfather on my father's side, read this book and fell in love with the name Zyanya. He bribed my mom with a ruby ring and got her to agree to name me Zyanya if I turned out to be a girl. Zyanya is a Mexican Indian name meaning 'Always.' Later when my mom had her sonogram, they told her I was a boy. Apparently my finger had been dangling in a strategic spot. My parents modified the name to Zyan. When I was born, clearly minus a Y chromosome, they were surprised but quite hooked on Zyan. Gramp was furious. He called me Zyanya for years. Should I leave the box screen on the dancing fountains, or should we switch channels?"

"The fountains are good," Sheela said, "but let's lower the music a little. I wonder if Zyan is like a male version of 'Always'."

"Nobody knows. My grandfather isn't even sure if Zyanya was a real name or if it was just made up by the book's author."

"Anyway, Zyan is a beautiful name," Sheela said, "and it suits you."

"Thanks, I sort of like it myself. I've been thinking about adding an Anya in the middle. It would thrill my grandfather. How does Zyan Anya Reuven sound to you?"

"It's neat, except it gives away your gender."

"Yeah, that's the problem," Zyan agreed. "I like the indeterminate gender."

"You had me wondering like crazy," Sheela admitted, "with your being hoarse and all."

"I didn't realize I even *sounded* like a guy! Anyway, Sheela is a lovely name and there are pluses to people knowing you are female right up front. Sheela Landau has a nice ring to it and the spelling, with the two e's is neat."

"It's an Indian from India spelling," Sheela explained. "Sunita's grandmother suggested it at my baby shower. In Hindi the name means having a beautiful nature. Later on, when my horoscope came from India, it gave some sounds that my name could start with for good luck, and one of them was Sh."

"Coolifical! How did Anjali Khanna end up at your baby shower?" Zyan asked.

"Her son, Sunil, and his wife Jaya—those are Sunita's parents—have been my parents' friends since before my mom and daddy got married," Sheela replied. "The Khannas used to live in Houston and Anjali, Mrs. Khanna, was visiting them when they gave my mom the shower. How about your grandparents? What's their connection with Sunita's grandmother?"

"Gramp Jake was a jeweler before he retired. He and his brother Daniel used to travel to India to buy stones and to get designs and settings made. They met the

Khannas on one of his trips there years ago and they hit it off. I'm not exactly sure how they got in touch in the first place. My grandfather adores India. He's into Hindu philosophy and stuff like that. He's something else."

"What about his brother, your grand-uncle?" Sheela asked.

"He died long before I was born in a skiing accident. According to Gramp, Danny was a little wild, always taking that extra risk. I'm starved. They certainly take their time around here bringing out the food."

"The waiter said we should buzz when we were ready," Sheela reminded her.

"Oh," Zyan said. "As usual I wasn't paying attention."

"Excuse me, ladies." A funky-looking waiter materialized at their table even before Sheela pressed the hand buzzer that was dangling from the entertainment box.

"Is this telepathy or something?" Sheela asked. "I was just going to buzz."

"No, it's a note I have been asked to deliver to you."

"Well, thanks," Sheela said, taking the folded piece of paper. Before she could ask the waiter to please take their order, he disappeared.

"You'll have to buzz after all," Zyan said, "but what's with the note?"

Sheela opened it up. "It's from this guy I thought might be you," she explained. "He said his name is Bryan. He was waiting for a blind date."

"So what does the note say or is it private?" Zyan asked.

"It's not private. It says, 'I don't know your name. Please tell me who you are. I'm Bryan Thomas Temple and I'm a Junior and God willing a future medical student. My address is bryt3@prod.edu. Don't vanish!'"

"Hmn! That's certainly an interesting development resulting from your not knowing whether I was male or female."

The waiter's return interrupted further discussion. "As you see on my button, my name is Boris," he said. "I recommend the shepherd's pie or the nopal and black bean chili with corn bread if you're into vegetarian. This is our menu," he added, reaching into his pocket for two 3 X 5-inch index cards that said:

Clementine's Menu

House Specials: Shepherd's Pie with Grilled Tomatoes
                Black Bean Chili with Nopales and Corn Bread
Other items: Standard fare: 40 to 50 minutes for preparation.
Desserts: Upside Down cakes
                Puddings

"I'll go for the black been chili," Zyan said.

"Me too," Sheela echoed.

"Good choice," Boris said.

That evening when Sheela fell into bed, she said to Aa-Oo, "This has been my best evening ever at UT."

"What about Bryan?" she imagined Aa-Oo asking. "Is he cool or what?"

"He's or what," Sheela answered. "I'll give him a chance, but why, oh why, can't they make guys like Zyan?"

⸭⸭⸭⸭⸭

The evening at Clementine's impacted Zyan and Bryan as much as it did Sheela. Zyan couldn't put her finger on what it was about Sheela that made her feel so special and at the same time caused her to want to protect the girl. She was bright, poised, and clearly competent, but there was something lonely and vulnerable about her. She wondered what it was. I hope, Zyan thought, she likes me as much as I like her.

As for Bryan, he didn't know how he could have become so taken by a person he saw and spoke with for less than a minute. Cynthia droned on and on and Bryan tuned out thinking that he had to find out who the woman with eyes as blue and deep as the ocean was. He wished he were Zyan. Mumbling something about the restroom, he walked to the front of Clementine's to find out where and with whom Sheela was seated. What a surprise to discover Zyan was another female! He scribbled his note on a napkin. Then he pointed out Sheela's table to a passing waiter and, slipping him a hefty tip, asked him to deliver it.

Cynthia was just sitting down when he returned to the table. She had a gaping grin on her face.

"I love it when they play music in restrooms," she said. "It's a very classy touch, don't you think? No wonder this is *the* in place."

"Yeah," Bryan answered.

"So, what did you think of the music?" Cynthia asked.

"Excuse me?" Bryan asked.

"I thought it was terrifical. You know *Clementine*, don't you?"

"I'm not sure; I mean we're here," Bryan said, thinking this is a date from hell.

"It's a real old song," Cynthia explained. "My grandmother used to sing it to me. I think there's a channel on this entertainment box that plays it. Here it is," Cynthia said gleefully. "Channel 77." In seconds the music began:

> In a cavern
> In a canyon,
> Excavating for a mine
> Dwelt a miner, forty-niner,
> And his daughter, Clementine.
> Light she was and like a fairy
> And her shoes were number nine,
> Herring boxes without topses
> Sandals were for Clementine.

"That's *Clementine*!" Bryan blurted.

"That's what I said, *Clementine*," Cynthia repeated. "What's wrong with you?"

Bryan didn't answer and the song played. Mercifully the screen did not depict Clementine or her big feet or her tragic fate. However, the duo dressed in western garb looked absurdly cheerful hopping about as they sang on:

312

Drove she ducklings
To the water
Every morning, just at nine.
Hit her foot against a splinter,
Fell into the foaming brine.
Oh my darling, oh my darling,
Oh my darling, Clementine.
You are lost and gone forever,
Dreadful sorry, Clementine.

"Let's play it again," Cynthia proposed.

"No, we'd better order. I have an early class tomorrow. Are you having the chili or the shepherd's pie?"

"I want the southern fried chicken. They make the greatest southern fried chicken here," Cynthia insisted.

"But that's a long wait."

"No problem. I adore southern fried chicken, especially when it's made with hand crushed corn flake crumbs, like Clementine's does it. You should try it."

"No," Bryan said. "I'll have the shepherd's pie."

"And I'd like the pear upside down cake for desert," Cynthia added.

By the time Bryan and Cynthia left Clementine's, Zyan and Sheela were gone.

Spring Break presented Sheela with a dilemma: she had three options. One was to spend it in Houston organizing a shower for Bernie and helping her do wedding stuff. Bernie was going to be a June bride and her parents were going all out. Her second option was to go to Chicago. In that case she would spend half of her time with Zyan and her family and the other half with the Khannas. Her third choice was to spend the break right in Austin where career workshops were being held for students interested in law, medicine, and social work. The University of Texas was running a pilot program for undergrads to enable them to explore their interests while gaining hands-on experience and performing valuable services to the needy. Bryan was staying for the medical program and he urged Sheela to participate in the legal workshop.

"I know you have experience from working with your mother," he said, "but this will be different. It'll be stuff their office doesn't handle."

Sheela had indeed contacted Bryan as she intended, though not right away. What happened was that she had misplaced his note and it took her about two weeks after their brief meeting to find it. She was sure she had put it in her purse, and she emptied it out to find it, but it wasn't there. Perhaps, she considered, she had lost it accidentally on purpose because her inner self was giving her a warning. But then she remembered that it might be in her pocket and there it was.

Bryan was an OK guy. He was friendly and bright and he didn't come on to her at all. She had no idea that he was head-over-heels in love with her.

He was a good listener and when Sheela let him know without telling him in so many words that she had no interest in him beyond friendship, he took her message to heart. Sheela's attitude and body language warned him that the only way he could be part of her life was to become a steadfast friend. Some day, he hoped, things might change, and he was prepared to wait for as long as it would take. Thus Bryan carefully avoided intimacy. He didn't tell her how he felt. Nor did he accidentally brush against her or bump into her or smooth her hair or try to hold her hand. Instead, he let her define the parameters of their relationship. As a result Sheela shared her smiles, her time, and sometimes even her thoughts with him.

He wondered what made her tick. Once she jumped all over him for calling her Sheel. It sounded so sweet to him.

"Please, Bryan," she told him, "never shorten my name. I hate what you just called me."

"Sure," Bryan said. "I won't make that blunder again." He didn't ask her what was so awful about Sheel and he was rewarded for his forbearance a few minutes later. Sheela saw that her criticism crushed him and she apologized for making him feel bad.

"I didn't mean to get mad," she explained. "It's just that, well, I just somehow don't like the abbreviation Sheel." After a brief pause she added, "There was this jerk who said it in a disparaging way and well, anyway, he was a creep. I'm sorry. It's not your fault that it makes me feel so yucky."

⁕⁕⁕

In the end Sheela decided to go to home and spend Spring Break with her family and Bernie. Her parents did not applaud her decision. They wanted her to go to Chicago. They thought she would meet some nice young men through Zyan. If not, they thought she should participate in the legal workshop and get to know other undergrads whose interests were compatible with her own. Bryan hadn't factored in their recommendation because Sheela didn't say much about him. She didn't want her mother or father to read more into that friendship than there was. They would want to know what his background was and Sheela had no idea. The question hadn't come up and Sheela didn't want to ask, lest he might think it mattered.

"That's not fair," Sheela said, when Natalya argued that Houston was a 'cop out.' "This is my last chance to really hang out with Bernie."

"Why?" Natalya asked. "She is getting married, not buried."

"It won't be the same," Sheela explained.

"Nothing stays the same," Nat pointed out. "You aren't the same today as you were when you were in high school. We grow and change. Life is change. But your friendship will survive. There is no point in clinging to the past."

"It's not only that," Sheela said. "I also wanted to spend the week home and be with Gappa. I worry about him."

"I know," Nat conceded. "It's just . . ."

"It's just that you think I should mix more. I get it. But Ma, I can't chase my destiny. I have to let it come to me. I'm making some really good friends at college and who knows what else is in store for me? You don't have to worry any more. OK?"

"OK, sweetheart," Natalya agreed. "As long as you're happy."

"I am," Sheela replied. "I'm fine."

49

"I must be getting older," Sheela said to Bernie on her conferencer." Ma says that as you mature, time goes by faster and this year has zoomed by at the speed of light. I have to pinch myself to make myself realize that finals have already descended upon us."

"I must be a rubber band, growing and shrinking at the same time, because time is both speeding and crawling." Bernie sighed. "The days don't have enough hours in them for me to cope and I feel as if I have been and will be eternally crazy-busy and frustrated. It's like being in a time jam: my life is stuck in a pre-wedding plus finals warp."

"I thought your parents were taking care of all the wedding stuff. How can you be busy up in Cambridge?"

"Don't even ask," Bernie said. "My mother has a knack for finding jobs that only I can do: shopping, reviewing lists, getting addresses, and looking at photographs of flower arrangements, ice sculptures, table settings, and whatever else she or the wedding consultant dreams up. I couldn't care less about any of it. You're right. It doesn't make any sense. Nothing makes any sense. I've had to fly home twice for fittings for my wedding dress. And I'm supposed to buy cream shoes with heels. I don't want heels; no one can see them anyway, but my Mom says that people can tell from my walk and every time I try to say no to her she gets hysterical and sends me on a guilt trip."

"Why can't you do all that when you go home after finals?" Sheela asked. "The wedding isn't until June 22nd."

"Don't ask me. My mother can't handle leaving stuff until the last minute. If I don't get comfortable shoes in the right color, I have to get white and get them shipped in time for her to get them dyed. I don't know. I'm surviving on four hours of sleep. I'm managing. I'm going to get on the Dean's list if it kills me."

"You don't look as frazzled as you sound," Sheela noted. "So how is Will holding up?"

"I haven't seen him for three days. When we meet it's all madness. But as far as I can tell he's fine. He's pretty steadying. He's arranged to get all our stuff put in a mini-storage for the summer. And he already rented a place for next year. Would you believe I haven't even seen the apartment? And William is surprising me with

"

the honeymoon plans too. I told him that my only requirement was curtains that blocked out the morning sun so we could sleep in."

"I guess it's normal for weddings to be mad," Sheela said. "I better let you go. I wish I could help more."

"You will, once school is over and we're back in Houston. You've already done tons. So thanks and luv," Bernie concluded.

"Luv," Sheela echoed and signed off.

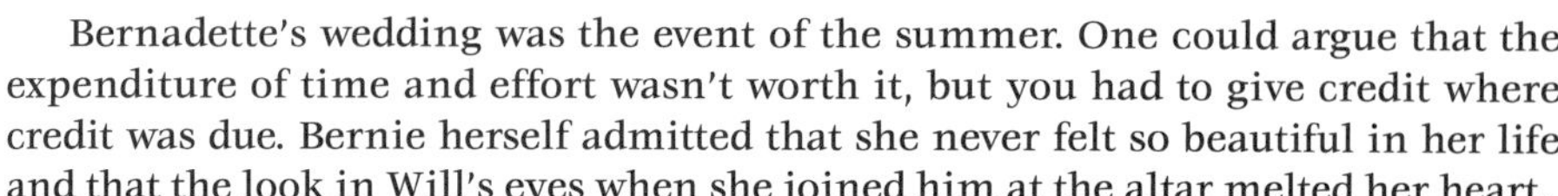

Bernadette's wedding was the event of the summer. One could argue that the expenditure of time and effort wasn't worth it, but you had to give credit where credit was due. Bernie herself admitted that she never felt so beautiful in her life and that the look in Will's eyes when she joined him at the altar melted her heart.

"Thank you," she whispered to her mother, giving her a huge tight embrace just after she made a slice in the five-tiered cake. "I didn't know it could be like this. You're right about marriage being more than sharing a bed and bath. It's a holy thing."

Sheela tingled throughout the ceremony. This was the first Catholic wedding she had ever seen. Come to think of it, it was just the second wedding she had ever attended and it was the only wedding in which she ever actually took part. When Bernadette admitted, "Now I'm glad I'm really a virgin," Sheela could see she meant it.

"You mean you waited all this time after all?"

"Well," Bernadette replied, "we didn't practice *total abstinence.*"

In the wedding party, Sheela was paired with her high school friend Sydney and they had a fine time reminiscing and dancing their feet off. Sydney was studying marine biology in Florida and working as a lifeguard. He remembered that Sheela couldn't swim and tried to persuade her to take lessons from him over the summer.

"No," Sheela said. "Don't you remember we had this conversation before?"

"I guess I do," he replied, "but I thought maybe I could get you to change your mind. It's weird that you can't swim. It's a fundamental part of life. What's with you that you won't give it a shot?"

"I just can't make myself try," Sheela answered. "The idea gives me the creeps. But trust me, this isn't . . . Oops, Bernie is going to throw her bouquet. Let's go."

"Are you going to try to catch it?" Sydney asked.

"Sure," Sheela said. "Wish me luck."

Sheela made a valiant dash for the bouquet, fragrant lilies of the valley, but William's cousin Evelyn virtually snatched it out of her hand. Then she apologized profusely explaining, "I had to catch it. I'm engaged to be married and we've set the date for Christmas Eve. Even though this is just a silly superstition, I guess I took it too seriously. I mean I forgot my manners totally. Please forgive me."

"That's OK," Sheela said. "Congratulations. I don't have any plans or prospects to get married for years."

During the months of June and July Sheela worked *pro bono* at the Federal Public Defender's office, helping with mundane tasks like filing and copying as well as with more challenging ones like preparing discovery requests. Everything was done in a frazzled, enthusiastic rush. The place was nothing like the firm of Jordan and Landau. Rather it was reminiscent of excerpts from a movie on fast-forward. These excerpts raised penetrating questions that whirled in Sheela's mind: Did indigent federal criminals get a fair shot? Was the protection of technical rights in criminal cases really essential to protect the rights of the public at large? Why were white-collar criminals treated in the same way as violent criminals? Did the adversarial system of justice have to be so adversarial? In theory, if two sides argued vigorously—the government for prosecution and the defense for acquittal—the truth came out. But why not simply seek the truth? The inquisitorial or investigative system seemed to work in other countries.

Although Sheela was stimulated by her work, she was looking forward to August. This year finally, at Victor and Nat's urging, she signed up for a seventeen-day student tour to Latin America. The group—limited to college kids who could hold their own in Spanish—was visiting Cuba, Mexico, Guatemala, and Peru. The group of fifteen was meeting with their guide in Miami on August 2.

Gappa was holding his own, and Sheela realized she couldn't hover over him and put her life on hold any longer for fear that something might happen. He was arthritic and far from chipper, but he was hanging in there. He told her that her worrying over him bothered him. He had said what had to be said to her and he had to learn to accept his life as it was given to him. He wanted her to travel with a lightened heart open to possibilities. Sheela promised that she would and she promised to bring him back a special present that would give him pleasure.

"That's a fine how do you do," Gappa said. "You will be a silly goose running around all over the place looking for something to give me pleasure. What could you find? It will be such a job that you won't have time for anything else."

"I like challenges," Sheela insisted. "Don't you worry. I'll have fun looking and I'll find something."

But Sheela didn't take her trip after all. She was stopped by tragedy that struck from a totally unexpected source.

On July 29, after dinner, Pappa had a stroke, which paralyzed his right side. Natalya flew to New York the next day. Forgetting how she felt years ago when her father had his heart attack, she told her daughter, "Don't cancel your trip. The doctors give your grandfather a better than fifty/fifty chance. Anyhow, this is not your responsibility."

"Why not?" Sheela asked. "Isn't my responsibility something I have to determine?"

"Of course, honey, but you are young and you have to live your life. We're all here for Pappa and Door."

"Since I'm young, I have a long life to live, God willing. Unless there is a reason for me to stay back, I'd prefer to come. Hopefully I'm not dispensable because the rest of you are there. Tell me, if Pappa does pull through, what are his hopes for rehabilitation?"

"It's too soon to tell," Nat answered.

"That sounds like the doctors don't want to admit they aren't good."

"The thing is that while Pappa isn't technically unconscious, he is non-responsive."

"Then Daddy and I should come to New York," Sheela said.

"It isn't necessary," Natalya insisted. "Door is all right. I'm here, and Ronald and Cecily are on call. The boys have been by."

In the end, Dora admitted that she would be happy if Sheela could come to spend some time with her.

Harold Rosenbaum never recovered sufficiently to speak with his family. But when Sheela came to his room in intensive care, straight from the airport, she thought she saw the shadow of a smile on the left side of his mouth. She whispered in his ear, "I love you," and she took both his husky hands in her delicate ones. She held on tight, and after a few moments she felt a gentle squeeze coming from his left hand. Then she left him with her parents and her grandmother to go to the flower shop. Pappa, she knew, loved violets and she was hoping that she could find them there. She couldn't. By the time she came up again, her grandfather on her mother's side had passed away.

⚬⚬⚭○◉○◉◉⚬⚭

Sheela remained in New York after her parents left and her aunt and uncle and her cousins returned to their routines. She stayed until just before college started again. Door said that her visit was a godsend.

"Instead of becoming despondent," she said, "I've found peace and acceptance. You've made me see and feel how much I have to live for and how important it is for me to be strong. We've even managed to have a few laughs. That's what Pappa would have wanted. Thank you."

"I had a pretty good time too, Door," Sheela told her grandmother. "I'm glad Pappa was so happy when he went: after a terrific dinner and a terrific life. It was so hard with Beca, and Gappa is so sad," she added.

"I know," Door said. "I guess death has as many qualities as life. I'm thankful that Pappa's was easy. I suppose if he had wanted to hang on he might have made some sort of a recovery, but I can't imagine him living an incomplete life. It isn't going to be easy, but I'll find the will and the energy to go on. I want to be a fun grandmother, maybe even a fun great-grandmother. And I want you to take that tour you missed. Next summer, OK?"

"I don't know," Sheela said. "I was happy about going, but not thrilled. We'll see. Remember you promised to come to stay with me in Austin. I'm out of the dorm. I have an apartment. It's an efficiency, but it's still an apartment and I've got it all to myself."

"Won't you be lonely?" Dora asked.

"No, I don't think so. I like being alone to study and relax, and I can have visitors like you. You'll be comfortable, I promise. And you've got to meet Zyan. She's terrifical."

⚬⚬⚭○◉○◉◉⚬⚭

Sheela flew straight to college from New York. Her parents had gone a couple of days early with her stuff to set up her little apartment for her. It was unfurnished so they purchased two futons and other essentials that were too bulky to transport. They were pleased with their efforts and eager to see Sheela's reaction.

"Wait until you see your place," they told their daughter at the airport. "We think you're going to like it."

"I'm going to love it. Your taste is perfect and you know what I like."

"Now you're grown up. You have your own style," Natalya said. "I hope we got it right. But anything you don't like, we can change."

"There won't be anything to change."

Sheela was indeed thrilled to see her fairly spacious room, big enough for two futons. One was set up as a daybed and the second as a sofa with a coffee table. The room was bright and cheerful, done in yellows and cream. She had a kitchenette behind a Chinese screen and a large dresser. There was also a small round dining table with two chairs. A bookcase and a study station that accommodated her conferencer completed the furnishings.

That room became Sheela's aerie. It was on the third floor of a garden apartment complex, shaded by an oak tree just outside her window. During the days when she wasn't in class or in the physical library, she sat at her study station and worked on notes or papers. During the evenings when she needed a break from working and wasn't ready for bedtime reading, she communicated on her conferencer or connected it to her small entertainment center and relaxed over a cup of tea or coffee. On weekends when she wasn't out, she sometimes entertained Zyan, Bryan, and other friends. They sat on her futons and ate on bamboo trays. She would order in or try her hand at simple cooking in her kitchenette. Spaghetti with a variety of sauces and casseroles became her specialties. She wondered how people made casseroles before the new speed ovens came into existence.

At night, Sheela dreamt more profusely and vividly than she remembered dreaming in the dorm. During sleep, her mind reawakened to the longings that clouded her otherwise happy life. Her dreams were frequently sexually explicit and she invariably awoke from them feeling unfulfilled and unhappy. Her inner core throbbed with emptiness. Her hollowness hurt. Sometimes her anguish lingered for hours or days almost bubbling at the surface of her consciousness. Other times it receded to the back of her mind. But it never went completely away. Yet Sheela could not satisfy her hunger with Bryan or with anyone else she could think of. Her body rejected coupling with the men she knew like a starving person rejects poisonous fruit.

One morning, after an unsettling night, Sheela gave up Karmatica for good. Her visits had become few and far between, but she had been reluctant to sign off completely. Finally she realized that it was pointless for her to cling to a make-believe family which she had outgrown. So she made her farewells and signed off.

∗ ∗ ∗

Sheela's favorite class was Modern Philosophy. Her professor, Dr. Myra Scanlon, opened her mind to thoughts that had never crossed it before. Dr. Myra, as she liked to be called, was a wrinkled ageless-looking old physicist who always pointed out that the distinctions between physics and philosophy were blurry. No one really knew the limits of either discipline.

"The main difference between science and philosophy," she said, "is that it's a damn sight easier to make a living as a scientist."

⸺ ◦◦◖◗◌◖◗◦◦ ⸺

It felt like Sheela's sophomore year was half over even before it began. It was chilly in Austin and the tree outside her window turned orange and then brown and then became bare. Thanksgiving came and went. Door had spent it with the Landaus and changed Gappa's future. Gappa paid attention when she told him that it was time for him to think about doing something worthwhile with himself instead of just waiting to die.

"What do you expect me to do?" he asked. "I'm old, my bones creek and I'm lonely. My children don't need me and my only granddaughter is fine. I have nothing more to accomplish in this life."

"If you had nothing more to accomplish," Dora asked, "don't you think God would have arranged for you to be dead by now?"

"I've been wondering about that," Gappa replied, "but I can't imagine what there is left for me."

"As I see it," Dora said, "there is work you have to do on yourself and there is work you have to do for others. The two go hand in hand. You know, Dr. Landau, that when we set out to do something for someone, we always get more than we give. This may sound like a silly little truism to you, but it is a valid one, nonetheless."

"But what could I do? What do you do?" Henry asked.

"Right now," Door replied, "I'm making sure that I keep my health and spirits up so I can be of some value to my family, even if it's just sharing bits and pieces of what I know. Then I'm keeping myself open for anything that might come my way. You know I haven't been a widow very long and it's taken me until about now to organize my affairs so that I can carry on without Harold."

Thanksgiving melted into finals followed by the year end holidays. This year Sheela and her parents remained in Houston. Memories of the past year's festivities in New York were too crowded with pictures of Harold, full of life and vigor. No one wanted to deal with those images, still so fresh in their minds. Thus the Landaus decided to arrange Chanukah festivities for a group of youngsters at the Children's Hospital and to celebrate Sheela's birthday/New Year with a small party at home including only Gappa, Steve Jordan, and the Singers. In New York, the Rosenbaum clan, faced with the same dilemma, decided to welcome 2020 in the suburbs in private.

Bobby Singer was grown up and settled down. He understood that his feelings for Sheela were one-sided, and without saying anything, he let Sheela know that he would always be there for her as a brother.

The Khannas stayed home in Chicago. Sunil was working through the New Year on a special project, so Sunita and Jaya took three days to do a mother-daughter thing. They went to Toronto to see the New Year show at Niagara Falls.

"Didn't you freeze your butts off?" Sheela asked.

"No," Sunita said. "They set up heaters and gave us thermoses of hot chocolate and hot buttered rum."

"Did it snow?"

"Yes, but they had these special inventions."

"Really, what?" Sheela asked, amazed.

"Umbrellas and waterproof raincoats," Sunita said.

"Very funny," Sheela remarked. "If my cousin Alex were here, you would have come to Houston in a heartbeat."

"That's not true," Sunita said.

"Ha!" Sheela retorted.

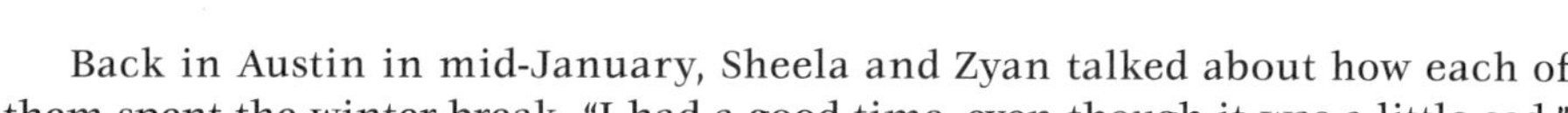

Back in Austin in mid-January, Sheela and Zyan talked about how each of them spent the winter break. "I had a good time, even though it was a little sad," Sheela admitted.

"I can understand this year was tough," Zyan said. "Generally though, isn't having your birthday right in the middle of New Year's Eve fantastical?"

"It has its pluses and minuses," Sheela replied, "but mostly I like it."

"Now you are a sorry nineteen," Zyan said. "Your last year as being a teenager. So what did you get?"

"That was the weirdness part of the holidays," Sheela answered. "Everything I got had to do with travel. My parents gave me this around the world ticket, which starts June 15. It has no special routing. Then I got a suitcase, one of the new ones that weighs under two pounds and is indestructible, and I got some travelers' checks. Oh, and then I got this gadget that you program to retrieve images from your conferencer. It works from anywhere on the planet. I feel pressured to go somewhere and there isn't really any place I want to go."

"That does seem odd," Zyan agreed, "but there has to be a logical explanation. It's got to be that something really cool is in the works. Keep the faith."

"Yeah," Sheela said. "I figured maybe that's what it is. Anyway I didn't say I was freaked. I thanked everyone and all. So, how was your vacation? Did anything new and exciting happen?"

"Potentially," Zyan said. "My generally absentee brother made an appearance this year and he made me forget how mad I've been at him. This friend of his, Jonathan, came to visit. He's new, but I'm not sure yet about exciting."

50

Bernie's marriage subtracted from the intimacy she used to enjoy with Sheela. The new Mrs. Bernadette Jenkins adopted her husband's name as well as many of his opinions and she no longer shared questions about life and love with her friend. Meanwhile Sheela's friendship with Zyan blossomed, but those two had no history. Moreover something about Zyan—Sheela couldn't put her finger on what it was—made her hold back her most private thoughts and emotions. It was almost as if, in some uncanny way, Zyan was tangled up in them. As a result, Sheela felt alone.

Sheela also felt that the vacuum left by Beca's death got bigger, not smaller with time. The hole in her soul didn't hurt as much as it had before, but it was more there. When she lost Beca, Sheela lost an anchor that kept her from drifting with the waves that swelled in her soul. Beca had given substance to the vague forms that lived like ghosts within Sheela's being and she validated the shadows that troubled Sheela like no one else ever could. Natalya and Victor were wonderful parents, but they were incapable of acknowledging shadows.

Gappa, on the other hand, was the biggest positive surprise in Sheela's life. His spirits had lifted almost miraculously. Recently Dr. Landau had begun to visit the Children's Hospital on a regular basis. He played with the sick youngsters and consulted with their physicians. To make himself more appealing to them, he went to Houston Community College and enrolled himself in a magic course. So now he was an amateur magician.

Pappa's absence made a different kind of hole from the one Beca left behind. Pappa's hole was in Sheela's life, not in her soul. It was hard to believe that he would never put his arms around her again. Door's positive mood, though, was a blessing. She was determined to preserve her home as the place where you always went to celebrate.

"Just because Pappa is in another world is no reason to mourn," Door said. "Our duty is to honor him with happy memories. He had a good long life."

"I feel bad for Re," Sheela told her grandmother. "She's not really going to know what he was like."

"Sure, she will," Door argued. "If we tell her."

Sheela had spent Spring Break in New York with Door and her cousins and with Bernie and Will who were also in the Big Apple for the week. She had fun with the Jenkins. She managed to do some catching up with Bernie—though not nearly enough—and she established a warm rapport with William. Notwithstanding his maturity and brilliance, Dr. Jenkins had his feet on the ground and managed to make you want to cuddle him, like a teddy bear.

With Door, Sheela explored old and new corners of New York City: reading cafés, museums, galleries, and shops. Her grandmother introduced her to the new Futuristic Theater, a genre that was just beginning to catch on and presented her with a copy of Pearson Marble's latest and, according to Door, greatest work, *New Balance*. Door thought Marble, who wrote spiritual mysteries, was the first true literary master of the twenty-first century.

⁓ ·•◎◉◍◉◍◉◉•· ⁓

Overall, Sheela's college years were an upward journey on a path that meandered through hills and valleys. On that path, her nineteenth birthday travel gift was a high hill. She didn't discover its details until after Spring Break when an express package arrived at her Austin apartment. The package contained a ticket, brochures, and a letter from Sunita. The letter, dated April 2, 2020, said:

Hi, Sheela,

I wanted to write you yesterday, but I didn't want you to think this was an April Fools' joke. I've been working on my plan since before your birthday.
I've been dying to go to India for the summer with YOU.
I figured that a) you would love to come with me (am I presuming too much?) and b) my parents would trust you and let me do whatever you think is OK (I hope they are presuming you are MUCH MORE CONSERVATIVE than I presume you are).
I know that India will be special for you. You will LOVE it.
The thing about India is that people are true individualists like you are and like I want to be.
I just read *A Prayer for Owen Meany* for English Lit. I really adored it. Hence my capitalization. It was my first Irving book. Now I am going to read *A Son of the Circus,* set in India in the sixties.
My grandmother says it's great.
I want to major in English Literature and become a writer but my parents say I'll never earn a living that way. I will write everything like e.e.cummings and/or JOHN IRVING. I'll make my own rules about capitalization, punctuation, and even grammar. Yes, I have read a book by Marble. It's the one called *Unsafe Harbor* and I liked it, but it rattled me. I'm into older classics now.
When we go to India you can give me your opinion about stuff like should I try to find out who my birth parents are and how long do I have to wait to have SEX?

Love,

323

Sunita

P.S. Your mother arranged most of our holiday. I had a fantastical time plotting with her.

After reading Sunita's letter, Sheela looked over the brochures about the Taj Mahal, about the Jain temples at Mount Abu, and the erotic temples at Khajurao. Finally she reviewed the ticket that had been left "open" in Houston. Now it was routed, dated, and accompanied by an itinerary. She was due to fly from Houston to New York to London to Delhi and to return to Houston via Singapore, Hong Kong, and San Francisco. She left on June 17 and returned on July 20. My God, she thought, is this something else or what? And she closed her eyes to quietly thank her parents, Sunita, Sunita's family, and everyone else who obviously knew about this when they gave her all those travel presents. It wasn't just for the wonderful trip that she was grateful. It was for all those people who cared so much about her having a good time.

⸻ ·•❈●❈•· ⸻

The India trip left Sheela rich with memories to savor for the rest of her days. Beyond that, it provided her with fodder for her spirit. In an intangible way it provided answers to unarticulated questions about her existence and gave direction to her life. In the recesses of her mind Sheela had an image of the universe as a fluid interwoven network, and India sharpened this vision.

"I felt like I was part of a giant whole and that my part was very important," she told her parents after she returned. She had started speaking on the drive home from the airport and ideas and tales rushed out of her with such excitement that they wiped out her jet lag. At home, hours later, she was still going strong.

"That makes sense," Natalya said. "I suppose your network is the tapestry of destiny. It fits with the Hindu idea that things happen as a result of karma and karma surely encompasses more than a single individual."

"Right! My destiny isn't mine alone. We are all dancers and our movements are intertwined, so whatever happens to anyone touches upon everyone else."

"That's an interesting analysis," Victor said. "Did it arise out of any particular discussions?"

"Not really, it came to me more as a picture than as a thought."

"I've read that Hinduism is a philosophy and a way of life more than a religion," Natalya pointed out. "Is that right?"

"I don't think so," Sheela answered. "Hinduism is a voyage that leads to enlightenment. That's its whole point. The thing is that while most Hindus believe in reincarnation and karma, they don't *have to* believe in those concepts. Belief is personal and Karma is just taken for granted. Hindus view it as logical. It reconciles the existence of misery with the existence of God. Actually though, karma doesn't require God. Or maybe in a way it *is* God."

"I suppose," Victor said.

"And you know what else?" Sheela continued. "I never realized that Hinduism is really monotheistic. Hindus believe in just one formless God, but since God is everything you can bestow divinity on any object or representation you wish. That's why there are so many religious images all over the place. Some come from mythology, some are incarnations, and some are symbols."

"It sounds to me," Victor said, "that anyone can be a Hindu. You and I could be Jewish and be Hindu too, if there are no limits on what Hindus believe."

"That may be true in theory," Sheela said, "but in practice it doesn't work that way. I'm Jewish and I wouldn't call myself a Hindu, even if I agree with Hinduism."

"Going back to God," Sheela continued, "Sunita told me that she didn't believe in God, but that she was afraid to tell her parents even though Hinduism is broad enough to tolerate atheism. I had to do some really quick thinking."

"What did you say?" Natalya asked.

"I asked Sunita what it was she didn't believe in when she claimed not to believe in God," Sheela replied.

"That's smart," Victor said. "So what was her answer?"

"She couldn't give a direct answer. She just said that if there were a God, the world wouldn't be such a horrible place, so there probably was no God. Then I suggested that God might be the force of order and purpose. I couldn't believe the world was purposeless and random. I mentioned how my physics professor said that the universe tends to chaos, and I think the fact that it resists chaos is a sign of God. At the same time, even chaos is a part of the order of things so that is divine too."

"So did Sunita buy your idea?" Victor asked.

"Yeah, I think she did. She said that Hinduism described three aspects of God: creation, preservation, and destruction, and I said that fitted right in with what I thought."

"You are persuasive," Natalya told her daughter. "You are going to make one hell of a lawyer."

"It's nothing really," Sheela said, but her expression showed she was pleased. "Actually I don't think Sunita really meant what she said about not believing in God. She was probably testing the waters for my reaction and trying to clarify her own thinking. Either that or else she was trying to sound intellectual and coolifical like her friends."

"I hope this next generation doesn't make a fashion of skepticism," Natalya said. "Like everything else, it comes and goes, but faithlessness can lead to pain."

"Not to change the focus of this conversation," Nat went on, "but tell me did you meet any fun people on your trip?"

"As in fun young men?"

"Yes," Nat replied. "Is that a taboo question?"

"No, I'll answer it," Sheela replied. "Sure, I met lots of nice young men. The Khannas have friends and relatives everywhere. They made sure I was well entertained in both Bombay and Delhi. I went to parties, bars, the whole works."

"So was there anyone special?" Natalya persisted.

"How could there be?" Sheela asked in turn. "You know I'm only interested in Jewish men. There were no Jewish men. The Indian Jewish community has more or less ceased to exist. Everyone migrated to Israel or America or Australia in the last century."

"Why does a man have to be Jewish for you to be interested?" Nat persisted. "I understand you want to marry a Jew, but you can still have fun with someone you aren't necessarily going to marry."

"Excuse me?" Sheela became flustered and angry. "Am I hearing you correctly? Are you actually suggesting I have an affair with a man I don't intend to marry?"

"Not exactly," Nat replied.

"Please explain to me," Sheela said, "how you would like me to go about having fun by not exactly having an affair."

"You're twisting my words around." Natalya flushed. "It is possible to enjoy an attractive man up to a point without planning to marry him. And you needn't look at me as if I am proposing you turn into a tramp."

"OK Ma," Sheela said. "I'm sorry. Maybe I did get you wrong. But I don't think it's possible for me to enjoy a man up to a point. In fact, I tried my damnedest to persuade Sunita that sexual relations were not essential to making the most of your teen-age years. I didn't think that 'enjoying a man' to use your expression was something that you had to do by any specific age. So now it seems that I've been dispensing wrong advice. Maybe something is wrong with me," she concluded.

"There is nothing wrong with you, honey," Victor told his daughter. "Your mother sees flirtation as a joy all its own. Most people do, you know. As a matter of fact most people don't think too much of having an affair even when marriage is not in the offing."

"Unfortunately, most people don't think period," Natalya interjected.

"That's neither here nor there," Victor snapped, annoyed at being interrupted. "The point I was trying to make is that while having an affair is going too far and selling yourself short, your way is somewhat extreme; still, it is worthy of respect."

"I think there is only one man in the world for me," Sheela explained, "and I don't believe second best would interest me in the slightest. I can't help myself if that is 'extreme' in you guys' view."

"God help you," Natalya said, "if the person you decided is right for you doesn't reciprocate your feelings."

"Yeah," Sheela agreed. "Or if I never meet him, God help me."

No one quite knew how to break the pause that weighted down the air in the heretofore cheerful room. Finally Sheela said, "So anyway let me tell about the funnest thing I did in India."

"What was that?" Nat asked.

"Actually, my story goes with two presents I brought you. So, just give me a sec and I'll get them."

"More presents?" Victor asked, surprised.

"I was finished shopping when I saw them and couldn't resist." Sheela walked toward her carry-on that was still sitting in the middle of the living room with its contents half-spilled on the floor. She fumbled a bit and then brought back two miniscule drawstring purses. "I spent days looking for the inlaid box and embroidered Kashmiri shawl and then I went to this jewelry shop and saw these tiny statues. The Ganpati with the elephant trunk is for Daddy. You know why Ganpati is so popular in India?" Sheela asked, still clutching the red silk bags.

"I bet because he is so cute," Victor replied. "In the nineties they had stories about him actually drinking milk through his trunk. It happened in temples, in houses, and everywhere. People in the West thought it was a big hoax but Sunil said it even happened to someone in his family. Sunil called him Ganesh."

"Right," Sheela said. "I heard the same story in India. Ganesh and Ganpati are the same god. And maybe Ganpati's popularity does stem from his cuteness. What I meant, though, was do you know why everyone always puts up pictures or statues of him?"

"No, why?" Victor asked.

"There is a legend that Lord Shiva, Ganpati's father, came home after a very long trip and Ganpati refused to let him in the house because Parvati, his Mom, was taking a bath and she had told him to keep everyone out. Ganpati and Shiva didn't recognize each other. Shiva got furious and summarily severed Ganpati's head. Parvati started to cry and Shiva said not to worry, I'll give him a new head. Thus, Shiva had an elephant's head cut off and he put it on Ganpati. Then Parvati got even more upset.

'Nobody will love or respect my son with this stupid elephant head,' she said.

'Don't worry,' Shiva repeated. 'I'll make sure everyone honors him.' So Shiva created a requirement that everyone had to pray to Ganesh before praying to God. That's why Ganpati is everywhere."

"How seriously do people take this legend?" Natalya asked.

"I think no one believes it, but no one disbelieves it," Sheela said. "After all what proof do we have it isn't true? And since the milk thing, who knows? Anyway the little Krishna is for Ma. It's called a Bal Krishna or baby Krishna. There are tons of stories about Krishna. As a kid he used to steal butter all the time so they call him 'Butter Thief.' Then when he got older he was a huge flirt. All the milkmaids were in love with him. Both statues are twenty-two karat gold. Here!" Sheela handed both bags to her mother. "I don't know which is which."

"They're beautiful," Nat said, admiring first her crawling Krishna and then Victor's Ganesh.

"Look at the detail," Victor said. "I'm getting a magnifying glass to see better."

"First listen to what happened in the jewelry store," Sheela said. "That's what I started to tell you. There's this fantastic store in Delhi to which Sunita's Aunt Meera took me. It's called Maneklal Javeri. Manek means ruby and Javeri means jeweler. Her aunt said I could look all I wanted and didn't have to buy anything because the store belonged to an old friend and she had been a customer forever. It turns out that Zyan's family used to buy stones from Maneklal Javeri ages ago. Remember, I told you that's how I met Zyan. Her grandmother knew Sunita's grandmother and the store has been there forever. Anyway, they had the most exquisite jewelry I've ever seen in my entire life. Not just bangles and rings, but all sorts of elaborate necklaces and armlets and gold knitted hand gloves which brides wear. So the owners kept bringing out tray after tray of jewelry like you can't believe. Sunita said people wear gold and jewels to weddings and parties all the time.

While we were looking at everything, guys kept bringing us cokes and snacks. And no one was stuffy like they are in expensive shops here. Everybody was laughing and talking so much that I wondered how they kept track of trays coming and going, but they managed. Then they showed me the miniature statues that they said were made by a special goldsmith. I couldn't resist so I bought the Bal Krishna and the Ganpati. It was toward the end of the trip and I figured I wouldn't need all the money I still had left because no one let me pay for anything.

After I saw the gold and inlaid pieces, the owner, Hareshbhai who is Maneklal's grandson or great-grandson, asked if we'd like to see precious stones and Sunita said absolutely. So I said I'd love to see blue sapphires and you know what? They didn't have any. The store wouldn't keep them because they were bad luck unless they suited you. Hareshbhai said that only certain people could wear blue sapphires without getting into trouble and he told me that Prince Charles gave Lady Di a huge blue sapphire. Instead he showed me rubies and diamonds and emeralds. Some were set and others were just plain. I I almost fainted. But then this eerie thing happened. They brought out one last tray and I saw a yellow stone that I wanted more than I ever wanted anything in my life. I figured maybe I'd return the little statues and get it, if it wasn't too expensive. I thought it was a yellow topaz and it wasn't all that big. But guess what? It was called a pokhraj, which is a yellow sapphire, and it cost $28,000.00. Hareshbhai said it would bring me good luck and insisted I borrow it over night. He said I had to put it under my pillow when I went to sleep.

I was really scared I would lose it or something would happen, but Meera Auntie said it would be fine. When I woke up, I thought I was in heaven and it took me the longest time to figure out who and where I was. I felt wonderful. I tried and tried to remember what I dreamt, but it had all evanesced. So the next day we took the stone back and Hareshbhai gave me this little 33 point yellow sapphire for a gift. He said it was left over from a bracelet they had made and they wouldn't be able to sell it for very much. So could you make it into a ring for me, please?"

"Well, let's see it," Victor said.

"Here it is," Sheela said unpinning a third miniature silk bag from her bra. "I haven't risked leaving it anywhere. When I shower I put it with my watch and at night I sleep with it pinned to my nightgown. It makes me feel happy. Hareshbhai said tiny stones aren't as powerful as larger ones. But I still adore it and I can feel its vibrations. It's not too small to make a ring out of, is it?"

"It might be better as an earring," Victor suggested. "Maybe for one of the upper holes in your ear."

"No, I really want a ring so I can look at it," Sheela insisted.

"I'm sure that would work too," Nat agreed. "It's very pretty and sparkly."

"I'll take care of it before you go back to school," Victor promised.

"And Ma? Daddy?"

"What?" Natalya and Victor asked together.

"Don't say anything about what all I told you, OK?"

"Of course we won't, Sheela," Nat readily agreed. "What would we say? But why is this a secret?"

"I don't know. Normally I'd be blabbing to Bernie and Zyan, but this feels too personal. Except I had to tell you."

51

Bryan, already a first year student at the University of Texas Medical School in Galveston, was depressed. His relationship with Sheela had gone nowhere. From day one he tried to tell himself he was prepared to remain a friend forever, but that was bullshit. The reality was that he had never expected this. He had been sure that sooner or later he would eventually find the key to Sheela's heart, but today he was as far away from figuring out where she kept it as he had been the moment he had laid eyes on her at Clementine's. Furthermore, his chances of success were slimmer than ever now that he was in Galveston and Sheela was in Austin.

Some months after meeting Sheela, Bryan recognized that her Jewishness was a barrier to his getting closer, so he resolved to convert. When he first mentioned his interest in Judaism to her, she seemed uncomfortable, but in time she acted as if she were OK with it.

"Why are you concerned about the Jewish religion?" she had asked. "Aren't you more interested in who you are?"

"Well," Bryan answered, honestly but not fully, "Right now I don't know who I am. I'm not really anything. I'm impressed with what your religion has contributed to you and I'd like the benefit of that dimension."

"How were you raised?" Sheela asked.

"As an agnostic, I guess," he replied. "My mom is a Unitarian. She is extremely liberal and open-minded. My dad is a reluctant Baptist. Religion has never played much of a role in our family, and I guess seeing the depth it has given you makes me feel like I'm missing something."

"I don't know," Sheela had butterflies in her stomach, "The idea that you may be thinking about converting because of me disturbs me."

"I'm not doing it because of you," Bryan said. Technically he was telling the truth. He was planning on conversion because he wanted it. Sheela didn't ask it of him. And he did feel that his life had no core.

Even though becoming Jewish hadn't produced the result he expected, Bryan didn't regret the rather drastic step he had taken. He had taken it for the wrong reasons and it didn't work out the way he had hoped, but it gave him satisfaction.

Rabbi Lubovsky, who guided his instruction, explained to him that conversion would not and should not re-invent him, but that it should give his life new meaning and perhaps new direction. Bryan confessed that his as yet unrequited love for a Jewish girl was the original reason for his interest in Judaism, but he explained that he also was attracted to this faith for other reasons. Mercifully, Rabbi Lubovsky didn't pry. Although Bryan's comment regarding "other reasons" was a stretch, in time it became more accurate.

The educational process had lasted nearly a year. Bryan studied the Old Testament, the Talmud, and Jewish prayers, and he became familiar with Jewish customs and history. After his Rabbi was satisfied that Bryan understood what he was about to undertake and that his commitment would endure, he told Bryan that further formal learning was not necessary. Although Bryan was becoming a reform Jew, Rabbi Lubovsky suggested an Orthodox conversion ceremony.

"It will make you feel more deeply," was what he said.

Thus Bryan appeared before a triumvirate of three rabbis and declared that he knew the responsibilities of Jewish law, that he would fulfill those responsibilities and that he would eschew those tenets of his former faith that were in conflict with Judaism. He also took the ritual bath called the "mikvah." Fortunately, he had been circumcised at birth so he was spared dealing with that issue at this late age. Perhaps because Bryan didn't have anyone he cared for present at the ceremony, the rituals didn't really make him feel anything. On a conscious level they seemed anticlimactic.

After the conversion, Bryan invited Sheela to dinner. He appeared wearing a Star of David.

"You're wearing a Jewish Star," Sheela said, stating the obvious. She didn't wear one. She had on her heart locket and the gold ring with the tiny yellow stone that she never took off. She had taken to rubbing the ring whenever she was pensive and she was rubbing it now.

"Yes, I'm now officially Jewish. I converted last week," Bryan explained.

"I hope you find happiness," Sheela said. "It's not so easy to be a Jew."

"What do you mean?" Bryan asked.

"I'm not exactly sure how to put it. Maybe the best way is to say that our miracles don't drop down like gifts from heaven. We work to make them happen, one deed at a time. Sometimes it's tough work."

"I understand," Bryan said. "Mitzvahs, not epiphanies."

Sheela's reaction had struck Bryan as promising. He felt he had impressed her with his grasp of his new faith and he expected that this common ground would lead to meaningful conversations that in turn would engender intimacy. However, nothing of the sort occurred. Without exactly brushing him off, Sheela skillfully deflected future discussions that touched upon Jewishness. Thus, although Bryan's Judaism gave him faith and self-definition, it brought him no closer to Sheela.

Now, sitting in the anatomy room at UT Med, Bryan struggled to figure out what had gone wrong. He analyzed one possibility after another. Eventually he settled on the idea that he had a made a serious and foolish mistake by not romancing Sheela more aggressively from the outset and that he had gone about this so-called courtship backwards. He was an idiot to have believed that an emotional relationship should precede a physical one. The more he pursued this line of thinking, the more sense it made. Sheela was wounded and shy and she protected herself by building a fortress around her feelings. Waiting for her to open a window in that fortress was like waiting for hell to freeze over. Bryan concluded he would have to storm the fortress in order to propel their relationship to another level.

From now on Bryan intended to pursue Sheela actively. No more walking on eggshells around her. His attentions would be hands on, and more, a great deal more. He would visit her in Austin as frequently as his demanding schedule allowed, even more frequently than it allowed if need be. His medical career wasn't nearly as important as his life and he couldn't picture his life being worth a damn without Sheela in it. The bottom line was that he saw Sheela wasn't content either and he was determined to make her happy. He would do whatever it took.

⁂

It wasn't easy for Sheela to appreciate the fact that she was already a junior. Her college years were half over. Her life as a student was changing. Bryan had already graduated and she missed him. He had turned out to be an enjoyable and gallant companion. For a while she had worried because he seemed to care for her too much, and his conversion exacerbated this concern. She wasn't up to coping with intensity. However, Judaism seemed to work for him and Bryan had stayed cool. No one could say that she didn't give Bryan a chance. It wasn't her fault that the idea of going beyond friendship was utterly unpalatable to her. If Zyan weren't already involved with someone else, she would have tried to set those two up. Now she hoped he would meet someone in Galveston because even though Bryan's absence made a dent in her life, she was glad he was gone.

Zyan was a senior. Sheela could see that she had already begun to cut her bonds with the undergraduate scene of which Sheela was still very much a part. Zyan's mind was on the LSAT and on Jonathan. To get a sense of what the law school experience would be like at UT, she was auditing a course in constitutional Law.

"Sitting in that class is like running backwards on a treadmill," Zyan told Sheela. "Professor Carson is brilliant. But he is also somewhat bitter. He was on the short list of nominees for the United States Supreme Court. I think he was crushed at not being appointed and he appears to consider teaching first year law students something of a step down. The entire class is terrified of him."

"Why is everyone terrified?" Sheela asked. "Now that grades have been abolished, what can happen?"

"Apart from being publicly humiliated, the students' future careers can be ruined by evaluations. Maybe not their careers, but certainly their first shot at a decent job. The evaluations are worse than grades used to be. Every nuance counts. A comment or the absence of a comment can make or break you. And the evaluations consider the quality of class participation, not just exams and papers. So the pressure never lets up."

"Do you think that's good or bad?" Sheela asked.

"I guess it's both," Zyan replied. "It's realistic anyway. There's a competitive world out there, so law school is a good place to start facing the music. But Carson is brutal. Students have broken down in tears under his badgering. Over 10 percent have already dropped out, including some of the brightest people in the class. The worst thing is that students are missing the fun of the intellectual challenge because they are so focused on performance. Surprisingly, I hear things aren't that tough in the ivy leagues."

"That's odd," Sheela said. "I should think they'd be tougher, although Will—that's Bernie's husband—never said anything about evaluations or about Harvard Law being like a pressure cooker."

"It's not," Zyan said. "It's just murderously hard to get in. However, once you're in, you are automatically a member of an elite club. It's a given that being admitted confirms you are the crème de la crème. There are no evaluations and no grades. Only pass or fail. And no one ever fails. Potential failures quietly disappear. They probably either jump into the Charles River or go on to shine at other institutions."

"So are you going to try to get into Harvard?" Sheela asked Zyan.

"I don't know, I don't think I'd get in. Even if I did, my family couldn't afford it. I like it here, but . . . ."

"What?" Sheela asked.

"Nothing," Zyan said. After a pause, she finally admitted, "Well, you know Texas is far from Cambridge and Jonathan is going to be there for quite a long time."

"I always wondered," Sheela asked, "what made you come to UT in the first place?"

"I was just tired of Chicago and of freezing all the time. I felt like I needed a change. I love my family, but at the same time I wanted to be on my own. I have a real overbearing family: parents, grandparents, the whole lot of them. And my brother was in Cambridge at MIT. I adore him, but he is too protective. Besides, I thought he needed to not have me around. I mean he compared everyone with me and so he never had any serious girlfriends. Then UT came along and offered me this terrific scholarship. Texas sounded like a lark. You know, refreshingly unlike Chicago and yet not all that far away.

"How come your family can afford MIT for your brother?"

"Actually they can't. They are just helping out a little. Ari worked and saved money between college and grad school and he has a grant."

"What are you doing over the holidays and for your birthday this year?" Zyan asked Sheela a few days later. The friends were taking a Friday afternoon break at the commissary. They were each drinking amaretto cappuccinos and splitting a lemon cheesecake.

"Don't know yet, what about you?"

"I don't know either. Jonathan is going sailing in the Caribbean with a bunch of guys. He felt a little guilty about leaving me, but he said he didn't know when he'd ever get another chance like this again."

"And you said?"

"I said fine, I understood. I do, to some extent," Zyan replied. "I mean he felt guilty, but not guilty enough to say no."

"Maybe he's getting nervous about getting really involved and is looking upon this as a final fling," Sheela suggested. "Not that I'm an expert, but from what I read it seems some guys get serious pre-commitment jitters."

"I don't know. We haven't talked about anything like a long-term commitment, but you might be right. It's in the air. Anyway my brother isn't coming home either. He says he can't spare the time."

"I should be in the gym burning calories, not here consuming them," Sheela remarked, "but what the hell. I'll equalize tomorrow."

"Funny you should say that when I'm the one who gained three pounds," Zyan pointed out.

"If so, it's all muscle," Sheela said. "You look terrific. Jonathan would be crazy to let you slip away."

"There isn't much risk of that," Zyan said. "He's pretty much of a looker himself. Actually he's just about the handsomest guy I've ever seen. And he's in great shape. I think he works out in his sleep because he doesn't go to a gym."

"You know you never showed me any pictures of Jonathan or your family," Sheela said. "Now I'm curious about what he looks like."

"I don't have any photographs with me," Zyan said. "They're all in Chicago. No, I take that back. There's this one snapshot in my apartment of Jonathan, Ariel and me. We took it over the last holidays in front of one of the giraffes on Michigan Avenue. Last year they did giraffes."

"Who is Ariel?"

"That's Ari, my brother. His name is really Ariel."

"So what exactly does Jonathan do?" Sheela asked. "I know he's teaching and getting some kind of a post doc., but in what?"

"His doctorate is in Robotics, but this post doc is in a new or more expanded field. It's the same thing in which Ari is getting his Doctor of Science. They call it A-In."

"That's as clear as mud," Sheela remarked. "So what's A-In?"

"It stands for Artificial Intelligence," Zyan explained. "From what I understand, it's a combination computer science, robotics and space degree. It has to do with all man-made intelligence."

"That's super coolifical," Sheela said. "It sounds like science fiction come true."

"I've got to get going." Zyan picked up her back pack. "Duty calls. I have an on-line session with Princeton Review in exactly forty-nine minutes."

"I need to get home and gargle and take vitamin C," Sheela said. "My throat is scratchy." As they got up and headed for the cashier Sheela asked, "How are you doing with Princeton?"

I scored in the 84 percentile in the year-before-last's LSAT. It's not enough. I've got to get past 93 percent, but I think I can make it. I ran out of time and couldn't review so I made some dumb mistakes."

"Your life is a preview of the coming attractions in store for me. It's better than consulting a fortune teller," Sheela remarked. "The Law School Admission Test and Professor Carson. So are you sure you can't come to the movies with us tonight?"

"Absolutely. Scalp my ticket," Zyan answered. "I'll take care of the check. This break is on me."

"Is it the LSAT or Carson that is primarily responsible for keeping your nose to the grindstone?" Sheela asked as the girls walked to the check out line.

"First time I've heard that expression used by a live person," Zyan commented. "I've read it though. Now I have a sense of what it actually means. It's a good image. But is my nose polishing the stone or vice versa? To answer your question, it's Carson. We're reviewing Supreme Court decisions that have to do with the rights of the unborn. It's a neat approach, going issue by issue."

"I thought you were just auditing and not getting graded."

"Full participation is mandatory or I get kicked out of the audit. And I get an evaluation even though it doesn't . . ."

"Excuse me," the cashier interrupted sarcastically, "whenever you girls are ready. The line behind you is growing, but don't let that worry you."

"Sorry," Zyan mumbled. She fumbled in her purse until she found her wallet.

"It would be nice if you stepped away from the counter so I can help the person behind you," the cashier said because Zyan kept on talking.

Zyan moved to the right before continuing, "Like I was saying, even though it doesn't count. And there is another benefit. Next year, assuming I stay at UT, I'm automatically out of the section that has Carson for constitutional law."

When Sheela got back to her apartment she was very surprised to find Bryan sitting on her stairwell.

"My God! What are you doing here?" she asked. "Are you OK?"

"I'm good," Bryan replied. His palms were getting sweaty and he was beginning to wonder how he was going to pull off the Tarzan act he had played out in his head. He had planned to greet Sheela with a hug that would merge into a kiss, but the sight of her looking more stunned than pleased scared him off. "It's the weekend and I thought I could spare tonight and tomorrow," he replied. "I missed you. I guess coming without making a date was dumb, huh?"

"You really should have called," Sheela said. It wasn't until after she blurted out her reproach that she softened it with a smile.

"I was afraid you'd tell me not to come," Bryan admitted. "So I figured if you were busy, I'd entertain myself and maybe you'd have time tomorrow. I'm not leaving until tomorrow night. In a pinch I could stay until Sunday. I brought plenty of work. I'm staying with Rudolph Collins and I was thinking of meeting Rabbi Lubovsky tomorrow."

"The thing is," Sheela said, "a bunch of us are going to the movies to see *Intergalactica* with Shannon Blake and Thor Cornwall. Why don't you come along?"

"Couldn't you maybe skip it and go another time? I was really hoping to get to talk to you."

"I can't because we already have the tickets. They are harder to come by than tickets to heaven. Joshua stood in line over three and a half hours for them. Zyan was going to join us and she backed out so we have an extra ticket. I was planning to scalp it."

"I don't know," Bryan said. "Maybe I should study instead."

"Come on! Now that you're here, come along. It'll be fun," Sheela said. "Look we can have lunch tomorrow and talk then."

Bryan hesitated before he said, "I better not. I have to cram tons of anatomy. This way I won't be so rushed tomorrow. Say, is there any way we can have dinner tomorrow night instead of lunch?"

"Sorry," Sheela replied. "My political history group is doing a marathon review."

Sheela regretted having let Bryan leave with a promise to meet for brunch the next day. It wasn't something she wanted to do. And her throat was getting worse. She had hoped to take a nap before the movie in order to shake off whatever she might be coming down with. Now she had to study instead since her plan to sleep in tomorrow morning and then work to prepare for the evening study session was shot. There was no way she was going to skip *Intergalactica*. It had rave reviews and she hadn't been to the movies in over six months.

On the other hand, what else could she have done? Bryan might have a problem. He did say he really wanted to talk and she owed him a chance to tell her what was on his mind. Her best bet now was to drink a non-drowsy anti-flu and get busy. She'd come straight home from the movie and set her alarm for 8:45 in order to get as much outlined as possible before Bryan showed up at 12:30.

The effects of the anti-flu held out for most of the evening. Sheela was OK until the last half-hour of the show, which was, if anything, even more exciting and artistic than she had expected, but by the time she got home, she was sick. Before bed, she took some night anti-flu and fell into a deep sleep.

Just before dawn Sheela became troubled. She was on trial before the Supreme Court of the United States. Something was very wrong because the Supreme Court never heard live testimony. It only reviewed the record to decide whether a lower court had erred. Nevertheless there she was. Chief Justice Jonathan Cartwheeler was yelling like a madman.

"You have no right to chose celibacy! You have a duty to the unborn! You must have a child or have your head chopped off. That's your choice."

"With all due respect, Your Honor," Zyan, her advocate, said, "may it please this honorable court . . . ."

"You displease this court!" Justice Cartwheeler said, still yelling. "This Supreme Court is supremely displeased and holds you in contempt!"

"In all fairness to the defendant and her counsel," Justice Shannon Blake interjected, "we must offer the defendant a list of potential mates."

"Very well," Cartwheeler agreed, lowering his voice. "We do not wish to go down in intergalactic history as an unfair institution. We will provide such a list."

As soon as he made that statement the justice turned three cartwheels. His robes flew up in the air, leaving him in his underwear. When he stood upright again, he clapped his hands. His robes turned into a black crow with a folded sheet of paper in its beak. It was flapping about the courtroom noisily.

"Deliver the paper to defendant's counsel," Cartwheeler said, turning toward Zyan with a fiendish grin. "Read the list out loud."

"Now?" Zyan asked.

"Hear Ye, Hear Ye," Cartwheeler replied. Then he screamed "NOW!" at the top of his lungs.

"Baby Bobby, Joshua, Bryan, Thor, Dwayne, Jonathan, the Honorable Chief . . . ." Zyan began.

"You, your Honor?" Sheela blurted just before she woke up in a sweat, with a full bladder and a very sore throat. It took her a half-hour to settle down. She swallowed two aspirins and changed her nightgown. Since she was wide awake, she started to work on her political history. At 8:45 when her alarm rang she went back to sleep.

As agreed the previous day, Bryan called at noon to say he would be by to pick Sheela up in about 15 minutes. The call woke her up.

"Would you mind terribly if we had brunch in?" Sheela asked in a sleepy tone of voice that sounded sexier than anything Bryan had ever heard. Yes! Yes! Yes! he told himself.

"No, no problem. That would be fine," he replied.

"Thanks, I'd really appreciate it," Sheela mumbled. "Pick up whatever you want. I have orange juice and coffee."

"OK, I'll come as soon as I can," Bryan agreed.

"Great," Sheela said and promptly fell back asleep.

When her doorbell rang, Sheela stirred herself into wakefulness and ran a hand through her hair before answering. The delay worried Bryan. He was about to ring again when he heard a weak "Who is it?"

"It's room service a la Bryan."

Sheela opened the door.

Bryan saw her flushed, with no make up on, her hair tousled and her eyes gleaming. Her nightgown was not quite transparent, but revealing enough to make him lose his composure. However there wasn't much he could do because his hands were full of boxes and bags.

"I'll help with these," Sheela offered. Her voice was shaky.

"No, I can take care of it," Bryan said. "Just relax. I'll be right with you."

It wasn't until he sat on the sofa beside his love and took her exquisite face in his hands, that Bryan realized Sheela was burning with fever.

52

The unsettling effect of Bryan's visit outlasted Sheela's flu. She felt heavy-hearted because she didn't know in whom to confide. Besides, what could she say?

Thanksgiving and the holidays came and went without further visits from Bryan. He was distraught over his trip to Austin, and he was unsure about what to do next. He continued to e-mail, phone, and conference with Sheela but her responses seemed strained, and she was becoming increasingly unavailable. Thus he couldn't bring himself to ask if he might visit again, nor could he chance another surprise appearance. He had hoped to inquire about her vacation plans and to try to include himself in them but Sheela closed every loophole Bryan tried to open.

After a period of brooding, Bryan decided to get help. He found that the Denver School of Emotional Intelligence offered a course entitled "Winning Strategies in Romance" and he enrolled. The bulk of the course could be taken by teleconference and he arranged to attend the requisite five days of live classes between January 2 and January 7. Once the spring semester rolled around, he expected to be ready to make his moves. This time he vowed they would be the right moves. As long as Sheela remained unattached, he figured he had hope.

The Landaus went to New York for Thanksgiving. They would have preferred to stay in Houston, but Ronald and Cecily wanted them to come very badly. They had never hosted Thanksgiving before. It took some doing to persuade Dora to go to the suburbs, and the job was delegated to Sheela.

"I feel like I'm being replaced. Does everyone think that because I'm single, I'm incapable of entertaining my own family?" Dora Rosenbaum asked Sheela.

"No way," Sheela said. "It's just that the kids complained that Cecily has never given a proper Thanksgiving dinner. This year Cecily's mother and aunt are coming to New York and the boys want to be with you *and* them. Alex dared his mom to come up with a meal that would turn out to be even half as good as yours always is. You never minded coming to Houston for Thanksgiving. So why not make the trip to the suburbs instead?"

"We won't all fit at Ronald's house and it's no fun to drive home after dinner." Dora replied.

"Mrs. Roth and her sister are staying in the Vacation Home Resort," Sheela said, "so we'll have enough room to sleep over."

"I didn't think Cecily had any interest in going to the trouble of preparing a full-fledged Thanksgiving dinner," Dora went on. "It's not her style."

"It didn't used to be, but since she switched from professional theater to teaching drama at the Community College, Aunt Cecily has excess energy. Some of it is going into cooking and entertaining."

"And the rest of it into redecorating," Dora added. "In five years, Cecily has redone her home three times. Now everything is aqua with ripples. It's the underwater look designed around Ronald's new aquarium that takes up half of the living room. Those two are great kids, but they're nuts."

"Look who's talking," Sheela said.

Later when Dora Rosenbaum called Cecily to accept her invitation, she learned that making a Thanksgiving turkey wasn't the only thing up her daughter-in-law's sleeve.

"Friday, we'll all drive into the city to see *The Cat That Never Meowed,*" Cecily said.

"You told me you already saw it," Dora pointed out.

"I did, but I'm thinking of adapting it for my class' final production this spring and I want to know what you think. Actually, I was wondering whether you would consider playing a small role in it. There is a part that's made to order for you."

"Gosh," Dora said. "I don't know. Wait a sec. Is this some scheme to keep me gainfully employed and out of trouble?"

"Not at all, scout's honor!"

"You've never been a scout," Dora said. "Besides, I've never heard you mention that you use outside actors for your performances."

"You never asked," Cecily explained.

For the second year in a row Sheela celebrated the arrival of the New Year and her birthday quietly in Houston. It was already 2021 and Sheela was going to be twenty. She had insisted they have a private dinner at home.

"Anything you would like," Natalya agreed. "But who may we include in this private dinner?" Nat was worried. In the past her daughter's disinterest in festivities tended to coincide with troubled feelings.

"Just the immediate family," Sheela said. "Door told me she would like to come to Houston this year because Uncle Ronald and those guys are going to Colorado to ski. Maybe Uncle Steve and the Singers. Sunita and her parents are going to California."

"OK," Natalya said, "but Steve is going out of town and the Singers said something about the Houston Symphony Concert. Maybe some of your friends from school would like to join us. We could show them a good time. Are you sure there isn't someone you would like to invite?"

"I'm totally sure," Sheela insisted.

After that conversation, Natalya called her mother.

"Why is Sheela being so anti-social? Do you suppose she has a problem?"

"What kind of problem?" Dora asked in turn. "She seemed fine over Thanksgiving, although now that you mention it she didn't share much about what was happening in her life. Usually she has more to say."

"Did she tell you anything at all?"

"Not really," Dora answered, "other than she misses Bernie and Zyan is preoccupied with getting into law school and with some new boyfriend."

"Same stuff she told me," Nat said. "I half think she has an interest in this Bryan who graduated, but Sheela insists that he is only a friend. She told Victor's dad about him, but all Gappa said is that I should take Sheela at her word."

"I wonder why she would talk to her grandfather and not to me." Dora felt slighted.

"Because Bryan was considering converting to Judaism or maybe he already converted and Sheela wanted Gappa's opinion. So do you think Sheela is OK?"

"I hope so," Door told Natalya. "Gappa is right though. We have to take Sheela at her word. If there's more to Bryan, she will tell us in due course."

When Sheela got home for the Christmas break, it became obvious to her parents that their worries over her state of mind were not without foundation. She struggled to seem more cheerful than she felt. Victor chanced a passing question.

"Is everything going well with you, sweetheart?"

"Pretty OK," Sheela answered.

"But not great, huh?" Victor continued.

"I guess not. You know how you always said life alternates between change and balance. Right now I'm in change, not balance. I feel like something is going to happen and I don't know what. But I don't want to think about it. I just want to hang out and spend time at the Children's Hospital with Gappa, OK?"

"OK, you got it," Victor said. "No discussions about your state of mind."

"Thanks, Daddy. So let's talk about your new book."

"What would you like to know?" Victor asked.

"Does it have a title yet?"

"No. All I can think of is *The History of Communication* and I don't like that."

"How about *The Evolution of Communication*?" Sheela proposed.

"That could be better, but the book is also about achieving excellence in communication. I considered *Excellence in Communication*, but that misses the history angle."

"So, what are you guys up to?" Natalya asked, walking in on her husband and daughter. "Can I get us all some cappuccinos?"

"No," Victor answered. "You can help us with the title of my new book though."

"I didn't realize you were ready for the title yet," Nat said.

"Neither did I," Victor concurred. "But Sheela asked. We were considering *The Evolution of Communication* or *Excellence in Communication*."

"You always talked in terms of 'development' rather than 'evolution.' I think 'development' might be better," Nat suggested.

"You need a title and a subtitle," Sheela said.

"That's right," Nat agreed. "Look in the mission summary you sent Merrit House and see what works."

"I don't have to now," Victor said. "I got it: *Excellent Communication: The Development of a Discipline.*"

⁂

Three days before Sheela's birthday, her parents and grandparents were still unsure about what gifts to give her. The packages from Steve Jordan, from the Khannas, from Lulu, and from the Singers were wrapped and waiting. "If we knew what this stuff was," Dora said, feeling the packages, "we might get some ideas."

"They all seem to be clothes. They're soft," Nat said.

"So let's do clothes," Dora said. "We can't go wrong with a new wardrobe."

Sheela opened her presents, just after midnight. As she unwrapped package after package, her mood began to brighten, almost against her will. The fact that pretty clothes had the power to change her state of mind made her feel decadent.

She tackled the boxes and packages at random and wound up with an embroidered Kashmiri outfit, a cream Tempco blazer that warmed in winter and cooled in summer, and Dora's gift, a long maroon coat made out of silvera, a shimmery new fiber that had just come on the market. Sheela noticed that one of the boxes was harder and she picked it next.

"That one is from us," Victor said. "Hope you like it."

"Wow!" Sheela said when she saw the contents: two pairs of Milani shoes in black and brown with matching purses. "These cost a fortune. Remember when we decided that no sane person would spend so much on shoes. I adore them!"

"Well," Natalya said, "they are too elegant to ever go out of style and they come with a lifetime guarantee. Milani reconditions them if they ever scuff or lose their shape. And see, the purses are versatile. They have zip-on compartments to make them bigger and three sets of straps. That way you don't have to change over from day to evening or for travel."

Next Sheela unzipped a bag containing a black dress with white stripes, a knitted tank and sweater set, and a hot pink body suit. Fashion in the twenties was an eclectic mix of throwbacks to antiquity like crinolines and braids and ultra modern styles like the body suits introduced by a fourteen year old designer, Horace Brinkle. Sheela had wanted one, but hadn't mustered the courage to get it. "So who is all this from?" she asked, because the package had no identification.

"It's from me," Gappa said. "I hope you don't think the body suit is too much; I got it on the web."

"It is too much," Sheela said, "but I adore it."

The last package to be opened had just arrived that morning by Globe Express. It was a huge box from the Rosenbaum clan. When Sheela finished removing layers of tissue paper, she found it contained a sleek ankle-length navy blue dress with silver trim. Underneath there was more tissue paper and a layer of corrugated cardboard. Under that there was a round box with still more tissue around a wide rimmed navy blue hat and a smaller square box containing a pair of high heeled sling-back navy shoes.

"Is this for real or for the theater?" Sheela asked.

"It's for real," Dora replied. "People are dressing again. It's what you wear *to* the theater."

"How do the folks behind someone in that hat see?" Sheela asked.

"It's polite to remove your hat when you are seated," Dora explained. "You check it in. New York has hat and coat check booths in movies now. Remember how many felt hats we saw men wearing over Thanksgiving? An industry that was thought dead and cremated is coming back to life."

"I don't think hats will catch on in Texas," Sheela said.

"What do you mean?" Victor asked. "What about cowboy hats? They're practically the symbol of the Lone Star State. I think that pretty soon you'll see people wearing all kinds of headgear around here."

"This weekend," Gappa said, "I'm inviting all of us to The Londoner for dinner. Sheela, you wear your dress and hat. And Nat, dear, I'd like you to go to Celebrité and buy a hat that goes with something you like, or buy something you like *and* a hat from me."

"Maybe not Celebrité," Natalya said. "I know this boutique in The Village that's much more reasonable. I've actually tried on some hats there, although I never seriously considered buying one."

"To think I left my only bonnet in New York," Dora said. "But it's brown. Maybe I'll splurge and get something in black with a veil or colored feathers. I brought my long black and green dress along just in case something like this came up."

"No new hat for me," Victor said. "I'm sticking to my cowboy hat and boots."

"And I," Gappa said "will sport my bare head. I'm proud of my white hair."

"As you should be." Sheela got up to give her grandfather a hug and to pat his head. "It's not white," she said. "It's silver and getting shinier and fuller by the day."

<hr>

The next day Sheela was the first person up. It was a little before ten and considering that everyone had been awake until nearly three a.m., she expected no company for a while. She padded into the kitchen and made herself a cup of tea. It was much too early to start brunch. In any case, her grandmother was looking forward to making cottage cheese pancakes with sour cream and baked apples.

Carrying her mug, Sheela wandered into her parents' study and started leafing through their albums. Even now, at twenty, she was bothered by the fact that she starred in most of them. Her parents got their kicks from snapping, sorting, viewing and reviewing the progression of photos that began with her birth—except luckily her father's camera broke the moment she emerged because he fainted—and always ended yesterday. It made no sense, but it was a constant in their lives and therefore in her own.

Of much greater interest to her were the older photographs, the ones buried behind the brightly colored ones produced by modern technology. Those were less life-like, but more real. Sheela sat on the floor and pulled out an odd-shaped brown book with pictures dating back to the first half of the last century. Deliberately she turned the pages until she came to the specific photograph she was looking for. It was one she remembered without really knowing that it existed. It was unlabeled. There were two girls in the photo, sisters. The little one was clutching the older one's hand. Neither child was smiling, perhaps because in those days you had to keep still too long to hold a smile. Or perhaps they were simply sad or fearful. The bigger girl had dark pigtails and a dimple on her cheek, just like her own dimple. The younger one had Beca's eyes. Sheela looked at the picture for some time and tasted bittersweet in her mouth. Her eyes became damp and she wiped them on the corner of her nightgown. Then Sheela put the album back exactly where she found it and went back to the kitchen for more tea.

In Houston Sheela stopped thinking about the absence of intimacy and romance in her life at college or about potential problems with Bryan. When the holidays were over, she was content to return to UT and to resume her studies. How could she know that less than a week into the new semester, her world would crash?

Zyan had invited her for supper. She wanted to give her a belated birthday gift and to chat because she was in the dumps. Her vacation had been a drag. She had spent it moping over Jonathan.

"Can you believe," Zyan asked Sheela, even before inviting her to sit down, "that when he finally got back from the Caribbean and called, Jonathan never even told me he missed me?"

"You didn't hear from him on New Year's?" Sheela asked in turn, arranging herself on the sofa.

"Nope," Zyan replied. "He claimed there were no communication facilities on the boat and he wasn't taking his detachables. But he had warned me about that part. What burned me up was that when he finally did get back, it took him two days to get around to conferencing with me. It was like no big deal. And then all he had to say was what a wonderful and exciting experience he'd had. Evidently they ran into some bad weather and were in some danger. It sounded like he loved every second of it. So what do you think?"

"I don't know what to think," Sheela answered. "But . . . ."

"What can I get you, a glass of wine or a Dr. Pepper?" Zyan interrupted.

"Just sit. You're making me nervous," Sheela said. "I'm trying to answer your question. I was about to say maybe Jonathan just wanted to impress you. He wouldn't admit that he missed you, even if he did. My point is maybe you're overreacting. So where is that picture of him you were going to show me?"

"It's in the alcove. I'll get it," Zyan answered, hopping up again.

She returned seconds later with a five by seven snapshot in a clear plastic frame. "Here he is," she said, a smile making its way back into her eyes.

There were three people in the picture: Zyan, Jonathan standing with his arm on her shoulder, and her brother who was staring into the camera looking totally out of place. Sheela stared at the three of them and thought she would faint, if not die. Her heart began to pound in her chest and her chin quivered. Her eyes became covered with a glaze that impeded her vision. She used every ounce of strength she could muster to act normal. At first she couldn't make her vocal cords work, but after concentrating for a few moments, she managed to say, "He's awfully handsome."

Handsome! That was the understatement of the millennium. Jonathan was the most beautiful man she had ever seen. She knew him. She had dreamed of him her whole life. She wanted to be with him always. She couldn't bear being apart from him. He was the incarnation of everything her heart and soul wanted for as long back as she could remember, even before she could remember. It was strange that until now she had never thought of giving a physical form to the person with whom she was so desperately in love. How could she have forgotten what he looked like and how it felt to be locked in his embrace? But now she recognized him. She remembered every detail about him: his brown eyes as warm as the sun, that shock of wavy chestnut hair that smelled of orange and musk and fell into his eyes, the strong shoulders that carried her as if she were a feather. How could she live another day without tasting his full lips or without feeling the ripples of muscles that strained under his T-shirt. She wanted to tear that shirt off and run her fingers over his chest and to. . . "God help me, please!" Sheela begged in silence.

"Are you OK?" Zyan asked.

"Sure," Sheela said. "I'm fine."

"Something's the matter," Zyan insisted. "What happened?

"It's just a twinge. A spasm in my leg. I've been having them for a couple of days. Maybe I'll have that glass of wine, please." Anything to get Zyan out of the room so she could breathe.

By the time her friend returned, Sheela had inhaled deeply, held her breath, and exhaled twice. Now she looked flushed, but her voice was normal and she wasn't visibly trembling.

"Thanks," she said, accepting the Chardonnay.

"Cheers," Zyan said. "I guess you may be right. I'll wait and see what Jonathan does next. Hey, I almost forgot. Here's your gift," she added reaching into her pocket.

Sheela opened the small velvet box that Zyan handed her and took out a small cloisonné pin shaped like a parrot. "It's lovely," she said, looking at the piece but not seeing it, not appreciating its uncanny resemblance to Aa-Oo. She was focused on maintaining her sanity and her decorum until she could manage her escape.

Nearly two hours later, Sheela heard herself taking Zyan's leave. For the life of her she couldn't remember anything that had transpired after the moment she laid eyes on Jonathan. She had been hypnotized by the thumping in her chest that kept pace with rhythms of the modern jazz Zyan had been playing throughout the evening. Zyan didn't appear to have noticed anything out of the ordinary.

"This has been a really good visit," Zyan said. "I'm so much better. You've made me feel as if everything is going to work out."

"I'm sure it will," Sheela agreed. "Dinner was yummy. Take care."

"You too." Zyan hugged her friend and closed the door.

53

As soon as Sheela entered her apartment, she collapsed on the floor. Relieved that she no longer had to pretend she was all right, she curled up in a heap to indulge the anguish that ravished her being and made her alive. At Zyan's she had been a zombie: walking, talking, and smiling as if she were human. Indeed, it dawned on Sheela that until now she had always been a virtual zombie, a shadow of her actual self. The true Sheela was a miserable tortured creature. The Sheela others perceived as someone who excelled in her studies, loved her family and friends, worried about love, and looked good was a mere phantom with no substance.

A phantom would not lay on the ground like she did, huddled with a pillow that she alternately crumpled and held against her face to muffle the screams that came out of her mouth, nor would it pound the floor until its fists began to ache. It was the real Sheela whose misery caused her to hurry to the bathroom to throw up and to make dry hacking noises until she felt that her body was emptied of everything but pain.

Too dry for more tears, Sheela sat motionless on a chair and watched the second hand on her clock go round and round and round until the dark starless night turned gray. She had sat so still that her joints became stiff and she stared with such fixedness that her eyes became grainy.

At dawn she took off her crumpled clothes and stepped into the shower. With her body brush she scrubbed herself until she was red. Then she patted herself dry.
She had an early morning class but she was in no condition to face another human being so she put on an old T-shirt and climbed into bed. She had been awake now for nearly 24 hours. Still sleep eluded her, but she unclenched her limbs and tried to block her consciousness.

In the early afternoon, twinges of hunger registered themselves in Sheela's brain in spite of her sore stomach and raspy throat. It was strange, she thought, that a person could have a death wish and yet feel the urge to ingest food. She got up, brushed her teeth, and prepared herself a cup of oriental noodle soup. Then she returned to her bed and, after a few moments, succumbed to exhaustion.

She slept deeply and woke up disoriented until she turned toward her clock radio and saw that it was 4 p.m. Then the events of the previous evening rushed back into her mind. However, she had no more strength for hysteria. Her thoughts were spent. She closed her eyes again and sought oblivion.

In the silence, she heard a fluttering and saw Aa-Oo flying to her bed.

"The secret," Aa-Oo said, "is to go backwards."

"I can't," Sheela told him. "I have to go forward."

"Then go forward," the parrot cawed. "It's all one and the same."

She was lying in the sun on a patch of grass not far from a body of water. She had taken off her clothes because they made her feel hot and bothered. Aa-Oo was perched on a tree above her.

"Turn around," Sheela told him. "I am not properly dressed."

Sheela stared at her swollen breasts and her erect nipples and felt to see if they were hard to the touch. As soon as her fingers brushed her chest, a young man materialized before her. He wore a hooded purple body suit that covered his head and he had on a silver mask that hid his eyes, except that hot brown sparks flashed through the slits. He was kneeling on one knee as though he were about make a medieval marriage proposal.

"They are very beautiful," he told her.

"This is the wrong fairy tale," Sheela said.

"Still, you are so very beautiful," the man insisted.

Sheela wanted to tell him to leave her alone, but she lacked the power to do so. If he stays, I'll have to go, she thought and tried to get up. But his penetrating gaze kept her pinned to the ground.

Silently she watched the masked apparition watching her. His intensity made her loins throb as they exuded perfumed moisture. Her limbs glistened from the tangy sweat released by her pores.

The beams that shot out from behind the young man's mask caused Sheela to smolder. Her body expelled all its juices and she became drained and parched. She wanted to tell the man to take her to the water, but heat befuddled her mind and dryness thickened her tongue. She began to moan and the man lowered himself to soothe her. Instead, his nearness set her on fire. The blaze roared and rose up and up until it extended beyond the galaxies and burned beyond the reach of time. When the flames died down, eons later, Sheela and her lover were gone. Not even ashes were left to show that either of them had ever existed.

⎯⎯ ⋅⊙⋅⊙⋅⊙⋅⊙⋅⊙⋅ ⎯⎯

Sheela remained ensconced in her apartment for three days trying to comprehend her reaction to the photograph of Zyan's boyfriend. The more she thought about it, the crazier it seemed. At the same time, whenever she permitted that photograph to sweep before her eyes, despair overwhelmed her. It was not a transient sensation, but a deep hollow sickness that sapped her energy and left her without the volition to go on with her life. "What's the point?" she thought.

The question she asked herself was the one Gappa had asked himself when he fell apart after Beca died. Gappa had pulled himself together after Door pointed

345

out his responsibilities to those who love him. He healed himself by undertaking more responsibilities in order to make life better for the sick children in Houston's Children's Hospital. The children adored him and he found a well of happiness in serving others. She would have to serve as well.

Sheela knew she could not tell a living soul about the picture and she knew she had to keep her emotions hidden. If she were to try to explain the truth, she would be viewed as unbalanced if not certifiable. Her parents would beg her to submit to therapy and if she refused—which she definitely would do—they would wind up so upset that God only knew what would happen.

She wished her family would stop taking her problems personally. Her parents always tried to fix whatever was wrong with her. Her father still thought he could wave a magic wand over her head and make her sorrows go away. He didn't realize he couldn't fix what ailed her or force happiness upon her. Her mother was something else too. Nat had an intrusive sixth sense. Between the two of them, they never let her just be. That's why Sheela would have to hide distress by turning her existence into a performance, one where she would play herself as a happy normal young woman. In the performance of her life, Sheela would pretend "The Picture" didn't exist. She would *not* try to win the man of her dreams away from her friend and she would smile and laugh as if everything were fine.

The first days after the picture, time was so heavy with sorrow that it barely crawled. Yet Sheela forced herself to resume her life. She turned on her message bank and halfway listened to what the people in her world had to say. Satisfied that there were no emergencies, she pushed the delete button. Then she drafted a short note and sent it off to everyone in her priority address book:

Sorry, but somehow all my messages got deleted. I'm bogged down, and so will not try to retrieve them from never-never land. Please re-send or update.
Hope I have not created a problem for you. I'm fine.
Love and hugs and stuff always.

Sheela

Zyan called back instantly. Sheela braced herself and took the call.
"What happened?" Zyan asked. "I've been trying to reach you for three days. How come you were switched off? Should I be worried? Did I do or say something wrong or did my cooking make you sick?"
"Nothing like that," Sheela said, forcing a chuckle. "I've had these spasms I told you about. And I needed to take some personal time out."
"Bryan, huh?" Zyan acknowledged.
"In a way," Sheela said. "But . . . ."
"I understand," Zyan quickly said. "You don't want to talk about it. But if you ever need an ear, use mine."
"Thanks," Sheela said as brightly as she could.
"And you're fine, right?"
"Completely. I've sorted myself out. And the spasms are gone. I think they were tension spasms. But now I have lots of catching up to do."
"I can take a hint; I'm out of your hair," Zyan said.
"That's not what I meant. We can talk a little. Have you heard from Jonathan?" Sheela almost choked on the words.

"He tried to conference, but I was out. Anyway, I'll let you get back to work. Call me when you catch your breath."

"OK, bye," Sheela said.

"Bye," Zyan echoed.

Sheela wondered what Zyan thought. Did her normalcy act convince her friend? Could she tell that Sheela nearly lost her voice when she uttered the name "Jonathan?" How long could a farce like this go on? The months ahead were going to be a nightmare.

⸺⸺ ❊❊❊❊✦❊❊❊ ⸺

Sheela didn't really care about school any more, but her role mandated dedication so she contacted her colleagues and teachers and asked them for help in assembling the materials and lectures she had missed. She told them all that she had been unwell. That was no lie. It took more than a week for her to bring her level of readiness back to its pre-picture level, but Sheela did it. If anything, her work was better than ever before. Her detachment seemed to have improved her concentration.

Although she was pressed, Sheela kept up with her messages. Her parents were fine. They were sorry to know that she had been under the weather and were glad she was better. Was she taking her vitamins? Gappa sent love. He also sent her a poem written by one of his children:

You said time would teach me what I need to know,
but you taught me all I need.
Your eyes, your words and your smile
were my teachers.
The love you gave me when you ruffled my hair
with your gentle hands was my teacher.

The world may not miss my shouts,
or my kites flying in the wind
or my favorite words, w hen I grow up.
And I will not miss the world, because I take it with me.
Everything I need is with me.
My memories are written in my heart with capital letters
like the A s you circled on my report cards.

Tomorrow you may not see me waving from my window,
or chasing Puff away from your feet,
or throwing my ball over the fence.
But I will be with you in every tree that shades your head,
in every breeze that blows on your face,
in every bird chirping in our garden.
And every tear that falls on your wrinkled cheek
will be a kiss I send you from heaven.

The tears that came to Sheela's eyes when she read the poem were not part of her performance.

Door recommended more calcium and yoga for leg cramps and Bernie said she had a horrible fight with William but was now reconciled. Sheela e-mailed Bernie and asked what her fight was about. Bernie replied saying that neither of them knew exactly what started it. It was something Will said about a former female colleague of his who recently got divorced from their former professor. "It ended up," she wrote, "with Will calling me an 'irritating, immature prima donna' and me calling him a 'priggish prick.' But we had such a marvelous time making up that the fight was almost worth it."

Then there was Bryan's message. He said he wanted to make a conference appointment whenever Sheela could give him thirty minutes of her undivided attention. She agreed to visit with him on Sunday afternoon. On Sunday morning she canceled the appointment because there was a live program, Time Travel, she had to watch for her Future of Physics class.

"When did you find out about this program?" Bryan asked.

"Just now. It was something that had been discussed when I was out sick."

"So, when can we reschedule?"

"I'm not sure," Sheela said.

"How about after the show?"

"That won't work," Sheela said. "I have to compile a critique while the stuff is still fresh in my mind."

"Look, if the truth is that you want me to disappear, please tell me that and I won't bother you again. OK?"

"That's not fair. I've always been a good friend and I resent your saying that."

"Well, I'm sorry," Bryan pressed on, "but you have been avoiding me and if you care about our friendship, you have to make a little effort. It's not like I'm asking anything extraordinary. All I'm asking is for thirty minutes of your undivided attention. So, when you are ready, please call. If you don't, I'll draw my own conclusions."

"I'm sorry," Sheela apologized. "I promise I'll call you within the next three or four days. And we'll conference within the week. I give you my word."

"I'd appreciate it," Bryan said. He was pleased at this outcome. One point for emotional intelligence! He had been open and stopped sulking. His honesty changed the dynamics of his dialogues with Sheela. He had the courage to throw the ball squarely in her court and now she was committed to the volley.

A week later to the hour Sheela received Bryan's visit on her conferencer. She was seated on her sofa, dressed in a pair of jeans and a snug sweater that looked as if it were painted on her. Bryan was seated at his desk where his mind always worked best.

"Hi," Sheela said.

"Hello," Bryan echoed and went right to the point. "I want to discuss our friendship. It's something that means a great deal to me and so I may have a little bit of a hard time expressing myself. Will you bear with me?"

"Of course. Our friendship matters to me, too."

"But not in the same way it matters to me," Bryan explained.

"How is that?" The minute the words came out of Sheela's mouth, she wished she hadn't uttered them. She knew the answer to her question and it was an answer she didn't want to hear.

"I'm surprised you ask," Bryan replied. "I think you know perfectly well how but you are afraid to face the truth. What I don't understand is why you are afraid."

Bryan and Sheela spoke for more than the allotted thirty minutes. At the end of their talk the fact that Bryan was in love with Sheela was out in the open, as was the fact that Sheela's affection for him was not at all romantic.

"I don't want to lose you as a friend," Sheela said. "But we can't go on seeing each other when our feelings are diametrically opposed."

"Our feelings are not diametrically opposed," Bryan argued. "They are on different points along a continuum. Besides, we've been feeling this way for years. I just haven't had the courage to address how we are precisely because I was afraid you'd say what you just said. Who knows what would have happened if I had been braver."

"What do you want to do then?" Sheela asked.

"I want to go on like before, but I want us to go out," Bryan said.

"To go out as in to date?" Sheela asked.

"That's right," Bryan said. "It won't be horrible, I assure you."

"I'm not clear," Sheela said, "about what dating actually entails. I never dated."

"It entails nothing more than your knowing that I love you and that I will strive to make you love me too. You define all the parameters of our togetherness. Oh, and I guess it entails our not dating anyone else."

"What if you or I want to date someone else?" Sheela asked. She knew she never would, but Bryan should be free to find a girl who could reciprocate his feelings.

"Then our deal is over. We stop going out and go back to being friends."

Sheela did not respond for a few seconds. Then suddenly everything fell into place. She saw that if she agreed to "date" Bryan, it would be easier for her to carry out the role of a happy, balanced young lady. They wouldn't be seeing all that much of one another—Bryan had to stay in Galveston. She would have to leave Austin. She could not remain in the same city with Zyan because Jonathan would be part of Zyan's life. Somehow she'd have to manage matters until she graduated, but right after that, she'd be gone. With luck she might get into Harvard. Bryan would find someone else and forget all about her.

"So?" Bryan asked, "Shall we try dating on an experimental basis?"

"I don't know," Sheela was not yet sure that her plan made sense.

"What do we have to lose?" Bryan insisted.

"I don't know," Sheela repeated.

"I'll tell you what," Bryan said.

"What?" Sheela asked.

"I'm happy with 'I don't know.' In fact I'm delighted. 'No' would have devastated me, but 'I don't know' is good. Next weekend I'll come to Austin and we'll go to Clementine's and talk some more, that is if you agree. And now I'm begging you to say 'yes' Do you agree?"

"Next weekend my grandmother is coming to Austin to stay with me," Sheela replied, "but the weekend after that would be fine. So, yes, I agree."

54

Natalya and Victor were bursting with pride. Sheela had graduated from UT Summa; she had a boyfriend; she was going to Harvard.

This time, Sheela didn't resist participating in her own graduation like she did when she finished high school. She was happy and proud to invite her parents and Door and Gappa to the ceremony and when Zyan and Bryan asked if she had tickets for them, she graciously said yes. It was the first time Bryan had met her family.

"Don't read anything into the fact that Bryan is here," Sheela insisted. "We have been seeing one another, but we have no plans whatsoever. We're wide open. I'm going to Harvard and he's staying in Galveston."

"But neither of you are dating anyone else, are you?" Natalya asked.

"No, not at the moment," Sheela replied, "but that could change at any time."

At home in Houston, Nat and Victor talked about their daughter. "The Dean's Reception for Honors Students was beautiful," Nat said. "I'll never forget it."

"My favorite moment was listening to Sheela's speech," Victor said. "Sheela is right you know."

"About what?"

"About how important it is not to lose sight of history. We do tend to think that we have made unprecedented progress in our era, but, in fact, we have merely accelerated the speed of technological progress."

"I agree. It's like the old medical student joke," Nat said.

"What joke?" Victor asked.

"You know. The professor asks a student to what extent the death rate has declined within the past century. So the student says it hasn't. 'It's the same, sir,' she explains, 'one death per person.'"

"Do you think Sheela is happy?" Nat asked her husband a few moments later.

"I'm not sure," Victor answered, "actually I was going to ask you the same question."

"I think something is bothering her," Nat said. "There's an undercurrent to her apparent contentment that is troubling, but I can't put my finger on it; I keep thinking the only person who fully understood her was Beca."

"Yes," Victor agreed, "and my mother wasn't the world's most upbeat soul. Sheela is different though. She is peppy and outgoing. Bryan is a fine young man and he's devoted to her. Sheela apparently cares for him, but . . . you're right, something is missing."

"Passion." Natalya completed her husband's thought. "That's it, passion! At times Sheela appears to be going through the motions of life almost like a robot. It's hard to tell if the things she has are what she really wants. Like Harvard. I can't figure out what made her change her mind about going there."

"Did you ask her?' Victor inquired.

"I was going to, but then I didn't."

"Yeah, me too," Victor added.

"Maybe we're overreacting," Nat said.

"I certainly hope that's the case."

Sheela couldn't quite digest the fact that she was 21, a college graduate, and a soon-to-be student at Harvard Law. It was a lot to take in. All said and done, the last year and a half weren't as bad as she had feared. Time didn't zoom by painlessly, but neither did she spend 24 hours of every day thinking about her broken heart.

It had been a good family year. She had spent her 21st birthday in New York. Her family surprised her with a formal party in the newly built Hotel 222 on Park Avenue and she had truly enjoyed herself. She finessed the question of including Bryan and Zyan in the party by telling them she did not know what her parents had planned and hinted they might be going abroad. Then she told her parents that Bryan and Zyan had other holiday commitments.

Sheela managed to maintain a semblance of normalcy in her relationship with Zyan. She was buoyed by the knowledge that she would soon be gone and spared the agony of hiding the crazy truth: she was hopelessly in love with her best friend's boyfriend whom she knew only from a photograph. Since both girls were busy, they generally met at the gym where there was not much opportunity for meaningful conversation. When they occasionally found themselves in other settings and Zyan did mention Jonathan, Sheela tried to avoid hearing Zyan's words, or at least to avoid stringing them into coherent thoughts. She couldn't help learning that things were moving in the right direction but at a pace that was too slow for Zyan's liking. If Zyan asked for advice, Sheela simply said, "I don't know." And when Zyan inquired about Bryan, Sheela's reply was always, "It's too soon to tell whether this is going to be the real thing." Eventually Zyan saw that any discussion of men shook Sheela up, so she talked of other things.

"Dating" Bryan was fine, except Sheela felt guilty because she believed she was using him. He was witty, gracious, and true to his word. He let Sheela define the extent of their physical relationship. She worked out an acceptable level of closeness that was short of sex, but allowed for some intimacy. While she was never transported to other worlds, she was not repelled, and if Bryan hurt from her coolness, he never let on. His kisses were homage to her beauty.

"You are exquisite," Bryan would say.

"You aren't so bad yourself," Sheela tended to respond.

"I love you," Bryan always said, but Sheela could never bring herself to say those three potent words back.

"I don't deserve you," was her usual reply.

Sheela couldn't make up her mind about how she wanted to spend the summer before Harvard. The previous summer, after her junior year, she had returned to work at the Federal Public Defender's Office. She had also slogged to prepare for the LSAT, to get a jump on the UT law courses she would be taking in her senior yeear, to work on her Harvard application, and to prepare back-up applications to Yale and Stanford. This summer Sheela wanted time our. She wanted to be away from studies, away from work, away from family, and away from friends. The problem was that she couldn't say this to anyone without hurting their feelings. Finally, she confided in her Aunt Cecily.

"It sounds to me," Cecily told her, "like what you really want is to be away from yourself."

"I do," Sheela said, "but you know what Ma always says, 'wherever you go you take yourself with you.'"

"Not just your ma, everyone's mother says that," Cecily pointed out. "My mother said it, I say it to my kids, and you'll probably say it to your kids someday. And it is fundamentally true. Still I have an idea I think will give you a rest from yourself or at least from your life and your preoccupations."

"Really? What?" Sheela asked.

"The Summer Amateur Theater in Albuquerque," Cecily replied.

"Wow!" Sheela said. "Do you think they'd take me?"

"I think they might," Cecily answered. "If your request to audition looks good on paper, they'll ask you up in April. They have three rounds of auditions. If you get past the first two, they record round three and the board votes the first week of May. I can pull a few strings, if you'd like me to."

"I would rather get in on my own," Sheela said.

"Your chance of getting a foot in the door would be a whole lot better with a live recommendation from someone who is connected. This kind of thing is above board, trust me. And like I said, ultimately your performance would be what counts."

"Well then," Sheela said, "OK. I mean, please."

Sheela's official invitation to participate in the Summer Amateur Theater pleased her almost as much as her Harvard acceptance, and the summer turned out to be everything Sheela had hoped it would be, plus some. Throughout the months of June, July, and August she practically forgot who she was, so engrossed did she become in the role of Roxanne Planetaria in Spaced Out. Sheela was thrilled that her team, one of three that made up the Summer Amateur Theater, chose this comedy about travel to past and future worlds and she loved her part.

Spaced Out's lead character, Harvey Boswell, was an automobile mechanic with the ability to project himself into other universes. Although he attempted to keep his voyages through time and space secret, he often leaked information or unwittingly transported stuff that embroiled him in a series of misadventures. Sheela was his love interest in the future and a thorn in the foot of his present wife, Rose. Rose thought Roxanne was a waitress who slipped love potions to her husband.

The play was absurd, yet Harvey's escapades gave rise to provocative speculation. Did the playwright expect his actors and audience to believe that Harvey actually moved back and forth between multiple worlds, or rather that he imagined his trips? Were the alien objects he unwittingly brought to Iowa adequate material proof that his travel was real? Were the physicists who insisted that space/time travel was not only feasible but also that it already existed crazy, or were they right? Could people be transmitted by signals just like electronic messages? If so, what did that tell you about the essence of humanity? And if God was omnipotent, omniscient, and omnipresent, why couldn't people who were of God exist in more than one time or place as well?

Some of the actors talked about these things non-stop, but Sheela tried not to speculate. Melissa Lee who played Harvey's medieval lover, Lady Jane, thought Spaced Out was a huge joke.

"I don't know," Sheela said. "This is my summer to not think at all."

* * *

Sheela's parents came out to New Mexico to see the final performance of Spaced Out.

"Did you really like it?" Sheela asked.

"No," Victor answered. "I loved it. I laughed so much my stomach hurts. But when I stopped shaking, I started thinking."

"I just had fun," Nat said to her daughter, "and admired your performance. You were good. Very good."

"But if you had to say," Victor asked his wife, "would you say we are supposed to believe Harvey really took those trips?"

"If I had to say, my answer would be yes," Nat replied.

"What about you, Sheela?" Victor went on.

"I guess I'd say yes too," Sheela admitted, "but that's as far as I'd go because that question is just the tip of a huge iceberg."

The three of them spent two days enjoying Albuquerque and then returned to Houston to spend some peaceful time together before Sheela's departure for Cambridge. Those days were filled with a poignant sense of closure. It was hard to say what was ending and what was starting, but the feeling was that the nuclear Landau family was entering a new phase.

* * *

Several hours later Sheela was in Logan International Airport talking with Bernie at the baggage ramp.

"Everything is all set," Bernie told her. "So look at the bright side of our moving to New York. I left you just about everything you're going to need."

"I'd rather have you staying here," Sheela said. "Are you sure you're OK with NYU?"

"Absolutely," Bernie said. "Will's job is a big step up and to tell you the truth, four years at any university is more than enough. NYU is at the heart of what's

353

happening in real life. As New York's heart beats, so beats the heart of the world. Harvard is really an ivory tower."

"So when are you leaving?" Sheela asked.

"Not until Sunday," Bernie replied. "Orientation doesn't start until Wednesday and I have everything at home all set. But I gave up our apartment this morning, so I'm staying with you until then."

"Thanks," Sheela said, squeezing Bernadette. "That's great."

By Sunday, Sheela felt like she'd always lived in her first floor one bedroom apartment with the dresser and table lamp she fell in love with and bought at an antique/junk shop. By Thursday, she was completely oriented and getting acquainted with the freshlaws in her section.

By the following Monday, Harvard University felt like home. Sheela was studying twelve hours a day and loving it. Her mind was so engrossed in the cases she dissected that there was no time to worry about anything more than sleeping and trying to squeeze in some exercise. Socializing was an extension of studying. All she and her colleagues talked about were their classes. But there was no real pressure in the air, just excitement and the feeling that you were at Harvard because you were destined to make a mark in the world.

Bryan visited for a day and a half in October and Sheela managed to take a few hours off to show him around campus and to have dinner at Durgan Park. The rest of the time she studied at the Law Center while he visited the Medical School.

Before she knew it, it was Thanksgiving and then Chanukah and then she was in Los Cabos spending her 22nd birthday with her parents and the Khannas.

"How come you never go swimming?" Sunita asked her one afternoon when Sheela was sitting in the shade reading the United States Constitution for the 27th time.

"I don't know, but I know why you shouldn't immerse yourself in public waters."

"Why not?" Sunita asked.

"Because the way you look in a bathing suit the ninety percent of the life guards who are male won't watch the other swimmers and someone may drown."

"I think you won't go in the water because you drowned in your past life," Sunita said.

"That conclusion is quite a leap," Sheela said.

"Is it really?" Sunita asked. "Why else would you be afraid to swim? Anyway I've been waiting to talk to you about something."

"Talk away," Sheela said.

"I decided something and I wanted to know what you think before I tell my parents. It's about my being adopted."

"Yes?" Sheela asked.

"Remember when we were in India and I asked you what you thought?"

"Yup. I said that at the right time you'd know whether you wanted to find out who your birth parents are."

"Well, I stopped thinking about it and then suddenly one day I realized I never want to know. After all, what difference does it make? I'm my parents' daughter and that's all I care about. Of course I know I'm not completely Indian from looking in the mirror, but I feel Indian and at the same time a little exotic and mysterious. And I don't want the mystery to go away. So I thought I'd tell my parents that they should destroy all the evidence of who my birth parents are. So don't you think that's a great idea?"

"Well, I'm not sure. Why would you want to destroy all the paperwork? What if you change your mind?"

"That's just it," Sunita said. "I don't want to change my mind and this way I'll never think about it again. Besides, I think my real parents would rather I didn't find out who my biological parents were and they'd be glad to know what I decided."

"Here's what I think," Sheela said. "You're probably right that your mom and dad would be happy to know the way you feel. At the same time they shouldn't destroy the information about your physical ancestry because one never knows what could come up. Some day you may need information about your genetic pool or your birth parents. That wouldn't change how you feel about whose daughter you really are. But there is another important factor to consider."

"What's that?"

"Some day your kids might want to know who their genetic ancestors were. Why take the option of their learning the truth away from them? So think about it."

"No, I don't need to think. You're right. I won't say that Mommy and Daddy should throw any papers away. I'll just say that I don't want to know who my birth mother was and that I don't think I'll want to know for a long time to come, if ever."

"I think something else too," Sunita added.

"What's that?" Sheela asked.

"I bet I know why you decided to go to Harvard."

"Bet you don't," Sheela argued.

"You're on," Sunita said. "What is the bet?"

"A box of Godiva chocolates?" Sheela suggested.

"No way," Sunita said. "Too fattening. Let's say silver earrings. I saw the cutest pair in the gift shop."

"Deal," Sheela replied. "For your sake I hope they're not too expensive." Sheela was sure she'd win this bet. There was no way on earth that Sunita could know that she went to Harvard to get away from Zyan because of a photograph. "So, what made me go to Harvard?"

"There is someone in Cambridge you hope you might run into."

Sunita's words made Sheela turn red and hot. Could Sunita be right? she asked herself.

"You're all flushed," Sunita said. "Does that mean I win?"

"I don't know," Sheela said. "I mean, I don't think so. At least I didn't think so. I mean I didn't think I wanted to run into him. Not consciously anyway. Actually I wanted to not run into him in Austin."

"That's a yes," Sunita concluded. "You can get me the earrings. And don't worry, I won't talk about this anymore and I won't say anything to anyone. OK?"

Sheela hesitated, rubbing her ring and turning it round her finger. Then she said, "OK."

<h1 style="text-align:center">55</h1>

Ariel Reuven couldn't get the dark-haired girl out of his head. He saw her from half a block away. She was walking out of Durgan Park while he was heading into the restaurant. It was a little after nine. One of his professors and her husband had invited him out to dinner.

"You need fattening up," Dr. Jane Crawford had said. "And you need to get out and talk to human beings. You can't spend your whole life buried in a laboratory making conversation with artificial intelligence."

If he hadn't been with Dr. Crawford, if the girl hadn't been holding hands with a very attractive man, if he'd had the courage to chase after her, if he'd realized that he would be unable to forget her. He couldn't really see but he was sure she would have deep blue eyes—the color of the ocean—and perhaps a dimple. If only he'd gotten a better look. If, if, if. . . .

Never before had Ariel thought about a girl with such longing. Not that he hadn't dated plenty of them; he had gone out with scores, perhaps hundreds. He was a womanizer who never had a girlfriend. Invariably, after one or two outings, Marsha—or Janet or Brianna or whoever—wanted to become close, while he wanted to keep looking for the girl with the elusive something without which his life was incomplete. His sister was forever scolding him.

"You wear broken hearts on your sleeve like stripes, and you've never had a real relationship with a single girl, ever," Zyan said.

"I'm just trying to find someone half as attractive and fun to be around as you are," he always replied.

After returning from Los Cabos, Sheela often caught herself walking to town and scanning the streets of Cambridge as if she thought Jonathan would suddenly appear. In her mind she played and replayed potential scenes that might occur when, at last, they would see one another face to face. Their meeting would be a reunion, except they had never met before. Then, in the midst of a reverie, she would be overcome with guilt. Jonathan belonged to Zyan. But did he really? Zyan told her more than once that he was dragging his feet. The reason had to be that he didn't love her. What other reason could there be? Wasn't what was meant to be, meant to be? Thus Sheela's mind wavered and teased her. Her escape was in the cases she studied and outlined, cases that read like mysteries to which she gave colorful names: the case of the hairy hand, the case of the ugly fountain, the case of mistaken identities, the case of the undelivered telegram.

When Sheela became conscious of her quest for Jonathan, it was cold and snowy, but soon the last snows melted and the weather turned rainy and then balmy. Frapuccinos and Italian ices replaced hot cider, hot chocolate, and lattes in the coffee shops. The next thing she knew, it was the end of April and she was cramming for finals and then it was May, and Sheela's first year in Harvard was over. Instead of going home to Houston, she remained on campus for a summer program on the European legal system. Summer passed in no time and Sheela had ten days off which she spent in New York. In late August, she returned to her apartment, transformed from a wide-eyed freshlaw to a seasoned second year law student ready to tackle a heavy class load along with work on the Law Review and resigned to the process of interviewing for summer clerkships. As Sheela was thus occupied, the crisp fall months sped by. Thanksgiving in Houston came and went, and the holiday season was upon her once again.

The year 2024 was about to be born and Sheela was going to be twenty-three years old. Twenty-three, she considered, an incipient lawyer struggling not to become a blasé young woman. 'Why is it that nothing enthuses me?' she asked herself. 'Is it that I've done and had too much?'
'No,' her inner voice replied, 'it's that you won't let go of an impossible dream.'
'Well,' she thought, 'I can't. My dream is what keeps my soul awake.'

The Landaus intended to go to the Napa Valley for the holidays. It was now a given that Sheela would celebrate her birthday and New Year with her parents and whomever else they hooked up with, but without her college friends. This year it would be just the three of them. But their plan was disrupted because a hit and run driver ran Lulu down on December 23rd. Lulu was rushed to Hermann Hospital's intensive care unit where she teetered on the brink of death for two days. She was pronounced out of danger on Christmas day, but she remained in a coma for another three days. When she regained consciousness Lulu spoke only Spanish and didn't appear to recognize Sheela or her parents. She rambled on like an agitated teenager still living in Monterrey, Mexico. Sheela decided to have a small party in Lulu's hospital room on the night of December 31 in hopes of bringing Lulu to the present. She decorated the room and brought in a small live Christmas tree and she placed Aa-Oo by Lulu's pillow. She tuned the radio to a station that was playing holiday music in English.
"Hola," she said at the stroke of midnight. "Aquí estamos, Aa-Oo y yo en Houston. Y aquí están mis papás y mi abuelito el Dr. Mágico y tu hermana Margarita."
"Hi Sheela," Lulu replied. "I am back."
"Yes," Sheela said with a big smile on her face, "You are back."
"Why do we have a party?" Lulu asked.
"It's New Year," Sheela answered.
"Happy Birthday," Lulu said.

Lulu reported that hovering between this world and the hereafter had been a blissful experience. She couldn't stop repeating how beautiful heaven was, but Sheela couldn't get any details out of her.
"It's yust beautiful," she said.
"What did you see?" Sheela persisted.

"I saw the everything, the whole ooniverse," Lulu answered "with God's eyes. Now I'm tired; let me esleep."

"I love you," Sheela said.

"I know. I love you too," Lulu replied.

The group left the hospital just before daylight. When they got home, Natalya gave Sheela her birthday gift. It came in a flat largish rectangular box and was wrapped in plain brown paper with a gold ribbon.

"This present is from everyone," Nat said. "Read the card."

"So many people," Sheela said. "How did you organize this?"

"It just came about," Natalya answered. "Open the box."

"Oh!" Sheela said. "Oh! It's magnificent." What she saw was an oil of a desert sunset painted by Virginia Stone.

"Your grandmother told us how much you liked Stone's work when she took you to her exhibit in New York," Victor said.

"She did this picture when she was 23," Nat told Sheela. "So we thought it would be appropriate."

"It makes me tingle," Sheela said. "It glows. Don't you think it makes the whole room glow? It has every color of the world in it and it keeps changing. It's alive. There isn't a single place where it wouldn't fit perfectly. I love sunsets. Look! Can you see the little animals scurrying around the saguaros?"

When she returned to school, Sheela found clerkship offers from six law firms and from one appellate judge awaiting her. She didn't know what to do so she conferenced with her mother.

"I'd say you are in a rather agreeable quandary," Nat remarked.

"Maybe," Sheela said, "but it's still a quandary."

"The thing to do," Nat said, "is to zero in on where you'd like to be and on the kind of work that interests you most."

"I'd like to be in Houston."

"And are any of the firms who offered you a position in Houston?"

"Fulbright and Jaworski have a big Houston office. But they invited me to New York."

"I suppose you could ask them if you could work in Houston instead."

"I didn't like the who interviewed me from Fulbright," Sheela said.

"Personalities shouldn't control a decision like this," Natalya countered.

"It's not a question of personalities. It's a question of culture. I don't think I'd fit in well."

"What firm appealed to you work-wise?" Nat asked.

"Corbin, Franklin and Zolmar," Sheela said. "They're a boutique that associates with lots of solos and small firms on a case by case basis, but they're in Connecticut and I have no desire to go to Connecticut."

"So why did you interview with them?" Nat asked.

"I don't know. The placement office sent out my resume and a bunch of firms invited me to interview, so I just did."

"I don't know what to tell you," Nat said.

"Then can I talk to Uncle Steve?" Sheela asked.

"What for?"

"I'd like to know if I can work for you guys," Sheela replied.

"All right," Natalya said, chuckling. "I'll give him a copy of your resume and have him call you back. He's in a meeting now. What's the going salary for a summer clerk from Harvard?"

"In the range of thirty thousand dollars for the summer, plus expenses. And," Sheela added, "they invite you to lunch a lot and to the country club and all. You know, they want you to like the firm so you go to work there after graduation."

"That's pretty steep," Nat commented.

"Yeah, but we could probably work out something a little more reasonable," Sheela said. "We can skip the expenses, but I do want to be taken out and courted, just like any other clerk."

"Fine, see what Steve says," Natalya told her daughter.

One Saturday in early March when the weather in the Northeast was unseasonably mild, Bryan and Sheela went out for a walk. Bryan visited every two or three months. On this occasion he was between rotations.

Sheela stressed over the visits beforehand. She was afraid that in some subtle way Bryan would demand more from her emotionally or physically than she was prepared to give. But then he never did. When he came he entertained her and made her feel looked after. It was a good feeling. However, as a rule she felt upset again after Bryan left. Then she was troubled by the knowledge that the equities in their relationship were badly unbalanced.

This particular Saturday the two of them went for a stroll along the banks of the Charles River immediately after a brief but heavy downpour. The earth had a clean renewing smell, which gave Sheela a sense of well-being. She looked at Bryan and thought how good a man he was, and she tried to envision a life with him by her side. But no matter how hard she strained to imagine the two of them together, all she saw were ghosts.

There was little conversation between them as they walked. Each of them was living in the moment, but the moments were different. Only their linked pinkies created a tenuous bond. Suddenly Sheela felt something warming her shoulder. She stopped and looked back and inadvertently tugged at Bryan. He turned as well.

Before them the sky began to change colors until it became resplendent with a perfectly formed, breathtaking rainbow. Its arc was complete, beginning on the ground just at their feet and ending across the riverbank. Its colors were brilliant: violet, indigo, blue, green, yellow, orange, and red, the same colors that played hide and seek in the Virginia Stone sunset. Never before had either Sheela or Bryan seen anything like it.

Both young people stood unmoving and watched in silence. After an immeasurable interval the colors began to blend and to pale and Bryan put his arm around Sheela's shoulder. When the rainbow faded completely away, Bryan lowered his arm and looked into Sheela's eyes where he saw the sparkle of unshed tears.

"Let's go back now," Sheela whispered.

"Something happened to me out there," Sheela said to Bryan when they were home in her apartment.

"Yes," Bryan agreed, "to me, too. That rainbow was magnificent. We had a once in a lifetime experience, and it came upon us so unexpectedly. If you hadn't turned around, we would have missed it. What made you turn?"

"I'm not sure. Something felt funny," Sheela said, "but that's not what I meant. What happened was I had a revelation, or maybe it was a coming together of lots of little revelations that were building up inside me."

"A revelation?" Bryan was taken aback.

"Maybe a vision. I think the rainbow radiated a magnetic energy that brought it about. It became so bright that it blinded me and for a split nanosecond I was able to see beyond my present life."

"I don't understand," Bryan said.

"I don't really understand either," Sheela told him and she began to weep.

Bryan took her hands in his and gently asked, "Would you like to try to explain?"

"Yes," Sheela replied, "I want to try, but it may take some time."

"I have more than all the time in the world, but don't cry. I can't stand it when you cry."

Sheela pulled her right hand out of Bryan's hands and rubbed her eyes with her palm. Then she blinked and began, "As we were walking, I kept thinking about how much I care for you and about how much you love me and I tried to work out whether there was any chance at all that things could come together for us. I tried to picture us as a couple and I tried to picture myself loving you in a romantic way, but I only saw emptiness. It made me very sad.

Then I felt something behind me and I turned around and saw the sky turning from grayish to blue. The clouds blew away and the rainbow began to come out. The colors made me forget myself completely. Suddenly a whole life flashed before me. I wasn't here in Cambridge, Massachusetts with you. I was somewhere entirely different and I was someone entirely different. There was a man with me, a man who looked very familiar. I recognized him and I realized that I am in love with him."

"Are you saying that looking at the rainbow made you think you are in love with someone you haven't met but that you recognize?" Bryan tried to keep his amazement out of his voice.

"Not exactly. Like I said it's a long story. Ever since I can remember I have had dreams about a man . . . ."

"Dreams like when you are asleep or dreams like when you wish for something?" Bryan was unable to stop himself from interrupting.

"Both," Sheela said. "But they weren't clear and I couldn't always remember what this man looked like."

"And now you suddenly remember?"

"Yes. It sounds strange, but it's true. And there is more. You know how I never want to go swimming?"

"Yes?"

"When I was in Los Cabos, Sunita Khanna, you know who she is, said the reason going into the water freaks me is because I drowned in my past life. When she made that statement, I told her she was leaping to conclusions. Still she put the idea in the back of my mind. Actually that's not exactly true. The idea already was there, but I couldn't face it. By putting the thought into words, Sunita brought it out into the open. Today I discovered for sure that I was very much in love when I drowned and that I could never forget the man I loved."

Sheela paused, waiting for some comment from Bryan, but he remained silent. Finally she concluded, "This is why I can never become romantically involved with you or with anyone else. Don't you see?"

"Sheela, this is a fantasy," Bryan finally responded.

"I don't think so," Sheela argued, "but even if it is a fantasy, it is a fantasy that has colored my life and it is a fantasy from which I can never escape. In any case I don't see a true difference between fantasy and reality. The play I did in Albuquerque made me think our physical and imagined experiences are both equally real; they merely exist at different levels of consciousness. When I was in high school, Bernie told me that the reason I didn't like any guys was because I was waiting for the person who stole my heart to return it. In a way she was kidding, but in a way she meant it. And she was right."

"However you look at it," Bryan said, "if you let this fantasy or this idea control your thinking, it will kill your chances of having a normal, happy life."

"It's not a question of my letting it do anything to my thinking or to my life," Sheela explained. "It has a life of it's own. It exists and makes me who I am. Only one person in the whole world ever understood."

"Who?" Bryan asked.

"My grandmother Rebecca. She was my father's mother. She and I were on the same wavelength. We had a connection before I drowned. There was sadness in my grandmother that no one could explain. It always made my father angry."

"Maybe your grandmother did know stuff that no one else could figure out, but it made her unhappy."

"She wasn't unhappy," Sheela responded. "She was tinged by sadness because of something that happened when she was little, not because of what you call a fantasy."

"Please," Bryan asked. "Don't misunderstand me. You may be right, but my point is that you shouldn't be sad because of a belief that may or may not have substance."

"There is another thing," Sheela volunteered.

"What?" Bryan asked.

"I never wanted to tell you or anyone about it," Sheela said. "But now I have to and you have to promise that you will never ever repeat this to a living soul."

"I promise," Bryan said. "Hey, you've started trembling."

"This is very difficult," Sheela said.

"It's OK," Bryan urged. "Go ahead. Getting everything off your chest will help."

"I don't know what you're going to think. You already think I've lost it."

"I don't think you lost it," Bryan said. "I am afraid of losing you to a phantom. In any case, it makes no difference what I think because I don't judge you."

"Right after you came to Austin, when I was sick, I had a weird experience, a horrible experience actually," Sheela started and then she stopped talking.

"What exactly happened?" Bryan prompted.

"This is going to sound stupid," Sheela said.

"I told you I'm not going to judge you. Don't you trust me?"

"OK. I saw the man I'm in love with in a photograph and it made me crazy."

"Where did you see the picture?"

"At Zyan's."

"So why didn't you just ask Zyan who the man in the photo was?"

"Because I already knew. He's Jonathan, Zyan's boyfriend. And I can never tell Zyan. She is madly in love with him too. So you see, I can't do anything at all."

"And you've never seen this Jonathan before, just his picture," Bryan said.

"That's right," Sheela confirmed, "but I know him. He was the man who was with me in the rainbow."

Bryan put his arms around Sheela and held her for a long time. Finally he spoke.

"I can't say that any of this makes sense to me, but it doesn't matter. I can see how shaken you are, but Jonathan and Zyan are in love, so what you think is destined to be, is not. Here's what does matter: as far as I'm concerned nothing between us is different. What you have told me doesn't change the way I feel about you and I don't see how it has changed the way you have always felt about me. The ghosts you saw when you imagined us together are fantasies. I'm going to fight for you, not lose you to them. Besides, you're going to need me when your dreams crumble."

"You deserve someone who loves you," Sheela argued. "You are very lovable and totally handsome, not to mention bright and potentially prosperous. You have to get on with your life. I'm a dead end."

"Possibly so," Bryan said. "But until the day comes that you either find your love or tell me that you absolutely want me out of your life, I'm not going anywhere."

"But you can't be happy that way. It's not fair."

"We all know life isn't fair. I can't be happy any other way. Whatever happens," Bryan continued, "I'm a survivor. I'll be fine."

"At least promise me," Sheela said, "that you'll see other girls."

"I see other girls all the time like you see other guys, but neither of us has met anyone else. I guess we're both in love with shadows."

"You haven't given any other girl a chance. Promise me you'll give other girls a chance."

"I promise," Bryan said, "that when you give other real men a chance, I'll start dating other girls."

56

In the year after the rainbow vision, Sheela met Zyan only once when Zyan had stopped in Houston en route to New Orleans. Sheela was clerking for Jordan and Landau then and Zyan came to spend a day and a night. Zyan bubbled. She had graduated from UT Law, she had passed the Texas as well as the Louisiana Bar exams, and she had her dream job at the United States Court of Appeals for the Fifth Circuit.

"I know the Napoleonic Code backwards and forwards," she told Sheela, "but I still can't imagine why Louisiana insists on upholding French Law. It's an anachronism. You'd think by now they would have gotten in step with the rest of the country."

Although she seemed pleased to see Zyan, Sheela was reserved. She never once inquired about Jonathan or Zyan's family and she avoided the subject of Bryan as well. She didn't invite her friend to visit at Harvard. Zyan wanted to say a million and one things, but Sheela deftly steered all conversation away from personal subjects and future plans. The visit perplexed Zyan. Sheela was a mystery Zyan knew she could not solve. She only hoped that in time it would solve itself and that the solution would be a happy one for her friend.

After that visit, Zyan and Sheela interacted sporadically, but their communications were directed toward the study and practice of law. Thus Sheela had no warning of Zyan's upcoming marriage until just before graduation when she found herself holding a wedding invitation in her hand. Sheela's heart pounded and her hands shook as she was about to open it. Then she put the cream colored envelope from Mr. Lawrence Reuven and Ms. Selma Samuels Reuven in her drawer. She decided not to read its contents until after her last final, exactly four days from today on May 14th.

Ten days after that, on May 24, she would graduate from Harvard. Only her parents were coming up for the ceremony. Then they would help her dissolve her little household and drive her back home to Houston. Perhaps in between they would take a few days to go to Cape Cod. Neither Door nor Gappa were coming. Her grandparents were slowing down. Moreover, finding convenient lodging was next to impossible. The town would be a zoo. The Landaus hadn't known that hotel reservations had to be made months, if not a year or more, in advance.

Sheela was all set to begin her life as an associate in her mother's firm. The bar exam was comfortably behind her. She had spent her winter vacation holed up in her Cambridge apartment doing a review course, taking only three days off when her parents came up to celebrate her becoming twenty-four and the arrival of 2025. They were snowbound on December 31 and had a fun time eating brunch at 2 a.m., dressed in pajamas with Sheela wearing the elaborate American Indian turquoise jewelry that Nat and Victor gave her for her birthday. Then, during spring break, Sheela took the Texas bar and passed with no problem. The day she got her score, she called home to brag.

"I'm in the 97 percentile," she told Natalya.

"I expected no less," Nat replied. "You worried for nothing."

"You don't get it Ma. That exam is not a test of reasoning. You'd be surprised how many Harvard students failed it. If anything, people from easier schools do better because their classes train them for the exam in their own state. I really crammed. It was all short-term memory."

"Do you think the test was a philosophy of law test in my day?" Nat asked. "The Harvard students who flunked were those who were too conceited to prepare. But I didn't mean to disparage your accomplishment. You did well, sweetheart."

Victor had urged Sheela to wait before starting work.

"You should spend a year in Oxford," he said, "and maybe get a post grad or study philosophy. It would broaden you. Or go to the Sorbonne. They have law courses for English speaking students. You're only 24. What's your rush?"

"Maybe after a few years of working," Sheela responded. "My whole life has been geared toward becoming a lawyer, and the minute I get my license, I want to do the real stuff lawyers do. I want to stand up before a judge or jury and I want to sign my name to my pleadings."

"It will be awhile before you're ready for a jury," Nat pointed out.

"All the more reason for me to get started," Sheela argued.

"Once you get bogged down, it will be hard to get away," Victor said. "This is an opportunity you may regret you let pass by."

"Perhaps, but there is no point in doing something that my heart wouldn't be into. Besides Ma is working too hard. I want her to start taking it a little easier. You have to realize she's not so young any more."

And that was the end of that.

Zyan enclosed a hand-written letter in the envelope that contained the invitation to her forthcoming marriage to Jonathan Mark Friedman on the thirteenth of July, 2025, at 6:00 p.m. In it she asked Sheela if she would please be her maid of honor and wrote, "Jonathan finished his project and turned down a job at the Aerotronic Research Bureau, because the job precluded the possibility of his being married. So that was the reason he took so long to propose and that's why he never agreed to my coming to see him at MIT. Although he didn't tell me in so many words, his work was linked to a top secret military program."

As she stared at the paper filled with Zyan's words, words meant to be read more than once rather than clicked into instant nothingness, Sheela expected she would suddenly disappear from the face of the earth. But no. Although she felt like a non-person, here she was sitting at her table, sipping iced tea and trying to disentangle her emotions and decide what to do. For a split second the idea that Jonathan would not go through with the marriage flitted through her mind, but then Sheela realized that would not happen and she saw she had no choice but to accept her friend's invitation and agree to be her maid of honor. Although it would be the most difficult thing she had ever done, she would stand by Zyan on the happiest day of her life. 'Please, God, help me,' her heart prayed, 'help me get through Zyan's wedding with grace.'

Thoughts swirled in her mind all that day: things Beca told her, books she read, micro discs she watched as a child, her horoscope, photographs, the vision she had when she saw the rainbow. At night, exhausted and tortured, Sheela finally went to bed to seek oblivion, but even before she closed her eyes, a loud voice startled her.

"No, no, a thousand times no," the life-sized figure in the huge photograph shouted out at her. "You don't know me!"

"Stop shouting. I know you very well," Sheela said. "You are a huge snapshot and you are engaged to be married."

"No, I am not," he shouted even louder. "See?" he asked, jumping out of the frame.

"Get back in the picture where you belong," Sheela said. "Now you left a white space. I hate white spaces in pictures."

"Don't look at the space, look at me," he said.

"What for?" Sheela asked. "Now you aren't even a space. You are a negative."

"That's because photographs are misleading. You never liked being photographed either, did you?" the negative's voice asked.

"What's that to you? And what are you saying 'no, no, no' to anyway?" Sheela asked back, but before she got an answer she was asleep.

Zyan and her family planned a small but elegant wedding in a beautiful new temple in Oak Park, outside Chicago. She and Jonathan could manage only a week's honeymoon, which they were spending in Jamaica. After that Zyan was returning to New Orleans and Jonathan was going to Bryn Mawr College in Pennsylvania to set up the department of Artificial Intelligence which he would chair. The newlyweds would have a commuter marriage for two years, after which they intended to establish themselves in the Philadelphia area.

Because of time constraints as well as her preferences, Zyan opted against holding any pre-wedding festivities. Only a handful of out of town guests would be coming: Sheela, Bryan, one of Zyan's UT Law colleagues, and the groom's immediate family.

"Jonathan says he has no one else to invite since he only has two human friends, both of whom will be here anyway," Zyan explained when she conferenced with Sheela.

"How come?" Sheela asked.

"Because my brother is one of his friends and I'm the other. The only other contacts he has had lately have been with his own artificial intelligence creations."

"Was he kidding?" Sheela asked.

"Not really," Zyan answered.

"Well, when is the rehearsal?" Sheela inquired.

"We're not having a rehearsal," Zyan said. "The wedding party isn't all that large and I think we can manage to walk down the aisle without prior practice."

"I talked at length with our Rabbi who is performing the ceremony," Zyan added. "He said that we didn't need to plan everything down to the minutest detail because the most important part of a Jewish wedding is *simchah* which has to be spontaneous."

"Joyousness?" Sheela asked.

"That's right."

The word *simchah* made Sheela acutely aware that her own heart was filled with rocks. Where would her joyousness come from?

"Yes," Sheela agreed, trying to concentrate on her friend's words and on keeping her facial expression unaltered.

"The rabbi went over the actual wedding with me too," Zyan explained. "In the first part of the ceremony we become sanctified to one another before God, and promise to pursue our commitment to Judaism together by doing things like keeping a Jewish home and raising our children to become responsible Jews. The second part is the benedictions. There are seven blessings that praise God, but I'm not sure what they say."

"I didn't really know that," Sheela mumbled when Zyan stopped talking. The truth was she didn't register anything her friend had said.

"Me neither," Zyan said. "Maybe I'll talk to Rabbi Markowitz some more and print a short explanation of the ceremony for the guests."

"What did he say about why the groom stamps on the glass to break it after you sign the marriage contract?" Sheela asked. She didn't think Zyan had mentioned that.

"He said it's to symbolize the sorrows of Israel. He explained that even though the ceremony has to be happy, we should remember those who have suffered. But he said there are also other interpretations."

"Bryan told me he was surprised that your wedding was on a Saturday. He learned you're not supposed to get married on the Sabbath," Sheela volunteered.

"I know. Technically, Sabbath starts at sunset on Friday and ends at sunset on Saturday. Since six is before sunset, we're stretching a bit, but the rabbi said it would be all right. He didn't think God would mind."

"I'd better let you sign off," Sheela said at the next lull in their visit. "You must have hundreds of things to do and lots of people to contact."

"I just want to say one more thing," Zyan added.

"What's that?" Sheela inquired.

"I hope you have a marvelous time at my wedding. Maybe something wonderful will happen."

"I don't know," Sheela responded. She was in the throes of figuring out how to tell Bryan that she didn't want to see him any more. She wished he hadn't been invited to the wedding. "I mean I don't know what will happen," she clarified, "but of course I will love your wedding."

⁕

Sheela drove to the synagogue with Zyan's grandparents, Jake and Sophie Reuven. Bryan was making his own way over.

"You are a beautiful girl," Jake told Sheela in the car. "My granddaughter can't stop talking about how brilliant and kind-hearted you are. But Zyan said you have an ache locked in your soul."

"Zyan spoke in confidence," Sophie said, chastising her husband. "Please forgive Jake his bluntness."

"No, it's OK," Sheela said. "But it's Zyan who is kind and beautiful."

Sheela saw Zyan gingerly seated on a chair in the bride's waiting room at the temple flanked by her parents. She was lovely. Her grandmother's cream colored wedding dress embroidered with seed pearls fit her like a glove and brought out the sheen in her hair and her complexion. Her happiness filled the space around her. Her mother and father's happiness was palpable too, although it was covered by a layer of nervous excitement. Her mother fiddled with Zyan's dress and veil, while her father looked on and stroked Zyan's cheek or squeezed her hand or straightened his cummerbund.

"I was waiting for you," Zyan said to Sheela. "You look magnificent. Your dress matches the color of your eyes."

"Today is about how magnificent and radiant you look," Sheela said. "No, it's actually about how magnificent and radiant you truly are. Jonathan is lucky."

As Sheela spoke, the man whose face was engraved in her heart and whose name she had just uttered with such difficulty walked into the room. His beauty was blinding and forced Sheela to turn away from him and toward Zyan.

"The groom is not supposed to see you before the wedding," she said.

"I know," Zyan replied with a smile. "Jonathan just got here. He's waiting out back. This is Ariel, my brother. He's the best man. You and he walk together behind my father and me. The bridesmaids follow you and then . . . ."

Sheela became pale and then flushed and then pale again. She felt faint. She couldn't speak or think or move and her sudden paralysis frightened her.

"What's the matter?" Zyan asked. For a few seconds Sheela was unable to answer. She clasped the back of Zyan's chair so she wouldn't fall.

"Please, say something," Zyan urged. She too was becoming afraid. "Are you all right?"

"No," Sheela finally said.

"What is it?" Zyan asked.

"I mean yes. Nothing's wrong," Sheela mumbled, "I just need to sit. I'm out of breath. I'm sorry; I'll be fine. I don't understand what's happening."

"She has blue eyes!" Ariel said. "And a dimple."

"Please, Ari," his mother said. "Stop talking nonsense. Sheela is a real person, not one of those artificial creations of yours. It's rude to make comments about someone who is in the room as if she weren't present. Get a glass of water."

"I'm sorry," Sheela apologized.

367

"It's all right, dear." Selma comforted Sheela and settled her in the chair Ariel brought over. "Weddings do this to people. They pull out all kinds of unexpected feelings."

"I'm sorry," Sheela repeated after she sipped the water that Ariel handed to his mother who handed it to her. "Something came over me; I'm feeling better."

In the seconds that followed, Sheela's brain tried to sort out what her senses were recording. How could Zyan not be marrying the man in the picture? She knew him the second she saw him in the photograph with his arm around her friend. There was no doubt about that. This wedding had to be a dream. In a minute she would wake up and everything would sort itself out. She arranged her hands so no one would see her pinching the inside of her arm and she wiggled her toes. They felt frozen and tingly, as if she had frostbite. Was it really that cold in the room?

Sheela looked up again and her eyes fell squarely upon Ariel. He met her gaze and she began to tremble. If she wasn't asleep, then she was having delusions, there was no question about it. She crossed her arms over her chest and clasped herself to stop herself from shaking and stamped her feet so the pins and needles would go away.

"Do you remember Ariel's picture?" Zyan asked. "Remember when I showed you that snapshot of Jonathan, looking into the camera like a goofball? So, is my brother handsome or what? Not that Jonathan isn't pretty good looking too."

"Your brother looks a lot like you," Sheela replied.

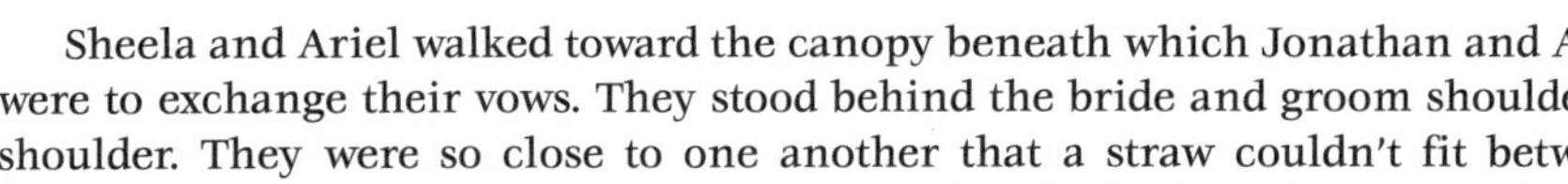

Sheela and Ariel walked toward the canopy beneath which Jonathan and Ariel were to exchange their vows. They stood behind the bride and groom shoulder to shoulder. They were so close to one another that a straw couldn't fit between them. They watched the ceremony and listened to the bride and groom and to the rabbi with a single intensity. Later, at the reception, they exchanged only a few sentences. The tension that filled them was so exquisitely thrilling that it virtually blocked their capacity to think. They danced and feasted their eyes upon one another and absorbed one another's joy.

Neither Sheela nor Ariel noticed when Betsy, Jonathan's younger sister, grabbed the bride's bouquet and scanned the crowd for Bryan, her eyes gleaming. Bryan saw her and raised his hand making a V for victory with his fingers.

After Zyan and Jonathan left, Ariel took Sheela's hand and asked, "Can we go now too?"

Sheela nodded, "I'm staying with the Khannas. I'll tell them not to expect me back."

"I'll tell my parents I'm spending the night in the city," Ariel said

Sheela went into the bathroom in their room at the Drake Hotel to undress. She wanted Ariel to see her naked all at once. She came out a short while later and found him sitting on the bed fully clothed, just as she had left him. When he saw Sheela, he stared, unable to move a muscle.

"You are perfect," he finally said. "I've wanted you my whole life and now I don't know what to do."

Sheela smiled and began to take off his clothes. When she was finished, she took his right hand with the yellow sapphire ring on his fourth finger and looked into the stone's light and rubbed it against her cheek. Its color was the same as that of the smaller stone she wore on the same finger and its feel was familiar. Ariel watched and then he traced his fingers around the tiny heart shaped pendant that rested in the hollow of Sheela's neck and around the familiar mole above her belly button.

When the sun rose, Sheela and Ariel were still not sated. In the brightness of the morning they crossed the barriers made by sound and by light and entered the dimension where they were one. Then, finally, they fell asleep in each other's arms.

Later they had breakfast in a French bakery and went for a walk along Lake Michigan.

"I want to marry you," Ariel said.

"You kept your promise," Sheela told him. "That's all that matters."

"I just signed a four-year contract with the ARB, that's the Aerotronic Research Bureau. They will send me to space stations. Everything is secret. I'm not allowed to have a wife."

"I'll wait," Sheela said. "We'll meet whenever it's possible."

"Do you take anything, you know, not to get pregnant?" Ari asked.

"No. Do you?" Sheela asked him.

"No. If we get pregnant we'll keep the baby right? I mean you aren't going to take the morning after pill, are you?"

"No, I couldn't do that. But I think a woman knows when she's started a baby, and I'm pretty sure I didn't."

"My contract doesn't begin until September 15 so I'll get an anti-dad shot today."

"You know I saw you once in Boston. It was from a distance and I didn't realize that you were you. But I was sure you had ocean-colored eyes and your dimple. And then I could never forget you," Ari told Sheela.

"I've never forgotten you either. I was born wanting you," Sheela told him.

"Do you know why?"

"I think I do, but it doesn't matter any more."

57

"I don't get it," Natalya said when Sheela called Sunday evening, the day after Zyan's wedding. "You are extending your stay in Chicago until September, and you hope we don't mind?"

"I'm having a wonderful time. I met some people. Like you and Daddy said, what's the rush?"

"The rush is that as of today a large pile of documents is sitting on your brand new desk at Jordan and Landau waiting for your attention. It wouldn't be there if we had hired someone else instead of you. There are deadlines to be met. We employed you as a professional at a competitive salary and we agreed to the starting date you wanted. Does that answer your question? This cavalier attitude is not what Steve or I would have expected of a new associate."

"Ma, you don't understand."

"That's precisely correct. I don't." Nat was angry. Then she heard a muffled sob over the phone, so she softened her tone. Her daughter's behavior was entirely out of character. There had to be a good reason for it.

"Perhaps something is going on that you cannot discuss over the phone. Why don't you come home and talk more openly? Then we can decide how to proceed."

"Would it be OK if I come on Tuesday instead of tomorrow?"

"I suppose so," her mother agreed, utterly perplexed.

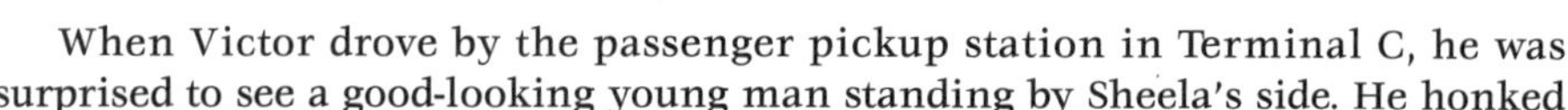

When Victor drove by the passenger pickup station in Terminal C, he was surprised to see a good-looking young man standing by Sheela's side. He honked and both of them got in the car.

"I'm Ariel Reuven," the man said. His voice was gentle but firm. "I'm here to help Sheela explain why she has to be in Chicago for a few weeks. She doesn't want you to be upset."

"Please Daddy, can he stay with us, please?" Sheela pleaded.

What could Victor do?

"I have been in love with Ariel my whole life," Sheela said. Once she started speaking, the words cascaded out of her mouth. "I didn't realize it, but he is the man I was waiting for. He is the reason I could never be happy with anyone else. And I recognized him when Zyan showed me his picture, only I thought he was Jonathan and that he loved Zyan. His arm was around Zyan's shoulder and Jonathan was standing to the side. I thought I would die. Then at the wedding when it turned out that Ariel was Zyan's brother and he wasn't Jonathan after all, I couldn't believe it. I nearly fainted. But it's true."

"There was never anyone else for me either," Ariel told the Landaus.

"And look Ma! Look Daddy!" Sheela sparkled. "See his ring. It's the same color as mine. It's a yellow sapphire from India! A pokhraj! Ariel's grandfather gave it to him."

Nat and Victor thought Sheela made very little sense, but it didn't take them long to understand that their daughter had redefined herself over the weekend. She was self-assured, even in her excitement and in her nervousness. And she had a new rounder beauty that spoke out her fulfillment. Seeing her thus they felt afraid. The man she introduced to them now held Sheela's happiness in the palm of his hands. What if he crushed it?

"I admit I don't understand you, Sheela," Victor acknowledged, "but I am a man open to the possibility that the surreal may be real. However, I cannot comprehend why you and your . . . uh, friend wouldn't enjoy a normal courtship. Get on with your lives, get engaged, and get married if that's what you want. A meaningful relationship is one that develops gradually. It incorporates your life; it doesn't require you to cast your life aside. Frankly I'm concerned that your intention to propel yourselves into this . . . trip to la-la land with utter disregard for your responsibilities doesn't bode well for a future together."

"It's hard to explain, Dr. Landau," Ari said, "but I will try. Our relationship cannot develop gradually. We cannot go through the motions of a courtship, because we are beyond courting. But we do intend to get married and to live responsible lives. The problem is I have accepted a four-year assignment with the Aerotronic Research Bureau beginning mid-September. I'm contractually bound to stay single for four years and during that period of time I be will away and out of touch. Vacation days will be few and far between. You know the Bureau's existence is not a secret, but the truth is that most of its activities are well hidden from the public eye."

"Four years is a long time and contracts are agreements that can be broken," Natalya interjected. "That's what damages are for. If Sheela is so important to you, surely you could find a way out."

"Perhaps I could," Ariel answered. "But the damages for my unexcused failure to perform as agreed could ruin me. More importantly, I am morally bound to honor my commitment. I must complete a project that matters a great deal to me and that I think could be of critical importance to the human race. Had I met Sheela a year ago, we would have decided what to do about ARB together," Ariel said, "but I didn't know her then. My colleague, Jonathan, turned down Aerotronic's offer because of Zyan. I, on the other hand, accepted it because I had no reason not to. My work was all I had in life."

"What about your commitment, Sheela?" Nat asked her daughter. "Don't you think you are bound to honor it?"

"I can't," Sheela answered. "I would die without these months with Ariel. I died once before. If I'm dead I can't honor my commitment anyway."

Natalya wanted to reject Sheela's remarks as dramatic and absurd, but something about the way she spoke and looked held her back. Neither she nor Victor knew what to say. They only knew that nothing they could say would make a difference.

"After September I'll do anything I can to make this up to you, Ma; please don't be angry," Sheela pleaded. "If it were any other law firm, I wouldn't care. But I do care about Jordan and Landau. I love you."

Nat covered her eyes with her hands. "I don't know. Your staying away for so long will create problems for us. I don't know, but I guess we'll manage somehow. Steve will understand. He's a pushover where you are concerned. Even though you think I'm not so young, I suppose I have enough stamina left in me to handle a few more months of pressure."

"And I suppose," Victor told his wife, "this means our trip to Bali is off."

On Thursday Sheela and Ariel flew back to Chicago, and by Friday noon they were settled in a little furnished apartment over Jake and Sophie Reuven's garage.

"So," Sophie declared, "when you don't feel like cooking or going out, you'll eat with us. Dinner is at 7:00. My specialties are stuffed peppers, chicken and rice, and Anjali Khanna's lamb curry. I've put a tuna casserole in your refrigerator in case you get hungry. It's made with olive oil and herbs, not that creamy guck. And there are brownies in the cupboard and some basic groceries. Tonight you'll come down for Shabbat. Usually we go to my son's or daughter's house, but this is an exception. There will just be the four of us so we can talk."

"Maybe Ari and Sheela would prefer to go home to Lawrence and Selma or maybe they want to be alone," Jake suggested.

"They wouldn't prefer anything like that; they would definitely prefer to talk with us. Right?"

"Right, Gran," Ari said.

"So there!" Sophie grinned triumphantly.

Jake Reuven shrugged his shoulders and pretended he wasn't glad.

"My brother Daniel was seven years older than I," Jake Reuven began, sipping an after dinner cup of tea generously laced with rum. "He was a handsome and jovial fellow, but his joviality was a mask that hid a deep sorrow. He was driven. He lived life frenetically so that he wouldn't have to pause to reflect upon it. He traveled all over the world and took crazy risks. He drove race cars, sky-dived on lonely beaches, and he flew helicopters in snowstorms.

"'The gods won't get me,' he used to say. 'I'm going to live to be a hundred. Only those who love life meet death.' But he was wrong. The gods got him after all. He was only thirty-five."

"Zyan told me Daniel died in a skiing accident," Sheela said. She rubbed her ring as she spoke.

"We think so," Jake replied. "His body was found at the foot of an alpine ski slope, frozen. The funny thing was that there was no injury."

Sophie broke the silence that filled the room. "Danny was a charmer and so handsome. But his heart was locked shut and there wasn't a woman in the world who had a key that could open it. Sometimes when he was in our house and there was silence, the depth of the pain in his eyes brought tears to mine.

"He loved India and he was always telling me that I should go there with Jake, but the children were small and there was no one to handle our business here. Later, when Jake retired, our children, Lawrence and Leah, tried to persuade us to take a trip around the world, but we never made it. We've become homebodies."

"Then how did you become friends with Anjali Khanna?" Sheela asked.

"I met her when she came to America for the first time. She was very close to our associates, the Javeris. Anjali and I hit it off and we stayed in touch over the years. Then, once her son moved to Chicago she started visiting regularly. She told me about you and I told Zyan to look you up."

"About Uncle Daniel," Ari asked his grandfather, "Did you ever find out why he was so unhappy?"

"He never talked about it," Jake said, "and I never did either, but I figured out bits and pieces."

"Tonight might be a good time to tell us," Sophie said.

"Yes, this could be the right time." Jake blinked his eyes. To resurrect the past was not an easy thing. "When I was about ten, which would make Danny about seventeen, my brother had a terrible experience. He went away for the summer and after he returned, he could no longer sleep at night. I'd wake up and see his bed empty and then I'd wander all over the house looking for him. Sometimes he was out and I waited up until I heard his key unlock the door. At other times I'd find him in the living room or in the kitchen with all the lights switched on. I'd climb into his lap and hug him and feel his face wet with tears.

"This went on for a long time, maybe a year. Then one night I went into Danny's room around ten o'clock to say good night. He was sitting on his bed clutching a little box.

"What's inside that box? I asked.

"It's a heart," he said. "Tomorrow I'm going to give it to Mrs. Gershwin. I don't need it any more."

"In the morning by the time I woke up, Danny was gone. He didn't get back until suppertime, but when he finally came home he was different. He roughed up my hair, like he hadn't done in months, and said, 'I've neglected you kiddo. Tomorrow we'll play a game of catch.'

"Did Mrs. Gershwin like the heart?" I asked Daniel.

"I don't know," my brother answered. "She told me to keep it, but her little girl said they had to save it for when her sister Sarah came back, so she took it."

"What was the little girl's name?" Sheela asked.

"I don't remember, I think it was Ruth or Rose." Jake said.

"Are you sure the lady's name was Mrs. Gershwin?" Sheela asked.

"Oh yes," Jake replied. "I remember Daniel saying that name and then years later I met a scientist who worked with her. The gentleman told me Mr. Gershwin was her second husband. Her first husband, Myron Fine, died before her eldest daughter was born and then that daughter, Sarah, died at about sixteen. I made the connection, but I never said anything to Daniel. What good would it have done? I kept thinking about the mother and I wondered how she survived such tragedies. And sometimes I wondered what happened to the little girl who was waiting for her sister to come back."

"My grandmother gave me the heart that I'm wearing. Her name was Rebecca Gershwin before she married my grandfather," Sheela said. "But Gappa, that's my grandfather, told me that Rebecca was really her middle name. She didn't like to be called by her first name, Ruth."

"I noticed your heart when we were riding to the wedding," Jake said. "It's very delicate and it fits right in the hollow of your neck. Your ring drew my attention too. The stone is very beautiful. It has the same color and brilliance as Ariel's. Where did you get it?"

"In India. I took a trip with Sunita, Anjali Khanna's granddaughter. When I saw it, I had to have it. It's a yellow sapphire. Mr. Javeri said it's called a pokhraj."

Jake nodded.

"May I ask you a question?"

"There is no need, Jake said. "I'll answer without your asking. "Yes, Ariel's ring belonged to his uncle. I gave it to my grandson on his eighteenth birthday." Jake turned to Ari. "Do you remember?"

"How could I forget? You told me that your grandfather gave it to Daniel and the original stone had been given as a gift to Rabbi Daniel Reuven."

"So it was," Jake mused. "Although the stone came from India, it was originally mined in Sri Lanka—Ceylon—in the old days. It has been in the family for centuries. We were told it brings good luck. After Daniel's death, I thought otherwise. I wasn't going to give it to you. I was going to sell it, but then I decided I had to speak to your father about it first. Lawrence believed it was your birthright. He wanted you to have it. 'Ari's destiny is his destiny' he said, so I gave it to you."

"You are so very much like Danny." Sophie smiled at her grandson. "You have his charm, his chestnut hair and his expressions. When your father told me he wanted to name you Ariel Daniel, I was afraid. I thought it was bad luck to name a child after someone who died young, but Lawrence insisted that his uncle's memory be kept alive. He pointed out that Daniel was also the name of the famous Rabbi Daniel Reuven from whom you are descended. Your forefather was a great scholar and he lived to be nearly ninety. But all these years I noticed how you had the same way about you that Danny had. I saw Danny's restlessness in your eyes and my heart was not at ease."

"I worried too," Jake said, "but now your eyes gleam like Danny's did before the summer that took away their luster."

At night, Sheela and Ariel celebrated the Sabbath again in the bed that would be theirs until September. It was the seventh night in a row they slept together, barely sleeping at all. This night the music in their hearts was subdued. Shyness overcame Sheela. She undressed with her back to Ari and she covered her body with a gown before slipping between the sheets. She and Ari remained apart for some time and when they turned toward each another, their caresses were soft and gentle. They touched only with their hands. They kept their eyes open and watched each other's features swell with pleasure. As their bodies overtook their minds, Ari raised Sheela's negligee. For a long time he and Sheela kept pace with the symphony that was inside them and all around them. The orchestra played slowly and softly at first. Gradually its rhythm quickened and its notes became louder and louder. When the lovers' faces contorted with passion and their senses could not endure another instant of the relentless pounding concert, the music exploded into a crashing silent finale.

Ariel waited for the silence to pass and for his breathing and Sheela's to become normal once again. Then he softly asked, "What do you remember about Sarah?

"I remember how she yearned for Daniel. She burned with longing, but Daniel denied her. They were too young, he said. It wasn't the right time, he said. He had thought it over and realized that succumbing to what they wanted just then, without considering the consequences, would be an irresponsible act. He didn't want to make love with one of those . . . you know, a rubber shield. He was afraid they would be caught and Sarah would shame her family. He had a million reasons to not give in to her. Instead he gave her this." Sheela lifted her locket to her mouth and kissed it. "He told her it was his heart and he promised it would always be hers. But he broke his promise to take her heart and make it his. Instead, Daniel took her rowing on a lake. It was dark, but your ring—his ring— was still bright and hot from the sun, even though the sun had set hours ago. The flames in the pokhraj lit a fire in Sarah's soul. She jumped in the water to cool herself off. She started to swim, but she tired quickly. Daniel jumped in after her. He tried to save her, but there was no way. They were too far from the shore."

"And you, what do you remember about Daniel?"
"Nothing," Ariel replied. "Nothing at all. My only memories are of you. But there is one strange thing I can't understand."
"What?"
"Your eyes were different; they were hazel and had gold flecks in them."
"Are you sure?"
"Yes, because they mirrored the golden flecks in my ring."
"So what don't you understand?"
"How did I know, without seeing them, that this time your eyes were blue?"

Select Bibliography

Wisdom from scores if not hundreds of books and articles are reflected in this work. Writings of our predecessors are our heritage. The list below cites the books that were consulted extensively for the purpose of writing *The Pokhraj.*

Bowman, Carol. *Children's Past Lives.* Bantam, 1998.

Corcoran, Diane K. *When Ego Dies.* Emerald Ink, 1996.

Cowan, Paul A. *An Orphan in History.* Quill-William Morrow, 1996.

Crichton, Michael. *Timeline.* Random House, 1999.

Gajjar, Irina. *You Know Me—The Gita,* Emerald Ink, 2000.

Kertzer, Rabbi Morris N. *What is a Jew?* Revised by Rabbi Lawrence A. Hoffman. Touchstone, 1996.

Nilsson , Lennart and Lars Hamberger. *A Child is Born.* Dell Publishing, 1993.

Scranton, Roger. *Modern Philosophy.* Penguin Books, 1994.

Spock, Benjamin and Michael B. Rothenberg. *Baby and Child Care.* Simon & Schuster, 1992.

Weiss, Brian L. *Many Lives, Many Masters.* Simon & Schuster, 1988.